John W. (John Wesley) Hales, Frederick James Furnivall

Ballads and Romances

Bishop Percy

I0592359

John W. (John Wesley) Hales, Frederick James Furnivall

Ballads and Romances
Bishop Percy

ISBN/EAN: 9783743306776

Manufactured in Europe, USA, Canada, Australia, Japa

Cover: Foto ©Andreas Hilbeck / pixelio.de

Manufactured and distributed by brebook publishing software
(www.brebook.com)

John W. (John Wesley) Hales, Frederick James Furnivall

Ballads and Romances

Bishop Percy's

Folio Manuscript.

Ballads and Romances.

EDITED BY

JOHN W. HALES, M.A.

FELLOW AND LATE ASSISTANT-TUTOR OF CHRIST'S COLLEGE, CAMBRIDGE

AND

FREDERICK J. FURNIVALL, M.A.

OF TRINITY HALL, CAMBRIDGE.

(ASSISTED BY PROF. CHILD, OF HARVARD UNIV., U.S.; W. CHAPPELL, ESQ., &c. &c.)

Vol. II.

LONDON:

N. TRÜBNER & CO., 60 PATERNOSTER ROW.

1868.

PREFACE

THE SECOND VOLUME.

As the first volume was specially that of Arthur and Gawaine, of Robin Hood and his great compeer, now almost forgotten, 'Randolph, Erl of Chestre,' so this second volume is specially that of· Sir Grey, who did such mighty deeds for England, and the pathos of whose death in his hermit's cell near Warwick has never yet been worthily sung.

But the Arthur and Gawaine stories are here continued in *The Grene Knight*, the *Boy and Mantle*, and *Libius Disconius*; and we have besides, in the present volume, versions of some of the best of our English ballads, *Chevy Chase*, *Childe Waters*, *Bell my Wiffe*, *Bessie off Bednall*, &c. Of one of the best of them, *King Estmere*, Percy's ruthless hands (p. 200, note) have prevented us giving the MS. version of the folio. We have been unable to find any other MS. or printed copy of this ballad, and have therefore been obliged to put side by side in an appendix Percy's two printed versions of it, with all their differences from each other marked in italics, so that readers may judge for themselves as to his probable amount of alteration in the other parts.

The folio version of *Bell my Wiffe*—a ballad to which Shakspere's quotation of it in *Othello* has secured immortality—is believed to be the earliest known; and as it just filled a page in the MS. it was chosen for photolithographing, and an impression of it will be given with Vol. III. for Vol. I.

John de Reeue is (among other pieces) here printed for the first time, and if it can be taken in any degree as a picture of the bondman's condition at the time it represents, or even the time it was written, it is of considerable historical value. At any rate, it shows us a merry scene of early English life. *Conscience's* tale is of a darker tint, but is valuable for its sketch of the corruptions of its times. The other historical ballads treat of fights and plots abroad and at home—of Agincourt, Buckingham's Fall, the Siege of Cadiz, Durham Field, Northumberland besieged by Douglas, &c. &c.,—but none of them are of more than average merit.

Mr. Hales has written all the Introductions, except those to *Cales Voyage* (for which the Editors are indebted to Mr. John Bruce, the Director of the Camden Society), to *Earle Bodwell* (which is reprinted from the first edition of Bishop Percy's *Reliques*), to *Boy and Mantle* (which is reprinted from Professor Child's *Ballads*), and the following by Mr. Furnivall: *Come, Come ; Conscience; Agincourte Battell;* and *Libius Disconius*. Mr. Hales has also written the Introductory Essay on The Revival of Ballad Poetry in the Eighteenth Century.

For the text Mr. Furnivall is, as before, mainly responsible, and has to thank Mr. W. A. Dalziel for his help in reading the copy and proof with the MS. The contractions of the MS. are printed in italics in the text.

To the Revs. Alexander Dyce, W. W. Skeat, J. Roberts, and Archdeacon Hale; to Messrs. Chappell, Bruce, T. Wright, Planché, and Jones, the Editors tender their thanks for help in divers ways.

February 4, 1868.

CONTENTS

OF

THE SECOND VOLUME.

———◆———

p. 9, l. **68**, *for* armour *read* armor.

p. 16, l. **253**, *for* and *read* &.

p. 23, l. **9**, *for* [and] *read* &.

p. 28, l. **6**, *for* with *read* with.

    l. **22**, *for* between *read* betweenu.

p. 29, l. **77**, *for* thein *read* them.

p. 41, l. **9**, *for* up *read* vp.

p. 46, l. **7**, *for* bells *read* bell.

p. 60, note **8**, *for* theye *read* they.

p. 63, l. **134**; p. 66, l. **203, 215**; *for* and *read* &.

p. 72, note **3**: *the* r *has fallen out of the A.-Sax. Gram.*

p. 77, note, col. **1**, l. **2**; *for* missed. As *read* missed, as.

p. 140, l. **109**, *add* witt *at the end of the line.*

    note **1**, *for* Strowt yu *read* Strowtyn.

p. 159, l. **7**, *for* 1569 *read* 1659.

p. 164, note **2**, *for* terme *read* tenne.

p. 254, l. **12**, *for* Robert *read* Richard.

p. 379, notes, col. **2**, for " 1867 " read " *Babees Book*, &c. 1868."

N.B. The reading of the vol. with the MS. was stopt at p. 74 by the return of the MS. to its owners.

THE REVIVAL OF BALLAD POETRY IN THE EIGHTEENTH CENTURY.

THE last century in England was in more respects than one a valley of dry bones. About the middle of it, " they were very many," and "they were very dry." Shortly afterwards, "behold, a noise," and the bones began to come together. These signs of life were followed by a growing animation. From the four quarters came the wind, and breathed on the quickening mass. From the north it came in its strength ; from the east and the west it blew vigorously ; from the south it rushed with a wild furious sweeping blast that changed the face of the valley. So at last the century revived—its dull lack-lustre eyes brightened—its stagnant pulse leapt—it lived.

I do not now propose to attempt a full description of this mighty revival. But I propose confining myself to one particular feature of it—the appreciation of our older literature, and especially of our ballad poetry. The century that had long been fully satisfied with its own productions, at last recognised that the English literature of ages that had preceded it was not wholly barbarous. The century that had given up itself to rules, and reduced the art of poetry to a mechanical trick, at last acknowledged graces beyond the reach of its art. At last it was brought to see that there were more things in heaven and earth than were dreamt of in its philosophy.

It discovered that there were innumerable beauties around it to which it had long been blind. It left its gardens and its elaborate manipulations of nature to see Nature herself. It gave over refining the lily and gilding the rose to look at the flowers in their simple beauty. It became conscious of the exquisite beauties and glories of Switzerland, of the English lakes, of Wales. New worlds of splendour, and of noble enjoyment, dawned upon it. Not greater discoveries were made by Columbus and his followers four centuries before than were then made. The age, with all its self-complaisance, had been living in a prison. The doors were thrown open, and it came forth to feel and enjoy the fresh breezes and the gracious sunshine. A huger, more dismal, more cramping Bastile than that of Paris fell along with it. The age saw at the same time that, besides the beauties of nature, there were beauties that the art of former days had bequeathed it. It began to discern the subtle loveliness of old cathedral churches that studded the country. It had long eyed them with much disfavour. It had sadly disfigured them with adornments of its own devising, and according with its own notions. It had deplored them as monstrous relics of a profound barbarism. But at last the scales fell from its eyes, and it saw that these " tabernacles of the Lord of Hosts " were " amiable." It awoke to their supreme, lavish, refined beautifulness. So with respect to other branches of Gothic art, other fruits of the old Romantic times, they came to a better appreciation of them. Poets and poems that had for many a day been relegated to neglect and oblivion, were more frankly and fairly valued. Voices that had long been silenced or ignored began to find a hearing and a heeding audience. As Greek literature was revived in the fifteenth, so was Romantic in the eighteenth.

A fair criterion of the progress of the century in the recognition of the Romantic age is its appreciation of Chaucer. The most important event of the century regarding him is the appearance of Tyrwhitt's edition of him in 1775. Then at last an attempt was made to vindicate his fame from the imputation of rudeness ; to show that he, no less than the eighteenth-century poets, had some sense of melody, some talent for character-drawing, some power of language. Spenser was more readily and continuously accepted. The age sympathised with the moralising part of his genius, and found pleasure in imitating him. But, as I have said, I propose now considering the history of our ballad poetry ; and to it I turn.

The most signal event regarding it is the publication of Percy's *Reliques of Ancient English Poetry* in 1765. Let us see how the century was prepared, or had been preparing, for that famous publication.

Our English ballads, though highly popular in the Elizabethan age, as innumerable allusions to them in Shakespeare and the other dramatists, and in the general literature of the time, show, were yet never collected into any volume, save in *Garlands*, till the year 1723. They wandered up and down the country without even sheepskins or goatskins to protect them. They flew about like the birds of the air, and sung songs dear to the heart of the common people—songs whose power was sometimes confessed by the higher classes, but not so thoroughly appreciated as to induce them to exert themselves for their preservation. They were looked down upon as things that were very good in their proper place, but which must not be admitted into higher society. They were admired in a condescending manner. They were much better than could be expected. But no one thought of them as popular lyrics of great intrinsic value. No one put forth a hand to save them from perishing. The custom of covering the walls of houses with them that happily prevailed in the seventeenth century did something for their preservation. So secured, they had a better chance of keeping a place in men's memories, and meeting some day appreciative eyes. Towards the end of the said century were made one or two collections of the broad sheets containing them. The black-letter literature of the people was collected rather for its curiousness than its power or beauty, by antiquaries rather than by poets or enjoyers of poetry. Whatever their motives, let us praise Wood and Harley, Selden [1] and Pepys, Rawlinson, Douce, and Bagford, for their services in gathering together and protecting the frail outcasts from destruction. They were as great benefactors of the old ballads as Captain Coram was of foundlings. Be their names glorified!

There can be no doubt that the powerful mind of Dryden justly appreciated the strength of our old literature, although he so far bows before the spirit of his age as to deface it for the reception of that age. Even when he revised and spoiled Chaucer's works, he felt the power of them. But he resigned his own judgment to that of his contemporaries. This Samson in his captivity consented to make merry and carouse with his captors—to translate the songs he loved into the Philistine dialect. He had a fine appreciation of the old ballads. "I have heard," says a *Spectator*, "that the late Lord Dorset, who had the greatest wit tempered with the greatest candour, and was one of the finest critics as well as the best poets of his age, had a numerous collection of old English ballads, and took a particular pleasure in the reading of them. I can affirm the same of Mr. Dryden, and know several of the most refined writers of our present age who are of the same humour." He is, I think, the first collector of poems who conceded to popular ballads their due place,—who admitted them into the society of other poems—poems by the most Eminent Hands,—who perceived their excellence, and welcomed them accordingly. To other collectors of that date it was as disgraceful to a poem as to a man to have no father,

---

[1] Tradition says that Pepys "borrowed" a part of his Collection from Selden, and forgot to return it.—W. C.

or to be suspected of a common origin. Dryden rose above
this prejudice. He showed one or two ballads the same hospitality as he extended to the poetasters of Oxford and Cambridge,
whose name was Legion at this time. In the *Miscellany Poems*,
edited by him, of which the first volume appeared in 1684, the
last in 1708, eight years after his death, are to be found " Little
Musgrave and the Lady Bernard," certainly one of the most
vigorous ballads in our language; " Chevy Chase," with a
rhyming Latin translation; " Johnnie Armstrong," " Gilderoy,"
" The Miller and the King's Daughters." But the evil that men
do lives after them. Dryden, in his " Knight's Tale " and other
works, had set the fashion of imitating and modernising our old
poems. That fashion survived him. For more than half a
century after his death, with the exception of the insertion of
two or three in Playford's [1] *Wit and Mirth, or Pills to purge
Melancholy*, and of the *Collection of Old Ballads* above referred
to, we have produced in England imitations or adaptations of
ballads—no faithful reprint of the genuine thing. The wine
that the age had given it to drink was a miserable dilution, or
only coloured water. Conspicuous amongst these imitators or
adapters were Parnell, Prior, and Tickell. But there were two
men in Queen Anne's time who had a genuine relish for old
ballads, and who said a good word for them. These were
Addison and Rowe. Addison's taste for them had been awakened
during his travels on the Continent. " When I travelled," he
writes, " I took a particular delight in hearing the songs and
fables that are come from father to son, and are most in vogue
among the common people of the countries through which I
passed; for it is impossible that anything should be universally
tasted and approved by a multitude, though they are only the
rabble of a nation, which hath not in it some peculiar aptness

---

[1] This Collection, though generally
called D'Urfey's, was Henry Playford's.
D'Urfey edited only the last edition
(1719), in six volumes. Five were
printed in 1714; the first volume in
1699.—W. C.

to please and gratify the mind of man." He gives, as is well
known, two numbers of the *Spectator* to a consideration of
" Chevy Chase," one to that of the " Children in the Wood."
" The old song of ' Chevy Chase,' " he writes, " is the favourite
ballad of the common people of England, and Ben Jonson used
to say he had rather have been the author of it than of all his
works." Then he quotes Sir Philip Sidney's famous words ; and
then adds, " For my own part I am so professed an admirer of
this antiquated song that I shall give my reader a critick upon
it, without any further apology for so doing." And he proceeds
to investigate the poem according to the critical rules of his
time. He compares it with other heroic poems, and illustrates
it from Virgil and Horace. He read the old ballad in the light
of his age—viewed and reviewed it in a somewhat narrow spirit.
But he did read it—he did look at it. In spite of the confining
criticism and hypercriticism of the day, he did feel and recognise
its power. " Thus we see," his *examen* concludes, " how the
thoughts of this poem, which naturally arise from the subject,
are always simple, and sometimes exquisitely noble ; that the
language is often very sounding, and that the whole is written
with a true poetical spirit." In another paper he calls attention
to and expresses the " most exquisite pleasure " he had received
from " The Two Children in the Wood," which he had en-
countered pasted upon the wall of some house in the country.
He describes it as " one of the darling songs of the common
people," and as having been "the delight of most Englishmen
in some part of their age ;" and then he discusses it after his
manner. " The tale of it is a pretty tragical story, and pleases
for no other reason but because it is a copy of nature. There
is even a despicable simplicity in the verse ; and yet because the
sentiments appear genuine and unaffected, they are able to
move the mind of the most polite reader with inward meltings
of humanity and compassion." But he could not bring his

contemporaries to sympathise with him. They would not hear, charmed he never so wisely. His " Chevy Chase" papers were ridiculed and parodied by Dennis and Wagstaff and kindred spirits. To them perhaps he alludes in the concluding words of his notice of the other ballad he reviews : " As for the little conceited wits of the age," he writes, " who can only show their judgment by finding fault, they cannot be supposed to admire those productions which have nothing to recommend them but the beauties of nature, when they do not know how to relish even those compositions that, with all the beauties of nature, have also the additional advantages of art." He fought a losing battle. What appreciation of the old things there was at the beginning of the century was rapidly decaying. An age of elaborate artificiality, and studied affectation, was dawning.

I have mentioned Rowe as sharing Addison's appreciation of the old ballads. He takes for one of his plays a subject that was the theme of a widely popular ballad, and in introducing his tragedy, deprecates the adverse prejudices of his audience, and speaks boldly in favour of the elder literature, and against the wretched affectations of his time. The Prologue to his " Jane Shore," first acted in 1713, opens thus :

> To-night, if you have brought your good old taste,
> We'll treat you with a downright English feast,
> A tale which, told long since in homely wise,
> Hath never failed of melting gentle eyes.
> Let no nice sir despise the hapless dame
> Because recording ballads chaunt her name ;
> Those venerable ancient song-enditers
> Soared many a pitch above our modern writers.
> They caterwauled in no romantic ditty,
> Sighing for Philis's or Cloe's pity ;
> Justly they drew the Fair, and spoke her plain,
> And sung her by her Christian name—'twas Jane.
> Our numbers may be more refined than those,
> But what we've gained in verse, we've lost in prose ;
> Their words no shuffling double-meaning knew,
> Their speech was homely, but their hearts were true.

In such an age immortal Shakespear wrote.
By no quaint rules nor hampering critics taught,
With rough majestic force they moved the heart,
And strength and nature made amends for art.
Our humble author does his steps pursue;
He owns he had the mighty bard in view;
And in these scenes has made it more his care
To rouse the passions than to charm the ear.

But this advocacy, too, of a better taste was doomed to fail. Rowe, as Addison, spoke in vain. The literary dominion of France was growing more and more supreme. Protests in behalf of our old masters were urged fruitlessly. The charms of our ballad poetry were disregarded, were despised.

There were, however, others besides Addison and Rowe who had some slight sense of those charms, as for instance those whom we have named—Parnell, Tickell, Prior. Parnell's acquaintance with our older literature is shown in his "Fairy Tale in the Ancient English Style." It is but a feeble piece, written in a favourite Romance metre—the metre of Chaucer's "Tale of Sir Topas"—and decorated with occasional bits of bad grammar to give it an antique look. Tickell's friendship with Addison could not but have conduced to some familiarity on his part with the old ballads. He seems to have been inspired by them in no ordinary degree. Apropos of his "Lucy and Colin," Goldsmith remarks: "Through all Tickell's works there is a strain of ballad-thinking, if I may so express it; and in this professed ballad he seems to have surpassed himself. It is perhaps the best in our language in this way." The writer of it has evidently drunk from the old wells. The story is simple. It is told in a queer style—a sort of strange compromise between the simplicity of the old ballad language and the superfine verbiage that was rising into esteem in Tickell's own day. Lucy, the reader may remember, is deserted by her lover for a richer bride. She cannot survive this cruelty. She says, to quote well-known lines,

> I hear a voice you cannot hear,
> Which says I must not stay.
> I see a hand you cannot see,
> Which beckons me away.

She is buried on the day of her false lover's marriage. The funeral cortège encounters the hymeneal. The bridegroom's old passion, too late, revives.

> Confusion, shame, remorse, despair
> At once his bosom swell;
> The damps of death bedew his brow;
> He shook, he groaned, he fell.

There is not the true note here, but there is a distant echo of it. In the handsome folio volume of poems published by Matthew Prior in 1718 was printed the "Not-Browne Maide," not for its own sake, but for the sake of a piece called "Henry and Emma," an extremely loose paraphrase of it, that the reader might see how magic was Mr. Prior's touch, who could transmute so rude an effort into a work so finely polished. However, Prior deserves some credit for having brought the old poem forward at all. His "Henry and Emma" won great applause. What a strange, instructive, significant fact, that when it and its original were placed before them, men should deliberately choose it! A morbid taste was prevailing with a vengeance. No plea that the language was obscure can be advanced in this case, as for Dryden's and Pope's versions of the *Canterbury Tales*. There is no obscurity in these words :

> O Lorde, what is
> This worldis blisse,
> That chaungeth as the mone!
> The somers day
> In lusty may
> Is derked before the none.
> I hear you say
> Farewel! Nay, nay.
> We departe not soo sone :
> Why say ye so?
> Wheder wyle ye goo?

Alas! what have ye done?
Alle my welfare
To sorow and care
Shulde chaunge yf ye were gon;
For in my mynde
Of all mankynde
I loue but you alone.

But Prior's age did not care for their simple beauty. It could not value that art *quæ celat artem*. It could not enjoy wild flowers. To the above delightful speech it preferred the following:

What is our bliss, that changeth with the moon,
And day of life, that darkens ere 'tis noon?
What is true passion, if unblest it dies?
And where is Emma's joy, if Henry flies?
If love, alas! be pain, the pain I bear
No thought can figure, and no tongue declare.
Ne'er faithful woman felt, nor false one feign'd
The flames which long have in my bosom reign'd;
The god of love himself inhabits there,
With all his rage, and dread, and grief, and care,
His complement of stores and total war.
O! cease then coldly to suspect my love,
And let my deed at least my faith approve.
Alas! no youth shall my endearments share,
Nor day nor night shall interrupt my care;
No future story shall with truth upbraid
The cold indifference of the nut-brown maid;
Nor to hard banishment shall Henry run,
While careless Emma sleeps on beds of down.
View me resolved, where'er thou lead'st, to go,
Friend to thy pain, and partner of thy woe;
For I attest fair Venus and her son,
That I, of all mankind, will love but thee alone.

Early in the reign of George I., then, the old ballads had grown insipid. Men had no longer eyes to see their wild graces. An age of rules was shocked by their fine irregularity. A moralising and sentimentalising age was horrified at their plain-spokenness and objectivity. A didactic age could conceive no interest in such spontaneous songs. It had narrow ideas of what is instructive, and it wanted instructing. It did not understand the singing as the linnet sings. It wanted its theories illustrated, discussed, enforced. In a word, it confounded poetry and morality. It did not cultivate, and it lost the faculty of pure enjoyment. No wonder then, if, finding no response to its ideas in the old ballads, it turned away from them, and would not answer when they called, would not dance when they piped.

But even at this time, when they were rapidly nearing the *nadir* of their popularity, the ballads found a friend. In 1723 appeared a volume of collected ballads, followed three years afterwards by a second, in 1727 by a third. These three volumes formed that first collection of English ballads (there is only one Scotch [1] ballad among them) to which we have above adverted. Denmark had made collections of its ballads in 1591 and in 1695; Spain in 1510, 1555, 1566, and 1615. England—save the earlier Garlands—first did so in 1723. Scotland, without, so far as we know, any knowledge of what had been done in England, in the following year, when Allan Ramsay, a great student of "the Bruce," "the Wallis," and Lyndsay's works,

---

[1] Songs and ballads of rustic and of humble life were called "Scotch" from about the middle of the 17th century, and without any intention of imputing to them a Scottish origin, or that they were imitations. The same had before been called "Northern." Mr. Payne Collier repeatedly reminds the readers of the Registers of the Stationers' Company that this word "northern" means "rustic." (See *Notes and Queries*, Dec. 28, 1861, p. 514; Feb. 8, 1862, p. 106; Feb. 21, 1863, p. 145.) The substitution of "Scotch" seems to have commenced during the civil war, and perhaps only after Charles II. had been crowned King of Scots, when "Scotch" at length became a popular, and even a party word with the Cavaliers. The first writer in whom I have noted the change is Martin Parker, author of the famous Cavalier ballad "When the King shall enjoy his own again." (See, for instance, "A pair of turtle doves, or a dainty new Scotch dialogue between a yong man and his mistresse," subscribed Martin Parker, *Pop. Music*, p. 452.) After him came Tom D'Urfey, and many more. The use extended till, at length, even ballads relating to the northern counties of England, and so, in every sense "northern," were reprinted as Scotch. (See, for instance, "Nanny O," *Pop. Music*, p. 610, note *a*.) This conventional meaning of "Scotch" seems to have been accepted in Scotland as well as in England, for in no other sense could Allan Ramsay claim, among others, Gay's ballad, "Black-ey'd Susan," in the very first part of "A miscellany of Scots Sangs," or W. Thomson appropriate songs by Ambrose Phillips and other well-known Englishmen, in his *Orpheus Caledonius*. This remark is necessary because Percy has, throughout, taken the words "northern" and "Scotch" only in their literal local sense. —W. C.

having "observed that Readers of the best and most exquisite Discernment frequently complain of our modern Writings as filled with affected Delicacies and studied Refinements, which they would gladly exchange for that natural strength of thought and simplicity of stile our Forefathers practised," published his " Ever-Green, being a collection of Scots Poems wrote by the Ingenious before 1600," and in the same year " The Tea-Table Miscellany, or a Collection of Scots Sangs, in three volumes." All three collections seem to have enjoyed a fair success. Who was the author of the English one is not known.[1] It is called " A collection of Old Ballads corrected from the best and most ancient copies extant, with Introductions, Historical, Critical, or Humorous, illustrated with copper plates." The editor adopts an apologetic motto for his book—some of the above-quoted words of Rowe. He writes, too, in an apologetic vein. " There are many," he says, " who perhaps will think it ridiculous enough to enter seriously into a Dissertation upon Ballads." He is evidently rather afraid of being thought a frivolous creature by his lofty-minded contemporaries. He is a little uneasy in introducing his protegées to the polished public. But he does his duty by them bravely, only indulging himself now and then in a little superior laugh at their expense. He gives what account he can of the theme of each one, and shows always a thorough interest in his work. But the time was not yet ripe for his labours. The popularity that attended the first appearance of his collection soon ceased. The predominant character of the age was not changed. The old voices could not yet secure a hearing. The age clung to its idols. Its Pharisaic spirit was too strong to be restrained. It could not yet believe that out of the mouth of the common people there was ordained strength.

After the middle of the century some promise was shown of

---

[1] Dr. Farmer ascribes it to Ambrose Phillips. See Lowndes, under "Ballads."
— W. C.

a better era. In Capell's "Prolusions, or Select Pieces of Antient Poetry, compil'd with great care from their several Originals, and offer'd to the Publick as Specimens of the Integrity that should be found in the Editions of Worthy Authors," published in 1760, appeared the "Not-browne Mayde," no longer accompanied by a modernised version. This book gives hints of the reaction that was coming against the old manipulating method. "Fidelity to the best Texts," is its watchword. In the same year (1760) appeared Macpherson's Ossian, and produced an immense sensation. Bishop Percy, with the good wishes and assistance of many then distinguished men—of Shenstone, Garrick, Joseph Warton, Farmer—was supplementing the treasures of his wonderful Folio MS. from other quarters, and preparing the materials of his *Reliques of Ancient English Poetry*. About the same time (1764) appeared Evans's "Specimens of the Poetry of the Antient Welsh Bards." Mallet's work on "the remains of the Mythology and Poetry of the Celtes, particularly of Scandinavia," had already been published some years.[1] About the same time Gray was writing his Welsh and Scandinavian pieces.[2] At the same time Chatterton was striving to satisfy the new taste that was spreading with forgeries of old poems.[3] The first decade, then, of George III.'s reign is most memorable in the history of the

[1] Mallet (P.-H.) Introduction à l'histoire de Dannemark, où l'on traite de la religion, des mœurs et usages des anciens danois etc. *Copenhague*, 1755-56. *Les Monumens de la Mythologie et de la Poesie des Celtes* (trad. des *Edda*) ouvrage qui fait partie de cette introduction, ont aussi paru séparément avec un titre particulier, en 1756. *Brunet.* Percy's translation was published in 1770.—F.

[2] In 1767 he [Gray] had intended a second tour to Scotland. At Dr. Beattie's desire, a new edition of his poems was published by Foulis at Glasgow; and at the same time Dodsley was also printing them in London. In both these editions, the "Long Story" was omitted. Some pieces of Welch and Norwegian poetry, written in a bold and original manner, were inserted in its place. *Mitford's Life of Gray, Works,* i. xlix.-l.—F.

[3] Published in 1777. He died Aug. 25th, 1770. His first article, purporting to be the transcript of an ancient MS. entitled "A Description of the Fryers' first passage over the Old Bridge," appeared in Farley's Journal, Bristol, Oct. 1768. *Penny Cycl.*—F.

revival of our ballad poetry. Then commenced an appreciation
of it which has grown stronger and stronger with the lapse of
years. Then it found itself so well supported that it was able
to hold up its head in spite of peremptory contemptuous
criticism. It feared no more the frowns of the great. Its
beauty was no longer to be hid—its light no longer veiled away
from men's eyes. " Even from the tomb the voice of nature
cried." In the midst of conventionalisms and artificialities,
Simplicity and Truth asserted themselves. The age was growing
sick and weary of its old darlings ; growing sensible that there
was no salvation in them, no infallibility, no supreme delight in
their worship :

Naturam expellas furcâ, tamen usque recurret.

Cinderella had sat by the kitchen fire for many a day. For
many a day the elder sisters, tricked out in all the modish
finery of the time, every attitude studied, every look elaborated
every movement affected, had possessed the drawing-room in all
their fashionable state. Cinderella down in the kitchen had
heard the rustle of their fine silks and satins, and the sound of
their polite conversation. She had been perplexed by their
polished verbiage, and felt her own awkwardness and rusticity.
She had never dared to think herself beautiful. No admiring
eyes ever came near her in which she might mirror herself.
She had never dared to think her voice sweet. No rapt ears
ever drank in fondly its accents. She felt herself a plain-
faced, dull-souled, uninteresting person, not worthy to receive
any attention from any one of the fine gentlemen who adored
her sisters, or to enter their well-mannered society. But her
lowliness was to be regarded. The songs she had sung in the
kitchen to the servants—her humble, unpretentious songs—
they were to find greater favour than ever did those of her
much-complimented sisters. She too was to be the *belle* of
balls. It was about the year 1760 when the possibility of so

great a change in her condition became first conceivable. She
met with many enemies, who clamoured that the kitchen was
her proper place, and vehemently opposed her admission into
any higher room. The Prince was long in finding her out.
The sisters put many an obstacle between him and her. They
could not understand the failure of their own attractions.
They could not appreciate the excellence of hers. But at last
the Prince found her, and took her in all her simple sweetness
to himself. At last, to lay metaphors aside, England acknowledged the power and beauty of the ballads that had
suffered for so long a time such grievous neglect.

At the accession of George III., William Whitehead was in
the third year of his adornment of the Poet Laureateship.
" The Pleasures of Imagination," " The Schoolmistress," " The
Complaint, or Night Thoughts on Life, Death, and Immortality"—works which had been given to the world some
sixteen or eighteen years before—were at the zenith of their
fame. The general character of our literature at this time
was wholly didactic. We cannot wonder, then, if the appearance of a poetry that was weighted with no overbearing moral,
or other purpose, produced a tremendous effect. We may be
prepared to understand the prodigious excitement caused by the
publication in 1760 of " The Works of Ossian the Son of Fingal,
translated from the Gaelic language by James Macpherson."
With all their magniloquence, they did not sermonise ; they
expressed some genuine feeling. Amidst all their affected cries
there was a true voice audible. Three years subsequently,
Bishop Percy, moved by Ossian's popularity, published a translation from the Icelandic language of five pieces of Runic poetry.

In the following year, 1764, appeared " Some Specimens of
the Poetry of the Ancient Welsh Bards translated into English,
with Explanatory Notes on the Historical Passages, and a short
Account of Men and Places mentioned by the Bards, in order

to give the Curious some Idea of the Taste and Sentiments of
our Ancesters and their Manner of Writing, by the Rev. Mr.
Evan Evans, curate of Glanvair Talyhaern in Denbighshire"
—a work with which Gray was familiar. Shortly afterwards
appeared Gray's own translations, made from translations,
of Norse and Welsh pieces : "The Fatal Sisters," "The
Descent of Odin," "The Triumphs of Owen," and "The Death
of Hoel." About the time, then, of the appearance of the
Reliques in 1765, there was dispersed over the country some
slight knowledge of the old Celtic and of Scandinavian poetry.

And now the age was ripe for the reception of such a collection of old ballads as had been published some forty years, but
had then, after a short-lived circulation, fallen into neglect.
Thomas Percy, the son of a grocer at Bridgenorth, Shropshire,
a graduate of Oxford, vicar of Easton Maudit, Northampton-
shire, was by nature something of an antiquarian. When "very
young," he became possessed of a folio MS. of old ballads and
romances. "This very curious old MS." he says in a memo-
randum made in the old folio itself, "in its present mutilated
state, but unbound and sadly torn, I rescued from destruction,
and begged at the hands of my worthy friend Humphrey Pitt, Esq.
then living at Shiffnal in Shropshire, afterwards of Prior Lee
near that town ; who died very lately at Bath ; viz. in Summer
1769. I saw it lying dirty on the floor under a Bureau in ye
Parlour: being used by the maids to light the fire." "When I
first got possession of this MS." he says in another entry in the
same place, "I was very young, and being in no degree an
Antiquary, I had not then learnt to reverence it; which must
be my excuse for the scribble which I then spread over some
parts of its margin; and in one or two instances, for even
taking out the leaves, to save the trouble of transcribing. I
have since been more careful." Besides this famous folio, he
possessed also a quarto MS. volume of similar pieces, supposed

to be the same as one still in the hands of his family, and containing only copies of printed poems. The folio has remained in the hands of the Bishop's family in the greatest privacy hitherto; Jamieson and Sir F. Madden being (I believe) the only editors who have printed from it, though Dibdin was allowed to catalogue part of it. It is now at last, as our readers know, being printed just as it is. These volumes had in Percy a (for that time) highly appreciative possessor. He determined to introduce to the public some specimens of their contents. This proposal was promoted by the sympathy of many then distinguished men: of Shenstone, Bird, Grainger, Steevens, Farmer, and by others of still greater and more enduring note—Garrick and Goldsmith. At last, in 1765 appeared *Reliques of Ancient English Poetry, consisting of Old Heroic Ballads, Songs, and other pieces of our earlier poets (chiefly of the Lyric kind) together with some few of later date.* The editor, even as the editor of the collection of 1723, of whom we have spoken, has, manifestly, some misgivings about the character of his protégées. He is not quite sure how they will be received by his polite contemporaries. He speaks of them, in his Dedication of his volumes to the Countess of Northumberland (he was extremely ambitious to connect himself with the great Percies of the North), as "the rude songs of ancient minstrels," "the barbarous productions of unpolished ages," and is troubled for fear lest he should be guilty of some impropriety in hoping that they " can obtain the approbation or the notice of her, who adorns courts by her presence, and diffuses elegance by her example. But this impropriety, it is presumed, will disappear when it is declared that these poems are presented to your Ladyship, not as labours of art but as effusions of nature, shewing the first efforts of ancient genius, and exhibiting the customs and opinions of remote ages." In his Preface he says that "as most of " the contents of his folio MS. " are of great simplicity, and seem to have

been merely written for the people, the possessor was long in
doubt, whether in the present state of improved literature they
could be deemed worthy the attention of the public. At length
the importunity of his friends prevailed." "In a polished age,
like the present, he adds, "I am sensible that many of these
reliques of antiquity will require great allowances to be made
for them. Yet have they, for the most part, a pleasing simplicity, and many artless graces, which in the opinion of no mean
critics [a foot-note cites Addison, Dryden, Lord Dorset &c., and
Selden] have been thought to compensate for the want of higher
beauties, and if they do not dazzle the imagination [Did "The
School-mistress," "The Sugar-cane," dazzle the imagination?]
are frequently found to interest the heart." Still more striking
are the following words : "To atone for the rudeness of the more
obsolete poems, each volume concludes with a few modern
attempts in the same kind of writing." And then he buttresses
his volumes with eminent names—Shenstone, Thomas Warton,
Garrick, Johnson (we shall see presently how far Johnson was
likely to smile on his undertaking), which "names of so many
men of learning and character, the editor hopes will serve as an
amulet, to guard him from every unfavourable censure for
having bestowed any attention on a parcel of Old Ballads. It
was at the request of many of these gentlemen, and of others
eminent for their genius and taste, that this little work was
undertaken. To prepare it for the press has been the amuse-
ment of now and then a vacant hour amid the leisure and
retirement of rural life, and hath only served as a relaxation
from graver studies. It hath been taken up and thrown aside
for many months during an interval of four or five years." With
such apologies and antidotes did the Reliques make their début !
How strange—what a wonderful tale of altered taste it tells—
that in order to make "Chevy Chase," "Edom o' Gordon,"
"Little Musgrave and Lady Barnard," endurable, to reconcile

the reader to their rudeness, such charming *chaperones* should be assigned them as " Bryan and Pereene, a West Indian ballad by Dr. Grainger," " Jemmy Dawson, by Mr. Shenstone " ! " Bryan and Pereene," " founded on a real fact," narrates how Pereene, " the pride of Indian dames," went down to the sea-shore to meet her lover, who, after an absence in England of one long long year one month and day, was returning to St. Christopher's and his mistress.

> Soon as his well-known ship she spied
> She cast her weeds away,
> And to the palmy shore she hied
> All in her best array.
>
> In sea-green silk, so neatly clad
> She there impatient stood ;

Bryan, seeing her in the said sea-green silk, impatient also, leapt overboard in the hope of reaching her sooner.

> The crew with wonder saw the lad
> Repell the foaming flood.
>
> Her hands a handkerchief display'd,
> Which he at parting gave ;
> Well-pleas'd the token he survey'd,
> And manlier beat the wave.
>
> Her fair companions one and all
> Rejoicing crowd the strand ;
> For now her lover swam in call,
> And almost touch'd the land.
>
> Then through the white surf did she haste,
> To clasp her lovely swain ;
> When ah ! a shark bit through his waist,
> His heart's blood dy'd the main.
>
> He shriek'd ! his half sprang from the wave,
> Streaming with purple gore,
> And soon it found a living grave,
> And ah ! was seen no more.

Now haste, now haste, yo maids, I pray,
Fetch water from the spring;
She falls, she swoons, she dies away,
And soon her knell they ring.

And so the doleful ditty ends with an injunction to the "fair,"
to strew her tomb with fresh flowerets every May morning, to
the end that they and their lovers may not come to similar
distress." Jemmy Dawson was one of the Manchester rebels
who took part in the '45, and was hanged, drawn, and quartered
on Kennington Common in 1746.

Their colours and their sash ho wore,
And in the fatal dress was found ;
And now he must that death endure,
Which gives the brave the keenest wound.

How pale was then his true love's cheek,
When Jemmy's sentence reach'd her ear ;
For never yet did Alpine snows,
So pale, nor yet so chill appear.

With faltering voice she weeping said,
Oh! Dawson, monarch of my heart,
Think not thy death shall end our loves,
For thou and I will never part.

Poor Kitty inflexibly witnesses his execution.

The dismal scene was o'er and past,
The lover's mournful hearse retir'd ;
The maid drew back her languid head,
And sighing forth his name expir'd.

Such were the pieces whose elegance was to make atonement
to the readers of a century ago, for the barbarousness of the
other components of the *Reliques*.

This barbarousness was further mitigated by an application
of a polishing process to the ballads themselves. Percy performed the offices of a sort of tireman for them. He dressed
and adorned them to go into polite society. To how great an
extent he laboured in their service, is now at last manifested by
the publication of the Folio. The old MS. contained many

pieces which, it would seem, were considered hopeless. No amount of manipulation could ever make them presentable. It contained many pieces and many fragments—thanks to the anxiety of Mr. Humphrey Pitt's servants to light his fires!—which the art of the editorial refiner of the eighteenth century deemed capable of adaptation; and Percy adapted them. The old ballads could reckon on no genuine sympathy. They were, so to speak, the songs of Zion in a strange land.

Percy, as the extracts we have quoted from his Dedication and Preface have shown, was not free from the prejudices of his time. He was but slightly in advance of them; but he *was* in advance of them. He *did* recognise the power and beauty of the old poetry, more deeply, perhaps, than he ever dared confess. And, though unconscious of the greatness of the work he was doing, did for us—for Europe—an unutterable service. He was, to the end, curiously unconscious of it. He had given a deadly blow to a terrible giant, and freed many captives from his thraldom, without knowing. Men are often reminded to be delicately careful in their actions, because they know not what harm they may do. They might sometimes be encouraged by the thought that they know not what good they do. Certainly Percy performed for English literature a far higher service than he ever dreamt of. He always regarded the *Reliques* as something rather frivolous. " I read ' Edwin and Angelina' to Mr. Percy some years ago," writes Goldsmith, in 1767, to the printer of the *St. James' Chronicle*, who had assigned Goldsmith's ballad to Percy, " and he (as we both considered these things as trifles at best) told me, with his usual goodhumour, the next time I saw him, that he had taken my plan to form the fragments of Shakespeare into a ballad of his own. He then read me his little cento, if I may so call it, and I highly approved of it." " I am so little interested about *the amusements of my youth*," writes Percy to his

publisher in 1794, " that, had it not been for the benefit of my
nephew, I could contentedly have let the *Reliques of Ancient
Poetry* remain unpublished." The great effect the memorable
work produced came " not with observation."

With all the consideration Percy showed for the prevailing
taste, he did not succeed in winning over to his support certain
great leaders of it. He was extremely solicitous to secure
the approval of the leader of the leaders of it—of that supreme
potentate, Dr. Johnson. In his Preface he twice mentions him :
first, as having urged him to publish a selection from the Folio
(" He could refuse nothing," he says, " to such judges as the
author of the *Rambler*, and the late Mr. Shenstone,"); and
secondly, as having lightened his editorial task with his assistance (" To the friendship of Mr. Johnson," he writes, " he owes
many valuable hints for the conduct of his work "). But, for all
these complimentary mentions, Johnson seems to have liked
neither the work nor its author, as may be seen in *Boswell*
again and again ; thus : " The conversation having turned on
modern imitations of ancient ballads, and some one having
praised their simplicity, he treated them with that ridicule
which he always displayed when that subject was mentioned."
The 177th number of the *Rambler* gives a satirical account of a
Club of Antiquaries. Hirsute, we are told, had a passion for
black-letter books ; Ferratus for coins ; Chartophylax for
gazettes ; " Cantilenus turned all his thoughts upon old ballads,
for he considered them as the genuine records of the natural
taste. He offered to show me a copy of The Children of the
Wood, which he firmly believed to be of the first edition, and
by the help of which the text might be freed from several
corruptions, if this age of barbarity had any claim to such
favours from him." In his Life of Addison, after a sarcastic
reference to his *Spectators* on " Chevy Chase," and Wagstaff's
ridicule of them, he adds, in modification of Dennis's *reductio*

ad absurdum of Addison's canon—that " Chevy Chase " pleases, and ought to please, because it is natural—" In Chevy Chase there is not much of either bombast or affectation, but there is chill and lifeless imbecility. The story cannot possibly be told in a manner that shall make less impression on the mind." With what horror the ghost of Sir Philip Sidney must have been struck if ever it was aware of this crushing dictum ! Still more suggestive are his observations on another old ballad. " The greatest of all his amorous essays," he remarks in his Life of Prior, " is Henry and Emma — a dull and tedious dialogue, which excites neither esteem for the man nor tenderness for the woman. The example of Emma, who resolves to follow an outlawed murderer wherever fear and guilt shall drive him, deserves no imitation [would Johnson have said that the " Laocoon," or the " Venus de Medici," deserved an imitation ? how could his critical rules have been applied to them ?], and the experiment by which Henry tries the lady's constancy is such as must end either in infamy to her or in disappointment to himself." With these terrible sentences in our ear, let us read these stanzas :

> Though it be songe
> Of old & yonge,
> That I shold be to blame,
>   Theyrs be the charge
> That speke so large
> In hastynge of my name ;
> *For I wyll prove*
> *That faythfulle love,*
> *It is devoyd of shame ;*
> In your dystresse,
> And hevynesse,
> To part with you the same ;
> And sure all tho
> That do not so
> True lovers are they none.
> For in my mynde
> Of all mankynde
> I love but you alone.

And,

> I thinke nat nay
> But as ye say,
> It is no mayden's lore ;
> But love may make
> Me for your sake,
> As I have sayd before,
> To come on foote
> To hunt, to shote
> To gete us mete in store ;
> For so that I
> Your companey
> May have, I ask no more.
> From which to part,
> It makyth my hart
> As colde as ony stone ;
> For in my mynde
> Of all mankynde
> I love but you alone.

Read these high passionate words, and think of Johnson's criticism.[1] He misses, evidently, the point of the poem—does not see how one noble idea permeates and vivifies every line, and glorifies the self-abandonment confessed.

> Here may ye see
> That women be
> In love, meke, kynde, and stable ;
> Late never man
> Reprove them than,
> Or call them variable ;
> But rather pray
> God that we may
> To them be comfortable.

His criticism of the " Nut-brown Maid " makes his dislike of the old ballads intelligible enough. We can understand now how he came to despise and abuse them, and parody their form in this wise :

---

[1] Cf. Mr. Gilpin's (Saurey-Gilpin, an artist, 1733–1807,) remark, *apud* Nichols and Steevens' *Hogarth*, on the seventh plate of the Rake's Progress : "The episode of the fainting woman might have given way to many circumstances more proper to the occasion. This is the same woman whom the Rake discards in the first print, by whom he is rescued in the fourth, who is present at his marriage, who follows him into jail, and lastly to Bedlam. The thought is rather unnatural, *and the moral certainly culpable.*"

The tender infant, meek and mild,
Fell down upon a stone;
The nurse took up the squealing child,
But still the child squeal'd on.

Warburton, Hurd, and others heartily concurred in his opinion. Warburton thought that the old ballads were utterly despicable by the side of the exalted literature of his own and recent times. He called them "specious funguses compared to the oak."

But in the face of this contumely, looked down on and sneered at by the learning and refinement of the age, the old ballads grew dear to the heart of the nation. They stirred emotions that had long lain dormant. They revived fires that had long slumbered. The nation lay in prison like its old Troubadour king; in its durance it heard its minstrel singing beneath the window its old songs, and its heart leapt in its bosom. It recognised the well-known, though long-neglected, strains that it had heard and loved in the days of its youth. The old love revived. The captive could not at once cast off its fetters, and go forth. But a yearning for liberty awoke in it; a wild, growing, passionate longing for liberty, for real, not artificial flowers; for true feeling, not sentimentalism; for the fresh life-giving breezes of the open country, not the languid airs of enclosed courts.

As one who long in populous city pent,
Where houses thick and sewers annoy the air,
Forth issuing on a summer's morn, to breathe
Among the pleasant villages and farms
Adjoin'd, from each thing met conceives delight,
The smell of grain, or tedded grass, or kine,
Or dairy, each rural sight, each rural sound,

so did the nation issue forth from its confinement, and conceive truer, more comprehensive joys.

The publication of the *Reliques*, then, constitutes an epoch in the history of the great revival of taste, in whose blessings we now participate. After 1765, before the end of the century, numerous collections of old ballads, in Scotland and in England, by Evans, Pinkerton, Hurd, Ritson, were made. The noble reformation, that received so great an impulse in 1765, advanced thenceforward steadily. The taste that was awakened never slumbered again. The recognition of our old life and poetry that the *Reliques* gave, was at last gloriously confirmed and established by Walter Scott. That great minstrel was profoundly influenced by the *Reliques*, both directly and indirectly, through Burger and others who had drunk deep of its waters.

"Among the valuable acquisitions," says Scott in his Autobiography, writing of his studies after his leaving Edinburgh High School, "I made about this time, was an acquaintance with Tasso's 'Jerusalem Delivered' through the flat medium of Mr. Hoole's translation. But above all I then first became acquainted with Bishop Percy's *Reliques of Ancient Poetry*. As I had been from infancy devoted to legendary lore of this nature, and only reluctantly withdrew my attention from the scarcity of materials and the rudeness of those which I possessed, it may be imagined, but cannot be described, with what delight I saw pieces of the same kind wheih had amused my childhood, and still continued in secret the Delilahs of my imagination, considered as the subject of sober research, grave commentary, and apt illustration by an editor who showed his practical genius was capable of emulating the best qualities of what his pious labour preserved. I remember well the spot where I read these volumes for the first time. It was beneath a huge plantaine tree, in the ruins of what had been intended for an old-fashioned arbour in the garden I have mentioned. The summer day sped onwards so fast that, notwithstanding the sharp appetite of thirteen, I forgot the hour of dinner, was sought for with anxiety, and was still found entranced in my intellectual banquet. To read and to remember was in this instance the same thing, and henceforth I overwhelmed my schoolfellows and all who would hearken to me with tragical recitations from the ballads of Bishop Percy. The first time too I could scrape a few shillings together, which were not common occurrences with me, I bought unto myself a copy of these beloved volumes; nor do I believe I ever read a book half so frequently or with half the enthusiasm."

ON "BONDMAN,"

THE NAME AND THE CLASS,

WITH REFERENCE TO THE BALLAD OF "JOHN DE REEVE."

By F. J. FURNIVALL.

— ◦✦◦ —

JOHNSON's definition of *bondman* is "a man slave." To it his latest editor, Dr. Latham, puts neither addition nor qualification; and the popular notion undoubtedly is, that whenever the word is used, of Early English times or modern, a *slave* is understood, one whose person, wife, children, and property, are wholly in his owner's power. We have to ask how far this popular notion is true with regard to our Bondmen, John de Reeue, Hobkin or Hodgkin long, and Hob o' the Lathe, and their class.

I do not find the word *bondman* in English till about 1250 A.D., taking that as the date of the *Owl and Nightingale*:

> Moni chapmon and moni cniht
> Lureþ and halt [1] his wif ariht;
> And swa deþ moni *bondeman*.
> (*Owl and Nightingale*, l. 1575, p. 49, ed. Stratmann, 1868.)

The earlier word was *bonde*, and the earliest the Anglo-Saxon *bonda*, which Thorpe rightly derives and defines as follows in his glossary to the *Ancient Laws*:

Bonda, boor, paterfamilias. This word was probably introduced by the Danes, and seems occasionally to have been used for *ceorl*; its immediate derivation is from O. N. *búandi*, contr[acted to] *bóndi*, villicus, colonus qui foco utitur proprio; part. pres. used substantively of *at búa*. Goth. *gabaúan* habitare; modern Danish *bonde*, peasant, husbandman.

Bosworth on the other hand defines *Bonda* as

1. One bound, a husband, householder. 2. A proprietor, husbandman, boor: *Bonde-land* land held under restrictions, copyhold.

[1] MS. Cot. *l/lad.*

Whether ' one bound ' (as if from *bond*, and -*a* one who has ; like *wæd* a garment, *wædu* one who has a garment,) is the original sense of the word, is more than doubtful ; and till the proof is produced, I reject the meaning as original,[1] though no doubt at a later period this sense prevailed over the Scandinavian one. Mr. Wedgwood says under Husband :

From Old Norse *bua* (the equivalent of G. *bauen*, Du. *bowen*, to till, cultivate, prepare) are *bu* a household, farm, cattle ; *buandi*, *bondi*,[2] N. *bonde* the possessor of a farm, husbandman ; *husbond* or

---

[1] *bóndi* (*d. i.* *bóandi* = *búandi*, *der Bonde*, *freier Grundbesitzer*, *Hausvater*, *pl. bœndr* mariti.—Möbius.

[2] Mr. Cockayne says " The word *Bond* bound has no existence but in Somner, whence others have copied it. Bosworth has built on *Bond* a guess, *Bonda* one bound, which is a delusion. For Bound, the true word is *bunden*, and for a Bond, *bend*." Mr. Earle also rejects the derivation from *bond*, and the meaning "one bound." Mr. Thorpe says that Ettmüller (p. 293) questions the *búandi, bóndi* derivation, but without sufficient grounds, in Mr. Thorpe's opinion. Haldorson accepts it "*Bondi* m. paterfamilias (quasi *bóandi, búandi*) en Husfader, Husbande, L. Colonus, ruricola, en Bonde, *Stórbœndr* prædicatores (Bonds with a large house and extensive ground), *Smabœndr* villici (Bonds with a small house and little yard)." Mr. Skeat notes " Bosworth also gives *Buend, bugend, bugigend*, as meaning an inhabitant, a farmer, from *búan*, to dwell, cultivate. This comes nearer to the Dan. and Sw. *bonde* as regards etymology, though it is not so near in form. Cf. A.-Sax. *búan*, Mœso-Goth. *bauan, gabauan*, to dwell, *bauains*, a dwelling-place. The G. *bauer*, peasant, is the Du. *boer*, and our *boor*. It is curious that the Du. *boer*, as well as the Sw. and Dan. *bonde*, signifies ' a pawn at chess.' I do not see how you distinguish between A.-Sax. *bonda* and A.-Sax. *buend*, unless you call the former a Danish word. In modern Danish the *d* is not sounded, and the *o* has an *oo* sound, so that *bonde* is called *boon-ne* (Lund's Danish Grammar)."

Professor Bosworth has kindly sent me the following note in support of the first meaning he assigns to *bonda*. It unfortunately came too late—in consequence of the illness of his amanuensis—to be worked up or noticed in the text. " Bunda, bonda, an ; *m.* I. *A wedded or married man, a husband* ; maritus, sponsus. II. *The father or head of a family, a householder* ; paterfamilias, œconomus. Then follow numerous examples, in proof of these meanings. I've gone over again all the examples, and I have enlarged what I had previously written, as to the origin of ' Bunda, bonda,' and given the detail in the following pages.—J. B." " Every word has its history by which its introduction and use are best ascertained. Bede tells us [Bk. I, 25, 2.] that Ethelbert king of Kent married a Christian, Bertha, a Frankish princess. The Queen prepared the way for the friendly reception of Augustine and his missionary followers, by Ethelbert in A.D. 597, who was the first to found a school in Kent, and wrote laws which are said to be "*ásette on Augustinus dæge*," *established in the time of Augustine*, between A.D. 597 and 604. The cultivation and writing of Anglo-Saxon [Englisc] began with the conversion of Ethelbert. Marriage, and the household arrangements depending upon it, were regulated by the law of the Church, and indigenous compound words were formed to express that law :—thus *æ̇ law, divine law* ; Cristes *æ̇ Christi lex*. Rihte *æ̇ legitimum matrimonium Bd.* 4, 5—*æ̇w wedlock, marriage, æ̇w-boren lawfully born, born in wedlock*—*æ̇w-brica m. wedlock breaker, m. an adulterer, æ̇w-brice f. an adultress, æ̇w-fæst-mann marriage-fast-man a wedded man, a husband* ; *æ̇w-nian to wed, take*

husband the master of the house. *Dan. bonde* peasant, countryman, villager, clown.

Where the word occurs in the Anglo-Saxon Laws, Thorpe translates it " proprietor," and then " husband," meaning " husband who is a proprietor."

Swa ymbe friðes-bóte, swa þam *bondan* si selost, ꝫ þam þeófan si laðost.—*Æthelredes Domas*, vi. xxxii.[1]

So concerning " frithes-bot," as may be best to the *proprietor* and most hostile to the thief.—*Ancient Laws*, i. 322–3.

---

a wife—ǽw-nung *wedding, marriage*—ǽw-wíf *a wedded woman.*—Hús-buuda, --bonda *a house binder, husband, householder.* This expressive compound is one of the oldest in the language. It is found in the interpolated passage of Matt. xx. between v. 28 and 29. The passage is in all the Anglo-Saxon MSS. of the Gospels, except the interlineary glosses. The *A.-Sax.* is a literal version of the Augustinian MS. in the Bodleian Library, Oxford [*Codex. August.* 857, *D.* 2, 14], from the Old Italic version, from which the Latin Vulgate of the Gospels was formed by St. Jerome about A.D. 384. Though we do not know the exact dates when the Gospels were translated from Latin into A.-Sax., Cuthbert assures us that Bede finished the last Gospel, St. John, on May 27, 735, [See Pref. to Goth. and A.-Sax. Gos. Bos. p. ix–xii]. As the three preceding Gospels were most likely translated before St. John, then the following sentence was written before 735, Se hús-bonda [hús-bunda in *MS. Camb. Ii.* 2, 11,] háte ðé árisan and rýman ðam óðrum, *the householder bid thee rise and make room for the other.* *Notes to Bosworth's Goth. and A.-Sax. Gos. Mt. xx.* 28 ; *p.* 576. Hús-bonda is also used by Ælfric in his version of the Scriptures about 970 [Ex. 3, 22.] Bunda, bonda *one wedded or bound, a husband,* from bindan ; *p.* band, bundon ; *pp.* bunden ; *to bind,* must have been of earlier origin than the compound hús-bunda. It is a well-known rule that in *A.-Sax. a person or agent* is denoted by

adding a,* as bytl *a hammer,* bytla *a hammerer,* ánweald *rule, government,* ánwealda *a ruler, governor,—*bunden, bund *bound,* bunda, bonda *one bound, a husband.* Bunda might be banda, as well as bonda, for *a* is often used for *o,* as monn for mann *a man.* The early use of hús-bunda, -bonda would at once indicate, that it was not likely to be of Norse or Icelandic origin. It could not be derived from the Norse búa *to dwell, part,* búandi bóandi *dwelling,* nor even from the cognate A.-Sax. búan *to dwell,* because the ú and ó are long in the *Norse* búa *to dwell,* búandi, bóandi *dwelling,* and the *A.-Sax.* búan *to dwell,* búende *dwelling,* búend, búenda *a dweller,* while the ú and o are always short in bunda and bonda. So in other compounds from bindan *to bind,* as bunde-land *bond or leased land, land let on binding conditions.* Bunda then is a pure Anglo-Saxon word, derived from bindan *to bind.* Búan *to dwell, with the part.* búende *dwelling,* and the noun búend, es ; *m. a dweller,* is quite a distinct word. Búend has its own numerous compounds ; as,—Land-búend *a land dweller, a farmer* ; agricola. An-búend *one dwelling alone, a hermit* : ceaster-, eg-, corp-, feor-, fold-, grund-, her-, ig-, land-, neah-, sund-, woruld- and þeódbúend."

[1] Ethelred, son of Edgar, succeeded to the throne, on the murder of his brother Edward, in the year 978, and died in 1016.—Thorpe's note in *Laws and Inst. of England,* vol. i. p. 280.

---

* To a substantive, not a verb or participle.—F.

Again, in the same sentence nearly repeated in *Cnutes Domas*, viii. (Canute died 12 Nov. 1035) " þam *bondan*, for the *proprietor*," p. 380–1. At p. 414–15, *Cnutes Domas*, lxxiii.

Conjux incolat eandem Sedem quam Maritus.

LXXIII. And pær se *bonda* sæt unwyd ꝛ unbecrafod, sitte þ wif ꝛ þa cild on þan ylcan unbesacen. And gif se *bonda* ær he dead wære, beclypod wære, þonne andwyrdan þa yrfenuman, swa he sylf sceoldo þeah he lif hæfde.

And where the *husband* dwelt without claim or contest, let the wife and the children dwell in the same, unassailed by litigation. And if the husband, before he was dead, had been cited, then let the heirs answer, as himself should have done if he had lived.

So the Laws of King Henry the First (who reigned 1100–35 A.D.), repeating the last provision, say :

§ 5 Et ubi *bunda* manserit sine calumpnia, sint uxor et pueri in eodem, sine querela &c.—*Ancient Laws*, i. 526.

In 1048 A.D. the Saxon Chronicle uses *bunda* for a householding cultivator or farmer :

Đa he [Eustatius] wæs sume mila oððe mare bebeonan Dofran . þa dyde he on his byrnan . and his ge-feran ealle . and foran to Dofran . þa hi þider comon . þa woldon hi innian hi þær heom sylfan gelicode . þa com an his manna . and wolde wician æt anes *bundan*[1]. huse, his undances . and gewundode þone *husbundon* . and se *husbunda*[2] ofsloh þone oðerne. Đa weard Eustatius uppon his horse . and his ge-feoran uppon heora . and ferdon to þan *husbundon* . and ofslogon hine binnan his agenan heorðæ . and wendon him þa up to þære burge-weard . and ofslogon ægðer ge wiðinnan ge wiðutan . ma þanne xx manna.—*Saxon Chronicle*, ed. Earle, p. 177 (A.D. 1048.)

When he [Eustathius] was some miles or more beyond Dover, then put he on his armour, and all his companions (did likewise), and went to Dover. When they came thither, then would they lodge where they pleased. Then came one of his men, and would dwell at the house of a *cultivator* (or householder) against his will, and wounded the *cultivator*; and the *cultivator* slew the other. Then Eustathius got upon his horse, and his companions on theirs, and went to the *cultivator*, and slew him within his own hearth ; and

---

[1] bundan, *gen. sing. goodman*, 1048. *Glossarial Index*.

[2] The equivalence of the *husbunda* with the *bunda* here is enough to ex-

plode the "moral-etymology" of a *husband* being so called because he is the band or binder-together of the house, even if Dr. Bosworth be right.

went then up to the guard of the city, and slew both within and without more than 20 men.

In a passage in *Hickes* the (no doubt) free *bunda*, paying a fine, is contrasted with the *thrœll* who gets a flogging :

And ȝif hwa ðis ne ȝclæste . þonne ȝebete he ꝥ swa swa hit ȝelaȝod is . *bunda* mid xxx pen. ðræl mid his hyde . peȝn mid xxx scill.—From Hickes's *Dissertatio Epistolaris*, p. 108.

And if any one does not perform this, then let him make amends for that as is laid-down-by-law : the *bonde* with xxx pence, the thrall with his hide, the thane with xxx shillings.

Thus far then the evidence—for I do not admit Bosworth's " one bound " as right—points to the *bonde* being a freeman, and if not a landed proprietor, still a free tenant. The evidence of the freedom is strengthened if we may regard the Danish-named *bonde* as a Saxon-named *churl*—the name of one seeming to be used for the other, as Mr. Thorpe observes, for the *ceorla* was a free man, the " ordinary freeman " of Anglo-Saxon society, though obliged by " the feudal system " which " may be traced throughout all Anglo-Saxon history, to provide himself with a lord, that he might be amenable to justice when called upon." [1] Still, this vassalage was no *bondage* in the later or the modern sense of the term ; the vassal churl was a freeman still, if we may trust Heywood.

In Alfred's time, and later, the *ceorl* had slaves. Sec. 25 of Alfred's Laws (translated) is :

If a man commit a rape upon a *ceorl's* female slave (mennen), let him make bōt (amends) to the *ceorl* with 5 shillings, and let the *wíte* (fine) be 60 shillings. *Anc. Laws*, i. 79.

The A.-S. laws of Ranks enact that,

if a *ceorl* thrived, so that he had fully five hides of his own land, church and kitchen, bell-house, and " burh"-gate-seat, and special duty in the king's hall, then was he thenceforth of thane-right worthy.—*Anc. Laws*, i. 191.

Thorpe defines *ceorl* thus :

Ceorl. O.H.G. *charal*. A freeman of ignoble rank, a churl, twy-hinde man, villanus, illiberalis.

Twyhynde (*Man*), a man whose '*wér-gild*' was 200 shillings. This was the lowest class of Anglo-Saxon aristocracy. *Twelf-hynde*

---

[1] Heywood's *Distinctions in Society*, 1818, p. 325.

(*Man*), a man whose *wér-gild* was 1200 shillings. This was the highest class of Anglo-Saxon aristocracy.

The slave was a þræl or þeow. Mr. Thorpe considers þræl to be a Scandinavian word.

Next comes the question, did these bondes or ceorls continue free till the time of the Conquest? Kemble says not:

‘ Finally, the nobles-by-birth themselves became absorbed in the ever-widening whirlpool ; day by day the freemen, deprived of their old national defences, wringing with difficulty a precarious subsistence from incessant labour, sullenly yielded to a yoke which they could not shake off, and commended themselves (such was the phrase) to the protection of a lord ; till a complete change having thus been operated in the opinions of men, and consequently in every relation of society, a new order of things was consummated, in which the honours and security of service became more anxiously desired than a needy and unsafe freedom ; and the alods being finally surrendered, to be taken back as *beneficia*, under mediate lords, the foundations of the royal, feudal system were securely laid on every side.—Kemble, *The Saxons in England*, vol. i. p. 184.

The very curious and instructive dialogue of Ælfric numbers among the serfs the *yrðling* or ploughman,[1] whose occupation the author nevertheless places at the head of all the crafts, with perhaps a partial exception in favour of the smith's.—Ibid. p. 216.

Mr. C. H. Pearson also says not :

Not only were slaves increasing, but freemen were disappearing. The ceorl is never mentioned in our laws after Edward the elder's time. If he became the villan of a later period, he was already semi-servile before the Norman conquest. If he passed into the freeman,[2] sometimes holding in his own right, and sometimes under a lord's protection, the class did not number 5 per cent. of the population at the time when Domesday was compiled, was virtually confined to Norfolk and Suffolk, and had not even a representative in the counties south of the Thames. It is evident that the bulk of the Saxon people was in no proper sense, and at no time free. Even the free in name were virtually bound down to the soil with the possession of which their rights were connected, and from which their subsistence was derived ; . . . the idea that any man might go where he would, live as he liked, think or express his thoughts freely, would have been repugnant to the whole tenour of a constitution which started from the Old Testament as a model, preserved or incorporated the traditions of Roman law, and regarded the regulation of life as the duty of the legislator.

---

[1] This should be compared with the second extract from *Havelok* below.

[2] Had he not always been free?

The mention of *villan* brings us to the Conquest[1] and to Domesday-book. On every page of the latter *villani* are mentioned, and the articles of enquiry for the composition of it show that the enquiry into the population and property of each district " was conducted by the king's barons, upon the oaths of the sheriff of each county, and all the barons, and their French-born vassals, and of the hundredary (reeve of the hundred), priest, steward, and *six villeins of every vill*," &c. (Heywood, p. 290, note). The question for us is, are we to take as free men or not these villans, who were to help in settling what " served for centuries as the basis of all taxation, and the authority by which all disputes about landed tenures and customs were decided," who were to state " on oath what amount of land there was in the district, whether it was wood, meadow, or pasture, what was its value, what services were due from its owners; and generally the numbers of free and bond on the estate " (*Pearson*, i. 374).

The arguments of Serjeant Heywood for the identity [2] of the *villein* with the *ceorl* or *twihynde man* seem to me very strong indeed; and Mr. Pearson tells me that in the earlier use of the word *villanus*, the first which he knows,—namely, that in the preamble to the Decree of the Bishops and Witan of Kent about keeping the peace under Athelstan, which speaks of *Thaini, Comites, et Villani*,—he thinks that " villan " means " ceorl " very literally.

Serjeant Heywood first shows that the *Textus Roffensis*, in explaining a passage from the *Judicia Civitatis Lundoniæ* like that quoted above from the Anglo-Saxon Laws [3] " makes it

---

[1] Of the name *villanus* Serjt. Heywood says, " I have not met with it in any authentic documents till about the time of the Conquest, but it is found in the laws of Edward the Confessor, William the Conqueror, and Henry the first. Among the Saxons were many words descriptive of persons engaged in husbandry, as ceorls, cyrlisc men, geneats, tunesmen, landsmen, &c., but the proper appellation for a villan has not been ascertained."—Pp. 290-1. But see the next paragraph above.

[2] Mr. Pearson says we must " understand it with the reservation that while the vast majority of the ceorl class had degraded into the position of villans, others were distributed in the different ranks of society as freemen, socmen, and perhaps in some cases bordars and cottars. It must be remembered that the *Rectitudines Singularum Personarum* use the word *villanus* to translate the Saxon *geneat*, and that the word *ceorla* does not occur in the whole document."

[3] De gentis et legis honoribus. Fuit quondam in legibus Anglorum ea gens et lex pro honoribus, et ibi erant sapientes populi honore digni, quilibet pro sua ratione; comes et *colonus*, thanus et rusticus (*corl and ceorl, thegen and theowen*).

Et si colonus tamen sit, qui habeat integras quinque hydas terræ, ecclesiam et culinam, turrim sacram (*bell hus*) et

relate to villan and not to ceorls (L. *coloni*), whence we may infer that the author considered them as the same persons " (*Disser- tation*, p. 185). He next shows that the eighth law of William the Conqueror, which makes the were of a villan only 100 shillings, was probably wrongly transcribed ; and that the seven- tieth law of Henry I. expressly defines the free twihind as a villan :—" the were of a twihind, that is, a villan, is five pounds : *twyhindi, i. villani, wera est IV lib'*;"—and the 76th law classes the twihinds among the free men. Also that

in other parts of the laws, villans are ranked with ceorls and twihinds. Moreover the weres of a cyrlisc man & [that is, or] a villan are ex- pressly mentioned, and required to be regulated in the same manner as that of a twelfhind.[1]—*Heywood*, p. 295.

Another proof may be adduced from their being liable to the pay- ment of reliefs which never were called for from the servile class. When, therefore, provision was made in the laws of William the Conqueror for the exaction of a relief from every villan, of his best beast, whether a horse, an ox, or a cow, we must conclude that, at the time of compiling those laws, namely, about four years after the Conquest, a villan was a freeman,

and this notwithstanding the concluding words of the law, *et postea sint omnes villani in franco plegio*, which must be taken as confirming an old truth, for the payment of one relief —which villans before the Conquest had paid—could not have turned an unfree man into a free one. Serjeant Heywood adds :

Another powerful argument in favor of the supposition that villans ranked among freemen, arises from the consideration that, unless this had been the case, the bulk of the population of England must have been found in the servile class. We cannot imagine that the farmers, who held at the payment of rent, either in money or kind, could be so very numerous as to furnish victuals for the armies which were collected, provide members for all the tythings, and crowd the public assemblies which were held for judicial purposes. But upon the demesne lands of almost every lord, villans might be found, and if they were admitted to bear the name, and partake of the privileges of freemen, and rank with ceorls or twihinds, the difficulty vanishes (p. 300).

atrii sedem (*burhgeat setl*) ac officium distinctum (*sunder note*) in aula regis, ille tunc in posterum sit jure thani (*thegen rihtas*) dignus.—*Heywood*, p. 184. *Text. Roff.* 46 has for *colonus* of the above, *villanus*. " Et si *villanus* ita crevisset sua probitate, quod pleniter habere quinque hidas de suo proprio allodii &c. *ib.* p. 185.

[1] Eodem modo per omnia *de cyrlisci vel villani* wera fieri debet secundum modum suum, sicut de duodecies cen- teno diximus.—*Ll. Hen.* i. 76; *Wilkins*, 270, in *Heywood*, p. 295 n.

Professor Pearson looks on the villans as 'bond upon bond land,' and as to the numbers of them and the freemen and the population generally at Domesday, gives Sir Henry Ellis's and Sir James Macintosh's calculations as follows:

We may probably place it [the population] at rather over than under 1,800,000; a number which may seem small, but which was not doubled till the reign of Charles II., six hundred years later. Reverting to the actual survey, we find about two thousand persons who held immediately of the king (E 1400, M 1599), or who were attached to the king's person (M 326), or who had no holding, but were free to serve as they would (M 213). The second class, the free upon bond-land, comprised more than 50,000; under-tenants or vavasors (E 7171, M 2899); burghers (E 7968, M 17,105); soc-men (E 23,072, M 23,404); freemen, holding by military service, or having been degraded into tenants to obtain protection (E 14,284); and ecclesiastics (E 994, M 1564). The largest class of all was the semi-servile. Of these villeins (E 108,407, M 102,704), and bordars,[1] or cottiers (E 88,922, M 80,320), make up the mass, about 200,000 in all. They were bond upon bond-land, that is to say, their land owed a certain tribute to its owner, and they owed certain services to the land; they could not quit it without permission from their lord. But they were not mere property; they could not be sold off the soil into service of a different kind, like the few slaves who still remained in England, and who numbered roughly about 25,000.

The large number of the middle classes, and the small number of slaves, are points in this estimate that deserve consideration. It is clear that the conquest did not introduce any new refinement in servitude. In a matter where we have no certain data, all statements must be made guardedly; but the language of chroniclers and laws, and the probabilities of what would result from the anarchy and war that had so long desolated England under its native kings induce a belief that the conquest was a gain to all classes, except the highest, in matters of freedom. In Essex the number of freemen positively increased, and the change may probably be ascribed to the growing wool-trade with Flanders, as we find sheep multiplying on the great estates, and with the change from arable to pasture-land fewer labourers would be required. The fact that the large and privileged class of soc-men was especially numerous in two counties, Norfolk and Suffolk, in which a desperate revolt had been pitilessly put down, seems to show that existing rights were not lightly tampered with. In Bedfordshire, however, the soc-men were degraded to serfs, probably through the lawless dealing of its Angevine sheriff, Raoul Taillebois, and the county accordingly fell off in rental beyond any other in

---

[1] Heywood draws a distinction between the villans and bordars. cottars, &c., who are generally mentioned after them in Domesday.

England south of Humber, though it had enjoyed a singular exemption from all the ravages of war.

The concluding paragraph of the foregoing extract is printed because in it is, for me, pointed out the true cause of the villan's hardships, of the exactions of which his class so bitterly complained, the character of the Norman baron, and his power over his dependants. The thirtieth law of Henry I. speaks in moderated phrase the spirit of the earlier time. It calls the villans with the *cocseti* and *pardingi* (probably bondmen inferior to the villans) *hujusmodi viles vel inopes personæ*, declares them disqualified to be reckoned among judges, excludes them from bringing any civil suits in the county or hundred courts, and refers them, for the redress of injuries, to the courts of their own barons (Heywood, p. 291).[1]

And it is (I believe) precisely because Edward I. made a resolute attempt to break down this power of the barons over their villans,[2] which must have often been awfully abused,—and not only tried to, but did to some extent substitute his own judges' court for the barons' one[3]—thereby rescuing many a villan from a bondman's fate; it is for this reason that he is the hero of our ballad of *John de Reeve*. Not only for the long shanks with which he strode against Wales, or the hammer he wielded against Scotland, was the first king who conceived and fought for the unity of Great Britain dear to the villans of

---

[1] Villani vero, vel cocseti vel pardingi vel qui sunt hujusmodi viles vel inopes personæ, non sunt inter legum judices numerandi, unde nec in hundredo vel comitatu pecuniam suam, vel dominorum suorum forisfaciunt, si justitiam sine judicio dimittant, sed summonitis terrarum dominis inforcietur placitum termino competenti, si fuerint vel non fuerint antea summoniti cum secuti jus æstimatis.— *LL.Hen.*i.c.30; *Wilkins*,248, in *Heywood*. p. 292.

[2] One of the first Acts of his (Edward I.'s) Administration, after his Arrival from the Holy Land, was to inquire into the State of the Demesnes, and of the Rights and Revenues of the Crown, and concerning the Conduct of the Sheriffs and other Officers and Ministers, who had defrauded the King and grievously oppressed the People (Annals of Waverley, 235) *Hundred Rolls*, i. 10. On the

inquiries of this Commission the first chapter of the Statute of Gloucester, relating to Liberties, Franchises and Quo Warranto (by what warrant the Parties held or claimed) was founded (*ib.*).

[3] See below, and also the Statute of 4 Edw. I. A Statute concerning Justices being assigned, called Rageman. "It is accorded by our Lord the King, and by his Council, that Justices shall go throughout the Land to inquire, hear, and determine all the Complaints and Suits for Trespasses committed within these twenty-five years past, before the Feast of Saint Michael, in the fourth year of King Edward ; as well by the King's Bailiffs & Officers as by other Bailiffs, & by all other Persons whomsoever. And this is to be understood as well of outrageous Takings, and all Manner of Trespasses, Quarrels, and Offences done unto the King and others,

his own [1] and after times. His steps and his blows came nearer their homes, and did something to clear oppressors out of their path. When in easier days they could sing of olden time, they gave the long king a merry night with three of their kin, and remembered with gratitude England's "first thoroughly constitutional" sovereign. This I gather from one of a series of interesting articles on the "Rights, Disabilities, and Wages of the English Peasantry" in the new Series of the *Law Magazine and Review*. But I am anticipating.

In the time of Edward I. bondage was looked upon as no part of the common law ; it existed by sufferance and by local usage, and was recognised, but only barely tolerated by the law. The law was on the side of freedom. A leaper or land-loper, as a fugitive was called, could rarely be recovered in a summary manner ; if he chose to deny his bondage, the writ of niefty did not give the Sheriff authority to seize him ; the question of his condition had to stand over until the Assizes, or had to be argued in the Court of Common Pleas.— *Law Mag.* 1862, vol. xiii, p. 38-9.

We need not attribute a long range of foresight, or very enlightened views of freedom, to the counsellors of Edward I. Their resistance to villenage was instinctive rather than deliberate. Villenage in their eyes appeared to be a consequence of those powers of local jurisdiction which had been indispensable in former times on account of the weakness of the central power, but were no longer wanted since the central power had become truly imperial. The same landlords who claimed a right to keep their dependents in bondage, usually claimed some degree of judicial power ; they claimed to have a more or less extensive cognizance over crimes committed, and criminals arrested within their precincts. Such a claim could only rest upon prescription ; any such pretension not

touched in the Inquests heretofore found by the King's command, as of Trespasses committed since. And the King willeth, that for Relief of the People (*pour le allegaunce del poeple*) and speedy execution of Justice, That the Complaints of every one be heard before the aforesaid Justices, & determined, as well by Writ as without, according to the Articles delivered unto the same Justices ; & this is to be understood as well within Franchise as without. Also the King willeth that the same Justices do hear and determine the Complaints of those who will complain of Matters done by any one contrary to the King's Statutes, as well of what concerneth the King as the people." See also the Statutes of Gloucester or *Quo Warranto* of 6 Edw. I.

"And the Sheriffs shall cause it to be commonly proclaimed throughout their Bailliwicks, that is to say, in Cities, Boroughs, Market towns, and elsewhere, that all those who claim to have any Franchises, by the Charters of the King's Predecessors, Kings of England, or in other manner, shall come before the King, or before the Justices in Eyre, at a certain day and place, to show what sort of Franchise they claim to have, and by what Warrant."

[1] I do not forget the groans of "The Song of the Husbandman" (temp. Edw. I.) printed in Wright's *Political Songs* for the Camden Society.

supported by immemorial usage would soon be upset by the King's attorney. The general Government struggled hard to extend its jurisdiction, to extinguish the private courts, to bring as many cases as possible before the Courts at Westminster, and before the Justices in Eyre. The private courts were not abolished, but gradually superseded. After all that the lords could do to keep their villeins from Assizes, villeins constantly became jurors, and bond-lands were constantly drawn into the King's Courts, and were thus in the way to be drawn into freeholds. Perhaps every circuit of the judges emancipated a number of bondmen.—*Ib.* p. 40.

In seeking for the light in which the Norman baron would regard his Saxon villans, I think that Mr. Thomas Wright[1] is justified in his adduction of the following instances,

The chronicler Benoit (as well as his rival Wace) extols Duke Richard II. for the hatred which he bore towards the agricultural or servile class : " he would suffer none but knights to have employment in his house ; never was a villan or one of rustic blood admitted into his intimacy ; for the villan, forsooth, is always hankering after the filth in which he was bred."—p. 237,

þe þridde cumeð efter, & is wurst likclare, ase ich er seide : vor he preiseð þene vuele, & his vuele deden, ase þe þe seið to þe knihte þet robbeð his poure men, " A, sire ! hwat tu dest wel. Uor euere me schal þene cheorl pilken & þeolien : nor he is ase þe wiði, þet sprutteð ut þe betere þat me hine ofte cropped."	The third flatterer cometh after, and is the worse, as I said before, for he praiseth the wicked and his evil deeds ; as he who said to *the knight that robbed his poor vassals*, "Ah, sire ! truly thou doest well. For *men ought always to pluck and pillage the churl* ; for he is like the willow, which sprouteth out the better that it is often cropped.

—*Ancren Riwle* (? ab. 1230 A.D.) p. 87, Camden Soc. 1853 (quoted in part by Wright).

and in referring to those most interesting Norman-French satires on the villans that M. Francisque Michel published, and which contain such passages as the following :

> Que' Diex lor envoit grant meschief,
> Et mal au cuer, et mal au chief,
> Mal ès bouche, et pis ès dens,
> Et mal dehors, et mal dedens . . .
> Et le mal c'on dist ne-me-touche.
> Mal en orelle, et mal en bouche !
> (*Des XXIII Manières de Vilains*, Paris, 1833, p. 12.)

---

[1] Paper on the political condition of the English Peasantry during the Middle Ages, in *Archæologia*, vol. xxx. p. 205-44.

" Why should villans eat beef, or any dainty food ? " inquires the writer of *Le Despit au Vilain* ; " they ought to eat, for their Sunday diet, nettles, reeds, briars, and straw, while pea shells are good enough for their every-day food. . . . They ought to go forth naked, on bare feet in the meadows to eat grass with the horned oxen. . . . The share of the villan is folly, and sottishness and filth ; if all the goods and all the gold of this world were his, the villan would be but a villan still."—*Wright*, p. 238.[1]

Though Mr. Wright's conclusion as to " the condition of the English peasant or villan during the 12th, 13th, and 14th centuries " may be exaggerated, yet much truth in it there must be :

Tied to the ground on which he was born in a state of galling bondage, exposed to daily insult and oppression, he served a master who was a stranger to him both by blood and language. The object of his lord's extortions, frequently plundered with impunity, and heavily taxed by the king, he received in return only an imperfect and precarious security for his person or his property. The villan was virtually an outlaw ; he could not legally inherit or hold " lordship," and he could bring no action, and, as it appears, give no testimony in a court of law. He was not even capable of giving education to his children, or of putting them to a trade, unless he had previously been able to obtain or purchase their freedom, which depended on his own pecuniary means, and on the will and caprice of the lord of the soil.

All Norman barons were not brutes of the Ivo Taillebois [2] type, but I look on it as certain that the bitter cry of the villans which reaches us from the pages of the old chroniclers and writers is not a mere bit of rhetoric, but speaks what the villans and poor really suffered and felt.

I also look to the generations immediately succeeding the Conquest for the growth of the legal view of villanage and its consequences which is stated by Littleton (ab. 1480 A.D.) and

[1] On the property needed for a Norman villan to marry on, see the tract *De l' Oustillement au Villain* (xiiie siècle) Paris 1863.

[2] He was one of the most cruel and hateful scoundrels who ever defaced God's earth. He used to make the poor Saxons serve him on bended knee, and then in requital burned their houses, drowned their cattle, and set his bulldogs to torment them. With diabolical cruelty he made them incapable of work by breaking their limbs and backs ;— and as the Chronicle declares, " he twisted, crushed, tortured, tore, imprisoned and excruciated them." See also Henry of Huntingdon's account of Robert de Belesme, Earl of Shropshire. " He preferred the slaughter of his captives to their ransom. He tore out the eyes of his own children, when in sport they hid their faces under his cloak. He impaled persons of both sexes on stakes. To butcher men in the most horrible manner was to him an agreeable feast." (*Farrar*.)

Coke, among others, from Bracton, Fleta, &c. and which justified any amount of rapacity and exaction on the part of the
feudal superior.   There were two classes of villans, 1. *regardant*,
attached to the soil of a manor, and sold with it like a cowshed
or an ox, but seemingly not liable to be removed from it, though
Littleton's words allow the removal ; 2. *in gross*, landless, and
attached to the person of a lord, and saleable or grantable to
another lord, like a chattel.

Littleton translated (ed. 1813). § 181.   Also there is a villein regardant, and a villein in gross.   A villein regardant is, as if a man
be seised of a manor to which a villein is regardant, and he which
is seised of the said manor, or they whose estate be both in the
same manor, have been seised of the villein and of his ancestors
as villeins and neifs[1] regardant to the same manor, time out of
memory of man.   And villein in gross is where a man is seised of
a manor, whereunto a villein is regardant, and granteth the same
villein by his deed to another ; then he is a villein in gross, and not
regardant.

§ 172.   Tenure in villenage, is most properly when a villein
holdeth of his lord, to whom he is a villein, certain lands or tenements according to the custom of the manor, or otherwise at the
will of his lord, and to do his lord villein service, as to carry and
recarry the dung of his lord out of the city, or out of his lord's
manor, unto the land of his lord, and to spread the same upon the
land, and such like.

Or as Coke puts it, fol. 120 *b.*

He is called regardant to the mannour, because he had the
charge to do all base or villenous services within the same, and to
gard and keepe the same from all filthie or loathsome things that
might annoy it : and his service is not certaine, but he must have
regard to that which is commanded unto him.   And therefore he
is called regardant, *a quo præstandum servitium incertum et inde-
terminatum, ubi scire non potuit respere quale servitium fieri debet
mane, viz. ubi quis facere tenetur quicquid ei præceptum fuerit*
(Bract. li. 2, fo. 26, Mir. ca. 2, sect. 12) as before hath beene observed (vid. sect. 84).

He says also at fol. 121 *b.*

Things incorporeall which lye in grant, as advowsons, villeins,
commons, and the like, many be appendant to things corporeall,
as a mannour, house, or lands.

As illustrations of the truth and the working of these legal

---

[1] A woman which is villein is called a *neif*, § 186.

doctrines, take the following instances out of many. About 1250 A.D., says Mr. Wright in *Archæol.* vol. xxx, quoting Madox's Formulare Anglicanum 318–418,

The abbot and convent of Bruerne sold "Hugh the shepherd, their naif or villan of Certelle, with all his chattels and all his progeny, for 4*s.* sterling;" and the abbot bought of Matilda, relict of John the physician, for 20*s.*, "Richard, son of William de Estende of Linham, her villan, with all his chattels and all his progeny;" and for half a mark of silver, a villan of Philip de Mandeville "with all his chattels and all his progeny."
: Early in Henry III. (1216–72 A.D. his reign) Walter de Beauchamp granted by charter "all the land which Richard de Grafton held of him, and Richard himself, with all his offspring." . . In 1317 Roger de Felton gave to Geoffry Foune certain lands, tenements &c. in the town and territory of Glanton, "with all his villans in the same town, and with their chattels and offspring."

We may also note the dictum of Cowel's Institutes: "Villaines are not to marry without consent of their patrons."—*W. G.'s translation*, 1651, p. 24.

But the sharpest pinch of the matter lay in the theory—and practice often, I do not doubt—that all the villan's goods were his lord's,[1] that whatever the lord took from him, he had no remedy against the lord for.

Sect. 189, fol. 123 *b.* Also, every villein is able and free to sue all manner of actions against everie person, except against his lord, to whom he is villeine.

On which Coke says:

For a villeine shall not have an appeale of robberie against his lord, for that he may lawfully take the goods of the villeine as his own (18 Edw. 3, 32; 11 Hen. 4, 93; 1 Hen. 4, 6; 29 Hen. 6, tit. Coron. 17). And there is no diversitie herein, whether he be a vilein regardant or in grosse, although some have said the contrary.

And look at what early book you will,—Homilies, Political Songs, Robert of Brunne[2], Chaucer, Gower, &c.—if it touches the subject at all, you are sure to find the lords' and their stewards' arbitrary extortions complained of and reproved.

Before quitting this branch of the subject it may be well to quote on it the words of the editor of Domesday, Sir Henry

---

[1] Cp. the extract from Chaucer, p. 554–5 below.

[2] See the quotation from his *Handlyng Synne* below.

Ellis. After a longish quotation from Blackstone's Commentaries upon the villani, he says (*General Introduction to Domesday Book*, vol. i. p. 80):

There are, however, numerous entries in the Domesday Survey which indicate the Villani of that period to have been very different from Bondmen. They appear to have answered to the Saxon Ceorls, while the Servi answered to the Deowas or Esnen. By a degradation of the Ceorls and an improvement in the state of the Esnen, the two classes were brought gradually nearer together, till at last the military oppression of the Normans thrusting down all degrees of tenants and servants into one common slavery, or at least into strict dependance, one name was adopted for both of them as a generic term, that of *Villeins regardant*.

The next questions are, how long were the words *bonde* and *bondman* used for the villan class; and when did their bondage cease; or at least, did it continue, and if so, with what amelioration did it continue, up to the time when our ballad may be supposed to have been written?

As the names require extracts, the two questions may be treated together.

Archdeacon Hale, writing of the land and villans of the Priory of St. Mary's, Worcester, in or about 1240 A.D. says:

The quantity of land in villenage in each manor being fixed, and the quantity of labour due from it fixed also, it follows that the lords of manors were not arbitrary masters who had unlimited power over the person and property of these tenants. There is, however, too much reason to believe that, taking into account the labour of various kinds to which the holder of a small quantity of villan land was liable, he paid what was equivalent to a high rent. His position as a holder of land, which would descend to his family, was superior to that of the modern labourer; and yet he might not be better off in a pecuniary point of view. His place in society was marked also by the obligation to give "Thac et Thol, auxilium et merchet, et in obitu melius catallum." (*Thac* was "Pig-money, a payment made by the villans to the lord in the autumn for every pig (the sows excepted), of a year old one penny, and under the year a halfpenny. *Thol*, the Penny paid by the villans for licence to sell a horse or ox." *Hale*, p. xx, xli. On *Thol*, see also p. lii.)

This fixity of rent, and Professor Rogers's pleasant view of things, make one side of the question; the legal power of the lord over all his villan's property, and the exactions out of him complained of by preachers, poets, and writers, the other.

In *Layamon* the word *bonde* is used once, in the description of the treacherous slaughter of Vortiger and his companions by Hengest and his:

Earlier text, 1200–20.	Later text, bef. 1300.
þer wes ot Salesburi	þar was a *bond* of Salusburi,
an oht *bonde* icumen;	þat bar on his honde
ænne muchelne mein clubbe	ane mochele club,
he bar on his rugge.	for to breke stones.

The earlier text Sir F. Madden translates:

There was a bold *churl* [1] of Salisbury come; he bore on his back a great strong club.

In one of a series of interesting articles on the "Rights, Disabilities, and Wages of the Ancient English Peasantry," in the *Law Magazine and Review*, New Series, xi. 259, &c., I find at p. 263, under the date of 1279 A.D.

At the same place [Mollond at Castle Camps, in the south-eastern corner of Cambridgeshire] there were several [27] tenants, [four of whom are women,] described as *Bondi*, bondmen.[2] One of them [i.e. each, except 12 who held in couples] held 16 acres of land in villenage. It does not appear that he paid any mail or gable. He returned a goose and a hen, worth 3d., 20 eggs worth $\frac{1}{2}$d., and a quarter of oats worth 12d. He worked for the lord twice a week from Michaelmas to Pentecost, and thrice a week from Pentecost to Michaelmas, and ploughed nine acres in the year. It is plain that this man was an operative tenant.[3]

Havelok the Dane comes next, and in it the bondman is the peasant or ploughman:

Thider komen bothe stronge and wayke;
Thider komen lesse and more,
That in the borw thanne weren thore;
Champiouns, and starke laddes,
Bondemen with here gaddes,
Als he comen fro the plow;
There was sembling inow:
(ed. Madden, p. 39, l. 1012–1018.)

Another drem dremede me ek,
That ich fley over the salte se
Til Engeland, and al with me
That euere was in Denemark lyues,

---

[1] *Ceorl* is used in the book in the general sense of *man*.

[2] ? Bondes, who might be freemen. They are given between the Customary Tenants and the Cottars.

[3] *Bondi*. Hugo Ruge tenet xvi. acras terre in villenagio, & dat j aucam et j gallinam, & valent iij d.; xx. ova quæ valent obolum [$\frac{1}{2}$d.], & j quarterium avenæ quod valet xijd., & facit a festo Sancti Michaelis usque Pentecostam, etc. —2 *Hundred Rolls* (ed. 1818), 425, col. 1.

But *bondcmen*, and here wines,
And that ich kom til Engelond,
Al closede it intil min hond,
And Goldeboro y gaf the :—
       (*The same*, p. 50, l. 1304-1311.)

In the *Song of the Husbandman*, of the reign of Edward I.
(1272–1307 A.D.) in Wright's *Political Songs*, Camden Soc.
p. 150, *bonde* represents the " peasant " class.

Thus me pileth the pore, and pyketh ful cleno,
The ryche raymeth withouten euy ryht ;
Ar londes and ar leodes liggeth fol leno,
Thorh b[i]ddyng of baylyfs such harm heth hight.
Meni of religione we halt hem ful hone,
Baroun and *bonde*, the clere and the knyght.
       (MS. Harl. 2253, leaf 64.)

In 1297, taking that as Robert of Gloucester's date, he says
of William the Conqueror and his ' high men : '

Hii to-draweth þe sely *bonde men*, as wolde hem hulde ywys.—
ii. 370.

which the latter reading gives as

Hii tormenteth hure *tenauntes*, as hulde hem they wolde.

Again in one of the *Lives of Saints*, said to have been written
by Robert of Gloucester, is this passage :

If a *bondeman* hadde a sone : to clergie idrawe,
He ne scholde, without his loverdes leve : not icrouned beo.
       (ab. 1300-10 A.D. *Life of Beket*, l. 552.)

Robert of Brunne, in the lifelike sketch which he gives us of
the England—or, at least, the Lincolnshire—of 1303, as he
tells the men of his day of their sins, of course does not forget
the bondman and his lord, of course remembers the poor :

Blessyd be alle poorë men,
For God almyȝty loueþ þem.
       (*Handlyng Synne*, p. 180, l. 5741-2.)

One tale that he tells shows a certain independence on the
part of a bondman, and I therefore take that first, from the
Handlyng Synne, p. 269-70. In a Norfolk village a knight's
house and homestead (manor) were near the churchyard,
into which his herdsmen let his cattle, and they defiled the
graves. A *bonde man* saw that, was woe that the beasts
should there go, went to the lord, and said, "Lord, your herdsmen do wrong to let your beasts defile these graves. Where

men's bones lie, beasts should do no nastiness." The Lord's
answer was "somewhat vile," "A pretty thing indeed to honour
such churls' bones! What honour need men pay to such churls'
livid bodies?" And then the bonde-man said him words full
well together laid :

> The lord that made of earth-e, earls,
> Of the same earth made he churls :
> Earlès might, and lordès stut, (strut)
> As churlès shall in earth be put,
> Earlès, churlès, all at ones ; (once)
> Shall none know your, from our, bones.

Which reproof the lord took in good part (few would have
done so, says Robert of Brunne [1]), and promised that his beasts
should no more break into the churchyard.

But still there is evidence enough in the *Handlyng Synne*
that if a lord wanted a bondman's wife or daughter, he would
not only carry her off, but brag of it afterwards (p. 231, l.
7420–7) ; and as to the treatment of the poor by their superiors,
Robert of Brunne asks—he is not here translating Wadington—

> Lord, how shul þese robbers fare,
> Þat þe pore pepyl pelyn ful bare,—
> Erlès, knygtès, and barouns
> And ouþer lordyngës of tounnes,
> Justyses, shryues and baylyuys,
> Þat þe lawès alle to-ryues,
> And þe pore men alle to-pyle ?
> To ryche men do þey but as þey wylle.—
> (p. 212, l. 6790–7.)

He goes on denouncing them who " pyle and bete many pore
men," and contrasts their conduct with that of Dives to Lazarus,
whom Dives did not rob of gold or fee,

> He dyde but lete an hounde hym to :
> Ye rychë men, weyl wers ʒe do !
> Ye wyl noun houndes to hem lete,
> But, ʒo self, hem *sle and bete*.
> He ne dyde but wernede hym of hys mete ;
> And ʒe robbe al þat ʒe mow gete.
> Ye are as Dyues þat wyl naghte ʒgue ;
> And wers : for ʒe robbe þat þey [the poor] shulde by lyue.
> (*Handlyng Synne*, p. 213, l. 6812–19.)

In a previous passage the lords' arbitrary exactions from

---

[1] þyr are but fewë lordës now
Þat turne a wrde so wel to prow ;
But who seyþ hem any skylle, .
Mysseye aʒen fouly þey wylle.

Lordynges,—þyr are ynow of þo ;
Of gentyl men, þyr are but fo
[few].

men in bondage—or *vileynage* as Wadington has it—are expressly mentioned:

> And ʒyf a lorde of a tounne
> Robbe his men oute of resoune,
> þoghe hyt be yn *bondage*,
> Aʒens ryʒt he doþe outrage.
> He shal so take þat he [the bondman] may lyue,
> And as lawe of londe wyl forʒyue ;
> For ʒyf he take ouer mesure,
> Lytyl tymé shal hyt dure.
> þoghe God haue ʒeue þe seynorye,
> He ʒaf hym no leue to do robborye ;
> For god haþ ordeyned al mennys state,
> How to lyue, and yn what gate ;
> And þoʒt he ʒyue one ouer oþer myʒt,
> He wyl þat he do hym but ryʒt.
> þys ys þe ryʒt of Goddys lokyng :
> ʒelde euery man hys owne þyng.
> But God takeþ euermore veniaunce
> Of lordys, for swych myschaunce,
> For swych robbery þat þey make,
> þat ofte of þe poure men take.

He then tells a tale of what a Knight suffered in Purgatory
(or hell) fire, for robbing a poor man of a cloth, and winds
up with the moral :

> Certys þefte ryʒt wykkede ys . . .
> Namly[1] pore men for to pele
> Or robbe or bete wyþ-oute skyle.[2]

The next reference to the word in Stratmann's *Dictionary* is
to *William and the Werwolf*, (better, *William of Palerne*:
E. E. Text Soc. 1868, *Extra* Series,) of ab. 1340 A.D. l. 216.

> do quickliche crie þurth echo cuntre of þi king-riche
> þat barouns burgeys & bonde[3] & alle oþer burnes
> þat mowe wiʒtly in any wise walken a-boute
> þat þei wende wiʒtly as wide as þi reaume.
>
> (*William and Werwolf*, p. 77, ed. Madden.)

In William of Malvern's[4] *Vision of Piers Ploughman*, about
1362 A.D. we have :

[1] especially.

[2] reason.

[3] Bonde, *n*. S. Bondsmen, villains ; as
opposed to the orders of barons and
burgesses, 77.—*Glossary to the above*.
But the *bonde* are still one of the three
principal orders of men, as shown by
the " other burnes " who are not worth
specifyiug.—Skeat.

[4] Mr. Hales's name for the author of
the *Vision*, who is sometimes called
Langland. As there is no real evidence
for the name Langland, I prefer the
vaguer title William of Malvern, though
Malvern is only mentioned in the first
of the poems of which the *Vision* is
composed.

> Barouns and Burgeis · and *Bonde-men* also
> I sanȝ in þat Semble.—(p. 6, l. 96, ed. Skeat.)

In Wright's edition of the *Vision*, i. 88, l. 2859 is—

> And as a *bonde*-man of his bacon his berde was bidraveled.

And part of the knight's duty is—

> And misbeode þou not þi *bondemen* · þe beter þou schalt spede.
> (Pas. vii. l. 45, Vernon Text, ed. Skeat, p. 76.)

In the third text of the *Vision* we read—

> *Bondmen* and bastardes · and beggers children,
> These bylongeth to labour · and lordes children sholde serven,
> Bothe God and good men · as here degree asketh
>
>   ·   ·   ·   ·   ·   ·   ·
>
> And sith, *bondemenne* barnes · han be made bisshopes,
> And barnes bastardes · han ben archidekenes ;
> And sopers and hero sones · for selver han be knyghtes,
> And lordene sones here laboreres.—(ab. 1380. *Vision of Piers Plowman.*
>   Whitaker's text. Passus Sextus.)

Mr. Skeat says that the various readings in the MSS. of the *Vision* show that *bondage* or *bondages* was used for *bonde-men*, and that *bonde* is thus connected with the verb to *bind*. Chaucer uses *bondemen* and *bondefolk* [1] as the equivalents of *cherls* and *thralles* in his Persones Tale, *de Avaritia* (p. 282 ed. Wright, quoted below, p. 554-5), while in The Frere's Tale the use is of one bound :

> Disposith youre hertes to withstonde
> The fend, that wolde make yow thral and *bonde*. [2]

The year 1394, or thereabouts, gives us that wonderful picture of a bondeman or ploughman whom its painter *saw*,

---

[1] And fortherover, ther as the lawe sayth, that temporel goodes of *bondefolk* been the goodes of her lordes ; ye, that is to understonde, the goodes of tho imperour, to defende hem in here righte, bent *not to robbe hem ne to reve hem.*

[2] In the Elegy on the Death of King Edward III. the phrase "bide her bonde" is glossed "remain as their captive."

> This goode schip, I may remene
>   [so]
> To the Chilvalrye of this londe,
> Sum time thei counted nouȝt a bene.
> Beo al Ffrance Ich understonde

> Thei tok & slouȝ hem with heore honde
> The power of Ffrance both smal and grete,
> And brouȝt ther Kyng hider to bide her *bonde*.
> And nou riȝt sone hit [the ship] is forȝete.

Myre's use of *bonde* is this:

> Fyrst þow moste þys mynne,
> What he ys þat doth þe synne,
> Wheþer hyt be heo or ho,
> Ȝonge or olde, *bonde*, or fre,
> Pore or ryche, or in offys.
> (Ab. 1430, Myre, *Instructions for Parish Priests*, p. 47.)

and which will not be out of the mind of anyone who has studied it:

> And as y wente be þe waie · wepynge for sorowe,
> [1] seiȝ a sely man me by · opon þe plow hongen.
> His cote was of a cloute · þat cary was y-called,
> His hod was full of holes · & his heer oute,
> Wiþ his knopped schon · clouted full þykke;
> His ton tuteden out · as he þe londe treddede,
> His hosen ouerhongen his hokschynes · on eueriche a side,
> Al beslombred in fen · as he þe plow folwede;
> Twey myteynes, as mete · maad all of cloutes;
> Þe fyngers weren for-werd · & ful of fen honged.
> Þis whit waseled in þe [fen] · almost to þe ancle,
> Foure roþeren hym by-forn · þat feble were [worþen];
> Men myȝte reken ich a ryb · so reufull þey weren.
> His wijf walked him wiþ · wiþ a longe gode,
> In a cutted coto · cutted full heyȝe,
> Wrapped in a wynwe schete · to weren hire fro weders,[1]
> Barfote on þe bare ijs · þat þe blod folwede.
> And at þe londes ende layo · a litell crom-bolle,
> And þeron lay a litell childe · lapped in cloutes,
> And tweyne of tweie ȝeres olde · opon a-no þer syde,
> And alle þey songen o songe · þat sorwe was to heren;
> Þey crieden alle o cry · a carefull note.
>
> (*Pierce the Ploughman's Crede,* l. 420–441, ed. Skeat, 1867.)

Those last two lines sum up for me the English history of the English poor (as has been said elsewhere), it was "full of care."

Frater Galfridus, about 1440, has in the Promptorium

> Bonde, as a man or woman, *Servus, serva.*
> Bondman . *Servus, nativus* [neif.]
> Bondschepe . *Nativitas*: but Bondage . *Servitus.*

That the lord's power over his bondmen was a reality, and that he "frequently took advantage of his power to tyrannize, is proved by the example of Sir Simon Burley, the tutor of Richard II., who seized forcibly an industrious artizan at Gravesend, on the plea of his being his escaped bondsman, and, when his exorbitant demand was refused, threw him into the prison of Rochester Castle."—(Wright in *Archæol.* xxx. 235.) And that the Lord's power over his bondman existed into the 16th century is shown by the following extracts.[2]

---

[1] It is a wyues occupation, to *vynowe all manner of cornes*, to make malte, to washe and wrynge, to make heye, shere corne, and in time of nede to helpe her husbande to fyll the mucke-wayne or dounge-carte, *dryue the ploughe*, to loode hay, corne, and suche other. ? 1523.—Fitzherbert's *Husbandry,* ed. 1767, p. 92.

[2] Mr. Wright says, "We can trace these charters of manumission [of villans] down to a very late period. In 2

In 1519 among the Duke of Buckingham's payments in Prof. Brewer's *Calendar*, iii., Pt. i. p. 498, is—

25 March, to Walter Parker, 40£, " restored to him for a fine by him made to me, for that he was my *bondman*, and made free during his life, for that I gave him a patent."

In 1521 on

"The Duke's Lands . . at Caurs (in Wales) are " Many *bondmen* both rich and poor.—*ib.* p. 509.

In 1523 (?), Fitzherbert says :

Customary tenauntes/ are those that holde their landes of their lorde by copye of courte role/ after the custome of the manere. And there may be many tenauntes with-in the same manere y[t] have no copyes/ and yet holde be lyke custome and seruyce at the wyll of the lorde. and in myne opinyon/ it began soone after the conquest/ whan Wyllyam Conquerour had conquered this realme/ he rewarded all those that came with hym in his voyage royall accordyng to their degre. And to honourable men he gaue/ lordshippes/ maners/ landes/ and tenementes/ with all the inhabytauntes/ men and women dwellyng in the same/ to do with them at their pleasure. And those honourable men thought y[t] they must nedes haue seruauntes and tenauntes/ and their landes occupyed with tyllage. Wherfore they pardoned the inhabytauntes of their lynes/ and caused them to do all maner of seruyce that was to be done/ were it neuer so vyle/ and caused them to occupye their landes and tenementes in tyllage and toke of them suche rentes/ customes/ and seruyces/ as it pleased them to haue. And also toke all their goodes & catell at all tymes at their pleasure/ and called them their *bonde men*, and sythe that tyme/ many noble men bothe spirytuall and temporall, of their godly disposycion/ haue made to dyuers of the sayd *bonde men* manumissions, and graunted them fredome and lybertie. and set to them their landes and tenementes to occupy/ after dyuers maners of rentes/ customes/ and seruyces, the whiche is vsed in dyuers places vnto this daye. how be it in some places the *bonde men* contynue as yet/ the whiche me semeth is the grettest inconuenyent that nowe is suffred by the lawe. That is, to haue any christen man bonden to another/ and to haue the rule of his body/ landes and goodes/ that his wife chyldren and seruauntes haue laboured/ for all their lyfe tyme/ to be so taken/ lyke as and it were extorcion or bribery. And many tymes

---

Ric. II., just before the peasants' insurrection, John Wyard or 'Alspach' manumits a female villan, and gives her, with her liberty, her goods and chattels, and the liberty of all her offspring : and we have a charter of affranchisement by the priory of Beauvalle in 6 Hen. V. A.D. 1419, and another by George Nevile, lord Bergevenny, as late as 2 Hen. VIII., A.D. 1511."

by colour therof/ there be many fre men taken as *bonde men*/and
their landes and goodes taken fro them/ so that they shall not be
able to sue for remedy to prove them selfe fre of blode. And that
is moost commenly where the fre men have the same name as the
bonde men haue/ or that his auncestors of whome he is comen/ was
manumised before his byrthe. In suche cause there can nat be to
great a punysshement. for as me semeth there shulde no man be
bonde but to god/ and to his king and prince ouer hym. Quia deus
non facit exceptionem personarum. For god maketh no excepcyon
of any person.—Fitzherbert's *Boke of Surveycny & Improumentes*
Cap. xiii. fol. xxvi.

I do not carry these extracts further, because those that have
been given—and they might be ten-folded with ease—sufficiently prove the reality of the hardships which the bondmen
suffered, and that certain of these hardships were in being as
late as Fitzherbert's time, about 1520. Vague talk that the
doctrine of the law-books was never carried out in practice,
that monkish writers exaggerated a molehill into a mountain
&c., will not do in the face of the evidence that literature
supplies. "Master Fitzherbarde" was not a sentimentalist, but
a practical horsebreeder, farmer and surveyor,[1] and spoke of the
bondmen's evils as he would speak of his broodmares' ailments.
There is no need for us then to imagine—as Professor Rogers
does, in his very valuable and interesting *History of Prices*, i.
81—a cause, of which no trace has come down to us, for Wat
Tyler's rebellion. Cause enough, and to spare, there was in
the condition of the men, if only that shown in their demand
"that we, our wives and children, shall be free." Granted that
the students of literature and charters alone get from them too
dark a view of the state of the early poor,—as Mr. Wright may
have done—yet we must declare that the student of prices on
college lands alone gets a too rose-coloured view, and that the
wrongs of the bondmen were real and deep; even Chaucer and
Froissart witness it.

On this *bonde* and *bondeman* question I conclude then, though
with much diffidence, and acknowledging the insufficiency of the
evidence for some points: 1, that the *bonde* was originally free,
that he was the Saxon ceorl or twihind, with a Danish name;
2, that if not partially before, yet wholly after, the Conquest,
his class, or the greater part of it, became bondmen or villans,
bond on bond-land; 3, that gradually they threw off their ser-

---

[1] It must be a mistake to identify him with Sir Anthony Fitzherbert.

vice and signs of bondage, taking the first decided step in advance in Edward I.'s time, the second and more decided one in Edward III. and Richard II.'s time; 4, that in 1520 the burden of bondage was still heavy. (It gradually disappeared,[1] except so far as our present copyhold fines and heriots represent it. Slavery was abolished by a statute of Charles II. The attempt to abolish it in 1526 proved a vain one. *Wright.*)

But our bondman was John *the Reeve*, though no special duties of his as Reeve are alluded to in the Ballad. On those duties in Anglo-Saxon times the reader may consult the references in Thorpe's Index to the *Ancient Laws*, vol. i., and section 12 of the *Institutes of Polity*, in vol. ii. p. 320–1. The office of Reeve was one that every villan was bound to serve, and although the *Law Magazine* says it was one which the villan rather declined and avoided,[2] it must have been one which, in later times at least, helped to fill its holder's pockets. The Reeve's duty was to manage his lord's demesne, to superintend the service-tenant's work on it, to collect the lord's dues and rent in money and kind, and submit his accounts yearly to the auditor. As the Sloane MS. *Boke of Curtesye* says of the greve or reve—

Granys, and baylys and parker,
Schone come to acountes euery yere
Byfore þo auditour of þo lorde onone,
Þat schulde be trew as any stone,
Yf he dose hom no ryȝt lele,
To a baron of chekker þay mun hit pele.
(*Babees Book*, p. 318, l. 589–94.)

And as William of Malvern says—

[1] The name seems to have lasted longer in Scotland than in England; see Jamieson's Dictionary, 4to, 1825, Supplement:
"BONDAGE, Bonnage, *s.* Tho designation given to the services due by a tenant to the proprietor, or by a cottager to the farmer. [Used in] Angus."
"Another set of payments consisted in services, emphatically called *Bonage* (from bondage). And these were exacted either in seed-time, in ploughing and harrowing the proprietor's land,—or in summer, in the carriage of his coals, or other fuel; and in harvest, in cutting down his crop."—*Agricultural Survey of Kincardineshire*, p. 213.

The late abridgement of Jamieson gives "*Bonday Warkis*, the time a tenant or vassal is bound to work for the proprietor."
[2] The chief incidents of base tenure which affected the villein's person are collected in one of Edward II.'s Yearbooks, (5 Ed. II.) They were,—1. The blood fine, or marriage ransom; 2. the taille or tallage, a variable charge, supplanted by regular taxation, unless it endured under tho name of chevage; 3. the obligation of undertaking the office of reeve or bailiff, an invidious dignity which the villein rather declined and avoided.—*Law Mag. & Rev.* xiii. 41.

I make Piers the Plowman my procuratour and my reve,
And registrar to receyve.[1]

Redde quod debes (v. ii. p. 411, ed. Wright).

And again—

Thanne lough ther a lord, and "by this light" seide,
"I holde it right and reson, of my reve to take
Al that myn auditour, or ellis my steward
Counseileth me bi hir acounte and my clerkes writyng.
With *spiritus intellectus* thei seke the reves rolles ;
And with *spiritus fortitudinis* feeche it I wole after."

(*Vision*, ii. 423.)

Need one quote Chaucer's sketch of the Reeve—

Wel cowde he kepe a gerner and a bynne ;
Ther was non auditour cowde on him wynne.
Wel wiste he by the drought, and by the reyn,
The yeeldyng of his seed, and of his greyn.
His lordes scheep, his neet, [and] his dayerie,
His swyn, his hors, his stoor, and his pultrie,
Was holly in this reeves governynge,
And by his covenaunt yaf the rekenynge,
Syn that his lord was twenti yeer of age ;
Ther couthe noman bringe him in arrerago.
Ther nas baillif, ne herde, ne other hyne,
That they ne knewe his sleight and his covyno ;
They were adrad of him, as of the deth.
His wonyng was ful fair upon an heth ;
With grene trees i-schadewed was his place.
He cowde bettre than his lord purchace.
Ful riche he was i-stored prively,
His lord wel couthe he plese subtilly,
To geve and lene him of his owne good,
And have a thank, a cote, and eek an hood.
In youthe he lerned hadde a good nester ;
He was a wel good wright, a carpenter.
This reeve sat upon a wel good stot,
That was a pomely gray, and highte Scot.
A long surcote of pers uppon he hadde,
And by his side he bar a rusty bladde.

Our Reeve too has "a rusty bladde," rides a good horse, has a
fair dwelling, and is "ful riche istored prively," but Hodgkin Long
and Hob of the Lathe are "not adrad of him as of the deth."
As he was the King's reeve and should have collected taxes [2] as
well as dues and rents,[3] he ought to have been a good scribe and
summer-up, but the ballad does not read as if he was. His

---

[1] See the extract at the end of this paper, line 12 from foot.
[2] If Mr. Toulmin Smith be right in his view, p. 557 note below.

[3] Toulmin Smith's *Parish*, p. 506, refers to a rentcharge paid to the King's reeve.

enemy is not the auditor, of whom we hear nothing, but the courtier or purveyor who could report his wealth to the King, and get leave, or take it, to put the screw on him. He sells his wheat (l. 144) to get it out of sight (?);—money could be more easily hidden ;—and he has a thousand pounds and some deal more.

The supper of his pretended poverty—bean-bread, rusty bacon, broth, lean salt beef, and sour ale, may well have been bondman's food in Edward I.'s time, better than many got in Edward III.'s, as William of Malvern shows (*Vision*, Passus VII. l. 267–82, ed. Skeat, p. 88–9, text A) ; but could the supper of his actual wealth, boar's head and capons, woodcocks, venison, swans, conies, curlews, crane, heron, pigeons, partridges, and sweets of many kinds, have been ever Reeve's food then ? I trow not. Chaucer's Frankeleyn couldn't have given a better spread in Richard II.'s time, and John Russell's Franklen in Henry VI.'s days (ab. 1450–60 A.D., say,) hardly exceeded it :

A Fest for a Franklin.

" A Franklen may make a feste Improberabille,
brawne *with* mustard is concordable,
bakon *ser* ued *with* pesoñ,

beef or motoñ stewed scruysable,
Boyled Chykoñ or capoñ agreable,
convenyent for þo sesoñ ;

Rosted goose & pygge fulle profitable,
Capoñ / Bakemete, or Custade Costable,
wheñ eggis & craymo be gesoñ.

þerfore stuffe of houschold is behoveable,
Mortrowes or lusselle ar delectablo
for þe second course by resoñ.

Thañ veel, lambe, kyd, or cony,
Chykoñ or pigeoñ rosted tendurly,
bakemotes or dowcettes *with* alle.

þeñ followynge frytowrs, & a leche lovely ;
suche seruyse in sesonn is fulle semely
To serue *with* bothe chambur & halle.

Theñ appuls & peris *with* spices delicately
Aftur þe terme of þe yere fulle deynteithly,
with bred and chese to calle.

Spised cakes and wafurs worthily
withe bragot & methe, þus meñ may meryly
plese welle bothe gret & smalle."

(Babees Book, p. 170-1.)

Edward I.'s order for his own coronation feast was 380 head
of cattle, 430 sheep, 450 pigs, 18 wild boars, 278 flitches of
bacon, and 19,660 capons and fowls (Macfarlane, *Cab. Hist.* iv.
11, referring to Rymer). Only in bacon, boar, and capons
could the king have come up to his reeve. To what date
then are we to bring the ballad down? I don't know, and,
if the reason I have assigned for its being tacked on to
Edward I. be the right one, I don't care; for the main
point to me is its connection with him. But taking the ballad
as it stands, the mention of the *Galliard* in it, l. 530, p. 579,
shows that it was recast, if not composed, after 1541, when that
dance was introduced. Also the Northern forms *baine*, l. 504,
gonge, l. 209, 343, 864, *strang*, l. 332, *seile*, l. 502, *ryke*, l. 263,
farrand, l. 353, 358, &c., the present no-rhymes of *both* and *lath*,
l. 623–4, 641–2, *arse* and *worse*, l. 668–9, *kneele* and *soule*, l.
806–7, &c., show that our version is an altered copy of a Northern
original, or Northern copy. I say copy, because if *lathe* is the
Anglo-Saxon *laδ*, a division of the county peculiar to Kent,
the scene of the ballad must have been Kent; but Chaucer's use
of the word in its sense of barn, in his *Reeve's Tale*—

> Why nad thou put the capil in the *lathe?* [1]

and Brockett's in his *Glossary of North Country Words*,

> *Lathe* or *Leathe*, a place for storing hay and corn in winter—a
> barn.

saves us from the necessity of supposing a double transformation
of the ballad, though this would be authorised by the ascription
of it to "the south-west country" in l. 909. The Northern
saint sworn by in l. 744, St. William, Archbp. of York in the
12th century, tends to confirm the Northern origin, as does the
"clerke out of Lancashire" who read the roll that contained the
tale, l. 8–12.

---

[1] The *Promptorium* gives "Berno of
lathe (or lathe P.), *Horreum*," p. 33, and
Mr. Way says, "Lathe, which does
not occur in its proper place in the
Promptorium, is possibly a word of
Danish introduction into the eastern
counties," Lade, *horreum*, Dan. Skinner
observes that "it was very commonly
used in Lancashire." At p. 288 he also
says that Bp. Kennett notices it also as
a Lincolnshire word, and that Harrison,
speaking of the partition of England
into shires and lathes, says "Some, as
it were roming, or rouing at the name
Lath, do saie that it is derived of a
barn, which is called in Old English a
lath, as they coniecture." "*Horreum est
locus ubi reponitur annona*, a barne, a
lathe. *Grangia*, lathe or grange.—Ou-
tus. *Orreum, granarium*, lathe."—Vo-
cab. Roy. MS., 17, C. xvii. Way.

If asked to guess a date for the composition of the ballad, I should guess the earlier half of the 15th century, while for the recast of it I should guess the latter half of the 16th, or the former half of the 17th. The tradition embodied in it is, I doubt not, of the 13th century.

Let me add, before ending this long rigmarole,[1] that John the Reeve was a well-known typical personage, like Piers Plowman, &c., as is shown by the following extract from a discussion on the Real Presence in the Harleian MS. 207 :

[*leaf* 1],

Bonum est sperare in domino quem et sperare
[1532.]

The Banckett of Iohan the Reve. Vnto peirs ploughman. Laurens laborer. Thomlyn Tailyor. And hobb of the hille. with other.

[*leaf* 2]

[A] relacion maide. by hobb of the hille vnto Sir Iohañ the pariche preste vpon A comminicacion. Betwene. Iacke Iolie Servyngman of thone partie. And. Iohañ the reve. Peirs plowghman. Lawrence Laborer. Thomlyn tailyor. And hobb of the hille of thother partie. Wherin the said Sir Iohan wold maike none Awnswer vnto he knewe the olde vecar mynde. the wiche saide vecar wrote lyenge in his bedd veray seeke. and delyuerde hys mynde in wrytynge. vnto his pariche preste. And the said prest delyuerd the same booke to hobb of the hille. counsellynge hym to learne it. wherebye he myght be more able to maike better Answere to suche light fellows if he channced to here any suche Comminicacion in tyme to comme. Hobb of the hille said vnto sir Iohañ .;. Good morow Sir Iohan .;. And he Answered .;. Good morrowe hobb .;. Hobb said .;. Sir Iohan I am veray glade of our metynge .;. For I am desirouse of your counselle in a weightie matter Sir Iohañ said. Marie ye shalle haue the beste councelle that is in me .;. What is your matter Bie my faithe Sir .;. yesterdaie My master [*leaf* 2 b.] and Iohan the reve maid a feaste. And piers plowghman. Laurence laboror. And Thomlyn tailyor was at dyner at our house, And I serued them at dyner. And or halfe dyner was done. comme in a Servynge man called Iacke Iolie. Rent getherar vnto my ladie. For my master Iohan the reve was Receuor this yeare : And when Iack[e] Iolie was sett downe. He demaunded whether we had any messe or no .;. And my master saide

---

[1] I ought to apologise for its shortcomings. It has been put together in great haste, Mr. Hales having been unfortunately unable to treat its subject, for which Part II. has been kept back four months. Feeling obliged to say something on the question to excuse the delay named, I have set down opinions, many of which, though hastily expressed, have not been hastily formed, as my long connection with working men and with Early English may guarantee.

we hadde, and trustede to haue .;. Than saide Iacke Iolic that we war blynded for wannt of teachynge. for it is plane ydolatrie to beleue *that* the bodie and blonde of criste ar in firme of breade and wyne ministrede in the alter, And for his purpose he Aleged Many Sayenges, As of Marty*n* luther. Eocolampadius. Caralstadij. Iohan Firtz Malangton, with many dynerse other .;. Than peirs ploughman waxed woundrus Angric. and called Iacke Iolic. fals heritike. Than my master desired them bothe to be content in his house. and to reason the matte*r* gentlic. And thei warre bothe contente So to doo.;.

NOTES.

———◆———

p. **xxx.** " Evans, Pinkerton, Hurd, Ritson." Here *Hurd* is a mistake for *Herd*, who published two vols. of Scottish Ballads.—D. (= Alexander Dyce.)

p. **1,** *Chevy Chase.* See Mr. Maidment's comments on this "modern version" in his *Scotish Ballads*, 1868, i. 81.—F.

that "expliceth," quoth Richard Sheale, does *not* mean that Sheale was the *author*, but the *scribe.* So one of the Piers Plowman MS., (Harl. 3954) ends—*quod* Herun, &c.—Skeat.

p. **2,** " *That day* " &c. In the " Complaynt of Scotland," which was not written before 1547, mention is made of the " Hunttiss of Chevot," and of " The persee and mongumrye met," as if these were the titles of two separate ballads. That these were two distinct ballads founded on the battle of Otterbourne, and known in Scotland by the above titles, is extremely probable ; for though, in the Scottish ballad of the " Battle of Otterbourne " the line " The Percy and Montgomery met " occurs, the name of Cheviot is never mentioned. Dr. Percy, in quoting the above line from the " Complaynt of Scotland," gives " That day, that day, that gentil day " as the following one ; but that is, in fact, the title of another ballad or song. Dr. Rimbault. *Musical Illustrations*, p. 1.

p. **5,** *Battle of Otterbourne.* See Mr. Robert White's full account of it, with an appendix and illustrations. London, 1857.—F.

p. **6,** l. **7** from foot: *for* Wold *read* Henry Bold. Another edition, says Mr. E. Peacock, is a fcp. 8vo. of 39 pages. " Chevy Chase, a ballad, in Latin Verse, by Henry Bold, accompanied by the original English Text. London, Printed by Henry Bryer, Bridge St. Blackfriars, 1818."

p. **8,** l. **30,** read *fat buckes.*—Ch. (= F. J. Child.)

p. **11,** l. **123,** lyons *woode,* beyond doubt.—Ch. *layd on lode* (= a load), as Skeat explains, is, I think, certain.—Ch.

p. **12,** l. **143,** " *which struck,*" (as in Old Ballads, 1723) is certainly the reading.—Ch.

p. **14,** l. **198** : sorry you left *too full* : no doubt of *doleful.*—Ch.

p. **17,** *When Loue with vnconfined wings.* This version is very corrupt, and inferior to the printed copy of 1649. See my edition of Lovelace, 1864.—Hazlitt.

p. **20,** l. **8, 16, 24,** *enioyes.* This is exactly the reverse of what the poet meant and wrote.—Hazlitt. The right burden is, " Know no such Liberty," but the 4th or last stanza has " Injoy such Liberty."—F.

p. 21, *Cloris.* See my communication to *Notes and Queries*, 3rd Series viii. 435, and Bell's edition of Waller.—Hazlitt.

p. 24, l. 3. The Percy Society reprinted the edition of 1686, but imperfectly.—Hazlitt.

p. 28, l. 13, *read* yeelded.—Ch.

p. 30, In Scots poems, &c., as Percy says, we find "Hollow, my Fancie:" but there are 17 stanzas, and many differences. The last 9—including only the last of those in the MS. which is also the last in the Scots Poems copy—are said to have been " writ by Colonel Cleuland of my Lord Angus's regiment, when he was a student in the College of Edinburgh, and 18 years of age."—Ch.

p. 35, l. 2. 1639 as the date of Carew's death is only conjectural.—H. (= W. C. Hazlitt.)

p. 37, l. 6. 1731. This *Collection* was printed in 1662, 8vo, and again, with some changes, in 1731, 2 vols. 12mo.—H.

p. 38, l. 22, for *soine* read *sinne* (the idea is that the Lower House sinnes when it *does* sit).—Ch.

p. 39, note. Percy's *Lumford* is of course a penslip for *Lunsford*. Sir Walter Scott, in a note to chap. xx. of *Woodstock*, gives another version of the 2nd verse of this Ballad, and an account of Lunsford, but there are mistakes in it. Scott's verse is—

> The post who came from Coventry
> Riding in a red rocket,
> Did tidings tell, how Lunsford fell,
> A childs hand in his pocket.

The same child-eating scandal is noticed in *Rump Songs*, pt. i. p. 65:

> From Fielding and from Vavasour,
> Both ill-affected men ;
> From Lunsford eke deliver us,
> That eateth up children.

The best account of Lunsford that I know is in *The Gentleman's Magazine*, vol. 106, pt. i. 350, 602; pt. ii. 32, 148; vol. 107, pt. i. 265. Cf. *Rushworth Hist. Col.*, vol. iii. pt. i. p. 459; Add. MSS. 1519 f. 26, 6358 f. 50, 5702 p. 118.

There is an engraving among the King's Pamphlets in the British Museum – I cannot give the press mark—representing Sir Thomas Lunsford at full length. In the background is a church in flames, and a soldier with a drawn sword pursuing a woman ; a companion is catching another woman by her hair. Under the engraving are these lines : .

> I'll helpe to kill, to pillage, and destroy
> All the opposers of the Prelacy.
> My fortunes are grown small, my friends are less,
> I'll venture, therefore, life to have redress ;
> By picking, stealing, or by cutting throntes,
> Although my practise cross the kingdom's votes.

p. 45, l. 32, for *witt* read *woe.*—Ch.

p. 50, *How fayre shee be.* The earliest appearance of this song of Wither's was in *A Description of Love*, 1620 ; then again it appeared at the end of *Faire Virtue* &c., 1622, unless the undated sheet in the Pepysian Library be older, which is more than possible.—Hazlitt.

p. **52**, l. **2**, read *hollydom* (halidom): Note the rhyme.—Ch.

l. **3**, omit *I*.—Ch.

p. **53**, l. **12**, Percy is right, and Mr. Chappell wrong: the rhyme is with *braines*, not *square*.—Ch.

l. **19**, *drouth*, for rhyme, as Percy suggests.—Ch.

l. **25**, drop *of*, hurts metre and sense: 'will you be the taster?' is the meaning.—Ch.

l. **28**, Exus = Naxos of course: 29, coyle, *rare*.—Ch.

l. **29**, *coyse* should be *coyle*: compare l. 2.—D.

l. **34**, for *of* read *on*.—Ch.

p. **54**, l. **42**, read *toward*: 50, *sword's*.—Ch.

l. **54**, read *Cynthia's fellow, Muses' deere*, i.e. (Diana's mate, darling of the Muses).—Ch.

p. **55**, l. **72**, *grace*: some word like *care* is wanted.—Ch.

p. **56**, *The Grene Knight*. Gascoigne the poet, when he was on service in the Low Countries, tells us that he acquired the nickname of *The Green Knight* under circumstances of a peculiar character.—Hazlitt.

p. **63**, l. **123**, note, Percy's *'gan* is wrong.—Ch.

l. **126**, *thy* should be *thee*: you can do nothing with the Sax. *þy*.—Ch.

l. **146, 147**, read *praye, blin*; (transpose the ; and ,).—Ch.

p. **64, 168** (he had *sayd* nothing), qy. *hele*? (i.e. so have I *hele*).—Ch.

p. **65**, note 4, read *Egilsson*: *braid* is well enough explained by the A.·Sax. *brǽdan*, here, *gripe*.—Ch.

p. **67**, l. **255**, *kell*, i.e. caul, net-work for a lady's head. The note on this word is quite from the purpose. [So it is]. Compare—

> Faire be thy wives, right lovesom, white, and small:
> Clere be thy virgyns, lusty under *kellys*.
> London! thowe art the flowre of cities all.
> Dunbar. *Reliq. Ant.* i. 206.—F.

The line describes *Bredbeddle's wife*, not Sir Gawaine: see it referred to in Madden's *Glossary*, to *Syr Gawayne*, under "kell."—D.

p. **67**, l. **236**, *rought* = were sorry for, Sax. *hreówian*.—Ch.

p. **71**, l. **349**, *frauce*, apparently from French *froisser*, clash, dash, &c.—Ch.

l. **355** and note. How *could* "beleeue" be right? To say nothing of l. 478, the rhyme required proves it to be wrong.—D.

p. **72**, l. **364**, *tho* seems to me more likely to be right.—Ch.

p. **74**, l. **429**: the meaning can hardly be *proved* about Gawaine: *proved by* is gone through by, performed by, I should say.—Ch.

p. **75**, l. **461**, *throe*: rightly explained in note. Icel. *þrár* has the same meaning as *thra* in G. Doug.: and so Sax. *þreá*, found only in composition.—Ch.

p. **76**, l. **496**, *other* = second, as in Sax. So l. 523.—Ch.

p. **82**, l. **68**, "& heard them speake" should be "& heard *him* speake."—D. and Ch.

p. **83**, l. **75**, *the* = thy.—Ch.

p. 86, l. 177, *noe more*, read *noe moe.*—D.

p. 88, l. 211, *some spending money*. The author must have written something like *money for spending.*—D. Read *money for spending.*—Ch.

l. 214, *you heyre*, read *your heyre.*—D.

p. 90, l. 273, drop *&* (caught from l. 271 or 268); *thereto* makes sense.—Ch.

p. 92, l. 336, for *said* read *had.*—Ch.

p. 94, l. 399, *fone* should be *foe* (unless in the concluding line of the stanza *goe* be an error for *gone*).—D.

l. 402, read *go[n]e.*—Ch.

p. 98, l. 523, *other* = second : cf. l. 496.—Ch.

l. 534, *soe bee*, read *soe beene.*—D.

p. 99, l. 556, " for to his graue he rann " ought manifestly to be " for to his *mas-ters* graue he rann " : compare l. 543.—D.

l. 557, read *followed.*—Ch.

p. 104, l. 693, *thither wold he wend*, ? read *thither wold he right.*—D.

p. 108, l. 800, read *rest.*—Ch.

l. 807, why not read *shiver? shimmer* makes no sense.—Ch.

p. 111, l. 895, *noe more*, read *noe moe.*— D. and Ch.

p. 112, l. 919, *in the crye*, an undoubted error for *in the stowre.*—D.

p. 113, l. 964, *was past*, read *was gane*, or *gaen* (i.e. gone).—D.

p. 117, l. 1048, read *with thee.*—Ch.

l. 1067, I should understand *yerning* as eager, &c. It is very expressive of the noise of a dog who wants a thing very much.—Ch.

p. 119, l. 1125, for *his heire*, read *is neire.*—Ch. I took it for *is here.*—F.

p. 120, l. 1165, read *come.*—Ch.

p. 122, l. 1202, *busted*, ? bustled, made a stir, made a " towre."—Ch.

l. 1207, read *fyery* wood ?—Ch.

p. 125, l. 1300, read *moe.*- Ch.

l. 1305, *feilds*, certainly *fells.*—D.

p. 128, l. 1403, *blithe*, read *bliue* (i.e. quickly).—D.

p. 132, l. 1496, *affrayd* should be *aghaste*—Copland's ed. having the right reading in l. 1494, *wonder faste*, and *brast* being the final word of l. 1500.—D.

p. 133, l. 1528, *Sir Marrockee the hight*. If this be right, it means " they called him Sir Marrock " : but qy. *he hight* (i.e. he was called)?—D. Why not, *he hight* ?—Ch.

p. 136, *Guye and Amarant*. This is a portion of *The Famous Historie of Guy Erle of Warwicke*, &c., by S. Rowlands; and I cannot but think that Mr. F. mistakes the nature and intention of it. Rowlands is evidently imitating the serio-comic romance poetry of Italy, a kind of writing which has been popular in that country, from Pulci down to Fortiguerra.— D.

p. **136.** I do not understand note 3, " torn out &c."—Ch. Page 253 of the MS. was torn out, Percy said, to send *King Estmere*, which was on it, to press.—F.

p. **137**, l. **45**, *recovers* = *recover his*, of course.—Ch.

p. **139**, l. **92**, *this coward art*, read *this coward act.* —D.

p. **140**, l. **135**, (probably) *den*[*a*]*yd*.—Ch.

p. **145**, l. **2**, *Rhé.* " The Duke of Buckingham's Manifestation of Remonstrance, with a Journal of his Proceedings in the Isle of Ree, 1627, 4to." An unhappy View of the whole Behaviour of my Lord Duke of Buckingham at the French Island called the Isle of Rhee, discovered by Colonel William Fleetwood, an unfortunate commander in that untoward service, 1648. This most fierce and prejudiced impeachment of an expedition, ill planned and unhappily terminated, is reprinted in the fifth volume of the *Somers Collection of Tracts.* Lowndes. *The Expedition to the Isle of Rhe,* by Edward, Lord Herbert of Cherbury. Edited by Lord Powis for the Philobiblon Soc. 1860.—F.

p. **147**, *King and Miller.* the first *known* edition was imprinted at London, by Edward Allde [*circâ* 1600].—Hazlitt.

p. **148**, l. **2**, read *the* Reeve.—Ch.

p. **155**, l. **186**, read *a botts.*—Ch.

p. **160**, l. **1**, for *is* read *It is.*

l. **2**, for *differen* read *different.*

p. **163**, l. **13**,
p. **169**, l. **72**, } 60,000 is evidently the right reading, as the metre shows.—Ch.

p. **168**, l. **57**, *and last*, read *at last.*—D.

p. **172.** the last line of notes, *hurms* should be *harms.*—D.

l. **135.** In Rymer, ix. 317–18, is Robert Waterton's petition to be repaid the costs of the Duke of York, and the prisoners (1) Count de Ewe, (2) Arthur de Bretaigne, (3) le Mareschall Buchecaud, Perron de Lupe, and Cuchart de Sesse, these 3, at s. 23, 4d. a day, and other travelling expenses. At p. 334, Rymer, ix, are " Beds, curtains, &c. for the Dukes of Orleans and Burbon, at Eltham, the Tower of London, Westminster, Windsor, and diverse other places." p. 360 is, de Domino de Lyne, prisonaris. —F.

p. **174**, *Conscience.* Compare *The Booke in Meeter of Robin Conscience*, ? about 1550 ; and Allde's edition before 1600, printed in Halliwell's *Contributions to Early English Literature,* 1849, and with 4 additional stanzas in Hazlitt's *Early Popular Poetry,* iii. 221. Compare also *A piece of Friar Bacons Brazen-heads Prophesies,* 1604, (Percy Society, 1844.) Lauder's poem on the *Nature of Scotland twiching the Intertainment of virtewus men that lacketh Ryches, &c.,* and Martin Parker's *Robin Conscience,* or Conscionable Robin. His Progresse thorow Court, City, and Countrey: with his bad entertainement at each severall place. Very pleasant and merry to bee read. Written in English by M. P.

> Charitie's cold, mens hearts are hard,
> And most doores against Conscience bard.

London 1635, 8vo., 11 leaves. *Bodleian.* (Burton's Books) *Hazlitt's Handbook.*— F.

p. **186**, l. **49**, read *denide.* —Ch.

p. **188**, l. 104, *sore* should be dropped and the line not indented: *sore* is evidently caught from the line above.—Ch.

p. **190**, Harl. MS. 4843 (paper). Article 11 is "Anno *Domini* millesimo cccxlvi die Martis, in vigilia Lucæ Evangelistæ, hora *Matutina* ix. commissum fuit bellum inter Anglos et Scotos non longe a Dunelmia, in loco ubi nunc stat crux vulgariter dictus Nevillcrosse" Poema rhythmicum, [leaf] 241. *Harl. Catal.*

p. **191**, l. 2, hearken to me a litle [while?]—Ch.

p. **199**. l. 245, read *brother*, ("to the King of ffrance" is a marginal gloss).—Ch.

l. 245, &c., *brothers* should be *brother*; and the words *to the King of ffrance* is a gloss crept into the text.—D.

p. **200**, last line but two of note, for 63-6 read 63-8. (Durham Feilde is likely enough by the author of Flodden Field).—Ch.

p. **201**, See the "Discendants from Guy, Earl of Warwick; i.e. of the family of Arden of Parke-Hall in Com. Warwic. who were indeed descended from the Great Turchil, who lived at the time of the Conquest." Harl. MS. 853, leaf 113. Mr. Halliwell in his *Descriptive Notices of Early English Histories*, p. 47-8, says of the story of Guy: "This tale was dramatized early in the 17th century, and Taylor mentions having seen it acted at the Maidenhead of Islington." "After supper we had a play of the life and death of Guy in Warwicke, played by the Right Honourable the Earle of Darbie his men." *Pennilesse Pilgrimage*, ed. 1630, p. 140." Dr. Rimbault prints the tune of the ballad at p. 46-7 of his *Musical Illustrations*, from the Ballad Opera of "Robin Hood," performed at Lee and Harper's Booth in 1730. The ballad, he says, "was entered on the Stationers' books, 5th January, 1591-2."—F.

p. **202**, l. 37, *the grave* is a ridiculous blunder for *the cave*.—D.

l. 47, *ingrauen in Mold* should be *ingrauen ins tone*. Here the scribe repeated by mistake the word *Mold* from the first line of the stanza.—D.

p. **203**, last line but 4, read "Mangertoun."—Ch.

p. **203**, l. 5 from foot. *Nephew to the Laird of Mangertoun* (misprinted Margertoun). This reference to the nephew of the Lord of Mangerton, the chief of the Armstrongs, leads to the inference that the circumstances on which the ballad is founded had occurred previous to the rescue of William Armstrong of Kinmont, as Sir Richard Maitland was born in 1496, and died at the advanced age of ninety, on the 20th of March, 1586. Jock, in 1569, gave protection to the Countess of Northumberland, after the unfortunate rising and defeat of her husband and the Earl of Westmoreland, when they were both compelled to fly from England. After an unsuccessful attempt to take refuge in Liddesdale, they were compelled to put themselves under the protection of the Armstrongs of the Debateable land. The Countess, who did not accompany them, her tire-woman and ten other persons who were with her, were unscrupulously despoiled by the Liddesdale reivers of their horses, so that the poor lady was left on foot at John of the Side's house, a cottage not to be compared to many a dog-kennel in England." Maidment's *Scotish Ballads*, i. 182-3. Maidment also gives the ballad of *Hobbie Noble* at p. 191, showing how he was betrayed into the hands of his enemies by the Armstrongs, whose Jock he had rescued.—F.

p. **204**, l. 4, *he is gone*, read *he is gane* or *gaen* (i.e. gone).—D.

l. 6, (of Maitland) read *ane* for *and*.—Ch.

p. **217**, l. **14**, *has received*, read *had received.*—D.

p. **222**, l. **106**, *ffacc* seems to be an error for *eye.*—D.

    l. **126**, . after "yee."—Ch.

p. **226**, l. **214**, for *land* read *man?* (Percy has *laird*, but that reading is not likely in this English ballad).—Ch.

p. **235**, note **5**, "and *delend.*" Perhaps so; but in old ballads *and* is sometimes redundant.—D.

p. **237**, l. **232**, *soe fast runn*, read *soe fast rinn.*—D.

p. **240**, l. **63**, *with speares in brest.* This, of course, should be *with speares in rest.*—D. (?—F.)

    l. **64**, . after "ffight."—Ch.

p. **279**, *Bessie off Bednall.* There are several plays on this subject. The earliest is *The Blind Beggar of Bednal-Green, with the merry humor of Tom Strowd the Norfolk Yeoman, as it was divers times publickly acted by the Princes Servants. Written by John Day*, 1659, 4to. The latest was by my friend Sheridan Knowles.—D.

p. **292**, l. **56**, for *shinne*, read, as in the next stanza, *shoone.*—D.

p. **297**, l. **35**, *pinn.* I prefer *pin* as a corruption of *point*, as in "He's but one *pin* above a natural." Cartwright. Cf. our use of *peg.*

        The calendar, right glad to find
        His friend in *merry pin.*
                       John Gilpin.—Skeat.

p. **306**, l. **43**, *wadded.* Surely the context, "gaule" and "greene" and "black." shows that "*wadded*" should be "*watchet*" (i.e. pale blue).—D. (? woaded. —F.)

p. **313**, l. **13**, *sonne.* Here, to be consistent, we must read *sonne*[s].—D.

p. **315**, l. **70**, "*scarlett and redd*," a blunder for "*scarlett redd.*"—D.

p. **319**, l. **200**, *giusts*; of course, "giusts" should be "*giufts*" (gifts).—D.

p. **323**, l. **30**, "itt is now but a *sigh* clout, as you may see." The note on this line is strangely wrong. "*A sigh clout*" is a clout for *sighing* (or, more properly, *sieing*), i.e. straining milk.—D. I only know *siling* for straining.—F.

p. **328**, l. **22**, for *Lay*, ? read *he laines* (i.e. conceals).—D.

p. **341**, *Sir Eglamore.* "Sir Eglamore" must have been originally written in Northern rather than in Southern English, as appears from internal evidence. We find innumerable rimes which are *no* rimes, but which become so at once when translated into a Northumbrian dialect. Is it not clear that such rimes as *taketh* and *goeth* should be *tais* and *gais*? That for *tane* and *bone* we should read *tane* and *bane?* So, too, *rore* (riming to *were*) ought to be *rair.* *Drueth* and *cliffes* should be *driffis* and *cliffis.* *Drew* and *loughe* (laughed) should be *dreuch* and *leuch.* *Abode* must be *abaid*, if it is to rime with *made* (or *maid*). And finally, as a crucial instance, it is almost impossible to believe that the *four* words in stanza 75— *pace, rose, was*, and *taketh*, were not intended to rime together in the forms *pas, ras, was*, and *tais* or *tas.* To take one more case, for *rest, trust, cast*, and *last* (st. 4), read *rest, trist, kest. lest.* And when we further observe that the rimes may be thus emended throughout the *whole poem*, surely the inference that it was of Northern origin becomes almost a certainty.—Skeat.

p. **343**, l. 65, for "& show your hart & love," ? read "— hart and love *her to*"?—D.

p. **344**, l. 93,

p. **345**, l. 132,

p. **352**, l. 320, } In these lines, *more* should be *mair*.—D.

p. **355**, l. 403,

p. **359**, l. 505, for *home* read *hame*.—D.

p. **367**, l. 702, *head*. There the rhyme determines that for "head" we must substitute the A.-S. *heved*.—D.

p. **369**, l. 766, for *yedde* read *yode* (not, as Percy says, *yeede*).—D.

p. **369**, *A Cauileere*. See Gervase Markham's chapter " Of Hawking with all sorts of Hawkes," &c., in his *Countrey Contentments*, 1615, Bk. I, p. 87–97. " The pleasure of hawking . . is a most Princely and serious delight."—F.

p. **373**, l. 856, for *rose* read *rase*.—D.

p. **382**, l. 1119, for *more* read *mor*.—D.

p. **384**, l. 1117, for *went hee* read *hee gone*.

p. **387**, note 1. As the true reading is undoubtedly "*man*," why say anything about the meaning of "*May*"?—D.

p. **388**, l. 1285, for *dwell* read *wend*.—D.

p. **390**. *The Emperour and the Childe*, or Valentine & Orson. See Halliwell's *Descriptive Notices*, 1848, p. 29–30, as to the Romance, and the prose story.

p. **401**, l. 12, " that *ginnye* his ffilly wold haue her owne will." Here " *Ginnye*" is the name of " his ffilly." If the MS. has " grimye," it is an error.—D.

p. **419**, l. 106, for *young* read *ying*.—D.

p. **432**, l. 439,   " & said, Cozen will !
                  who hath done to you this shame ? "

Here "will" sounds very ridiculously, as if the 3 knights were using the familiar abbreviation of their cousin's name ! Read undoubtedly (comparing Ritson's text of the passage),

" & said, Cozen *William*,
   who hath done to you this shame ? "—D.

p. **454**, l. 1078. " both old & young." } In both places " young " should be
p. **496**, l. 2223. " both old and young." } " *ying*."—D.

p. **493**. note 1. *Wiere*. See a drawing of one at p. 9 of the *Bestiaire d'Amour* of Richard de Fournival, Paris, 1860 ; and Mons. Hippeau's note at p. 103–4. —F.

p. **500**. *Childe Maurice*. See R. Jamieson's notes to this ballad in his *Pop. Bal. and Songs*, i. 16–21.—F.

p. **505**, l. **98**, *and dryed it on the grasse.* Jamieson compares

> Hom gan his sword gripe
> Ant *on his arm hit wype*:
> The Sarazyn he hit so,
> That his hed fel to ys to.
> *Ritson's Met. Rom.* vol. ii. p. 116.—F.

p. **506**, l. **117**, *wicked be my merry men all.* Jamieson compares with this the last 3 stanzas of Little Musgrave (i. 122, note): " Woe worth you, woe worth my merry men all." and says, " The same kind of remonstrance with those about him occurs in Lee's tragedy of ' Alexander the Great' after the murder of Clitus." Most men want to put their sins on other people's shoulders.—F.

p. **521**, the extract from Lane's MS. Harl. 5243, is only his address to the reader, before his Poem on Guy.—F.

p. **536**, l. **284**, for *noone* read " noone *time.*" (Compare, *ante*, p. 468, l. 1441,—

> " ffro: the hower of *prime*
> till it was *euensong time.*")—D.

p. **536**, l. **290**, for *there* read *thore.*—D.

p. **541**, l. **432**. There is a church in Winchester called St. Swithin's, which is merely a large room over the archway of King's Gate, but it has no pretensions to the antiquity mentioned in your letter. The sword and axe of the giant were probably ordered to be hung up in the cathedral church, which was originally dedicated under the title of St. Peter and St. Paul; but the body of St. Swithin having been transferred from the churchyard into the sumptuous shrine built for its reception, the cathedral from thenceforth down to the time of Henry VIII. was distinguished by the name of *Saint Swithin*, and this is no doubt the church alluded to.—Walter Bailey.

p. **579**, l. **529**, *John de Reeve.* The mention of the *galliard* here, a dance not introduced into England till about 1541, confirms what the language shows, that our version of the poem is a late one.—F.

p. **582**, l. **606**, On *Chape*, see Wedgwood's Dict. i. 321.

Bishop Percy's Folio MS.

Ballads and Romances.

———∞⚬⚭⚬∞———

Cheup Chase : [1]

THERE are two principal versions of this well-known ballad—
an old, and a modern one. The copy preserved in the Folio is
a slightly various form of the latter.

The oldest copy of the old version is preserved in a MS. in
the Ashmolean Collection at Oxford. This was printed by
Hearne, in 1719, in the Preface to his edition of Gulielmus
Neubrigiensis. "To the MS. copy," says Percy, " is subjoined the
name of the author, Rychard Sheale [expliceth quoth Rychard
Sheale]; whom Hearne had so little judgement as to suppose to
be the same with a R. Sheal, who was living in 1588." The
general character of the language, if there were no other proof,
proves that the ballad is of a much earlier date than 1588 ; but
probably Hearne is right in identifying the subscribed "R. Sheale"
with the well-known ballad-singer of that name, who flourished,
or more truly withered, in the reign of Queen Elizabeth. This
Sheale was in some sort the last of the minstrels. There are

---

[1] In *the* printed Collection of Old
Ballads. 1727. Vol. 1. p. 108. No. xiv.
N.B. The Readings in the Margin
[here transferred to the foot-notes] are
taken from the Scotch Edition printed at
Glasgow 8vo 1747.—Which is remarkable
for the wilful Corruptions made in all
ye Passages which concern the two
Nations.—P.

extant some lines of his, of very inferior merit, wherein he bewails his miserable condition. He narrates with many sighs and groans how he has been robbed, left destitute, and no man gave unto him. Certainly, if these lines are a fair specimen of his talents, one cannot wonder that he found the world somewhat cold. And certainly the author of those lines could never have written "The Hunting of the Cheviot." But he may have sung it many and many a time, and passed with many an audience for the author. And hence, perhaps, the subscription of his name to the Ashmolean copy. The ballad in his time was extensively popular. Sir Philip Sidney refers to it in a well-known passage (though, as Prof. Child suggests, it is not impossible that he may mean the "Battle of Otterbourne"), as commonly sung by "blind crowders." Many years before Sidney wrote his *Defence of Poetry*, the *Complaint of Scotland*, written in 1548, speaks of "The Huntis of Chevot," and quotes the line,

> That day, that day, that gentill day,

which is apparently a memory-quotation, or perhaps a Scotch version of

> That day, that day, that dredfull day.

This evidence of its popularity in the middle of the sixteenth century, coupled with the antiquity of the language (though much of that "antiquity" belongs to the dialect in which, rather than to the time at which, it was written), justify the assigning of the ballad to the fifteenth century.

This ballad is historically highly valuable for the picture it gives of Border warfare in its more chivalrous days, when ennobled by generosity and honour. The hewing and hacking lose their horrors in the atmosphere of romance thrown around them. And the main incidents of the piece are no doubt generally true.

Such fierce collisions as here represented must often have

occurred, and from the same cause here given. " It was one of the Laws of the Marches frequently renewed between the two nations, that neither party should hunt in the other's borders without leave from the proprietors or their deputies." This permission the high-spirited Borderer was not always disposed to ask. He did not care to beg for favours. He would make no secret of his purposed sport, so that if the warden of the March about to be trespassed upon chose to oppose him, he was not prevented from doing so by ignorance of his intention. In this way the proclamation of a hunting expedition across the Borders was in reality a challenge to a contest. An excellent illustration of the perpetual possibility of an encounter, which attended and recommended these defiant expeditions, is to be found in the *Memoirs of Carey, Earl of Monmouth*. Carey was Warden of the Marches in Queen Mary's time, and gives the following account :

"There had been an ancient custom of the borders, when they were at quiet, for the opposite border to send the warden of the Middle Marche, to desire leave that they might come into the borders of England, and hunt with their greyhounds for deer, towards the end of summer, which was denied them. Towards the end of Sir John Foster's government, they would, without asking leave, come into England and hunt at their pleasure, and stay their own time. I wrote to Farnehurst, the warden over against me, that I was no way willing to hinder them of their accustomed sports; and that if, according to the ancient custom, they would send to me for leave, they should have all the contentment I could give them ; if otherwise, they would continue their wonted course, I would do my best to hinder them. Within a month after, they came and hunted as they used to do, without leave, and cut down wood, and carried it away. Towards the end of summer, they came again to their wonted sports. I sent my two deputies with all the speed they could make, and they took along with them such gentlemen as were in their way, with my forty horse, and about one o'clock they came up to them, and set upon them. Some hurt was done, but I gave especial order they should do as little hurt, and shed as little blood as possible they could. They took a dozen of the principal gentlemen that were there, and brought them to me to Witherington, where I then lay; I made them welcome, and gave them the best entertainment I could; they lay in the castle two or three days, and so I sent them home, they assuring me that they would never hunt again without leave. The Scots king complained to Queen Elizabeth very grievously of this fact."

"Mr. Addison, in his celebrated criticism on that ancient ballad of Chevy Chase, *Spect.* No. 20, mistakes the ground of the quarrel. It was not any particular animosity or deadly feud between the two principal actors, but was a contest of privilege and jurisdiction between them, respecting their offices, as lords wardens of the marches assigned." Extract from the Report of Sir Thomas Carlton, of Carlton Hall, 1547, in Hutchinson's *History of Cumberland*, pp. 28–9.

The general spirit of the ballad then is historical. But the details are not authentic. "That which is commonly sung of the Hunting of Cheviot," says Godscroft, writing in his James VI.'s time, and apparently referring to a version of the ballad then circulating in Scotland, "seemeth indeed poetical and a mere fiction, perhaps to stir up virtue; yet a fiction whereof there is no mention, either in Scottish or English Chronicle." An event to which it might possibly refer according to Collins, in his *Peerage*, was the Battle of Pepperden, fought in 1436, as Hector Boethius informs us, "not far from the Cheviot hills, between the Earl of Northumberland, and Earl William Douglas of Angus, with a small army of about four thousand men each, in which the latter had the advantage. As this seems to have been a private conflict between these two great chieftains of the Borders, rather than a national war, it has been thought to have given rise to the celebrated old ballad of Chevy Chase; which to render it more pathetic and interesting, has been heightened with tragical incidents wholly fictitious." But in any case these were great Border names. Percy and Douglas were typical chieftains. Moreover on the field of Otterbourne a Percy and a Douglas had fought fiercely together, man against man, under very similar circumstances. That field was much celebrated in Border poetry, and elsewhere. The ballad on the Hunting of the Cheviot,—borrowed largely from that on the Battle of Otterbourne,—was, in fact, in course of time believed to celebrate the same event. Observe these lines of it :

> This was the Hontynge of the Cheviat ;
>   That tear began this spurn :
> Old men that knowen the grownde well yenough ;
>   Call it the Battell of Otterburn.

This attempt made at the identification of two actions is noticeable. We are afraid that the " old men " scarcely knew the ground well enough. Otterbourne is but some 30 miles from Newcastle. Douglas met Percy, the " Hunting " tells us, in Teviotdale. In 'a word, the two ballads represent two different features of the old Border life—the Raid and the defiant Hunt. But they had much in common, and so were soon confused together.

Of the battle of Otterbourne, fought in 1388, there are historical accounts in abundance—Fordun's, Froissart's, Holinshed's, Godscroft's. See *Minstrelsy of the Scottish Border*. Of the ballad concerning it—whose account is mainly accurate—indeed the facts somewhat trammel the poet's wings,—there are three versions: the English one, given by Percy in his *Reliques*, from a Harl. MS. in the earlier editions, from a more perfect Cotton MS. (Cleop. iv. f. 64) in the fourth, and two Scotch ones, to be found, one in the *Minstrelsy*, the other in Herd's *Scottish*

Songs. The differences between the English and Scotch versions are such as might be expected—are of a patriotic kind. The main difference between the two Scotch versions relates to the death of Douglas.

Of the versions of "the Hunting of the Cheviat," that preserved in the Folio is, as we have said, the modernised one ; not that heard by Sidney, who calls what he heard "the rude and ill-apparelled song of a barbarous age ;" a description not applicable to the present version. When this modernisation was made, cannot be said exactly. "That it could not be much later than Queen Elizabeth's time," says Percy, " appears from the phrase ' doleful dumps ;' which in that age carried no ill sound with it, but to the next generation became ridiculous. We have seen it pass uncensured in a sonnet that was at that time in request, and where it could not fail to have been taken notice of, had it been the least exceptionable [in " a song to the lute in Musicke " from the *Paradise of Daintie Devises,* 1596], yet in about half a century after, it was become burlesque. *Vide* Hudibras, Pt. i. c. iii. v. 95." Its presence in the Folio MS. shows that it was not made later than the first half of the seventeenth century. It soon became the current version. Addison in his *critique* in the *Spectator* knows of no other. A comparison of it with the old versions will show, besides one or two verbal blunders, that much of its vigour has been lost in the process of translation.

Of all our ballads this perhaps has enjoyed the widest popularity, both North and South of the Tweed. This popularity has scarcely ever decayed. It was translated into rhyming Latin verses by a Mr. Wold of New College, Oxford, at the instance of Dr. Compton, Bishop of London, in 1685.

> Vivat Rex noster nobilis,
> Omnis in tuto sit ;
> Venatus olim flebilis
> Chevino luco fit.

It circulated on many a broad sheet. It was eulogised in

the *Spectator* in Queen Anne's reign. It was printed wherever anything of the kind was printed in the succeeding years, when such things were held in but slight esteem. It is as it were the *Epic* of Border poetry.

GOD Prosper long our noble K*ing*,　　　[page 188]
　　our liffes & saftyes all !
a woefull hunting once there was
4　　in Cheuy Chase befall.

A woeful hunt was held in Chevy Chase.

to driue the deere with hound and horne
　　Erle Pearcy took the way :
the Child may rue *that* is vnborne
8　　the hunting of *that* day !

Earl Percy

the stout Erle of Northumberland
　　a vow to god did make,
his pleasure in the Scottish woods
12　　3 sommers days to take ;

vowed to kill Scotch deer for three days.

the cheefest harts in Cheuy C[h]ase
　　to kill & beare away.
these tydings to Erle douglas came
16　　in Scottland where he Lay,

Douglas

who sent Erle Pearcy present word
　　he wold prevent his sport.
the English Erle, not fearing that,[1]
20　　did to the woods resort

said he'd stop that sport.

But Percy went to his hunt

with 1500 [2] bowmen bold,
　　all chosen men of Might,
who knew ffull well in time of neede
24　　to ayme their shafts arright.

with 1500 bowmen,

---

[1] this.—P.　　　　　[2] 2000.—P.

the Gallant Greyhound [1] swiftly ran
   to Chase the fallow deere ;

on Munday they began to hunt
28   ere [2] daylight did appeare ;

& long before high noone thé had
   a 100 fatbuckes slaine.

then hauing dined, the drouyers went
32   to rouze the deare [3] againe ;

The Bowmen mustered on the hills,
   well able to endure ;
theire backsids all with speciall care
36   *that* they [4] were guarded sure.

the hounds ran swiftly through the woods
   the Nimble deere to take,

that with [5] their cryes the hills & dales
40   an Eccho shrill did make.

Lord Pearcy to the Querry [6] went
   to veiw the tender deere ;

quoth he, " Erle douglas promised once
44   this day to meete me heere ;

" but if I thought he wold not come,
   noe longer wold I stay."
with *that* a braue younge gentlman
48   thus to the Erle did say,

" Loe, yonder doth Erle douglas come,
   hÿs men in armour bright,

full 20 hundred [7] Scottish speres
52   all Marching in our sight,

---

[1] greyhounds.—P.
[2] when.—P.
[3] them up.—P.
[4] that day.—P.

[5] And with.—P.
[6] Quarry.—P.
[7] 15,00.—P.

"all pleasant men of Tiuydale [1]
fast by the riuer Tweede."

"O ceaze your sportts!" [2] Erle Pearcy said,

Percy calls
on his men

56   "and take your bowes with speede,

"& now with me, my countrymen,
your courage forth advance!
for there was neuer Champion yett [3]

to be brave;

60   in Scottland nor in ffrance

"that euer did on horsbacke come,
& if my hap [4] it were,

he will fight
anyone,

I durst encounter man for man,

man to man.

64   with him to breake a spere."

Erle douglas on his [5] Milke white steede,
Most Like a Baron bold,
rode formost of his company,

Douglas

68   whose armour shone like gold: [page 189]

"shew me," sayd hee, "whose men you bee
that hunt soe boldly heere,

asks whose
men they are
that hunt

that without my consent doe chase

72   & kill my fallow deere."

his deer.

the first man that did [6] answer make
was noble Pearcy hee,

Percy

who sayd, "wee list not to declare,

will not tell,

76   nor shew whose men wee bee, .

"yett wee will [7] spend our deerest blood

but will
fight for the
right to
hunt.

thy cheefest [8] harts to slay."
then douglas swore a solempne oathe,

Douglas

80   and thus in rage did say,

declares

---

[1] men of pleasant Tiviotdale.—P.
[2] Then cease sport.—P.
[3] For ne'er was there a champion.—P.
[4] but if my hap.—P.
[5] a.—P.
[6] man that first did.—P.
[7] will we.—P.
[8] the choicest.- P.

that one of
them must
die,

"Ere thus I will outbraued bee,
 one of vs tow shall dye !
I know thee well ! an Erle thou art,
84 Lord Pearcy ! soe am I ;

and as it
would
be wrong to
kill their
guiltless
men,

"but trust me, Pearcye, pittye it were,
 & great offence, to Kill
then any of these our guiltlesse [1] men,
88 for they haue done none ill [2] ;

he chal-
lenges Percy
to single
combat.
Percy
accepts.

"Let thou [3] & I the battell trye,
 and set our men aside."
"accurst bee [he !] " Erle [4] Pearcye sayd,
92 "by whome it is denyed."

A squire,

Withering-
ton,
protests

then stept a gallant Squire forth,—
 witherington was his name,—
who said, " I wold not haue it told
96 to Henery our King, for shame,

that he'll
not look on
while Percy
fights :

"that ere my captaine fought on foote,
 & I stand looking on :
you bee 2 Erles," [5] quoth witheringhton,
100 "& I a Squier alone,

"Ile doe the best that doe I may,[6]
 while I haue power to stand !
while I haue power to weeld my [7] sword,

he'll fight
too.

104 Ile fight with hart & hand ! "

The English
archers
shoot, and
kill 80 Scots.

Our English archers bend [8] their bowes—
 their harts were good & trew,—
att the first flight of arrowes sent,
108 full foure score scotts [9] thé slew.

[1] harmless.—P.
[2] no ill.—P.
[3] thee.—P.
[4] he, Lord.—P.
[5] Lords.— P.

[6] that e'er I may.—P.
[7] a.—P.
[8] Scottish bent.—P.
[9] they 4 score English.—P.

to driue the deere with hound & horne,
　　dauglas [1] Bade on the bent;
2 Captaines [2] moued with Mickle might,[3]
112　　their speres to shiuers went.

they closed full fast on euerye side,
　　noe slacknes there was found,
but [4] many a gallant gentleman
116　　Lay gasping on the ground.

O Christ! it was great greeue [5] to see
　　how eche man chose his spere,[6]
& how the blood out of their brests [7]
120　　did gush like water cleare! [8]

at last these 2 stout Erles [9] did meet
　　Like Captaines of great might;
like Lyons moods [10] they Layd on Lode,[11]
124　　thé made a cruell fight.

thé fought, vntill they both did sweat,
　　with swords of tempered steele,
till blood [a-]downe their cheekes like raine
128　　thé trickling downe did feele.[12]

" O yeeld thee, Pearcye! " [13] Douglas say'd,
　　" & [14] infaith I will thee bringe
where thou shall high advanced bee
132　　by Iames our scottish King;

[1] The Scotch Editor thinks this sh⁴ be
Piercy.—P.
　[2] a cap⁴ --P.
　[3] pride.—P.
　[4] and.—P.
　[5] grief.—P.
　[6] And likewise for to hear.—P.
　[7] The Cries of Men lying in their
gore.—P.
　[8] And lying here & there.—P.

[9] Lords.—P.
[10] mov'd.—P. ? for woode, wild.—F.
or 'the mood or pluck ' of lions.—Skeat.
[11] ? A.-S. leód, a man ; or for hlude,
loudly.—F. or (a)load, laid on heavily.
—Skeat.
[12] Until the blood like drops of rain
　　They trickling down did feel.—P.
[13] yield the Lord P.—P.
[14] d.---P.

"thy ransome I will freely giue,
  & this [1] report of thee,
thou art the most couragious K*night*
136   [that ever I did see.[2]]"

**Percy will
never yield
to a Scot.**

"Noe, Douglas!" quoth Erle[3] Percy then, [page 190
  "thy p*r*ofer I doe scorne;
I will not yeelde to any scott
140   *that* eue*r* yett was borne!"

**An English
arrow**

w*i*th *that* there came an arrow keene
  out of an english bow,

**kills
Douglas.**

who [4] scorke Erle douglas on the brest [5]
144   a deepe and deadlye blow;

**exhorting
his men to
fight.**

who neue*r* sayd [6] more words then these,
  "fight on, my merrymen all!
for why, my life is att [an] end,
148   Lor*d* Pearcy sees my [7] fall."

Percy

then leauing liffe, Erle Pearcy tooke
  the dead man by the hand;

**laments
over his
dead foe;**

who [8] said, "Erle dowglas! for thy [9] sake
152   wold I had lost my Land!

"O christ! my verry hart doth bleed
  for [10] sorrow for thy sake!

**a braver
knight ne'er
died.**

for sure, a more redoubted [11] K*night*,
156   Mischance cold [12] neue*r* take!"

---

[1] thus.—P.
[2] That ever I did see.—P.
[3] Lord.—P.
[4] which.—P. *scorke.* for *storke*, stroke,
struck; *skorke* means scorch; see
skorche in Halliwell's Gloss.—F.
[5] to y*e* heart.—P.

[6] spake.—P.
[7] me.—P.
[8] And.—P.
[9] life.—P.
[10] with. —P.
[11] renowned.—P.
[12] did.—P.

a K*night* amongst the scotts there was,
which [1] saw Erle Douglas dye,
who streight in hart did vow revenge
160   vpon the Lord [2] Pearcye ;

A Scotch
knight,
Sir Hugh
Montgom-
ery, vows
revenge on
Percy,

[Part II.]

2ᵈ parte.

Sir Hugh Mountgomerye was he called,
  who, with a spere full bright,
well mounted on a gallant steed,
  ran feircly through the fight,

gallops to

And [3] past the English archers all
  without all dread or feare,
& through Erle Percyes Body then
168   he thrust his hatfull spere

*him, and
runs him*

with such a vehement force & might
  that his body he did gore,[4]
the staff ran [5] through the other side
172   a large cloth yard & more.

*right
through the
body.*

thus [6] did both those Nobles dye,
  whose courage none cold staine.
an English archer then perceiued
176   the Noble Erle was slaine,

*An English
archer*

he had [a] good bow [7] in his hand
  made of a trusty tree ;
an arrow of a cloth yard long [8]
180   to the hard head haled [9] hee,

[1] that.—P.
[2] Earl.—P.
[3] He.—P.
[4] His body he did gore.—P.
[5] spear went.—P.
[6] So thus.—P.
[7] a bow bent.—P.
[8] length.—P.
[9] unto the head drew.—P.

shoots Mont-
gomery

against Sir Hugh Mountgomerye [1]
     his shaft full right [2] he sett ;
the grey goose winge *that* was there-on,

through the
heart.

184   in his harts bloode [3] was wett.

The fight
lasts all day.

this fight from breake of day did last [4]
     till setting of the sun,
for when thé rung the Euening bell

188   the Battele scarse was done.

Names of
the English
knights
slain.

with [5] stout Erle Percy there was slaine [6]
     Sir Iohn of Egerton,[7]
Sir Robert Harcliffe & Sir William,[8]

192   Sir Iames that bold barron ;

& with Sir George & [9] Sir Iames,
     both Knights of good account ;
& good Sir Raphe Rebbye [10] there was slaine,

196   whose prowesse [11] did surmount.

Withering-
ton fights on
his stumps
when his
legs are cut
off.

for witherington needs must I wayle
     as one in too full [12] dumpes,
for when his leggs were smitten of,

200   he fought vpon his stumpes.

Names of
the Scotch
knights
slain.

And with Erle dowglas there was slaine
     Sir Hugh Mountgomerye,
[13] & Sir Charles Morrell [14] *that* from feelde

204   one foote wold neuer flee ;

---

[1] then.—P.
[2] so right his shaft.—P.
[3] heart-blood.—P.
[4] did last from break.—P.
[5] the.—P.
[6] There is a dot for the *i*, but nothing more in the MS.—F.
[7] Ogerton.—P.
[8] Ratcliffe & Sir John.—P.
[9] Sir George also & good.—F.
[10] Good . . . . Rabby.—P.
[11] courage.—P.
[12] doleful.—P.
[13] d.—P.
[14] Murray.—P.

Sir Roger Heuer of Harcliffe tow,—[1]
  his sisters sonne was hee,—
Sir david Lambwell well[2] esteemed,
208   but saved he cold[3] not bee;

& the Lord Maxwell in like case[4]
  with Douglas he did dye;[5]
[6] of 20[7] hundred scottish speeres,

Of 2000 Scotch scarce 55 were left;

212   scarce 55 did flye;

of 1500 Englishmen

of 1500 English, only 53.

  went home but 53[6];
the rest in Cheuy chase were slaine,
216   Vnder the greenwoode tree.   [page 191]

Next day did many widdowes come

Next day the widows come, and weep,

  their husbands to bewayle;
they washt[8] their wounds in brinish teares,
220   but all wold not[9] prevayle.

theyr bodyes bathed in purple blood,

and carry the corpses off

  thé bore with them away,
they kist them dead a 1000 times
224   ere thé[10] were cladd in clay.

to the grave.

the[11] newes was[12] brought to Eddenborrow
  where Scottlands King did rayne,
that braue Erle Douglas soddainlye
228   was with an arrow slaine.

[1] Sir Cha. Murray of Ratcliffe too.—P.
[2] Lamb so well.—P.
[3] yet saved could.—P.
[4] wise.—P.
[5] did with Earl D! die.—P.
[6]—[6] Of 1500 Scottish spears
    went home but 53,

Of 20,00 Englishmen
    scarce 55 did flee.—P.
[7] 15.—P.
[8] MS. they washt they.—F. d.—P.
[9] could not. –P.
[10] when they.—P.
[11] These.—P.   [12] were.—P.

King James
laments the
loss of
Douglas.
No such
captain has
he left.

"[1] O heauy newes!" King Iames can say,
  " Scottland may wittenesse bee
I haue not any Captaine more
232   of such account as hee! "

like tydings to King Henery came
  within as short a space,

that Pearcy of Northumberland
236   in Cheuy chase was slaine.[2]

"Now god be with him!" said our King,
  " sith it will noe better bee,[3]

I trust I haue within my realme
240   500 as good as hee!

"[4] yett shall not Scotts nor Scottland say

  but I will vengeance take,
& be revenged on them all

244   for braue Erle Percyes sake."

[4] this vow the King did well performe
  after on humble downe;

in one day 50 Knights were slayne,
248   with Lords of great renowne,

& [5] of the rest of small [6] account,
  did many hundreds dye :
thus endeth the hunting in [7] Cheuy Chase
252   made [8] by the Erle Pearcye.

God saue our [9] King, and blesse this [10] land
  with plentye, Ioy, & peace;

& grant henceforth that foule debate
256   twixt noble men may ceaze!
            ffinis.

---

[1] Now God be with him, cried our king,
   Sith will no better be!
   I trust I have &c.—P.
[2] Was slain in Chevy Chase.—P.
[3] O heavy news, K. Henry said,
   Engl[d] can witness be.—P.

[4] These 2 stanzas omitted in y[e] Scotch
   Edition.—P.   See note, p. 1.—F.
[5] Now.—P.   [6] mean.—P.
[7] of.—P.   [8] led.—P.
[9] the.—P.   [10] the.—P.

When Love with unconfined.[1]

LOVELACE'S songs were in great request in his day. They were set to music by popular composers of the time,—by Dr. John Wilson, by Mr. John Laniere, by Mr. Henry Lawes whom Dante was to give Fame leave to set higher than his Casella—and circulated widely in Royalist Society. Till 1649—the author was born in 1618—they led a scattered and wandering life. In that year they were gathered together and published in a volume entitled " Lucasta, Epodes, Odes, Sonnets, Songs, &c. to which is added Aramantha a Pastorall, by Richard Lovelace, Esq." Meanwhile there were, no doubt, in vogue many versions of the greater favourites, more or less inaccurate. The copy of the exquisite song beginning "When Love with unconfined wings," here printed from the Folio MS., is one of these.

Of all the Cavalier poets Lovelace is the most charming. He is a true cavalier ; he is a true poet. The world, that has long turned away its ear from Cowley and Cleveland, still listens to his sweet voice. Are there any gems brighter than his song " to Lucasta on going to the Wars," or that to " Althea from Prison " ? How chivalrous the thought of them ! How tremulously delicate the expression !

His life was full of sadness. The son of a Kentish knight, educated at the Charterhouse and at Gloucester Hall, Oxford,

[1] Written by Col. John Lovelase [t.i. Richard Lovelace]. See Wood's *Athenæ Oxon*. Vol. 2ᵈ Written by *the* Author when imprison'd.—P.

"the most amiable and beautiful person that eye ever beheld, a person also of innate modesty, virtue and courtly deportment, which made him then [at Oxford], but especially after, when he retired to the great city, most admired and adored by the female sex." Thus physically endowed, thus happily circumstanced, he was yet crossed in love, and died in a state of destitution.

Lucy Sacheverell—the Lux Casta or Lucasta of his poems, from the nunnery of whose chaste breast and quiet mind he had fled to war and arms, that "dear" whom he loved so much because he loved honour more—misled by a report that he had died of wounds received at Dunkirk while commanding a regiment, of his own forming, in the service of the French king, became the wife of somebody else. The close of the civil war, in which he had devoted both his services and his fortunes to his king's cause, found him beggared. His loyalist zeal got him twice into prison. "During the time of his confinement," says Wood of the first imprisonment, "he lived beyond the income of his estate, either to keep up the credit and reputation of the king's cause by furnishing men with horses and arms, or by relieving ingenious men in want, whether scholars, musicians, soldiers, &c.; also by furnishing his two brothers Colonel Franc. Lovelace, and Capt. Will. Lovelace (afterwards slain at Caermarthen) with men and money for the king's cause, and his other brother called Dudley Posthumus Lovelace with monys for his maintenance in Holland to study tactics of fortification in that school of war." "After the murther of King Charles I., Lovelace was set at liberty [from his second captivity], and having by that time consumed all his estate, grew very melancholy (which brought him at length into a consumption), became very poor in body and purse, was the object of charity, went in ragged cloaths (whereas when he was in his glory he wore cloth of gold and silver), and mostly lodged in obscure and dirty places, more befitting the worst of beggars and poorest of servants, &c. . .

He died in a very mean lodging in Gunpowder alley near Shoe-lane, and was buried at the west end of the church of St. Bride alias Bridget in London, near to the body of his kinsman, Will. Lovelace of Gray's Inn, Esq."—"Richard Lovelace, Esq.," says Aubrey, "obiit in a cellar in Long Acre, a little before the restauration of his ma^{tie}. Mr. Edm. Wyld, &c., had made collections for him and given him money. . . . . . Geo. Petty, haberdasher, in Fleet Street, carryed XXs to him every Munday morning from Sir ——— Many, and Charles Cotton, Esq., for months, but was never repay'd." He died in 1658, and so was saved from experiencing Stuart gratitude. These accounts of his dismal indigence may perhaps be coloured. But there can be no doubt he ended in extreme poverty, in a sad contrast to the brilliancy of his early days.

The following song was written during his first captivity. He had been chosen by his county to present a Petition to the House of Commons " for the restoring of the king to his rights, and for setling the government." He presented it, and by way of answer was committed to the Gate House at Westminster. But his mind, innocent and quiet, took his prison for a hermitage. His gaolers heard him singing in his bonds. Love with wings that brooked no confinement hovered near him. Brought by that chainless spirit, the divine Althea came to visit him in his durance. She led away the captive into a second captivity. With her fair hair she wove fresh bonds for him ; she laid on new fetters with her eyes. But he revelled in these chains. Having freedom in his soul, angels alone that are above enjoyed such liberty.

———

WHEN Love with vnconfined wings
　　hovers within my gates,
& my divine Althea brings
　　to whisper at my grates,

When my love visits my prison.

4

c 2

I am free
as a bird.

when I lye tangled in her heere
    & fettered with her eye,
the burds *that* wanton in the ayre
8   enioyes [1] such Lybertye.

When I,
continued,
sing my
king's
goodness,

When, Lynett like confined, I
    with shriller note shall sing
the mercy, goodnesse, maiestye
12   & glory of my kinge,
when I shall voice aloud how good
    he is, how great shold bee,

I am free as
the winds.

the enlarged winds *that* curles the floods [2]
16   enioyes such Lybertye.

When I
drink with
boon com-
panions

When flowing cupps run swiftly round
    with woe-allaying theames,
our carlesse heads with roses crowned,

to our cause,

20   our harts with Loyall flames,
when thirsty soules in wine wee steepe,
    when cupps and bowles goe free,

I am as free
as a fish.

ffishes *that* typle in the deepe
24   enioyes such Lybertye.

Though in
prison,

Stone walls doe not a prison make,
    nor Iron barrs a cage,

yet with a
pure soul

the spotlesse soule an[d] Innocent [3]
28   Calls this an hermitage. [3]   [page 192]

and free
love,

if I haue freedome in my loue,
    & in my soule am free,

I am free as
an angel.

angells alone *that* sores aboue
32   enioyes such Lybertye !

ffins.

---

[1] This final *s* and several others have
been marked through by a later hand.
— F.

[2] flood. — P.
[3] These lines differ from the usual
reading. — Skeat.

Cloris.[1]

SEVERAL collections of Waller's Poems appeared as early as 1645, while he was living in France. The first edition "corrected and publish'd with the approbation of the Author" came out in 1664. "When the Author of these verses," says the Printer to the Reader in this one, " (written only to please himself and such particular persons to whom they were directed), returned from abroad some years since, He was troubled to find his name in print, but somewhat satisfied to see his lines so ill rendered, that he might justly disown them, and say to a mistaking Printer, as one did to an ill Reciter, *male dum recitas, incipis esse tuum.* Having been ever since pressed to correct the many and gross faults (such as use to be in impressions wholly neglected by the authors) his answer was, That he made these when ill verses had more favour and escaped better than good ones do in this age, the severity whereof he thought not unhappily diverted by these faults in the impression, which hitherto have hung upon his Book, as the Turks hang old raggs (or such like ugly things) upon their fairest Horses, and other goodly creatures, to secure them against fascination ; and for those of a more confind understanding (who pretend not to censure) as they admire most what they least comprehend, so his Verses (mained to that degree that himself scarce knew what to make of many of them), might that way at least have a title to some Admiration, which is no small matter, if what an old Author observes be true, that the

---

[1] An elegant old song written by Mr. Waller. See his Poems.—P.

aim of Orators is Victory, of Historians Truth, and of Poets Admiration: He had reason, therefore, to indulge those faults in his Book whereby It might be reconciled to some, and commended to others." But the considerations expressed in this longwinded and somewhat confusing manner, were overcome by the importunity of the worthy Printer, and the Poet at last gave leave "to assure the Reader, that the Poems which have been so long and so ill set forth under his name, are here to be found as he first writ them, as also to add some others which have since been composed by him." The following song does not occur in this edition; nor in that of 1682, "the Fourth Edition with several Additions never before printed." It appears in that of 1711, "the eight edition, with additions," and no doubt in several of the preceding editions.

The song is a fair specimen of Waller's average style. It exhibits his faults, and his merits—his affectation, and strained gallantry, with something of his elegance and grace.

His life was not a noble one. He was not inspired by that spirit which enabled Lovelace to sing that

Stone walls do not a prison make, Nor iron bars a cage.

He lived from 1605 to 1687, from the year of the Gunpowder Treason to the year before the Revolution. He sat in Parliament, for various places, from his nineteenth year to his death, except from 1643 to the Restoration, in which period his connection with the Royalist Plot of 1643 suspended his public life.

Cloris. I
must go,

or lose my
sight.

CLORIS, farwell! I needs must goo!
  for if with thee I longer stay,
  thine eyes prevayle upon me soe,
4 I shall grow blynd & lose my way.[1]

[1] Lines 2. 3. 4, are almost all eaten away by the ink of the title at the back.—F.

ffame of thy bewty & thy youth,
 amongst the rest me hither brought ;
but finding fame fall short of truth,
8 made me [1] stay longer then I thought.

Report
brought me
hither ;

your beauty

keeps me.

ffor I am engaged by word [and] othe
 a servant to anothers will ;
but for thy loue wold forfitt both,
12 were I but sure to keepe itt still.

Though I
am be-
trothed,

I'd break
my troth if
I could
secure you ;

But what assurance can I take,
 when thou, fore-knowing this abuse,
for some [more [2]] worthy louers sake
16 mayst leaue me with soe Iust excuse.

but how
could I ?

You'd jilt
me, and

ffor thou wilt say it, " it was [3] not thy fault
 that I to thee [4] vnconstant proue,
but were by mine [5] example taught
20 to breake thy othe to mend thy loue."

plead my
example as
your excuse.

Noe, Cloris, Noe ! I will returne,
 & rayse thy story to that height
that strangers shall att distance burne,
24 & shee distrust thee [6] reprobate.

No ! I'll go,
and praise
your beauty
from afar,

Then shall my loue this Doubt displace,
 & gaine the trust *that* I may come
& sometimes banquett on thy face,
28 but make my constant meales att home.

seeing you
sometimes
but loving
my own
love.

---

[1] my. Qu.—P.
[2] more.—P. A *may* that precedes *for* in the MS. is crossed out.—F.
[3] is.—P.
[4] thou to me. Qu.—P.
[5] One stroke too few in the MS.—F.
[6] mee. Qu.—P.

The kinge enioyes his righ[ts againe.][1]

THIS song occurs in the *Roxburghe Collection of Ballads*, iii. 256, in the *Loyal Garland containing choice Songs and Sonnets of our late Revolution* (London, 1671, Reprinted by the Percy Society), in a *Collection of Loyal Songs*, in Ritson's *Ancient Songs*. Mr. Chappell, in his *Popular Music of the Olden Time*, ii. 434–9, gives the air to which it was sung, along with much information concerning it (which should be read), and nine more stanzas than are included in our Folio. It was written by Martin Parker, as appears from the following extract from the *Gossips' Feast or Morall Tales*, 1647: "The gossips were well pleased with the contents of this ancient ballad, and Gammer Gowty-legs replied 'By my faith, Martin Parker never got a fairer brat; no, not when he penn'd that sweet ballad, *When the King injoyes his own again*.'" It was an extreme favourite with the Cavaliers.

Booker, Pond, Rivers, Swallow, Dove, Dade, and Hammond, were eminent astrologers and almanack-makers. See *Ritson*, and *Chappell*, ii. 437, note [a].

WHAT Booker can prognosticate,
consider[i]ng now the kingdomes state?
I thinke my selfe to be as wise
4 as he that gaseth [2] on the skyes;
my skill goes beyond the depth of Pond [3]
or Riuers in the greatest raine,
wherby I can tell *tha*t all things will goe well
8 when the Ki*ng* enioyes his rights againe.

Marginal notes: Who can foretell — when the King will enjoy his own again?

---

[1] An old Cavilier Song.—P.   [2] gazeth.—P.   [3] ponds.—P.

There is neither swallow, doue nor dade,
can sore more high, or deep*er* wade
to shew a reason from the starres,
12 what causeth these our ciuill warres.

No stargazer
can tell
what causes
our civil
wars.

the man in the moone may weare out his shoo[ne [1]]
in running after Charles his wayne;
but all is to noe end, for the times will not me[nd [2]]
16 till the K*ing* enioyes his right againe.

The times
won't mend
till the King
has his own.

ffull 40 yeeres his royall crowne
hath beene his fathers and his owne,
& is there any more nor [3] hee
20 that in the same shold sharrers [4] bee,
or who better may the scepter sway
then he that hath such rights to raine?
there is noe hopes of a peace, or the war to ce[ase [5]],
24 till the K*ing* enioyes his right againe.

Who has
better right
to the crown
than our
King?

Although for a time you see Whitchall   [page 193]
w*i*th cobwebbs hanging on the wall
insteed of silkes & siluer braue
28 wh*i*ch fformerly ['t] was [6] wont [to] haue,
w*i*th a sweete p*er*fume in eue*r*ye roome
delightfull to *that* princely traine:
wh*i*ch againe shalbe when the times you see
32 *that* the King enioyes his right againe. [7]
ffins.

Though
Whitchall is
all cobwebs
now,
soon it will
be silks

and per-
fumes,

when the
King enjoys
his right
again.

[1] shoone.—P.   [6] formerly 't was.—P.
[2] mend.—P.   [7] This fourth stanza is put before the
[3] than.—P.   third in the copy that Mr. Chappell
[4] sharers.—P.   [5] cease.—P.   prints, ii. 438.

The Ægiptian Queue.[1]

THIS song under the title of *Mark Anthony* is found, *minus*
vv. 13–20 inclusive, in *Poems by J. C.* 1651, the first edition
of Cleveland's Poems, and in such of the many subsequent ones
as we have examined, those of 1654 (B. in the notes below), of
1677 (C. in the notes), and of 1687 (D. in the notes). Our copy
is probably a bad one of the verses before they were printed,
when lines 13–20 were cut out. The song is marked by Cleveland's characteristic vigour and tendency to "conceits."

John Cleveland sang and suffered much in the Royal cause.
Educated at Christ's College, elected a Fellow of St. John's
College, Cambridge—"To cherish such hopes," says an old
biographer of him, "the Lady Margaret drew forth both her
breasts"—he joined the King at Oxford when the breach with
the Parliament became irreparable, and gallantly adhered to the
King's fortunes to the end. After the capture of Newark, when
he was Judge Advocate, he seems to have led, for some years, a
life of wretched vagrancy. In 1655 he was taken prisoner. He
made an appeal to Cromwell, which was heard. He did not live
to see the restoration of the race which he had served with all his
trenchant wit, with the truest devotion. April 29, 1659, is the
date of his death.

As the copy in our folio MS. is corrupt in many places, we
give here the copy from the first edition of 1651, collated with
the editions of 1654, 1677, and 1687.

MARK ANTHONY.

WHEN as the Nightingale chanted her Vespers,
And the wild Forester couch'd on the ground.
Venus invited me in th' Evening whispers,
4 Unto a fragrant field with Roses crown'd:

---

[1] Not an inelegant old song. Corrected by an Edition in Cleveland's Poems.
12mo 1687. p. 65.—P.

Where she before had sent
My wishes complement,
Unto my hearts content
8   Plaid with me on the Green,
Never Mark Anthony
Dallied more wantonly
With the fair Egyptian Queen.

12 First on her cherry cheeks I mine eyes feasted,
Then [1] fear of surfeiting made me retire :
Next on her warm [2] lips, which when I tasted,
My duller spirits made [3] active as fire.
16   Then we began to dart
Each at anothers heart,
Arrows that knew no smart :
Sweet lips and smiles between,
20   Never Mark, &c.

Wanting a glass to plate her amber tresses,
Which like a bracelet rich decked mine arm,
Gawdier then *Juno* wears when as she graces
24 *Jove* with embraces more stately than warm.
Then did she peep in mine
Eyes humour Christalline ;
I in her eyes was seen,
28   As if we one had been.
Never Mark, &c.

Mystical Grammar of amorous glances,
Feeling of pulses the Physick of Love,
32 Rhetorical courtings and Musical Dances ;
Numbring of kisses Arithmetick prove.
Eyes like Astronomy,
Streight limb'd Geometry :
36   In her heart's ingeny
Our wits are sharp and keen.
Never Mark, &c.

WHEN as the Nightingale chanted her vesper, [4]   At eve
  & the wyld fayryes lay coucht [5] on the ground,
Venus invited me to an euening Wisper, [6]   my Love
                                  invited me
4 to fragrant feelds [7] with roses crounde   to toy with

---

[1] Thence.—B. C. D.
[2] warmer.—B. C. D.
[3] made me.—C. D.
[4] her vespers.—P.
[5] forrester coucht. I wd read here

forresters, *i.e.* the deer, the Inhabitants
of the forrest.—P.
[6] in th' evening whispers.—P.
[7] Unto a fragt field.—P.

her in the fields.

which [1] shee before had sent her cheefest complement,
Vnto my [2] harts content sport [3] with me on the greene ;

We dallied like Antony and Cleopatra.

8   Neuer marke Anthony dallyed more wantonly
With his fayre Ægiptian queene [4] !

I looked at her cheeks,

flirst on her Cherry cheekes I my eyes [5] feasted ;
thence feare of surffetting made me retyre,

kissed her lips,

then to her warmed [lips], [6] which when I tasted,

12   my spiritts duld were made actiue by [7] fyer.

pressed her hand,

[8] this heat againe to calme, her moyst hand yeelderd balme ;
whilest wee Ioyned [9] palme to palme as if wee one had beene,
Neuer marke Anthony dallyed more wantonly

16   with his fayre Cor [10] egiptian queene !

twined mine in her hair,

Then in her golden heere [11] I my hands twined ;
shee her hands in my lockes twisted againe,
as if her heere had beene fetters assigned,

20   Sweet litle Cupid [12] Loose captiue [13] to chayne ;

gazed in her eyes.

soe did wee often dart one at anothers hart
arrows *that* felt [14] noe smart, sweet lookes and smiles [15] betweene.
Neuer, &c.

Her tresses deckt my

24   Wa[yting a glass to platt] those amorus tresses [16]
which like a [bracelet] deckt richly mine arme,

---

[1] Where.—P. *For* her cheefest *Percy puts* my wishes.—F.

[2] And to my. query.—P.

[3] Play'd.—P.

[4] Only half the *n* in the MS.—F.

[5] mine eyes.—P.

[6] warmer lips.—P.

[7] actiue as.—P.

[8] N.B. from hence to [So did we often dart] is wanting in the printed Copy.—P.

[9] A *t* is between *Ioyned* and *palme* in the MS. *as if wee one had heene* has been first written as a separate line, then struck out and written after *palme* ; then one had beeⁿ was struck out, and copied in again by Percy.—F.

[10] ? MS.—F.

[11] haire.—P.

[12] After the *d* Percy puts *'s.*—F.

[13] After the *e* Percy adds *s.*—F.

[14] fett, fetch'd.—query : it is know no sm! in print.—P.

[15] Lipps and smiles.—P.

[16] Wayting a glass to platt (plait) her amber tresses.—P. The ink of the heading *The king enioyes* on the back has eaten the MS. away.—F.

gaudyer then Iuno was *which* [1] when shee blessed [2]   arm like a bracelet ;
  Ioue with Euers races [3] more richly [4] thein warme.

28 shee sweetely peept in eyne *that* was more cristalline,
  which by reflection shine ech eye and eye was seene. she peept sweetly at me,
  Neuer, &c.

Misticall gram*mers* [5] of [6] amorus glances,
32 feeling of pulses, the phisicke of loue, and in her glances
  Retoricall courtings & musicall dances,
  numbring of kisses arithemeticke proues [7] ;
  Eyes like astronomy, strayght limbes geometry, I saw kisses alone.
36 in her harts enginy [8] ther eyes & eyes were seene.[9]
  Neuer, &c.

ffins.

[1] Juno wears.—P.
[2] presses (graces) Pr. Copy.—P.
[3] So in the MS.—F. embraces.—P.
[4] stately. P.C.—P.
[5] *grammars*; grammar of: pr. Copy. —P. Note the Seven Sciences—Grammar, Physic, Rhetoric, Music, Arithmetic, Astronomy, Geometry.—Skeat.
[6] are. query.—P.
[7] proue. p.c.— P.
[8] Arts Ingeny.—P.
[9] our wits were sharp and keen. Printed Copy.—P.

["*The Mode of France,*" *and* "*Be not affrayd,*" *printed in* Lo. *and* Hum. Songs, *p.* 45–8, *follow here in the MS.*]

ℌollowe me ffancye.

This song, says Percy's marginal note, is "printed in a collection of Scots Poems, Edingboro', 1713, pag. 142." *Mens prætrepidans avet vagari.* Led by Fancy, it throws off for the nonce the fetters of the body, and "dances through the welkin." It inspects the phenomena of cloudland, rejoices *rerum cognoscere causas.* Then, turning its gaze downwards, it studies that great ant-hill the earth. It sees mankind rushing to and fro upon it, with all their various pursuits, humours, passions. At last the much-travelled spirit wearies. Its wings droop, and it implores its ever-vigorous guide to lead it no further. The great world-prospect, with its tumult and turmoil, is too tremendous a vision. So the spirit hies it back to its home, the body.

Melancholy,	IN: a Melancholly fancy, out of my selfe,
I dance	thorrow the welkin dance I,
	all the world survayinge, noe where stayinge ;
like an elf	4 like vnto the fierye elfe,[1]
over moun- tains, plains, and woods.	over the topps of hyest mountaines skipping,
	ouer the plaines, the woods, the valleys, tripping,[2]
	ouer the seas without oare of[3] shipping,
	8 hollow, me fancy ! wither wilt thou goe ?

[1] fairy elfe.— P.   [2] Only half the *n* in the MS.—F.   [3] oare or.— P.

Amydst the cloudy vapors, faine wold I see
what are those burning tapors
which benight vs and affright vs,   *I'd like to see what the stars and meteors are;*
12 & what the Meetors [1] bee.

ffaine wold I know what is the roaring thunder, [page 195]
& the bright Lightning which cleeues the clouds in *what the thunder,*
    sunder, *lightning,*
& what the cometts are att which men gaze & wonder. *and comets.*
16 Hollow, me &c.

Looke but downe below me where you may be bold, *I'd like to look down*
where none can see or know mee ; *on the bust-*
all the world of gadding, running of madding, *ling world,*
20 none can their stations hold :
One, he sitts drooping all in a dumpish passion ; *and see one man in the*
another, he is for Mirth and recreation ; *dumps,*
the 3ᵈ, he hangs his head because hees out of fassion. *another all mirth ;*
24 Hollow, &c.

See, See, See, what a bustling !
Now I descry one another Iustlynge ! *others jost-ling their*
how they are turmoyling, one another foyling, *fellows,*
28 & how I past them bye !
hee thats aboue, him thats below [2] despiseth ; *high de-spi-ing low,*
hee thats below, doth enuye him [2] that ryseth ; *low envying high ;*
euerye man his plot & counter [2] plott deviseth.
32 Hollow.

Shipps, Shipps, Shipps, I descry now ! *shipmen*
crossing the maine He goe too, and try now
what they are proiecting & protecting ; *projecting*
36 & when thé turne againe.
One, hees to keepe his country from inuadinge ; *defence from foes*
another, he is for Merchandise & tradinge ; *or gain in*
the other Lyes att home like summers cattle shadding.[3] *trade.*
40 Hollow.

✤

[1] meteors.—P.   [2] MS. blotted.—F.   [3] ? getting into a shed or the shade.—F.

Hollow, me fancy, hollow !

I can't go
on.
Fancy, come
back to me ;

I pray thee come vnto mee, I can noe longer follow !

I pray thee come & try [me] ; doe not flye me !

44 Sithe itt will noe better bee,

leave off
soaring,
and keep to
your book.

come, come away ! Leave of thy Lofty soringe !

come stay att home, & on this booke be poring !

for he *that* gads abroad, he hath the lesse in storinge.

48 welcome, my fancye ! welcome home to mee !

ffins.

Newarke.[1]

THIS song may very well have been written, as Percy suggests, by Cleveland to cheer the garrison of Newark; when, during the Royalist occupation of it, he was Judge Advocate. See Introduction to " Egyptian Queen."

" In the reign of Charles I. Newark was garrisoned for the King, and held in subjection the whole of this country, excepting the town of Nottingham; and a great part of Lincolnshire was laid under contribution; here that unfortunate sovereign established a mint. . . . During this contest the town sustained three sieges: in the first, all Northgate was burnt by order of the governor, Sir John Henderson; in the second, when under the government of Sir John, afterwards Lord, Byron, the town was relieved by the arrival from Chester of Prince Rupert, who, according to Clarendon, in an action between his forces and the parliamentarians under Sir John Meldrum, on Beacon Hill, half a mile eastward of the town, took four thousand prisoners and thirteen pieces of artillery; in the third siege, after the display of much prowess and several vigorous sallies, the fortress remained unimpaired; afterwards Lord Bellasis, then governor, surrendered the town to the Scottish army, by the King's order, on the 8th of May, 1646. At the close of this siege, the works and circumvallations were demolished by the country people, with the exception of two considerable earth-works, which are now nearly perfect, and are called the King's Sconce and the Queen's Sconce; about this time the castle also was destroyed." (Lewis' *Topogr. Dict. of England.*)

[1] Very probably writ by Jack Cleveland during the siege of Newark upon Trent: to Chear the Garrison: where he was judge advocate.—P.

Fill us a cup!

Our : braines are asleepe, then fyll vs [1] a cupp
    of cappering sacke & clarett ;

Here's a health to King Charles.

here is a health to *King* Charles ! then drinke it all vp,
4   his cause will fare better for itt.
    did not an ould arke saue noye [2] in a fflood ?

We dread not our foes.

    why may not a new arke to vs be vs [3] good ?
    wee dread not their forces, they are all made of wood,
8   then wheele & turne about againe.

Though all beyond trent be sold to the Scott,
    to men of a new protestation
    if Sandye come there, twill fall to their Lott
12   to haue a new signed possession ;

If Leslie gets hold of 'em he'll play the devil and all.

but if once Lesly gett [them] in his power,
    gods Leard ! heele play the devill & all !
but let him take heed how hee comes there,
16   lest Sweetelipps ring him a peale in his eare.

Then tosse itt vp merrilye, fill to the brim !
    wee haue a new health to remember ;

Drink to our garrison.

heeres a health to our garrisons ! drinke it to them,
20   theyle keepe vs all warme in December.

I fear no foe,

I care not a figg what enemy comes;
    for wee doe account them but hop-of-my-thumbes ;

for our Maurice is coming.

for Morrise [4] our prince is coming amaine
24   to rowte & make them run againe.

                           ffins.

---

[1] MS. vis *or* vus.—F.   [3] us.—F.
[2] Old Ark—Noë.—P.   [4] Maurice.—P.

Amongst the mirtles.[1]

THE first collection of Carew's poems was made in 1640, the year after his death. But many of them had been set to music during his life; others no doubt had circulated in MS.

"He was a person," says Clarendon, "of a pleasant and facetious wit, and made many poems (especially in the amorous way), which for the sharpness of the fancy and the elegance of the language in which that fancy was spread, were at least equal, if not superior to any of that time: but his glory was that after fifty years of his life spent with less severity or exactness than it ought to have been, he died with great remorse for that license, and with the greatest manifestation of Christianity, that his best friends could desire."

AMongst the Mirtles as I walket,
loue & my thoughts sights this [2] inter-talket:
"tell me," said I in deepe distresse,
4   "Where may I find [my sheperdesse.[3]]

> Where can I find my shepherdess?

"Thou foole!" said loue, "knowes thou not this?
in cuerye thing thats good shee is.
in yonder tulepe goe & seeke,
8   there thou may find her lipp, her cheeke;

> [page 196]
> She's in all that's good, her hue in the tulip,

"In yonder enameled Pancye,
there thou shalt haue her curyous eye;
in bloome of peach & rosee [4] budd,
12   there waue the streamers of her blood;

> her eye in the pansy,

---

[1] A very elegant old song. Writ by Mr. Thomas Carew. See his poems, 8? L. 1640.—P.
[2] thus.—P.; and sights markd for omission by Percy.—F.
[3] The MS. is cut away.—F.
[4] rosee.—P.

D 2

her hand in
the lily.

" In [1] brightest Lyllyes *that* heere stand,
the [2] emblemes of her whiter hands ;

the scent of
her bosom
on the hills.

in yonder rising hill, their smells [3]

16   such sweet as in her bosome dwells."

I went to
pluck these
flowers.

" It is trew," said I ; & therevpon
I went to plucke them one by one

but all
vanished.

to make of parts a vnyon ;

20   butt on a sudden all was gone.

So shall pass
my joy!

With *that* I stopt, sayd, " loue,[4] these bee,
fond man, resemblance-is of thee [5] ;
& as these flowers, thy Ioyes shall dye

24   Euen in the twinkling of an eye,

" And all thy hopes of her shall wither
Like these short sweetes soe knitt together."

ffi[ns.]

---

[1] The.—P.
[2] are.—P.
[3] there smells.—P.

[4] stop'd. S⁴ Love &c.—P.
[5] resemblances of thee.—P.

𝔗𝔥𝔢 𝔴𝔬𝔯𝔩𝔡𝔢 𝔦𝔰 𝔠𝔥𝔞𝔫𝔤𝔢𝔡.[1]

Songs of a very similar kind are common enough in the collections of Royalist poems : as, for instance, "The Humble Petition of the House of Commons" in *A Collection of Loyal Songs written against the Rump Parliament between the years* 1639 *and* 1661, 1731.

> If Charles thou wilt but be so kind
> To give us leave to take our mind,
>   Of all thy store ;
> When we thy Loyal Subjects, find
> Th'ast nothing left to give behind
>   We'll ask no more.

and " Pym's Anarchy " in the same collection :

> Ask me no more, why there appears
> Daily such troops of Dragooners ?
> Since it is requisite, you know,
> They rob *cum privilegio*.
>
> Ask me no more, why from Blackwall
> Great Tumults come into Whitehall ?
> Since it's allow'd, by free consent,
> The Privilege of Parliament.
>
> Ask me no more, for I grow dull,
> Why Hotham kept the Town of Hull ?
> This answer I in brief do sing,
> All things were thus when Pym was King.

The : world is changed, & wee haue choyces, *Not Reason, but most voices rule.*
not by most reason, but most voyces ;
the Lyon is trampled by the Mouse,
4   the lower is the vpper house, *The lower house is the upper.*
& thus from laus [2] orders come,
but now their orders laus [2] frome.

[1] A good old Cavilier song.—P.

[2] qu. Caus.—F.

In all humilitye they craue
8   theire soueraigne to be their slaue,
beseeching him *that* hee wold bee
betrayd to them most Loyallye ;

for it were Meeknesse soe in him
12   to be a vice-Roy vntoy Pyim.[1]

If *that* hee wold but once Lay downe
his scepter, maiestye, & crowne,
hee shalbe made in time to come
16   the greatest prince in christendome.

Charles, att this time hauing noe neede,
thankes them as much as if they did.

Petitions none must be presented
20   but what are by themselves inuented,
that once a month thé thinke it ffitting
to fast from soine [2] because from sittinge ;
Such blessings to the Land are sent
24   by priuiledge of Parlaiment.

ffins.

---

[1] unto Pym.—P.   [2] ? MS. *sone,* with a dot over the first stroke of the *n*.—F.

The tribe off Banburye.[1]

THIS song, not before printed so far as we know, gives an insolent Cavalier account, put in the mouth of a Puritan, of the occupation of Banbury by a Royalist force. Banbury was visited more than once by such a force during the Civil War of 1642-6. The visit here referred to was paid in the very beginning of the disturbances, some seventeen days before the Royal Standard was set up at Nottingham. When the King and the Parliament each insisted on having the management of the militia, the former appointed the Earl of Northampton to "array" it in Warwickshire, the latter Lord Brook. In July the Parliament granted its deputy six pieces of ordnance to strengthen his castle, at Warwick. These were conveyed as far as Banbury by the 29th. The attempt to convey them on to Warwick was barred by Lord Northampton. The two lords at last agreed that they should be carried back to Banbury, and that neither party should remove them without giving the other three days' notice. On the 6th and 7th of August great alarm began to prevail in the town, that the enemy was meditating an assault, and a seizure of the said ordnance. On Sunday night, the 7th, the enemy was discovered by a scout, coming down Hardwick lane in great force. But "the night growing extreme dark, they forbare all that night." Then next morning a parley was held, when the Cavaliers by turns cajoled and threatened the fearful citizens. At last :—

The town being in a sad case, not knowing how they would deal with them, exposed themselves and town on Munday morning [the 8th], and in a while after they came in with about 5 or 600 horses,

[1] An old Cavilier Song on the Taking of Banbury by Colonel Lumford.—P.

but 300 good ones, and the rest sorry jades, anything [they] could get from the poor countrey men, some at work; and as beggarly riders set on them, though for the present they flourished with money, yet their cloths bewrayed them to be neither gentlemen nor Cavaliers. And having fil'd the town with horses the chief of them came to the Red Lion Inne, and desired to speak with Colonell Feines and Captaine Vivers, who were in the Castle, to whom reply was made, they should, if they would send two as considerable men in lieu, which they did; then they produced the Commission of Array, and required them to deliver the Ordnance, otherwise they would take them by force, and fire the town. And having obtained that they came for, the ordnance and ammunition thereunto belonging, they clear'd the town againe, and were all departed before night, who carried them to the E. of Northamptons house [Compton Wyngate], and it was thought they intended to goe to Warwicke castle the next day, but the Lord Brooke had noe notice from the Earle of three dayes warning, as was agreed between them ; There was also Colonell Lunsford, and divers Lords too long to name ; There was the Lord Wilmot, who kept backe the town of Atherbury from coming in to aide Banbury, and threatned he would hang up the men and send the souldiers to their wives and children; There was also the Lord Dunsmore.—"Proceedings at Banbvry since the Ordnance went down for the Lord Brooke to fortifie Warwick Castle," 4to, 1642. Among the King's Pamphlets in the Brit. Mus. *apud Beesley's* "*History of Banbury,*" p. 302.

On July 7

the Cavi- liers took Banbury.

We had news of Lunsford's coming,

ON : the 7th day on the 7 month,
    most Lamentablye
the men of Babylon did spoyle
4   the tribe of Banburye.

A brother post from conentry
    ryding in a blew rockett,[1]
sayes, " Colbronde Lunsford comes, I saw,
8   with a childs arme hang in his pockett."

---

[1] A.-S. *roc*, clothing, an outer garment, a coat, jacket. vest ; Bosworth. Germ. *rock*, a coat. Chaucer describes dame Fraunchise in a *rocket*, see Fairholt's Glossary :

Fullo wel [y-] clothed was Fraunchise, For ther is no cloth sittith bet On damyselle, than doth *rocket*. A womman wel more fetys is

Then wee called up our men of warr,
   younge Viuers, Cooke & Denys,[1]
whome our Lord Sea[2] placed vnder
12   his Sonne *Master* ffyenys.[3]

and called
out our men
of war,

When hee came neere, he sent vs word
   that hee was coming downe,
& wold, vnles wee lett him in,
16   Granado[4] all our towne.

but Lunsford
said he'd

grenado our
town,

Then was our Colb*ronde*—fines,[5]—& me,
   in a most woefull case ;
for neither he nor I did know
20   who this granado was.

wee had 8 gunnes called ordinance,[6]
   & foure score Musquetiers,[7]
yett all this wold not serue to stop
24   those Philistime cauileeres.

and our guns
and men

[page 197] couldn't stop
him.

Good people, thé did send in men
   from Dorchester & Wickam ;
but wher this Gyant did them see,
28   good Lord, how he did kick han[8] !

In *roket* than in cote, ywis.
The whyte *roket* rydled faire, &c.
Romaunt of the Rose, l. 1238-43, Poet.
Works, ed. Morris, vi. 38.
"Rocket, a surplys:" Palsgrave.
"Skelton describes Elinor Rumming
the Alewife in a gray russet *rocket*.
Rocket, a cloak without a cope: Randle
Holme;" in Fairholt.
Rocket, a frocke ; loose gaberdine, or
gowne of canuas or course linnen, worne
by a labourer over the rest of his clothes ;
also, a Prelates Rocket: Cotgrave. See
the woodcut in Fairholt, p. 220.—F.
[1] There is a dot over the stroke following the *e* in the MS.—F.
[2] Say.—P.
[3] Fiennes.—P.
[4] Fr. *Grenade*. A Pomegranet; also,
a ball of wild-fire, made like a Pomegranet: Cotgrave. An iron case filled
with powder and bits of iron, like the
seeds in a pomegranate: Wedgwood.
—F.
[5] Fiennes.—P.
[6] Ordinance, all sorts of Artillery, or
great Guns us'd in War. Phillips.—F.
[7] Musquetiers.—P. The last *e* is made
over a *y* in the MS.—F.
[8] kick 'em.—P.

He swore
and threat-
ened us so

"You round heads, rebells, rongs,[1]" quoth hee,
"Ile crop & slitt eche eare,
& leaue you neither arme nor lege
32   much longer then your heere[2]!"

that we
opened our
gates,

Then wee sett ope our gates[3] full wyde;
they swarmed in like bees,
& they were all arraydd in buffe
36   thicker then our towne cheese.[4]

and his
blood-
thirsty men

Now god deliuer vs, we pray,
from such blood-thirstye men,
forom[5] Leayathan Lunsford
40   who eateth our children!

hung us and
plundered
us.

ffor Banburye, the tinkers crye,
you hanged vs vp by twelues;
now since Lunsford hath plundred you,
44   you may goe hang your selues.

ffins.

---

[1] rogues.—P.
[2] haire. N.B. The Roundheads were
so called from wearing their hair cropt
short.—P.

[3] gater in the MS.—F.
[4] Banbury Cheese.—P.
[5] this.—P.

["*Doe you meane to overthrowe me,*" and "*A Maid & a Younge Man,*"
printed in Lo. and Hum. Songs, *p.* 49–52, *follow here in
the MS.*]

𝔄𝔶 : 𝔪𝔢 : 𝔄𝔶 𝔪𝔢 :

The Editors have not found any printed copy of this song. Mr. Chappell informs them that there is a tune in the *Dancing Master* of 1657 entitled "Ay me, or the Symphony," but it requires words of a different metre to that of this song.

"A fling at the Scots, probably writ in James I. time" is Percy's MS. note; or, as Mr. Halliwell says of *Joky will prove a gentillman*,[1] a "satire . . doubtlessly levelled against the numerous train of Scotch adventurers who wisely emigrated to England in the time of James I., in the full expectation of being distinguished by the particular favour and patronage of their native sovereign." Poor Sisly, the chief speaker in the piece, laments the dropping off of her suitors. She once had twelve, and now she has but one. The first was handsome; the ten following were all well-to-do in the world in one way or another; the one that yet remains has no merit of either sort. The others were Welsh, Dutch, French, or Spanish; this one is a sorry Scotchman. A doleful state of things; but the best must be made of it. At any rate, as this last lingering wooer is a beggar, he can never be declared bankrupt. But indeed begging is the way to wealth now-a-days—begging for appointments, &c. In *Joky will prove* such begging is introduced as the cause of the marvellous change of the hero's cowhide shoes into Spanish-leather ones decked with roses, of his twelvepenny stockings into "silken blewe," of his list garters into silk tasselled with gold and silver, &c.

---

[1] Reprinted from *The Archæologist* in *Satirical Songs* (Percy Society). p. 127.

Thy hose and thy dublett, which were full plaine,
Whereof great store of lice [did] containe,
Is turned nowe. Well fare thy braine
That can by begginge this maintayne!
By my fay, and by Saint Ann,
Joky will prove a gentilman!

Moved by this disinterested consideration—that begging is the
winning game—Sisly resolves to give the constant Scot the right
to beg for her as well as himself.

Oh dear!
I had twelve
suitors,

"AY: me, ay me, pore sisley, & vndone [1]!
I had 12 sutors, now I have but one!
they all were wealthy; had I beene but wise;

and all are
gone but
one,
the worst of
all,

4   now haue all left me since I hauę beene soe nice,[2]
but only one, and him all Maidens scorne,
for hees the worst I thinke *that* ere was borne."
"peace good sisley! peace & say noe more!

8   bad mends in time; good salue heales many a sore."

"ffaith such a one as I cold none but loue,[3]
for [4] few or none of them doe constant proue;
a man in shape, proportion, looke, and showe,

a regular
weed.

12   much like a Mushroome in one night doth grow;
proud as a Iay *thats* of a comely hew,
cladd like a Musele in a capp of blew.[5]"
"peace, good sisley! peace, & say noe more!

16   be Merry, wench, & lett the welkin rore!"

The rest
were good,

"The first I had was framed in bewtyes mold,
the second: 3[d] and 4th had store of gold,
the 5. 6. 7. 8th had trades eche one,

20   the best had goods & lands to liue vpon;
Now may I weepe, sigh, sobb, & ring my hands,

this one's
naught,

since this hath neither witt, trade, goods, nor Land[s.]"

-----

[1] I'm vndone.—P.
[2] Particular; not Fr. *niais*, a simple,
witlesse, vnexperienced gull. *Nice*, dull,
simple: Cotgrave.—F.

[3] As none but I *could* love.—P.
[4] But.—P.
[5] The Scotch cap. See *Blew-cap for
me* in *Sat. Songs*, p. 130, &c.—F.

"peace, good sisley; peace & take *that* one
24 *that* stayes behind when all the rest are gone!"

"He [is,] as [1] turkes doe say, noe renegatoe,[2]
noe Portugall, Gallowne, or reformato [3];
but in playne termes some say he is a scott,   n Scot,
                                                            in a cast-off
28 *that* by his witts some old cast suite hath gott,   suite.
& now is as [4] briske [5] as my [6] Bristow Taylor,
& swaggers like a pander or a saylor.[7]"
"kisse him, sisley, kisse him, he may proue the best,
32 & vse him kindly, but witt bee all the rest."

"One was a welchman, her wold [8] scorne to crye;   My other
                                                           suitors were
& 3 were Dutchmen *that* sill [9] drunke wold bee;   Welch,
                                                           Dutch, &c.
& 6 were frenchemen *that* were pockye proude;
36 & one a spanyard *that* cold bragg alowd.
Now all are gone, & way [10] not me a figge,
but one poore Scott who can doe nought but begg."   This one is a
                                                           poor begging
"take him, sisley! take him, for itt is noe doubt,   Scot.
40 his trades *that* beggs, heele neuer proofe [11] banquerout."

"Nay, sure, Ile haue him, for all people say   But I'll take
                                                           him;
that men by begging grow rich now a day,   begging's a
                                                           good trade
& *that* oftentimes is gotten with a word   now;
44 att great mens hands *that* neuer was woone by sword.
then welcome Scotchman, wee will weded bee,
& one day thou shalt begg for thee and mee."   and he'll beg
                                                           for us both.
"well sayd, sisley! well said! on another day,
48 by begging thou maist weare a garland gay!"

---

[1] He is, as, &c.—P.
[2] renegado.—P.
[3] reformado.—P. Sp. *reformádo*, reformed. Minsheu. *Reformado*, or *Reformed
Officer*, an Officer whose Company or
Troop is disbanded, and yet be continu'd
in whole or half Pay; still being in the
way of Preferment, and keeping his
Right of Seniority: Also a Gentleman
who serves as a Volunteer in a Man of
War, in Order to learn Experience, and
succeed the Principal Officers. Phillips.
—F.
[4] It may be *al* in the MS.—F.
[5] And now's as brisk.—P.
[6] any.—P.
[7] ? MS. Jaylor.—F.
[8] hur wold, &c.—P.
[9] still.—P.
[10] weigh.—P.
[11] The Man that begs will ne'er prove.
—P.

ffaine : wolde : I change : [page 199]

THIS is the song of one who entertains a supreme horror of living and dying an old maid. She has been told by old wives, no doubt well informed on the subject, that those who do so are employed subsequently in " leading apes in hell;"[1] after which singular occupation she feels no great hankering. "To the church," then, is the word. Ding-dong away, Marriage bells.

———— · —

"FAINE wold I change my maiden liffe
   to tast of loues true Ioyes."

I want to change my maiden life,

"What ? liffe ! woldest[2] thou chuse to bee a wiffe ?
4 maids wishes are but toyes."
"how can there bee a greater hell then liue a maid
   soe long,[3]
  a mayd soe long ?
to the church ring out the Marriage bells,
8 ding dong, ding dong, ding dong !"

"Beffore that 15 yeeres were spent,
  I knew, & haue a sonne."

for I'm nearly sixteen,

"how old art thou ? " " sixteene next Lent."
12 "alas, wee are both vndone ! "
how can there bee &c.

---

[1] Mr. Dyce says : " The only instances of the expression *leading apes in* (or *into*) *hell*, which at present occur to me, are these :—

" ' — and he that is less than a man, I am not for him : therefore I will even take sixpence in earnest of the bear-ward, and *lead his apes into hell.'*—Shakespeare's *Much ado about Nothing*, act. ii. sc. 1.

" ' — but keeping my maidenhead till it was stale, I am condemned to *lead apes in hell.'*—Shirley's *Love-Tricks*, act iii.

sc. 5 ; *Works*, vol. i. p. 53, ed. Gifford and Dyce.

" This phrase, which is still in common use, never has been (and *never will be*) satisfactorily explained. Steevens suggests, 'That women who refused to bear children, should, after death, be condemned to the care of apes in leading-strings, might have been considered as an act of posthumous retribution.' "—F.

[2] why would'st.—P.

[3] ? MS.—F. so long.—P.

"Besides, I heard an old wiffe tell
　　that all true maids must dye."
16　"what must they doe ? " "lead apes in hell !
　　a dolefull destinye."

　"& wee will lead noe apes in hell ;
　　¹ weele change our maiden song, our maiden song ;
20　to the church ring out the Marriage bells,
　　wee haue liued true mayds to ² longe."

　　　　　　ffins.

and true
maids die
and lead apes
in hell.

I won't do
that,

but will off
to church.

---

¹ "Weele change" is in the 18th line in the MS.—F.　　² too.—P.

When first I sawe.

THIS song occurs, as Mr. Chappell remarks, in the *Golden Garland of Princely Delight*, 3rd edition, 1620. Mr. Chappell adds a fourth stanza from later copies, " such as *Wit's Interpreter*, third edition, 8vo. 1671 : "

> If I have wronged you, tell me wherein,
> And I will soon amend it ;
> In recompense of such a sin,
> Here is my heart, I'll send it.
> If that will not your mercy move,
> Then for my life I care not :
> Then, O then, torment me still,
> And take my life and spare not.

He gives the tune to which the song was sung, composed by Thomas Ford (one of the musicians in the suite of Prince Henry, the eldest son of James I.), who published it in his *Musick of Sundrie Kindes*, in 1607.

I loved you
at first sight,

WHEN first I saw her face, I resolued [1]
to honor & renowne thee ;
but if I be disdayned, I wishe
4   *tha*t I had neuer knowne thee.

and you bade
me love ;

I asked leaue ; you bade me lone ;
is itt now time to chyde mee ?
O : no : no : no ! I loue you still, what fortune euer
betyde mee !

8 If I admire or praise you too much,
    *tha*t fortune [you] might [2] forgiue mee ;
or that my hand hath straid but to touch,[3]
    thenn might you iustly leaue mee,

---

[1] thee I resolv'd. P.   [2] that fault you might.—P.   [3] MS. teach.—F. to touch.—P.

12 but I that liked, & you *that* loued,
  is now a time to wrangle?
 O no: no: no, my hart is flixt, & will not new <small>will you</small>
   entangle.   <small>now quarrel
with me?</small>

 The sun, whose beames most glorious are,
16 rejecteth [1] noe beholder;
 your faire face, past all compare,   <small>Your beauty</small>
  makes my faint hart the bolder.
 when bewtye likes, & witt delights,
20 & showes of Loue doe bind mee;
 there, there! O there! whersoeuer I goe, <small>has stolen</small>
  Ile leaue my hart behind mee!   <small>my heart.</small>

         ffinis.

[1] MS. & reacheth.—F.

["*A Creature for Feature,*" and "*Lye alone,*" *printed in*
 Lo. and Hum. Songs, *p.* 53–56, *follow here in the MS.*]

How fayre shee be.[1]

This well-known song by George Wither (1590–1667) appeared in 1619, appended to his *Fidelia*, and again in *Juvenilia*, in 1633, in "Fair Virtue the Mistress of Philarete." It was reprinted again and again, sometimes with another stanza. The version here given is slightly corrupt. "A copy of this song," says Mr. Chappell, "is in the Pepys collection, i. 230, entitled A new song of a young man's opinion of the difference between good and bad women. To a pleasant new tune. It is also in the second part of the Golden Garland of Princely Delights, third edition 1620, entitled The Shepherd's Resolution. To the tune of The Young Man's Opinion."

SHALL: I, wasting in dispayre,

    dye because a womans fayre?

or make pale my cheekes with care [2]

4   because anothers rose-yee [3] are?

Be shee fairer then the day

    or the flowry Meads in may,

    if shee thinke not well of mee,

8   What care I how fayre shee bee?

Shall my foolish hart be pind

    because I see a woman kind,

    or a well disposed nature

12   with [4] a comlye feature?

Marginal notes:

Shall I kill myself

because my love doesn't care for me?

Not I.

----

[1] An elegant old Song by Withers. This song is in *the* Tea Table Miscellany of Allan Ramsay, 1753, *page* 304. But the Printed Copy wants the 2d stanza:— it containing only three. It is also in Dryden's Misc. V. 6, p. 335, with the omission of St. 2d.—P.

[2] shall my Cheeks look pale with care (printed Copy).—P.

[3] rosie are.—P.

[4] matched or joined.—P.

Be shee Meeker, kinder, then
  the turtledoue or Pelican,
if shee be not soe to me,
16   what care I how kind shee bee ?

If she's not
kind to me,
let her go.

Shall a womans vertues ¹ moue
  me to perish for her loue,
or her worthy merritts knowne
20   make me quite forgett mine owne ?
were shee with *that* goodness blest,
  as may meritt name of best,
if shee be not soe to me,
24   what care I how good shee bee ?

Shall I
perish for
her love ?

Not I.

²Be shee good or kind or fayre,
  I will neuer more disp[air ;]
if shee loue me, this beleeue,
28   I will dye ere shee shall g[reiue ;]
if shee slight me when I woe,
  I will scorne & lett her goe.
or if shee be not ³ for mee,
32   what care I ⁴ for whom shee bee ?

If she slight
me,
let her go.

What care I ?

---

¹ goodness (printed Copy).—P.
² The following four lines are written
in two in the MS.—F.

³ Percy inserts *fit*.—F.
⁴ A *whom* struck out follows *I* in the
MS.—F.

["*Downe sate the Shepard*," and "*Men that more*," *printed in
Lo. and Hum. Songs, p. 57–60, follow here in the MS.*]

Come : Come : Come : [1]   [page 202]

This is, says Percy in his marginal note in the Folio, " A curious
old drinking song, supposed to be sung by an old gouty Baccha-
nal." Not content with fellow mortal topers, the old roisterer
calls on all the Gods to join him in his carouse. Not his the
Lotus-eater's conception of the Deities. He does not think
that " careless of mankind they lie beside their nectar . . where
they smile in secret, looking over wasted lands," smile at the
music centred in the doleful song of lamentation, the ancient
tale of wrong, from the " ill-used race of men that cleave the soil."
He sees them madding their brains for " a little care of the
world's affair," " utterly consumed with sharp distress " at the
world's misery ; and he calls on them to be such fools no longer—
to " let mortals do as well as they may "—while they, the Gods,
take up their wine and drink with him. Mars, Momus, Mercury,
Apollo, Vulcan, the great Jove himself, dread Juno, and Venus,
Goddess of Love—none are excused—all must join ; the grape
is sweet, and wine for them as well as men : let all quaff, and
sing fa la la !—F.

Let's be jolly!

COME: Come, come ! shall wee Masque or mum ?
by my holly day,[2] what a coyle is heere !
some must [3] sway, & some obay I,
4   or else, I pray, who stands in feare ?

Though we have the gout,

though [4] my toe, *that* I limpe on soe,[5]
doe cause my woe & wellaway,

wine'll make us sing.

yett this sweet spring & another thing
8   will make you sing fa.la.la.la.la.

---

[1] A curious old drinking song, supposed to be sung by an old gouty Bac-
chanal.—P.
[2] Dame.—P.

[3] *mist* in the MS.—F.
[4] what tho'.—P.
[5] sc. with the Gout.—P.

ffellow gods, will you fall att odds ?

what a fury madds your morttall [1] braines !

Don't bother about business.

for a litle care of the worlds affare,

12   will you frett, will you square,[2] will you vexe, will you vai[r ?] [3]

No, gods ! no ! let fury go,[4]

& Morttalls doe as well as they may !

for this sweet &c.

16 God of Moes,[5] with thy toting Nose,

    with thy mouth *that* growes to thy Lolling care,

stretch thy mouth from North to south,

    & quench thy drought[6] in vinigar !

20 though thy toung be too Large & too Longe

    to sing this song of fa la la la la,

Ioyne Momus grace to vulcans pace,

    & with a filthy face crye " waw waw waw ! "

Momus,

drink vinegar!

Sing with us somehow !

24 Brother Mine, thou [7] art god of wine !

    will you tast of the wine [8] to the companye ?

King of quaffe, carrouse & doffe

    your Liquor of, and follow mee !

28 [9] Sweete soyle of Exus Ile,

    wherin this coyse [10] was euery day,

for this sweet &c.

Bacchus,

join me in a bowl!

Mercurye, thou Olimpian spye !

32   wilt thou wash thine eye in this fontaine cleere ?

when [11] you goe to the world below,

    you shall light of noe such Liquor there,

Mercury,

drink!

---

[1] immortal, qu.—P.

[2] i. e. quarrel.—P.

[3] will you vex your vaines.—P. *Fair* for *ver*, turn. It should rhyme with *square.*—Chappell.

[4] ? MS. *gutt*, with *t t* blotched out.— F.

[5] Mows, i. e. Mockery. Se. Momus. P.

[6] drowth.—P.

[7] that.—P.

[8] vine.- P.

[9] To the. P.

[10] ? MS. coyle.—F. ? *coyse*, body.— Halliwell.

[11] whene'er.— P.

though [1] you were a winged stare

36   & flyeth [2] farr as shineth day ;

Wine'll wing your heart.

yett heeres a thing your hart will wing,

    & make you sing &c.

Mars,

You *that* are the god of warr,

40   a cruell starr perverse & froward,

Mars ! prepare thy warlicke speare,

    & targett ! heers a combatt towards !

[3] then fox [4] me, & Ile fox thee ;

stop strife, and drink.

44   then lets agree, & end this fray,

    since this sweet &c.

Venus,

Venus queene, for bewtye scene,

    in youth soe greene, & loued soe young,

48   thou *that* art mine owne sweet hart,

you drink too!

    shalt haue a *part* in Cuppe [&] songe [5] ;

though my foot be wrong, my swords full long

    & hart full strong; cast care away,

52   Since this sweet &c.

Apollo,

Great Appollo, crowned with yellow, [6]

    Cynthius, fellow [7]-muses deere !

here's wine for you ! It will refine your music.

heere is wine, itt must be thine,

56   itt will refine thy Musicke cleere ;

to the wire of this sweet lire

    you must aspire another day,

    for this sweet &c.

Juno,

60   Iuno cleere, & mother deere,

    you come in the rere of a bowsing feast ;

---

[1] Altho', or even tho', or perhaps

  What tho' you are a winged star
  And fly as far.—P.

[2] and flew as, as. That flyeth.—P.

[3] Do thou fox me. P.

[4] a toping Word. P. *Fox*, to make tipsy. A cant term. See Hobson's Jests, 1607, repr. p. 33. Halliwell.—F.

[5] Cup & song.—P.

[6] Cloath'd in yellow.—P.

[7] Cease to follow, *or* Quit thy fellow, *or* With thy fellow.—P. Apollo was surnamed *Cynthius*, and Diana *Cynthia*, as they were born on Mount Cynthus, which was sacred to them. Lempriere.—F.

thus I meet, your grace to greet ;
the grape is sweet & the last is best.

64 now let fall your angry brawlee [1]
for from immortall & wayghtye sway ;
tis a gracious thing to please your King,
& heare you sing &c.

leave your anger,

drink and sing!

68 Awfull sire, & king of fire !
let wine aspire to thy mighty throne,
& in this quire of voices clere
Come thou, & beare an imorttall drame [2] ;   [page 203]

72 for fury ends, & grace d[e]sends
with Stygian feinds to dwell for aye.
lett Nectur spring & thunder ring
when Ioue [3] doth sing &c. &c.

Jove,

drink, and join our song!

76 Vulcan, Momus, hermes, Bacchus,
Mars & Venus, 2 and tooe,
Phebus brightest, Iuno rightest,
& the mightyest of the crew,

80 Ioue, and all the heauens great [4] hall,
keepe festiuall & holy-day !
since this sweete spring with her blacke thing
will make you sing fa la la la.

Vulcan and all you gods,

rejoice and drink wine.

ffinis.

---

[1] brawle.—P.
[2] drone, i. e. bass.—P.

[3] Jove.—P. MS. Iohue, with perhaps the *h* marked out.—F.
[4] *full* here, struck out.—F.

The Grene Knight.[1]

[In 2 Parts.—P.]

THIS is a late, popular version of the old romance of "Sir Gawain and the Green Knight," preserved amongst the Cottonian MSS. (Nero A. X. fol. 91) edited by Sir Frederick Madden for the Bannatyne Club in 1839 and by Richard Morris Esq. for the Early English Text Society in 1864.[2] The old romance, written, according to Mr. Morris, about 1320 A.D., by the author of the Early English Alliterative Poems also printed by the E. E. Text Society, is lengthy, is written in alliterative metre, and is as difficult as the old alliterative poems usually are. To dissipate this besetting obscurity, to relieve this apparent tediousness, the present translation and abridgement was made. The form is changed; the language is modernised. In a word, the old romance was adapted to the taste and understanding of the translator's time. Moreover, it was made to explain a custom of that time—a custom followed by an Order that was instituted, according to Selden and Camden, some three-quarters of a century (A.D. 1399) after the time when, according to Mr. Morris, the poem first appeared. It explains why

> Knights of the bathe weare the lace
> Untill they have wonen their shoen,
> Or else a ladye of hye estate
> From about his necke shall it take
> For the doughtye deeds hee hath done.

On this point SOMERSET HERALD has kindly furnished us with the following note :

---

[1] A curious adventure of Sir Gawaine, explaining a custome used by the Knights of the Bath.—P.

N.B. See a Fragment p. 29 [of MS.; vol. i. p. 70, l. 213 of text] wherein is mention of a Green Knight & decapitation p. 29-31 [of MS.; pp. 70-3 of text]. —P.

[2] In his edition of *Syr Gawayne*, Sir F Madden printed the present poem as No. III. in his Appendix, p. 224-242.

College of Arms, June 8.

It appears to have been the custom of Knights of the Bath, from at least as early as the reign of Henry IV., to wear a lace or shoulder knot of white silk on the left shoulder of their mantles or gowns, ("theis xxxii nw kni3tes preceding immediately before the king in theire gownis,[1] and hoodis, and tookins of whi3te silke upon theire shouldeirs as is accustumid att the Bath:" MS. *temp.* Edw. IV., fragment published by Hearne at the end of Sprott's Chronicle, p. 88). This lace was to be worn till it should be taken off by the hand of the prince or of some noble lady, upon the knight's having performed "some brave and considerable action," vide Anstis's History of the Order. What this custom originated in does not appear, and the writer of the poem has only exercised the allowed privilege of his craft, in attributing the derivation to the adventure of Sir Gawaine and "the Lady gay" in this legend of "The Green Knight."

In the Statutes of the Order, 11th of George I. 1725, it is commanded that they shall wear on the left shoulder of their mantle "the lace of white silk antiently worn by the said knights," but there is no mention of its being taken off at any time for any reason.

J. R. Planché.

The recast belongs then to an age which was beginning to study itself, and to enquire into the origin of practices which it found itself observing. It is an infant antiquarian effort. But the poem has lost much of its vigour in the translation. It is in its present shape but a shadow of itself. Moreover, the following copy appears much mutilated. Several half-stanzas have dropped out altogether, probably through the sheer carelessness of the scribe.

The two leading persons of the romance are the well-known Sir Gawain, of King Arthur's court, and Sir Bredbeddle of the West country—the same knight who appears in *King Arthur and the King of Cornwall*, vol. i. p. 67. The main interest rests upon Sir Gawain. His "points three"—his boldness, his courtesy, his hardiness—are all proved. He is eager for adventures; he unshrinkingly pursues them to the end; he bears extreme hardships patiently; his courtesy is shown in his nobly

[1] Froissart says, "un double cordeau de soÿe blanche a blanches louppettes pendans."

resisting the overtures made him by his host's wife, whom Agostes
has brought to his bedside.

> The ladye kissed him times three,
> Saith, " Without I have the love of thee,
>   My life standeth in dere."
> Sir Gawaine blushed on the Lady bright,
> Saith, " Your husband is a gentle Knight,
>   By Him that bought mee deare!
> To me itt were great shame,
> If I shold doe him any grame,
>   That hath beene kind to mee."

All these provings are given much more fully in the original
romance. But enough is given here to uphold the fame of the
chivalrous knight. See the *Turk and Gowin.*

When
Arthur
lived, he
ruled all
Britain,

LIST! wen [1] Arthur he was K*i*ng,
  he had all att his leadinge
    the broad Ile of Brittaine;
4 England & Scottland one was,
  & wales stood in the same case,
    the truth itt is not to layne.[2]

  he drive allyance [3] out of this Ile,

and lived, for
a time, in
peace.

8 soe Arthur lived in peace a while,
    as men [4] of Mickle maine,

To stop his
knights con-
tending for
precedency,

  kn*i*ghts strong of [5] their degree
  [strove] w*h*ich of them hyest shold bee;
12   therof Arthur was not faine;

he made the
Round
Table,

  hee made the round table for their behoue,
  *tha*t none of them shold sitt aboue,

that all

    but all shold sitt as one,[6]

---

[1] when.—P.
[2] without layne, i.e. without lying.—
or with*out* altering the line (only dele *it
is*) it is " Not to conceal the truth."—P.
Old Norse *leyna,* to hide.—F.
[3] drave aliens.—P.

[4] man.—P.
[5] K*n*ts strove of (about) &c.—P.
[6] at one.—P.   Compare *Arthur,* E. E.
Text Soc., p. 2, l. 43-53:
    At Cayrlyone, wythoute fable,
    he let make þe Rounde table:

16   the King himselfe in state royall,
    Dame Gueneuer our queene withall,
      seemlye of body and bone.

    itt fell againe the christmase,
20   many came to *that* Lords place,
      to *that* worthye one
    with helme on [1] head, & brand bright,
    all *that* tooke order of knight;
24   none wold linger att home.

    there was noe castle nor manour free
    that might harbour *that* companye,
      their puissance was soe great.
28   their tents vp the pight [2]
    for to lodge there all *that* night,
      therto were sett to meate.

    Messengers there came [&] went [3]
32   with much victualls verament
      both by way & streete ;
    wine & wild fowle thither was brought,
    within they spared nought
36   for gold, & they might itt gett.

    Now of King Arthur noe more I mell [4] ;
    'but of a venterous knight I will you tell [5]
      that dwelled in the west countrye [6] ;
40   Sir Bredbeddle, for sooth he hett [7] ;
    he was a man of Mickele might,
      & Lord of great bewtye.

Side notes:
might be equal.

One Christmas many knights came to Arthur's court.

No house could hold all of them,

so they pitched their tents,

and food was served to them.

But I shall leave Arthur, and tell you about Sir Bredbeddle.

And why þat he maked hyt þus,
þis was þe resoun y-wyss,
þat no man schulde sytt aboue oþer,
ne haue indignacioun of hys broþer ;
And alle hadde .oo. seruyse,
For no pryde scholde aryse
Oþer for any degree of syttynge
Oþer for any seruynge. -F.

[1] MS. &.—F.
[2] pitched, or put.—P.
[3] and went.—P.
[4] mell, meddle, fr. mêler. Urry.—P.
[5] I tell.—P.
[6] See line 515.—F.
[7] hight, was called.—P. The earlier
romance makes the knight's name " Bern-

He loved his
wife dearly,

but she
loved Sir
Gawaine.

Her mother
Agostes
dealt in
witchcraft,

could trans-
form men,

and told
Bredbeddle
to go, trans-
formed,

to Arthur's
court to see
adventures.

This was in
order to get

Gawaine

he had a lady to his [1] wiffe,

44 he loued her deerlye as his liffe,
  shee was both blyth and blee [2] ;
  because Sir Gawaine was stiffe in stowre,
  shee loued him priuilye paramour,[3]
48 & [4] shee neuer him see.

  itt was Agostes *that* was her mother ;
  itt was witchcraft & noe other
   *tha*t shee dealt with all ;

52 shee cold transpose k*nigh*ts & swaine
  like as in battaile they were slaine,
  wounded [5] both Lim & lightt,[6]
  shee taught her sonne the k*nigh*t alsoe
56 in transposed likenesse he shold goe [7]
  both by fell and frythe ;

  shee said, "thou shalt to Arthurs hall;
  for there great aduentures shall befall
60 That euer saw K*ing* or Knight."   [page 204]
  all was for her daughters sake,
  *that whi*ch she [8] soe sadlye spake
  to her sonne-in-law the K*nigh*t,
64 because Sir Gawaine was bold and hardye,

lak de Hautdesert " (p. 78, l. 2445); it does not make his wife fall in love with Gawain, but Bernlak sends her to tempt him (p. 75, l. 2362). Gawain comes out of the temptation as one of the most faultless men that ever walked on foot, and as much above other knights as a pearl is above white pese (l. 2364). The enchantress is *Morgne la Faye*, Arthur's half-sister and Gawaine's aunt ; and she sends Bernlak to Arthur's court in the hope that his talking with his head in hand would bereave all Arthur's knights of their wits, and grieve Guinevere, and make her die (p. 78, l. 2460). The description of Morgne la Faye (p. 30-1) is very good, with her rough yellow wrinkled cheeks, her covered neck, her black chin muffled up with white vails, her forehead enfolded in silk, showing only her black brows, eyes, nose, and lips " sowe to se and selsyly blered."—F.

[1] MS. wis.—F.

[2] so bright of blee, *blee* is colour, complexion, bleo S. Color. Urry.—P.

[3] I w? read par amour.—P.

[4] and yet.—P.

[5] and wound.—P.

[6] lythe, a joint, a limb, a nerve, Sax. li*x*, artus. Urry.—P.

[7] to go.—P.

[8] MS. *that* theye wh*ich*.--F.

& therto full of curtesye,[1]
  to bring him into her sight.

the knight said " soe mote I thee,
68 to Arthurs court will I mee hye
    for to praise thee right,
  & to proue Gawaines points 3 ;
  & *that* be true *that* men tell me,
72 by Mary Most of Might."

earlye, soone as itt was day,
  the K*night* dressed him full gay,
    vmstrode[2] a full good steede ;
76 helme and hawberke both he hent,
  a long fauchion verament
    to fend them in his neede.

that[3] was a Iolly sight to seene,·
80 when horsse and armour was all greene,
    & weapon *that* hee bare.
  when *that* burne was harnisht still,
  his countenance he became right well,
84 I dare itt safelye sweare.

that time att Carleile lay our K*ing* ;
  att a Castle of flatting was his dwelling,
    in the fforrest of delamore.[4]
88 for sooth he[5] rode, the sooth to say,
  to Carleile[6] he came on Christmas day,
    into *that* fayre countrye.[7]

---

[1] " þat fyne fader of nurture " the old romance calls him, p. 29, l. 919.—F.
[2] and strode, i. e. bestrode.—P. *um* = round. See the elaborate description of the knight, his armour and horse, in the old romance, p. 5-6, l. 151-202.—F.

[3] Yt, i.e. *it*.—P.
[4] Delamere.—P. In Cheshire.—H.
[5] for soe hee.—P.
[6] Camylot, in the old romance.—F.
[7] countrye faire.—P.

The porter
asks
him where
he's going to.
when he into *that* place came,[1]

92   the porter thought him a Maruelous groome:

he saith, " S*i*r, wither wold yee ? "

hee said, " I am a venterous K*n*ight,

" To see
King Arthur
and his
lords."
& of *your* K*ing* wold haue sight,

96   & other Lo*r*ds *that* heere bee."

The porter
noe word to him the porter spake,

but left him standing att the gate,

& went forth, as I weene,

tells Arthur
100   & kneeled downe before the K*ing* ;

saith, " in lifes dayes old or younge,

such a sight I haue not seene !

of the Green
Knight's
arrival,
" for yonder att *your* gates right; "

104   he saith, " hee is [2] a venterous K*n*ight ;

all his vesture is greene."

and the
king
orders him
to be let in.
then spake the K*ing* proudest in all,[3]

saith, " bring him into the hall ;

108   let vs see what hee doth meane."

Dredbeddle
comes,
when the greene K*n*ight came before the K*ing*,

he stood in his stirrops strechinge,

& spoke with voice cleere,

wishes
Arthur God
speed,
112   & saith, " K*ing* Arthur, god saue thee

as thou sittest in thy prosperitye,

& Maintaine thine honor [4] !

and says he
has come
" why [5] thou wold me nothing but right ;

116   I am come hither a venterous [Knight,[6]]

& kayred [7] thorrow countrye farr,[8]

to challenge
his lords to
a trial of
manhood.
to proue poynts in thy pallace

that longeth to manhood in euerye case

120   among thy Lo*r*ds deere."

---

[1] come or was come.--P.
[2] there is.—P.
[3] first or foremost of all.--P.
[4] honnore.—P.
[5] for why, because.—F.

[6] Knight.—P.
[7] have gone; A.-S. *cérran, cirran*, to turn, pass over or by.—F.
[8] farre, or perhaps faire.—P.

the King, he sayd [1] full still [2]   Arthur

till he had said all his will ;

certein thus can [3] he say :

124 " as I am true knight and King,

thou shalt haue thy askinge ! consents to

I will not say thy nay, [4]   let him try

" whether thou wilt [5] on foote fighting, on foot,

128 or on steed backe [6] iusting or horse-

for loue of Ladyes gay.   back.

If & thine armor be not fine,

I will giue thee part of mine."

132 " god amercy, Lord ! " can he say,

" here I make a challenging Bredbeddle

among the Lords both old and younge challenges

that worthy beene in weede, Arthur's
lords :

136 which of them will take in hand [7]— he'll let any

hee that is both stiffe and stronge one

and full good att need—

" I shall lay my head downe, [page 205] cut his head

140 strike itt of if he can [8]   off,

with a stroke to garr [9] itt bleed,

for this day 12 monthe another at his : for a return

let me see who will answer this, cut at his
executioner's

144 a knight [10] that is doughtye of deed; head a year
hence

" for this day 12 month, the sooth to say,

let him come to me & seieth his praye ;

rudlye, [11] or euer hee blin, [12]

---

[1] satt.—P.

[2] quietly.—P.

[3] certes then 'gan.—P.

[4] say thee nay.—P. þy is the abla-
tive of the A.-Sax. demonstrative pro-
noun, se, seo, þæt.—F.

[5] wilt be.—P. wilt = wishest, pre-
ferest.—H.

[6] on steed-back, i.e. on horse-back.
—P.

[7] hond.—P.

[8] con.—P.

[9] gar, cause.—F.

[10] perhaps To a kt.—P.

[11] redlye, i.e. readily. Vid. G.D.—P.

[12] blin, linger, delay.—P.

at the
Greene
Chappell.

148   whither to come, I shall him tell,
        the readie way to the greene chappell,
        that place I will be in."

        the K*ing* att ease sate full still,
152   & all his lords said but litle [1]
        till he had said all his will.

Kay

        vpp stood S*ir* Kay *that* crabbed *knight*,
        spake mightye words *that* were of height,
156   *that* were both Loud and shrill ;

accepts the
challenge.

        " I shall strike his necke in towe,
        the head away the body froe."

The other
knights tell
Kay to be
quiet ;
he's always
getting into
a mess.

        the bade him all be still,
160   saith,[2] " Kay, of thy dints make noe rouse,[3]
        thou wottest full litle what [4] thou does [5] ;
        noe good, but Mickle ill."

        Eche man wold this deed haue done.

Sir Gawaine

164   vp start S*ir* Gawaine soone,
        vpon his knees can kneele,

says it will
be too bad if
Arthur
doesn't let
him take the
adventure.

        he said, " *that* were great villanye
        w*i*thout you put this deede to me,
168   my leege, as I haue sayd ;

        " remember, I am yo*ur* sisters sonne."

Arthur
consents,

        the K*ing* said, " I grant thy boone ;
        but mirth is best att meele ;
172   cheere thy guest, and giue him wine,

but not till
after dinner.

        & after dinner, to itt fine,
        & sett the buffett well ! "

---

[1] littel.—P.
[2] i. e. they say.—P.
[3] praise, extolling, boast.—Jun. per-

haps *roust*, noise. G. Doug.—P.
[4] that. – P.
[5] doest.—P.

now the greene Knight is set att meate,
176 seemlye [1] serued in his seate,
   beside the round table.
to talke of his welfare, nothing he needs,
like a Knight himselfe he feeds,
180   with long time reasnable. [2]

Bredbeddle dines.

when the dinner, it was done,
the King said to Sir Gawaine soone,
   withouten any fable
184 he said, "on [3] you will doe this deede,
I pray Iesus be your speede!
   this knight is nothing vnstable."

Arthur wishes Gawaine

God speed.

Bredbeddle is a stiff one.

the greene Knight his head downe layd;
188 Sir Gawaine, to the axe he braid [4]
   to strike with eger will;
he stroke the necke bone in twaine,
the blood burst out in euerye vaine,
192   the head from the body fell.

Gawaine

chops off Bredbeddle's head.

the greene Knight his head vp hent, [5]
into his saddle wightilye [6] he sprent,
   spake words both Lowd & shrill,
196 saith: "Gawaine! thinke on thy couenant!
this day 12 monthes see thou ne want
   to come to the greene chappell!"

Bredbeddle picks it up, jumps into his saddle,

reminds Gawaine to meet him twelve months hence,

---

[1] MS. *seemlye*, with a horizontal line and two vertical strokes over the *n*, denoting a contraction, and showing that I ought to have read as *in* the similar *n* in the heading of "Eger and Grine," vol. i. p. 341. The title would then have corresponded with the text; but never having noticed the contraction before, I hesitated to alter the MS.—F.

[2] reasonable.—P.

[3] an.—P.

[4] See Herbert Coleridge's *Glossary* on this word, Old Norse *bregða*. He abstracts from Egilson. As a neuter verb it is used "of any violent motion of body, as to leap."—F.

[5] took.—P. The old romance makes some of the knights kick the head with their feet, l. 428.—F.

[6] actively.—P.

All had great marnell, *that* the see
200 *that* he spake so merrilye
& bare his head in his hand.

forth att the hall dore he rode right,
and *that* saw both King and knight
204 and Lords *that* were in land.

without the hall dore, the sooth to saine,
hee sett his head vpon againe,[1]

saies, " Arthur, haue heere my hand !
208 when-soener the Knight cometh to mee,
a better buffett sickerlye
I dare him well warrand."

the greene Knight away went.
212 all this was done by enchantment   [page 206]
that the old witch had wrought.

sore sicke fell Arthur the King,
and for him made great mourning
216 that into such bale was brought.

the Queen, shee weeped for his sake ;

sorry was Sir Lancelott dulake,
& other were dreery in thought
220 because he was brought into great perill ;
his mightye manhood will not availe,
that before hath freshlye fought.

Sir Gawaine comfort King and Queen,
224 & all the doughtye there be-deene [2] ;
he bade the shold be still;
said, " of my deede I was neuer feard,[3]
nor yett I am nothing a-dread,

228 I swore by Saint Michaell ;

---

[1] The old romance makes the head
open its eyelids and speak while it's on
the knight's hand, l. 446.—F.

[2] immediately.—P. or all together.—
F.

[3] fraid.—P.

"for when draweth toward my day,
I will dresse me in mine array
   my promise to fulfill.

232 Sir," he saith, " as I haue blis,
I wott not where the greene chappell is,
   therfore secke itt I will."

the royall Couett [1] verament
236 all rought [2] Sir Gawaines intent,
   they thought itt was the best.

they went forth into the feild,
knights that ware both speare and sheeld
240   thé priced [3] forth full prest [4];

some chuse them to Iustinge,
some to dance, Reuell, and sing;
   of mirth thé wold not rest.

244 all they swore together in fere,
that and Sir Gawaine ouer-come were,
   thé wold bren all the west.

Now leaue wee the King in his pallace.
248 the greene Knight come home is
   to his owne Castle;
this folke frend [5] when he came home
what doughtye deeds he had done.
252   nothing he wold them tell;

full well hee wist in certaine
that his wiffe loued Sir Gawaine
   that comelye was vnder kell. [6]
256 listen, Lords [7]! & yee will sitt,
& yee shall heere the second ffitt,
   what adventures Sir Gawaine befell.

---

[1] royall Courtt.—P. ? covey, Fr. couvée.—F.
[2] ? reached, took in.— F.
[3] pricked.—P.
[4] ready.—P.
[5] His folke freyn'd, i. e. inquired.—P.

[6] A child's caul, any thin membrane. " Rim or kell wherein the bowels are lapt." Florio, p. 340. Sir John " rofe my kell " (deflowered me) MS. Cantab. Ff. v. 48, fo. 111, Halliwell's Gloss.—F.
[7] Lordings.—P.

[Part II.]

2ᵈ. parte.

The year is
up, and
Gawaine
must go.

260

The king
and court
grieve.

264

> The day is come *that* Gawaine must gone ;
> Kn*igh*ts & Ladyes waxed wann
>   *that* were without in *that* place ;
> the K*ing* himselfe siked ill,
> ther Q*uee*n a swounding almost fell,
>   to *that* Iorney when he shold passe.

When he was in armour bright,
he was one of the goodlyest Kn*igh*ts
    that euer in brittaine was borne.

His steed
was dapple-
grey,

268

they brought S*i*r Gawaine a steed,
was dapple gray and good att need,[1]
    I tell w*i*thouten scorne ;

his bridle
jewelled,

272

his bridle was w*i*th stones sett,
with gold & pearle oue*r*frett,
    & stones of great vertue ;
he was of a furley[2] kind ;

his stirrups
silk ;

276

his stirropps were of silke of ynd ;
    I tell you this tale for true.

when he rode ou*er* the Mold,

he glittered
like gold.

his geere glistered as gold.
    by the way as he rode,

280

many furleys[3] he there did see,
fowles by the water did flee,
    by brimes & bankes soe broad.

---

[1] Gryngolet is the steed's name in the old romance, but his colour is not given. All the jolly bits about his trappings, and Gawaine's armour, with its pentangel devised by Solomon, and called in English "the endeles knot," are omitted here.—F.

[2] *ferlie*, wonder, wonderful ; Sax. *ferlic*, repentinus, horrendus, Gl. ad G.D.—P.

[3] ? MS. *furlegs*, for ferlies, wonders. —F.

many furleys there saw hee

284 of wolues & wild beasts sikerlye;
on hunting hee tooke most heede.
forth he rode, the sooth to tell,
for to seeke the greene chappell,

288 he wist not where [1] indeed.

[page 207]

As he rode in an eue[n]ing late,
riding downe a greene gate,[2]
a faire castell saw hee,[3]

292 *that* seemed a place of Mickle pride;
thitherward S*i*r Gawaine can ryde
to gett some harborrowe.[4]

thither he came in the twylight,

296 he was ware of a gentle Kn*ight*,
the Lo*rd* of the place was hee.
Meekly to him S*i*r Gawaine can speake,
& asked him, "for K*ing* Arthurs sake,

300 of harborrowe I pray thee!

"I am a far Labordd Knight,
I pray you lodge me all this night."
he sayd him not nay,

304 hee tooke him by the arme & led him to the hall.
a poore child [5] can hee call,
saith, "dight well this palfrey."

into a chamber thé went a full great speed;

308 there thé found all things readye att need,
I dare safelye swere;

Marginal notes: Gawaine sees wondrous beasts; discerns a castle, rides to it, and asks its lord lodging for the night. The lord leads him in,

---

fier in chambers burning bright,
candles in chandlers [1] burning light;

and they go
to supper.

312   to supper thé went full yare.[2]

The lord's
wife

he sent after his Ladye bright
to come to supp with *that* gentle Knight,
& shee came blythe with-all;

316   forth shee came then anon,
her Maids following her eche one
in robes of rich pall.[3]

sups with
them,

as shee sate att her supper,
320   euer-more the Ladye clere
Sir Gawaine shee looked vpon.

when the supper it was done,

and then
retires.

shee tooke her Maids, & to her chamber gone.[4]

324   he cheered the Knight & gaue him wine,

The lord
asks Ga-
waine

& said, "welcome, by St. Martine!
I pray you take itt for none ill;
328   one thing, Sir, I wold you pray;

what he has
come there
for.

what you make soe farr this way?
the truth you wold me tell;

"I am a Knight, & soe are yee;

He will keep
his counsel.

332   Your concell, an you will tell mee,
forsooth keepe itt I will;
for if itt be poynt of any dread,
perchance I may helpe att need
336   either lowd or still."

for [5] his words *that* were soe smooth,

Gawaine
tells him all,
not knowing
he was in

had Sir Gawaine wist the soothe,
all he wold not haue told,

---

[1] Candlesticks.—P.
[2] *Yare*, acutus, ready, eager, nimble.
—P.
[3] any rich or fine Cloth, but properly purple: taken from the Robe worn by Bishops.—P. See the description of the Ladye in the old romance, with "Hir brest & hir bry3t þrote bare displayed," (p. 30–1).—F.
[4] Next line wanting in the MS.—F.
[5] for all.—P. The old romance keeps the secret till the end.—F.

340 for *that* was the greene K*n*ight
that hee was lodged with that night,
& harbarrowes [1] in his hold.

he saith, "as to the greene chappell,
344 thitherward I can you tell,
itt is but furlougs 3.

the Master of it is a venterous K*n*ight,
& workes by witchcraft day & night,
348 with many a great furley.[2]

" if he worke with neu*er* soe much frauce,[3]
he is curteous as he sees cause.

I tell you sikerlye,
352 you shall abyde, & take your rest,
& I will into yonder fforrest
vnder the greenwood tree."

they plight their truthes [4] to beleeue,[5]
356 either with other for to deale,
whether it were siluer or gold ;
he said, " we 2 both [sworn[6]] wilbe,
what soeu*er* god sends you & mee,
360 to be parted on the Mold."

The greene K*n*ight went on hunting [7] ;
Sir Gawaine in the castle beinge,
lay sleeping in his bed.

---

[1] harberow'd, lodged.—P.
[2] wonder.—P.
[3] perhaps *frais*—to make a noise, crash. G. ad G.D.—P.
[4] trothes.—P.
[5] be leil.—P. See Leele, l. 478. But if the text is right, see Wedgwood on *be-lieve* in his *English Etymology*. " The fundamental notion seems to be, to approve, to sanction an arrangement, to deem an object in accordance with a certain standard of fitness."—F.

[6] ? See l. 481, "wee were *both.*" The old romance sets out the agreement at length, l. 1105-9 : What the Green Knight wins hunting in the wood, Gawaine is to have ; what Gawaine gets at home, the Green Knight is to have— " Sweet, swap we so, swear with truth, whether, man, loss befall, or better."—F.
[7] The spirited accounts in the old romance of the three-days' hunt of the deer, wild boar, and fox, are all left out here. All the go is taken out of the poem.—F.

[page 208]

364 Vprose the old witche with hast throwe,[1]
   & to her dauhter can shee goe,
     & said, " be not adread ! "

(margin: Bredbeddle's witch mother-in-law)

   to her daughter can shee say,
368 " the man *that* thou hast wisht many a day,
     of him thou maist be sped ;
   for Sir Gawaine *that* curteous Kn*ight*
   is lodged in this hall all night."
372 shee brought her to his bedd.

(margin: tells his wife)

(margin: that Gawaine is in the castle, and takes her to him,)

   shee saith, " gentle Kn*ight*, awake !
   & for this faire Ladies sake
     that hath loued thee soe deere,
376 take her boldly in thine armes,
   there is noe man shall doe thee harme ; "
     now beene they both heere.

(margin: and tells him to embrace her.)

   the ladye kissed him times 3,
380 saith, " without I have the loue of thee,
     my life standeth in dere.[2] "
   Sir Gawaine blushed on the Lady bright,
   saith, " your husband is a gentle Kn*ight*,
384   by him *that* bought mee deare !

(margin: The wife kisses him thrice, and asks his love.)

(margin: Gawaine)

   " to me itt were great shame
   if I shold doe him any grame,[3]
     that hath beene kind to mee ;
388 for I haue such a deede to doe,
   that I can neyther rest nor roe,[4]
     att an end till itt bee."

(margin: refuses to shame his host.)

---

[1] tho, then.—P. Se. *thro, thra,* eager, ernest, Isl. *thrá,* pertinax. Jamieson. The old romance makes the Green Knight's wife go to Gawaine of herself, and on three successive nights.—F.

[2] *Dere,* lædere, nocere. Lye.—P.
[3] *Grame*—Chaucer. Grief, sorrow, vexation, anger. madnes, trouble, affliction. S. G, am [or *Gram,*] furor. Urry.—P.
[4] A.-Sax. *row,* quiet, repose.—F.

then spake *that* Ladye gay,

392 saith, "tell me some [1] of your Iourney,

your succour I may bee ;

if itt be poynt of any warr,

there shall noe man doe you noe darr [2]

396 & yee wilbe gouerned by mee ;

"for heere I haue a lace of silke,

it is as white as any milke,

& of a great value."

400 shee saith, "I dare safelye sweare

there shall noe man doe you deere [3]

when you haue it [4] vpon you."

Sir Gawaine spake mildlye in the place,

404 he thanked the Lady & tooke the lace,

& promised her to come againe.

the Knight in the fforrest slew many a hind,

other venison he cold none find

408 but wild bores on the plaine.

plentye of does & wild swine,

foxes & other ravine,

as I hard true men tell.

412 Sir Gawaine swore sickerlye

"home [5] to your owne, welcome you bee,

by him *that* harrowes hell ! "

the greene Knight his venison downe Layd ;

416 then to Sir Gawaine thus hee said,

"tell me anon in heght, [6]

what noueltyes *that* you haue won,

for heers plenty of venison."

420 Sir Gawaine said full right,

The wife

offers to help Gawaine in his adventure,

and will give him a silk lace

that will protect him from all harm.

Gawaine takes the lace.

Bredbeddle, after hunting,

is welcomed home by Gawaine.

He shares his venison with Gawaine,

[1] Sir.—P.
[2] A.-S. *dar*, injury, hurt.—F.
[3] hurt, vid. supra [p. 72, n. 2].—P.
[4] on you.—P. There is a bit of a *p* or & in the MS. between *it* and *upon.*—F.
[5] to your own home welcome, &c. —P.
[6] speed; like *highing*, from to *high.*—F.

Sir Gawaine sware by S! Leonard,[1]
"such as god sends, you shall haue *part*:"

in his armes he hent the K*night*,
424 & there he kissed him times 3,
saith, "heere is such as god sends mee,
by Mary most of Might."

euer priuilye he held the Lace :
428 *that* was all the villanye *that euer* was
prooued by [2] Sir Gawaine the gay.
then to bed soone thé went,
& sleeped there verament
432   till morrow itt was day.

then Sir Gawaine soe curteous & free,
his leaue soone taketh hee
att [3] the Lady soe gaye ;
436 Hee thanked her, & tooke the lace,   [page 209]
& rode towards the chappell apace ;
he knew noe whitt the way.

euer more in his thought he had
440 whether he shold worke as the Ladye bade,
that was soe curteous & sheene.
the greene k*night* rode another way ;
he transposed him in another array,
444   before as it was greene.

as Sir Gawaine rode *ouer* the plaine,
he hard one high [4] vpon a Mountaine
a horne blowne full lowde.

---

[1] November 6.—S. Leonard or Lionart
may be termed the Howard of the sixth
century. He was .. probably receiued into
the Church at the same time as his royal
master, Clovis, with whom he was in
high fauour, and who gaue him permission
to set many of the prisoners at liberty
who were confined in the dungeons which
his charity prompted him to visit. *Notes
on the Months*, p. 341.
[2] on.—P. A.-Sax. *be, bi*, of, concerning.—F.
[3] of.—P. *Att* is right.—F.
[4] on high.—P.

448 he looked after the greene chappell,
    he saw itt stand vnder a hill
      couered with euyes [1] about;

and sees the Green Chapel,

    he looked after the greene Knight,
452 he hard him wehett a fauchion bright,
    that the hills rang about.

and the Green Knight;

    the Knight spake with strong cheere,
    said, " yee be welcome, S[ir] Gawaine heere,
456   it behooveth thee to Lowte." [2]

who calls him to lay down his head,

    he stroke, & litle perced the skin,
    vnneth the flesh within.
    then Sir Gawaine had noe doubt ;

then strikes,

but hardly cuts through the flesh.

460 he saith, " thou shontest [3] ! why dost thou soe ? "
    then Sir Gawaine in hart waxed throe [4] ;
    vpon his ffeete can stand,
    & soone he drew out his sword,

He reproaches Gawaine for shrinking.

464 & saith, " traitor ! if thou speake a word,
    thy liffe is in my hand [5] ;
    I had but one stroke att thee,
    & thou hast had another att mee,
468   noe falshood in me thou found ! "

Gawaine threatens to kill him.

    the Knight said withouten laine,
    " I wend I had Sir Gawaine slaine,
    the gentlest Knight in this land [6] ;
472 men told me of great renowne,
    of curtesie thou might haue woon the crowne
    aboue both free & bound,[7]

Bredbeddle answers that Gawaine

---

[1] I suppose *Ivyes* or perhaps *Eughes*, *i.e.* yews.—P.

[2] some great omission. Note in MS. *Sir Gawayne and the Green Knight* makes Gawaine answer that he is ready and will not shrink. " Then the grim man seizes his grim tool," strikes, and as it comes gliding down, Gawaine shrinks a little. Bredbeddle (that is, Bernlak de Hautdesert) reproaches him for his cowardice. Gawaine promises not to shrink again, stands firm, and Bredbeddle strikes. (ed. Morris, E. E. Text Soc. p. 72-4.)—F.

[3] shuntest, flinchest, shrinkest.—F.

[4] forte idem ac *Thra,* apud G. Doug: ferox, acer, audax, vel potius pertinax. Vide Lye.—P.

[5] hond.—P.

[6] Londe.—P.

[7] bond.—P.

has lost his three chief virtues, of truth, gentleness, and courtesy.

He has concealed the lace,

" & alsoe of great gentrye;

476 & now 3 points [1] be put fro thee,

    it is the Moe pittye:

Sir Gawaine! thou wast not leele [2]

when thou didst the lace conceale

480 *that* my wiffe gaue to thee!

and should have shared it.

" ffor wee were both, thou wist full well,

for thou hadst the halfe dale [3]

    of my venerye [4];

484 if the lace had neuer beene wrought,

to haue slaine thee was neuer my thought,

    I swore by god verelye!

Yet Bred-beddle will

" I wist it well my wiffe loued thee;

488 thou wold doe me noe villanye,

    but nicked her with nay;

forgive him if he'll take him to Arthur's court.

but wilt thou doe as I bidd thee,

take me to Arthurs court with thee,

492   then were all to my pay.[5] "

Gawaine agrees. They go back to Hutton Castle, and next day on to Arthur's court.

now are the Kn*igh*ts accorded there [6];

to the castle of hutton [7] can thé fare,

    to lodge there all *that* night.

496 earlye on the other day

to Arthurs court thé tooke the way

    with harts blyth & light.

All rejoice at Gawaine's return.

all the Court was full faine,

500 aliue when they saw S*i*r Gawaine;

    they thanked god aboue.[8]

---

[1] perhaps these points, q. d. thou hast forfeited these qualities.—P.

[2] *i. e.* loyal, honourable, true.—P.

[3] A.-S. *dǽl*, part.—F.

[4] venison, or rather hunting. So in Chauc*r*. Fr. Venerie. Urry.—P.

[5] content, liking.—P.

[6] there.—P.

[7] Hutton Manor-house, [Somerset-shire]: the hall, 36 feet by 20, is of the fifteenth century, with arched roof and panelled chimney-piece. *Domestic Archi-tecture*, iii. 342. The scene is laid "in the west countrye," see l. 39, l. 515.—F.

[8] ? MS. aboue.—F. aboone, abone, idem.—P.

that is the matter & the case

why K*nigh*ts of the bathe weare the lace

504 vntill they haue wonen their shoen,[1]

or else a ladye of hye estate

from about his necke shall it take,

for the doughtye deeds *that* hee hath done.

508 it was confirmed by Arthur the K[ing ;]

thorrow Sir Gawaines desiringe

The K*ing* granted him his boone.

Thus endeth the tale of the greene K*night*. [page 210]

512 god, *that* is soe full of might,

to heauen their soules bring

that haue hard this litle storye

that fell some times in the west countrye

516 in Arthurs days our King !   ffiins.

---

[1] See p. 123, l. 1232.—F.

[It may be noted, that as the story is told here, the point of it is missed. As the agreement of Bredbeddle and Gawaine is here only to *share* with the other what each gets, p. 71, l. 356, not to *change* it, as in the old romance. Bredbeddle gives Gawaine only half his venison, p. 76, l. 482, and Gawaine gives Bredbeddle half his gettings, three kisses, out of three kisses and a lace. As he couldn't cut three kisses in half, to go with the half of the lace, he divided the gift fairly in another way,—the three kisses to Bredbeddle, the lace to himself. Rather hard measure to lose one's "3 points" for that.—F.]

Sir: Triamore.:[1]

THE earliest known existing copy of this Romance is preserved at Cambridge. It is of the time of Henry VI., according to Mr. Halliwell, who has edited it for the Percy Society. There is, too, an old MS. copy preserved in the Bodleian Library. The Romance once enjoyed a wide popularity. It was twice printed by William Copland. From one of these editions Mr. Ellis draws the outline he gives in his *Early English Metrical Romances*. One of the old printed versions was reprinted by Mr. Utterson in 1817. The copy here given differs but slightly from Copland's and from the Cambridge version. The more important of what differences there are, are mentioned in the notes.

The piece is a fair specimen of the old Romances, with all their vices and their virtues; with their prolixity, their impro-bability, their exaggeration; with their wild graces also, their chivalrousness, their pageantry.

The story tells how a good lord and his gentle lady were estranged by the treachery of their steward; how their son, con-ceived in honour, was born in shame; how, after many a weary year, the execrable fraud was discovered; and how, at last, the son (who has in the meantime won himself a wife) and his mother are happily reunited to the grieving husband. These various incidents are described with much power and feeling.

King Arradas was blessed with a wife, Margaret, " comely to be seen, and true as the turtle-doves on trees." As their union was not followed by the birth of any child, the King determines to

---

[1] 271 Stanzas.—P.

go and fight in the Holy Land, so to propitiate Heaven and per-
suade it to grant him an heir.   On the very eve of his departure
his desire is granted.   But he sets forth to the wars not knowing.
During his absence his steward Marrock evilly solicits the
Queen.   "But she was steadfast in her thought."   When the
King returned from heathenness, and

> at last his Queen beheld,
> And saw her go great with child,
>   He wondered at that thing.
> Many a time he did her kiss,
> And made great joy without miss,
>   His heart made great rejoicing.

The wicked steward avails himself of the King's wonder to
insinuate, and more than insinuate, that the child is none of his.
The King unhappily listens.   The Queen is presently, at the
steward's advice, banished the country.

> So now is exiled that good Queen,
> But she wist not what it did mean,
>   Nor what made him to begin.
> To speak to her he nay would;
> That made the Queen's heart full cold,
>   And that was great pity and sin.
>   *   *   *   *   *
> For oft she mourned as he did fare,
>   And cried and sighed full sore.
>
> Lords, knights, and ladies gent
> Mourned for her when she went,
>   And bewailed her that season.

In this way came to pass the sad schism that was to bring so
many years of forlornness and anguish, the source of so many
bitter tears and poignant self-reproaches.   The child whom the
dishonoured lady then bore in her womb was to be a full-grown
man, and a warrior even more formidable than his father himself,
ere Arradas and Margaret kissed conjugally again.   Who does
not rejoice when the fair fame of this true wife is vindicated, the
iniquity of her tempter made bare?   When at last, at the
marriage of their son, Sir Triamour, to the beautiful Helen of
Hungary, she and her husband are again brought face to face:

King Arradas beheld his Queen ;
Him thought that he had her seen,
 She was a lady faire.
The King said, " If it is your wish,
Your name me for to tell,
 I pray you with words fair."

" My lord," said she, " I was your Queen ;
Your steward did me ill teen. .
 That evil might him befall ! "
The King spake no more words
Till the cloths were drawn from the boards,
 And men rose in hall,
And by the hand he took the Queen,
So in the chamber forth he went,
 And there she told him all.

Then was there great joy and bliss
When they together gan kiss ;
 Then all the company made joy enough.

But we do not propose here to gather the wild flowers of this
poem for our readers. They shall wander through the meadows
and cull for themselves. They will easily find them blowing
and blooming, if they have any care for the blossoms of Romance.

God bless
you all !

LOW [1] Iesus christ, o [2] heauen King !
 grant you all his deare blessing,
  & his heauen for to win !

If you'll
listen,
I'll tell you
a tale

4 if you will a stond [3] lay to your care,
 of adventures you shall heare
  that wilbe to your liking,

of King
Arradas

 of a King & of a queene
8 that had great Ioy them betweene ;
  Sir Arradas [4] was his name ;

and Queen
Margaret,

 he had a queene named Margarett,
 shee was as true as steele, & sweet,

who was
defamed by

12 & full false brought in fame [5]

[1] Now.—Cop. (or Copland's edition.   [4] Ardus.—Ca. (or Cambridge text,
Collated by Mr. Hales.)   ed. Halliwell.—F.)
[2] our.—Cop.   [5] evil report, disrepute ; L. *fama* (in
[3] stounde.—Cop.   a bad sense), ill-repute, infamy, scandal ;

by the Kings steward *that* Marrocke hight,

a traitor & a false knight :

   hcrafter yee will say all the same.

16 hee looued well *that* Ladye gent ;

& for shee wold not *with* him consent,

   he did *that* good Queene much shame.

Sir Marrock

because she would not yield to him.

this King loued well his Queene

20 because shee was comlye [1] to be seene,

   & as true as the turtle on tree.

either to other made great Moane,

for children together had they none

24   begotten on their bodye ;

Arradas and Margaret

lament that they are childless,

therfore the King, I vnderstand,

made a vow to goe to the holy land,

   there for to fight & for to slay [2] ;

28 & praid god *that* he wold send him tho

grace to gett a child be-tweene·them tow,

   that the right heire might bee.

and Arradas

vows to go to the Holy Land,

praying God to send him an heir.

for his vow he did there make,

32 & of the pope the Crosse he did take,

   for to seek the land were god him bought.

the night of his departing, on the Ladye Mild,

as god it wold, hee gott [3] a child ;

36   but they both wist itt naught.

He begets a child on his wife,

& on the morrow when it was day

the King hyed on his Iourney ;

   for to tarry, he it not thought.

and next day starts on his journey.

---

famosus, infamous. (White.) Compare

For yf it may be founde in thee

That thou them *fame* for enmyte,

Thou shalt be taken as a felon,

And put full depe in my pryson.

The Squyr of Lowe Degre. l. 392 (Ritson iii. 161, Hall!).—F.

[1] semely.—Cop.

[2] sle.—Cop.

[3] gate.—Cop.

40   then the Queene began to mourne
      because her Lord wold noe longer soiourne ;
      shee sighed full sore, & sobbed oft.

      the King & his men armed them right,
44   both Lords, Barrons, & many a knight,
      with him for to goe.

      then betweene her & the King
      was much sorrow & mourninge
48   when thé shold depart in too.

      he kissed & tooke his leaue of the Queene,
      & other Ladies bright & sheene,
      & of Marrocke his steward alsoe ;

52   the King commanded him on paine of his life
      for to keepe well his queene & wiffe
      both in weale & woe.

      now is the King forth gone
56   to the place where god was on the crosse done,
      & warreth there a while.

      then bethought this false steward—
      as yee shall here after[ward,[1]]—
60   his lord & King to beguile ;

      he wooed [2] the Queene day & night
      for to lye with her, & he might ;
      he dread no creature thoe.
64   ffull fayre hee did that Lady speake,   [page 211]
      that he might in bed with that Ladye sleepe ;

          thus full oft he prayed her thoe.

      but shee was stedfast in her thought,
68   & heard them speake, & said nought
      till hee all his case [3] had told.

---

[1] MS. hereafter. P. has added *ward.*—F.   [2] wowed.—Cop.   [3] tule.—Cop.

then shee said, "Marrocke, hast thou not thought
all *that thou* speakcest is ffor nought?

72   I trow not *that* thou wold[1] ;

and re-proaches Marrock.

"for well my Lord did trust thee,
when hee to you deliuered mee
    to haue me vnder the[2] hold ;
76   & [thou] woldest full faine
    to doe thy Lord shame !
    traitor, thou art to bold ! "

Her lord trusted him,

and he betrays his trust.

then said Marrocke vnto *that* Ladye,
80 "my Lord is gone now verelye
    against gods foes to ffight ;
&, w*i*thout the more wonder bee,
hee shall come noe more att thee,
84   as I am a true knight.

Marrock

tells the Queen

that Arradas is sure never to return ;

"& Madam, wee will worke soe priuilye,
that wethere[3] he doe liue or dye,
    for of this shall[4] witt noe wight.[5] "
88 then waxed the Queene wonderous [wroth,[6]]
& swore many a great othe
    as shee was a true woman,

and promises to keep their sin secret.

Margaret angrily

shee said, "traitor ! if euer thou be soe hardiye
92 to show me of such villanye,
    on a gallow tree I will thee hange !
  if I may know after this
  that thou tice me, I-wis[7]
96   thou shalt haue the law of the land."

threatens to hang Marrock,

if he says another word to her.

---

[1] I didn't think you were capable of this.—F.
[2] they.—Cop.
[3] After the first *e* an *h* is marked out. —F.
[4] there shall.—Ca.
[5] man.—P.
[6] Added by Percy.—F.
[7] tyce me to do a mysse.—Cop.

Marrock
assures her
he meant
her no
wrong,

Sir Marrocke said, "Ladye, mercye !
I said itt for noe villaine,
by Iesu, heauen Kinge !

but only to
try her
truth.

100 but only for to proue your will,
whether *that* you were good or ill,
& for noe other thinge ;

Now he
knows she is
true,

" but now, Madam, I may well see
104 you are as true as turtle on the tree [1]
vnto my Lord the King ;
& itt is to me both glad & leefe ;

she must not
be vexed.

therfore take it not into greefe
108 for noe manner of thinge."

Margaret
believes him.

& soe the traitor excused him thoe,
the Lady wend itt had beene soe
as the steward had said.

But
Marrock,

112 he went forth, & held him still,
& thought he cold not haue his will ;

disgusted,

therfore hee was euill apayd.

[2] soe with treason & trecherye
116 he thought to doe her villanye ;
thus to himselfe he said.

schemes how
to betray
her,

night & day hee laboured then
for to betray [3] *that* good woman ;

and does it.

120 soe att the last he her betraid.

now of this good Queene leaue wee,
& by the grace of the holy trinitye
full great with child did shee gone.

Arradas

124 now of King Arradas speake wee,
that soe farr in heathinnesse is hee
to fight against gods fone [4] ;

---

[1] as stele on tree.— Ca.
[2] This stanza is not in Ca.—F.
[3] deceyue.—Cop.
[4] fonne.—Cop.

there with his army & all his might
128 slew many a sarrazen [1] in fight.
   great words of them there rose
   in the heathen Land, & alsoe in Pagainé [2];
   & in euerye other Land that they come bye,
132 there sprang of him great losse.[3]

   when [he [4]] had done his pilgrimage,
   & labored all *that* great voyage [5]
   with all his good will & lybertye,— [page 212]
136 att fflome Iorden & att Bethlem,[6]
   & att Caluarye beside Iernsalem,
   in all the places was hee ;—

   then he longed to come home
140 to see his Ladye *that* liued at one ;
   he thought euer on her greatlye.
   soe long thé sealed on the fome
   till att the last they came home ;
144 he arriued ouer the Last [7] strond.

   the shippes did strike their sayles eche one,
   the men were glad the King came home
     vnto his owne Land.
148 there was both mirth & game,
   the Queene of his cominge was glad & faine,
   Eche of them told other tydand.[8]

   the King at last his Queene beheld,
152 & saw heer goe great with childe:
   [& [9]] hee wondred att that thinge.

[1] sarzyn.—Cop.
[2] Pagany.—Cop.
[3] Loos or fame, *Fama.* Promptorium. —F.
[4] he.—Ca.
[5] vayge.—Cop.
[6] Bedleem.—Cop.
[7] salte.—Cop.
[8] tydynge.—Cop.
[9] A hole in the MS.—F.

many a time he did her kisse,
& made great ioy without misse ;
156   his hart[1] made great reioeeinge.

soone after the *King* hard tydinges newe

by Marroecke : *that* false knight vntrue
w*i*th reason his lord gan fraine,
160   " my lord," he sayd, " for gods [2] byne [3] !

for of *that* childe *that* neue*r* was thine,[4]
why art thow soe fayne ?

" you wend *th*at itt yo*ur* owne bee ;

certainly
not his. His
Queen has
been fal*s*e;
another
knight begot
the child.

164   but," he said, " S*i*r, ffor certaintye
yo*ur* Q*ueen*e hath you betraine ;
another K*nigh*t, soe god me speed,
begott this child sith you yeed,
168   & hath thy Q*ueen*e forlaine."

" Alas ! " said the K*ing*, " how may this bee ?
for I betooke her vnto thee,
her to keepe in waile & woe[5] ;
172   & vnder thy keeping how fortuned this
*th*at thou suffered her doe amisse ?
alas, Marroecke ! why did thou soe?"

" S*i*r," said the steward, " blame not me ;
176   for much mone shee made for thee,
as though shee had loued noe more ;

" I trowed on her noe villanye
till I saw one lye her by,
180   as the Mele [6] had wrought.
to him I came w*i*th Egar mood,

& slew the traitor as he stood ;
full sore itt [me] forethought.

---

[1] First written *halt.*—F.
[2] G*o*ddes.—Cop.
[3] Goddys pyne.—Ca.
[4] MS. thine was.—F.

[5] weal & woe.—P.
[6] ? Fr. *mal*, evil ; or *meslée*, a mixture,
mingling, melling. Cotgrave.—F.

184   " then shee trowed shee shold be shent,   *and the*
       & promised me both Land & rent ;   *Queen pro-*
         soe fayre shee me besought   *mised him*
         to doe with her all my will   *herself for*
188   if *that* I wold [keepe] me still,   *his silence.*
         & tell you naught."

       " of this," said the K*ing*, " I haue great wonder ;   *Arradas*
       for sorrow my hart will breake assunder [1] !   *sorrows.*
192   why hath shee done amisse ?
       alas ! to whome shall I me mone,   *He has lost*
       sith I haue lost my comlye Queene   *his Queen*
         that I was wont to kisse ? "

196   the K*ing* said, " Marroccke, what is thy read ?   *What can he*
       it is best to turne to dead [2]   *.do ? He'll*
         my ladye *that* hath done me this [2] ;   *kill her.*
       now because *that* shee is false to mee,
200   I will neue*r* more her see,
         nor deale with her, I-wisse.[3] "

       the steward said, " Lo*rd*, doe not soe ;   *Marrock*
       thou shalt neither burne ne sloe,[4]   *advises*
204   but doe as I you shall you tell."
       Marroccke sayd, " this councell I :
       banish her out of *your* Land priuilye,   *him to*
         far into exile.   *banish her,*

208   " deliuer her an ambling [5] steede,   [page 213]   *give her a*
       & an old K*nigh*t to her lead ;   *horse*
         thus by my councell see [6] yee doe ;

---

[1] asonder.—Cop.
[2] ? *turne* is for *burne*, cp. 1. 203.—F.
   brenne her to ded.—Cop.
   Whether that sche be done to dedd
   That was my blysse ?—Ca.

[3] ywys.—Cop.
[4] flo.—Cop.
[5] ambelynge.—Cop.   oolde.—Ca.
[6] loke.—Cop.

and money,   & giue them some spending money

and let her
go.   212 *that* may them out of the land bring ;
                                         I wold noe better then soe.

                                    " & an other mans child shalbe you heyre,
                                         itt were neither good nor fayre
                                    216   but if itt were of *your* kin."

Arradas
agrees.   then said the K*ing*, "soe mote I thee,
                                         right as thou sayest, soe shall it bee,
                                         & erst will I neu*er* blin.[1]"

Queen
Margaret is
to be exiled ;   220 Loe, now is exiled *that* good Queene ;
                                         but shee wist not what it did meane,
                                         nor what made him to begin.

the King
will not   to speake to her he nay wold ;
speak to her.   224 *that* made the Queenes hart full cold,
                                         & *that* was great pittye & sin.

He gives her
an old steed,   he did her cloth in purple [2] weede,
                                         & set her on an old steed
                                    228   *that* was both crooked & almost blinde ;
an old
knight,   he tooke her an old Knight,
Sir Roger,
to look after   kine to the Queene, Sir Rodger [3] hight,
her,   *that* was both curteous [4] & kind.

and three
days to quit   232 3 dayes he gaue them leaue [5] to passe,
the land in,   & after *that* day sett was,
                                         if men might them find,
(or the
Queen will   the Queene shold burned [6] be starke dead
be burnt,)   236 in a flyer with flames redd :
                                         this came of the stewards [7] mind.[8]

---

[1] blyne.—Cop.   [5] And gaf them twenty dayes.— Ca.
[2] He let clothe hur in sympulle.—Ca.   [6] brenned.—Cop.
[3] Roger.— Cop.   [7] stuardes.—Cop.
[4] curteyse.—Cop.   [8] mimd, in the MS.—F.

40^{ty} florences for their expence [1]
the *King* did giue them in his presence,

240   & comaunded them to goe.
the Ladye mourned as shee shold dye ;
for all this shee wist not whye
hee fared with her soe.

al\~o forty
florins.

Queen
Margaret
mourns.

244   *that* good K*night* comforted the Queene,
& said, " att gods will all must beene ;
therfore, Madam, mourne you noe more."
Sir Rodger for her hath much care,

248   [For ofte she mourned as she dyd fare,[2]]
& cryed & sighed full sore ;

Sir Roger
comforts her,

Lords, Knights, & ladyes gent
mourned for her when shee went,

252   & be-wayled [3] her *that* season.
the Queene began to make sorrow & care
when shee from the K*ing* shold fare
with wrong, against all reason.

256   forth they went, in number [4] 3,
Sir Rodger, the Queene, & his greyhound trulye ;
ah ! o [5] worth wicked treason !

but she
wails still,

and they set
off.

then thought the steward trulye

260   to doe the Queene a villanye,
& to worke with her his will.
he ordained him a companye
of his owne men prinilye

264   *that* wold assent him till ;

Marrock

gets his men
together,

all vnder a Wood [6] side they did lye
wheras the Queene shold passe by,
& held them wonderous still ;

and lies in
ambush for
the Queen,

---

[1] Thretty florens to there spendynge.
—Ca.
[2] This line is from Copland's text.—H.
[3] MS. he wayled.—F.

[4] nunnber, in the MS.—F.
[5] wo.— Cop.
[6] wodes.—Cop. The *W* is made like
rv in the MS.—F.

to work his
lust on her.
268 & there he thought verelye
his good Queene for to lye by,
his lusts [1] for to fulfill.

& when hee came into the wood,

The Queen
and Sir
Roger
272 Sir Rodger & the Queene soe good,
& there [2] to passe with-out doubt;

perceive
Marrock's
with that they were ware of the steward,
how hee was coming to them ward
276 with a ffull great rout.

treason.
" heere is treason ! " then said the Queene.
" alas ! " said Roger, " what may this meane ?
with foes wee be sett round about."

Sir Roger
prepares
280 the Knight sayd, " heere will wee dwell ;
Our lille wee shall full deere sell,   [page 214]
be they neuer soe stout.

for defence.
" Madam," he sayd, " be not affrayd,
284 for I thinke heere with this sword
that I shall make them lowte."

Marrock
threatens to
kill him.
then cryed the steward to Sir Rodger on hye,
& said, " Lord,[3] traitor ! thou shalt dye !
288 for that I goe about."

Sir Roger
defies him,
Sir Rodger said, " not for thee !
my death shalt thou deare abye;
for with thee will I fight."
292 he went to him shortlye,
& old Sir Rodger bare him manfullye [4]
like a full hardye Knight;

attacks his
men,
he hewed on them boldlye ;
296 there was none of that companye
soe hardye nor sow [5] wight.

---

[1] lustes.—Cop.
[2] ? construction. Is there miswritten
for thought, or is thought understood. or

is thereto one word ?—II.
[3] olde.—Cop.   [4] manly.—Cop.
[5] so.—Cop.

Sir Rodger hitt [1] one on the head

that to the girdle the sword yeed,

300   then was hee of them quitte [2];

splits one to
the girdle,

he smote a stroke with a sword [3] good

that all about them ran the blood,

    soe sore he did them smite ;

304 trulye-hee,[4] his greyhound *that* was soo [5] good,

did helpe his m*aster*, & by him stood,

    & bitterlye can hee byte.

wounds
others,

and his
greyhonnd,
Trulyhee,
helps.

  then *that* Lady, *that* fayre foode,[6]

308 she feared Marrocke in her mood ;

    shee light on foote, & left her steede,

    & ran fast, & wold not leave,

    & hid her vnder a greene greaue,[7]

312   for shee was in great dread.

Queen
Margaret

dismounts,

runs away,

and hides
herself.

Sir Rodger then the Q*ueene* can behold,

  & of his liffe he did nothing hold ;

    his good grayhound did help him indeed,

316 &, as itt is in the romans [8] told,

    14 he slew of yeomen [9] bold ;[10]

    soe he quitted him in *that* steade.

Sir Roger

kills fourteen
yeomen,

  if hee had beene armed, I-wisse [11]

320 all the Masterye had been his ;

    alas hee lacked weed.

    as good Sir Rodger gaue a stroake,

    behind him came Sir Marroccke,—

324   *that* euill might he speed,—

but Marrock

[1] hyt.—Cop.
[2] quyte.—Cop.
[3] swerde.— Cop.
[4] Trewe-loue.—Ca.
[5] *de* at the end has been marked out of the MS.—F.
[6] fode.—Cop. person.—F.
[7] greve.—Cop. grove.—F.
[8] Romaynes.—Cop.
[9] yemen.—Cop.
[10] xl^ti Syr Roger downe can folde.— Ca.
[11] ywis.—Cop.

stabs him in the back

he smote Sir Rodger with a speare,
  & to the ground he did him beare,
    & fast *that* Knight did bleed.

328   Sir Marroccke gaue him such a wound
  that he dyed there on ground,

and kills him.

    & *that* was a sinfull deede.

Marrock

now is Rodger slaine certainlye.

332   he rode forth & let him Lye,

searches everywhere for the Queen,

  & sought after the Queene.
fast hee rode, & sought euerye way,
yet wist he not where the Queene Laye.

336   then said the traitor teene ; [1]

ouer all the wood hee her sought ;

but cannot find her ; he

but as god wold, he found her nought.
    then waxed he wrath, I weene,

gets wroth,

340 & held his Iourney euill besett,
that with the Queene had not mett
  to haue had his pleasure, the traitor keene.

& when he cold not the lady finde,

and goes home,

344 homeward they began to wend,
  hard by where Sir Rodger Lay.

stabbing Sir Roger's corpse on the way,

the steward [2] him thrust throughout,
for of his death he had noe doubt,

348   & this the storye doth say.

& when the traitor had done soe,
he let him lye & went him froe,
  & tooke noe thought *that* day ;

352 yett all his companye was nye gone,

and having lost fourteen men.

14 he left there dead for one ;
  there passed but 4 away. [3]

---

[1] If a stanza is not omitted, *said* must mean *assayed*, tried.—F.
[2] stuarde.—Cop.

[3] xl. he had chaunged for oone. Ther skaped but two away.—Ca.

then the Queene was ffull woe,   Queen
Margaret
356 And shee saw *that* they were goe,   [page 215]
    shee made sorrow & crye.
    then shee rose & went againe
    to Sir Rodger, & found him slaine ;   laments over
360   his grey-hound by his feet did lye.

    " alas," shee said, " *that* I was borne !
    my trew k*night* *that* I haue lorne,   Sir Roger's
corpse.
      they haue him there slaine ! "
364 full pitteouslye shee mad her moane,
    & said, " now must I goe alone ! "
      the grey-hound shee wold haue had full faine ;

    the hound still by his *Master* did lye,   The grey-
hound will
not leave the
corpse.
368 he licked his wounds, & did whine & crye.
      this to see the Queene had paine,
    & said, " Sir Roger, this hast thou for me !
    alas *that* [it] shold euer bee ! "
372   her hayre shee tare in twayne ;

    & then shee went & tooke her steed,   The Queen
    & wold noe longer there abyde
      lest men shold find her there.
376 shee said, " Sir Roger, now *thou* art dead,   laments
again the
loss of Sir
Roger,
    who will the right way now me lead ?
      for now thow mayst speake noe more."

    right on the ground there as he lay dead,
380 shee kist him or shee from him yead.[1]   kisses his
corpse,
      god wott her hart was sore !
    what for sorrow & dread,
    fast away shee can her speede,   and speeds
away.
384   shee wist not wither nor where.

    [1] This incident is not in Ca.—F.

The hound	the good grayhound for waile & woe
	from the Knight hee wold not goe,
licks his master's wounds, to heal them.	but Lay & licked his wound ;
	388 he waite [1] to haue healed them againe,
	& therto he did his paine :
What love!	loe, such loue is in a hound [2] !
	this knight lay till he did [3] stinke ;
The hound	392 the greyhound he began to thinke,
	& scraped a pitt anon ;
scrapes a grave, and buries his master.	therin he drew the dead [4] corse,
	& couered itt with earth & Mosse,[5]
	396 & from him he wold not gone.
	the grayhound lay still there ;
Margaret	this Queene gan forth to fare
	for dread of her fone ;
	400 shee had great sorrow in her hart,
	the thornes pricked her wonderous smart,[6]
	shee wist not wither to goe.
rides on into Hungary.	this lady forth fast can hye
	404 into the land of Hugarye [7] ;
	thither came shee with great woe.
	at last shee came to a wood side,
The pains of labour come on,	but then cold shee noe further ryde,
	408 her paynes tooke her soe.
	shee lighted downe in that tyde,
	for there shee did her trauncell [8] abyde ;
	god wold that it shold be soe.
	412 then shee with much paine
	tyed her horsse by the rayne,
	& rested her there till her paynes were goe.

---

[1] expected.—F.
[2] Grete kyndenes ys in howndys.—Ca.
[3] The last *d* is made over an *s* in the MS.— F.   [4] deed.—Cop.
[5] And scraped on hym bothe ryne and mosse.—Ca.
[6] wonder smert.—Cop.
[7] Hongarye.—Ca.   Hongrye.—Cop.
[8] *for* trauell, *travail.*—F.   trauayll.—Cop.

shee was deliuered of a manchild sweete;

416 & when it began to crye & weepe,

it ioyed her hart greatlye.

soone after, when shee might stirr,

shee tooke her child to her full neere,

420 And wrapt¹ itt full softlye. [page 216]

What for wearye & for woe,

they fell a-sleepe both towe;

her steed stood her behind.

424 then came a *knight* rydand there,²

& found this ladye soe lonelye of cheere

as hee hunted-after the hind.

the *Knight* hight Bernard Mowswinge,³

428 *that* found the *Queene* sleepinge,

vnder the greenwoode lyande.⁴

softlye he went neere & neere;

he went on foot, & beheld her cheere,

432 as a *Knight* curteous & kind.

he awaked *that* ladye of beawtye⁵;

shee looked on him pitteouslee,

& was affrayd⁶ full sore.

436 he said, "what doe you here, Madame?

of whence be you, or whats *your* name?

haue you *your* men forlorne⁷?"

"*Sir*," shee sayd, "if you will witt,⁸

440 my name is⁹ called Margerett;

in Arragon I was borne;

heere I sufferd much greefe;

helpe me, *Sir*,¹⁰ out of this Mischeefe!

444 att some towne *that* I were."

Marginal notes:
and she is delivered of a male child.

She joys,

takes her baby to her,

and falls asleep.

A knight

finds her,

Sir Bernard Mowswinge,

wakes her,

and asks her what she does there, what is her name?

"Margaret;

help me!"

---

¹ wrauped.—Cop.
² nere.—Cop.
³ Sir Barnarde Messengere.—Ca. Barnard Mausewynge.—Cop.
⁴ lynde.—Cop.
⁵ beaute.—Cop.
⁶ aferde.—Cop.
⁷ MS. forlorme.—F. forlore.—P.
⁸ wete.—Cop.
⁹ MS. is is; ? *for* it is.—F.
¹⁰ There appears a word like *it* marked out here in the MS.—F.

Sir Bernard

the Knight beheld the Ladye good ;
hee [1] thought shee was of gentle blood
that was soe hard bestead [2] ;

takes her

448 he tooke her vp curteouslye,

and her
baby home,

& the child that lay her bye ;
them both with him he led,

gets a
woman to
tend her,

& made her haue a woman att will,

452 tendinge of her, as itt was skill, [3]
all for to bring her a-bedd.

and gives
her all she
wants.

whatsoeuer shee wold haue,
shee needed itt not long to craue,

456   her speech was right soone sped.

She christens
her boy
Triamore,

thé christened the child with great honour,
& named him Sir TRYAMORE.
then they were of him glad ;

460 great gifts to him was giuen
of Lords & ladyes by-deene,
in bookes as I read.

and stays
with her
new friends.

there dwelled *that* Ladye longe

464 with much Ioy them amonge ;
of her thé were neuer wearye.
the child was taught great nurterye [4] ;

Triamore is
taught
courtesy,

a *Master* had him vnder his care,

468 & taught him curtesie. [5]
this child waxed wonderous well,
of great stature both of fleshe & fell ;
euerye man loued him trulye,

and all folk
love him.

472 of his companye all folke were glad ;
indeed, noe other cause they had,
the child was gentle & bold.

---

[1] MS. shee.—F. And.—Ca.
[2] bestadde.—Cop.
[3] skell.—Cop. reason.—F.

[4] nurture.—P. norture.—Cop.
[5] Sche techyd hur sone for to wyrke,
And taght hym evyr newe.—Ca.

Now of the *Queene* let wee bee,

476 & of the grayhound speake wee

that I erst of told.

Sir Roger's
greyhound

long 7 yeeres, soe god me saue,

he did keepe his *Masters* graue,

480   till *that* hee waxed old ;

this Gray-hound *Sir* Roger kept [1] long,

& brought him vp sith he was younge,

in story as it is told ;

keeps to his
master's
grave seven
years,

for Sir Roger
had brought
him up.

484 therfore he kept soe there

for the [2] space of 7 yeere,

   & goe from him he ne wold.

euer vpon his *Masters* graue he lay,

488 there might noe man haue him away

for heat neither for cold,   [page 217]

The hound
never leaves
the grave,

without it were once a day

he ran about to gett his prey [3]

492 of beasts that were bold,

conyes, when he can them gett ;

thus wold he labor for his meate,

   yett great hungar he had in how.[4]

except

to get food.

496 & 7 yeeres he dwelled there,

till itt beffell on *that* yeere,

   euen on christmasse day,

the gray-hound (as the story sayes)

500 came to the K*ings* palace [5]

   without any [6] delay.

One Christ-
mas
the hound

goes to
Arradas's
palace,

---

[1] had kepte.—Cop.
[2] By the.—Cop.
[3] praye.—Cop.

[4] holde.—Cop. *How*, care. Halliwell.
—F.
[5] palayes.— Cop.
[6] ony.—Cop.

when they Lords were [1] sett at meate, soono
the grayhound into the hall runn
504   amonge the knights gay ;

all about he can behold,

cannot find
what he
seeks,

but he see not what hee wold ;
then went he his way full right
508 when he had sought & cold not find ;
ffull gentlye he did his kind,
speed better when he might.

and goes
back to Sir
Roger's
grave.

the grayhound ran forth his way
512 till he came where his *Master* Lay,
as fast as euer he mought.

Arradas

the king marueiled at *that* deed,
from whence he went, & whither he yeed,
516   or who him thither brought.

thinks he
has seen the
dog before.

the King thought he had seene him ere,
but he wist not well where,
therfor he said right nought.
520 soone he bethought him then
*th*at he did him erst ken,
& [2] still stayd in *th*at thought.

Next day

the other day, in the same wise,
524 when the King shold from his meate rise,

the hound
returns,

the Grayhound came in thoe ;
all about there he sought,

but cannot
find
Marrock.

but the steward found he nought ;
528 then againe he began to goe.

Arradas says
it is Sir
Roger's dog,

and perhaps
the Queen
has come
back ;

the[n] sayd the King in *th*at stond,
"methinkes it is S*i*r Rogers hound
*th*at went forth with the Queene ;
532 I trow they be come againe to this land.
Lords, all this I vnderstand,
it may right well soe bee ;

---

[1] The first *e* is made over an *h* in the MS. — F.   [2] sate styll in a. — Cop.

"if *that* they be into this Land come,
536 we shall haue word therof soone
      & within short space;
for neu*er* since thé went I-wisse
I saw not the gray hound ere this;
540   it is a marueilous case!

"when he cometh againe, follow him,
fo[r] eu*er*more he will run [1]
    to his Mas*te*rs dwelling place;
544 run & goe, looke ye not spare,
till *that* yee come there
    to S*i*r Rodger & my Queene."

then the 3.ᵈ day, amonge them all
548 the grayhound came into the hall,
    to meate ere thé were [2] sett.
Marrocke the steward was within,
the grayhound thought he wold not blin
552   till he w*i*th him had mett;

he tooke the steward by the throte,
& assunder he it bote [3];
    but then he wold not byde,
556 for to his graue he rann.
there follolwed him many a man,
    some on horsse, some beside;

& when he came where his Mas*te*r was,
560 he Layd him downe beside the grasse
    And barked at the men againe.   [page 218]
there might noe man him from the place gett,
& yett with staues thé did him beate,
564   *that* he was almost slaine.

Side notes:
when the dog comes again, some lords are to follow him
to Sir Roger and the Queen.
Next day the dog comes again,
finds Marrock,
and bites him through the throat.
Men follow the dog
to Sir Roger's grave,
which he will not quit.

---

[1] renne.—Cop.
[2] werere, in the MS.—F.
[3] MS. *o* over a *y*.—F. The hovnd wrekyd hys maystyrs dethe.—Ca.

H 2

They return.

& when the men saw noe better boote,
then the men yeed home on horsse & foote,
with great wonder, I weene.

and Arradas says that Marrock has slain Sir Roger.

568   the King said, " by gods paine,
I trow Sir Marrocke hath Sir Rodger slaine,
& with treason famed [1] my Queene.

He orders a search for his corpse.

" goe yee & seeke there againe ;
572   for the hounds Master there is slaine,
some treason there hath beene."
thither they went, soe god me saue,

They find the body,

& found Sir Roger in his graue,
576   for *that* was soone seene :

and take it to Arradas.

& there they looked him there vpon,
for he was hole both flesh & bone,
& to the court his body they brought.
580   for when the King did him see,

who weeps.

the teares ran downe from his eye,
full sore itt him forethought.

the grayhound [2] he wold not from his course [3] fare :
584   then was the King cast in care,

laments over Marrock's treachery,

& said, " Marrocke hath done me teene ;
slaine he hath a curteous Knight,
& fained [4] my Queene with great vnright,
588   as a traitor keene."

the King let draw anon-right
the stewards bodye, *that* false Knight,
with horsse through the towne ;

and hanged.

592   then he hanged him on a tree,
that all men might his body see,
that he had done treason.

---

[1] defamed.- F. flemed. Cop.
[2] grehound. Cop.
[3] corse.—Cop.

[4] *for* famed, *defamed*. F. flemyd.
—Ca. flemed.—Cop.

Sir Rogers Body the next day
596 the King buryed in good array,
   with many a bold baron.[1]

the Grayhound was neuer away
by night nor yet by day,
600   but on the ground he did dye.
the King did send his messengere
in euerye place far & neere
   after the Queene to spye ;
604 but for ought he cold enquire,
he cold of that Ladye nothing heare ;
   therfore the King was sorrye.[1]

the King sayd, " I trow noe reed,
608 for well I wott that shee is dead ;
   for sorrowe now shall I dye !
alas, that euer shee from mee went !
this false steward hath me shent
612   throughe his false treacherye."

this King lined in great sorrow
both euening & morrow
   till that hee were brought to ground.
616 he lined thus many a yeere
with mourning & with euill cheere,
   his sorrowes lasted long :

& euer it did him great paine
620 when hee did thinke how Sir Roger was slaine,
   & how helped him his hound ;
& of his Queene that was soe Mylde,
how shee went from him great with child ;
624   for woe then did hee sound.[2]

---

[1] Percy marks the three last lines as separate stanzas, but I add them to those that precede them.—F.

[2] swoon.—F.

[page 219]

He mourns

long time thus lined the King
in great sorrow & Mourning,
   & oftentime did weepe ;

and is sad at heart.

628 he tooke great thought more & more,
It made his hart verrye sore,
   his sighs were sett soe deepe.

Meantime

now of the King wee will bline,
632 & of the Queene let vs begin,
   & Sir [1] Tryamore ;

Triamore

Is fourteen,

for when he was 14 yeere old,
there was noe man soe bold
636   durst doe him dishonor [2] ;

strong,

in euerye time [3] both stout & stronge,
and tall,

& in stature large & longe,
   comlye of hye color ;

640 all *that* euer he dwelled amonge,
and well-doing.

he neuer did none of them wronge,
   the more *that* was his honor.

in *that* time sikerlye
The King of Hungary dies,

644 dyed the King of Hungarye [4]
   that was of great age I-wiss [5] ;

leaving only a daughter, fair Helen, of fourteen,

he had no heire his land to hold
but a daughter was 14 yeers old [6] ;
648   faire [Hellen [7]] shee named is.

white as a lily.

shee was as white as lilye [8] flower,
   & comely, of gay color,
     the fairest of any towne or tower ;

[1] her sonne.—Cop.
[2] dysshonoure.—Cop.
[3] lymme.—Cop.
[4] Hungry.—Cop.
[5] The second *s* is made over an *e* in the MS.—F.
[6] of vij. yerys elde.—Ca.

[7] See l. 775. Hellene, l. 1587 below.—F. Her name Helyne ys.—Ca. Elyne.—Cop.
[8] The top of a long *s* whose bottom is marked through, is left in the MS. before the first *l*.—F.

652 shee was well shapen of foote & hand,
peere shee had none in noe land,
   shee was soe fresh & soe amorous.

  for when her father was dead,

Her land is invaded;

656 great warr began to spread
   in *that* land about ;
  then the Ladyes councell gan her reade,

her council tell her to marry a lord to protect her.

  ' gett her a lord her land to lead,
660   to rule the realme without doubt ;
  some mightye prince *that* well might
  rule her land with reason & right,
   that all men to him might Lout.'

664 & when her councell had sayd soe,
  for great need shee had therto,
   shee graunted them without Lye :

She consents,

  the Lady said, "I will not feare
668 but he [be] prince or princes peere,
   & cheefe of all chiualrye."

  therto shee did consent,
  & gaue her Lords commandement
672   a great Iusting for to crye ;

proclaims a jousting,

  & at the Iustine, shold soe bee,
  what man *that* shold win the degree,[1]

the winner at which shall win her too.

   shold win *that* Ladye trulye.

676 the day of Iusting then was sett,

The day is fixed.

  halfe a yeere without lett,
   without any more delay,
  because thé might haue good space,
680 Lords, *knights*, dukes, in *euerye* place,
   for to be there *that* day.

[1] Fr. *degré*, a degree, ranke, or place of honour. Cotgrave.—F.

The best lords

Lords, the best in euerye Land,
hard tell of *that* rydand,

prepare to contend.

684   & made them readye full gay ;
of euerye land there was the best,[1]
of the States *that* were honest [2]
attyred [3] many a Lady gay.

688   great was *that* chiualrye
that came *that* time to HUNGARYE,
there for to Iust with might.

Triamore hears of the jousting,

and resolves to go to it,

at last TRIAMORE hard tyding
692   that there shold be a Iusting ;
thither wold he wend.

if he wist *that* he might gaine   .
with all his might, he wold be faine [4]
696   *that* gay Ladye for to win ;
hee had noe horsse nay noe other geere,

but he has no horse or arms.

Nor noe weapon with him to beare ;   [page 220]
that brake his hart in twaine.

700   he thought both euen & morrow
where he might some armour borrowe,
therof wold hee be faine.

He asks Sir Bernard to lend him some,

to Sir Barnard then he can wend,[5]
704   *that* he wold armour lend [6]
to iust against the knights amaine.[7]

and the knight tells him he knows nothing about it.

Triamore asks to be tried.

then said Sir Barnard, " what hast thou thought ?
perdew ! of iusting thou canst nought !
708   for yee bee not able wepon to weld."
" Sir," said TRIAMORE, " what wott yee
of what strenght *that* I bee
till I haue assayd in feeld ? "

---

[1] bestee.—Cop.
[2] moost honasty.—Cop.
[3] dressed herself: parallel to l. 681.
States may mean " nobles." F.

[4] He wolde purvey hym fulle fayne.
—Ca.
[5] mene.—Cop.
[6] lene.- Cop.   [7] of mayne.—Cop.

712 then Sir Barnard *that* was full hend,
said, "Triamor, if thow wilt wend,
thou shalt lacke noe weed ;
I will lend thee all my geere,

Sir Bernard then promises to lend

716 horsse & harneis, sheild & spere,
thou art nothing [1] to dread ;

him horse and arms,

"alsoe thither with thee will I ryde,
& euer nye be by thy side

go with him,

720 to helpe thee if thou haue need ;
all things *that* thow wilt haue,
gold & siluer, if thow wilt craue,
thy Iourney for to speed."

and provide him money.

724 then was Triamore glad & light,
& thanked Barnard with all his might
of his great proferinge.
that day the Iusting shold bee,

On the day of the joust,

728 Triamore sett him on his knee
& asked his mother blessinge.

Triamore asks his mother's blessing,

at home shee wold haue kept him faine ;
but all her labor was in vaine,
732 there might be noe letting.
shee saw it wold noe better bee,
her blessing shee gaue him verelye
w[i]th full sore weepinge.

and she gives it him sorrowfully.

736 & when it was on the Morrow day,
Triamore was in good array,
armed & well dight ;
when he was sett on his steed,

In the morning, Triamore

740 he was a man both [2] lenght & bread,[3]
& goodlye in mans sight.

---

[1] nothenge.—Cop.   [2] in.—Cop.   [3] brede.—Cop.

starts with
Sir Bernard.

then TRIAMORE to the feeld can ryde,
  & Sir Barnard by his side;
744 they were Iocund & light;
there was none in all the feild
that was more seemlye vnder sheild;
  he rode full like a knight.

Queen Helen
of Hungary
looks from a
turret

748 then was the faire **Lady** sett
full hye vppon a turrett,[1]
  for to behold *that* play;

on the gay
scene of

there was many a seemlye **K**night,
752 princes, Lords, & dukes of Might,
  themselues for to assay,

helmed
knights.

with helme on theire heads bright
that all the feelds shone with light,
756 they were soe stout & gay:

Triamore

then Sir TRIAMORE & Sir BARNARD
thé pressed them into the feeld forward,[2]
  there durst noe man say nay.

760 there was much price [3] & pride
when euerye man to other can ryde,
  & lords of great renowne;

happens to
choose his
father, King
Arradas's
side.

it beffell TRIAMORE *that* tyde
764 for to be on his fathers side,
  the King of Arragon.

A big Lom-
bard lord
rides forth;

the first *that* rode forth certainlye
was a great Lord of Lumbardye,
768 a wonderfull bold Barron.

Triamore
throws him,

TRIAMOR rode him againe:
for all *that* lord had Might & maine,
  the child bare him downe.

[page 221]

---

[1] Hye up in a garett.—Ca. [2] warde.—Cop. [3] prees.—Cop.

772 [1] then cryed S*i*r Barnard w*i*th honor,
    "A TRIAMOR, a TRIAMORE !"
      for men shold him ken.
    Mayd Hellen [2] *that* was soe mild,
776 more shee beheld TRIAMORE the child
      then all the other men.

and Sir Bernard shouts "A Triamore" to make him known. Queen Helen views him with favour.

    then the K*i*ngs sonne of Nauarrne [3]
    wold not his body warne [4];
780   he pricked forth on the plaine.
    then young Triamore *that* was stout,
    turned himselfe round about,
      & fast rode him againe;

The Prince of Navarne rides out; Triamore charges him;

784 soe neither of them were to ground cast,[5]
    they sate soe wonderous fast,
      like men of much might.
    then came forth a Bachelour,[6]
788 a prince proud w*i*thout peere;
    S*i*r Iames, forsooth, he hight;

neither is thrown.

Sir James of Almaigne

    he was the Emperours sonne of Almaigne [7];
    he rode S*i*r TRIAMORE [8] againe,
792   w*i*th hard strenght to fight.
    S*i*r Iames had such a stroake indeed
    that he was tumbled from his steed;
      then failed all his might.
796 there men might see swords brast,
    helmes ne sheilds might not last;
      & thus it dured till night;

next charges Triamore, and is un-horsed.

The joust lasts till night.

---

[1] Ca. puts this stanza after the next. —F.
[2] Elyne.—Cop.
[3] Armony.—Ca. Nauerne.—Cop.
[4] A.-S. *warnian*, to take care of, beware. —F.

[5] Ca. makes Triamore bear him down, and transfers this to Sir James in the next stanza.—F.
[6] batchelere.—Cop.
[7] Almaine.—Cop.
[8] ? MS. Triamoir.—F.

but when the sun drew neere[1] west,

800 and all the Lords went to rest,

[Not so the maide Elyne.[2]]

Next day, the Kni*gh*ts attired them in good arraye,

on steeds great, with trappers[3] gaye,

before the sun can[4] shine ;

it begins
again, 804 then to the feeld thé pricked prest,

& everye man thought himselfe best

[As the mayden faire they paste.[2]]

and the
knights
charge
fiercely. then they feirelye ran together,

great speres in peeces did shim*m*er,[5]

808 their timber might not last.

& at *that* time there did run[6]

King
Arradas the Ki*ng* Arradas of Arragon :

his sonne Triiamore mett him in *that* tyde,

is thrown by
his son
Triamore, 812 & gaue his father such a rebound

that harse & man fell to the ground,[7]

soe stoutlye gan he ryde.

who also
vanquishes
Sir James. then the next K*nigh*t *that* hee mett

816 was S*i*r Iames ; & such a stroake him sett

vpon the sheild ther on the plaine

that the blood brast out at his nose & eares,

his steed vnto the ground him beares ;

820 then was S*i*r Barnard faine.

Queen Helen
falls in love
with
Triamore. *that* Maid of great honor

sett her loue on younge TRIAMORE

that fought alwayes as a feirce[8] Lyon.

---

[1] ferre.—Cop.

[2] This line is from Copland's text. —H.

[3] The trappings of horses. Halliwell. — F.

[4] gan.—Cop.

[5] shyner.—Cop.

[6] dyde ronne.—Cop.

[7] Tryamore must be supposed to have changed since the first day, when he was on his father's side : see l. 763. In l. 920, Arradas is accused of killing the Emperor's son. whom Triamore slays (l. 860-1), but he (Arradas) declares he had nothing to do with it, l. 974-9. He only rescues his son from the Emperor's men. l. 866-7.—F.

[8] fyers.—Cop.

824   speres *that* day many were spent,
   & with swords there was many a stripe lent,
      till the[re] failed light of the sunn.

   on the Morrow all they were faine   *Next day*
828   for to come into the feild againe
      with great spere & sheild.
   then the Duke of Sinille, Sir Phylar,[1]   *the Duke of*
   that was a doughtye knight in euerye warr, *Seville*
832   he rode first into the feild ;

   & Triamore tooke his spere,   *is charged*
   against the Duke he can it beare,   *by Triamore,*
      & smote him in the sheild ;   *and his*
836   a-sunder in 2 peeces it went ;   *shield split.*
   & then many a louelye Lady gent,
      full well they him beheld.

   then came forth a *Knight that* hight Terrey, *Sir Terrey*
840   hee was a great Lo*r*d of Surrey,[2]   [page 222] *of Syria*
   he thought Noble TRIAMORE to assayle ; *charges*
   & TRIAMORE rode to him blithe   *Triamore,*
   in all the strenght *that* he might drine,
844   he thought he wold not fayle ;

   he smote him soe in *that* stond
   that horsse & man fell to the ground,[3] *and gets*
   soe sore his stroke he sett.   *thrown.*

848   then durst noe man att TRIAMORE [ride,[4]] *No one else*
   for fortune held all on his side   *will try*
   all those dayes 3.[5]   *Triamore ;*

---

[1] Syselle, sir Sywere.—Ca. Cycyll,
sir Fylar.—Cop.
[2] The dewke of Lythyr, sir Tyrre.
—Ca.

[3] . . . the dewke, bothe hors and man,
Turnyd toppe ovyr tayle.—Ca.
[4] to Tryamoure ryde.— Cop.
[5] The Cambridge text makes Triamore

Sir Iames, sonne vnto the Emperour,
852 had enuye to Sir Triamore,
   and laid wait [1] for him priuilye.

att the last TRIAMORE came ryding bye.
Sir Iames said, "Triamore! thou shalt dye,
856   for thou hast done me shame."

he rode to Triamore with a spere,
& thorrow [2] the thigh he can him beare;
   he had almost him slaine.

860 but Tryamore hitt him in [3] the head
that he fell downe starke dead.
   then was all his men woe;
then wold they haue slaine Tryamore
864 without he had had great succour [4];
   they purposed to doe soe.

with that came King Arradas [5] then,
& reschued Tryamore with all his men,
868   that stood in great doubt.
then Sir Barnard was full woe
that Tryamore was hurt soe;
   then to his owne house he him brought.

872 but when the Mother saw her sonns wound,
shee fell downe for sorrow to the ground,
   & after a Leeche shee sent.
of [6] this, all the Lords that were [7] Iustinge,
876 to the pallace [8] made highinge,[9]
   & to that Ladye went.

truly, as the story sayes,
thé [1] pricked forth to the pallace
880   the Ladyes will to heare,   *to hear*
Bachelours & kni*gh*ts prest,
   that shee might choose of them the best   *whom she*
   w*hi*ch to her faynest were.   *will choose.*

884   the Ladye beheld all *that* fayre Meanye,
but Tryamore shee cold not see :
   tho chaunged all her cheere,
   then [2] shee sayd "Lo*rd*, where is hee [3]   *She chooses*
888 *that* eue*r*ye day wan the degree ?   *Triamore.*
   I chuse him to my peere.[4] "   *Where is he?*

al about [5] thé Tryamore sought ;   *He can't be*
he was ryddn home ; thé found him nought ; *found,*
892   then was *that* Ladye woe. ·
   the K*ni*g*h*ts were afore her brought,
   & of respite shee them besought,   *so Helen*
    a yeare & noe more :   *asks for a*
                                    year's delay.

896 shee said, " Lords, soe god me saue !
he *that* wan me, he shall me haue ;
   ye wot well *that* my cry was soe."
   thé all consented her vntill,
900 for shee [6] said Nothing ill,
   thé said it shold be soe.

for when they had all sayd,
then answered *that* fayre Mayd,
904   " I will haue none but Tryamore."   *she will have*
then all the Lo*rd*s *that* were p*r*esent   *none but*
tooke their Leaue, & home went ;   *Triamore.*
   there wan thé litle honor.

[1] they.—Cop.   [4] fere.—Cop.
[2] Tho.—Cop.   [5] All aboute.—Cop.
[3] he.—Cop.   [6] had *inserted*.—Cop.

908 Sir Iames men were nothing faine
     because their *Master*, he was slaine,
       That was soe stout in stowre ;   [page 223]
     in chaire his body thé Layd,

912 & led him home, as I haue sayd,
     vnto his father the Emperour ;

     & when *that* hee his sonne gan see,
     a sorrye man then was hee,
916 & asked ' who had done *that* dishonor [1] ? '
     thé sayd " wee [ne] wott who it is I-wisse,[2]
     but Sir Tryamore he named is,
       soe thé called him [3] in the crye ;

920 " the *King* of Arragon alsoe,
     he helped thy [4] sonne to sloe,
       with all his companye."
     they said, " thé be good warryoirs ;
924 they byte [5] vs with sharpe showers [6]
       with great villanye.[7] "

     " Alas ! " said the Emperour,
     " till I be reuenged on *that* traytour,
928 now shall I neuer cease !
     thé shall haue many a sharpe shower,
     both the *King* & Tryamore,
       they shall neuer haue peace ! "

932 the Emperour sayd thé shold repent ;
     & after great companye he sent
       of princes bold in presse,
     Dukes, Earles, & lords of price.[8]
936 with a great armye, the Duke sayes,
     thé yeed to Arragon without losse.

---

[1] dysshonour.—Cop.   [5] bete.—Cop.
[2] has ywys.—Cop.   [6] shoutes.—Cop.
[3] called thé him.—Cop.   [7] vilany.—Cop.
[4] MS. the.—F.   [8] pryse.—Cop.

King Arradas[1] was a-dread[2]   Arradas
for the Emperour such power had,
940   *that* battell hee wold him bid[3];
he saw his land nye one*r*-gon,
& to a castle hee fledd anon,   takes refuge
                                     in his castle,
& victualls[4] it for dread.

944 [5] the Emperour was bold & stout,   where the
& beseeged the castle about;   Emperor
                                      besieges him,
his[6] banner he began to spread,
& arrayd his host full well & wiselye,
948 with wepons strong & mightye
he thought to make them dread.

the Emperour was bold & stout,
& beseeged the castle about,
952 & his banner he gan to spread;
he gaue assault[7] to the hold.   and assaults
                                      it.
King Arradas was stout & bold,   Arradas
ordayned him full well.[8]

956 with gunes & great stones round   fires and
were throwne downe to the ground,   hurls stones
& on the men were cast;   on the
                                      besiegers.
they brake many backes & bones,
960 *that* they fought eue*r*ye[day[9]] ones   After seven
while 7 weekes did last.   weeks,

the Emperour was hurt ill therfore,
his men were hurt sore,
964 all his Ioy was past.

---

[1] Aragus.—Cop.
[2] a-dradde.—Cop.
[3] bydde.—Cop.
[4] vytaylled.—Cop. vetaylyd.--Ca.
[5] This stanza, which seems superfluous, is not in the Cambridge text. —F.

[6] A letter like *t*, seemingly blotched out, precedes *his* in the MS.—F.
[7] assalte.—Cop.
[8] And defendyd hym full faste.—Ca. And ordered it full welle. Rawlinson MS. (Percy Soc., p. 62).—F.
[9] day.—Cop.

Arradas

King Arradas thought full longe
that hee was beseeged soe stronge,
with soe much might & maine :

sends to
the Emperor

968   2 Lords forth a Message he sent,
  & straight to the Emperour thé [1] went.
    soe when they cold him see,
    of peace [2] they can him pray,[3]
972   to take truce [4] till a certaine day.
    thé kneeled downe on their knee,

to say that
he did not
slay his son,

  & said, " our *King* sendeth word to thee
  that he neuer your sonne did slay,[5]
976   soe he wold quitt him faine ;
    he was not then present,
    nor did noe wise [6] consent
    that your sonne was slaine.

980   That [he] will prone, if you will soe,   [page 224
    your selfe and he betweene you tow,

and to
propose a
settlement
of their
quarrel by
single
combat :.

    if you will it sayne ;

  " or else take your selfe a Knight,
984   & he will gett another to fight
    on a certaine day :

if the
Emperor's
knight wins

  if *that* your Knight hap soe
  ours for to discomfort or sloe,
988   as by fortune itt may,

Arradas will
give in ;

  our *King* then will doe your will,
  be att your bidding lowde & still
    without more delay ;

if Arradas's
knight wins,

992   " & alsoe if it you betyde
  that your knight on your syde
    be slaine by Mischance,

---

[1] yᵉ.—Cop.   [2] peas.—Cop.   [4] treues.—Cop.
[3] Only the long part of the *y* is in the   [5] sle.—Cop.
MS.—F.   [6] noe wise did.—Cop.

My Lord shall make your warr to cease,[1]
[and we shall after be at pease,[2]]
996 without any distance.[3] "

the Emperour said[4] without fayle
" sett a day of Battell
 by assent of the King of france ; "
1000 for he had a great Campiowne,[5]
in euerye realme he wan[6] renowne ;
 soe the Emperour ceased his distance.

when peace was made, & truce came,[7]
1004 then King Arradas were[8] a Ioyfull man,
 & trusted vnto Tryamore.
Soe after him he went without fayle,
for to doe the great battelle
1008 to his helpe & succour.

his Messengers were come & gone,
tydings of him hard[9] thé none.
 the King Arradas thought him long,
1012 " & he be dead, I may say alas !
who shall then fight with Marradais
 that is soe stout & stronge ? "

when Tryamore was whole[10] & sound,
1016 & well healed of his wound,
 he busked him for to fare ;

---

[1] sense.—Cop.

[2] This line is from Copland's text. —H.
He preyeth yow that ye wyll cese,
And let owre londys be in pees.—Ca.

[3] " Dystaunce, supra in Debate vel
Dyscorde (discidia)." Promptorium.
Fr. distance, difference. Colgrave.—F.

[4] We keep the said of the MS., though

it is not wanted, and the Cambridge text
has not got it.—F.

[5] Champion. MS. campanye.—F.
Company.—Cop.

[6] the.—Cop.

[7] treues tane.—Cop.

[8] was.—Cop.

[9] herde.—Cop. [10] hole.—Cop.

and asks his
mother who
his father is.

he sayd, "mother," with mild cheere,
"& 1 wist what my father were,
1020   the lesse were my care."

His mother
will not tell
him till he
marries,

"sonne," shee said, "thou shalt witt;
when [1] thou hast Marryed *that* Ladye sweet,
thy father thou shalt ken."
1024 "mother," he said, "if you will [soe,[2]]
haue good day, for now I goe
to doe my Masteryes if I can.[3] "

so he starts
for Arragon.

then rode he ouer dale & downe
1028 vntill he came to Arragon,
ouer many a weary way.
aduentures many him befell,
& all he scaped full well,
1032   in all his great Iourney.

On his way

he saw many a wild beast
both in heath & in forrest ;

he sets his
greyhounds
at a hart,

he had good grey-hounds 3 ;
1036 then to a hart he let them run
till 14 fosters spyed him soone,
soe threatened him greatlye ;

and is
attacked by
fourteen
foresters.

Triamore
tries to
pacify them,

they yeede to him with weapons on euerye side ;
1040 it was noe boote to bid them byde ;
Tryamore was loth to flye,
& said vnto them, "Lords, I you pray,
lett me in peace wend my way
1044   to seeke my grayhounds 3."

offers them
all his
money.

then said Tryamore as in this time,
"gold & siluer, take all mine
if [4] *that* 1 haue tresspassed ought."

---

[1] Wham.—Cop.   [3] and speke wyth my lemman.—Ca.
[2] soo.—Ca.   [4] Of.—Cop.

1048 Thé said, " wee will meete with thy anon,   [page 225]   They refuse it,
    there shall noe gold borrow thee soone,[1]
      but in prison thou shalt be brought,   and threaten
      Such is the law of the ground ;[2]   to prison him.
1052 Whosoever therin may be found,
    other way goe thé nought."

    then Sir Tryamore was full woe   Triamore
    that to prison he shold goe ;
1056   hee thought the flesh to deare bought.
    there was no more to say,
    the fosters att him gan lay   is attacked by the foresters,
      with strokes sterne and stout.

1060 there Tryamore with them fought ;
    some to the ground be brought ;   and soon discomfits them,
      he made them lowe to looke ;
    some of them fast gan pray,
1064 the other fled fast away
    with wounds wyde that they sought.[3]

    Tryamore sought & found[4] his gray-hounds ;   but finds two of his greyhounds
    he hear[k]ned to their yerning[5] sounds,
1068   & thought not for to leaue them soe.
    at last he came to a water side ;
    there he saw the beast abyde   slain by a hart,
    that had slaine 2 of his grayhounds ;

1072 the 3d. full sore troubled the hind,
    & he hurt him with his triude[6] ;   and the other wounded.
    then was Tryamore woe.
    if the battaile had lasted a while,
1076 the hart wold the hound beguile,[7]
    & take his life for euermore.

[1] ? MS.: it may be meant for *frome* ; but one stroke of the *m* is missing.—F.
[2] Ca. has "ye must lese yowre ryght honde."—F.
[3] ? tooke.—F.
[4] rod and sought.—Cop.
[5] ? running.—F.
[6] One stroke of the *u* is wanting in the MS. Ca. has *Tyndys*, branches of the antlers.—F.
[7] begyle.—Cop.

Tryamore smote att the deere,

and [1] to the hart went the spere ;

1080   then his horne he blew full sore.

the King Lay there beside

at Mannour [2] *that* same tide ;

he hard a horne blowe ;

1084   they had great wonder in hall,

both Knights, Squiers,[3] & all,

for noe man cold it know.

w*i*th *that* ran in a foster

1088   into the hall w*i*th euill cheere,

& was full sorry, I trow.

the King of tydings gan him fraine ;

he answered, " Sir King, your Keepers be slaine,

1092   and lye dead on a rowe.

there came a knight *that* was mightye,

he let 3 grayhounds *that* were wightye,

& laid my fellowes full lowe : "

1096   he sayd, it was full true

that the same *that* the horne blew

that all this sorrow hath wrought.

King Arradas said then,

1100   " I haue great need of such of a man ;

god hath him hither brought."

the King commanded Knights 3,

he said, " goe [4] feitch yond gentleman to me

1104   *that* is now at his play ;

looke noe ill words w*i*th him yee breake,

but pray him with me for to speake ;

I trow he will not say nay."

1108   Euerye knight his steed hent,   The knights
      & lightlye to the wood ¹ thó went
      to seeke Tryamore *that* child.
      thó found him by a water side   find
                                     Triamore,
1112   where he brake the beast ² *that* tyde,
      that hart *that* was soe wylde.

      thó said, " S*i*r ! god be at yo*ur* game ! "   salute him,
      he answered them euen the same ;
1116   then was he frayd of guile.
      " S*i*r K*night* ! " they said, " is itt yo*ur* will   and ask if he
                                   will come to
      to come & speake our K*i*n*g* vntill   their king,
      w*i*th word[e]s meeke & mylde ? "   [page 226]

1120   Tryamore asked shortlye,³
      " wh*a*t hight your K*i*n*g*, tell yee mee,
      that is lord ⁴ of this land ? "
      " this Land hight Arragon,   Arradas of
                                     Arragon.
1124   & our K*i*n*g*, Arradas, w*i*th crowne ;
      his place his heire att hand."

      Tryamore went vnto the K[*i*n*g*,]   Triamore
                                     comes,
      & he was glad of his cominge,
1128   he knew him att first sight ;
      the K*i*n*g* tooke him by the hand,   Arradas
                                   welcomes
      & said, "welcome into this land ! "   him,
      & asked ⁵ him what he hight.

1132   " S*i*r, my name is Tryamore ;   and
                                     Triamore
      once you helpt me in a stowre   tells him
                                     who he is.
      as a noble man of might ;
      & now I am here in thy Land ;
1136   soe was I neue*r* erst, as I vnderstand,
      by god full of might."

¹ wodde.—Cop.
² The top of some letter over the *a* is marked out in the MS. *brake* means "cut up."—F.
³ shortely.—Cop.
⁴ There is a round blot like an *o* after the *r* in the MS.—F.
⁵ axet.—Cop.

Arradas
Is very glad.

when the King wist it was hee,
his hart reioced greatlye ;

1140   3 times he did downe fall,
     & [said] " Tryamore, welcome to me !
     great sorrowe & care I haue had [1] for thee ; "

and tells
Triamore

     and he told him al ;

of the day
set for the
fight with the
Emperor's
champion.

1144   " with the Emperour I [2] tooke a day
     [to] defend me if *that* I may ;
     to Iesu I will call ;
     for I neuer his sonne slew ;

1148   god he knoweth I speake but true,
     & helpe me I trust he shall ! "

then said Tryamore thee, [" I am fulle woe [3]]
that you for me haue beene greeued soe,

1152   if I might it amend ;

Triamore
agrees to
fight for
Arradas,

     & att the day of battell
     I trust to proue [4] my might as [5] well,
     if god will grace me send."

of which the
latter is
glad.

1156 then was King Arradas very glad,
     and of Marradas was not adread :
     when he to the batteile shold wend,
     he ioyed [6] *that* he shold well speed,

1160 for Tryamore was warry [7] at neede
     against his enemye to defend.

there Tryamore dwelled with the King
many a weeke without lettinge ;

1164 he lacked right nought.

On the day
fixed, the
Emperor

     & when the day of battayle was came,
     the Emperour with his men hasted full soone,
     & manye wonder thought ;

---

[1] Cop. omits *had*.—H.
[2] MS. he.—F.   [3] From Ca.—F.
[4] proue, in the MS.— F.

[5] This word is blotted in the MS.—F.
[6] joyed.— Cop.
[7] ware.—Cop.

1168   he brought thither both K*ing* & K*night*;
    & Marradas, *that* was of might,
      to battcillc hc him brought.
    there was many a scemclyc man,
1172   moo then I tcll you can;
      of them all hc nc wrought.

brings his champion, Marradas;

  both p*a*rtycs *that* ilke day
  into thc fccld tookc thc way,
1176   they were already [1] dight.
  thc K*ing* there kisscd Tryamore,
  & sayd, " I make thec mine [hcyre [2]] this hower,
    & dubb thee a k*night*."

the King brings

Triamore,

1180   " S*ir*," said Tryamore, " take no dread ;
  I trust Icsus will mc speedc,
    for you bc in thc right ;
  therforc through gods grace
1184   I will fight for you in this placc
    with thc helpe of our Lords might ! "

who trusts in Christ's help.

  both p*a*rtycs were full swore
  to hold the p*r*omisc *that* was madc before ;
1188   to Iesus can hce [3] call.
  S*ir* Tryamore & S*ir* Marradas
  both wcll armed was
    amonge the Lords all ;

Both partics swear to abide by thc result.

1192   cchc of them were sett on stecdc ;
  all men of Tryamorc had drccdc,
    that was soc hind in all.[4]
  Marradas was stiffe & surc,[5]
1196   their [6] might noc man his stroakc endure,
    But *that* he made them fall.   [page 227]

Triamore

and Marradas

---

[1] al rcdy.—Cop.
[2] hcyrc.—Cop.
[3] thcy.—Cop.

[4] Ther was none so hyndc in hallc.—Ca.
[5] so styff in stourc.—Ca.
[6] then.—Ca.

charm,

then rode they together [1] full right;
with sharpe speres & swords bright

1200   they smote together sore ;

break their
speers and
shields,

thé spent speres & brake sheelds,
thé busled [2] fowle in middest the feelds,
either fomed as doth a bore.

1204   all thé [3] wondred that beheld

and fight
marvel-
lously.

how thé fought in the feeld ;
there was but a liffe. [4]
Marradas fared fyer [5] wood

1208   because Tryamore soo long stood ;
sore gan hee smite.

Triamore
kills Mar-
radas's horse,

Sir Tryamore fayled of Marradas,
that sword lighted vpon his horsse,

1212   the sword to ground gan light.

Marradas said, " it is great shame
on a steed to wreake his game !
thou sholdest rather smite mee ! "

1216   Tryamore swore, " by gods might
I had lener it had on thee light !
then I wold not be sorye [6] ;

and then
offers him
his own.

" but here I giue thee steede mine

1220   because I haue slaine thine ;
by my will it shalbe soe."

Marradas
refuses it.

Marradas sayd, " I will [him] nonght
till I haue him with stroakes bought,"

1224   [and won him from my foe. [7]]

& Tryamore lighted from his horsse,
& to Marradas straight he goes,

Both alight

for both on foote they did light.

---

[1] the longer.—Cop.
[2] powsed.—Cop.
[3] they.—Cop.
[4] ? a life to be lost.—F. lyte (little).
—Cop.
[5] fare.—Cop.
[6] sore.—Cop.
[7] ?; a line is wanting in the MS. Cop.
has "And wonne hym here in fyght."
—F.

1228   Sir Tryamore spared him nought,
     [But evyr in his hert he thoght [1]]
      "this day was I made a Knight!"

     & thought *that* hee himselfe wold be slaine soone,
1232   "or else of him I will win my shoone [2]
     throughe gods might."
     thé laid eche at other with good will   *and fight on foot*
     with sharpe swords made of steele ;
1236   *that* saw [3] many a knight.

     great wonder it was to behold
     the stroakes *that* was betwixt them soe bold ;   *fiercely.*
     all men might it see.
1240   thé were weary, & had soe greatlye bled ;
     Marradas was sore adread,   *Marradas grows faint.*
      he fainted then greatlye ;

     & *that* Tryamore lightlye beheld,
1244   & fought feercelye in the feeld ;
      he stroke Marradas soe sore
     that the sword through the body ran.   *Triamore kills him.*
     then was the Emperour a sorry man ;   *The Emperor*
1248   he made thenn peace for euer-more ;

     he kissed the King, & was his freind,   *kisses Arradas,*
     & tooke his leauce homewards to wend ;   *and goes home.*
     noe longer there dwell wold hee.
1252   then King Arradas & Tryamore   *Arradas and Triamore return*
     went to the palace with great honor,
     into *that* rych citye.   *to the city,*
     there was ioy without care,
1256   & all they had great welfare,
      there might no better bee ;

---

[1] From Ca.—F.   euer in hys herte he thought.—Cop.
[2] See p. 77, l. 504.   [3] sauce.—Cop.

hunt, ride,
and enjoy
themselves.

they hunted & rode many a where,
full great pleasure they had there.

1260   among the knights of price

the K*ing* profered him full fayre,

Arradas
offers to
make
Triamore his
heir,

& sayd, "Tryamore, Ile make thee mine heyre,
for thou art strong & wise."

but Triamore
declines, and

1264   Sir Tryamore said, "Si*r*, trulye
into other countryes goe will I;

asks only a
steed;

I desire of you but a steed,
& to other lands will I goe

he means to
do adven-
tures.

1268   some great aduentures for to doe,
thus will I my liffe lead."

the K*ing* was verry sorry tho;
when *that* hee wold from him goe,

Arradas
gives him

1272   he gaue him a sure weede,[1]

money

& plenty of siluer & gold,

and a fearless
steed,

& a steed as hee wold,
that nothing wold feare.

1276   hee tooke his leaue of the King,
And mourned at his depa*r*ting,   [page 228]
then hasted he him there;

and promises
him all

the K*ing* sayd, "Tryamor! *that*[2] is mine,

1280   when thou list it shall be thine,

his realm.

all my kingdome lesse & more."

Triamore

Now is Tryamore forth goe;
Lords & ladyes were full woe,[3]

1284   euerye man loued him there.

rides to

Hungary.

Tryamore rode in hast trulye
into the Land of Hungarye,
aduentures for to seeke.[4]

---

[1] *steede* is marked out in the MS.—F.
[2] whatever, all that.—F.
[3] for him were woe.—Cop.

[4] The Cambridge text sends him
generally everywhere before going to
Hungary.—F.

1288 betweene 2 mountaines, the sooth to say,
 he rode forth on his way;
  with a palmer he did meete;

On his road
a palmer

 he asked almes for gods sake,
1292 & Tryamore him not forgate,
  he gaue him with words sweete.
 the palmer said, "turne yee againe,
 or else I feare you wilbe slaine;

warns him
to turn back

1296 you may not passe but you be beat."

 Tryamore asked "why soe?"
 "Sir," he said, "there be brethren towe
  that on the mountaine dwells."

for fear of
two brothers
there.

1300 "faith," said Tryamore, "if there be no more,
 I trust in god *that* way to goe,
  if this be true *that* thou tells."
 he bade the palmer good day,

Triamore

1304 & rode forth on his way
  ouer heath & feelds;

rides on,

 the palmer prayed to him full fast,
 Tryamore was not agast,
1308   he blew his horne full shrill.
 he had not rydden but a while,
 not the Mountenance of a mile,

and soon
meets

  2 knigh*t*s he saw on a hill:

two knights,

1312 the one of them to him gan ryde,
 they other still gan abyde

who order
him to go
back.

  a litle there beside.
 & when thé did Tryamore spye,
1316 thé said, "turne thee traytor,[1] or thou shalt dye,
  therfore stand & abyde!"

    [1] traytor turne.—Cop.

*One charges
him,*
either againe other [1] gan ryd fast,

theire strokes mad their speres to brast,

1320   & made them wounds full wyde.

the other
the other knight *that* houed [2] soe,

wondred *that* Tryamore dared soe :

he rode to them *that* tyde

*separates
them,*
1324   & departed them in twaine,

& to speake fayre he began to fraine

with words *that* sounded well :

*asks
Triamore
his name,*
to Tryamore he [3] sayd anon,

1328   "a doughtyer Kn*ight* I neuer saw none ! [4]

thy name *that* thou vs tell."

Tryamore said, "first will I wett

why *that* you doe keepe this street,

1332   & where *that* you doe dwell."

*and says
that their
brother
Marradas*
thé said, "wee had a brother hight Marradas,

with the Emperour forsooth he was,

a stronge man well I-know. [5]

1336   in Arragon, before the Emperour,

*was slain by
one
Triamore,*
a kn*ight* called S*ir* Tryamore

in battel there him slew [6] ;

*and their
elder brother
Burlong*
" & alsoe wee say another,

1340   Burlong [7] our elder brother,

as a man of much might ;

he hath beseeged soothlye

the K*ings* daughter of HUNGARYE ;

1344   to wed her he hath height ;

---

[1] other than.—Cop.   *ryd* has a tag at
the end.—F.

[2] houed, *i.e.* hovered on the hill, qu.—
P.   *houd* is common in the sense of
halted.—F.

[4] they.—Cop.

[4] so doughty a knight knowe I none.
—Cop.

[5] y-nough (enough).—Ca.

[6] There is something like another *e*
before the *w* in the MS.—F.

[7] Burlonde.—Ca.

. " & soe well hee hath sped
that hee shall *that* Lady wedd
but shee may find a K*night*
1348 *that* BURLONGE ouercome may ;
to *that* they haue tooke a day,
wage battel & fight ;

is to wed
Queen Helen
of Hungary
unless she
can find a
knight to
beat him,

" for *that* same Tryamore
1352 loued *that* Ladye paramoure,
as it is before told ;
if he will to Hungarye,
needs must he come vs by ;
1356 to meete with him wee wold."

and she is
Triamore's
love.

[page 229]

They'd like
to catch him.

Tryamore said, " I say not nay,
but my name I will tell this day,
in faith I will not Laine :
1360 thinke your Iourney well besett,
for with Tryamore you haue mett
that your brother hath slaine."

Triamore
says

" here he is."

" welcome ! " thé said, " Tryamore !
1364 his death shalt thou repent sore ;
thy sorrow shall begin.
yeeld thee to vs anon,
for thou shalt not from vs gone
1368 by noe manner of gin.[1] "

They call on
him to yield.

thé smote feirely att him tho,
& Tryamore against them 2
without more delay.
1372 Sir Tryamore proued him full prest,
he brake their spere on their brest,
hee had such assay ;

He fights
them,

[1] gynne.—Cop.   wile.—F.

they split
his shield
and kill his
horse,

his sheeld was broken in peeces 3,
1376   his horsse was smitten on his knee,
soe hard att him thé thrust.[1]
Sir Tryamore was then right wood,
but he slays
one of them.
& slew the one there as he stood
1380   with his sword full prest.

The other
that other rode his way,
his hart was in great affray,
yet he turned againe that tide,—
1384   when Tryamore had slaine his brother,
a sorry man then was the other,—
rides at him,
& straight againe to him did rydde ;

then they 2 sore foughte
but Tria-
more kills
him too.
1388   that the other to the ground was brought
then were thé both slaine.

Helen
wonders
where
Triamore is.
tho the Ladye on Tryamore thought,
for of him shee knew right nought,
1392   shee wist not what to say.
The day to
win her is
come ;
the day was come that was sett,
the Lords assembled without lett,
all in good array.

Burlong
calls for her
knight.
1396   Burlonge was redye dight,
he bade the Lady send the Knight.
She has
none.
shee answered " I ne may : "
for in that castle shee had hight
1400   to keepe her with all her might,
as the story doth say.

thé said, " if Tryamore be aliue,
hither[2] will hee come blithe ;
1404   god send vs good grace to speed ! "

---

[1] thrast.— Cop.   [2] MS. either.—F.

with *that* came in Sir Tryamore
in the thickest of *that* stower,
into the feild without dread.

But just
then
Triamore

rides into
the field,

1408 he asked 'what all *that* did meane.'
the people shewed *that* a battel there shold beene
for the loue of *that* Ladye.
he saw BURLONG on his steede,
1412 & straight to him he yeede ;
that Ladye challengeth hee.

goes straight
to Burlong,

Burlong asked him if he wold fight.
Tryamore said, " with all [my] might
1416 to slay thee, or thou me."
anon thé made them readye,
& none there knew him sikerlye,
thé wondred what he shold bee.

and says he'll
fight him.

1420 high on a tower stood *that* good Ladye ;
shee knew not what Kni*ght* verelye
that with Burlong did fight.
fast shee asked of her men
1424 'if *that* Kni*ght* they cold ken
that to battell was dight ;

Helen
does not
know him ;

'a griffon he beareth all of blew.'[1]
a herald of armes soone him[2] knew,
1428 & said anon-right,
"Madame ! god hath sent you succor ;
for yonder is Tryamore
That with Burlong will fight."

but a herald
recognises
his crest,

and tells her
it is
Triamore.

[page 230]

1432 to Iesus gan the Ladye pray
for to speed him on his Iourney
that hee about yeed.

She prays for
his success.

---

[1] A kreste he beryth in blewe.—Ca.   [2] Syr Barnarde.—Ca.

Triamore
and Burlong
fight

1436   then those *Knights* ran together,
       the speres in peeces gan shiuer,
           the fought full sore indeed ;

       there was noe man in the feild tho
       who shold haue the better of them tow,
1440   soe mightilye they did them beare.
for a long   the Battel lasted wonderous long ;
while,   though Burlong was neuer soe stronge,
           there found he his peere.

till Triamore 1444   Tryamore a stroke to him mint,[1]
loses his   his sword fell downe at *that* dint
sword.   out of his hand him froe.
                       then was Burlong verry [2] glad,
1448   & the Ladye was verry sad,
           & many more full woe.

He asks for   Tryamore asked his sword againe,
it,   but Burlong gan him fraine
and Burlong
agrees to   1452   to know first his name ;
give it him   & said, " tell me first what thou hight,
if he'll tell   & why thou challengeth the Ladye bright,
his name.   then shalt thou haue thy sword againe."

Triamore   1456   Tryamore sayd, " soe mote I thee,
tells him.   My name I will tell trulye,
                       therof I will not doubt ;
                       men call me Si̇r Tryamore,
1460   I wan this Ladye in a stowre
           among Barrons stout."

Burlong   then said Burlong, " thou it was
reproaches   *that* slew my brother Marradas !
him with
killing   1464   a faire [3] hap thee befell ! "
Marradas

---

[1] mynt.—Cop. minded, meant, intended.—F.
[2] wonder.—Cop.   [3] ? fowle.—F.

Sir Tryamore sayd to him tho,
" soe haue I done thy Brethren 2
that on the Mountaines did dwell."

1468 Burlong said, " woe may thou bee,
for thou hast slaine my brethren 3 !
sorrow hast thou sought !
thy sword getts thou neuer againe
1472 till I be avenged, & thou slaine ;
now I am well bethought ! "

Sir Tryamore sayd, " noe force [1] tho,
thou shalt repent it ere thou goe ;
1476 doe forth ! I dread thee nought ! "
Burlong to smite was readye bowne,
his feete slipt,[2] & hee fell downe,
& Tryamore right well nought,[3]

1480 his sword lightlye he vp hent,
& to Burlonge fast he went ;
for nothing wold he flee ;
& as he wold haue risen againe,
1484 he smote his leggs euen in twaine
hard fast by the knee.

Tryamore bade him "stand vpright,
& all men may see now in fight
1488 wee beene meete of a size."
Sir Tryamore suffered him
to take another weapon,
as a knight of much prize.

1492 Burlong on his stumpes stood
as a man *that* was nye wood,
& fought wonderous hard.[4]

Marginal notes:
and his other brothers,

and refuses to let him haue his sword.

Burlong makes ready to strike ; his foot slips, and he falls.

Triamore gets his sword again,

cuts big Burlong off at the knees,

to make him his equal in height,

and lets him get a sword.

Burlong fights well on his stumps,

---

[1] matter.—F.
[2] his fote schett.—Ca.
[3] wylyly wrought.—Ca.   wrought.—Cop.
[4] wonder faste.—Cop.

K 2

& S*ir* Tryamore strake stroakes sure,
1496   for he cold well endure ;
of him hee was not affrayd,

but
Triamore
cuts his head
off,
& vnder his ventale
his head he smote of without fayle ;
1500   with *that* in peeces his sword brast.

Now is Burlong slaine,
& Triamore with maine
and goes to
his love.   into the Castle went,
1504   to the Ladye *that* was full bright;
Helen   & att the gates shee mett the K*night*,
& in her armes shee him hent.

welcomes
him.
Shee said, " welcome s*ir* Tryamore !   [page 231]
1508   for you haue bought my loue full deere,
my hart is on you lent! "
The barons
agree to hold
their lands
of him.
then said all the Barrons bold,
" of him wee will our lands hold ; "
1512   & therto they did assent.

and the
wedding-day
is fixed.
there is noe more to say,
but they haue taken a certaine day
that they both shalbe wed.
Triamore
sends for his
mother, 1516 S*ir* Tryamore for his mother sent,
a Messenger for her went,
& into the castle he[r] led.

Tryamore to his mother gan saine,
1520   " my father I wold know faine,
sith I haue soe well sped."
and she
tells him
that King
Arradas is
his father,
shee said, " K*ing* Arraydas of Arragon,
is thy father, & thou his owne sonne ;
1524   I was his wedded Queene ;

"a leasing was borne me in hand,[1]
& falsely fleamed me out of his land
 by a traitor Keene,

that she was
banished
wrongfully,

1528 Sir Marrockee the hight[2]: he did me woe,
 & Sir Rodger my knight he did sloe,
  that my guide[3] shold haue beene."

through Sir
Marrock.

 & when that Tryamore all heard,[4]

Triamore

1532 & how his mother shee had[5] sayd,
 letters he made & wrought;

writes and
begs
Arradas

 he prayd King Arradas to come him till,
 if that it were his will,

1536 thus he him besought:

'if hee will come into HUNGARYE
 for his Manhood & his Masterye,

to come to
Hungary.

  & that he wold fayle in nought.'

1540 then was King Arradas verry glad;
 the Messengers great guifts had
  for they tydings that they brought.

the day was come that was sett,

On the
wedding-
day,

1544 the Lords came thither without let,
 & ladyes of great pryde;
 then wold they noe longer lett;
 shortlye after[6] they are fett,

1548 with 2 dukes on euerye side;

they lady to the church the led;

Queen Helen
is married to
Triamore,

a Bishopp them together did wed,
 in full great hast the hyed.

1552 soone after that weddinge
 Sir Tryamore was crowned King,

who is then
crowned
king.

  they wold noe longer abyde.

---

[1] forced on me.—F.
[2] ? the wight.—F.
[3] gyder.—Cop.
[4] herde.—Cop.
[5] to him.—Cop.
[6] after forthe.—Cop,

the *Queene*, his mother Margarett,

1556 before the *King* shee was sett

in a goodlye cheare.[1]

Arradas sees
Margaret,

King Arradas beheld his Queene,

him thought *that* hee had her scene,

1560   shee was a ladye fayre ;

the *King* said, "it is *your* will   .

and asks her
what her
name is.

your name me for to tell,

I pray you w*i*th words fayre."

She says she
was his
queen, and
Marrock
defamed her. 1564

" my Lord," sayd [she,] " I was *your* Queene ;

your steward did me ill [2] teene ;

that euill might him befalle ! "

the *King* spake noe more words

After dinner 1568

till the clothes were drawen from the bords,

& men rose in the hall.

& by the hand he tooke the *Queene* gent ;

she tells him
all her
history.

soe in the chamber forth he went,

1572   & there shee told him all.

They kiss,
and all
rejoice.

then was there great Ioy & blisse !

when they together gan kisse,

then all they companye made Ioy enough.

1576   the younge Queene [was] full glad

Helen is
glad too,

that shee a *Kings* sonne to her Lord had,

shee was glad, I trowe ;

and both
couples live
long and
happily.

in Ioy together lead their liffe

1580   all their dayes w*i*thout striffe,

& lined many a fayre yeere.

Then king Arradas & his Queene   [page 232]

had ioy enough them betweene,

1584   & merrilye [3] lined together.

---

[1] For the preceding half-stanza the Cambridge text has a whole one :

Ye may welle wete certeynly
That there was a great mangery,
There as so many were mett :

Qwene Margaret began the deyse ;
Kyng Ardus wyth-owtyn lees,
Be hur was he sett.—F.

[2] mekyll.—Cop.
[3] merely.—Cop.

& thus wee leaue of Tryamore
that liued long in great honor
   with the fayre HELLENE.[1]

1588 I pray god giue their soules good rest,
  & all *that* haue heard this litle Iest,[2]
   highe heauen for to win!
  god grant vs all to haue *that* grace,
1592 him for to see in the celestyall place!
   I pray you all to say Amen!

Good bye, Triamore!

God send all my hearers to heaven! Amen!

ffins.[3]

[1] Elyne.—Cop.
[2] Gest. P.C.—P. gest.—Cop.
[3] Copland's colophon is, " ¶ Im- printed at London in Temes strete vpon the thre Crane wharfe. By Wyllyam Copland."—F.

Guye: & Amarant.[1]

[See the General Introduction to the Guy Poems, under *Guy & Colebrande* below.]

Guy jour-
neys in the
Holy Land,

GUYE : iourneyed ore the sanctifyed ground
whereas the Iewes fayre cityc someti[me] stood,
wherin our saviours sacred head was crowned,
4 & where for sinfull man he shed his blood.
to see the sepulcher was his intent,
the tombe *that* Ioseph vnto Iesus lent.

With tedious miles he tyred his wearye feet,
8 & passed desarts places [2] full of danger;

and meets
a woeful
man,

att last with a most woefull wight did meet,
a man [3] *that* vnto sorrow was noe stranger,

whose fifteen
sons are held
in bondage
by

for he had 15 sonnes made captiues all
12 to slauish [4] bondage, in extremest thrall.

the giant
Amarant.

A gyant called Amarant detained them,
whom noe man durst encounter for his strenght,
who, in a castle w*h*ich he held, had chaind them.

Guy under-
takes to free
them,

16 Guy questions w[h]ere,[5] & vnderstands at lenght
the place not farr. "lend me thy sword," quoth Guy ;
"Ile lend my manhood all thy sonnes to free."

and knocks
loudly at the
giant's door.

With that he goes & layes vpon the dore
20 like one, he sayes, *that* must & will come in.
the Gyant, he was neere soo rowzed before,

---

[1] By the elegance of Language &
easy Flow of *the* versification, this Poem
should be more modern than the rest.
—P. The first bombastic rhodomontade
affair in the book. Certainly modern,
and certainly bad, as bad as it well can
be, if it was meant seriously. One is
tempted in charity to think it a quiz of
the style it affects. Cp. st. 31, " but
did not promise you they should be fatt."
l. 186.—F. [2] desart-p[laces].—P.
[3] called Erle Jonas, p. 253 [of MS.
torn out for *King Estmere*].—P.
[4] There are two strokes in MS. after
the *u*, one is dotted.—F.
[5] where.—P.

for noe such knocking at his gate had beene ;

soo takes his keyes & club, & goeth out,

24 Staring with irefull countenance about :

"Sirra!" sais hee, "what busines hast thou heere ?

art come to feast my crowes about the walls [1] ?

didst [2] neuer heare noe ransome cold him cleere

28 *that* in the compas of my furye falls [3] ?

for making me to take a porters paines,

with this same club I will dash out thy braines."

and says
he'll dash
Guy's brains
out.

"Gyant," saies Guy, "*your* quarrelsome, I see ;

32 choller & you are something neere of Kin ;

dangerous at a club be-like you bee ;

I haue beene better armed, though now goe th[in.]

but shew thy vtmost hate, enlarge thy spite !

36 heere is the wepon *that* must doe me right."

Soe takes his sword, salutes [him [4]] with the same

about the head, the shoulders, & the sides,

whilest his erected club doth death proclaime,

40 standing with huge Collossous spacious strydes,

putting such vigor to his knotted beame

that like a furnace he did smoke extreme.

But on the ground he spent his stroakes in vaine,

44 for Guy was nimble to avoyde them still,

& ere he cold reconers [5] clubb againe,

did beate his plated coate against his will :

att such aduantage Guy wold neuer fayle

48 to beate him soundly in his coate of Mayle.

---

[1] wall.—P.

[2] ? MS. *didest* or the *e* has been altered
into part of the *s*.—F.

[3] fall.—P.

[4] him *with*.—P.

[5] There's an apostrophe in recent ink
over the *s* in the MS.—F.

Amarant
grows faint,

Att last through strength, Amarant [1] feeble grew,
  & said to Guy, "as thou art of humane race,

and asks
Guy to let
him drink at
a spring.

shew itt in this, since nature [2] wants her dew ;
52 let me but goe & drinke in yonder place ;
    thou canst not yeeld to [3] [me] a smaller thing
  then to grant life *tha*ts giuen by the spring."

Guy gives
him leave.

"I giue the leaue," sayes Guy, "goe drinke thy [4] last,
56 to pledge the dragon & the savage beare, [5]
    succeed the tragedyes *that* they haue past ;
  but neu*er* thinke to drinke [6] cold water more [7] ;
  drinke deepe to death, & after *that* carrouse
60 bid him receiue thee in his earthen house."

Amarant
drinks so
greedily

Soe to the spring he goes, & slakes his thirst,
  takeing in [8] the water in, extremly like
  Some wracked shipp *that* on some rocke is burst, [p. 233]
64 whose forced bulke against the stones doe stryke ;
  Scoping it in soe fast *with* both his hands

that Guy
wonders.

  that Guy, admiring, to behold him stands.

He calls on
Amarant to
fight again.

"Come on," quoth Guy, "lets to our worke againe ;
68 thou stayest about thy liquor ou*er* longe ;
  the fish w*h*ich in the riuer doe remaine
  will want thereby ; thy [9] drinking doth them
    wrong ;
  but I will [have] their [10] satisfaction made ;
72 w*i*th gyants blood thé must & shall be payd ! "

The giant

"Villaine," quoth Amarant, " Ile crush thee straight !
  thy life shall pay thy daring toungs offence !
  this club, w*h*ich is about some hundred waight,

[1] the strength of A : or thro' lacke of strength he.—P. This circumstance seems borrowed from song 104. p. 349, [of MS. *Guy & Colebrande*].—P.
[2] An *'s* has been added by P. in the MS.—F.
[3] unto.—P.

[4] One stroke too many for *thy* in the MS.—F.
[5] boar. Qu.—P.
[6] Only half the *n* in the MS.—F.
[7] here, Qu., or mair.—P.
[8] delend.—P.
[9] MS. their.—F. thy.—P.
[10] have their.—P.

76   has deathes commission to dispacth [1] thee hence !
dresse thee for Rauens dyett, I must needs,
& breake thy bones as they were made of reeds ! "

Inceused much att [2] this bold Pagans bosts,
80   which worthy Guy cold ill endure to heare,
he hewes vpon those bigg supporting postes
which like 2 pillars did his body beare.
Amarant for those wounds in choller growes,
84   & desperatelye att guy his club he throwes,

Which did directlye on his body light
soe heauy & soe weaghtye [3] there withall,
that downe to ground on sudden came the Knight ;
88   & ere he cold recouer from his fall,
the gyant gott his club againe in his fist,
& stroke a blow that wonderfullye mist.

" Traytor ! " quoth Guy, " thy falshood Ile repay,
92   this coward art to intercept my bloode."
sayes Amarant, " Ile murther any way ;
with enemyes, all vantages are good ;
o ! cold I poyson in thy nostrills blowe,
96 be sure of it, I wold destroy the soe ! "

" Its well," said Guy, " thy honest thoughts appear
within that beastlye bulke where devills dwell,
which are thy tennants while thou liuest heere,
100   but wilbe landlords when thou comest in hell.
Vile miscreant ! prepare thee for their den !
Inhumane monster, hurtfull vnto men !

" But breath thy selfe a time while I goe drinke,
104   for flaincing Pheabus with his fyerye eye
torments me soe with burning heat, I thinke

---

[1] Here again is tho cth for tch, noticed
in vol. i. p. 23, note [1].—F.

[2] MS. all.—F.   att this.—P.

[3] weightye.—P.

my thirst wold serue to drinke an Ocean drye.
forbear a litle, as I delt with thee."

108   Quoth Amarant, "thou hast noe foole of mee!

Amarant
refuses: he
is not such a
fool

"Noe! sillye wretch! my father taught more ·
how I shold vse such enemyes as thou.
by all my gods! I doe reioyce at itt,

112   to vnderstand *that* thirst constraines thee now;
for all the treasure that the world containes,
one drop of water shall not coole thy vaynes.

as to refresh
his foe.

"Releeue my foe! why, twere a madmans part!

116   refresh an aduersarye, to my wronge!
if thou imagine this, a child thou art.
no, fellow! I haue knowne the world to longe
to be soe simple now I know thy want;

120   a Minutes space to thee I will not grant."

Amarant
swings his
club round,

And with these words, heauing a-loft his club
into the ayre, he swinges the same about,
then shakes his lockes, & doth his temples rubb,

124   & like the Cyclops in his pride doth strout [1];
"Sirra," said hee, "I haue you at a lifte;
now you are come vnto your latest shift;

and promises
to kill Guy

"Perish for euer with this stroke I send thee,

128   a Medcine will doe thy thirst much good;
take noe more care of drinke before I end thee,

and drink
his blood.

& then weelle haue carowses of thy blood!
heeres at thee with a buchers downe-right blow,

132   to please my fury with thine ouerthrow!"

Guy abuses
the giant,

"Infe[r]nall, false, obdurat feend!" Guy said,[2]
"*that* seemes a lumpe of crueltye from hell!
ingratefull monster! since thou hast denyd [3]

---

[1] Strowt yñ, or bocyñ owte (bowtyn.
S.) *Turgeo*, Catholicon, Prompt.—F.

[2] cryd; [or] perhaps, 'said Guy.'—P
[3] dost deny.—P.

136 the thing to mee wherin I vsed thee [well,[1]]
  with more reuenge then ere my sword did make,
  On thy accursed head revenge Ile take! [page 234]

  " Thy gyants longitude shall shorter shrinke,
140 except thy sunscorcht sckin doe weapon proue.[2]
  farwell my thirst! I doe disdaine to drinke.
   streames, keepe you[r] waters to you[r] owne
   behoues,[3]
  or let wild beasts be welcome therunto;
144 with those pearle dropps I will not haue to doe.

bids the streams keep their waters for themselves,

  " Hold, tyrant! take a tast of my good will;
  for thus I doe begin my bloodye bout;
  you cannot chuse but like the greeting ill,—
148 it is not *that* same club will beare you out,—
  & take this payment on thy shaggye crowne,"
  a blow *that* brought him with a vengeance
  dow[ne].

strikes Amarant, fetches him down,

  Then Guy sett foot vpon the monsters brest,
152 & from his shoulders did his head devyde,
  which with a yawninge mouth did gape vnblest,—
  noe dragons Iawes were euer seene soe wyde
  to open & to shut,—till liffe was spent.
156 soe Guy tooke Keyes, & to the castle went,

cuts off his head,

  Where manye woefull captiues he did find,
  which had beene tyred with extremitye,
  whom he in ffreindly manner did vnbind,
160 & reasoned with them of their miserye.
  eche told a tale with teares & sighes & cryes,
  all weeping to him with complainning eyes.

sets free his captives,—

---

[1] well.—P.   [2] be weapon-proof.—P.   [3] behoue.—P.

some, ladies
There tender Laidyes in darke dungeon[1] lay,
164   *that* were surprised in the desart wood,
& had noe other dyett euery day
who had
been fed on
their dead
lovers and
husbands,—
then flesh of humane creatures for their food;
some with their louers bodyes had beene fed,
168 & in their wombes [2] their husbands buryed.

Now he bethinkes him of his being there,
to enlarge they [3] wronged Brethren from [4] their
and the
palmer's
fifteen sons,
w[oes;]
& as he searcheth, doth great clamors heare;
172   by w*hich* sad sounds direction, on he goes
vntill he findes a darkesome obscure gate,
armed strongly ouer all w*ith* Iron plate:

That [5] he vnlockes, and enters where appeares
176   the strangest obiect *that* he euer saw,
men *that* with famishment of many yeerres
who were
like the
pictures of
Death.
will [6] were like deaths picture, w*hich* the painters
dra[w;]
diuers of them were hanged by eche thumbe;
180 others, head downeward; by the middle, summe.[7]

With dilligence he takes them from the walls,
w*ith* lybertye their thraldome to acquainte.
Guy restores
the palmer
his sons,
then the p*er*plexed K*nigh*t the father calls,
184   & sayes, " receiue thy sonnes, thoo poore & faint!
I p*r*omised you their liues; eccept of *that* [8];
but did not p*r*omise you thé shold be fatt.

gives him
the giant's
castle,
" The castle I doe giue thee,—heere is the Keyes,—
188   where tyranye for many yeeres did dwell;
p*r*ocure the gentle tender Ladyes ease;

---

[1] Only half of the first *n* in the MS.
—F.
[2] ? MS. wombers.—F.
[3] the.—P.
[4] There is something like a blotched *o*
before the *r* in the MS.—F.

[5] Then.—P.
[6] delend.—P.
[7] some.—P. The *e*, and last stroke of
the *m*, have been cut off by the binder.
—F.
[8] accept of that.—P.

for pittye sake vse wronged women well!
men may easilye revenge the deeds men doe,

and charges
him to use
the women
well.

192   but poore weake women haue no strenght therto."

The good old man, euen ouerioyed with this,
    fell on the ground, & wold haue kist Guys fee[t.]

Guy refuses
to let the
palmer kiss
his feet.

"father," quoth hee, "refraine soe base a kisse!
196   for age to honor youth, I hold vnmeete;
ambitious pryd hath hurt me all it can,
I goe to mortifie a sinfull man."   ffins.

Cales: Voyage :[1]

THE allusions in these lines are principally to well-known incidents in the reign of Charles I., most of which occurred between 1625 and 1630.

"Cales," of course, means "Cadiz;" and the expeditions of Viscount Wimbledon to that place in 1625, of the Duke of Buckingham to Rhé in 1627, and of the Earl of Denbigh to Rochelle in 1628—all failures—are commemorated in lines 1, 2, and 3. Line 4 alludes to the grant of five subsidies made on the concession of the Petition of Right; lines 6, 8, and 9, refer to the death of Buckingham. The peace with Spain, mentioned in line 7, was proclaimed on the 5th of December, 1630. Lines 9 to 12 commemorate the recent passing of the Petition of Right, which took place on the 5th of June, 1628. Of lines 17 to 24 I take the meaning to be: "Do not meddle with the hierarchy for fear of the Inquisition, that is, the Star Chamber, where thou shalt find a crop-ear doom, cries Leighton." The allusion is to the dreadful sentence inflicted on Dr. Alexander Leighton, a portion of which was that he should have " one of his ears cut off, and his nose slit, and be branded in the face." (*State Trials*, vol. iii. p. 385.)

Line 25 alludes to the King's commission for extracting fines from those who, having 40*l.* a year in lands, did not attend at the coronation to be knighted. Lines 26 to 30 refer to the case of Walter Long, sheriff of Wilts, who was fined 2,000 marks for absenting himself from his county to attend his duty in parliament. (*State Trials*, vol. iii. p. 235.)

---

[1] A kind of State Satire on *the* abuses in Charles 1st time—very obscure.—P.

Lines 33 to 37 relate to a speech of Sir Dudley Carleton in the House of Commons in 1628, in which he warned the House of the fate of parliaments in foreign countries, where they had been overthrown by monarchs as soon as they began to know their own strength. Hence, he continued, the misery of the people on the continent, who look like ghosts and not men, being nothing but skin and bones, with some thin cover to their nakedness, and wearing only wooden shoes on their feet. *Rushworth,* vol. i. p. 359. Whitelocke substitutes " canvas clothes " for the thin covering, p. 6. Both agree in the wooden shoes.

The allusion in the closing lines, 39 and 40, is to the Lord Chief Justice Tresilian, in the reign of Richard II. He was one of that King's evil advisers, was impeached by parliament, found guilty of treason, and hanged at Tyburn [1]—which may be said to be the moral of this poem. J. BRUCE.

ATT cales wee latelye made affray,
att Ile of Ree [2] wee run away,
our shippes poore Rochell did betray.
4   5 subsiddyes for that,

We've been defented right and left,

but give us five subsidies

And then wee shall to sea againe,
all *that* [3] our generall was slaine,
& now wee haue made peace with spaine,
8   Iacke ffellton !

and we'll fight again.

Sir Artigall grand Torto [4] slew ;
now eue*r*ye man must have his dew
by vertue of a gracious new
12   Petition of right.

[page 235]

We've a new Petit on of Right. What a blessing!

[1] See *Political Poems and Songs,* ed. Wright, vol. i. p. 423, 460.

[2] See Marc Lescarbot's " La chasse aux Anglois en l'Isle de Rez et au Siege de la Rochelle." Paris. 1629.—F.

[3] Altho' or Albeit.—P.

[4] See Spencer's Fairy Queen. P.

The child of honor did deffye
In mortall fight his enemye,
& when he came to doo him dye,
16   cryes Sall : Brooke.

Don't talk
of Pope
John's
children,

Eleuen children had Pope Iohn,
Pope Iohn the twelft, an able man ;
heeres to the daffe, Ile pledge the don,
20   A pulpitt of sacke !

or the
Inquisition
will catch
hold of you.

Noe more of *that*, doe not presume,
ffor ffeare of the Inquisition at Rome,
where thou shalt find a cropeare dome,
24   Cryes Layston.

Don't leave
your county
when you're
Sheriff.

Ten poundes for not being made a K*night* ;
ffiue thousand Markes was deemed right
for being out of his countryes sight
28   In time o Shreaualltrye.

These & such like, as I you tell,
In fayrye land latelye befell,
where Iustice ffought with Iustice Cell
32   Att Gloster.

Be dutiful,
or else you'll
turn French-
men, and
have to wear
wooden
shoes.

Be dutifull, good people all,
the gouerment else alter shall,
& bring you to the state of Gaule,
36   Haire shirts & woodden shooes !

Hang bad
counsellers.

Noe habeas corpus shall be gott ;
but for all this damned plott
Tresilian went vnto the pott
40   Att Tyburne !   fins.

𝕶𝖎𝖓𝖌𝖊 & 𝕸𝖎𝖑𝖑𝖊𝖗 : [1]

THIS copy is given in the *Reliques* " with corrections," and " collated with an old black-letter copy in the Pepys Collection intitled ' A pleasant ballad of K. Henry II. and the Miller of Mansfield.' " "There are copies of this ballad," says Mr. Chappell, who prints the tune, "in the Roxburghe Collection, vol. i. p. 178, and p. 228 ; in the Bagford p. 25."

" It has been a favourite subject," says Percy, " with our English ballad-makers to represent our kings conversing, either by accident or design, with the meanest of their subjects. Of the former kind, besides this song of the King and the Miller, we have ' K. Henry and the Soldier,' ' K. James I. and the Tinker,' ' K. William III. and the Forester ' &c. Of the latter sort are ' K. Alfred and the Shepherd,' ' K. Edward IV. and the Tanner,' ' K. Henry VII. and the Cobbler ' &c."

" The earliest of these stories," says Professor Child in his Introduction to King Edward Fourth and the Tanner of Tamworth, " seems to be that of King Alfred and the Neatherd, in which the herdsman's wife plays the offending part and the peasant himself is made Bishop of Winchester. Others of a very considerable antiquity are the tales of Henry II. and the Cistercian Abbot in the *Speculum Ecclesiæ* of Giraldus Cambrensis (an. 1220) printed in *Reliquiæ Antiquæ* i. 147 ; *King Edward and the Shepherd,* and *The King* [Edward] *and the Hermit* in Hartshorne's *Metrical Tales* (p. 35. p. 293, the latter previously in *The British Bibliographer* iv. 81) ; *Ranf Coilzear,*

---

[1] In *the* printed Collection of Old Ballads, 1727, Vol. i. p. 53. No. VIII.—P.

how he harbreil King Charles in Laing's *Select Remains; John de Reere . . . .* and *the King and the Barker,* the original of the present ballad."

The idea of majesty compelled, or condescending to fraternise with low life has in foreign countries, too, excited the vulgar imagination. Such meetings of extremes—the fellowships of a power so high with a thing so low—have proved extremely fascinating. And while the stories of them show how tremendous was the interval between the king and his poor subjects, they show also how friendly was the popular conception of royalty. The king was far, far off; but he was kindly and genial. He could be imagined descending from his supreme height, and enjoying the humours of the humblest and vulgarest. Such descents were a kind of Avatars, which the people rejoiced to remember and celebrate. They served to kindle and fan their loyal affection; to bind the king and people, as showing that he was a man of like passions with themselves, not an alien unsympathetic being, scarcely human.

1

King Henry will go a hunting.

HENERY, our royall *King,* wold goe a huntinge
   to the greene fforrest soe pleasant & fayre,
   to haue the harts chased, the daintye does tripping;

Hawk and hound are let go.

4   to merry Sherwood his nobles repayre;
   hauke & hound was vnbound, all things prepared
   for the same to the game with good regard.

2

The King hunts all day,

All a longe summers day rode the *King* pleasantlye
8   with all his princes & nobles eche one,
   chasing the hart & hind & the bucke gallantlye,
   till the darke euening inforced them turne home.

and at night loses himself in the wood.

   then at last, ryding fast, he had lost quite
12   all his Lords in the wood in the darke night.

3

Wandering thus wearilye all alone vp & downe,
  with a rude Miller he mett att the Last,
asking the ready way vnto fayre Nottingham.
16 "Sir," Quoth the Miller, "I meane not to Iest,
  yett I thinke what I thinke truth for to say,
  you doe not lightlye goe out of your way."

He meets a Miller, and asks his way to Nottingham. The Miller

4

"Why, what dost thou thinke of me?" Quoth our
  King merrily,
20 "passing thy iudgment vpon ¹ me soe breefe."
"good faith," Quoth the Miller, "I meane ² not to
  flatter thee,
  "I gesse thee to bee some gentleman theefe;
stand thee backe in the darke! light not adowne,
24 lest I presentlye cracke thy knaues cro[wn]e!"

takes the King for a thiefe, and threatens to crack his crown.

5

"Thou doest abuse me much," quoth our King,
  "saying thus.
I am a gentleman, and lodging doe lacke."
"thou hast not," quoth the Miller, "a groat in thy
  pursse;
28 all thine inheritance hanges on thy backe."
"I haue gold to discharge for that I call;
if itt be 40 pence, I will pay all."

The King says he's a gentleman who wants lodging,

and can pay for it.

6

"If thou beest a true man," then said the Miller,
32 "I sweare by my tole dish Ile lodge thee all night."
"Heeres my hand," quoth our King, "that was I
  euer."
  "nay, soft," quoth the Miller, "thou mayst be a
  sprite;
better Ile know thee ere hands I will shake;
36 with none but honest men hands will I take."

The Miller offers to lodge him,

[page 236]

but won't shake hands with him.

---

¹ MS. vpom.—F.   ² Only half the *n* in the MS.—F.

7

They go into

Thus they went all alonge into the Millers house,

where they were seeding [1] of puddings & souce.[2]

the Miller's
smoky house,

the Miller first entered in, then after went the King ;

40 neuer came he in soe smoakye a house.[3]

" now," quoth hee, " let me see heere what you are."

Quoth our King, " looke you[r] fill, & doe not spare."

8

" I like well thy countenance ; thou hast an honest

fac[e] ;

44 with my sonne Richard this night thou shalt Lye."

and the wife
asks if the
King is a
runaway.

Quoth his wiffe, " by my troth it is a good hansome

yout[h] ;

yet it is best, husband, to deale warrilye.

art thou not a runaway ? I pray thee, youth, tell ;

Where is his
passport ? **48** show vs thy pasport & all shalbe well."

9

Then our King presentlye, making lowe curtesie,

with his hatt in his hand, this he did say :

He has none,

" I haue noe pasport, nor neuer was seruitor,

as he is a
ccurtier. **52** but a poore Courtyer rode out of the way ;

& for your kindnesse now offered to me,

I will requite it in euerye degree."

10

Then to the Miller his wiffe whisperd secretlye,

56 saing, " it seemeth the youth is of good kin

both by his apparell & by his Manners ;

The Miller
thinks the
King behaves
well to his
betters,

to turne him out, certainely it were a great sin."

" yea," quoth hee, " you may see hee hath some grace,

60 when as he speaks to his betters in place."

11

" Well," quoth the Millers wiffe, "younge man, welcome

heer[e] !

& tho I sayt, well lodged shalt thou be ;

---

[1] seething, boiling.—F.

[2] The head, feet, and ears of swine
boi'ed and pickled for eating.   Halli-

well.—F.

[3] See Forewords to *Babees Boke*, p.
lxiv. -F.

fresh straw I will lay vpon your bed soe braue,
64   good browne hempen sheetes likwise," Quoth shee.
"I," quoth the goodman, " & when *that* is done,
thou shalt lye noe worse then our owne sonne."

and he may therefore lie on straw and hemp sheets with their son,

12

"Nay first," quoth Richard, "good fellowe, tell me true,
68   hast thou noe creepers in thy gay hose ?
art thou not troubled with the Scabbado [1] ? "
"pray you," quoth the King, "what things are those ?
art thou not lowsye nor scabbed ? " quoth hee ;
72   "if thou beest, surely thou lyest not with me."

if he has no creepers in his breeches,

and is not scabbed.

13

This caused our King suddenly to laugh most hartilye
till the teares trickled downe from his eyes.
then to there supper were thé sett orderlye,
76   to hott bag puddings & good apple pyes ;
nappy ale, good & stale, in a browne bowle,
which did about the bord Merrilye troule.

They sup on bag-puddings, apple pies, and nappy ale.

14

"Heere," quoth the Miller, "good fellowe, Ile drinke to thee
80   & to all the courtnolls *that* curteous bee."
"I pledge thee," quoth our King, " & thanke thee heartilye
for my good welcome in euerye degree ;
& heere in like manner I drinke to thy sonne."
84   "doe then," saies Richard, " & quicke let it come."

The Miller drinks to the King,

and the King to him

and his son.

15

"Wiffe," quoth the Miller, "feitch me forth lightfoote,
that wee of his sweetnesse a litle may tast."
a faire venson pastye shee feiched forth presentlye.

The Miller calls for Lightfoot.

---

[1] MS. may be Scolloado. See Forewords to *Babees Boke*, 1868, p. lxiv.—F.

The King
like- it
immensely. 88

"eate," quoth the Miller "but first make noe wast;

heer is dainty Lightfoote." "infaith," quoth our *King*,

"I neuer before eate of soe dayntye a thinge."

16

" Iwis," said Richard, "noe dayntye att all it is,

92 for wee doe eate of it euerye day."

Where can
he buy some ?

"in what place," sayd our *King*, " may be bought lik

to th[is ?] "

"wee neuer pay peennye for it, by my fay;

It's the
King's deer
from
Sherwood. from merry Sherwood wee feitch it home heere;

96 now & then we make bold w*ith* our Kings deere."

17

" Then I thinke," qu*o*th our *King*, "*that* it is Venison."

"eehe foole," qu*o*th Richard, " full well may see *that*;

neu*er* are we w*i*thout 2 or 3 in the rooffe,

100 verry well fleshed & exellent flatt.

Don't tell
him. but I pray thee say nothing where-ere thou goe,

we wold not f*or* 2 pence the K*ing* shold it know."

18

"doubt not," saies [1] our *King*, "my promised secresye;

Certainly
not, says
the King. 104 the K*ing* shall neu*er* know more out for mee."

a cupp of lambes woole [2] they dranke vnto him,

& to their bedds th*é* past presentlye.

Next
morning the
nobles the Nobles next Morning went all vp & downe

108 for to seeke the K*ing* in euerye towne;

19   [page 237]

find the King
at the
Miller's
house,
and fall on
their knees
before him. At last, att the Miller's house soone th*é* did spye him

plaine,

as he was mounting vpon his faire steede;

to whome th*é* came presentlye, falling downe on their

knees,

---

[1] MS. saiy.- F.

[2] A favourite liquor among the common people, composed of ale and roasted
apples; the pulp of the roasted apple
worked up with the ale, till the mixture
formed a smooth beverage. Nares.—F.

112   which made the Millers hart wofullye bleed.   The Miller

     Shaking & quaking before him he stood,   quakes.

     thinking he shold be hanged by the rood.

20

     The K[ing] perceiuing him fearfully tremblinge,   The King draws his sword.

116   drew forth his sword, but nothing he said ;

     the Miller downe did fall crying before them all,   The Miller expects to have his head cut off,

     doubtinge [1] the King wold cut of his head.

     but he, his kind curtesie for to requite,

120   gaue him great liuing, & dubd him a Knight.   but is knighted.

21

     When as our noble King came from Nottingam,

     & with his nobles in westminster Lay,   At Westminster, afterwards,

     recounting the sports & the pastime thé had tane

124   in this late progresse along on the way ;

     of them all, great & small, hee did protest

     the Miller of Mansfeild liked him best ;

22

     "And now, my Lords," quoth the King, "I am de-   the King resolves to ask the Miller and his son up to a feast.

       termined,

128   against St. Georges next sumptuous feast,

     that this old Miller, our youngest confirmed Knight,

       with his sonne Richard, shalbe both my guest ;

     for in this merryment it is my desire

132   to talke with this Iollye Knight & the younge squier."

23

     When as the Noble Lords saw the Kings merriment,

       thé were right Ioyfull & glad in their harts.

     a Pursiuant thé sent straight on this busines,   A pursuivant is sent with the invitation,

136   the which oftentimes vsed those parts.

     when he came to the place where he did dwell,

     His message merrilye then he did tell.

---

[1] fearing.—F.

24

which he
delivers in
due form.

140

" God saue your worshippe," then said the messenger,
" & grant your Ladye [1] her owne harts desire ;
& to your sonne Richard good fortune & happinesse,
that sweet younge gentleman & gallant squier !
our King greets you well, & thus doth say,

144　' you must come to the court on St. Georges day ' ;

25

At first the
Miller is
half afraid,

148

" Therfore in any case fayle not to be in place."
　　" I-wis," quoth the Miller, " it is an odd Iest !
what shold wee doe there ? " he sayd, " infaith I am
　　halfe afraid."
　　" I doubt," quoth Richard, " to be hanged att the
　　least."

but on
hearing of
the feast

" nay," quoth the Messenger, " you doe mistake ;
our King prepares a great feast for your sake."

26

152

" Then," said the Miller, " now by my troth, Mes-
　　senger,
thou hast contented my worshipp full well :

gives the
pursuivant
three
farthings,

hold ! there is 3 farthings to quite thy great gentleness
　　for these happy tydings which thou dost me tell.
let me see ! hearest thou me ? tell to our King,

and promises
to come.

156　weele wayte on his Mastershipp in euerye thing."

27

160

The pursivant smyled at their simplicitye ;
& making many [2] leggs, tooke their reward,
& takeing then his leaue with great humilitye,
　　to the Kings court againe hee repayred,

The
pursuivant
reports all
to the King.

showing vnto his grace in euerye degree
the Knights most liberall giftts & great bountye.

---

[1] ? MS. Ladyes.—F.　　　　　　　　[2] Only half the *n* in the MS.—F.

28

When hee was gone away, thus can the Miller say,

164   "heere comes expences & charges indeed !

now must wee needs be braue, tho wee spend all wee
    haue ;

  for of new garments wee haue great need.

of horsses & serving men wee must haue store,

168 with bridles & sadles & 20ᵗʸᵉ things more."

The Miller
purposes to
buy new
clothes,
horses, &c.

29

  "Tushe, Sir Iohn," quoth his wiffe, "neither doe frett
    nor frowne !

  you shall bee att noe more charges of mee !

for I will turne & trim vp my old russett gowne,

172   with euerye thing else as fine as may bee ;

& on our Mill horsses full swift wee will ryd,

with pillowes & pannells as wee shall prouyde."

His wife
dissuades
him.

She'll trim
up the old
clothes,

and they'll
ride their
mill-horses.

30

In this most statelye sort thé rod vnto the court,

176   their lusty sonne Richard formost of all,

who sett vp by good hap a cockes fether in his cappe ;

& soe thé ietted downe towards the Kings hall,

the Merry old Miller with his hands on his side,

180 his wiffe like Maid Marryan did Mince at that tyde.

Thus they
go to court.

31

The King & his nobles that hard of their coming,

  meeting this gallant Knight with this braue traine,

"welcome, Sir Knight," quoth hee, "with this your
    gay Lady !

184   good Sir Iohn Cockle, once welcome againe ;

& soe is this squier of courage soe free ! "

Quoth dicke, "abotts on you ! doe you know me ? "

The King
welcomes
them,

32

Quoth our King gentlye, "how shall I forgett thee ?

188   thou wast my owne bed-fellow ; well that I wot,

and assures
Richard
that he

remembers him.

but I doe thinke on a tricke ; tell me, pray thee, dicke,
    how with farting we made the bed hott."

" thou horson happy knaue," the[n] quoth the Knight,
192 " speake cleanly to our [king now,] or else goe shite ! "

33   [page 238]

The king and his councellors hartilye laugh at this,

The King conducts them to table,

    while the King tooke them by the hand.
with Ladyes & their maids, like to the Queene of
    spades
196 the Millers wiffe did most orderlye stand ;
    a milkemaids curtesye at euerye word,
    & downe these folkes were set to the bord,

34

Where the King royally with princely Maiestye
200   sate at his dinner with Ioy & delight.

and after dinner drinks to the Miller,

when he had eaten well, to resting then hee fell ;
    taking a bowle of wine, dranke to the Knight,
" heeres to you both ! " he sayd, " in ale, wine, & beere,
204 thanking you hartilye for all my good cheere."

35

Quoth Sir Iohn Cockle, " Ile pledge you a pottle,
    were it the best ale in Nottingam-shire."

and wants some of his venison.

" but then," said our King, " I thinke on a thinge,
208   some of your lightfoote I wold we had heere."
" ho : ho : " Quoth Richard, " full well I may say it ;
    its knanerye to eate it & then to bewray it."

36

" What ! art thou hungry ? " quoth our King merrilye,
212   " infaith I take it verry vnkind ;

He asks Richard to pledge him.

I thought thou woldest pledg me in wine or ale
    heartil[y.]"

Dick says he must finish his dinner first ;

" yee are like to stay," quoth Dicke, " till I haue
    dind ,

he wants a black pudding,

you feed vs with twatling dishes soe small.
216 zounds ! a blacke pudding is better then all."

37

"I, marry," quoth onr King, "*that* were a daintye thing,
  if wee cold gett one heere for to eate."
with *that*, dicke straight arose, & plucket one out of
  his h[ose,]

220 which with heat of his breech began for to sweate.
the King made profer to snatch it away ;
  " its meate for your *Master*, good S*i*r, you shall stay ! "

(margin) and pulls one out of his breeches.

(margin) "That's meat for your master, Sir King."

38

Thus with great merriment was the time[1] wholy spent;
224   & then the Ladyes prepared to dance.
old S*i*r Iohn[2] Cockle & Rich*ar*d incontinent
  vnto this practise the King did advance,
  where-with the Ladyes such sport thé did make,
228 the Nobles with laughing did make their heads ake.

(margin) The Miller and Richard dance with the ladies,

(margin) and make the nobles laugh.

39

Many thankes for their paines the King did giue them
    then,
  asking young Richard if he wold be wed :
  " amongst these ladyes faire, tell me which liketh thee."
232 Quoth hee, " Iugg Grumball w*i*th the red head ;
shees my lone ; shees my liffe ; her will I wed ;
shee hath sworne I shall haue her maidenhead."

(margin) TheKing asks Dick which lady he'd like. " Jugg Grumball with the red head."

40

Then S*i*r Iohn Cockle the King called vnto him ;
236   & of Merry sherwood made him ou*er*seer,
  & gaue him out of hand 300ℓ yearlye,
  "but now take heede you steale noe more of my deere !
  & once a quarter lets heare haue your vow ;
240 & thus, S*i*r Iohn Cockle, I bid thee adew ! "

(margin) The King makes the Miller overseer of Sherwood, and warns him not to steal any deer.

ffins.

[1] A *y* has been altered into part of   [2] Only half the *n* in the MS. F.
the *m* in the MS.— F.

[" Panche," printed in Lo. and Hum. Songs, p. 61, follows here
in the MS.]

Agincourte Battell.[1]

AGINCOURT must have been a tempting theme to the ballad-writer and poet of its day. The splendid pluck with which the little English army, wasted by dysentery, ill-fed, and harassed by long marches and hostile skirmishers, nevertheless went at its enemies, facing the terrible odds of more than six to one, and put to ignominious rout the vaunting knights of France, must have appealed to the English heart and the English pride, and ought to have been worthily sung. The ballad-writer especially was bound to take it up, for the class he wrote for led the van and won the field. As at Crecy, as at Poictiers, so at Agincourt, the English yeomen humbled the gentlemen of France. Like the *feu d'enfer* of our rifles at Inkerman, the hail of yeomen's arrows gained England honour in the olden hard-fought field. But though at Agincourt the rout of the first division of the French army was due solely to our bowmen, against the second, squire and knight, noble and king did well their part too—none better than the Harry who said "WE WILL NOT LOSE," and gave the battle lastingly the name of *Azincourt*. To the valour of all was due the flight of the French third division, which, though more than double the number of the English host, feared to face their arrows and their swords, and gallopped off the field. That "the people of England were literally mad with joy and triumph" at the victory—rushing into the sea to meet Henry, and carrying him on shore on their shoulders—we do not wonder; but it is somewhat odd that no better ballad or poem on the battle should have come down to us, though in a play Shakspeare has done it justice. The ballads known to me are only—

---

[1] In the printed Collection of Old Ballads, 1726, vol. ii. p. 79, No. xii.

1. The *Deo gratias, Anglia, redde pro victoria!* printed by Percy in his *Reliques*, vol. ii. p. 24, " from a MS. copy in the Pepys collection, vol. i., folio," and to which the musical notes of the MS. are given in vol. ii. p. 24 of the second edition of the *Reliques*. 2. The present copy, having seven stanzas more than, but being otherwise nearly the same as, that in the Crown Garland of Golden Roses, ed. 1569 (p. 69 of the Percy Soc. reprint), the *Collection of Old Ballads*, 1726–38, vol. ii. p. 79, No. xii. ; *Evans*, vol. ii. p. 351, &c. 3. The *Three Man's Song*,—far the best of the lot,—the first verse of which is quoted in Heywood's *King Edward IV*. ed. 1600 (p. 52 of the Shakspere Soc. reprint), and the whole of which is printed from a black-letter copy (about 1665, Mr. Collier tells me) in Collier's Shakspere, ed. 1858, vol. iii. p. 538. Its title is " Agin Court, or the English Bowman's Glory : " to a pleasant new Tune. London, printed for Henry Harper in Smithfield. It is a broadside, and contains eleven seven-line stanzas. It begins " Agincourt! Agincourt! Know ye not Agincourt? " 4. The ballad No. 286 in the Halliwell Collection in Chetham's Library, Manchester, entitled, " King Henry V., his Conquest of France in Revenge for the Affront offered by the French King in sending him instead of the Tribute a Ton of Tennis Balls." It begins, " As our King lay musing on his bed ; " and two versions different from it and from one another are given in *Nicolas*, Appendix, p. 78, and p. 80, ed. 1832. 5. The *Cambro-Briton's Ballad of Agincourt*, by Michael Drayton, *ib.* p. 83. Nos. 3 and 4 will be printed at the end of this volume.

Of Poems, there are :

1. *a*. That attributed to Lydgate, in three Passus, in Harl. MS. 565, fol. 102–14, beginning " God þat alle þis world gan make," and printed among the illustrations of *The Chronicle of London*, 4to, 1827, and in *Nicolas*, p. 301–29. β. " The Siege of Harflet, & Batayl of Agencourt, by K. Hen. 5 : " another copy of Lydgate's poem, says Nicolas (p. 301), but differing from it so materially that it was necessary to print it as notes to the corresponding passages of the other. It was printed by Hearne at p. 359–75 of his edition of *Elmham's Life of Henry V.*, from the since burnt Cotton MS., Vitellius D. xii. fol. 214 b. Extracts from it are given by Nicolas, p. 301-29.

γ. The Batayll of Egyngecourt, and the great Sege of Rouen. Impryntyd by John Skot [about 1530 A.D.]. Reprinted in *Nicolas*, and in Mr. W. C. Hazlitt's *Remains of the*

Early Popular Poetry of England, vol. ii. p. 88–108.   is, says Nicolas (App. p. 69), " merely another, though a very differen version of the one " attributed to Lydgate.

2. Drayton's *Battaile of Agincovrt*, 1627. (Besides *The Lay of Agincourt*, Edinburgh, 1819 (a very poor performance), and possibly other modern productions.)

Of Dramas, we find :

1. The Famous Victories of Henry the Fifth : Containing the Honourabell Battell of Agin-court: as it was plaide by the Queene's Maiesties Players. London, Printed by Thomas Creede, 1598, 4to, 26 leaves. *Bodleian.* (Malone).[1]

2. The Chronicle History of Henry the Fift, With his Battell fought at Agin Court in France. Togither with auncient Pistoll. 1600 : the first cast of Shakspere's *Henry V.*[2]

In prose, a full and admirable account of the battle, with contemporary accounts and plentiful extracts from historians, is given by Sir Nicholas Harris Nicolas in his *History of the Battle of Agincourt, and of the Expedition of Henry V. into France in 1415*, (2nd ed., 1832; 3rd, 1838); and from this book it may be worth while just to run through the points of our ballad, and see how far they are borne out by facts. The Council of line 1, Nicolas thinks was the parliament which met in November 1514, which elected Chaucer's son Thomas its Speaker, and voted the King supplies for the defence of the kingdom of England and the safety of the seas. But it may have been a smaller Council, no doubt held before the Commission of the 31st of May, 1514, absurdly claiming the French crown, was issued to the Bishops of Durham and Norwich, the Earl of Salisbury, Richard Lord Grey, &c.—whom Monstrelet calls *le Comte d'Ourset, oncle du Roy d'Angleterre, le Comte de Grez, l'Admiral d'Angleterre, les Euesques du Damelin et de Noruegue, et plusieurs autres iusques au nombre de six cens cheuaux ou enuiron* (vol. i. p. 216, ed. 1595)—and who were so hospitably entertained in Paris. The great Council at which the arrange-

---

[1] Hazlitt's Handbook.   [2] Bohn's Lowndes. p. 2280, col. 2.

ments for the expedition were made was held at Westminster on three successive days, April 16, 17, 18, A.D. 1415, directly after the despatch of Henry's second letter to Charles.

The story of the scornful treatment of the ambassadors in l. 16–28 is belied by Monstrelet's account of the *moult notable feste dedans Paris en boyres, mangers, joustes, dances et autres esbatemens,* at which the English ambassadors were present; and there seems no foundation whatever for the present of the tennis balls, which would have gone directly counter to the French King's policy, letters, and interest. But still his young son may have been saucy, and have sent a saucy message to Henry. The story was believed to be true at the time or soon after; it is mentioned by Elmham in his Latin-verse life of Henry V [1] (though not in his prose life), and a long account of it is given in a middle fifteenth-century Cotton MS. (Claudius A. viii.) which Sir H. Nicolas prints, and which, as I had to refer to it to correct his *cornet* to the *MS. scorne,* I add here too :

And than the dolphine of Fraunce aunswered to our embassatours, and said in this maner, 'that the kyng was ouer yong and to tender of age to make any warre ayens hym, and was not lyke yet to be noo good werrioure to doo and to make suche a conquest there vpon hym. And somwhat in scorne and dispite he sente to hym a tonne fulle of tenys ballis, be-cause he wolde haue some-what for to play withalle for hym and for his lordis, and that be-came hym better than to mayntayn any werre. And than anone oure lordes that was embassatours token hir leue and comen in to England ayenne, and tolde the kyng and his counceille of the vngoodly aunswer that they had of the Dolphyn, and of the present the whiche he had sent vnto the kyng. And whan y⁰ kyng had hard her wordis, and the answere of the Dolpynne, he was wondre sore agreued, and righte euelle apayd towarde the frensshemen, and toward the kyng, and the Dolphynne, and thoughte to auenge hym vpon hem as sone as good wold send hym grace and myghte ; and anon lette make tenys ballis for tho Dolpynne in all the hast that the myghte be made, and they were grete gonne stones for the Dolpynne to play wythe-alle. (fol. 1, back.)

[1] Printed in Coles's *Memorials of Henry V*.

This Dauphin was Louis, eldest son of Charles VI., then between eighteen and nineteen years of age. He was born on January 22, 1396, and died before his father, without issue, on December 18, 1415, in his twentieth year (*Nicolas*). But as Henry V. was eight years older than the Dauphin, having been born in 1388, it is not likely that he would have taunted Henry with his youth.

Lines 33–40 : Henry exerted himself greatly to get his army together, and had to pledge his crowns, his jewels, plate, &c. to his men to guarantee them their wages. Nobody would move without taking security from him. He sailed from Southampton on August 7, 1415, with a fleet of between 1200 and 1400 vessels of various sizes, from 20 to 300 tons, according to Nicolas. Lingard makes the fleet 1500 sail, carrying 6000 men-at-arms and 2400 archers. The army landed at Clef de Caus, or Kideaux, on August 15 ; on the 19th arrived before Harfleur, and at once laid siege to it. On " the English balls," l. 34, and missiles, Labourewr states that, among other engines, the English had some which threw stones of a monstrous size, and projected entire millstones (*des meules toutes entières*), which threw down the walls with a frightful noise, so that by the Feast of the Assumption (August 15, a wrong date) all their batteries were destroyed. I find nothing about the "great gunn of Calais" of l. 49 ; but on September 17 at midnight the French messengers came to treat with Henry ; and as the town was not relieved by September 22, the Lord de Gaucourt and thirty-four of the noblest persons of the town then surrendered it to him. He turned out the inhabitants (l. 58) to the number of 2000, besides citizens, 60 knights, and more than 200 other gentry; left in the town more than the 300 Englishmen of our ballad, l. 59, even,[1] " under the captain [2] (Sir John Blount, says

---

[1] There is a muster-roll of the garrison of Harfleur, under the Earl of Dorset, taken in the months of January, February, and March, immediately following the battle. It consisted of 4 barons,

22 knights, 273 men-at-arms, and 798 archers. Most of these, we may presume, had been left behind when the King marched on to Agincourt. *Hunter*, p. 55.

[2] þe lord Beauford, Harl. MS. 575, f. 75 b.

Monstrelet), certain barons and knights skilful in affairs of war, with 300 lances, and 900 archers on pay " (*Nicolas*, p. 217), and marched out himself on October 7 with " not above 900 lances and 5000 archers," says a writer who was with him. Nicolas puts the force at from 6000 to 9000 fighting men. Lines 61–4 of the ballad are not true, for Henry's movements were watched, his stragglers cut off, and the country laid waste before him. He was repulsed in his first attempts to cross the Somme, between October 12 and 18 ; but on the 19th, finding a ford not staked, his army got over; on the 24th reached Maisoncelles, and on the 25th fought the battle.

The 600,000 French of l. 72 is of course an exaggeration, a 0 has been added for effect.[1] The message and answer of lines 73–88 are not historical, though the following particulars are nearly so, and the 10,000 killed of l. 137 is borne out by Nicolas's conclusion, that the whole of the French loss on the field was between 10,000 and 11,000 men.

The Duke of Yorke of line 117 was " Edward, Duke of York, son of Edmund of Langley, Duke of York, son of King Edward III., and cousin german to the King. He indented on April 29 to serve with 1 banneret, 4 knights, 94 esquires, and 300 mounted archers. His contingent, in the indenture of jewels, is said to have been 99 lances and 300 archers. He had one of the crowns in pledge. He went on with the King to Agincourt, where he lost his life " (*Hunter*, p. 22). On the Wednesday before the battle, says Monstrelet, i. 227, " le duc d'Yorch, son oncle, menant l'auantgarde, se logea à Frenench sur la riuiere de Cauche." This leadership of the vanguard the Duke kept on the 25th, and as the Cotton MS. already quoted from narrates his asking for it, and the events of the battle, I copy a page and a half of it from leaves 3 and 4.

[1] The highest number in any of the sixteen chronicles that Nicolas gives (p. 133, ed. 1832) is "3 Dukes, 5 Counts, 90 Barons, 1050 Knights, and 100,000 other persons. Note to Hardyng's Chronicle, 'according to the computation of the Heralds.'" 150,000 occurs in a doubtful list. *Nicolas*, p. 370.

And the duke of yorke felle on knees and besoughte the kyng of a bone, that he wold grawnte hym that day the avaunteward in his batayle. And the kyng grawnted hym his askyng, And sayd, "grawnte mercy, cosen of yorke," and prayd hym to make hym redy. And than he bad euery man to ordeyne a stake of tre, and sharpe bothe endes that the stake myghte be pyghte in the ye-[1]rthe a slope, that hir enemies shuld not ouer-come hem on horsbak, ffor that were hir fals purpose, and araide hem alle there for to ouer-ryde our meyne sodenly at the fyrst comyng on of hem at the fyrst brount: and al nyghte be-ffore the bataile þᵉ ffrenshemen made many grete fiers and moche reuelle, with howtyng and showtyng, and plaid oure kyng and his lordis at the dise, and an archer alway for a blanke [2] of hir money, ffor they wenden alle had bene heres. the morne arose, the day gan spryng, And the kyng by goode auise let araie his batayle [3] and his wenges, and charged euery man to kepe hem hole to-gedʳˢ, and praid hem alle to be of good chere. And whan they were redy, he asked what tyme of the day it was, And they sayd prime. Than said oure kyng, "now is good tyme! For alle England praythe for vs; and therfore be of good chere, and let vs goo to oure iorney." And than he said with an highe vois, "in the name [4] of almyghtey god and seynt George, avaunt Baner! and seint george this day be thyne helpe!" And than these ffrenshmen come prikyng doune as they wolde haue ouer-ridden alle oure meyne. But god and oure archers made hem sone to stomble; ffor oure archers shett neuer arow a-mys, but yt persshed and broughte to grounde man and hors; ffor they put day shoten for a wager. And oure stakes mad hem stoppe, & ouer-terned eche on oothir that they lay on hepes two spere lengthe of heyghte. And oure kyng with his meyne and with his men of armes and archiers that thakked [5] on theym so thykke with arowes, and leyd on with strokes, and oure kyng withe his owne hondes faughte manly. And thus almyghtey god and seynt George broughte oure enymies to grounde and yaf vs that day þᵉ victorie. and there were slayne of ffrenshmen that day in the felde of Agincourte mo thanne A xi Mˡˡ withe prisoners that were taken. And there were nombred that day of ffrenshmen in the felde mo than six score thou-

---

[1] MS. fol. 3, back.

[2] Fr. _Blanc_, the halfe of a _Sol_, a peece of money which we call also, a blanke. _Sol_, a _Sous_, or the French shilling, whereof terme make one of ours.—Cotgrave.

[3] The main body under his own command. The vanguard as the right wing under the Duke of York, the rearguard as the left wing under Lord Camois.

[4] MS. mame.

[5] thwacked, beat, pattered.

sand, and of Englishemen nat vij M^li; but god that day faughte for vs.
And after cam ther tydynges to oure kyng that there was a new
batayle of ffrenshemen redy to stele on hym, and comen towardis
[_fol._ 4.] hym. Anone our kyng let crie that euery man shuld
slee his prisoners that he had take ; and anon araid his bataille
ayenne to fighte _with_ the frenshmen. And whanne they sawe that our
men kylled doune her prisoners, thanne they w_ith_drowe hem, and
brake hir bataille and all_e_ hir Array. And this oure kyng, as a
worthy conqueror, had that day the victorye in the felde of Agencourt
in Picardie.[1]

The Duke of Orleance, l. 149, though he was taken prisoner
in the battle, is not named by Monstrelet as the leader of the
attack on Henry's camp :

Et adonc vindrent nouuelles au Roy Anglois, que les François les
assailloient par derriere : & qu'ils auoient desia prins ses sommiers
& autres bagues, laquelle chose estoit veritable : car Robinet de
Bournonuille, Rifflart de Clamasse, Ysambart d'Azincourt, & aucuns
autres hommes d'armes, accompagnez de six cens païsans, allerent
ferir au bagaige dudit Roy d'Angleterre. Et prindrent lesdites
bagues, & autres choses, auec grand nombre de cheuaux desdits
Anglois, entre-temps que les gardes d'iceux estoient occupez en la
bataille. _Monstrelet_, vol. i. p. 229.

The 200,000 French prisoners is an impossible number, and
Nicolas does not give any at all. The highest estimate of
the English loss is 1600 men. From Agincourt Henry marched
to Calais, where he arrived on October 29. On November 14
he crossed the Channel to Dover, and on the 24th entered
London in triumph :

the Cite of london, where þat there was shewed many a fayre
syghte at all the conduytes and at crosse in the chepe, as in heuenly
arraye of aungels, Archaungels, patriarches, prophites and Virgines,
w_ith_ dyuers melodies, sensyng and syngyng, to welcome oure kyng ;
And all_e_ the conduytes rennyng w_ith_ wyne. (Cott. Claud. A. viii.
leaf 4, back).

The last three verses of our ballad quicken and alter events

---

[1] Nicolas quotes this also, p. 277-8, at foot.

considerably. It was not till after many a weary siege and
fight, culminating with the fall of Rouen on January 16, 1419,[1]
that Henry saw his beautiful bride, and that for one day only,
on May 30, 1419. It was not till May 20, 1420, that he
married her at Troyes; not till December of that year that he
made his triumphal entry into Paris with his wife and his
father-in-law, the French King. He was never crowned in
Paris, King of France, but his wife was crowned in Westminster
Abbey, Queen of England, on St. Matthew's day, September 21,
A.D. 1421.

Henry V.	A councell braue[2] our *King* did hold with many a lord & knight, in[3] whom he trulye vnderstands 4 how ffrance withheld his right.
sends an ambassador to the French King	therefor a braue embassador vnto the *King* he sent, *that* he might ffully vnderstand 8 his mind & whole entente,
to yield him his right, or he'll take it.	desiring him, as[4] freindlye sort, his lawfull wright to yeeld, or else he sware[5] by dint of sword 12 to win the same in feild.
Charles VI. answers	the *King* of ffrance, with all his lords who[6] heard this message plaine, vnto our braue embassador 16 did answer in disdaine ;

---

[1] See the "Sege of Roan," *Archæol.*
xxi. 48 ; xxii. 361.—F.
[2] graue, P.C. (Print^d Copy).—P.
[3] Of. Conj[ecture].—P.

[4] in, P.C.—P.
[5] vow'd, P.C.—P.
[6] which, P.C.—P.

who sayd,[1] "our King was yett but [2] younge
   & of a [3] tender age ;
wherfor I way not for his warres,[4]

that he
cares not for
Henry's
threats,

20   nor care not for his rage,[5]

"whose [6] knowledge eke [7] in ffeats of armes,
   whose sickill [8] [is] but [9] verry small,
whose [10] tender ioynts more ffitter are
24   to tosse a Tennys ball."

a tunn of Tennys balls therfore,
   in pryde and great disdaine
he sends to Noble Henery the 5th,[11]

and sends
him a tun of
tennis-balls.

28   who recompenced [12] his paine.

& when our King this message hard
   he waxed wrath in his [13] hart,

Henry

& said "he wold such balls provyde
32   that [13] shold make all france to smart."

an army great [14] our King prepared,[15]
   that was both good & strong ;

prepares an
army,

& from Sowthampton is our King
36   with all his Nauye gone.

he landed in ffrance both safe [16] and sound
   with all his warlike traine ;

lands in
France,

vnto [17] a towne called Harffleete first [18]
40   he marched vp amaine.

---

[1] And feign'd, P.C.—P.
[2] too, P.C.—P.
[3] of too, P.C.—P.
[4] we weigh—of his war, P.C.—P.
[5] fear we his courage, P.C.—P.
[6] His, P.C.—P.
[7] is, P.C.—P.
[8] skill.—P.
[9] As yet but &c., P.C.—P.
[10] His.—P

[11] He sent unto our noble Kg, P.C.—P.
[12] To recompence, P.C.—P.
[13] d.—P.
[14] then, P.C.—P.
[15] did raise, P.C.—P.
[16] In France he landed safe, &c., P.C.—P.
[17] And to, P.C.—P.
[18] of Harfleur strait, P.C.—P.

and when he had beseeged the same,
 against these fensed walls
to batter downe their statlye towers
44 he sent his English Balls.

bids it sur-
ren ler

or he'll beat
it to the
ground.

[1] And he bad them yeeld [up to him [2]] [page 242]
 themselues & eke their towne,
or else he sware vnto the earth
48 with cannon [3] to beate them downe.

[1] the great gunn of Calcis was vpsett,[4]
 he mounted against those walls [5];
the strongest steeple in the towne,
52 he threw downe bells & all.

[1] then those *that* were the gouernors
 their woefull hands did wringe [6];
thé brought their Keyes in humble sort
56 vnto our gracious K*ing*.

[1] & when the towne was woone and last,
 the ffrenchmen out thé [7] threw,
& placed there 300 englishmen
60 *that* wold to him be true.

this being done, our Noble K*ing*[8]
 marched vp & downe *that* [9] land,—
& not a ffrenchman flor his liffe
64 durst once his fforce withstand,—

---

[1] These 4 stanz: not in print.—P.
[2] MS. cut away. It has more words.
—F. He bade the governors give up.
—P.
[3] guns. P.
[4] then.— P.

[5] was··'gainst their wall.--P.
[6] Only half the *n* in the MS.—F.
[7] he.—P.
[8] done our noble English K*ing*, P.C.
—P.
[9] the, P.C.—P.

till [1] ho came to Agincourt;
    & [2] as it was his chance,
to flind [3] the King in readinesse,
68   with him was all the power of ffrance,

Aginconrt,

where the
French King
is,

a mightye host they [4] had prepared
    off armed souldiers then,
which was noe lesse (the chronicle sayes) [5]
72   then 600000 [6] men. [7]

with 600,000
men.

the King of ffrance that well did know
    the number of our men,
in vanting pride vnto our King
76   sends one of his heralds [8] then

Charles
sends

a herald

to vnderstand what he wold giue
    for the [9] ransome of his liffe,
when in that feild he had taken him [10]
80   amiddst that [11] bloody striffe.

to ask Henry
what ransom
he'll pay for
his life.

& when [12] our King the Message heard, [13]
    did straight the [14] answer make,
saying, "before that thing shold [15] come to passe,
84   many [16] of their harts shold [17] ake!

Henry
answers

---

[1] Until, P.C.—P.
[2] Where, P.C.—P.
[3] He found.—P. *him was*, l. 68,
marked out by P. conj[ecturally].—F.
[4] He, P.C.—P.
[5] by just account, P.C.—P.
[6] 40,000, P.C.—P.
[7] Between 18 and 19th Stanza of ye
MS. is the following in Print:—
Which sight did much amaze our king,
    For he and * all his host
      Not passing fifteen thousand had,

Accounted at the most.—P.
[8] Did send a Herald, P.C.—P.
[9] *d.*—P.
[10] he in field sh'd . . . be, P.C.—P.
[11] their, P.C.—P.
[12] then . . .—P.
[13] with cheerful heart.—P.
[14] this.—P.
[15] *thing shold*, cut out by P.—F.
[16] some.—P.
[17] shall, P.C.—P.

* n.—P.

" My heart's
blood."

 " vnto your proud presumptuss prince
  declare this thing," quoth hee,
 my owne harts blood shall pay the price ;
88 nought [1] else he getts of me." [2] .

The French

 then all the night the frenchman Lyon,
  with triumphe, mirth, & Ioy ;
 the next morning they mad full accomp[t] [3]
92 our Armye to destroye.

play at dice
for the
English,

 & for our *King* & all his Lords
  at dice thé [4] playd apace,
 & for our comon souldiers coates
96 they set a prize but base,

and value
their red
coats at 8d.,
white at 4d.

 8 pence for a redd coate, [5]
  & a groate was sett to a white ; [6]
 because they [7] color was soo light,
100 they sett noe better buy itt. [8]

 the cheerfull day at last was come ;

Henry en-
courages his
men :

  our *King* with Noble hart
 did pray his valliant soldiers all
104 to play a worthye part,

 & not to shrinke from fainting foes,
  whose fearfull harts in ffeeld
 wold by their feirce couragious stroakes
108 be soone in-forced [9] to yeeld ;

[1] none.—P.
[2] Seven Stanz' following not in Print.
—P.
[3] Making account the next morning,
  or,
 They made &c.—P. *del.* full.—P.

[4] they.—P.
[5] coat was set.—P.
[6] And fourpence for a white.—P.
[7] The *y* put in brackets by P. *conj.*—F.
[8] by't.—P.
[9] enforced.—P.

"regard not of [1] their multitude,
　　tho they are more then wee,
　for eche of vs well able is
112　　to beate downe ffrenchmen 3 ;

" Don't mind the French numbers ; each of us can kill three of them ; but

"yett let euerye man provide himselfe [2]
　　a strong [3] substantiall stake,
　& set it right before himselfe,
116　　the horsmans force to breake."

let every archer get a stake to stop the horse-men."

& then [4] bespake the Duke of yorke
　　" O noble King," said hee,
　" the leading of that [5] battell braue
120　　vouch[s]afe to giue it [6] me ! "

The Duke of York

leads the vanguard.

" god amercy, cosen yorke," sayes hee,
　　" I doe [7] grant thee thy request ;
　Marche you [8] on couragiouslye,　　[page 243]
124　　& I will guide [9] the rest."

Henry

the rest.

then came the bragginge frenchmen downe
　　with cruell [10] force & might,
　with whome our noble King began
128　　a harde & cruell flight.

The French come on.

our English archers [11] discharged their shafts
　　as thicke as hayle in skye,[12]
　& [13] many a frenchman in that [14] feelde
132　　that happy day did dye ;

Our archers

kill many;

[1] you, or then.—P.
[2] himselfe is in l. 114 in the MS.　P. marks it to go to l. 113.　yett is marked out by P.—F.
[3] But yet let every man provide
　　A strong &c.—P.
[4] With that, P.C.—P.
[5] this (the), P.C.—P.
[6] to, P.C.—P.
[7] d[ele].—P.
[8] then—thou, P.C.—P.
[9] lead, P.C.—P.
[10] greater, PC.—P.
[11] d. English. [Insert] they, P.C.—P.
[12] from skye, P.C.—P.
[13] That, P.C.—P.
[14] the, P.C.—P.

their stakes
stop the
horse.

[1] ffor the horssmen stumbled on our stakes,
    & soe their liues they lost;
& many a frenchman there was tane
136   for prisoners to their [2] cost.

10,000
French are
slain,

10,000
taken,

10000 ffrenchmen [3] there were slaine
    of enemies in the ffeeld,
& neere as many prisoners tane [4]
140   that day were fforced to yeeld.

and Henry
wins the
day.

thus had our King a happy day
    & victorye ouer ffrance;
he brought his foes vnder his ffeete [5]
144   that late in pride did prance.

While the
fight is going
on, news
comes

[6] when they were at the Maine battell there
    with all their might & forces, then [7]
a crye came ffrom our English tents
148   that we were robbed all them [8];

that the
French have
plundered
the English
tents.

for the Duke of Orleance, with a band of men,
    to our English tents they came [9];
all [10] our Iewells & treasure that they hane taken,
152   & many of our boyes [11] hane slaine.

Henry

much greeved was King [12] Harry therat,—
    this was against [13] the law of armes then,—

orders all
the French
prisoners to
be slain,

comands euerye souldier on paine of death
156   to slay euerye prisoner then. [14]

[1] This stanza not in Print.—P.
[2] [prisoner··] his, [P.]C.—P.
[3] men that day, P.C.—P.
[4] (d. P.C.)—P.
[5] them quickly under foot, P.C.—P.
[6] The Nine Stanz² following not in print, but instead the annexed stanza vizt.:—
    The Lord preserve our noble King
    And grant to him likewise
    The upper hand and victory
    Of all his enemies! P.

[7] force and might.—P.
[8] they were robbed quite.—P.
[9] Of men unto them came.—P.
[10] And prefixed; Iewells &, and that marked out by P.—F.
[11] all our boys. so Shakesp!—P.
[12] the King.—P.
[13] Being 'gainst.—P. and then deleted.—F.
[14] And bade ym slay their Prisoners For to revenge these hurms.—P.

200000 [1] ffrenchemen our Englishmen had,
 some 2, & some had one [2] ;
en*e*ry*e* one was commanded by sound of trumpett
160 to slay his prisoner then. [3]

200,000 of them.

& then thé followed vpon the maine battell ;
 the ffrenchmen thé fled then [4]
towards the citye of Paris
164 as fast as thé [5] might gone.

The French flee towards Paris,

but then ther was neu*er* a peere with-in france [6]
 of all those [7] Nobles then,
of all those worthye Disse peeres,
168 durst come to King Harry [8] then.

and no Duzeper dares meet King Harry;

but then Katherine, the Kings fayre daughter there, [9]
 being proued apparant his heyre,
with her maidens [10] in most sweet attire
172 to King Harry did repayre ; [11]

but the Princess Katherine

& when shee came before our [12] King,
 shee kneeled vpon her knee,
desiring him [13] *that* his warres wold [14] ccase,
176 & *that* [13] he her loue wold bee.

comes and asks him

to marry her.

there-vpon our English Lords then agreed [15]
 with the Peeres of ffrance then [16] ;
soe he Marryed Katherine, the Kings faire daughter,
180 & was crowned King in Paris then. [17]

He does, and is crowned King in Paris.

ffinis.

[1] 10,000.—P. Both *men* deleted.—F.
[2] Some one and some had two.—P.
[3] And each was bid by Trumpets sound
 To slay his prisoner tho,
  (or)
 His Prisoner to slo.—P.
[4] anon.—P. *the*, l. 162, and *ƒ, the* and *vp* of l. 161 deleted by P.—F.
[5] they.—P.
[6] Then was there never a Peer in France. Conj.—P.
Then *could* there not be found in France
 Of their Nobles all or Some.—P.

[7] Not one of all those.—P.
[8] to Kg Harry come.—P.
[9] King's Daughter fair, [P.]C.—P.
[10] all—Maids.—P. *then*, l. 169, *his*, l. 170. *most*, l. 171, marked *d* by P.—F.
[11] Did to our King rep*te*, [P.]C.—P.
[12] our.—P.
[13] *d.*—P.
[14] might.—P.
[15] Our Kg & — Lords.—P.
[16] Soon with the French agreed.—P.
[17] So at Paris he fair Kath*ne* wed
 And crowned was with spee*d*.—P.

Conscience.[1]

THERE are two sides to Early English Literature; one gay, the other grave; one light, the other earnest: and a man who comes to the subject fresh from struggles in the cause of reform, social and political, and meets first with the grave and earnest side of our early writings, is struck with delight and surprise at finding that in the old days, too, protesters against wrong existed, and that English writers denounced from the depths of their soul, in words of sternest indignation, the oppressions and abuses from which the English poor of their days suffered. Having passed myself from those *Morning Chronicle* letters on "Labour and the Poor"—which in 1849–50 revealed so much of the sad state of our workmen,—from meetings of sweated tailors, over-worked bakers, and ballast-heavers forced into drunkenness, to the pages of Roberd of Brunne's *Handlyng Synne*, Langlande's *Vision of Piers Ploughman*, *Piers Ploughman's Crede*, and works of like kind from 1303 to 1560,—I can bear witness to the deep impression made on me by the noble and fervent spirits of our early men, rebuking the selfish, denouncing the hard-hearted, calling down God's judgment on the oppressor; striving, in their time too, to leave the land better than they found it. As one looked backward to these sources of the river of English life, one heard a great murmur of wrong rise from the torrents' currents, one saw the stream turbid with the woes of "humble folk;" but there were never wanting voices, ordering the one to be stilled in orderly channels, and the other cleared. Further

[1] This is a satirical Allegory: and seems not very ancient, vid. St. 13, v. 4.—P.

study of our early writers did not lessen this impression: for though the bright side came, though Chaucer's living sketches portrayed all that was merriest in early days, yet still there was method in his mirth; abuses in religion and social life were exposed, none the less effectively because with a joke; and when he spoke seriously, he too declared, "Thilke that thay clepe thralles, ben Goddes people; for humble folk ben Christes frendes: thay ben contubernially with the Lord: . . . certes, extorciouns and despit of our undirlinges is dampnable." (Persones Tale, *De avaritia*.) To their honour be it said, our early writers were on the weak man's side against the strong, and did what in them lay to lessen the vice of the world. It is this which makes the lovers of them not only surprised, but indignant, at the willing and wilful ignorance in which men of our day remain with regard to them. Our moderns will not take a few days' trouble to master their language; they care little for their thoughts: but when once the readers of the nineteenth—or is it to be the twentieth?—century awake to the recognition of the fact that there *is* an Early English Literature worth studying, they will be ashamed of their countrymen's long neglect, and gladly acknowledge the value of the treasures they will find—food for all the best impulses of the human soul. So far as I know, justice has never yet been done to this spirit of our early literature by any writer on it, except the latest—Professor Morley. He, a man of mind akin with that of our old men—fresh from half a life spent in struggles for reform in health-laws, education, politics, and religion, ever backing the right and fighting the wrong—has come to the old books and said to them, not only " what were you translated or altered from, what manuscripts are there of you ? " but first and mainly, " *what do you mean?* what has the spirit of your writer got to say to the spirits of me and men here now ? " And the old bones (that were nothing more to so many) have taken flesh again and answered him, have stretched out their hands

and gript his as a friend's; and he has put down their answer for
us in his own way in divers places of his genial and able book,[1]
one of which I quote. He is speaking of Gower's *Vox Clamantis*, written on Wat Tyler's rebellion.

"In that earlier work, though written with vigour and ease in
Latin, the language of literature which alone then seemed to be
lasting, John Gower spoke especially and most essentially the
English mind. To this day we hear among our living countrymen, as was to be heard in Gower's time and long before,
the voice passing from man to man that—in spite of admixture
with the thousand defects incident to human character—sustains
the keynote of our literature, and speaks from the soul of our
history the secret of our national success. It is the voice that
expresses the persistent instinct of the English mind to find
out what is unjust among us and undo it, to find out duty to
be done and do it, as God's bidding. We twist religion into
many a mistaken form. With thought free and opinions mani-
fold we have run through many a trial of excess and of its
answering reaction. In battle for main principles we have
worked on through political and social conflicts in which often,
no doubt, unworthy men rising to prominence have misused
for a short time dishonest influence. But there has been no
real check to the great current of national thought, the stream
from which the long line of our English writers, like the trees
by the fertile river-bank, derive their health and strength.
We have seen how persistently that slow and earnest English
labour towards God and the right was maintained for six
centuries before the time of Chaucer, from the day when
Caedmon struck the first note of our strain of English song with
the words: 'For us it is very right that we praise with our
words, love in minds, the Keeper of the Heavens, Glory King of
Hosts.' It was the old spirit still in Chaucer's time that worked
in the 'Vision of Piers Plowman,' and spoke through the Voice
of Gower as of one crying in the wilderness, 'Prepare ye the
way of the Lord.' It needed not in those days that a man
should be a Wicliffite to see the griefs of the Church and
people, and to trace them to their root in duties unperformed.
Gower's name is a native one, possibly Cymric, but derived probably in or near Kent, from the old Saxon word for marsh-

---

[1] *English Writers*, vol. ii. pt. i. p. 106-7.

country, of which there was much about the Thames mouth, Gyrwa-land. His genius is unmixed Anglo-Saxon, closely allied to that of the literature before the Conquest, in the simple earnestness of a didactic manner leavened by no bold originality of fancy. In his Latin verse Gower writes easily, and, having his soul in his theme, forcibly. But he tells that which he knows, and invents rarely. His few inventions also, as of the dream of transformed beasts that represent Wat Tyler's rabble, of the ship of the state at sea, of his landing at an island full of turmoil which an old man described to him as Britain, are contrivances wanting in the subtlety and the audacity of true imaginative genius. He does not see as he writes, and so write that all they who read see with him. But in his own old English or Anglo-Saxon way, he tries to put his soul into his work. Thus, in the 'Vox Clamantis' we have heard him asking that the soul of his book, not its form, be looked to ; and speaking the truest English in such sentences as that 'the eye is blind, and the ear deaf, that convey nothing down to the heart's depth ; and the heart that does not utter what it knows is as a live coal under ashes. If I know little, there may be another whom that little will help. Poor, I give of my scanty store, for I would rather be of small use than of none. But to the man who believes in God no power is unattainable if he but rightly feels his work ; he ever has enough whom God increases.' This is the old spirit of Cædmon and of Bede, in which are laid, while the earth lasts, the strong foundations of our literature. It was the strength of such a temper in him that made Gower strong. 'God knows,' he says again, 'my wish is to be useful ; that is the prayer that directs my labour.' And while he thus touches the root of his country's philosophy, the form of his prayer that what he has written may be what he would wish it to be, is still a thoroughly sound definition of good English writing. His prayer is that there may be no word of untruth, and that 'each word may answer to the thing it speaks of, pleasantly and fitly ; that he may flatter in it no one, and seek in it no praise above the praise of God. Give me,' he asks, 'that there shall be less vice and more virtue for my speaking.' "

So far as regards the spirit of our early literature, I believe that Professor Morley is justified in every word that he has said. Granted the occasional coarseness of expressions in it to us, granted many another shortcoming, the spirit of it is noble and worthy of honour, as its words are worthy of study, by every Englishman.

The present poem, *Conscience*, is one effort, a late one, in the strain of that "slow and earnest labour towards God and the right" of which Professor Morley speaks. Differing as it does in word and form from the *Ayenbite of Inwyt* (or *Remorse of Conscience*) which Dan Michel of North Gate, "ane brother of the cloystre of saynt Austin of Canterburi," fulfilled in the year of our lordes bearing, 1340, it has yet the same aim,

> þis boc is ywrite
> uor englisse men, þet hi wyte (may learn)
> hou hi ssolle ham-zelue ssriue,
> and maki ham klene ine þise liue.

With Richard Rolle of Hampole in 1345 (or thereabouts), its writer desires that by his *Pricke of Conscience* men may

> Be stird þar-by til ryghtwyse way,
> þat es, tille þe way of gude lyfyng,
> And at þe last be broght til gude endyng. (p. 258, l. 9611.)

With Langlande, our *Conscience* tries the Court, the Lawyers, the Landlords, the Merchants, the Clergy; and all he finds in the possession of his enemies. Covetousness, Lechery, Usury, Avarice, and Pride have their way with all; the husbandmen are left desolate so that they cannot help the poor, and Conscience is driven out to lodge in the wood, and eat hips and haws, his only comforters being Mercy, Pity, and Almsdeeds. In early times Langlande's *Conscience* fared better: he got the King on his side; stood his ground well; reproved Mede or Bribery; brought sinners to repentance, sent them seeking for truth, and remained master of the situation. (See *Langlande's Vision of Piers the Ploughman*, ed. Skeat, E. E. Text Soc. 1867, Passus 3–5.)

A contrast of the different evils complained of by reforming writers in different ages, and the comparative prominence given to each vice by each writer, could not fail to bring out the characteristics of the successive periods of our social history, and be of great interest. But though I have some material for it, want of space forbids my attempting it here. Still, the point may be illustrated by looking at the clergy's hinderers in their good work of giving, as mentioned in the present poem,

for their wiues & their children soe hange them vpon,
that whosoeuer giues almes deeds they will giue none,

when set beside Roberd of Brunne's complaints, in his *Handlyng Synne*, about the priest's mare or concubine, and the earlier one of the *Old English Homilies* (? about 1200 A. D.) that Mr. Richard Morris will edit, probably in 1869, for the Early English Text Society:

And oðre fele lerdemen spoken alse lewede alse ure drihten seide þurh anes prophetes muðe. *Erit sicut populus sacerdos.* Prest sal leden his lif alse lewede mæn . and swo hie doð nuðe : and sumdel werse. For þe lewede man wurðeð his spuse mid cloðes more þane mid him seluen . and prest naht sis (= so his) chireche, þe is his spuse : ac his daie, þe is his hore . awlencð hire mid cloðes . more þan him seluen. De chirche cloðes ben to-brokene : and calde . and his wiues shule ben hole : and newe . His alter cloð great and sole : and hire chemise smal and hwit . and te albe sol : and hire smoc hwit. Þe haued-line sward : and hire wimpel wit . oðer maked geleu mid saffran. De meshakele of medeme fustain . and hire mentel greue oðer burnet. De corporeals sole : and unshapliche . hire handcloðes . and hire bord cloðes maked wite and lustliche on to siene. De caliz of tin : and hire nap of mazere and ring of golde. And is þe prest swo muchele forenðere . þane þe lewede. Swo he wurðeð his hore more þan his spuse.—*Homilies in Trinity Coll. MS.* A.D. 1200.

Translation by Mr. Richard Morris.

And many other learned men speak as the unlearned, as our Lord spake through the mouth of a prophet, *Erit sicut, &c.* The priest shall lead his life as the laity; and so they do now, and somewhat worse, for the layman honoureth his spouse with clothes more than himself, and the priest not so his church, which is his spouse; but his day (maid servant), who is his whore, whom he adorneth with clothes more than himself. The church cloths are ragged and old, and his woman's shall be whole and new. His altar cloth great (coarse) and dirty (soiled), and her chemise small and white; and the alb soiled, and her smock white; the head linen black, and her wimple (neck-cloth) white, or made yellow with saffron. The masseloth of paltry fustian, and her mantle green or burnet; the corporas soiled and badly made, her hand-cloths and her table-cloths made white and pleasant to the sight. The chalice of tin, and her cup of maser (a sort of hard wood gilded or inlaid with jewels), and her ring of gold; and so the priest is much worse than the laity for he honoureth his whore more than his spouse.

On the question of the rents asked by grasping landlords, I may quote a passage from Ascham used in the Forewords to *The Babees Boke, &c.* (E. E. T. Soc., 1868).

" He says to the Duke of Somerset on Nov. 21, 1547 (*Works*, ed. Giles, i. 140–1).

" ' Qui auctores sunt tantæ miseriæ ? . . . Sunt illi qui hodie passim, in Anglia, prædia monasteriorum gravissimis annuis reditibus auxerunt. Hinc omnium rerum exauctum pretium; hi homines expilant totam rempublicam. Villici et coloni universi laborant, parcunt, corradunt, ut istis satisfaciant. . . Hinc tot familiæ dissipatæ, tot domus collapsæ . . Hinc, quod omnium miserrimum est, nobile illud decus et robur Angliæ, nomen, in-quam, *Yomanorum Anglorum*, fractum et collisum est. . . . . NAM VITA, QUÆ NUNC VIVITUR A PLURIMIS, NON VITA, SED MISERIA EST.'

(When will these words cease to be true of our land? They should be burnt into all our hearts.) "

Harrison, in 1577, speaks more easily about rents, and as he deals also with the question of Usury or Interest noted in our poem, I make a long quotation from his *Description of England,* a book invaluable to the student of the England of Shakespeare's days, and which I hope we shall soon reprint in the Extra Series of our Early English Text Society. Harrison is speaking of the " Three things greatlie amended in England " in his day : "(1.) Chimnies; (2.) Hard lodging; (3.) Furniture of household," and of the latter says :

The third thing they tell of, is the exchange of vessell, as of treene platters into pewter, and woodden spoones into siluer or tin. For so common were all sorts of treéue stuffe in old time, that a man should hardlie find foure péeces of pewter (of which one was peraduenture a salt) in a good farmer's house, and yet for all this frugalitie [1] (if it may so be iustly called) they were scarse able to liue and paie their rents at their daies without selling of a cow, or an horsse, or more, although they paid but foure pounds at the vttermost by the yeare. Such also was their pouertie, that if some one od farmer or husbandman had béene at the alehouse, a thing greatlie vsed in those daies, amongst six or seuen of his neighbours, and there in a brauerie to shew what store he had, did cast downe his pursse, and therein a noble or six shillings in siluer vnto them (for few such men then cared for gold bicause it was not so readie paiment, and they were oft inforced to giue a penie for the exchange of an angell) it was verie likelie that all the rest could not laie downe so much against it : whereas in my time, although peraduenture foure pounds of old rent be improued to fortie, fiftie, or an hundred pounds, yet will the farmer (as another palme or date tree) thinke his gaines verie small toward the end of his terme, if he haue not six or seuen yeares rent lieng by him, therewith to purchase a new lease, beside a faire garnish of pewter on his cupbord, with so much more in od vessell going about the house, thrée or foure featherbeds, so manie couerlids and carpets of tapistrie, a siluer salt, a bowle for wine (if not an whole neast) and a dozzen of spoones to furnish vp the suite. This also he taketh to be his owne cléere, for what stocke of monie soeuer he gathereth & laieth vp in all his yeares, it is often séene, that the landlord will take such order with him for the same, when he renueth his lease, which is commonlie eight or six yeares before the old be expired (sith it is now growen almost to a custome, that if he come not to his lord so long before, another shall step in for a reuersion, and so defeat him out right) that it shall neuer trouble him more than the haire of his beard, when the barber hath washed and shauen it from his chin. And as they commend these, so (beside the decaie of housekeeping whereby the poore haue beene relieued) they speake also of thrée things that are growen to be verie grieuous vnto them, to wit, the inhansing of rents, latelie mentioned; the dailie oppression of copiholders, whose lords sécke to bring their poore tenants almost into plaine seruitude and miserie, daily deuising new meanes, and sécking vp all the old how to cut them shorter and

---

[1] The sidenote here is "This was in the time of generall idlenesse."

shorter, doubling, trebling, and now & then seuen times increasing their fines, driuing them also for euerie trifle to loose and forfeit their tenures (by whome the greatest part of the realme dooth stand and is mainteined) to the end they may fléece them yet more, which is a lamentable hering. The third thing they talke of is vsurie, a trade brought in by the Iewes, now perfectlie practised almost by euerie christian, and so commonlie, that he is accompted but for a foole that dooth lend his monie for nothing. In time past it was *Sors pro sorte*, that is, the principall onelie for the principall; but now beside that which is aboue the principall properlie called *Vsura*, we chalenge *Fœnus*, that is commoditie of soile, & fruits of the earth, if not the ground it selfe. In time past also one of the hundred was much, from thence it rose vnto two, called in Latine *Vsura, Ex sextante*; thrée, to wit *Ex quadrante*; then to foure, to wit *Ex triente*; then to fiue, which is *Ex quincunce*; then to six, called *Ex semisse*, &c. : as the accompt of the *Assis* ariseth, and comming at the last vnto *Vsura ex asse*, it amounteth to twelue in the hundred, and therefore the Latines call it *Centesima*, for that in the hundred moneth it doubleth the principall; but more of this elsewhere. See *Cicero* against *Verres*, *Demosthenes* against *Aphobus*, and *Athenæus lib.* 13. *in fine:* and when thou hast read them well, helpe I praie thée in lawfull maner to hang vp such as take *Centum pro cento*,[1] for they are no better worthie, as I doo iudge in conscience. Forget not also such landlords as vse to value their leases at a secret estimation giuen of the wealth and credit of the taker, whereby they séeme (as it were) to eat them vp and deale with bondmen, so that if the leassée be thought to be worth an hundred pounds, he shall paie no lesse for his new terme, or else another to enter with hard and doubtfull couenants. I am sorie to report it, much more gréeued to vnderstand of the practise; but most sorowfull of all to vnderstand that men of great port and countenance are so farre from suffering their farmers to haue anie gaine at all, that they themselues become grasiers, butchers, tanners, shéepmasters, woodmen, and *denique quid non*, thereby to inrich themselues, and bring all the wealth of the countrie into their owne hands, leauing the communaltie weake, or as an idoll with broken or féeble armes, which may in a time of peace haue a plausible shew, but when necessitie shall inforce, haue an heauie and bitter sequele.—*Holinshed*, vol. i. p. 188–189, ed. 1586.

The date of the poem I cannot pretend to fix. "The new-found land" of l. 91—

[1] "By the yeare" is the sidenote.

> We banisht thee the country beyond the salt sea,
> & sett thee on shore in *the new-found land*—

cannot refer, I think, to the re-discovery of Newfoundland by John Cabot, then in the service of England, on the 24th of June, 1497 (*Penny Cycl.*). The date must be later than that.

The first three stanzas of the poem, which should contain twenty-one lines, in the Manuscript (which is written without divisions) contain only eighteen lines. Mr. Skeat has sent me two arrangements of them, of which the following seems the right one:

> As I walked of late by one wood side,
>   to god for to meditate was my entent,
> where vnder a hawthorne I suddenly espyed
> a silly poore creature ragged & rent,
> with bloody teares his face was besprent,
> his fleshe & his color consumed away,
> & his garments they were all mire, mucke, & clay;
>
> with turning & winding his bodye was toste,
>   *   *   *   *   *
> *   *   *   *   *   *
>   *   *   *   *   *
> "good lord! of my liffe depriue me, I pray,
> for I, silly wretch, am ashamed of my name;
> & I cursse my godfathers *that* gaue me the same."
>
> this made me muse & much desire
>   to know what kind of man hee shold bee;
> I stept to him straight, and did him require
> his name & his secretts to shew vnto me.
> his head he cast vp, & wooful was hee,
> "my name," q*uo*th hee, "is the causer of my care,
> & makes me scornd, & left here soe bare."—F.

As: I walked of late by one[1] wood side,
  [2] to god for to meditate was my entent,
where vnder a hawthorne I suddenly espyed
4 a silly poore creature ragged & rent;

As I walked out to meditate,

I spied

a poor

[1] an.—P.   [2] perhaps On God.- P.

ragged
creature
with bloody teares his face was besprent,

his fleshe & his color consumed away ;

[1] with turning & winding his bodye was toste,

mired all
over.
8   & his garments they were all mire, mucke, & clay.

He wished
himself dead,
" good lord ! of my liffe depriue me, I pray,

for I, silly wretch, am ashamed of my name !

his name
caused his
trouble.
[2] my name, " quoth hee, " is the causer of my care,

12   & I cursse my godfathers *that* gaue me the same ! "

this made me muse, & much desire

to know what kind of man hee shold bee ; [3]

I asked him
to tell it me.
I stept to him straight, & did him require

16   his name & his secretts to shew vnto me.   [page 244]

his head he cast vp, & wooful was hee,[4]

[" My name," quoth hee, is the causer of my care,]

& makes me scornd, & left [5] here soe bare."

then straight-way he turnd him & prayd him[6] sit
dow[ne]

He said his
name was
Conscience.
20   " & I will," saithe he, " declare my whole greefe.

my name is called Conscience ;" wheratt he did
fro[wne]

he pined to repeate it, & grinded his teethe.

.   .   .   .   [7]

When young
for while I was young & tender of yeeres,

24   I was entertained with *Kings*[8] & with Peeres,

---

[1] This verse is redundant.—P.

[2] To come in below.—P.

[3] Percy, in his *Reliques*, omits three of these lines, and transfers line 11 to line 18, where it must be, at least, repeated, without notice to the reader. The bishop warns his readers in his second and later editions that some corruptions in the old copy are here corrected, but not without notice to the reader, where it was necessary, by inclosing the corrections between inverted 'commas.' He must have therefore thought the omission of lines 9, 10, and 12, a correction not necessary to be noticed.—F.

[4] The verse
[" my name" quoth hee, " is the causer of my care,"]
to come in here.—P.

[5] The *f* is like an *ʃ* in the MS.—F.

[6] me. P.

[7] Thoughe now silly wretche, I'm deny'd all relief,
Yet . . .—*Reliques.*

[8] kinges. *Rel.*

"there was none in all[1] the court *that* liued in such
 fame ;

   he was honoured

for with the K*ings* councell he sate[2] in Commission ;

Dukes Erles & Barrons esteemed of my name ;

   by Dukes

28 & how *that* I liued there needs no repetition ;

 I was eu*er* holden in honest condition ;

for howsoeu*er* the lawes went in westminster hall,

when sentence was giuen, for me th*e* wold[3] call.

   and in Law Courts.

32 "noe Incombes[4] at all the landlord wold take,

 but one pore peny, *that* was their fine,

   Landlords obeyed him;

 & *that* they acknowledged to be for my sake ;

 the poore wold doe nothing w*i*thout councell mine ;

   the poor,

36 I ruld the world w*i*th the right line ;

   the world,

for nothing *that* was[5] passed betweene foe & freind,

but Conscience was called to bee at an[6] end.

"noe Merchandize nor bargaines the Merchants wold
 ma[ke],

   and merchants.

40 but I was called a wittenesse therto ;

   No usury was practised.

no vse[7] for noe mony, nor forfett wold take,

 but I wold controwle them if *that* they did soe ;

that makes me liue now in great woe,

44 for then came in pride, Sathans disciple,

   " Then came in Pride.

that now is[8] entertaind with[9] all kind of people ;

he brought w*i*th him 3, whose names they be these,[10]

   Covetous-ness,

that is couetousnes, Lecherye, vsury,[11] beside ;

   Lechery, and Usury

48 they neu*er* pr*e*uailed till they had[12] wrought my
 downe-fall.

   who over-threw me.

---

[1] *all* omitted.—*Rel.*
[2] I sate.—P.
[3] they wold.—P.
[4] Incomes.—P.
[5] (that was) seem redundant.—P.
[6] tho.—P.
[7] interest.—F.
[8] is now.—*Rel.*
[9] of.—P.
[10] thus they call.—*Rel.*
[11] ' & pride' was added here in the MS.,
then struck out with a heavy ink stroke,
the acid of which has eaten the paper
away.—F.
[12] *had* omitted.—*Rel.*

soe pride was entertained, but Conscience was
deride.[1]

I tried abroad,

yet st[i]ll[2] abroad haue[3] J tryed
to haue had entertainment with some one or other,
52   but I am reiected & scorned of my brother.

then the Court;

"then went J to the[4] court, the gallants to winn,
but the porter kept me out of the gates.

but was told to pack off to St. Bartholo- mew's.

to Bartlwew[5] spittle, to pray for my sinnes,[6]
56   they bad[7] me goe packe me; it was fitt for my state;
"goe, goe, threed-bare conscience, & seeke thee a
mate!"

good Lord! long preserue my King, Pirince, & Queene,
with whom euer more I haue esteemed[8] beene!

Next I tried London, but they

60   "then went I to london, where once I did wonne,[9]
but they bade away with me when thé knew my
name;
"for he will vndoe vs to bye & to sell,"

sent me off too.

they bade me goe packe me, & hye me for shame,
64   they lought at my raggs, & there had good game;
"this is old threed-bare Conscience *that* dwelt with
St. Peete[r];
but they wold not admitt me to be a chimney sweeper.

I spent my last penny in an awl and patches to cobble shoes,

"not one wold receiue me, the Lord god doth know.
68   I, hauing but one poore pennye in my pursse,
of an aule[10] & some patches I did it bestow;
I thought better to[11] cobble shooes then to doe worsse.

[1] perhaps decried.—P.
[2] now euer since.—*Rel.*
[3] Only half the u in the MS.—F.
[4] *the* omitted.—*Rel.*
[5] Bartlmew.—*Rel.*
[6] Sin.—P.
[7] *me* omitted in 1st edn, restored in

2nd—*Rel.*
[8] esteemed I've.—P.   I *euer* esteemed have.—*Rel.*
[9] perhaps dwell. (*idem*)—P.   dwell. *Rel.*
[10] On an awl.—P.
[11] For I thought better.—*Rel.*

straight then all they [1] Coblers they began to cursse,

72 & by statute *thé* wold proue me [2] I was a rouge &
forlor[ne,]
& they whipt [3] me out of towne to see [4] where I was
borne.

but the cobblers whipt me out of the town.

"then did I remember & call to my minde
they court [5] of conscience where once I did sit,

76 not doubting but there some favor I shold find,
for [6] my name & the place agreed soe fitt.
but therof my [7] purpose I fayled a whitt,
for the [8] iudge did vse my name in euerye condicion [9]

80 for Lawyers with their qu[i]lletts [10] wold get a [11]
dismission.

I tried the Court of Conscience,

but there the lawyers wheedled me out.

"then westminster hall was noe place for me ;
good god ! [12] how the Lawyers began to assemblee ;
& fearfull they were lest there I shold be !

84 the silly poore clarkes began to tremblee ; [13]
I showed them my cause, & did not dissemble.
soe then they gaue me some mony my charges to beare,
but they [14] swore me on a booke I must neuer come there.

Then I went to Westminster Hall, and the lawyers

gave me money, but made me swear to go.

88 "then [15] the Merchants said, 'counterfeite, get thee
away,
dost thou remember how wee thee found ? [16]
we banisht thee the country beyond the salt sea,
& sett thee on shore in the new-found land, [17]

The merchants too rejected me,

---

[1] the.—P.
[2] (I was) *defend.*—P.
[3] And whipp.—*Rel.*
[4] seeke.—*Rel.*
[5] The court.—P.
[6] Sith.—*Rel.*
[7] there of my.—P. sure of my.—*Rel.*
[8] usd.—*Rel.*
[9] For tho'—comission.—P.
[10] The Lawyers—quillets.—P.
[11] my.—*Rel.*
[12] lord.—*Rel.*
[13] tremble.—*Rel.*
[14] *they* omitted.—*Rel.*
[15] Next.—*Rel.*
[16] fond.—*Rel.*
[17] lond.—P. land.—*Rel.*

92   & there thow & wee most freindly shook hands ; [1]
      & we were verry [2] glad when thou did refuse vs,
      for when we wold reape profitt heere [3] thou wold [4]
          accuse vs.'

so I had to
go to Gentle-
men'shouses,
and tell them
I had made
their fore-
fathers grant
just leases.

      " then had I noe way but for to goe an [5]
96   to gentlemens houses of an ancyent name,
      declaring my greeffes; & there I made moane, [page 245]
      & [6] how there [7] forfathers had held me in fame,
          & in letting of their flarmes I alwayes vsed the same. [8]

They cursed
me.

100   thé sayd, " fye vpon thee ! we may thee cursse !
      they haue leases [9] continue, & we fare the worsse."

At last I was
driven to
husband-
men ;
but land-
lords had left
them no-
thing to give
away ;

      " & then I was forced a begging to goe
         to husbandsmens houses ; who greeved right sore,
104   who sware that their Landlords had plaged them so
          sore [10]
      that they were not able to keepe open doore,
          nor nothing thé [11] had left to giue to the pore.

so I am in
this wood,
and eat hips
and haws,

      therfore to this wood I doe repayre
108   with hepps & hawes ; that is my best fare.

but am
comforted
by Mercy,
Pity, and
Almsdeeds."

      " & yet within this same desert some comfort I haue
          of Mercy, of pittye, & of almes-deeds,
      who haue vowed to company me to my [12] graue.
112   wee are ill [13] put to silence, & liue vpon weeds ; [14]

      .   .   .   .

      our banishment is their vtter decay,
      the which the rich glutton will answer one day."

---

[1] hond.—P.
[2] right.—Rel.
[3] proffitt heere omitted. Rel.
[4] woldst.—Rel.
[5] on.—Rel.
[6] Telling.—Rel.
[7] their.—P.
[8] And at letting their farmes how
always I came.—Rel.

[9] their leases, i. e. the indulgent Leases
let by our forefathers.—P.
[10] sor.—Rel.
[11] (the) redundant.—P.
[12] my in the MS.—F.
[13] all.—Rel.
[14] and hence such cold housekeeping
proceeds.—Rel.

116 ‘ why then,” I said to him, “ methinkes it were best
to goe to the Clergee ; for dealye [1] thé preach
eche man to loue you aboue all the rest ;
of mercy & of Pittie & of almes they doe [2] teach.”
“O,” said he, “ no matter of a pin what they doe
preach,
120 for their wiues & their children soe hangs them vpon,
that whosoeuer giues almes deeds [3] they will [4] giue
none.”

then Laid he him downe, & turned him away,
prayd [5] me to goe & leaue him to rest,
124 I told him I might happen to [6] see the day
to haue [7] him & his fellowes to liue w*i*th the best ;
[8] “ first,” said hee, “ you must banish pride, & then
all England were blest,[9]
& [10] then those wold loue vs *that* now sells [11] their lands,[12]
128 & then good houses euerye where wold be kept [13] out of
hand.”

ffins.

Side notes:
“ Go to the Clergy,” said I.

It'd be no good ; their wiues and children stop their giving.

Banish Pride ; then England will be blest.

[1] daily.—P.
[2] *doe* omitted.—*Rel.*
[3] *deeds* omitted.—*Rel.*
[4] It ought in justice and Truth to be “ CAN.”—P.
[5] And prayd.—*Rel.*
[6] haplie might yet.—*Rel.*
[7] For.—*Rel.*
[8] This line written as two in the MS. — F.
[9] First said he, banish Pryde : Then all England were blest.—P. These make two lines in the MS.—F.
[10] For.—*Rel.*
[11] sell.—*Rel.*
[12] land.—P.
[13] house-keeping wold revive.—*Rel.*

Durham ffeilde.[1]

Says Shakespeare's Henry V.:

> You shall read, that my grandfather
> Never went with his forces into France,
> But that the Scot on his unfurnisht kingdom
> Came pouring, like a tide into a breach,
> With ample and brim-fullness of his force;
> Galling the gleaned land with hot assays;
> Girdling, with grievous siege, castles and towns,
> That England being empty of defence
> Hath shook and trembled at th' ill neighbourhood.

Perhaps the best account of the expedition celebrated in the following ballad is given by Fordun. "The local accuracy," observes Surtees, "with which Fordun describes the advance of the English army from Auckland, ... infers that his account must have been received from eye-witnesses." Other accounts are furnished by Knighton, Walsingham, Froissart. Harl MS. No. 4843 contains an ancient monkish poem on it.

The confidence of the Scotch King is amusingly represented in the First Part of the ballad.

Oddly enough, nothing is said of the Queen, who, though probably Froissart exaggerates the part she played, yet was certainly not remote from the scene of the conflict. One would have expected her presence to have been made much of by the ballad-writer.

John Copeland, who captured the King, was a Northumbrian esquire. He was afterwards Governor of Berwick and Sheriff of Northumberland.

---

[1] Fought Oct. 17, 1346, at St. Nevil's Cross, near Durham. "An excellent" [half scratched out].—P.
Old Ballad. The Subject is the inrode (sic) into England by the Scotts, & the taking of their King, while Edward 3d was in France.—P.

LORDINGES, listen, & hold yo[u] [1] still ;
   hearken to me a litle ;
I shall you tell of the fairest battell
4   *that* euer in England beffell.

                 Listen,

       and I'll tell
       you of a fair
       battle.

for as it befell in Edward the 3[d] dayes,[2]
   in England, where he ware the crowne,
then all the cheefe chiualry of England
8   they busked [3] & made them bowne [4] ;

       When Ed-
       ward III.
       was king,

       all his
       knights

they chosen all the best archers
   that in England might be found,
and all was to fight with the King of ffrance
12   within a litle stounde.[5]

       and archers

       went to fight
       the French.

and when our King was ouer the water,
   and on the salt sea gone,
then tydings into Scotland came.
16   *that* all England was gone ;

       Then the
       Scotch hear

bowes and arrowes they were all forth,
   at home was not left a man [6]
but shepards and Millers both,
20   & preists with shauen crownes.

       that no men
       are left in
       England

       but millers
       and priests.

then the King of Scotts in a study stood,
   as he was a man of great might ;
he sware 'he wold hold his Parlament in leeue [7]
   London
24   if he cold ryde there right.'

       The Scotch
       king

       swears he'll
       ride to
       London.

---

[1] ? MS. ; it may be *yo.*—F.

[2] when *Edward* the 3[d] —P.

[3] See P. 397, st. 46. (of MS.)—P.

[4] *bowne,* paratus, L.—P.

[5] *Stound,* signum, momentum, spatium, hora, tempus. Lye.—P.

[6] mon.—P. See vol. i. p. 217, l. 109. —F.

[7] *Leeve,* perhaps the same as leef, lief, leif, dear, beloved—A.-S. *leofa, belg. lief.* Teut. *lieb,* charus, amicus, gratus. Gloss? to Gaw[n] Douglas.—P.

A squire

then bespake a Sq*uier* of Scottland borne,
   & sayd, "my leege, apace,

tells him he'll rue his resolve,

before you come to leeue London
28   full sore youle rue *that* race !

"ther beene bold yeomen in merry England,
   husbandmen stiffe & strong ;
sharpes swords they done weare,
32   bearen bowes & arrowes longe."

for which the King

the K*ing* was angrye at that word,
   a long sword out hee drew,
and there befor his royall companye

kills him,

36   his owne squier hee slew.

so no one else dares say a word.

hard hansell had the Scottes *that* day
   that wronght them woe enoughe,
for then durst not a Scott speake a word
40   ffor hanging att a boughe.   [page 246]

James tells the Earl of Angus to lead the van,

" the Earle of Anguish,[1] where art thou ?
   in my coate armor [2] thou shalt bee,
and thou shalt lead the forward [3]
44   thorrow the English countrye.

" take thy [4] yorke," then sayd the K*ing*,
   " in stead wheras it doth stand ;

and promises him Northumberland.

Ile make thy eldest sonne after thee
48   heyre of all Northumberland.

To the Earl of Buchan he promises

" the Earle [5] of Vaughan,[6] where be yee ?
   in my coate armor thou shalt bee ;

Derbyshire ;

the high Peak & darbyshire
52   I giue it thee to thy fee."

---

[1] Earl of Angus.- P.
[2] Cote-Armour. A name applied to the tabard by Chaucer and others. Fairholt.—F.
[3] vaward. - P. There is a tag to the *d* in the MS.—F.
[4] thee. i. e. to thee. P.
[5] The *l* is made over an *e*. - F.
[6] It should be Baughan, i. e. Buchan. — P.

then came in famous Douglas,
   saies, " what shall my meede bee?
   & Ile lead the vawward,[1] Lord,
56   thorow the English countrye."

to Douglas,

" take thee Worster," sayd the King,
   " Tuxburye,[2] Killingworth, Burton vpon trent ;
   doe thou not say another day
60   but I haue giuen thee lands and rent.

Worcester ;

" Sir Richard of Edenborrow, where are yee ?
   a wise man in this warr !
   Ile giue thee Bristow & the shire
64   the time that wee come there.

to Sir Richard of Edinburgh, Bristol and its shire ;

" my Lord Nevill, where beene yee ?
   you must in this warres bee !
   Ile giue thee Shrewsburye," saies the King,
68   " and Couentrye faire & free.

to Lord Nevill, Shrewsbury and Coventry ;

" my Lord of Hambleton, where art thou ?
   thou art of my kin full nye ;
   Ile giue thee lincolne & Lincolneshire,
72   & thats enouge for thee."

to Lord Hambleton, Lincolnshire.

by then came in William Douglas
   as breeme [3] as any bore ;
   he kneeled him downe vpon his knees,
76   in his hart he sighed sore,

William Douglas

saies, " I haue serued you, my louelye leege,
   this 30 winters and 4,
   & in the Marches [4] betweene England & Scottland
80   I haue beene wounded & beaten sore ;

reminds the King of his long services,

---

[1] i. e. the Van, the Vanguard. Fr. avant-guarde. L.—P.
[2] qu. MS.—F.
[3] breme, ferox, atrox, cruel, sharp, severe. Lye.—P.

[4] Marches, confinia, limites, alicujus territorii : refer ad Mark Scotis. March, a landmark, &c. Vid. Lye, ad Jun.—P.

and asks
what his re-
ward is to be.

"for all the good service *that* I haue done,
        what shall my meed bee ?
& I will lead the vanward
84   thorrow the English countrye."

" Whatever
you ask,"
answers
James.
" Then I ask
for London."

"aske on, douglas," said the King,
        " & granted it shall bee."
"why then, I aske litle London," saies Wi*ll*iam
        Douglas,
88   " gotten giff' *that* it bee."

James
refuses that.

the K*ing* was wrath, and rose away,
        saies, " nay, *that* cannot bee !
for *that* I will keepe for my cheefe chamber,
92   gotten if it bee ;

but gives
Douglas N.
Wales and
Cheshire.

" but take thee North wales & weschaster,
        the cuntrye all round about,
& rewarded thou shalt bee,
96   of *that* take thou noe doubt."

makes 100
new knights

5 score k*nigh*ts he made on a day,
        & dubbd them w*i*th his hands ;

and gives
them the
English
towns.

rewarded them right worthilye
100   w*i*th the townes in merry England.

They make
ready for
battle,

& when the fresh k*nigh*ts they were made,
        to battell thé buske them bowne ; [1]
Iames Douglas went before,
104   & he thought to haue wonnen him shoone.

but the
English
Commons
meet them,
and let none
escape ;

but thé were mett in a morning of May
        w*i*th the com*m*inaltye of litle England ;
but there scaped neu*er* a man away
108   through the might of christes hand,

[1] See Page 397, st. 46 [of MS.].—P.

but all onely Iames Douglas ;
　　in Durham in the ffeild
an arrow stroke him in the thye.
112　　fast flinge[s he] towards the King.

except
Douglas,

who is
wounded
and flees to
the King.

the King looked toward litle Durham,
　　saies, "all things is not well !
for Iames Dowglas beares an arrow in his thye,
116　　the head of it is of steele.

"how now Iames ?" then said the King,
　　"how now, how may this bee ?
& where beene all thy merrymen
120　　That thou tooke hence with thee ?"　　[page 217]

James asks
where his
men are.

"but cease, my King," saies Iames [1] Douglas,
　　"aliue is not left a man ! "
"now by my faith," saies the King of scottes,
124　　"that gate [2] was euill gone ;

All dead.

James vows

"but Ile reuenge thy quarrell well,
　　& of that thou may be faine ;
for one Scott will beate 5 Englishmen
128　　if the meeten them on the plaine."

revenge ;

one Scot is a
match for
five English.

"now hold your tounge," saies Iames Douglas,
　　"for in faith that is not soe ;
for one English man is worth 5 Scotts
132　　when they meeten together thoe ;

"No," says
Douglas,

"one Eng-
lishman is
worth five
Scots ;

"for they are as Egar men to fight
　　as a faulcon vpon a pray.
alas ! if euer the winne the vanward,
136　　there scapes noe man away."

they let no
one escape
alive."

[1] *Iames* in the MS.—F.
[2] gate, *via* a way : march or walk. Lye.—P.

"O peace thy talking," said the King,
  "they bee but English knaues,
but shepards & Millers both,
140   & [mass] preists with their staues."

the King sent forth one of his heralds of armes
  to vew the Englishmen.

"be of good cheere," the herald said,
144   "for against one wee bee ten."

"who leades those Ladds?" said the King of Scottes,
  "thou herald, tell thou mee."

the herald said, "the Bishopp of Durham
148   is captaine of that companye;

for the Bishopp hath spred the Kings banner
  & to battell he buskes him bowne."
"I sweare by St. Andrewes bones," saies the King,
152   "Ile rapp that preist on the crowne!"

[Part II.]

The King looked towards litle Durham,
  & that hee well beheld,

that the Earle Percy was well armed,
156   with his battell axe entred the feild.

2ᵈ part

the King looket againe towards litle Durham,
  4 ancyents there see hee;
there were to standards, 6 in a valley,
160   he cold not see them with his eye.

My Lord of yorke was one of them,
  my lord of Carlile was the other;
& my Lord Fitzwilliams,
164   the one came with the other.

the Bishopp of Durham commanded his men,
   & shortlye he them bade,
'*that* neuer a man shold goe to the feild to fight
168   till he had serued his god.'

500 preists said masse *that* day
   in durham in the feild ;
& afterwards, as I hard say,
172   they bare both speare & sheeld.

the Bishopp of Durham [1] orders himselfe to fight
   with his battell axe in his hand ;
he said, "this day now I will fight
176   as long as I can stand!"

"& soo will I," sayd my Lord of Carlile,
   "in this faire morning gay ; "
"& soo will I," said my Lord flluwilliams,
180   "for Mary, *that* myld may."

our English archers bent their bowes
   shortlye and anon,
they shott ouer the Scottish Oast
184   & scantlye [2] toucht a man.

"hold downe your hands," sayd the Bishopp of Durham,
   "my archers good & true."
the 2.d shoote *that* the shott,
188   full sore the Scottes itt rue.

the Bishopp of Durham spoke on hye
   that both partyes might heare,
"be of good cheere, my merrymen all,
192   the Scotts flyen, & changen there cheere ! "

---

[1] Durham in MS.—F.   [2] scantly. scarcely.—P.

but as thé snidden, soe thé didden,

who fall in heaps.

they fell on heapes hye ;

our Englishmen laid on with their bowes

196   as fast as they might dree.

King James

[1] The King of Scotts in a studye stood   [page 248]

amongst his companye,

is shot through the nose,

an arrow stoke him thorrow the nose

200   & thorrow his armorye.

the King went to a marsh side

gets off his horse,

& light beside his steede,

he leaned him downe on his sword hilts

204   to let his nose bleede.

there followed him a yeaman of merry England,

and is summoned to yield by an English yeoman, Copland.

his name was Iohn of Coplande :

"yeeld thee Traytor !" saies Coplande then,

208   "thy liffe lyes in my hand."

"how shold I yeeld me ?" sayes the King,

James refuses,

"& thou art noe gentleman."

"noe, by my troth," sayes Copland there,

212   "I am but a poore yeaman ;

"what art thou better then I, Sir King?

tell me if that thou can !

what art thou better then I, Sir King,

216   now we be but man to man ?"

the King smote angerly at Copland then,

and strikes at Copland,

angerly in that stonde [2] ;

& then Copland was a bold yeaman,

who floors him,

220   & bore the King to the ground.

---

[1] Here a short leaf is inserted in the MS. in a more modern hand, Percy's late upright hand, differing from the early

small one of most of his notes.—F.
[2] stound.- ? Percy.

he sett the King upon a Palfrey,
himselfe upon a steede,
he tooke him by the bridle rayne,
224   towards London he can him Lead.

puts him on a palfrey.

and takes him to London.

& when to London that he came,
the King from ffrance was new come home,
& there unto the King of Scottes
228   he sayd these words anon,

where King Edward is.

"how like you my shepards & my millers,
my priests with shaven crownes?"
"by my fayth, they are the sorest fighting men
232   that ever I mett on the ground;

Edward asks James how he likes his millers and priests. "They're the hardest fighters I ever met."

"there was never a yeaman in merry England
but he was worth a Scottish knight!"
"I, by my troth," said King Edward, & laughe,
236   "for you fought all against the right."

but now the Prince of merry England
worthilye under his Sheelde
hath taken the King of ffrance
240   at Poytiers in the ffeelde.

The King of France is also taken at Poictiers

the Prince did present his father with that food,[1]
the lonely King off ffrance,
& fforward of his Iourney he is gone:
244   god send us all good chance!

by the Black Prince.

"you are welcome, brothers!" sayd the King of Scotts,
to the King of ffrance,
"for I am come hither to soone;
Christ leeve that I had taken my way
248   unto the court of Roome!"

and both he and the Scotch King

[1] feod or feodary. P. Person: see note 2, p. 456. vol. i.—F.

"& soe wold I," said the King of ffrance,

"when I came over the streame,

that I had taken my Iourney

252　unto Ierusalem."

Thus ends the battell of ffaire Durham　　　[page 249]

in one morning of may,

the battell of Cressey, & *the* battle of Potyers,

256　All within one monthes day.

then was welthe & welfare in mery England,

Solaces, game, & glee,

& every man loved other well,

260　& the King loved good yeomanrye.

but God *that* made the grasse to growe,

& leaves on greenwoode tree,

now save & keepe our noble King,

264　& maintaine good yeomanry!　　　ffinis.[1]

---

[1] (*Pencil note in Percy's late hand.*)
" This & 2 following Leaves being unfortunately torn out, in sending the subsequent piece [King Estmere] to the
Press, the conclusion of the preceding
ballad has been carefully transcribed;
and indeed the fragments of the other
Leaves ought to have been so."
The loss of *King Estmere* is much to
be lamented. It was, perhaps, the best
ballad in the Manuscript. Percy says
in the 2nd edition of the *Reliques*,
p. 59, that " this old Romantic Legend . .
is given from two copies, one of them in
the Editor's folio MS."; but we have not
been able to find the second copy. It is
not in the other small MS. in the possession of the Bishop's descendants now.
It is evident at a glance that Percy must
have touched up the ballad somewhat,
as in line 4 he has *y-were*, were, for a
perfect tense, *y* being the past participle
prefix; and a comparison of the first
three editions with the 4th shows what
liberties he took with the (supposed)
text of the MS. Some of these will be
pointed out in a note at the end of this
volume. The thing to be noticed here is

that Percy must have deliberately and
unnecessarily torn three leaves out of
his MS. when preparing his 4th edition
for the Press, and after he had learnt—to
use his own words—*to reverence* the MS.
These leaves were in the MS. till that
time, as he says in his note on "Ver. 253.
Some liberties have been taken in the
following stanzas; but wherever this
edition differs from the preceding, it
hath been brought nearer to the folio
MS." As the differences of the fourth
from the other editions, after v. 253,
are only in spelling *louked*, 'looked,' and
wyfe, 'wiffe,' we must take the latter
part of Percy's sentence to apply to the
whole ballad. By tearing out the leaves
he has prevented us from knowing the
extent of his large changes, and has
sacrificed not only the original of the
whole of *King Estmere* but also the first
22 (or more or less) stanzas of *Guy and
Phillis*, of which his version is printed
in the *Reliques* iii. 143, 4th ed., and
Child's *Ballads* i. 63–6. I calculate
Percy's additions to *Estmere* and the
lost part of *Guy* at 40 lines.—F.

Guy & Phillis.[1]

[A fragment.]

[See the General Introduction to all the Guy Poems in *Guy & Colebrande* below.
The beginning of this Poem was on one of the torn-out leaves of the MS.]

In winsor fforrest I did slay   [page 254]   In Windsor
    a bore of passing might & strenght,[2]   Forest I
                                                slew a big
whose like in England neuer was   boar,
4   for hugnesse, both for breadth & lenght ;

some of his bones in warwicke yett   some of
    within the Castle there doth [3] Lye ;   whose bones
                                              are in
one of his sheeld bones to this day   Warwick
8   doth hang in the Citye of Couentrye.   Castle

                                            and
                                          Coventry.
on Dunsmore heath I alsoe slewe   On Duns-
    a mightye wyld & cruell beast   more Heath
                                            I slew
calld the Duncow of Dunsmore heath,   the Dun
12   which many people had opprest ;   Cow,

some of her bones in warwicke yett   whose bones
    there for a monument doth [4] lye,   are also in
                                          Warwick.
which vnto euery lookers veue
16   as wonderous strange they may espye.

another dragon in this Land   Another
    in fight I alsoe did destroye,   Dragon I
                                          also slew,
who did bothe men & beasts opresse,
20   & all the countrye sore anoye ;

& then to warwicke came againe   and then
    like Pilgrim poore, & was not knowen ;   came back
                                          to Warwick,
& there I liued a Hermitts liffe   and lived a
                                          hermit's life,
24   a mile & more out of the towne ;

---

[1] Title written in by P.—F.   [2] strenght in the MS.—F.   [3] do.—P.   [4] do.—P.

in a cave
cut out of a
rock,

where with my hands I hewed a house
     out of a craggy rocke of stone,
& lined like a palmer poore
28   within the caue my selfe alone ;

and
begged my
food at my
own castle
of my wife.

& daylye came to begg my foode
     of Phillis att my castle gate,
not knowing [1] to my loued wiffe,
32   who daylye moned for her mate ;

At last I fell
sick,

till att the last I fell soe sicke,
     yea, sicke soe sore *that* I must dye.

sent her a
ring,

I sent to her a ring of gold
36   by w*hi*ch shee knew me presentlye ;

then shee, repairing to the graue,
     befor *that* I gaue vp the ghost

and she
closed my
dying eyes.

shee closed vp my dying eyes,
40   my Phillis faire, whom I loued most.

thus dreadfull death did me arrest,
     to bring my corpes vnto the graue ;

I died like a
palmer to
save my soul.

& like a palmer dyed I,
44   wherby I sought my soule to saue.

tho now it be consumed to mold,
     my body *that* endured this toyle,

You may
see my
statue now.

my stature ingrauen in Mold
48   this present time you may behold.

                            ffins.

[1] knowen.—P.

John : a : Side.

THE rescue of a prisoner was a favourite subject with the ballad-makers of the Borders. There are in the *Minstrelsy of the Scottish Border* " no fewer than three poems on the rescue of prisoners, the incidents in which nearly resemble each other; though the poetical description is so different, that the editor did not think himself at liberty to reject any one of them as borrowed from the others." These three are *Jock o' the Side, Kinmont Willie*, and *Archie of Ca'field*. The ballad here given for the first time is vitally the same with *Jock o' the Side*. The persons are partly changed: Sybill o' the Side takes the place of the Lady Downie of Scott's ballad; Much the Miller's Son answers to the Laird's Saft Wat, though as the Folio copy does not give the names of the five who accompany Hobbie Noble, the Laird's Saft Wat may have been one of them. The incidents differ very slightly: as at Culerton or Cholerford, when the rescuers are going and returning, at Newcastle where the *Minstrelsy* copy brings in "a proud porter" to be duly made away with, at the gaol on the way back, where that same copy gives the banter with which the heavy-ironed prisoner was assailed by his triumphant friends. The Folio copy is a very fresh, valuable version of the ballad.

" The reality of this story," says Scott, " rests solely upon the foundation of tradition. Jock o' the Side seems to have been nephew to the laird of Margertoun, cousin to the Laird's Jock, one of his deliverers, and probably brother to Chrystie of the Syde, mentioned in the list of border clans, 1597. Like the Laird's Jock, he is also commemorated by Sir Richard Maitland :

He is weil kend, Johne of the Syde.
A greater theif did never ryde;
He never tyris
For to brek byris,
Our muir and myris
Ouir gude and guide.

———   ————

PEETER a whifeild [1] he hath slaine ;

John-a-Side
is taken,

and sent
prisoner to
Newcastle.
   & Iohn a side, he is tane ;

& Iohn is bound both hand & foote,
4 & to the New-castle he is gone.

His mother,
Sybill,
but Tydinges came to the Sybill o the side,
   by the water side as shee rann ;
shee tooke her kirtle by the hem,

tells Lord
Mangerton.
8 & fast shee runn to Mangerton.

.   .   .   .   .

the Lord was sett downe at his meate ;
when these tydings shee did him tell,
neuer a Morsell might he eate.

Lords and
Ladies
lament,
12 but lords thé wrunge their fingars white,
   Ladyes did pull themselues by the haire,
crying "alas and weladay !
   for Iohn o the side wee shall neuer see more [2] !

and vow to
lose their all
16 "but weele goe sell our droues of Kine,
   & after them our oxen sell,
& after them our troopes of sheepe,

or rescue
him.
   but wee will loose him out of the New-castell."

Hobby Noble
offers to
fetch John,
with five
men.
20 but then bespake him hobby noble,
   & spoke these words wonderous hye,
sayes " giue me 5 men to my selfe,   [page 255]
   & Ile feitch Iohn o the side to thee."

[1] ? The first i may be t.   F.   [2] maire.—P.

24   " yea, thoust haue 5, hobby noble,
      of the best *that* are in this countrye!
      Ile giue thee 5000, hobby Noble,
      that walke in Tynidale trulye."

The lord promises 5000 ;

28   " nay, Ile haue but 5," saies hobby Noble,
      " *that* shall walke away with mee ;
      wee will ryde like noe men of warr ;
      but like poore badgers[1] wee wilbe."

but Hobby will only have five,

dressed as corn-dealers.

32   they stuffet vp all their baggs with straw,
      & their steeds barefoot must bee ;
      " come on my bretheren," sayes hobby noble,
      " come on your wayes, & goe with mee."

They start,

36   & when they came to Culerton[2] ford,
      the water was vp, they cold it not goe ;
      & then they were ware of a good old man,
      how his boy & hee were at the plowe.

but at Culerton Ford find the water up.

40   " but stand you still," sayes hobby noble,
      " stand you still heere at this shore,
      & I will ryde to yonder old man,
      & see were the gate[3] it Lyes ore.

Hobby

asks an old man

44   " but christ you saue, father," Quoth hee,
      " crist both you saue and see !
      where is the way ouer this fford ?
      for christs sake tell itt mee ! "

the way over the ford.

48   " but I haue dwelled heere 3 score yeere,
      soe haue I done 3 score and 3 ;
      I neuer sawe man nor horsse goe ore
      except itt were a horse of 3.[4] "

The old man won't tell it.

---

[1] corn-dealers, Fr. *bladiers.*—F.
[2] Challerton, probably.—P.
[3] way, ford.—F.
[4] Tree, qu.—P.

52 " but fare thou well, thou good old man ;
　　the devill in hell I leave with thee!
　　noe better comfort heere this night
　　　thow giues my bretheren heere & me."

56 but when he came to his brother againe,
　　& told this tydings full of woe,
　　& then they found a well good gate
　　they might ryde ore by 2 and 2.

60 and when they were come ouer the fforde,
　　all safe gotten att the last,
　　" thankes be to god !" sayes hobby nobble,
　　" the worst of our perill is past."

64 & then they came into HOWBRAME wood,
　　& there then they found a tree,

　　& cutt itt downe then by the roote ;
　　the lenght was 30 ffoote and 3.

68 & 4 of them did take the planke
　　as light as it had beene a fflee,

　　& carryed itt to the Newcastle
　　where as Iohn a side did lye ;

72 & some did climbe vp by the walls,
　　& some did climbe vp by [1] the tree,

　　vntill they came vpp to the top of the castle
　　where Iohn made his moane trulye :

76 he sayd, " god be with thee, Sybill o the side !
　　my owne mother thou art," Quoth hee,
　　" if thou knew this knight [2] I were here,
　　a woe woman then woldest thou bee !

---

[1] MS. eaten through by ink.—F.　　　　　　　[2] night.—P.

80   "& fare you well, Lord Mangerton!
    & euer I say 'god be with thee!'
    for if you knew this night I were heere,
    you wold sell your land for to loose mee.

of Lord Mangerton,

84   "& fare thou well, Much Millers sonne!
    Much Millars sonne, I say ;
    thou has beene better att Merke midnight
    then euer thou was att noone o the day.

of Much the Miller's son,

88   "& fare thou well, my good Lord Clough!
    thou art thy flathers sonne & heire ;
    thou neuer saw him [1] in all thy liffe,
    but with him durst thou breake a speare.

and of Lord Clough ;

92   "wee are brothers childer 9: or :10:
    & sisters children 10: or :11:
    we neuer come to the feild to fight,
    but the worst of us was counted a man."

and boasts that his family is large and brave.

96   but then bespake him hobynoble,
    & spake these words vnto him,
    saies, "sleepest thou, wakest thou, Iohn o the side,
    or art thou this castle within?"

Hobby tells him

100   "But who is there," Quoth Iohn oth side,   [page 256]
    "that knowes my name soe right & free?"
    "I am a bastard brother of thine ;
    this night I am comen for to loose thee."

he has come to free him.

104   "now nay, now nay," quoth Iohn othe side ;
    "itt ffeares me sore that will not bee ;
    ffor a pecke of gold & silver," Iohn sayd,
    "infaith this night will not loose mee."

I fear not, says John ;

[1] man.—F.

108   but then bespake him hobby Noble,
                            & till his brother thus sayd hee,
sayes, "I shall take this matter in hand,
                            and 2 shall tent our geldings ffree."

                     112   for I did breake one dore without,
then Iohn brake 5 himsell;
but when they came to the Iron dore,
                            it smote 12 vpon the bell.

116   "itt ffeares me sore," sayd much the Miller,
"that heere taken wee all shalbee."
                            "but goe away, bretheren," sayd Iohn a side,
                            "for euer, alas! this will not bee."

120   "but ffye vpon thee!" sayd Hobby Noble;
"Much the Miller! fye vpon thee!
                            "it sore feares me," said Hobby Noble,
                            "man that thou wilt neuer bee."

                     124   but then he had fflanders files 2 or 3,
& hee fyled downe that Iron dore,
& tooke Iohn out of the New-castle,
                            & sayd "looke thou neuer come heere more!"

                     128   when he had him fforth of the Newcastle,
                            "away with me, Iohn, thou shalt ryde."
                            but euer alas! itt cold not bee;
                            for Iohn cold neither sitt nor stryde.

132   but then he had sheets 2 or 3,
& bound Iohns boults fast to his ffeete,
& sett him on a well good steede,
                            himselfe on another by him scete.

136   then Hobby Noble smiled & longe,[1]
     & spoke these words in mickle pryde,
     " thou sitts soe finely on thy geldinge
     that, Iohn, thou rydes like a bryde."

woman-fashion.

140   & when they came thorrow ΠOWBRAME towne,
     Iohns horsse there stumbled at a stone ; [2]
     " out & alas ! " cryed much the Miller,
     " Iohn, thoule make vs all be tane."

Much the Miller gets into another fright.

144   " but fye vpon thee ! " saies Hobby Noble,
     " much the Millar, fye on thee !
     I know full well," sayes Hobby Noble,
     " man *that* thou wilt neuer bee ! "

and is again snubbed by Hobby Noble,

148   & when thé came into ΠOWBRAME wood,
     he had fflanders files 2 or 3
     to file Iohns bolts beside his ffeete,
     that hee might ryde more easilye.

who files off John's chains from his feet.

152   sayes Iohn, " Now leape ouer a steede,"
     & Iohn then hee lope ouer 5 :
     " I know well," sayes Hobby Noble,
     " Iohn, thy ffellow is not aliue ! "

Thereupon John leaps over five horses,

156   then he brought him home to Mangerton ;
     the Lord then he was att his meate ;
     but when Iohn o the side he there did see,
     for faine hee cold noe more eate ;

and goes home to Lord Mangerton.

160   he sayes " blest be thou, Hobby Noble,
     th at euer thou wast man borne !
     thou hast feitched vs home good Iohn oth side
     that was now cleane ffrom vs gone ! "

Lord Mangerton blesses Hobby Noble.

                      ffins.

[1] loughe.—P.   [2] stane.— P.

Risinge in the Northe: [1]

THIS ballad is printed in the *Reliques*, " from two MS. copies, one of them in the Editor's folio collection. They contained (*sic*) considerable variable variations, out of which such readings were chosen as seemed most poetical and consonant to history."

On the subject see the Introduction to "The Earle of Westmorelande," vol. i. p. 292, and Percy's, in the *Reliques*, i. 248, 1st ed.

Listen,	LISTEN, linely lordings all,
	& all *that* beene this place within !
and I'll tell all about it.	if youle giue eare vnto my songe,
	4 I will tell you how this geere did begin.

It was the good Erle of westmorlande,
   a noble Erle was called hee ;
& he wrought treason against the crowne ;
   8   alas, itt was the more pittye !

The Earl of Westmoreland turned traitor ;

& soe itt was the Erle of Northumberland,
   another good Noble Erle was hee,
they tooken both vpon one part,   [page 257]
   12   against their crowne they wolden bee.

so did the Earl of Northumberland.

Earle Pearcy is into his garden gone,
   & after walkes his awne ladye [2] ;
" I heare a bird sing in my eare
   16   *that* I must either flight or fllee."

Earl Percy tells his wife he must fight or flee.

---

[1] A.D. 1569. N.B.—To correct this by my other copy, which seems more modern.—P. The other copy in many parts preferable to this.—Pencil note.

[2] This lady was Anne, daughter of Henry Somerset, E. of Worcester.—*Rd.*

"god fforbidd," shee sayd, "good my lord,
   that euer soe *that* it shalbee!
but goe to London to the court,
20   & faire ffall truth & honestye!"

She advises him to go to court.

"but nay, now nay, my Ladye gay,
   that euer it shold soe bee;
my treason is knowen well enoughe;
24   att the court I must not bee."

He says

his treason is too well known.

"but goe to the Court! yet, good my Lord,
   take men enowe with thee;
if any man will doe you wronge,
28   your warrant they [1] may bee."

She again says, "Go to court with plenty of men."

"but Nay, Now Nay, my Lady gay,
   for soe itt must not bee;
If I goe to the court, Ladye,
32   death will strike me, & I must dye."

No, says the Earl,

it would be certain death.

"but goe to the Court! yett, [good] my Lord,
   I my-selfe will ryde with thee;
if any man will doe you wronge,
36   your borrow [2] I shalbee."

She offers to go with him.

"but Nay, Now nay, my Lady gay,
   for soe it must not bee;
for if I goe to the Court, Ladye,
40   thou must me neuer see.

He still refuses,

"but come hither, thou litle footpage,
   come thou hither vnto mee,
for thou shalt goe a Message to *Master* Norton
44   in all the hast *that* euer may bee:

but sends a page to ask

Master Norton

---

[1] altered from *them.*—F.   they.—P.   fide jussor, vadimonium, pignus. A.-S.
[2] *Borrow, borow, borge.* Sponsor, vas,   *lorge, borhoe,* Lye.—P.

" comend me to *that* gentleman ;
    bring him here this letter from mee,

to go with
him.
    & say, 'I pray him Earnestlye
48   *that* hee will ryde in my companye.' "

The page
hurries off

but one while the foote page went,
    another while he rann ;

to Master
Norton,
vntill he came to M*aster* Norton,
52   the ffoot page neuer blanne ; [1]

& when he came to M*aster* Nortton,
    he kneeled on his knee,

and gives
him the
letter.
& tooke the letter betwixt his hands,
56   & lett the gentleman it see.

& when the letter itt was reade
    affore all his companye,
I-wis,[2] if you wold know the truth,
60   there was many a weeping eye.

Norton asks
his son
Kester

he said, " come hither, Kester[3] Nortton,
    a fline ffellow thou seemes to bee ;

for advice.
some good councell, Kester Nortton,
64   this day doe thou giue to mee."

Kester tells

" marry, Ile giue you councell, ffather,
    if youle take councell att me,

him not to
draw back
from his
word.
that if you haue spoken the word, father,
68   *that* backe againe you doe not flee."

Norton

" god amercy, Christopher Nortton,
    I say, god amercye !
if I doe liue & scape with liffe,

promises
him reward.
72   well advanced shalt thou bee ;

---

[1] cessavit.—P.
[2] to *wis*, to know. Germ. *wissen*,
Johns.—P.

[3] Kester, Christopher. *Northern.* Halliwell's Glossary.—F.

" but come you hither, my 9 good sonnes,
    in mens estate I thinke you bee ;
how many of you, my children deare,
76   on my part *that* wilbe ? "

and asks his own nine sons

who will be on his side.

but 8th of them did answer soone,
    & spake ffull hastilye,
sayes " we wilbe on your part, ffather,
80   till the day *that* we doe dye."

Eight vow

to be with him to the death.

" but god amercy, my children deare,
    & euer I say godamercy !
& yett my blessing you shall haue,
84   whether-soeuer I liue or dye.   [page 258]

" but what sayst thou, thou ffrancis Nortton,
    mine eldest sonne & mine heyre trulye ?
some good councell, ffrancis Nortton,
88   this day thou giue to me."

He asks his eldest son, Francis,

for advice ;

" but 1 will giue you councell, ffather,
    if you will take councell att mee ;
for if you wold take my councell, father,
92   against the crowne you shold not bee."

and he answers

Don't go against the Crown.

" but ffye vpon thee, ffrancis Nortton !
    I say ffye vpon thee !
when thou was younge & tender of age
96   I made ffull much of thee."

Norton reproaches his son Francis,

" but your head is white, ffather," he sayes,
    " & your beard is wonderous gray ;
itt were shame ffor your countrye
100   if you shold rise & fflee away."

and calls him
a coward.

"but flye vpon thee, thou coward ffrancis!
thou neuer tookest *that* of mee!
when thou was younge & tender of age

104   I made too much of thee."

Francis
offers to go
vnarmed,
but invokes
death on
traitors,

"but I will goe with you, father," Quoth hee;
"like a Naked man will I bee;
he *that* strikes the first stroake against the
crowne,

108   an ill death may hee dye!"

Norton and
his men join
the Earls

but then rose vpp *Master* Nortton *that* Esq*uier*,
with him a ffull great companye;
& then the Erles they comen downe

112   to ryde in his companye.

at Wether-
by;

they have
13,000 men.

att whethersbye thé mustered their men
vpon a ffull fayre day;
13000 there were scene

116   to stand in battel ray.[1]

Westmore-
land's
standard is
the Dun
Bull.

the Erle of westmoreland, he had in his ancyent[2]
the DUNE bull in sight most hye,
& 3 doggs with golden collers

120   were sett out royallye.

Northum-
berland's the
half-moon.

the Erle of Northumberland, he had in his
ancyent[3]
the halfe moone in sight soe hye,
as the Lo*rd* was crucifyed on the crosse,

124   & sett forthe pleasantlye.

---

[1] array.—P.
[2] Ensign, standard. See vol. i. p. 304,
for the Dun Bull. That of Nevill
(Chevet, Co. York: granted 1513), is "A
greyhound's head erased or, charged on
the neck with a label of three points,
vert, between as many pellets, one and
two." The crest of Nevill (Ireland), is a
greyhound's head, erased argent, collared

gules, charged with a harp or. *Burke's
Armorie.*—F.

[3] Burke gives the Percy (Duke of
Northumberland) badge as 'A crescent
argent within the horns, per pale, sable
and gules, charged with a double
manacle, fesseways or.' *Armorie,* 1847.
—F.

    & after them did rise good Sir George Bowes,[1]
       after them a spoyle to make ;
    the Erles returned backe againe,
128   thought euer *that* Knight to take.

> Sir G. Bowes rises behind them.
>
> They turn back,

    this Barron did take a Castle then,
       was made of lime & stone ;
    the vttermost walls were ese to be woon ;
132   the Erles haue woon them anon ;

> take the outer walls of his castle

    but tho they woone the vttermost walls
       quickly and anon,
    the innermust[2] walles thé cold not winn,
136   thé were made of a rocke of stone.

> but can't win the inner.

    but newes itt came to leene London
       in all they speede *that* euer might bee ;
    & word it came to our royall Queene
140   of all the rebells in the North countrye.

> News of the rebellion reaches London.

    shee turned her grace then once about,
       & like a royall Queene shee sware,[3]
    sayes, "I will ordaine them such a breake-fast
144   as was not in the North this 1000 yeere!"

> Elizabeth swears she'll give the rebels a breakfast they won't stomach.

    shee caused 30000 men to be made
       with horsse and harneis all quicklye ;
    & shee caused 30000 men to be made
148   to take the rebells in the North countrye.

> She sends 30,000 men
>
> against them

    they tooke with them the false Erle of Warwicke,
       soe did they many[4] another man ;
    vntill they came to yorke Castle,
152   I-wis they neuer stinted nor blan.

> under Lord Warwick.
>
> They march to York,

---

[1] Bowes.—P.
[2] inermust in MS.—P.
[3] This is quite in character : her majesty would sometimes swear at her nobles, as well as box their ears. *Reliques,* i. 255.—F.
[4] Only half the *n* in the MS.—F.

[page 259]

but West-
moreland,

Northum-
berland,

and Norton
flee like
cowards.

"spread thy ancyent, Erle of Westmoreland!
    The halfe moone flaine wold wee see!"
but the halfe moone is fled & gone,
156   & the Dun bull vanished awaye;
& ffrancis Nortton & his 8 sonnes
    are flled away most cowardlye.

Ladds with mony are counted men,
160   men without mony are counted none;
but hold your tounge! why say you soe?
men wilbe men when mony is gone.

                           ffins.

𝕹𝖔𝖗𝖙𝖍𝖚𝖒𝖇𝖊𝖗𝖑𝖆𝖓𝖉 : 𝕭𝖊𝖙𝖗𝖆𝖞𝖉 𝖇𝖞 : 𝕯𝖔𝖜𝖌𝖑𝖆𝖘.[1]

[A Sequel to *the* preceding.—P.]

THIS ballad is printed in the *Reliques* (from another copy) and elsewhere.

After the dispersion of their forces, the rebel Earls of Westmoreland and Northumberland sought refuge in the Borders. See Introduction to *Earl of Westmoreland*, vol. i. p. 294. Neville found his trust in the Borderers justified; but Percy was betrayed to the Regent Moray by Hector Graham (not Armstrong, as the ballad, v. 209, calls him) of Harlaw; whose name became thenceforward infamous, to take *Hector's cloke* becoming a proverbial phrase for betraying a friend. Moray's successor, the Earl of Morton, who during his exile in England has received many kindnesses from Northumberland, "sold his unhappy prisoner to Elizabeth," in May 1572. He delivered him up to Lord Hunsdon, governor of Berwick, who sent him to York, where he was executed.

The extradition of the refugee by Morton gave as deep dissatisfaction to the country at large as his betrayal by Hector of Harlaw did to the Borderers. Many furious ballads made their appearance, as —'Ane exclamation maid in England upone the delyverance of the Erle of Northumberlan furth of Lochlevin, quho immediattlie thairefter was execute in Yorke, 1572 '--the answer to the English ballad, 'Ane schort inveccyde maid aganis the delyverance of the Erle of Northumberland.' The present

---

[1] Whose Sister being an enchantress would have saved him, from her Brother's treachery.—P.

This song seems unfinished.—P.

N.B. My other Copy is more correct than this, and contains much which is omitted here.—P.

N.B. The other Copy begins with Lines the same as that in pag. 112. [*Earle of Westmorelande* i. 300.] The minstrels often made such Changes. —Pencil note.

ballad so far recognises this national feeling as to introduce a
Scotch woman using her utmost endeavours to preserve the Earl,
from the snare laid for him. Mary Douglas[1] represents Scotia.
But the Earl will not listen. He goes away with her brother,
his keeper, to be the victim of a second betrayal, which was
finally to conduct him to the scaffold at York.

I'll tell you
how Douglas
betrayed
banished
Percy.

NOW list & lithe you gentlemen,
   & Ist tell you the veretye,
how they haue delt with a banished man,
4   driuen out of his countrye.

when as hee came on Scottish ground,
   as woe & wonder be them amonge,
ffull much was there traitorye
8   thé wrought the Erle of Northumberland.

At supper

when they were att the supper sett,
   beffore many goodly gentlemen

they ask
Percy

thé ffell a flouting & Mocking both,
12   & said to the Erle of Northumberland,

"what makes you be soe sad, my Lord,
   & in your mind soe sorrowffullye ?

to go to a
shooting in
Scotland.

in the North of Scottland to-morrow theres a shooting,
16   & thither thoust goe, my Lord Percye.

"the buttes are sett, & the shooting is made,
   & there is like to be great royaltye,
& I am sworne into my bill
20   thither to bring my Lord Pearcy."

[1] " The interposal of the WITCH-LADY
[1. 26, here] is probably his [the northern
bard's] own invention; yet even this
hath some countenance from history; for
about 25 years before, the Lady Jane
Douglas, Lady Glamis, sister of the earl
of Angus and nearly related to Douglas
of Loughleven, had suffered death for the
pretended crime of witchcraft ; who, it is
presumed, is the lady alluded to in verse "
[101 here]. Reliques, i. 258.—F.

" Ile giue thee my Land,[1] Douglas," he sayes,
    & be the faith in my bodye,
if *that* thou wilt ryde to the worlds end,
24   Ile ryde in thy companye."

Percy pro-
mises to go
with
Douglas.

& then bespake the good Ladye,—
    Marry a Douglas was her name,—
" you shall byde here, good English Lo*r*[7];
28   my brother is a traiterous man ;

Mary
Douglas

warns Percy
that her
brother is a
traitor

" he is a traitor stout & stronge,
    as Ist[2] tell you the veretye,
for he hath tane liuerance of the Erle,[3]
32   & into England he will liuor thee."

and will give
him up to
the English.

" now hold thy tounge, thou goodlye Ladye,
    & let all this talking bee ;
ffor all the gold *that*s in Long Leuen,[4]
36   william wold not Liuor moe !

Percy de-
clares that
he trusts
Douglas.

" it wold breake truce betweene England & Scottland,
    & freinds againe they wold neuer bee
if he shold liuor a bani[s]ht[5] Erle
40   was driuen out of his owne countrye."

" hold your tounge, my Lo*rd*," shee sayes,
    " there is much ffalsehood them amonge ;
when you are dead, then they are done,
44   soone they will part them freinds againe.

Mary
Douglas

" if you will giue me any trust, my Lord,
    Ile tell you how you best may bee ;
youst lett my brother ryde his wayes,
48   & tell those English Lords trulye

advises
Percy

to let
Douglas go
alone,

---

[1] hand. *Reliques.*—F.
[2] I'll. See note 4, p. 20, vol. i. —F.
[3] pay "of the earl of Morton:" James
Douglas, Earl of Morton, elected regent
of Scotland, Nov. 24, 1572. *Re'*. vol. i.
p. 251, 259.—F.
[4] Lough Leven.—P.
[5] banisht. —P.

" how *that* you cannot with them ryde
    because you are in an Ile of the sea[1] ;

and then
she'll see
him safe
then, ere my Brother come againe,

52   to Edenborrow castle[2] Ile carry thee,

Into Lord
Hume's
hands.
" Ile liuer you vnto the Lord HVME,
    & you know a trew Scotho Lord is hee,

for he hath lost both Land & goods

56   in ayding of *your* good bodye."

Percy says
that no
friend shall
suffer for
him again,
" marry ! I am woe ! woman," he sayes,
    " *that* any freind fares worse for mee ;

for where one saith ' it is a true tale,'

60   then 2 will say it is a Lye.

his old ad-
herents have
" when I was att home in my [realme,][3]   [page 260]
    amonge my tennants all trulye,

in my time of losse, wherin my need stoode,

64   they came to ayd me honestlye ;

suffered
enough.
" therfore I left many a child fatherlese,
    & many a widdow to looke wanne ;

& therfore blame nothing, Ladye,

68   but the woefull warres w*hi*ch I began."

Mary
Dowglas
offers to
prove her
words.
" If you will giue me noe trust, my Lo*r*d,
    nor noe credence you will give mee,

& youle come hither to my right hand,

72   indeed, my Lord,[4] Ile lett you see."

Percy will
have nothing
to do with
her witch-
craft.
saies, " I neuer loued noe witchcraft,
    nor neu*er* dealt w*i*th treacherye,

but euermore held the hye way ;

76   alas ! *tha*t may be scene by mee ! "

---

[1] *i.e.* Lake of Leven, which hath communication with the sea.—*Rl.* i. 261.
[2] At that time in the hands of the
opposite faction.--*Rl.*

[3] This line is partly pared away.—F.
[4] ? MS. Lorid, or Loue*r*d ; or Lord,
with one stroke too many.—F.

"if you will not come your selfe, my Lord,
   youle lett your chamberlaine goe with mee,
3 words *that* I may to him speake,
80   & soone he shall come againe to thee."

Mary Douglas shows the chamberlain

when Iames Swynard came *that* Lady before,
   shee let him see thorrow the weme [1] of her ring
how many there was of English lords
84   to wayte there for his *Master* and him.

through her ring the oliers in wait for Percy:

"but who beene yonder, my [2] good Ladye,
   that walkes soe royallye on yonder greene?"
"yonder is Lord Hunsden,[3] Iamye," she saye;
88   "alas! heele doe you both tree [4] & teene!"

Lord Huns-den,

"& who beene yonder, thou gay Ladye,
   that walkes soe royallye him beside?"
"yond is Sir william Drurye,[5] Iamy," shee sayd,
92   "& a keene Captain hee is, and tryde."

and Sir Wm. Drurye,

"how many miles is itt, thou good Ladye,
   betwixt yond English Lord and mee?"
"marry, 3 : 50 mile, Iamy," shee sayd,
96   "& euen to seale [6] & by the sea:

(150 miles off,

"I neuer was on English ground,
   nor neuer see itt with mine eye,
but as my witt & wisedome serues,
100   and as [the] booke it telleth mee.

"my mother, shee was a witch woman,
   and part of itt shee learned mee;
shee wold let me see out of Lough Leuen
104   what they dyd in London Cytye."

as her mother's witchcraft tells her.)

---

[1] weme, the Scottish word for the belly, i. e. womb.—P.
[2] ny in MS.—F.
[3] The Lord Warden of the East Marches.—*Rel.* i. 263.
[4] dre, dree, to suffer, endure.—P.
[5] Governor of Berwick.—*Rel.* i. 264.
[6] saile.—P.

" but who is yond, thou good Layde,
that comes yonder with an Osterne [1] ffacc ? "
" yonds Sir Iohn fforster,[2] Iamyc," shee sayd ;
108 " methinkes thou sholdest better know him
then I."
" Euen soe I doe, my goodlye Ladye,
& euer alas, soe woe am I ! "

he pulled his hatt ouer his eyes,
112 &, lord, he wept soe tenderlye !
he is gone to his *Master* againe,
& euen to tell him the veretye.

" Now hast thou beene with Marry, Iamy," he sayd,
116 " Euen as thy tounge will tell to mee;
but if thou trust in any womans words,
thou must refraine good companye."

has shown
him the
English
Lords wait-
ing to take
him,

" It is noe words, my Lord," he sayes,
120 " yonder the men shee letts me see,
how many English Lords there is
is wayting there for you & mee ;

" yonder I see the Lord Hunsden,
124 & hee & you is of the 3ᵈ. degree ;
a greater enemye, indeed, my Lord,
in England none haue yee,"

Percy says
that he's
been three
years in jail,

" & I haue beene in Lough Leven
128 the most part of these yeeres 3 :
yett had I neuer noe out-rake,[3]
nor good games *that* I cold see ;

---

[1] Austerne, austere, fierce. L. austerus.
Gloss. ad G.D.—P.
[2] Warden of the Middle March.—*Rel.*
i. 264.
[3] *rake raik*, ambulare, expatiari. As
Isl. *reika. Raik* gradus citatus, a long
raik, Iter longum, to *raik* home, ac-
celerato gradu domum abire; hinc a
Rake, homo dissolutus ; an *out-raik*, a
Riot, at large. Lye. See G.D. 224. 39.
P.

"& I am thus bidden to yonder shooting
132 by william Douglas all trulye;
therfore speake neuer a word out of thy mouth
That thou thinkes will hinder mee.[1] [page 261]

and he will go to the shooting with Douglas.

then he writhe the gold ring of his ffingar[2]
136 & gaue itt to *that* Ladye gay;
sayes, "*that* was a legacye left vnto mee
in Harley woods where I cold[3] bee."

He gives Mary a gold ring.

"then ffarewell hart, & farewell hand,
140 and ffarwell all good companye!
that woman shall neuer beare a sonne
shall know soe much of *your* priuitye."

She laments over him.

"now hold thy tounge, Ladye," hee sayde,
144 "& make not all this dole for mee,
for I may well drinke, but Ist neuer eate,
till againe in Lough Leuen I bee."

He says he shall soon be back,

he tooke his boate att the Lough Leuen
148 for to sayle now ouer the sea,
& he hath cast vpp a siluer wand,
saies "fare thou well, my good Ladye!"
the Ladye looked ouer her left sholder;
152 in a dead swoone there fell shee.

and gets into the boat to sail away.

Mary Dougl swoons.

"goe backe againe, Douglas!" he sayd,
"& I will goe in thy companye,
for sudden sicknesse yonder Lady has tane,
156 and euer, alas, shee will but dye!"

Percy asks her brother to return,

as she will die.

[1] Part cut away by the binder.—F.
Percy gives the verse as:
Therefore I'll to yond shooting wend,
As to the Douglas I have hight:
Betide me weale, betide me woe,
He ne'er shall find my promise light.
[2] A.-S. *wriðan* to twist: perf. *wráð* twisted.—F.
[3] did.—F.

"if ought come to yonder Ladye but good,
 then blamed fore *that* I shall bee,
 because a banished man I am,
160 & drinen out of my owne countrye."

Douglas
refuses ;

"come on, come on, my Lord," he sayes,
 "& lett all such talking bee ;

the ladies can
look after his
sister.

theres Ladyes enow in Lough Leuen,
164 & for to cheere yonder gay Ladye."

Percy a:ks
that his
Chamberlain
may go back
with him.

"& you will not goe your selfe, my lord,
 you will lett my chamberlaine goe w*i*th mee ;
wee shall now take our boate againe,
168 & soone wee shall one*r*take thee."

Douglas says

"come on, come on, my Lord," he sayes,
 "& lett now all this talking bee !

it's only his
sister's
tricks.

ffor my sister is craftye enoughe
172 for to beguile thousands such as you & mee."

They sail 50
miles ;

When they had sayled [1] 50 : myle,
 now 50 mile vpon the sea,
hee had fforgotten a message *that* hee
176 shold doe in lough Leuen trulye :

the Cham-
berlain asks
how far it is
to the
shooting.

hee asked 'how ffarr it was to *that* shooting.
 that w*illi*am Douglas promised mee.'

Douglas
says

now faire words makes fooles faine [2] ;
180 & *that* may be scene by thy Ma*ster* & thee ;

he'll never
see it.

ffor you may happen think [3] itt soone enoughe
 when-ener you *that* shooting see."

---

[1] There is no navigable stream between Lough-leven and the sea: but a ballad-maker is not obliged to understand Geography.— *Rel.* i. 266.

[2] *Belle promesse fol lie*: Prov. Faire promises oblige the fool ; or, are noe better than fopperies ; (for the words *fol lie* equivocate vnto *folie*.) *Douces promesses obligent les fols* : Prov. Faire promises oblige fools ; or, (as our) faire words make fools faine.—F.

[3] A Lancashire phrase.—F.

Iamye pulled his hatt now oucr his browe;   Jamie
184 I wott the teares fell in his eye;
  & he is to his *Master* againe,
  & ffor to tell him the veretye:

"he sayes, fayre words makes fooles faine,   tells Percy Douglas's words.
188 & *that* may be seene by you and mee,
  ffor wee may happen thinke itt soone enoughe
  when-euer wee *that* shooting see."

"hold vpp thy head, Iamye," the Erle sayd,   Percy says Douglas
192 & neuer lett thy hart fayle thee;
  he did itt but to proue thee w*ith*,   was only trying his courage.
  & see how thow wold take w*ith* death trulye."

when they had sayled other 50 mile,   After 100 miles' sail,
196 other 50 mile vpon the sea,
  Lo*rd* Peerey called to him, himselfe,   Percy asks Douglas what he'll do with him.
  & sayd, "Douglas what wilt thou doe w*ith*
    mee?"

"looke *that* your brydle be wight, my Lord,   Douglas tells him to have his bridle and spurs ready.
200 *that* you may goe as a shipp att sea;
  looke *that* your spurres be bright & sharpe,
  that you may pricke her while sheele awaye."

"what needeth this, Douglas," he sayth.   Percy asks "why this mockery?"
204 "*that* thou needest to ffloute mee?
  for I was counted a horsseman good
  before *that* euer I mett w*ith* thee.

"A ffalse Hector hath my horsse;   [page 262]   My horse and spurs are in others' hands."
208 & eu*er* an euill death may hee dye!
  & willye Armestronge hath my spurres
  & all the geere belongs to mee."

After 150
miles' sail,

212

Percy is
landed and
betrayed on
English soil.

when thé had sayled other 50 mile,

other 50 mile vpon the sea,

thé landed low by Barwicke side ;

a deputed land [1] Landed Lord Percye.

ffin[s [2]].

---

[1] So in MS. Percy prints 'The
Douglas' in *Rel.* i. 268, and winds up
with an added stanza:

Then he at Yorke was doomde to dye,

It was, alas! a sorrowful sight :
Thus they betrayed that noble earle,
Who ever was a gallant wight.—F.

[2] *s* pared off by the binder.—F.

Guye : of : Gisborne : [1]

[The fight between him and Robin Hood.—P.]

THIS ballad was printed from the Folio in the *Reliques*, and from the *Reliques* by Ritson, Child, and others.

"As for Guy of Gisborne," says Ritson, "the only further memorial which has occurred concerning him is in an old satirical piece by William Dunbar, a celebrated Scottish poet of the fifteenth century, on one Schir Thomas Nory (MS. Maitland, p. 3, MMS. More (l. 5. 10) where he is named along with our hero, Adam Bell, and other worthies, it is conjectured of a similar stamp, but whose merits have not, less fortunately, come to the knowledge of posterity.

> Was nevir Weild Robeine under bewch,
> Nor yitt Roger of Clekkinslowch
> So bauld a bairne as he ;
> Gy of Gisborne, na Allane Bell,
> Na Simones Sones of Qutrynsell
> Off thocht war nevir slie.

Gisborne is a market town in the west riding of the county of York, on the borders of Lancashire.

WHEN shales beene sheene, & shradds [2] full fayre,
   & leeues both Large & longe,
itt is merry walking in the fayre fforrest
4   to heare the small birds singe.[3]

It is merry to walk in the forest in spring.

---

[1] A very curious Old Song, much more ancient and perfect than the common printed Ballads of Robin Hood.— P.
[2] *Shale*, a husk. The *shales* or stalkes of hempe. Hollyband's *Diction-*ary, 1593, Halliwell. *Shradd* is a twig, either from "shred, to cut off the smaller branches of a tree," or "*schrags*, the clippings of live fences." Halliwell.— F.
[3] songe.—P.

the woodweete sang & wold not cease
amongst the leaues a lyne ; [1]
[*   *   *   *   *   *]

Robin Hood dreams that two yeomen 8

" [2]& it is by 2 [3] wight yeomen,
    by deare god *that* I meane :

beat him.

" me thought they did mee beate & binde,
    & tooke my bow mee froe :

He vows revenge on them, 12

If I bee Robin a-liue in this Lande,
    Ile be wroeken on both them towe."

" sweenens [4] are swift, *Master*," quoth Iohn,
    " as the wind *that* blowes ore a hill ;
ffor if itt be neuer soe lowde this night,

and orders his men to go with him. 16

to-morrow it may be still."

" buske [5] yee, bowne yee, my merry men all !
    ffor Iohn shall goe with mee ;
for Ile goe seeke yond wight yeomen

20

in greenwood where thé bee."

They all start,

thé cast [6] on their gowne of greene ; [7]
    a shooting gone are they
vntill they came to the Merry greenwood

24

where they had gladdest bee ;

and soon see one yeoman,

there were thé ware of [a] wight yeoman ;
    his body Leaned to a tree,

---

[1] of lime: I would read 'so greene.'—P.

[2] As the lines that follow are part of a Speech of Robin hood relating a dream: there are certainly some lines wanting and we can no where better fix the *hiatus* than between the 2d & 3d lines of st. 2d. N.B. In my printed Copy of this song in *the* Reliques, &c., Vol. I. I took the Liberty to fill up some of these *Lacunæ*, &c., from Conjecture, &c.—P.

Percy also alters lines 6 7 and 8 : his verses in the 1st edition are—

The woodweete sang, and wold not cese,
Sitting upon the sprayo,

Soe lowde, he wakend Robin Hood
  In the greenwood where he lay.
Now by faye, said jollye Robin,
  A sweaven I had this night ;
I dreamt me of tow mighty yemen
  That fast with me can fight.—F.

[3] of 2.—P.

[4] i. e. dreams.—P.

[5] i. e. get you ready.—P.

[6] *then* inserted by Percy.—F.

[7] Two lines wanting at *the* beginning of this St., if these 2 lines are not rather to be added to the next St.—P.

a sword & a dagger he wore by his side,
28   had beene many a mans bane,[1]
& he was cladd in his Capull [2] hyde,
    topp, & tayle, and mayne.

clad in a horse's hide.

"stand you still, *Master*," quoth litle Iohn,
32   " vnder this trusty tree,
& I will goe to yond wight yeoman
    to know his meaning trulye."

Little John tells Robin to stop while he asks who the man is.

"a, Iohn![3] by me thou setts noe store,
36   & *that*s a ffarley [4] thinge ;
how offt send I my men beffore,
    & tarry my-selfe behinde ?[5]

Robin Head is angry at John's wanting to keep him back,

" it is noe cunning a knaue to ken,
40   & a man but heare him speake ;
& itt were not for bursting of my bowe,
    Iohn, I wold thy head breake."

and threatens to break Little John's head.

but often words they breeden ball ;[6]
44   *that* parted Robin and Iohn ;
Iohn is gone to Barnsdale,
    the gates[7] he knowes eche one.

This parts them, and

Little John goes to Barnsdale,

& when hee came to Barnesdale,
48   great heauinesse there hee hadd ;
he ffound 2 of his own fellowes
    were slaine both in a slade,[8]

where he finds two mates slain,

& Scarlett a ffoote flyinge was
52   ouer stockes and stone,
for the sheriffe with 7 score men
    fast after him is gone.

and Scarlett flying

from the Sheriff.

[1] Of many a man tho bane.—P.
[2] Horse.—P.
[3] Ah ! John.—P.
[4] wonderous. Lye.—P.
[5] mean*ing* that he never did so.—P.
[6] bale.— P.
[7] passes, paths, ridings.—P. *in Red.*
[8] i. e., a parting between 2 Woods.—P.

56
"yett one shoote Ile shoote," sayes Litle Iohn ;
        " with crist his might & Mayne
    Ile make yond fellow *that* flyes soe fast
        to be both glad & ffaine.

Iohn bent vp a good veiwe [1] bow,[2]   [page 203]
60   & ffetteled [3] him to shoote :
    the bow was made of a tender boughe,
        & fell downe to his footee.[4]

"woe worth thee, wicked wood ! " sayd litle Iohn,
64   " *that* ere thou grew on a tree !
    ffor [5] this day thou art my bale,
        my boote when thou shold bee ! "

68
this shoote it was but looselye shott,
        the arrowe flew in vaine,
    & [6] it mett one of the Sheriffes men :
        good *william* a Trent was slaine.

72
it had beene better [7] for a *william* Trent
        to hange vpon a gallowe
    then for to lye in the greenwoode
        there slaine with an arrowe.[8]

& it is sayd, when men be mett,
76   6 [9] can doe more then 3 :
    & they haue tane [10] litle Iohn,
        & bound him ffast to a tree.

[1] Query MS : the word is partly pared away.— F.

[2] John bent up a good yew bow.—P.

[3] prepared, addressed him, verbum Salopiense.— P.

[4] foote.— P.

[5] ffor now.—P.

[6] or Yet.—P.

[7] as good.— P.

[8] Altered in the *Reliques*, 1st ed. i. 81, to

To have been abed with sorrowe,
Than to be that day in the green wood slade
To meet with Little Johns arrowe.—F.

[9] Fyve.—*Rd.*

[10] insert now.—P.

"thou shalt be drawen by dale and downe," quoth
the sheriffe,[1]

80 "& hanged hye on a hill."
"but thou may ffayle," quoth litle Iohn,
"if itt be christs owne will."

and the Sheriff vows he shall be hanged.

"Don't be too sure," says Little John.

let vs leaue talking of Litle Iohn,
84 for hee is bound fast to a tree,
& talke of Guy & Robin hood
in they [2] green woode where they bee ;

Let us turn to Guy and Robin.

how these 2 yeomen together they mett
88 vnder the leaues of Lyne,[3]
to see what Marchandise they made
euen at that same time.

"good morrow, good fellow !" quoth Sir Guy ;
92 "good morrow, good ffellow !" quoth hee ;
"methinkes by this bow thou beares in thy hand,
a good archer [4] thou seems to bee.[5]

Guy greets Robin

"I am wilfull [6] of my way," quoth Sir Guye,
96 "& of my morning tyde."
"Ile lead thee through the wood," quoth Robin,
"good ffellow, Ile be thy guide."

"I seeke an outlaw," quoth Sir Guye,
100 "men call him Robin Hood ;
I had rather meet with him vpon a day [7]
then 40 li of golde."

and tells him he seeks an outlaw, Robin Hood.

---

[1] These three words seem added by some explainer.—P.
[2] the.—P.
[3] perhaps Lime; tho' Line or Lyne is more common in these old ballads.—P.
[4] An e has been added at the end.—F.
[5] shouldest bee.—P.
[6] probably the same as "wilsome," page 357 [of MS.] st. 6.—P.
[7] this day.—P.

Robin pro-
poses some
sport.

" if you tow mett, itt wold be seene whether were
104   better
aforc yee did part awaye ;
let vs some other pastime find,
good ffellow, I thee pray.[1]

No doubt, as
they go on,
they'll meet
Robin Hood.

" let vs some other masteryes make,
108   & wee will walke in the woods euen,
wee may chance [2] mee[t] with Robin Hoode
att some vnsett steven." [3]

they cutt them downe the [4] summer shroggs [5]
112   which grew both vnder a Bryar, [6]

They make
pricks ready
to shoot at.

& sett them 3 score rood in twinn [7]
to shoote the prickes full neare. [8]

" leade on, good ffellow," sayd Sir Guye,
116   " lead [9] on, I doe bidd thee."
" nay, by my faith," quoth Robin Hood,
" the leader thou shalt bee."

[1] Percy alters this in his *Reliques*, i.
81, 1st ed., to
Now come with me, thou wighty yeman,
    And Robin thou soon shalt see:
But first let us some pastime find
    Under the greenwood tree.
[2] to.—P.
[3] See page 358, st. 16.—P. unfixed,
unexpected moment. There is a stroke
before the *v* of *steven* in the MS.—F.
[4] two.—Rel.
[5] *scrog*, a stunted shrub: Jamieson.
—F.
[6] pronounced Breer in some parts of
England.— P. *Bryor* is entered in
Levin's, 1570, under the words in *eare*.
[7] apart.—F.
[8] y-fere.—Rel. Threescore roods or
330 yards must have been a long range.
The *Pricke-wandes* were, I suppose,
willow wands or long thin branches stuck
in the ground to shoot at. *Prickes* seem

to have been the long-range targets,
butts the near.
Moll. Out upon him, what a suiter
have I got; I am sorry you are so bad
an Archer, sir.
Eare. Why Bird, why Bird?
Moll. Why, to shoote at *Buts*, when
you shou'd use *prick-shafts*, short-shoot-
ing vvill loose ye the game, I us[sure]
you, sir.
Eare. Her minde runnes sure upon
a *Fletcher*, or a *Bowyer*, ...
1633, Rowley. *A Match at Midnight*,
Act ii. sc. 1.

" Modern prick shooting is practised by
the Royal Archers at Edinburgh, and
is their favourite, at a small round target
fixed at 180 yards," says Mr. Peter Muir,
their Bowmaker. See my note on *pricks*
in *The Babees Boke &c.* 1868, p. ci.—F.
[9] *i. e.* begin to shoote.—P.

the first good shoot *that* Robin ledd,

120   did not shoote an inch the pricke [1] ffroc.

Guy was an archer good enoughe,

but he cold neere shoote soe.

the 2[d] shoote [2] S*i*r Guy shott,

124   he shott w*i*thin the garlande ;

but Robin hoode shott it better then hee,

for he cloue the good pricke wande.

" gods blessing on thy heart ! " sayes Guye,

128   " goode ffellow, thy shooting is goode ;

for on [3] thy hart be as good as thy hands,   [page 264]

thou were better then Robin Hood.

" tell me thy name, good ffellow," qu*o*th Guy,

132   " vnder the leaues of Lyne."

" nay, by my faith," qu*o*th good Robin,

" till thou haue told me thine."

" I dwell by dale & downe," qu*o*th Guye,

136   " & I haue done many a curst turne ;

& he *that* calles me by my right name,

calles me Guye of good Gysborne."

" my dwelling is in the wood," sayes Robin ;

140   " by thee I set right nought ;

my name is Robin Hood of Barnesdale,

a ffellow thou has long sought."

he *that* had neither beene a [4] kithe nor kin [5]

144   might haue seene a full fayre sight,

to see how together these yeomen went

w*i*th blades both browne & bright ;

---

[1] was not an Inch the prick.—P.   [4] *a* delend.—P.
[2] *that* inserted by P. —F.   [5] neither acquaintance nor relation.
[3] an, or and.—P.   —P.

to haue scene how these yeomen together foug[ht]
148 2 howers of a summers day :

itt was neither Guy nor Robin hood
 that ffettled them to flye away.

Robin was reacheles [1] on a roote,
152 & stumbled [2] at *that* tyde ;
& Guy was quicke & nimble w*i*th-all,
 & hitt him ore the left side.

"ah, deere Lady ! " sayd Robin hoode,
156 "thou art both Mother & may !
I thinke it was neu*er* mans destinye
to dye before his day."

Robin thought on our Lady deere,

160 & soone leapt vp againe ;
& thus he came w*i*th an awkwarde [3] stroke ;

good S*i*r Guy hee has slayne.

he tooke S*i*r Guys head by the hayre,
164 & sticked itt on his bowes end ;
"thou hast beene traytor all thy liffe,
w*h*ich thing must haue an ende."

Robin pulled forth an Irish kniffe,

168 & nicked S*i*r Guy in the fface,
that hee was neuer on [4] a woman borne
cold tell who S*i*r Guye was :

saies, "lye there, lye there, good S*i*r Guye,
172 & w*i*th me be not wrothe ;
if thou haue had the worse stroakes at my hand,
thou shalt haue the better cloathe."

·

---

[1] i.e. careless.--P.   [3] perhaps backward.—P.
[2] he stumbled.—P.   [4] of woman.—P.

Robin did on [1] his gowne of greene,
176   [on] Sir Guye [2] hee did it throwe ;
& hee put on *that* Capull hyde
   that cladd him topp [3] to toe.

"the [4] bowe, the [4] arrowes, & litle horne,
180   & [5] with me now Ile beare ;
ffor now I will goe to Barnsdale,
   to see how my men doe ffare."

Robin sett Guyes horne to his mouth ;
184   a lowd blast in it he did blow.
that beheard the Sheriffe of Nottingham
   as he leaned vnder a lowe [6] ;

"hearken ! hearken !" sayd the Sheriffe,
188   "I heard noe tydings but good ;
for yonder I heare Sir Guyes horne blowe,
   for he hath slaine Robin hoode :

"for yonder I heare Sir Guyes horne blow,
192   itt blowes soe well in tyde,
for yonder comes *that* wighty yeoman
   cladd in his capull hyde.

"come hither,[7] thou good Sir Guy !
196   aske of mee what thou wilt haue !"
"Ile none of thy gold," sayes Robin hood,
   nor Ile none of itt haue [8] ;

"but now I haue slaine the Master," he sayd, [page 265]
200   let me goe strike the knaue ;
this is all the reward I aske,
   nor noe other will I haue."

Margin notes:
throws his own green coat on the corpse, puts on Sir Guy's horse-hide,

and takes his horn,

and blows it.

The Sheriff hears it,

thinks Guy has slain Robin Hood,

and promises him whatever reward he asks. Robin asks

leave to kill Little John.

---

[1] off.—P.
[2] On Sir Guy.—P.
[3] from topp.—P.
[4] thy.—*Rel.*
[5] *and* defend.—P.
[6] perhaps bowe.—P. hill, A.-S. *hlœw.*

[7] come hither [repeated].—P.
[8] Perhaps
None of it I will have
   or
Nor nothing else Ill have.—P.

> " thou art a Madman," said the shiriffe,

> " thou sholdest haue had a knights ffee.

> seeing thy asking beene [1] soe badd,
>
> well granted it shall be."

Little John
knows
Robin's
voice,
and thinks
he shall be
freed.
> but litle Iohn heard his *Master* speake,

> well he knew *that* was his steuen [2];
>
> " now shall I be loset, [3]" quoth litle Iohn,
>
> " with Christs might in heauen."

> but Robin hee hyed him towards Litle Iohn ;

> hee thought hee wold loose him beliue.

> the Sheriffe & all his companye
>
> fast after him did driue.

> " stand abacke ! stand abacke ! " sayd Robin ;

> " why draw you mee soe neere ?
>
> itt was neuer the vse in our countrye
>
> ones shrift [4] another shold heere."

> but Robin pulled forth an Irysh kniffee,

> & losed Iohn hand & ffoote,
>
> & gaue him Sir Guyes bow in his hand,
>
> & bade it be his boote.

> [5] but Iohn tooke Guyes bow in his hand,

> his arrowes were rawstye by the roote ;
>
> the Sherriffe saw litle Iohn draw a bow
>
> & ffettle him to shoote ;

[1] hath been.—P.
[2] i. e. voice.—P.
[3] loosed. P.
[4] i. e. confession.—P.
[5] Then John he took Guyes bowe in his
        hand.

His boltes and arrowes echo one :
When the sheriffe saw Little John bend
        his bow.
He fettled him to be gone. —Rel.
? is *rawstye*, l. 224, rusty. *Rawly* is
rude ; unskilful. Halliwell.—F.

towards his house in Nottingam
228   he flled full fast away,—
& soo did all his companye,
not one behind did stay,—

The Sheriff
take- to
flight,

but he cold neither soo fast goe,
232   nor away soo fast runn,[1]
but litle Iohn with an arrow broade
did cleaue his heart in twinn.[2]

but can't get
away from
Little John's
arrow,
which
cleaves his
heart.

ffins.

---

[1] ryde.—*Rel.*
[2] He shott him into the 'backe'-syde.—*Rel.* Too bad, Bishop! And to put your inverted commas too, as if you'd only altered the one word 'backe.' —F.

Hereford & Norfolke.[1]

This ballad is to be found in Dryden's *Miscellany Poems*, in the 1727 *Collection of Old Ballads*, and elsewhere.

The subject is the well-known quarrel between the Earls of Hereford and Norfolk,[2] which finally resulted in their banishment in 1398. A full description of the Lists of Coventry (in September, not August) is given by Hall.[3] The ballad's account of the origin of the quarrel is not quite fair. Hereford accused Norfolk, not Norfolk Hereford, of treason. But the ballad goes with the winning side. Vox populi mostly shouts in favour of the successful. The cause pleases it that "pleases the gods."

The ballad is evidently written by a practised ballad-writer, some time about 1600 probably. But it may have been founded on some older one. The subject is not likely to have lain uncelebrated till late in Elizabeth's reign.

I sing the fall of two noble Dukes,

TOWE noble dukes of great renowne
    that long had liued in flame,
throng ffatall envye were cast downe
4   & brought to sudden bane :

Hereford

the Duke of Hereford was the one,
    a prudent prince & wise,
gainst whom such mallice there was showen,
8   w*hi*ch soone in fight did rise.

---

[1] In *the* printed Collection of old Ballads, 1727, Vol. i. p. 120. N. XV., and in Dryden's Misc. Vol. 5, 382.—P.

[2] See Shakspere's *Richard II.*—F.

[3] Hall's descriptions of armour and fashions before his time were his own fabrication, though adopted as genuine by Gough and Sharon Turner. *Planché, Hist. of Costume, p. 223.*—F.

the Duke of Norfolke most vntrue [1]   and Norfolk.
    declared to the King,   Norfolk de-
"the duke of Hereford greatly grew   nounces
12   in hatred of cche thinge   Hereford

which by his grace was acted still   to the King
    against both hye & lowe,
& how he had a traiterous will   as a traitor.
16   his state to ouerthrowe."

the Duke of Hereford then in hast   The King
    was sent for to the Kinge,   sends for
                                                           Hereford,
& by his lords in order placet   has him
20   examined in cche thinge ;   examined,

which being guiltelesse of *that* crime   and he is
    which was against him layd,   guiltless.
the duke of Norfolke at that time [2]   Norfolk
24   these words vnto him sayd :

"how canst thou with a shamelesse face   reproves him
    deny a truth soe stout,   for his
                                                           shamelesss-
& there before his royall grace   ness,
28   soe falselye faced itt out ?

"did not these treasons from thee passe   declares
    when wee together were,   [page 266]   Hereford has
                                                           talked
how *that* the King vnworthye was   treason,
32   the royall crowne to weare ?

"wherfore, my gracyous Lords," quoth hee,
    "& you, his Noble Peeres,
to whom I wish long liffe to bee,
36   with many happy yeeres,

" I doe pronounce before you all
    the duke of Hereford here,

a traytour to our Noble Kinge,
40   as time shall show itt clere."

the Duke of Herefford hearing *that*,
    in mind was greeved much,
& did returne this answer fllatt,
44   w*hich* did Duke Norfolke tuche ;

" the terme of Traytor, trothelesse Duke,
    in scorne & deepe disdaine,
with fllatt deffyance to thy face [1]
48   I doe returne againe !

" & therfore, if it please your grace
    to grant me grace," quoth hee,
" to combatt with my knowen ffoe
52   *that* hath accused mee,

" I doe not doubt but plainlye proue,
    that like a periured knight
hee hath most falslye sought my shame
56   against all truth & right."

the K*ing* did grant their iust request,
    & did therto agree,
att Couentry in August next
60   this combatt fought shold bee.

the Dukes in barbed steeds full stout,
    in coates of steele most bright,
with speares in brest did enter list,
64   the combatt feirce to flight

---

[1] There is a stroke between the *c* and *e* in the MS.—F.

the King then cast his warder downe,
  commanding them to stay ; but the King
stops the
combat,
& with his Lords some councell tooke
68 to stint *that* Mortall ffraye.

att lenght vnto the Noble Duke[s]
  the King of Heralds came, and a Herald
& vnto them with loftye speech
72 this sentence did proclaime : proclaims
his judg-
ment.

" with Henery Bullenbrooke this day,
  the Duke of Hereford here,
& Thomas Mawbray, Norfolkes Duke,
76 soe valyant did apeare,

" & haue in honourable sorte
  repayred to this place.
our noble King for specyall cause
80 hath altered thus the case :

" flirst, Henery Duke of Hereford, Hereford
  Ere 15 dayes were past
shall part this realme, on payne of death, is banished
for ten
years ;
84 while 10 yeeres space doth last.

" & Thomas, duke of Norfolke, thou Norfolk
  that hast begun this striffe,—
& therfore noe good prone can bring,
88 I say,—for terme of liffe, for life ;

" by iudgment of our soueraine Lord
  which now in place doth stand,
for eu[er] 'more I banish thee
92 out of thy Natiue Land,

" charging thee on payne of death, and both
must go in
fifteen days.
  when 15 dayes are past,
thou neuer treade on English ground
96 soe long as liffe doth last."

[page 267]

thus were they sworne before the King
ere they did further passe,

Each swears

the one shold neuer come in place
wheras the other was.

not to go
where the
other is.

100

then both the dukes with heainy hart
were parted presentlye,
the vncoth streames of froward chance
in forraine lands to trye.

104

the duke of Norfolke cominge then
where [he] shold shipping take,
the bitter teares fell from his cheekes,
& thus his moane did make :

Norfolk,
before
sailing off,

laments his
lot.

108

"now let me sob & sigh my fill
ere I from hence depart,
that inward panges with speed may burst
my sore afflicted hart !

" May grief
burst my
heart !

112

"accursed man, whose lothed liffe
is held soe much in scorne,
whose companye ¹ is cleane despised,
& left as one forlorne,

116

"Now take thy leaue & last adew
of this thy country deare,
w*h*ich neuer more thou must behold,
nor yett approache itt neere !

I bid adieu
to my loved
land.

120

"how happy shold I count my selfe,
if death my hart had torne,
that I might haue my bones entombed
where I was bredd and borne ;

Would I were
dead, that I
might be
buried here,

124

¹ In the MS. there is only one stroke for the *n.*—F.

"or *that* by Neptunes rathfull rage,
 I might be prest to dye,
while *that* sweet Englands pleasant bankes
128 did stand before mine eye.

or that I
might die
now!

" how sweete a sent hath Englands ground
 within my sences now !
how fayre vnto my outward sight
132 seemes euery branch & bowe !

How sweet
smells Eng-
land's
ground!

" the ffeeleds, the flowers, the trees & stones,
 seeme such vnto my minde,
that in all other countreys sure,
136. the like I shall not ffinde.

There are no
such fields
abroad.

" oh *that* the sun [1] his shining face
 wold stay his steeds by strenght !
that this same day might streched bee
140 to 20 yeeres of lenght ;

Oh that this
night could

last twenty
years,

" & *that* they true performed tyde
 their hasty course wold stay,
that Æolus wold neuer yeeld
144 to bring me hence away !

" *that* by the fountaine of mine eyes
 the ffeldes might wattered bee,
that I might graue my greevous plaints
148 vpon eche springing tree !

and that I
could grave
my plaints
on the trees!

" but time, I see, with Egles wings,
 I see, doth flee away,
& dusty clouds begin to dimm
152 the brightnesse of the day ;

But Time
flies,

---

[1] MS. or *that* the shaning.—F.

"the flatall hower draweth on,
  the winds & tydes agree ;
& now, sweet England, ouer soone
156   I must depart from thee !

the sailors
call me.

"the Mariners haue hoysed sayle,
  & call to catch me in,
& in [my] woefull hart doe [1] feele
160   my torments to begin.

Farewell,
sweet Eng-
land,

"wherfore, farwell for euermore,
  Sweet England, vnto thee !
& farewell all my freinds which I
164   againe shall neuer see !

I kiss thy
soil

" & England, heere I kisse the ground
  vpon my bended knee,

to shew how
I loved
thee."

herby to shew to all they world
168   how deere I loued thee."

Hereford
goes,

this being [2] sayd, away he went
  As fortune did him guide ;   [page 268]
and att the lenght, with greefe of hart,

and dies in
Venice.

172   in Venis [3] there he dyed.

Norfolk

the other duke in dolefull sort

lives in
France,

did lead his liffe in ffrance,
& at the last the mightye Lord

is promoted,

176   did him ffull hiye advance.

recalled to
England

the Lords of England afterwards
  did send for him againe,

while
Richard II.
wars in
Ireland,

while that King Richard [4] in the warres
180   in Ireland did remaine ;

---

[1] I.—F.
[2] A de follows in the MS., but is
crossed out.—F.
[3] or Veins, MS.—F.
[4] The d has a curl like s to it. F.

who thro ¹ the vile and great abuse
wh*i*ch through his deeds did springe,
deposed was, & then the duke
184   was truly crowned Kinge.

ffins.

and is
crowned
King.

¹ MS. tho. "The vile and great abuse" is dwelt on in the curious incomplete alliterative poem on the Deposition of Richard II., edited by Mr. Thomas Wright for the Camden Society in 1838 from the Cambridge MS. Ll. 4. 14. Take, among other passages, lines 88–106, pp. 4, 5:

Now, Richard the redeles, reweth on
  ȝou self,
That lawelesse leddyn ȝoure lyf and
  ȝoure peple bothe;
Ffor thoru the wyles and wronge and
  wast in ȝoure tyme,
ȝe were lyghtlich y-lyste ffrom that ȝou
  leef thouȝte,
And ffrom ȝoure willffull werkis, ȝoure
  will was chaungid,
And rafte was ȝoure riott, and rest, ffor
  ȝoure daieȝ
Weren wikkid thoru ȝoure cursid coun-
  ceill, ȝoure karis weren newed,

And coveitise hath crasid ȝoure croune
  ffor evere.
Of a-legeaunce now lerneth a lesson
  other tweyne
Wherby it standith and stablithe moste,
By dride, or be dyntis, or domes untrewe,
Or by creaunce of coyne ffor castes of
  gile;
By pillynge of ȝoure peple ȝoure prynces
  to plese,
Or that ȝoure wylle were wrouȝte, thouȝ
  wisdom it nolde,
Or be tallage of ȝoure townues without
  ony werre,
By rewthles routus that ryffled evere,
Be preysing of polaxis that no pete
  hadde,
Or be dette ffor thi dees, deme as thu
  ffyndist,
Or be ledinge of lawe with love well
  y-temprid.—F.

𝕷𝖆𝖉𝖞𝖊𝖘 : 𝖋𝖆𝖑𝖑.[1]

THIS ballad is given in the *Reliques* "(with corrections [2]) from the Editor's ancient folio MS. collated with two printed copies in black letter: one in the British Museum, the other in the Pepys Collection. Its old title is 'A lamentable ballad of the Lady's fall,' to the tune of 'In Peascod Time,'" (to which air "Chevy Chace," as Mr. Chappell informs us, was sometimes sung). There is also a copy of it in the Douce Collection. It appears in the 1727 Collection of Old Ballads, and many later Collections.

It is evidently of very much the same date as *The Children in the Wood* (which is certainly as old as 1595, as its name is entered in the Stationers' Registers of that year), and may possibly be by the same author. The same facility of language and of rhime, the same power of pathos, the same extreme simplicity characterise both ballads.

The story is who can say how old? Who was the first frail woman? who the first false man? It touchingly illustrates Goldsmith's pathetic lines:

> When lovely woman stoops to folly
> And finds too late that men betray,
> What charm can soothe her melancholy?
> What art can wash her guilt away?
>
> The only art her guilt to cover,
> To hide her shame from every eye,
> To give repentance to her lover
> And wring his bosom, is—to die.

The poor weak betrayed lady had looked in vain for the fulfilment of her lover's promises :

---

[1] In y⁰ printed Collection of Old Ballads, 1727, Vol. i. p. 244. N. xxxiv.—P.
[2] Noticed in the 4th edition only.— F.

If any person she had spied
Come riding o'er the plain,
She thought it was her own true love ;
But all her hopes were vain.

She gives birth to a child,

And with one sigh which brake her heart
This gallant dame did die.

Then, at last, repentance is given to her lover, and his bosom is wrung. He kills himself. And so the ballad ends with a word of admonition and warning to " dainty damsels all."

MARKE: well my heauy dolefull tale,
you loyall louers all,
& heedfully beare in your brest
4   a gallant Ladyes fall.

Hear the sad tale of a lady's fall :

long was shee wooed ere shee was woone
to lead a wedded liffe,
but folly rought her ouerthrowe
8   before shee was a wiffe ;

Long was she wooed,

to soone, alas ! she gaue consent,
& yeeleded to his will,
tho he protested to be true
12   & faithfull to her still.

but consented too soon.

shee felt her body altered quite,
her bright hue waxed pale,
her faire red cheekes changed color quite,[1]
16   her strenght began to fayle.

Her shape changed,

& soe [2] with many a sorrowfull sighe,
this bewtious Ladye Milde
with greeued hart perceiued her selfe
20   to be [3] conceiued with chyld.

and she found herself with child.

---

[1] Her lovelye cheeks chang'd color white.—*Rel.* 1st ed. (only partly collated. —F.)

[2] Soe that.—*Rel.*
[3] haue.—*Rel.*

She bid it
from her
parents,

shee kept it from her parents sight
   as close as close might bee,
& soe put on her silken gowne
24   none shold her swelling see.

but told her
lover,

vnto her louer secretly
   her greefe shee did bewray,
& walking with him, hand in hand,
28   these words to him did say :

"behold," quoth shee, "a Ladyes distresse
   by loue brought to your bowe ;
see how I goe with chyld with thee,
32   tho none thereof doth knowe !

"my litle babe springs in my wombe
   to heare it [1] fathers voyce ;

prayed him
not to let
her babe be
a bastard,

o lett itt not be a bastard called,
36   sith I make thee my choyce ! [2]

to remember
his promises,

"thinke on thy former promises,
   thy words & vowes eche one !
remember with what bitter teares
40   to mee thou madest thy Moane !

and marry
her
or kill her.

"conuay me to some secrett place,
   & marry me with speede,
or with thy rapyer end my liffe,
44   lest further shame proceede ! "

Her lover
makes ex-
cuses :

"alacke, my derest loue ! " quoth hee,
   "my greatest Ioy on earthe !
which way shold I connay you hence
48   to scape [3] a sudden death ?

---

[1] It preceded its as the gen. neuter of
he.—F.   its.—Rel.

[2] Rel. inserts four lines here.—F.
[3] without.—Rel.

"your freinds are all of hye degree,
    & I of meane estate ;
ffull hard itt is to gett you forthe   [page 269]
52   out of your ffathers gate."

how can he get her away from her home ?

"dread not your liffe to saue your fame !
    for if you taken bee,
my selfe will step betweene the sword
56   to take the harme of thee ;

She says

she will save him from harm,

"soe may you [1] scape dishonor quite.
    if soe you [2] shold be slaine,
what cold they say, but *that* true loue
60   had wrought a Ladyes paine [3] ?

"but feare not any further harme ;
    my selfe will soe deuise,
I will safelye ryd [4] with thee
6   vnknowen of Morttall Eyes.

and will come to him

disguised like some pretty page
    Ile meete thee in the darke,
& all alone Ile come to thee
68   hard by my ffathers parke."

disguised as a page.

"& there," quoth hee, "Ile meete my deere—
    if god doe lend me liffe—
on this day month without all fayle ;
72   Ile make thee then my wiffe."

He agrees to meet her that day month.

& with a sweet & louing kisse
    they parted presentlye,
& att their partinge brinish [5] teares
76   stoode in eche others eye.

They kiss and part.

---

[1] shall I.—*Rel.*
[2] ? I.—F. and if I.—*Rel.*
[3] bane.—P. and *Rel.*
[4] ryde away.—*Rel.*
[5] ? MS. ; perhaps it is *bainish.*—F.

On the day
fixed
the body is
ready,

att lenght the wished day was come
   wherin [1] this louely Mayd
with longing eyes & strange attire
80   for her true louer [2] stayd.

if any person shee had spyed [3]
   came ryding ore the plaine,
shee thought [4] itt was her owne true loue;
84   but all her hopes was vaine !

but her lover
never comes.

She weeps,

then did shee weepe, & soer bewayle
   her most vnhappy fate ;
then did shee speake these wofull words
88   when succourles shee sate :

reproaches
her false
lover.

" O ffalse, fforsworne, ffaithelesse man !
   disloyall in thy loue !
hast thou fforgott thy promise past,
92   & wilt thou periured prooue ?

" & hast thou now fforsaken mee
   in this my greate distresse,
to end my dayes in heauinesse [5]
96   which well thou might [6] redresse ?

and wishes
she had
never
trusted him.

" woe worth [7] the time I did beleeue [8]
   that flattering toung of thine !
wold god *that* I had neuer seene
100   the teares of thy false eyen ! "

Grieving, she
goes home,

soe *that* with many a grieuous groane [9]
   homewards shee went amaine.
noe rest came in her waterye eyes,
104   shee found [10] such priuy payne.

---

[1] On which.—*Rel.*
[2] ? MS. loues.—F.
[3] When any person she espyed.—*Rel.*
[4] hoped.—*Rel.*
[5] open shame.—*Rel.*
[6] thou mightst well.—*Rel.*
[7] be to ; A.-S. *weorthan*, to become, be.—F.
[8] I e'er believ'd.—*Rel.*
[9] sorrowful sigh.—*Rel.*
[10] felt.—*Rel.*

in tranell strong shee fell *that* night

    with many a bitter thraw [1] :—

what woefull paines shee felt *that* night [2]

108   doth ecke good woman knowe!—

is taken with childbirth pangs,

shee called vp her waiting mayds

    who lay att her bedds feete,[3]

and musing at her great [4] woe

112   began full fast to weepe.

calls up her maids,

"weepe nott," shee sayth, "but shutt the dores

    & windowes all about;

let none bewray my wretched state,

116   but keepe all persons out!"

has the doors shut,

and bids them keep out every one.

"O Mistrus! call your mother here;

    of women you hane neede;

& to some skilfull midwiffe helpe

120   the better may you speed."

The maids urge her to

have a mid-wife.

"call not my mother for thy liffe,

    nor ffeitch noe woman here!

The midwiffes helpe comes all to late;   [page 270]

124   my death I doe not feare."

She refuses.

with *that* the babe sprang from her wombe,

    noe creature being by,[5]

& with one sighe which brake her hart

128   this gallant dame did dye.

gives birth to a babe,

and dies.

the litle lonely infant younge,

    the pretty smiling babe,[6]

resigned itt new receiued berath

132   to him *that* had it made.

Her babe dies too.

---

[1] throwe.—*Rel.*

[2] then did feel.—*Rel.*

[3] A curl at the end like another *e.*—F.

[4] Who musing at her mistress.—*Rel.*

[5] nye.—*Rel.*

[6] The mother being dead.—*Rel.*

Her lover
comes, and

    next morning came her owne true loue
      affrighted with this newes,

kills himself.

    & he for sorrow slew himselfe,
136   whom eche one did accuse.

Mother and
babe are
buried
together.

    the Mother with her new borne babe
      were laide both in one grane;
    their parents, ouerworne [1] with woe,
140   noe Ioy *that* they [2] cold haue.

Damsels!
ware flat-
tering
words!

    take [heed] you dayntye damsells all ;
      of fllattering words beware ;
    & to the honor of *your* name
144   haue you a specyall care.[3]

                          ffins.

---

[1] overcome.—*Rel.*
[2] joy thenceforth.—*Rel.*
[3] The *Reliques* add :

        Too true, alas! this story is,
          As many one can tell.
        By others harmes learne to be wise,
          And you shall do full well.

Buckingam betrayd : by Banister.[1]

In the late autumn of 1483, the nobles who had previously
determined to put an end to the usurpation of Richard the
Third, and who had lately heard of the murder of the young
Princes, fixed on Henry of Richmond for their king. About the
middle of October the Marquess of Dorset proclaimed him at
Exeter. Men declared for him in Wiltshire, in Kent, in
Berkshire. The Duke of Buckingham made a rising at Brecon.
But the conspiracy failed. Richard was on the alert; Henry
could not land; the insurgents could not combine. From Brecon
the Duke " marched through the forest of Deane to the Severn;
but the bridges were broken down, and the river was so swoln
that the fords had become impassable. He turned back to
Weobley, the seat of the lord Ferrers; but the Welshmen who
had followed him disbanded; and the news of their desertion
induced the other bodies of insurgents to provide for their own
safety. Thus the King triumphed without drawing the sword.
Weobley was narrowly watched on the one side by Sir Humphrey
Stafford, on the other by the clan of the Vaughans, who for
their reward had received a promise of the plunder of Brecon.
Morton effected his escape in disguise to the isle of Ely, and
thence passed to the coast of Flanders; *the Duke, in a similar
dress, reached the hut of Banister, one of his servants in
Shropshire, where he was betrayed by the perfidy of his host.* If
he hoped for pardon on the merit of his former services, he had

---

[1] There is another Song on this Subject in *the* printed Collection 12mo 1738,
Vol. 3^d p. 38. N. 5.—P.

mistaken the character of Richard. That prince had already reached Salisbury with his army; he refused to see the prisoner, and ordered his head to be immediately struck off in the market-place." (Lingard).

There is another ballad on this same subject given in the *Collection of Old Ballads*, vol. iii. 1727, entitled "The Life and Death of the Great Duke of Buckingham, who came to an untimely End, for consenting to the deposing of the two gallant young Princes, King Edward the Fourth's children. To the tune of *Shore's Wife*." In point of style this is of much the same date with that here given from the Folio. It is the production of a thorough-bred ballad-writer, viz. Robert Johnson, and included in his *Crown Garland of Golden Roses*. It administers political justice in the same uncompromising manner :

> Thus Banister was forc'd to beg
> And crave for Food with Cap and Leg ;
> But none on him would Bread bestow,
> That to his Master prov'd a Foe.
>
> Thus wandring in this poor Estate,
> Repenting his misdeeds too late,
> Till starved he gave up his Breath,
> By no man pitied at his Death.
>
> To woful End his Children came,
> Sore punish'd for their Father's shame ;
> Within a channel one was drown'd
> Where water scarce could hide the ground.
>
> Another by the Powers divine
> Was strangely eaten up of swine ;
> The last a woful ending makes
> By strangling in an empty Jakes.

A third ballad, entitled " A most sorrowful Song, setting forth the miserable end of Banister, who betrayed the Duke of Buckingham, his Lord and Master," is in the Pepys Collection, vol. i. p. 64, and reprinted in Evans's *Old Ballads*, vol. iii. p. 23, 8vo, 1810. It begins thus :—

If ever wight had cause to rue
A wretched deed, vile and untrue,
Then Banister with shame may sing,
Who sold his life that loved him.

Perhaps all three ballads are founded on some common older
original.

YOU: Barons bold, ma[r]ke [1] and behold
  the thinge *that* I will rite [2];
a story strange & yett most true
4   I purpose to Endite.[3]

A strange true tale I tell.

ffor the Noble Peere while he liued heere,
  the duke of Buckingam,
he fflourisht in King Edwards time,
8   the 4ᵗʰ King of *that* name.

The Duke of Buckingham

in his seruice there he kept a man
  of meane & low degree,
whom he brought vp then of a chyld
12   from basenesse to dignitye;

has a servant

he gaue him lands & liuings good
  wherto he was noe heyre,
& then [4] mached him to a gallant dame
16   as rich as shee was fayre.

whom he enriches, and marries to a gallant dame,

it came to passe in tract of time
  his wealth did soe excell,
his riches did surpasse them all
20   *that* in *that* shire did dwell.

so that the man is very wealthy;

who was soe braue as Banister?
  or who durst with him contend?
wh*i*ch [5] wold not be desirous still
24   to be his daylye freind?

none dares strive with Banister.

[1] mark.—P. [2] write.—P. places are marked in red brackets, for
[3] Only half the *n* in the MS.—F. omission.—F.
[4] This and 19 other words in different [5] who.—P.

for then[1] it came to passe; more woe, alas!
for[2] sorrowes then began;
for why, the *Master* was constraind[3]
28   to seeke succour of his man.

Richard III.

then Richard the 3.^d swaying the sword,
cryed himselfe a kinge,[4]

murders
the princes;

murthered 2 princes in their bedds,
32   w*h*ich deede great striffe did bringe.

Buckingham
raises a host
to avenge
them;

& then the duke of Buckingam,
hating this bloody deede,
against the tyrant raysed an Oaste
36   of armed men indeed.

& when *King* Richard of this hard tell,
a mightye Ost he sent
against the duke of Buckingam,
40   his purpose to prevent.

but his men
flee from
Richard's
army,

& when the dukes people of this heard tell,
ffeare filled their hearts eche one;
many of his souldiers fledd by night,
44   and left him one by one.

in extreme need the Duke tooke a steede,[5]   [page 271]

and he flees

& posted night and day
towards Banister his man,

to Banister

48   in secrett there to stay.

" O Banister, Sweet Banister!

to hide him.

pitty thow my cause," sayes hee,
" & hyde me from mine[6] Enemyes
52   that here accuseth[7] mee."

[1] Now it.—P.
[2] such.—P.
[3] The M.^r was constrained to seek.
—P.
[4] Himself proclaimed king.—P.

[5] Part of the line pared off the MS.
—F.
[6] One stroke too few in the MS.—F.
[7] persueth (in red ink: by Percy in
his late hand.— F.)

"O, you be welcome, my Lord!" hee sayes,   Banister
  "your grace is welcome here!
& as my liffe Ile keepe you safe,   vows to keep
56   although it cost me deere!"   him safe,

"be true, sweete Banister!" sayes hee,
  O sweete Banister, be true!"
"christs curse," he sayd, "on me & mine   "Christ's
60   if euer I proue ffalse to you!   curse on
                                   me if I be
                                   false!"

then the Duke cast of his veluett sute,   Buckingham
  his chaine of gold likwise,   takes off his
                                   velvet
& soe he did his veluett capp,   clothes,
64   to blind the peoples eyes;

a lethern Ierkyn[1] on his backe,   dresses as a
  & lethern slopps[2] alsoe,   woodman,
a heidging bill vpon his backe,
68   & soe into the woods did goe!

an old felt hat vppon his head,
  with 20 holes therin;
& soe in labor he spent the time,   and works
72   as tho some drudge he had beene.   away

& there he lined long vnknowen,   in safety.
  & still vnknowne might bee,
till Banister for hope of gaine
76   betrayd him Iudaslye.

for a proclamation there was made,   But Richard
  'whosoeuer then cold bringe
newes of the Duke of Buckingam
80   to Richard then our Kinge,

---

[1] Languedoc *jhergaon*, an over-coat;
Fr. *Jargiot. Jergot.* a kind of course
garment worne by countrey people. Cot-

grave; in Wedgwood.—F.
  [2] slopps, A kind of open breeches,
trowsers. Johnson.—P.

'a 1000 markes shalbe his ffee
　　of gold & siluer bright,

& then be preferred by his grace,
84　　& made a worthy knight.'

& when Banister of *that* heard tell,
　　straight to the court sent hee,
& soe betrayd his *Master* good
88　　for lucre of *that* ffee.

a herald of armes there was sent,
　　& men with weapons good,
who did attach this noble Duke
92　　where he was labouring in the wood.

" Ah, ffalse Banister ! a, wreched man !
　　Ah, Caitiffe ! " then sayes hee ;
" haue I maintained thy poore estate
96　　to deale thus Iudaslye ?

" alas *that* euer I beleeued
　　that flattering tounge of thine !
woe worth the time *that* euer I see
100　　*that* false Bodye of thine ! "

then ffraught with feare & many a teare,
　　with sorrowes almost dead,
this noble Duke of Buckingam
104　　att Salsbury[1] lost his head.

then Banister went to the court,
　　hoping this gold to haue,
but straight in prison hee was cast,
108　　& hard his liffe to[2] saue.

---

[1] query Shrewsbury.—P.　　　　[2] hard his life could.—P.

small ffreinds he found in his distresse,
 nor any comfort in his need,
but euery man reuiled him
112 [for] this [1] his trecherous deede.

reviled by all,

& then, according to his wishe,
 gods Iudgments did on him fall ;
his children were consumed quite,
116 his goods were wasted all ;

and Christ's curse falls on him :

[page 272]

ffor one of his sones for greeffe Starke madd did fall ; [2]
 the other ffor sorrow drowned was
within a shallow runing streame
120 where euery man might passe.

one son turns mad, the other is drowned.

his daugter right of bewtye bright,
 to such lewde liffe did ffall
that shee dyed in great miserye ;
124 & thus they were wasted all.

His daughter becomes a strumpet.

Old Banister lined long in shame,
 & att the lenght did dye ;
& thus they Lord did plague them all
128 ffor this his trecherye.

He lives in shame and dies.

now god blesse our king & councell graue,[3]
 in goodness still to proceed ;
& send euery [4] distressed man
132 a better ffreind att need ! ffins.

God send

all in need a better friend !

---

[1] for this. Qu.—P.
[2] stark mad did fall.—P. This line is made two in the MS. *Starke* begins p. 272.—F.

[3] Our k^g G^d bless And grant his grace.—P.
[4] to each.—P.

Earle Bothwell.[1]

THIS ballad is printed in the *Reliques*, vol. ii. pp. 198–200, under the title of "The Murder of the King of Scots." Percy's Introduction, p. 197, is as follows:—" The catastrophe of Henry Stewart, lord Darnley, the unfortunate husband of Mary Q. of Scots, is the subject of this ballad. It is here related in that partial imperfect manner, in which such an event would naturally strike the subjects of another kingdom; of which he was a native. Henry appears to have been a vain capricious worthless young man, of weak understanding, and dissolute morals. But the beauty of his person, and the inexperience of his youth, would dispose mankind to treat him with an indulgence, which the cruelty of his murder would afterwards convert into the most tender pity and regret: and then imagination would not fail to adorn his memory with all those virtues, he ought to have possessed. This will account for the extravagant elogium bestowed upon him in the first stanza, &c.

"Henry lord Darnley, was eldest son of the earl of Lennox, by the lady Margaret Douglas, niece of Henry VIII. and daughter of Margaret queen of Scotland by the earl of Angus, whom that princess married after the death of James IV.— Darnley, who had been born and educated in England, was but in his 21st year, when he was married, Feb. 9, 1567–8. This crime was perpetrated by the E. of Bothwell, not out of respect to the memory of David Riccio, but in order to pave the way for his own marriage with the queen.

---

[1] On the Murther of David Riccio and of *the* king of Scotts. Written while *the* Queen of Scotts was in England.— P.

" This ballad (printed [1] from the Editor's folio MS.) seems to
have been written soon after Mary's escape into England in
1568, see v. 65.—It will be remembered at v. 5, that this princess
was Q. dowager of France, having been first married to
Francis II, who died Dec. 4, 1560."

WOE: worth thee, woe worth thee, false Scottlande !
   ffor thou hast euer wrought by a [2] sleight ;
   for [2] the worthyest Prince *that* euer was borne,
4   you hanged vnder a cloud by night !

Woe to you, Scottland, you've hanged the best of Princes!

   the queene of ffrance a letter wrote,
   & sealed itt [3] with hart and ringe ;
   & bade him come Scottland within,
8   & shee wold marry him [2] & crowne him King.

Queen Mary bade him come and marry her ;

   to be a King, itt [2] is a pleasant thing ;
   to bee [4] a Prince vnto a Peere ;
   but you haue heard, & so haue I too, [2]
12   a man may well by [5] gold to deere.

   there was an Italyan in that place,
   was as welbeloved as euer was hee ;
   Lord David [6] was his name,
16   chamberlaine [7] vnto the Queene was hee.

but she had an insolent Chamberlain, Rizzio,

   ffor [8] if the King had risen forth [2] of his place,
   he wold haue sitt [9] him downe in the cheare, [10]
   & tho itt [11] beseemed him not soe well,
20   altho the King had beene [12] present there.

[1] So in 2nd and 3rd editions too:
" printed with a few corrections," 4th ed.
—F.

[2] *Rel.* omits these.—F. 4th and 2nd
and 3rd editions restore *too*, l. 11.

[3] it.—*Rel.* itt.—*4th ed.*

[4] be.—*Rel.* bee.—*4th ed.*

[5] buy.—P.

[6] And Dav⁴ Rizzio - qu. Davi⁴ Rizzio.
—P.*

[7] Lord Chamberl⁰.—P.

[8] from.—P.

[9] sate.—*Rel.*

[10] i' th' chaire.—*Rel.* in the cheare. -
4th ed.

[11] although it.—*Rel.* And tho itt.—
4th ed.

[12] And tho . . . . were.—P.   *Rel.*
Although . . had biene.—*4th ed.*

* And David Riccio.—*Rel.* Lord David. *4th ed.*

and some
Scotch lords
some lords in Scottland waxed wonderous [1] wroth,
　& quarrelld with him for the nonce [2] :
I shall you tell [3] how itt beffell ;

stabbed him.   24
12 daggers were in him all [1] att once.

The Queene
was wroth,
when this queene see the [4] Chamberlaine was [1] slaine,
　for him her [5] cheeks shee did weete,
　& made a vow for a 12 month & a day [6]

28　the King & shee [7] wold not come in one sheete.

and other
Lords
then some of the Lords of Scotland [8] waxed wrothe,
　& made their vow [9] vehementlye,

vowed to
kill the
King.
' for death of the queenes [10] Chamberlaine [11]

32　the King himselfe he shall dye.' [12]

they strowed his chamber ouer with gunpowder,[13]
　& layd greene rushes in his way ;
ffor the traitors thought that [14] night

36　the [15] worthy king for to betray.[16]

to bedd the worthy King made [17] him bowne ; [18]
　to take his rest, that [19] was his desire ;

They set
fire to his
bedroom,
he was noe sooner cast on sleepee,[20]

40　but his chamber was on a blasing fyer.[21]

he jumped
out of
window,
vp he lope, & a glasse [22] window broke ;
he [23] had 30 foote for to flall.

[1] Rel. omits these.—F.
[2] ? MS. noncett, with tt blotted out.—F. nonce.—Rel.
[3] And I shall tell.—Rel.　4th ed. omits And.
[4] the queene she saw her.—Rel. 4th ed. omits she, and restores was.
[5] [her] fair.—P.
[6] year & a day.—P.
[7] shee'd ne'er.—P.
[8] lords they.—Rel.
[9] [vow] now.—P.
[10] That for the death of the.—Rel. For the death of the queenes.—4th ed.
[11] Queen's Lo. Chn.—P.
[12] How he, the king himself shd dye.—P. and.—Rel. The king himselfe how he shall dye.—4th ed.
[13] with Gunpowdr they strewd his room.—P.
[14] very.—P.　[15] this.—Rel.
[16] betraye.—Rel.　betray.—4th ed.
[17] the kg he made.—P.
[18] ready, paratus. Lye.—P.
[19] omitted.—Rel.
[20] sleepe.—Rel.
[21] it was all on fire.—P.
[22] and the.—Rel.　[23] And.—P.

Lord Bodwell kept a priuy wach
44   vnderneath [1] his castle wall.
"who haue wee [2] heere ? " sayd Lord Bodwell ;
"answer me, now I doe call." [3]

and was
caught by
Lord
Bothwell,

"King Henery the 8th my vnckle was ;
48   some pitty show for his sweet sake ! [4]
"Ah, Lord Bodwell ! I know thee well ;
some pitty on me I pray thee take ! "

whom he
prayed for
mercy.

"Ile [5] pitty thee as much," he sayd,
52   "& as much favor [6] Ile show to thee
As thou had on the Queenes Chamberlaine   [page 273]
that day thou deemedst [7] him to dye.[8] "

But Both-
well would
have none,

through halls & towers this [9] King they Ledd,
56   through castles & towers [10] that were hye,[11]
through an arbor into an orchard,
& there hanged him in a peare tree.[12]

and hanged
him on a
pear-tree.

when the gouernor of Scottland he [13] heard tell [13]
60   that [14] the worthye king he [13] was slaine,
he hath banished [15] the Queene soe bitterlye
that in Scottland shee dare not remaine ;

The Go-
vernor
cursed Mary,

---

[1] all und^r &c.—P. All vnderneath. —*Rel.* Underneath his.—*4th ed.*
[2] we.—*Rel.* wee.—*4th ed.*
[3] Now answer me that I may know. —*Rel.*
[4] For his sweete sake some pitty show.—*Rel.*
The next two lines Percy has altered into
Who haue we here? lord Bodwell sayd, Now answer me when I doe speake.—F.
[5] I'll.—*Rel.*
[6] favour.—*Rel.* favor.—*4th ed.*

[7] i. e. doomedst—deem, est opinari, censere, judicare. Jun.—P. l. 51 is partly pared off the MS.—F.
[8] dye.—*Rel.* die,—with the note " Pronounced after the northern manner *dee*" in ed^s 2, 3, 4.
[9] the.—P.
[10] thro' towers & castles, &c.—P.
[11] nye.—*Rel.*
[12] There on a peare-tree hangd him hye.—*Rel.*
[13] omitted.—*Rel.*   [14] how that.—P.
[15] He persued.—*Rel.* ? banish=ban, curse.—F.

and she fled
to England,

where she
now is.

64

but shee is fled into Merry England,

& Scottland to aside hath laine ; [1]

& through the Queene of Englands good [2] grace

now in England shee doth remaine. [3]

ffins.

---

[1] And here her residence hath tane.
—*Rel.* A change not for the better.
—F.

[2] omitted.—*Rel.*

[3] In Engl.^d now shee doth remain.
—P.

[Those readers (if any) who have looked at the notes will have noticed that the fourth edition of the *Reliques* has restored the reading of the MS. in several places where the first has altered it.—though in others it leaves the changes of the first edition untouched :—thus in lines

First three editions.		Fourth edition and MS.
6. it	*is changed into*	itt
15. And David Riccio	,,	Lord David
18. i' th' chaire	,,	in the cheare
19. Although it	,,	And tho itt
20. And though	,,	Altho
23. And 1	,,	1
25. queene shee	,,	queene
25. slaine	,,	was slaine
29. wroth	,,	wrothe
36. betraye	,,	betray
44. All underneath	,,	Underneath his
45. we	,,	wee
51. hee	,,	he
52. favour	,,	favor

while in lines 31–32 the manuscript

" for death of the queenes Chamberlaine,
the King himselfe he shall dye,"

which Percy altered in his first edition to

That for the death of the chamberlaine,
How hee, the king himselfe sholde dye,

he changed back in the fourth to,

For the death of the queenes chamberlaine,
The king himselfe, how he shall die."

I write *he* changed back, for Mr. David Laing says that a friend of Percy's and his assured him that Percy himself edited the fourth edition of the *Reliques*, and that with great care, though he let his nephew, in the Advertisement to that edition, take the responsibility of it off his own episcopal shoulders, supposed to be burdened with "more important" matters. It is, indeed, evident that the many changes made in the text of the fourth edition must have been carefully considered by Percy, for they are changes of lines sometimes as well as of words.
—F.]

Bishoppe & Browne.[1]

SEE Introduction to *King James & Brown*, vol. i. p. 135.

This piece is printed in the *Reliques*. "The original copy," says Percy, "(preserved in the archives of the Antiquarian Society, London) is entitled, 'A new Ballad, declaring the great treason conspired against the young King of Scots, and how one Andrew Browne, an Englishman, which was the King's Chamberlaine, prevented the same. To the tune of Milfield, or els to Green-sleeves.' At the end is subjoined the name of the author ' W. Elderton.' 'Imprinted at London for Yarathe James, dwelling in Newgate Market, over against Ch. Church,' in black-letter folio."

It is the work of the professional ballad-writer who could "rhyme you so eight years together, dinners and suppers and sleeping-hours excepted"; and it is well-executed work of its sort. The image is fairly well shaped; but there is scarcely a spark of Heaven's fire in it—no breath of life breathed into its nostrils.

It was written, no doubt, rather to give information than entertainment. At a time when there were no newspapers circulating through the country, the ballad was an ordinary vehicle of news. "Marry, they say that *the running stationers of London*, I mean *such as use to sing ballads*, and those that cry malignant pamphlets, &c." (*Knaves are honest men, or More Knaves yet*, apud Collier's Book of Roxburghe Ballads.)

---

[1] N.B. This Copy is very imperfect. See Page 58 & 59 [of MS.]. Stanza the last in that Page [vol. i. p. 141, l. 108-9 of print], where the subject of this ballad is alluded to.—P. The title in the *Re-* *liques*, vol. ii. p. 204, first edition, is the "King of Scots and Andrew Browne." The version there printed contains 15 stanzas, while the present one has only 10, and two of these are incomplete.—F.

IESUS god ! what[1] greeffe is this
   that Princes subiects cannot be true !
but still the devill &[2] some of his
4   doth play his part, as plaine is in shew.[3]

in Scottland dwelles a bony king,
   as proper a youth as any can bee ;
hee is giuen to euery happy[4] thing
8   *that* can be in a Prince to see.[5]

on whitsontyde, as itt befell,
   a possett was made to giue the King ;
& *that* his Ladye Nurse heard tell
12   *that* itt was made a poysoned thing.
shee cryed, & called pittiouslye,
   "helpe ! or else the King must dye ! "

& Browne being[6] an Englishman,
16   he did heare[7] *that* Ladyes pityous crye ;
but with his sword he besturred him then ;
forth att the dore he thought to fflee,
but euery dore was made full fast;
20   forth of a window hee lope at last.[8]

he mett the Bishopp att the dore,
   & with the possett in his hand.
the sight of Browne made the Bishopp agast ;

[1] Out alas ! what a.—*Rel.*
[2] hath.—*Rel.*
[3] Will play their parts, whatsoever
   ensue ;
Forgetting what a grievous thing
It is to offend the anointed kinge?
Alas for woe, why should it be so,
This makes a sorrowful heigh ho.
       —*Rel.*
The collation after this is not com-
plete.—F.

[4] The *y* is made over an *h* in the MS.
—F.
[5] *Rel.* adds :—

Yet that unluckie countrie still
Hath people giuen to craftie will,
  Alas for woe, &c.

[6] One Browne that was.—*Rel.*
[7] And hard.—*Rel.*
[8] MS. at last lope hee.—F. Out of a
window he got at last.—*Rel.*

24   he bade him soe boldleye stay & stand.
    with him were 2 *that* ran awaye
    for feare lest browne shold make a fray.

    " Bishopp," said Browne, " what hast thou there ?"
28   " nothing at all, my ffreinde,[1]" Quoth hee,
    " but a possett to make the King good cheere."   poisoned possett.
      " is itt soe ? " sayd Browne, " *that* will I see ;
    before thou goe any further inn,
32   of this possett thou shalt begin."

    " Browne," said the Bishopp, " I know thee well ;
    thou art a yong man both pore & bare ;
    & liuings [2] of [3] thee I shall bestowe ;
36   goe thou thy way, & take noe care."   rejected his bribes to be quiet,
    " noe ! " said Browne, " *that* shall not bee !
    Ile not be a traitor for all christentye !
    for be itt for wayle,[4] or for woe be itt,
40   drinke thou off this sorrowfull possett."   and made

    the Bishopp dranke ; then by & by   the Bishop drink the possett.
    his belly burst, & he ffell downe :   The Bishop burst and died.
    a iust reward for his traitorye.
44   " marry, this was a possett indeed ! " sayd Browne.
    he searched the Bishopp, & found they Kayes
    to goe to the King when he did please.

    & when the Kinge heard tell of this,   King James thanked God,
48   he meekelye fell downe on his knee,
    & thanked god *that* he did misse
    then of this false trecherye ;
    & then he did perceiue & know
52   *that* his clergye wold haue him betraid [so.[5]]

---

[1] The last *e* is made over an *s* in the MS.—F.
[2] Only half the *n* in the MS.—F.
[3] on.—*Rel.*
[4] i. e. sorrow : unless it be corruptly written for weal, welfare, good : written by the Scots weil, wele.—P.
[5] *Rel.* inserts another stanza here, and adds four after the next.—F.

rewarded
the nurse,

and knighted   56
Browne.

he called the nursse befor his grace,
& gaue vnto her 20ᵗʸᵉ pounds [a yeere.]
doughtye Browne, [i'] the like case,
he dubbd him K*night* w*i*th gallant cheere,
bestowed vpon him linings great
[For dooing such a manly feat.¹]

ffins.

¹ Last line cut away in the MS. ;
supplied here from the *Rel.*, which adds :
As he did showe, to the bishop's woe,
Which made &c.

and then four more stanzas about a fresh
attempt to make away with the King.
—F.

Childe Waters.[1] [page 274]

This ballad was printed in the *Reliques* from the Folio, with a few "corrections." These amount to the insertion of six new lines, and numerous minor changes. The copy is indeed somewhat mutilated, and needed a little patching to make it presentable to the general reader.

"Several traditional versions," says Professor Child in his *English and Scotch Ballads*, "have since been printed, of which we give *Burd Ellen* from Jamieson's, and in the Appendix *Lady Margaret* from Kinloch's Collection. Jamieson also furnishes a fragment, and Buchan[2] (*Ballads of the North of Scotland*, ii. 30) a complete copy of another version of *Burd Ellen*; and Chambers (*Scottish Ballads*, 193) makes up an edition from all the copies, which we mention here because he has taken some lines from a manuscript supplied by Mr. Kinloch."

The love and fidelity of a woman are here tried to the utmost limit. Worse sufferings than are even mentioned in the *Nut-brown Maid*, and in that feeble reflection of it, *A Jigge*, are here verily endured. Certainly "Burd Ellen" is the better, more expressive title for the ballad. She is the one centre of interest in it—the one living glory and delight. Child Waters appears but to introduce her—to "bring her out"—to furnish her with an opportunity for displaying her splendid trust and adherence. He must be regarded so, or he is intolerable. This part he performs excellently. He brings Ellen's faithfulness into glorious

---

[1] A Tryal of female Affection not unlike the Nut-brown Maid. Shewing how child Waters made his M.^s undergo many Hardships, & afterwards married her. It was not necessary to correct this much for the Press.— P.

[2] This Buchan (whom I once endeavoured to assist in his poverty by procuring purchasers for his books) was a most daring forger: scarcely anything that he has published can be trusted to as genuine.—A. Dyce.

relief. Let this and kindred ballads, then, be accepted as atone-
ments for the light doubting talk men sometimes hold about
women.

> Be it true or wrong
> These men among
> On women do complaine
> · Affermyng this
> How that it is
> A labour spent in vaine
> To love them wele
> For never a dele
> They love a man agayne.
> For lete a man
> Do what he can
> Ther favour to attayne
> Yet yf a newe
> To them pursue
> Ther furst trew lover than
> Laboureth for nought
> And from her thought
> He is a bannisshed man.
>
> I say not nay
> But that all day
> It is both writ & sayde
> That woman's fayth
> Is as who sayth
> All utterly decayed.

This and kindred ballads show how, in spite of many sad
scandals, in spite of suspicions and sneers, the heart of men
still nursed and cherished a precious fond belief in the truth
of women. Much frivolity there might be,[1] much hypocrisy,
much falseness; but ever here and there was one to be found
—one who, through good report and through evil, through all
extreme distresses and neglects and cruelties, would never withdraw her trust from him to whom once she had given it—would
never falsify the vows she had once uttered—would never
fail from her true-love's side—*una de multis face nuptiali*

---

[1] See the ballad in the metre of the
Notbrowne Mayd in Mr. Skeat's Preface
to *Partenay*, p. ii, (E. E. T. Soc. 1866)

beginning,

masteres anne,
I am your man.—F.

digna. Such an one is Ellen in this ballad. She illustrates how " many waters cannot quench love, neither can the floods drown it." She cares nothing for gold and fee ; had rather have one kiss of her love's mouth or one twinkling of his eye than " Cheshire and Lancashire both " ; will lay aside her woman's dress, sacrifice her long yellow locks, endure strange hardships —running barefoot through the broom and struggling through the water—invoke generous blessings on the head of her supposed rival, obey the most trying orders, that she may accompany and please the master of her heart. Her love never hesitates. When, after much ill usage, she gives birth to a child in the stable whither she has gone in the early morning to feed the Child's horse, she lets no murmur against the author of her miseries escape her.

> She said, " Lullaby, my own dear child,
> Lullaby, dear child dear !
> *I would thy father were a king,*
> *Thy mother laid on a bier."*

In the end her trust wins its reward.

> " Peace now," he said, " good fair Ellen,
> And be of good cheer, I thee pray ;
> And the bridal and the churching both
> They shall be upon one day."

CHILDE : watters in his stable stoode,
    & stroaket his milke white steede :
to him came a ffaire young Ladye
4   as ere did weare [1] womans wee[de [2];]

To Childe Waters

comes fair Ellen,

saies, " christ you saue, good Chyld waters ! "
    sayes, " christ you saue and see !
my girdle of gold which was too longe
8   is now to short ffor mee ;

says,

[1] ware.- P. ever ware.— *Rel.*   [2] weed. P.

" I am with
child by
you."

" & all is with one[1] chyld of yours,
     I ffeele sturre att my side.
my gowne of greene, it is to strayght ;
12   before it was to wide."

" If so,

take
Cheshire and
Lancashire,

" if the child be mine,[2] faire Ellen," he sayd,
     " be mine, as you tell mee,
take[3] you Cheshire & Lancashire both,
16   take them your owne to bee.

an I make
it a child
your heir."

" if the child be mine, ffaire Ellen," he said,
     " be mine, as you doe sweare,
take you Cheshire & Lancashire both,
20   & make that child your heyre."

" I'd rather
have a kiss

shee saies, " I had rather haue one kisse,
     child waters, of thy mouth,
then I wold haue Cheshire & lancashire both,
24   that lyes[4] by north & south.

and a look
from you,
than your
counties."

" & I had rather haue a twinkling,
     Child waters, of your eye,[5]
then I wold haue Cheshire & Lancashire both,
28   to take them mine owne to bee ! "

He says
he must take
the fairest
lady north
with him.

" to-morrow, Ellen, I must forth ryde
     soe ffarr into[6] the North countrye ;
the ffairest Lady that I can ffind,
32   Ellen, must goe with mee."[7]

Ellen asks
to be his
footpage.

" & ener I pray you, Child watters,
     your ffootpage let me bee ! "

---

[1] a.—P.
[2] Only one stroke for the m.—F.   be
mine.—P.
[3] Then take.—Rel.
[4] lye.—P.
[5] thine ee.—Rel.

[6] far into.—P.
[7] The Reliques inserts:
Though I am not that ladye fayre,
     Yet let me go with thee.—F.
Tho' I am not that fayre Lady,
     Yet let me go with thee.—P.

"if you will my ffootpage be, Ellen,
36   as you doe tell itt mee,
then you must cutt your gownne of greene
  an inche aboue your knee ;

   He agrees,

   if she'll cut her gown

"soe must you doe your yellow lockes,
40   another inch [1] aboue your eye ;
you must tell noe man what is my name ;
  my ffootpage then you shall bee."

   and hair.

all this [2] long day Child waters rode,
44   shee ran bare ffoote [3] by his side ;
yett was he neuer soe curteous a Knight,
  to say, "Ellen, will you ryde ?"

   She runs barefoot by his side

but all this day Child waters rode,
48   shee ran [4] barffoote thorow the broome !
yett he was [5] neuer soe curteous a Knight
  as to say, "put on your shoone."

   all day thro' the broom.

"ride softlye," shee said,[6] "Child watters ;
52   why doe you ryde soe ffast ?
the child, which is no mans but yours,[7]
  my bodye itt will burst.[8]"

   Ride softly, she says.

he sayes,[9] "sees thou yonder [10] water, Ellen,
56   *that* fflowes from banke to brim ?"
"I trust to god, Child waters," shee said,[11]
  "you will neuer [12] see mee swime."

but when shee came to the waters side,
60   shee sayled to the Chinne :
"except the [13] Lord of heauen be my speed,
  now must I [14] learne to swime."

   He makes her

---

[1] an inch.—P.
[2] Shee all the.—*Rel.* and omits 'shee' in the next line.—P.
[3] Shee all the long day (that) Ch. Wat. rode, ran barefoot.--P.
[4] She all *the* long day Ch. W. rode. Ran.—P.

[5] was he.—P.
[7] thine.—P.
[9] Hee sayth.—*Rel.*
[11] I trust in God O Child Waters.—*Rel.*
[13] but the.—P. Now the.—*Rel.* and P.

[6] O.—P.
[8] brast.—P.
[10] yond.—P.
[12] you'll never.—P. not.—P.
[14] For I must.—*Rel.*

[page 275]

the salt waters bare vp Ellens [1] clothes;

64   our Ladye bare vpp he[r] chinne;

& Child waters was a woe man,[2] good Lord,[3]

to ssee faire Ellen swime.

& when shee ouer the water was,

68   Shee then came to his knee :

he said, "come hither, ffaire Ellen,

loe yonder what I see!

"seest thou not yonder hall, Ellen ?

72   of redd gold shine the yates [4];

theres 24 ffayre ladyes,[5]

the ffairest is my wordlye make.[6]

"Seest thou not yonder hall, Ellen ?

76   of redd gold shineth the tower;

there is [7] 24 ffaire Ladyes,[8]

the fairest is my paramoure."

"I doe see the hall now, Child waters,

80   *that* of redd gold shineth the yates.[9]

god giue [10] good then of your selfe,

& of your wordlye make [11]!

"I doe see the hall now, Child waters,

84   *that* of redd gold shineth the tower.

god giue [12] good then of your selfe

and of your paramoure!"

---

[1] her.—*Rel.*

[2] i. e. a woeful man.—P.

[3] Ch. W. was a woo man good Lord.
—P.

[4] shines [the] gate.—P.

[5] Of twenty foure fayre ladyes there.
—*Rel.* of.—P.

[6] mate: so the rhyme seems to require,
but Make signifies also a Mate, match, or
equal, a familiar companion. from A.-S.

maca, gemaca, par, socius, conjux. Vid.
Jun. Gloss. Sax. Voc.—P. *Rel.* omits
'wordlye.'—F.

[7] There are . . . . there.—P.

[8] *Rel.* adds 'there.'—F.

[9] yate.—P.

[10] [insert] you.—P.

[11] worthy mate.—P.

[12] [insert] you.—P.

there were 24 Ladyes,[1]
88   were [2] playing at the ball;
& Ellen was [3] the ffairest Ladye,[4]
must bring his steed to the stall.

She stables his steed,

there were 24 faire Ladyes [5]
92   was [6] playing att the Chesse;
& Ellen shee was[7] the ffairest Ladye,[8]
must bring his horsse to grasse.

and takes it to grass.

& then bespake Child waters sister,
96   & [9] these were the words said shee;
" you haue the prettyest ffootpage, brother,
that euer I saw [10] with mine eye,

His sister

asks that his footpage

" but *that* his belly it is soe bigg,
100   his girdle goes [11] wonderous hye;
& euer I pray you, Child waters,
let him goe into the Chamber with mee.[12] "

may go to her room with her.

[13] " it is more meete for a litle ffootpage
104   *that* has run through mosse and mire,
to take his supper vpon his knee
& sitt downe [14] by the kitchin fyer,
then to goe into the chamber with any Ladye
108   that weares soe [rich] attyre.[15] "

Childe Waters says the page had

better sup by the kitchen fire.

---

[1] 'were playing' follows and is crossed out.—F.   There were 24 faire Ladies there.—P.   There twenty four ladyes were.—*Rel.*

[2] A.—*Rel.*   A.—P.

[3] that was, Qu.—P.

[4] the fayrest ladye there.—*Rel.*

[5] P. has written *there* at the end.—F.   *Rel.* omits 'were.'

[6] a.—P.

[7] that was, Qu.—P.

[8] the fayrest ladye there.—*Rel.*

[9] *Rel.* omits &.—F.

[10] I did see.—P.   I did see.—*Rel.*

[11] is.—P.

[12] in my chamber lie.—P.

[13] Percy turns the last two lines into another stanza, and prefixes it to the first four:—

It is not fit for a little foot page
  That has run through mosse and myre,
To lye in the chamber of any lady
  That weares soe riche attyre.

[14] And lye.—*Rel.*

[15] rich attyre, Qu.—P.

He sends

but when the had supped euery one,
    to bedd they tooke they [1] way ;

Ellen

he sayd, " come hither, my litle footpage,
112   hearken what I doe say !

to hire a
prostitute
for him

" & goe thy downe into [2] yonder towne,
    & low into the street ;
the ffarest Ladye *that* thou can find,
116   hyer her in mine armes to sleepe,

and carry
her up to
him.

& take her vp in thine armes 2 [3]
    for filinge [4] of her ffeete."

Ellen

Ellen is gone into the towne,
120   & low into the streete :

hires the
woman

the fairest Ladye *that* shee cold find,
    shee hyred in his armes to sleepe,

and carries
her up,

& tooke her in her armes 2
124   for filing of her ffeete.

and asks to
lie at his
bed-foot.

" I pray you now, good Child waters,
    that I may creepe in att your bedds feete ;. [5]
for there is noe place about this house
128   where I may say [6] a sleepe."

At daybreak

[7] this, & itt droue now affterward [8]
    till itt was neere the day :

Childe
Waters
orders Ellen
to feed his
steed.

he sayd, " rise vp, my litle ffoote page,
132   & giue my steed corne & hay ;
& soe doe thou [9] the good blacke oates,
    that he may carry me the [10] better away."

---

[1] their.—P. they = the.—F.
[2] thee into.—P. thee downe into.
—*Rel.*
[3] twaine.—*Rel.*
[4] i. e. for fear of defiling.—P.
[5] Let me lie at your feet.—P. Let
me lye at your feete.—*Rel.*
[6] Vide 'Liffe & Death.' Pag. 384,
lin. 36; pag. 390, lin. 453 [of MS.]—P.
say = essay, try.—F.

[7] In the *Reliques* a stanza is made of
the next two lines :—
He gave her leave, and faire Ellen
Down at his beds feet layc :
This done the nighte drove on a pace,
And when it was neare the daye.—F.
[8] This done, the night drove on apace.
—P.
[9] And give him nowe.—*Rel.*
[10] To carry mee.—*Rel.*

And vp then rose [1] ffaire Ellen,   [page 276]

136   & gaue [2] his steed corne & hay,   She does it,

    & soe shee did on [3] the good blacke oates,

      that he might carry him the better [4] away.

shee layned [5] her backe to the Manger side,

140   & greiuouslye did groane ; [6]   but groans, for her pains come on.

    & *that* beheard his mother deere,   Childe Waters's mother

      and [7] heard her make her moane.

shee said, " rise vp, thou Child waters !   tells him to get up,

144   I thinke thou art a [8] cursed man ;

    for yonder is a ghost in thy [9] stable   there's a ghost in his stable,

      that greiuouslye doth groane,

    or else some woman laboures of [10] child,   or a woman in labour.

148   shee is soe woe begone ! "

but vp then rose Child waters, [11]   He dresses,

    & did on his shirt of silke ;

    then he put on his [12] other clothes

152   on his body as white as milke.

& when he came to the stable dore,   goes to the stable,

    full still *that* hee did [13] stand,

    that hee might heare now faire Ellen,   and hears Ellen

156   how shee made her monand [14] :

shee said, " lullabye, my [15] owne deere child !   sing to her child :

    lullabye, deere child, deere !

    I wold thy father were a king,   would that his father were a king,

160   thy mother layd on a beere !   she dead !

---

[1] [insert] the.—P.   [2] to give.—P.

[3] *Rel.* omits on.—F.

[4] to carry him th' bet.—P.

[5] leaned.—P.

[6] The *Reliques* inserts and alters thus :
She leaned her back to the manger side
And there shee made her moane,
And that beheard his mother deare,
Shee heard her ' woeful woe ; '
Shee sayd, Rise up, thou Childe Watèrs,
And into thy stable goe.—F.

[7] she.—P.

[8] thee a.—P.

[9] the.—P.

[10] with.—*Rel.*

[11] 'soon' is written at the end by P. —F.

[12] and so he did his.—P.

[13] there did he.—P.

[14] monand, is moaning, i. e. moan. Lye. —P.

[15] mine.—*Rel.*

Childe
Waters
promises

to marry
her.

"peace now," he said, "good faire Ellen!

& be of good cheere, I thee pray;

& the Bridall, & the churching both,

161   they [1] shall bee vpon one day." [2]

ffins.

---

[1] *Rel.* omits they.— F.

[2] In the admiration bestowed on fair Ellen, Enid, and patient Grisild, it is doubtful whether disgust and indignation at their friends' conduct have been suf- ficiently expressed or felt. Anything more deliberately brutal, I find it hard to conceive. "Cursed man" is surely an epithet well deserved here.— F.

Perhaps the most poetical and finest version of this poem is to be found in Bürger's melodious German ballad, entitled *Graf Walter*, which he professes to have made *nach dem Alt-englischen*, and which follows Percy's edition pretty closely. He has made it into a very pleasing poem, having paraphrased it after his own fashion with great artistic skill.

Bürger concludes thus:

"Sammt deinem Vater schreibe Gott
   Dich in sein Segensbuch!
Werd' ihm und dir ein Purpurkleid,
   Und mir ein Leichentuch!"

"O nun, O nun, süss, süsse Maid,
   Süss, süsse Maid, halt ein!
Mein Busen ist ja nicht von Eis,
   Und nicht von Marmelstein.

"O nun, O nun, süss, süsse Maid,
   Süss, süsse Maid, halt ein!
Es soll ja Tauf' und Hochzeit nun
   In *einer* Stunde sein."

He has also translated "King John and the Abbot of Canterbury" as *Der Kaiser und der Abt*, and "The Child of Elle" as *Die Entführung.*—Skeat.

Bessie: off Bednall:[1]

There are copies of this ballad in the Roxburghe and the Bagford collections, and in the Collection of Old Ballads. It is printed in the *Reliques* chiefly from the Folio MS. "compared with two ancient printed copies." It appears in numberless recent collections, as Professor Child's, Mr. Bell's *Ballads of the Peasantry*, Mr. Dixon's *Ancient Poems, Ballads and Songs of the Peasantry of England*. The Folio copy, differing slightly from the current ones, is here printed faithfully for the first time; for the editor of the *Reliques* seems to have thought that to him too, as to painters and poets,

> Quidlibet audendi semper fuit æqua potestas,

and freely used his license in the case of this ballad. He was offended by the "absurdities and inconsistencies" of the old version, "which so remarkably prevailed" in that part of the song where the Beggar discovers himself. These were, we suppose, that a Montfort should be spoken of as serving in the wars,

> When first our King his fame did advance
> And fought for his title in delicate France,

and then that the blinded soldier, when at last he got back to his country, should resign himself to a beggar's life instead of at once declaring himself and appealing to the royal bounty, if he was possessed of no estate to support him. There seemed no hope of curing such grievous deformities as these; so the whole limb was lopped off, and a new one substituted, manufactured by Robert Dodsley, author of *The Economy of Human Life*. Eight new stanzas were substituted. "By the alteration of a

---

[1] In the printed collection of Old Ballads. 1726. Vol. 2, p. 202, N. 35.—P.

few lines," says Percy, "the story is rendered much more affecting, and is reconciled to probability and true history." Let those who think it profitable or possible to bring about such a reconciliation be thankful. The copy as now at last reproduced gives one stanza (vv. 228–32) not found in the ordinary versions.

The ballad was certainly not written later than Queen Elizabeth's reign ; for, as Percy points out, *Mary Ambree* was sung to the tune of it. One reason for which Percy attributes it to that reign seems odd—because the "Queen's Arms" are mentioned in v. 23 !

It was an extremely popular ballad, and no wonder. "This very house," writes Pepys in his Diary, June 25, 1663, of Sir W. Rider's place at Bethnal Green, "was built by the blind Beggar of Bednall Green, so much talked of and sung in ballads ; but they say it was only some outhouses of it." (*apud* Mr. Chappell's *Popular Music of the Olden Time,* where the tune is given.) The story is pretty, and is told unaffectedly. Each part has its own surprise : the one revealing the wealth, the other the high birth of the Beggar. These *dénouements* are not supremely noble ; but they are such as please the crowd. Such sudden reverses are always delightful. But what a bathos it would seem if, in the ballad of King Cophetua, the Beggar-maid should turn out to be a disguised Princess, or the village maiden, whom the Lord of Burleigh in Mr. Tennyson's poem leads home, a Lady of title ! The present ballad is not satisfied to represent Bessie as " pleasant and bright," " of favours most fair," " courteous." It crowns her with vulgarer honours—showers riches on her, and proves her of high lineage.

> Regium certe genus et penates
>   Mœret iniquos.
> Crede non illam tibi de scelesta
> Plebe dilectam.

ITT was a blind beggar *that* long lost his sight,
he had a faire daughter both pleasant & bright,
& many a gallant braue sutor had shee,
4 for none was soe comelye as pretty Bessye.

A blind
beggar had
a fair
daughter.

And tho shee was of ffavor most faire,
yett seeing shee was but a beggars heyre,
of aneyent houskeepe*rs* despised was shee,
8 whose sonnes came as sutors to prettye Bessye.

House-
holders
despised her,

Wherefore in great sorrow faire Bessy did say,
" good ffather & mother, let me goe away
to seeke out my fortune, where euer itt be."
12 this sute then they granted to pretty Bessye.

so she

Then Bessye *that* was of bewtye soe bright,
they cladd in gray russett, & late in the night
with teares shee lamented her destinye ;
16 soe sadd & soe heauy was pretty Bessye.

left her
parents,

Shee went till shee came to Stratford the bow,
then knew shee not whither nor w*hi*ch way to goe ;
ffrom ffather & mother alone p*ar*ted shee,
20 who sighed & sobbed for pretty Bessye.

walkt to
Stratford,

Shee kept on her Iourney till it was day,
& went vnto Rumford along the hye way,
& att the Queenes armes entertained was shee,
24 soe faire & welfavoured was pretty Bessye.

stopt at the
Queen's
Arms,
Rumford,

Shee had not beene there a month to an End,
but M*aster* & M*istre*ss, and all, were her ffreind ;
& euery braue gallant *that* once did her see,
28 was straight-way in loue w*i*th pretty Bessye.

and all the
gallants fell
in love with
her,

Great guifts they did giue her of siluer & gold,
& in their songs daylye her loue was extold ;
her beawtye was blessed in euery degree,
32 soe faire & soe comlye was pretty Bessye.

sang of her
beauty,

The yonng men of Rumford in her had their Ioy,
shee showed herselfe curteous, & neuer to coye ;

and did her
bidding.
and att her commandement wold they [euer] bee,
36 soe ffayre and soe comly was pretty Bessye.

Four suitors
sue her :
ffowre sutors att once thé vnto her did goe,   [page 277]
thé craved her ffavor, but still shee sayd noe ;
" I wold not wish gentlemen marry with mee : "
40 yett euer thé honored pretty Bessye.

1. a rich
London
Merchant,
A merchant of London, whose wealth was not small,
was there the ffirst sutor, & proper with-all ;

2. a Gentle-
man,
the 2^d a genteleman of good degree,
44 who wooed & sued ffor pretty Bessye ;

3. a Knight,
The 3^d of them was a gallant yonng Knight,
& he came vnto her disguised in the night ;

4. the Land-
lady's son,
who will die
for her.
her Mistress owne sonne the 4. man must bee,
48 who swore he wold dye ffor pretty Bessye.

The Knight
will make
her a lady ;
" And if thou wilt wedd with me," quoth the Knight,
" Ile make thee a Ladye with Ioy [and] delight ;
my hart is inthralled by thy bewtye !
52 then grant me thy ffavor, my pretty Bessye ! "

the Gentle-
man will
clothe her in
velvet ;
The gentleman sayd, " marry with mee ;
in silke & in velnett my bessye shalbee ;
my hart lyes distressed ; O helpe me ! " quoth hee,
56 " & grant me thy Loue, thou pretty Bessye ! "

the
Merchant
will give her
jewels.
" Let me bee thy husband ! " the Merchant cold say,
" thou shalt liue in London both gallant & gay ;
my shippes shall bring home rych Iewells for thee ;
60 & I will ffor euer loue pretty Bessye."

Bessy refers
them to her
father.
Then Bessye shee sighed, & thus shee did say,
" my ffather & mother I meane to obey ;
ffirst gett their good will, & be ffaithfull to me,
64 & you shall enioye your prettye Bessye."

To euery one this answer shee made,
wherfore vnto her they Ioyffullye sayd,
"this thing to ffulfill wee doe all agree ;

Who is he ?

68 & where dwells thy ffather, my pretty Bessy ? "

"My ffather," shee said, "is soone to be seene ;
he is the blind beggar of Bednall greene,
that daylye sitts begging ffor charitye ;

The Blind Beggar of Bednall Greene,

72 he is the good ffather of pretty Bessye ;

"his markes & his tokens are knowen ffull well,
he alwayes is led with a dogg and a bell ;
a silly blind man, god knoweth, is hee,

led by a dog with a bell.

76 yett hee is the good ffather of pretty Bessye."

"Nay then," quoth the Merchant, "thou art not for
mee ! "

The Merchant,

"nor," quoth the Inholder, "my Wiffe thou shalt bee!"

Innkeeper,

"I lothe," sayd the gentleman, "a beggars degree ;

and Gentle-

80 therffore, ffarwell, my pretty Bessye ! "

man cry off.

"Why then," quoth the knight, "hap better or worsse,
I way not true loue by the waight of my pursse,
& bewtye is bewtye in euery degree,

But the Knight says

84 then welcome to me, my pretty Bessye !

he'll have Bessy.

"With thee to thy ffather fforth will I goe."
"nay sofft," quoth his kinsman, "itt must not be soe ;
a beggars daughter noe Ladye shalbe ;

His kinsman says No :

88 therfore take thy due [leaue] of pretty Bessye."

But soone after this, by breake of the day,
the knight ffrom Rumfford stole Bessye away.
the younge men of Rumfford, as thicke as might bee,

but he carries off Bessy.
The Rum-ford men

92 rode affter to ffeitch againe pretty Bessye ;

As swift as they winde to ryd they were seene
vntill they came to Bednall greene ;
& as the knight lighted most curteouslye,

overtake him ;

96 thé ffought against him for pretty Bessye ;

but he is
rescued.

But rescew speedilye came on the plaine,
or else the young knight ffor his loue had beene slaine.
this ffray being ended, then straight he did see
100 his kinsman came rayling against pretty Bessye.

The Blind
Beggar

offers to
give his girl
as much
gold as the
Knight's
kin will.

Then spake the blind Beggar, "althoe I be poore,
yett rayle not against my child at my dore;
thoe shee be not decked in veluett & pearle,
104 yett will I dropp angells with you for my girle;

"And then if my gold may better her birthe,
& equall the gold you lay on the earth,
then neyther rayle, nor grudge you to see
108 the blind beggars daughter a Lady to bee.

[page 278]

Agreed.

"Butt flirst I will heare, & haue itt well Knowen,
the gold that you drop shall all be your owne."
with that they replyed, "contented wee bee."
112 "then here is," quoth the Beggar, "ffor pretty Bessye."

The Beggar
lays down
angels
against the
Knight's

With that an angell he dropped on the ground,
& dropped in angells 500ll
& oftentimes itt was proued most plaine,
116 ffor the gentlemans one the beggar dropt twayne,

Soe that the place wherin they did sitt,
with gold was couered euery whitt.
till the
latter's store
is gone,
the gentleman hauing dropped all his store,
120 said, "Beggar, hold! for wee haue noe more.

"Thou hast ffulfilled thy promise arright."
"then marry," quoth hee, "my girle to this Knight;
and then
gives 100l.
more.
& heere," quoth hee, "Ile throw you downe
124 a 100ll more to buy her a gowne."

The gentleman that all this treasure had seene,
admired the beggar of Bednall greene,
& those that were her sutors before,
128 their fllesh for verry anger they tore.

Then was ffaire Bessye mached to the knight,
& made a Ladye in others despite ;
a ffairer Ladye was neuer scene
132 then the Beggars daughter of Bednall gree[ne].

So fair Bessy is made a Lady,

But of their sumptuos marriage & ffeast,
& what braue Lords & Knights thither we[r]e prest,
the 2^d. flitt shall sett to sight,
136 with marueilous pleasure & wished delight.

and I'll tell you all about the Marriage in Fitt II.

[Part II.]

Off a blind beggars daughter most bright,
that late was betrothed vnto a younge Knight,
all the discourse ther-of you did see :
140 but now comes the wedding of pretty Bes[sye].

The wedding

2^d parte

within a gallant pallace most braue,
adorned with all the cost thé cold haue,
this wedding was kept most sumptuously,
144 & all ffor the creditt of pretty Bessye.

is held in a palace,

All kind of daintyes & delicates sweete
was brought ffor the banquett, as it most mee[t],
Partridge, plouer, & venison most ffree,
148 against the braue wedding of pretty Bessye.

and a grand banquet is made.

This marryage through England was sp[r]ead by
repor[t],
soe that a great number therto did resort
of nobles & gentles in euery degree ;
152 & all was ffor the ffame of pretty Bessye.

Nobles and gentles come to it.

To church then went this gallant younge knight ;
h[i]s bride ffollowed, an angell most bright,
with troopes of Ladyes, the like were neuer scene
156 as went with Sweet Bessye of Bednall greene.

Ladies follow Bessy to church.

This marryage being solempnized then
with musicke performed by the skillfullest men,

the Nobles & gentles sate downe at *that* tyde,
160 each one beholding the beautifull bryde.

But after the sumptuous dinner was done,
to talke & to reason a number begunn
of the blind Beggars daughter most bright,
164 & what with his daughter he gaue to the Knight.

Then spake the Nobles, "most maruell haue wee,

this Iolly blind beggar wee cannott here see."
"my Lord," said the Bride, "my father is soe base,
168 he is loth by his presence these states[1] to disgrace;

"The prayse of a woman in questyon to bringe ˙
before her fface heere, were a flattering thing."

"wee thinke thy ffathers basenesse," quoth they,
172 "might by thy bewtye be cleane put awaye."

They had noe sooner these pleasant words spoke,
but in comes the beggar cladd in a silke cote,
a velluett capp and a ffether had hee,
176 & now a Musityan fforsooth hee wold bee;

And being led in, ffor catching of harme   [page 279]

he had a daintye Lute vnder his arme,
saies, "please you to heare any Musicke of mee?
180 Ile sing you [a] song of pretty Bessye."

With *that* his lute he twanged straight-way,
& there begann most sweetlye to play,
& after a lesson was playd 2 or 3:

184 he strayned on this song most delicatelye:

---

[1] Nobles.—F.

"A Beggars daughter did dwell on [a] greene,
who ffor her ffaire might well be a queene;
a blithe bonny Lasse, & daintye, was shee,
189 & many a one called her pretty Bessye."

the Beggar's daughter,

"Her ffather hee had noe goods nor noe Lands,
but begd [1] for a penny all day with his hand[s] ;
yett to her marriage hee gaue thousands 3 :
192 & still he hath somewatt for pretty Bessye ;

Pretty Bessy,

whose father gave her 3,000l.,

"And if any one her birth doe disdaine,
her ffather is ready with might & with maine
to proove shee is come of a Noble degree ;
196 therfore neuer fflout att pretty Bessye."

and can prove she's of noble birth.

With that the Lords & the companye round
with harty Laughter were like to sound.
att last said the Lords, "full well wee may see,
200 the Bride & the Beggar is behouldinge to thee."

The Lords laugh.

With that the Bride all blushing did rise
with the salt water within her faire eyes :
"O pardon my ffather, graue Nobles," quoth shee,
204 "that thorrow blind affection thus doteth on mee."

Bessy begs them to excuse her father's praise of her.

"If this be thy ffather," the [2] noble[s] did say,
"well may he be proud of this happy day ;
yett by his countenaunce well may wee see,
208 his birth & his ffortune did neuer agree ;

The Lords ask

"And therfor, blind man, I pray thee bewray,
& looke that the truth thou to vs doe say,
thy birth & thy parentage, what itt may bee,
212 euen for the loue thou bearest to pretty Bessye."

the Blind Beggar to confess who he really is.

[1] The _g_ is made over a _d_ in the MS.
—F.

[2] The _e_ is made over a _g_ in the MS.
—F.

He tells
them.

"Then gine me leaue, you Gengells[1] eche one,
a song more to sing, then will I goe on ;
& if *that* itt may not winn good report,
216   then doe not gine me a groat for my sport.

With King
Henry,

"When ffirst our King his ffame did Advance,
& fought for his title in delicate ffrance,
in many a place many perills past hee :
220   then was not borne my pretty Bessye.

went to
France
young
Mountford.

"And then in those warres went over to fight
many a braue duke, a Lord, & a Knight,
& with them younge Mountford, his courage most free :
224   but then was not borne my pretty Bessye.

At Blois he
was
wounded,

"Att Bloyes there chanced a terrible day,
where many braue ffrenchmen vpon the ground Lay ;
amonge them Lay Mountford for companye :
228   but then was not borne my pretty Bessye.

"But there did younge Mountford, by blow on the
face,

lost both
his eyes,
and nearly
his life,
but for a
young
woman

loose both his eyes in a very short space ;
& alsoe his liffe had beene gone with his sight,
232   had not a younge woman come forth in the night

"Amongst the slaine men, as fancy did moue,
to search & to seeke for her owne true loue ;
& seeing young Mountford there gasping to bee,

who saved
him.

236   shee saued his liffe through charitye.

Together
they begged ;

"And then all our vittalls, in Beggars attire [page 280]
att hands of good people wee then did require.

came to
Bednall
Greene.

att last into England, as now it is seene,
240   wee came, & remained att Bednall greene ;

[1] Gentles.—F.

"And thus wee haue liued in ffortunes despite,
tho [1] poore, yett contented with humble delight ;
& in my young [2] yeeres, a comfort to bee,

244 god sent mee my daughter, pretty Bessye.

and begot
Pretty
Bessy.

"And thus, noble Lords, my song I doe end,
hoping the same noe man doth offend ;
full 40 winters thus I haue beene,

248 a silly blind beggar of Bednall greene."

That's the
Beggar's
tale.

Now when the companye euerye one
did heare the strange tale in the song he had show[n],
they were all amazed, as well thé might bee,

252 both at the blind beggar & pretty Bessye.

The Lords

wonder.

with *that* he did the fayre bride imbrace,
saying, "thou art come of an honourablle race ;
thy ffather likewise of a highe degree,

256 & thou art well worthy a lady to bee!"

The Beggar
embraces
Bessy,

Thus was the ffeast ended with Ioy & delight ;
a br[i]degrome [blissful] was the young knight,
who liued in Ioy & felicitye

260 with his ffaire Ladye, pretty Bessye.

ffins.

and she and
her Knight
live happily.

---

[1] MS. the.—F.   [2] ? old.—F.

𝕳𝖚𝖌𝖍 : 𝕾𝖕𝖊𝖓𝖈𝖊𝖗 : [1]

[His great atchievements on an Embassy to france.—P.]

THIS piece is now printed from the Folio for the first time. It is no very considerable addition to English literature. It gives, with average dulness, a ridiculously bragging account of the achievements of one Sir Hugh Spencer at the court of France, whither he was dispatched as ambassador—a truly Philistine piece, such as might have been told at Gath or published at Askalon. There does not seem to be any historical ground for it. Not even the most triumphant English history of England contains any account of the terrifying a French king into promises of peace by the prowess of an English ambassador, as here happens when Spencer, with four others, manages to kill " about two or three score " of the King's guards (p. 295, l. 134), after having slain " 13 or 14 score on a previous occasion (p. 294, l. 122). The piece is, indeed, nothing better than a tissue of coarse English braggadocio. An English " old hackney " outvalues any one of a French knight's war-steeds. An English staff is as stout as three French spears bound together. And as for an English man, why he is good for a French host. What a vulgar Philistine was this ballad-monger!

THE : Court is kept att lecue London,
  & euermore shall be itt ;

The King tells Sir H. Spencer the *King* sent for a bold Embassador,

4   & S*ir* Hugh Spencer *th*at he hight.

---

[1] The subject of this Ballad seems to be all-together fabulous.—P.

" come hither, Spencer," saith our Kinge,
  " & come thou hither vnto mee,
I must make thee an Embassadour
8   betweene the King of ffrance & mee.

to go to the King of France,

" thou must comend me to the King of ffrance,
  & tell him thus & now ffrom mee,
' I wold know whether there shold be peace in his land,
12   or open warr kept still must bee.'

and ask him whether he's for peace or war.

" thoust haue thy shipp at thy comande,
  thoust neither want for gold nor ffee,
thoust haue a 100 armed men
16   all att thy bidding ffor to bee."

they [1] wind itt serued, & they sayled,
  & towards ffrance thus they be gone ;
they [1] wind did bring them safe to shore,
20   & safelye Landed euerye one.

Spencer and his men

land in France.

the ffrenchmen lay on the castle wall [2]
  the English souldiers to be-hold :
" you are welcome, traitors, out of England ;
24   the heads of you are bought and sold !"

The French

count on their heads.

with that spake proud Spencer,
  " my leege, soe itt may not bee !
I am sent an Embassador
28   ffrom our English King to yee.

Spencer says he

comes from the English King

"the King of England greetes you well,
  & hath sent this word by mee ;
he wold know whether there shold be peace in your
   Land,
32   or open warres kept still must bee."

to ask whether it's to be peace or war.

---

[1] the.—P.   [2] There is a tag at the end of this word in the MS.—F.

[page 281]

War, says
the French
King ;

"Comend me to the English Kinge,
    & tell this now ffrom mee ;
There shall neuer peace be kept in my Land
36   while open warres kept there may bee."

and his
Queen

with *that* came downe the Queene of ffrance,
    and an angry woman then was shee ;

sneers at
him for
talking to
English
traitors.

saies, "itt had beene as ffitt now for a *King*
40   to be in his chamber with his ladye,
then to be pleading with traitors out of England
    kneeling low vppon their knee."

Spencer

But then bespake him proud Spencer,
44   for noe man else durst speake but hee :

calls her a
liar.

"you haue not wiped your mouth, Madam,
    since I heard you tell a lye."

She dares
him to fight
her knight.

"O hold thy tounge, Spencer !" shee said,
48   "I doe not come to plead with thee ;
darest thou ryde a course of warr
    with a knight *that* I shall put to thee ?"

Spencer says
he has

"but euer alacke !" then Spencer sayd,
52   "I thinke I haue deserued gods cursse ;

neither
armour nor
steed.

ffor I haue not any armour heere,
    nor yett I haue noe Iusting horsse."

The Queen
tells him he's
too spindle-
shanked,

"thy shankes," quoth shee, " beneath the knee
56   are verry small aboue the shinne
ffor to doe any such honourablle deeds
    as the Englishmen say thou has done.

and too
small-
thighed

"thy shankes beene small aboue thy shoone,
60   & soe thé beene aboue thy knee ;

for a
jouster.

thou art to slender euery way,
    any good Iuster ffor to bee."

"but euer alacke," said Spencer then,
64 " for one steed of the English countrye ! "
with *that* bespake & one ffrench knight,
" this day thoust haue the Choyce of 3 : "

A French
knight offers
him one of
three steeds :

the first steed he ffeiched out,
68 I-wis he was milke white.
the flirst lloot Spencer in stirropp sett,[1]
his backe did from his belly type.[2]

1. a white

(whose back
breaks ?),

the 2.ª steed *that* he ffeitcht out,
72 I-wis[3] *that* hee was verry Browne ;
the 2.ª ffoot Spencer in stirropp settt,
that horsse & man and all ffell downe.

2. a brown

(who
tumbles
down),

the 3.ª steed *that* hee ffeitched out,
76 I-wis *that* he was verry blacke ;
the 3.ª lloote Spencer into the stirropp sett,
he leaped on to the geldings backe.

3. a black

which
Spencer
jumps on,

"but euer alacke," said Spencer then,
80 " for one good steed of the English countrye !
goo ffeitch me hither my old hacneye
that I brought with me hither beyond the sea."

but soon
calls for his
old English
hack,

but when his hackney there was brought,
84 Spencer a merry man there was hee ;
saies, " with the grace of god & St. George of England,
the ffeild this day shall goo with mee !

and hopes to
win the
fight with
him.

" I haue not fforgotten," Spencer sayd,
88 " since there was ffeild foughten att walsingam,
when the horsse did heare the trumpetts sound,
he did beare ore both horsse & man."

---

[1] There is a curl between the *e* and *t* in the MS.—F.

[2] ? MS. tylpe, with the *l* crossed at top : no doubt for *tyte*, quickly, or Sc. *tyte* to snatch, draw suddenly, Du. *tijden* to draw, goe. —F.

[3] As the *I wis* is followed by *that*, it may mean here ' I know,' and not be the adverb ' certainly.'—F.

The joust
begins;

the day was sett, & togetther they mett
92 with great mirth & melodye,
with minstrells playing & trumpetts soundinge,
with drumes striking loud & hye.

Spencer
breaks his
French spear
on his
opponent;

the flirst race that spencer run,
96 I-wis hee run itt wonderous sore;
he [hit] the knight vpon his brest,
but his speare itt burst, & wold touch noe more.

asks for an
English one,

"but euer alacke," said Spencer then,
100 "for one stalfe of the English countrye!
without youle bind me 3 together,"   [page 282]
quoth hee, "theyle be to weake ffor mee."

with *that* bespake him the ffrench Knight,
104 sayes, "bind him together the whole 30ye,
for I haue more strenght in my to hands
then is in all Spencers bodye."

and Lets the
Frenchman
fiue to four
he'll beat
him.

"but proue att parting," spencer sayes,
108 "ffrench Knight, here I tell itt thee,
for 1 will lay thee 5 to 4
the bigger man I proue to bee."

So they joust
again,

but the day was sett, & together they mett
112 with great mirth & melodye,
with minstrells playing & trumpetts soundinge,
with drummes strikeing loud & hye.

and Spencer

the 2ᵈ race *that* Spencer run,
116 I-wis hee ridd itt in much pride,

unhorses the
French
knight,

& he hitt the Knight vpon the brest,
& draue him ore his horsse beside.

but he run thorrow the ffrench campe;
120 such a race was neuer run beffore;

kills about
280 men,

he killed of *King* Charles his men
att hand of 13 or 14 score.

but he came backe againe to the K[ing]
124   & kneeled him downe vpon his knee,
saies, "a knight I haue slaine, & a steed I haue woone,
the best *that* is in this countrye."

" but nay, by my faith," said the K*ing*,
128   " Spencer, soe itt shall not bee ;
Ile haue *that* traitors head of thine
to enter plea att my Iollye."

but Spencer looket him once about ;
132   he had true bretheren left but 4 :
he killed ther of [1] the K*ing*s gard
about 2 or 3 score.

" but hold thy hands," the K*ing* doth say,
136   " Spencer ! now I doe pray thee ;
& I will goe into litle England,
vnto *that* cruell Kinge w*i*th thee."

" Nay, by my ffaith," Spencer sayd,
140   " my leege, for soe itt shall not bee ;
for on [2] you sett [3] ffoot on English ground,
you shall be hanged vpon a tree."

" why then, comend [me] to *that* English Kinge,
144   & tell him thus now ffrom mee,
that there shall neu*er* be open warres kept in my Land
whilest peace kept *that* there may bee."
     ffins.

---

[1] MS. therof.— F.   [2] on = an, if.—F.   [3] ? MS. scitt *or* scttt.—F.

Kinge : Adler : [1]

THIS Adler may be the same with that one who appears in the ballad of *King Estmere*. As that ballad narrates the marriage of the elder brother Estmere, and how the younger Adler assisted to bring it about, so here the younger brother's wooing and winning are described, and how Estmere promoted them. Perhaps the lost second line made mention of Estmere. There seems to be an error in the eleventh verse: Estmere there should be Ardine. Both brothers are somewhat fastidious in their connubial tastes. "I know not," says Estmere in the ballad dedicated to him in the *Reliques*,

> "I know not that ladye in any lande
> That is able to marry with mee."

And here Adler insists on a wife silk-soft, milk-white, lithe and lissome.

In this ballad the comic element predominates. The narrative is humorous, and so is the narration. The piece reads like a nursery tale, as Mr. Furnivall suggests in the note.

King Adler

KINGE: Adler, as hee in his window Lay,
[unto a stranger knight he did say,]
"I wold my lands they were as broada
4 as the red rose is in my garden:

describes the wife he wants.

there were not that woman this day alive,
I kept to bee my wedded wiffe,
without thé [2] were as white as any milke
8 or as soft as any silke,

---

[1] Poor stuff.—P. No doubt meant for a nursery tale.—F.   [2] she.—F.

& they royall rich wine ran downe her brest bone,
& lord ! shee were & a leath [1] maiden."

"but Estmere our *King* has a daughter soe younge ;

12 god Lord ! shees as soft as any silke,
& as white as any milke,
the royall rich wine runes downe her brest bone,
& lord ! shee is a leath maiden."

16 "but will you goe vnto King Ardine,
& will *that* ffaire Lady *that* shee wilbe mine ? "
Hee tooke the flood, & the winde was good, [page 283]
vntill hee came vnto *that* Kings hall.

20 he grett them well both great & small :
"Kinge Adler hath sent me hither to thee,
& wills thy ffayre daughter, shee will his bee."
he sayes, "if King Adler will my daughter winne,

24 of another manner he must begin :
ifaith he shall bring Lords to the Mold,
100 Shippes of good red gold,
100 Shippes of Ladyes on the moure,

28 100 Shippes of wheat boulted flower,
100 Shippes of Ladyes bright,
100 Shippes of new dubbd knights.
yett he shall doe *that* is more pine,

32 he shall take the salt sea & turne itt to red wine ;
when hee has done all these deeds,
then my faire daughter shalbe his ;
but I haue sett her on such a pinn,[2]

36 King Adler shall her neuer winne."
he tooke the flood, & they wind was good,
& neuer stayd in noe stead
vntill he came to Kinge Adlers hall.

40 he greeted them well both great & small,

---

[1] *Leath*, soft, supple, limber, pliant, Denbighshire ; in Halliwell's Gloss. Lithe.—F.

[2] ? high point, station, or 'fancy, humour,' as in 'Each sett on a mery pin,' *Fryar & Boye*, l. 484, Lo. and Hum. Songs, p. 28.—F.

and gives
him

saies " I haue beene att yonder *Kings* place
to speake with his daughter fayre of face ;
he sayes, if you will his daughter winne,

44 of another manner you must begin :

King
Estmere's
message :
the ship-
loa Is he's to
bring him,

you must bring lords to the mold,
100 Shippes of good redd gold,
100 Shippes of Ladyes of the moure,

48 100 Shippes of wheat boulted flower,
100 Shippes of Ladyes bright,
100 Shippes of new dubdd knights ;

and then
turn the sea
into wine.

& yett you must doe *that* is more pine,

52 take the salt sea & turne it to red wine ;
but he hath sett her on such a pinne
that you can her neuer winne."

Adler says

" some thing you must doe for mee,

56 I tell you all in veretye ;

they must
dress him as
a woman,
and take him
to the
Princess's
court to
board with
her ladies.

in Ladyes [clothes [1]] will yee mee bowne,
& bring mee to *that* Ladyes towne,
& boaird me there one yeere or towe

60 amongst those Ladyes for to [2] goe,
& board [3] me there yeeres 2 or 3 :
amongst those faire Ladyes for to bee."

His
messenger
takes him,

he tooke the fllood, & the wind was good,

64 & he neuer stayd nor stoode
vntill he came to *that* Ladyes hall :
he greeted them well both great & small,

and tells
Estmere he
has brought
a lady to
board among
his ladies.

sayes, "heere I haue brought a fayre Ladye ;

68 from her owne ffreinds shee is comen to bee ;
I must board her a yeere or tow
amongst your Ladyes for to goo."
these Ladyes sate all on a rowe ;

72 some began to cut silke, some for to sowe ;

---

[1] clothes, qu.—P.

[2] a *K*, seemingly marked out, stands
between *to* and *goe*.—F.

[3] Mr. Gee, in his *Vocabulary of B.
Words*, gives *board* v. n. lodge, as early as
1390 A.D.—F.

the Kings daughter sayes, "your ffingars are too
 great,
or else your eyes beene out of seat,—
I tell you full soone anon,—
76 to sowe silke or Lay gold on."
but ere the 12 moneth was come & gone
he wan the farrest Ladye of euerye one.
thé cast the lot, & one by one,
80 & all the Ladyes euerye one
they cast it ouer 2 or 3 :
King Adler ffell with the Kings daughter to lye.
but when they were in bedd Laid,
84 these words vnto her then hee said;
saies, "Lady, were *that* man this day aliue
that you wold be his wedded wiffe,
& were *that* man soe highlye borne
88 *that* you wold be his bend lemman ?"
" there is noe man this day aliue
I kept to be his wedded wiffe,
without itt were King Adler, hee,
92 the noblest Kn*ight* in Christentye.
my father hath sett me on such a pinne,[1]
King Adler must me neuer winne."
"but, Ladye, how &[2] soe betyde
96 King Adler were in your bed hidd ?
wold you not call them all att a stowre,
none of the Ladyes within your bower ?
nor wold you not call them all at a call,
100 none of the Lords in your fathers hall ?
nor wold you not call them all by-deene,
your ffather the King, nor your mother the queene ?
but soe quickly you wold gett you bowne,
104 to goe with King Adler out of the towne ? "
sais shee, "if itt wold soe betyde
King Adler were in my bed hidd,

The Princess
tells Adler
his fingers
are too big.

One night
they cast
lots for bed-
fellows,

[page 284]

and Adler
wins the
Princess.

He asks her
whom she'd
like to
marry.

" King
Adler."

" Suppose he
were in your
bed,

would you
wake up
your ladies

and the
King and
Queen, or
elope with
Adler ? "

---

[1] MS. pinne.—F.   [2] an, if.—F.

x 2

" I wouldn't
call up my
ladies,

I wold not call them all in stowre,

108　none of the Ladyes in my bower;

nor I wold not call them all att a call,

none of the Lords in my fathers hall;

nor I wold not call them all by-deenee,

112　my ffather the King, nor my mother the Queene;

but would
go off with
Adler."

but soe quicklye I wold gett me bowne

to goe with King Adler out of the towne."

Adler
discovers
himself,

" but turne thee, Ladye, hither to mee !

116　for I am the K[ing] that speakes to thee ! "

"alacke ! King Adler ! I shall catch cold,

for I can neuer tread on the mold,

but vpon rich cloth of gold

120　that is 5 thousand fold."

carries his
love off
under his
arm, and
sails away
home.

"peace, faire Lady ! youst catch noe harme,[1]

for I will carry you vnder mine arme."

he tooke the fflood, & the winde was good,

124　& he neuer stinted nor stood

vntill he came to his owne hall;

he greeted them well both great & small.

May we all
prosper till
men wed so !

god send vs all to be well, & none to be woe,

128　vntill they wine their true loue soe !

ffins.

[1] harne in MS.—F.

Down the left margin of this p. 284
of the MS. is written :

my sweet brother sweet Cous　　*Edward
Revell*　*Bouke*　*Elizabeth Revell.*

And in the same hand are written on the
right of verse 3 of " Boy and Mantle "
the sam and *f henercy.*—F.

Boy and Mantle.[1]

This ballad was printed by Professor Child as the first in his *English and Scottish Ballads*, under the title of "The Boy and the Mantle," with the following Introduction :—

No incident is more common in romantic fiction, than the employment of some magical contrivance as a test of conjugal fidelity, or of constancy in love. In some romances of the Round Table, and tales founded upon them, this experiment is performed by means either of an enchanted horn, of such properties that no dishonoured husband or unfaithful wife can drink from it without spilling, or of a mantle which will fit none but chaste women. The earliest known instances of the use of these ordeals are afforded by the *Lai du Corn*, by Robert Bikez, a French minstrel of the twelfth or thirteenth century, and the *Fabliau du Mantel Mautaillé*, which, in the opinion of a competent critic, dates from the second half of the thirteenth century, and is only the older lay worked up into a new shape. (Wolf, *Ueber die Lais*, 327, sq., 342, sq.) We are not to suppose, however, that either of these pieces presents us with the primitive form of this humorous invention. Robert Bikez tells us that he learned his story from an abbot, and that "noble ecclesiast" stood but one further back in a line of tradition which curiosity will never follow to its source. We shall content ourselves with noticing the most remarkable cases of the use of these and similar talismans in imaginative literature.

In the *Roman de Tristan*, a composition of unknown anti-

---

[1] This seems to have furnish'd the Hint of Florimel's Girdle to Spencer. Lib. 4. Cant. 2. St. 25 seq. Lib. 5. Cant. 5.—P.

quity, the frailty of nearly all the ladies at the court of King
Marc is exposed by their essaying a draught from the marvellous
horn, (see the English *Morte Arthur*, Southey's ed. i. 297). In
the *Roman de Perceval*, the knights, as well as the ladies,
undergo this probation. From some one of the chivalrous
romances Ariosto adopted the wonderful vessel into his *Orlando*,
(xlii. 102, sq., xliii. 31, sq.,) and upon his narrative La Fontaine
founded the tale and the comedy of *La Coupe Enchantée*. In
German, we have two versions of the same story,—one, an
episode in the *Krone* of Heinrich vom Türlein, thought to have
been borrowed from the *Perceval* of Chrétien de Troyes, (*Die
Sage vom Zauberbecher*, in Wolf, *Ueber die Lais*, 378,) and
another, which we have not seen, in Bruns, *Beiträge zur kriti-
schen Bearbeitung alter Handschriften*, ii. 139; while in English,
it is represented by the highly amusing " bowrd," which we are
about to print, and which we have called *The Horn of King
Arthur*.[1] The forms of the tale of the mantle are not so
numerous. The *fabliau* already mentioned was reduced to
prose in the sixteenth century, and published at Lyons, (in
1577,) as *Le Manteau mal taillé*, (Legrand's *Fabliaux*, 3rd ed.
i. 126,) and under this title, or that of *Le Court Mantel*, is very
well known. An old fragment (*Der Mantel*) is given in Haupt
and Hoffmann's *Altdeutsche Blätter*, ii. 217, and the story is also
in Bruns' *Beiträge*. Lastly, we find the legends of the horn and
the mantle united, as in the German ballad *Die Ausgleichung*,
(*Des Knaben Wunderhorn*, i. 389,) and in the English ballad of
The Boy and the Mantle, where a magical knife is added to the
other curiosities. All three of these, by the way, are claimed by
the Welsh as a part of the *insignia* of Ancient Britain, and the
special property of Tegau Eurvron, the wife of Caradog with the
strong arm. (Jones, *Bardic Museum*, p. 49.)

In other departments of romance, many other objects are

---

[1] Child's Ballads, i. 17–27, from MS. Ashmole 61, fol. 59–62.

endowed with the same or an analogous virtue. In Indian and Persian story, the test of innocence is a red lotus-flower; in *Amadis*, a garland, which fades on the brow of the unfaithful;[1] in *Perceforest*, a rose. The *Lay of the Rose* in *Perceforest* is the original (according to Schmidt) of the much-praised tale of Senecé, *Camille, ou la Manière de filer le parfait Amour*, (1695),—in which a magician presents a jealous husband with a portrait in wax, that will indicate by change of colour the infidelity of his wife,—and suggested the same device in the twenty-first novel of Bandello, (Part First,) on the translation of which in Painter's *Palace of Pleasure*, (vol. ii. No. 28,) Massinger founded his play of *The Picture*. Again, in the tale of *Zeyn Alasman and the King of the Genii*, in the *Arabian Nights*, the means of proof is a mirror, that reflects only the image of a spotless maiden; in that of the carpenter and the king's daughter, in the *Gesta Romanorum*, (c. 69,) a shirt, which remains clean and whole as long as both parties are true; in *Palmerin of England*, a cup of tears, which becomes dark in the hands of an inconstant lover; in the *Fairy Queen*, the famous girdle of Florimel; in *Horn and Rimnild* (Ritson, *Metrical Romances*, iii. 301,) as well as in one or two ballads in this collection [ed. Child], the stone of a ring; in a German ballad, *Die Krone der Königin von Afion*, (Erlach, *Volkslieder der Deutschen*, i. 132,) a golden crown, that will fit the head of no incontinent husband. Without pretending to exhaust the subject, we may add three instances of a different kind: the Valley in the romance of *Lancelot*, which being entered by a faithless lover

---

[1] So also in the well-told story of *The Wright's Chaste Wife* (E. E. T. Soc. 1865) a garland is the test:

Haue here thys garlond of roses ryche,
In alle thys lond ys none yt lyche;
For ytt wylle euer be newe
(Wete þou wele withowtyn fable,)
Alle the whyle thy wyf ys stable

The chaplett wolle hold hewe;
And yf thy wyfe vse putry,
Or tolle eny man to lye her by,
Then wolle yt change hewe;
And by the garlond þou may see,
Fekyll or fals yf þat sche be,
Or ellys yf sche be trewe.
l. 53–66.—F.

would hold him imprisoned forever; the Cave in *Amadis of Gaul*, from which the disloyal were driven by torrents of flame; and the Well in *Horn and Rimnild*, (*ibid.*) which was to show the shadow of Horn, if he proved false.

In conclusion, we will barely allude to the singular anecdote related by Herodotus, (ii. 111,) of Phero, the son of Sesostris, in which the experience of King Marc and King Arthur is so curiously anticipated. In the early ages, as Dunlop has remarked, some experiment for ascertaining the fidelity of women, in defect of evidence, seems really to have been resorted to. "By the Levitical law," (*Numbers* v. 11–31,) continues that accurate writer, "there was prescribed a mode of trial, which consisted in the suspected person drinking water in the tabernacle. The mythological fable of the trial by the Stygian fountain, which disgraced the guilty by the waters rising so as to cover the laurel wreath of the unchaste female who dared the examination, probably had its origin in some of the early institutions of Greece or Egypt. Hence the notion was adopted in the Greek romances, the heroines of which were invariably subjected to a magical test of this nature, which is one of the few particulars in which any similarity of incident can be traced between the Greek novels and the romances of chivalry." See DUNLOP, *History of Fiction*, London, 1814, i. 239, sq.; LEGRAND, *Fabliaux*, 3d ed., i. 149, sq., 161: SCHMIDT, *Jahrbücher der Literatur*, xxix. 121; WOLF, *Ueber die Lais*, 174–177; and, above all, GRAESSE's *Sagenkreise des Mittelalters*, 185, sq.

The Boy and the Mantle was [said to be] "printed verbatim" from the Percy MS., in the *Reliques of Ancient English Poetry*, iii. 38.

A boy comes to Carlisle

IN the third day of May,
  to Carleile did come
a kind curteous child
4   *that* cold much of wisdome.

a kirtle & a Mantle
   this Child had vppon,
with branches [1] and ringes,   *richly*
8   full richelye bedone.   *dressed and*
                                   jewelled.

he had a sute of silke
   about his middle drawne ;
without he cold [2] of curtesye,
12   he thought itt much shame.

"god speed thee, *King* Arthur,   *He greets*
   sitting att thy meate!   *Arthur*
& the goodlye Queene Gueneuer!   *and*
16   I canott her fforgett.   *Guenevere, .*

" I tell you Lords in this hall,
   I hett you all heate,[3]   [page 285]
except you be the more surer
20   is you for to dread."

he plucked out of his potewer,[4]   *and pulls*
   & longer wold not dwell,   *out of his*
he pulled forth a pretty mantle   *bag*
24   betweene 2 nut-shells.   *a mantle*

" haue thou here *King* Arthure,   *which he*
   haue thou heere of mee ;   *tells Arthur*
giue itt to thy comely queene
28   shapen as itt is alreadye ;   *to give to*
                                    Guenevere.

" itt shall neuer become *that* wiffe
   that hath once done amisse."
then euery Knight in the Kings court
32   began to care for his wiffe.[5]

---

[1] Brooches.—P. ? MS. branches.—F.
[2] knew.—F.
[3] heed, qu.—P. heede.—*Rel.* hete,
a promise.—F.
[4] See pag. 382, ver. 98 [poteuere in

Sir Degree.]—P. poterrer.—*Rel.* The
first syllable must be *porte*, carry.—F.
[5] began to care for his.—P. ? *care* in
MS.—F

forth came dame Gueneuer;
   to the mantle shee her biled[1] :
the Ladye shee was new fangle,[2]
36   but yett shee was affrayd.

when shee had taken the Mantle,
   shee stoode as she had beene madd :
it was from the top to the toe
40   as sheeres had itt shread.[3]

one while was itt gaule,[4]
   another while was itt greene,
another while was itt wadded,—
44   ill itt did her beseeme,—

another while was it blacke
   & bore the worst hue.
"by my troth," quoth King Arthur,
48   "I thinke thou be not true."

shee threw downe the mantle
   that bright was of blee.[5]
fast with a rudd[6] redd
52   to her chamber can shee flee ;

shee curst the weauer & the walker[7]
   that clothe that had wrought,
& bade a vengeance on his crowne
56   that hither hath itt brought ;

and says
she'd rather
be in a wood
than
shamed.
"I had rather be in a wood
   vnder a greene tree,
then in King Arthurs court
60   shamed for to bee."

---

[1] Query the le in the MS.—F. hied.
—Rel.
[2] new fangle is fond of a new thing,
catching at novelties, ab. A.-S. fangan,
apprehendere, capere, corripere, hine
fang, Gloss. ad G. D.—P.

[3] i. e. divided.—P.
[4] gule, qu.—P. red.—F.
[5] colour. complexion, bleoh—idem,
Saxon.— P.
[6] Complexion.—P.
[7] Fuller, Jun.—P. A.-S. wealcere.—F.

Kay called forth his ladye,
    & bade her come neere;
saies, "madam, & thou be guiltye,
64   I pray thee hold thee there."

Kay calls forth his wife.

forth came his Ladye
    shortlye & anon;
boldlye to the Mantle
68   then is shee gone.

She tries the mantle,

when she had tane the Mantle
    & cast it her about,
then was shee bare
72   all aboue the Buttocckes.[1]

but it leaves her buttocks bare.

then euery Knight
    that was in the Kings court
talked, laug[h]ed, & showted,
76   full oft att *that* sport.

shee threw downe the mantle
    that bright was of blee :
ffast with a red rudd
80   to her chamber can shee flee.

She runs off with a red face.

forth came an old *Knight*
    pattering [2] ore a creede,
& he proferred to this litle boy
84   20 markes to his meede,

An old knight offers the boy a reward

& all the time of the Christmasse
    willignglye to ffeede ;
for why this Mantle might
88   doe his wiffe some need.

to try it on his wife.

---

[1] Before all the rout.—*Rd*.

[2] patter, obscuro murmure humilibus que susurris hypocritarum instar, coram populo preculas fundere—Junius. They say in Shropshire to *pather*, i. e. to make a noise, as when one rubs the feet against the ground, & scratches.—P.

She takes it,

When shee had tane the mantle   [page 286]
    of cloth *that* was made,

and has only a tassel and a thread on her.

shee had no more left on her
92   but a tassell & a threed.
then euery K*night* in the K*ings* court
    bade " euill might shee speed."

She rushes off shamed,

shee threw downe the Mantle
96   *that* bright was of blee,
& fast with a redd rudd
    to her chamber can shee flee.

Craddock tells his wife to try

Craddocke called forth his Ladye,
100   & bade her come in ;
saith, " winne this mantle, Ladye,
    with a litle dinne :

and win the mantle.

" winne this mantle, Ladye,
104   & it shalbe thine
if thou neuer did amisse
    since thou wast mine."

She comes,

forth came Craddockes Ladye
108   shortlye & anon,
but boldlye to the Mantle
    then is shee gone.

puts it on ;

when shee had tane the mantle
112   & cast itt her about,

It begins to crinkle up.

vpp att her great toe
    itt began to crinkle [1] & crowt ;
shee said " bowe downe, Mantle,
116   & shame me not for nought ;

[1] to crinkle, to go in & out, to run in flexures ; from krinckelen *Belg.* Johnson.   —P. *Crout,* a variant of *crowd,* to draw close together.--F.

" once I did amisse, She confesses
   I tell you certainlye,
when I kist Craddockes mouth that she
120 Vnder a greene tree, kissed
Craddock
when I kist Craddockes mouth
   before he marryed mee." before he
married her.

when shee had her shreeuen,[1] The mantle
124 & her sines shee had tolde, vncriukles.
the mantle stoode about her clothes her,
   right as shee wold,

seemelye of coulour, and glitters
128 glittering like gold. like gold.
then euery Kn*ight* in Arthurs court
   did her behold.

then spake dame Gueneuer Guenevere
132 to Arthur our King,
" she hath tane yonder mantle, maligns
   not w*i*th wright[2] but w*i*th wronge ! Craddock's
wife,

" see you not yonder woman
136 *tha*t maketh her selfe soe cleare[3] ?
I haue seene tane out of her bedd says she has
seen fifteen
   of men fiueteeene, men taken
out of her
bed.

" Preists, Clarkes, & wedded men
140 from her by-deene !
yett shee taketh the mantle
   & maketh her-selfe cleane ! "

then spake the litle boy The Boy
144 *tha*t kept the mantle in hold ;
sayes " K*ing* ! Chasten thy wiffe ! tells Arthur
   of her words shee is to bold. to restrain
his wife,

---

[1] i. e. confessed : shrive, fateri, confi-
teri. Hinc shrovetide. Jun.—P.

[2] right.—P.
[3] cleane.—P.

"shee is a bitch & a witch,
148　　& a whore bold !
King, in thine owne hall
　　thou art a Cuchold !"

A litle boy [1] stoode
152　　looking ouer a dore ;
he was ware of a wyld bore [2]
wold haue werryed a man.

he pulld forth a wood kniffe ;
156　　fast thither *that* he ran ;
he brought in the bores head,
　　& quitted him like a man.

he brought in the bores head,
160　　and was wonderous bold :
He said, "there was neuer a Cucholds　[page 287]
　　　　kniffe
carue itt that cold."

some rubbed their k[n]iues
164　　vppon a whetstone ;
some threw them vnder the table,
　　& said they had none.

K*ing* Arthus & the Child
168　　stood looking them vpon [3];
all their k[n]iues edges
　　turned backe againe.

Craddocke had a litle kniue
172　　of Iron & of steele ;
he birtled [4] the bores head

---

[1] The little boy.—P.
[2] And there as he was looking
　　He was ware of a wyld Bore.
　　　　　　　　　　Qu.—P.

[3] upon them, Qu.—P.
[4] birtled, or britled.—P. A.-S. *bryt-
tian*, to divide into fragments, distribute.
—F.

wonderous weele,
that euery K*night* in the K*ing*s court
176 had a morssell.

the litle boy had a horne
     of red gold *that* ronge ;
he said, "there was noe Cuckolde
180 shall drinke of my horne,
but he shold itt sheede
     Either behind or beforne."

The Boy
says no
cuckold can
drink out of
his horn
without
spilling.

some shedd on their shoulder,
184 & some [1] on their knee ;
he *that* cold not hitt his mouth
     put it in his eye;
& he *that* was a Cuckold,
188 euery man might him see.

Many try,

Craddoccke wan the horne
     & the bores head;
his ladye wan the mantle
192 vnto her meede.
Euerye such a louely Ladye,
     God send her well to speede !

but
Craddock
alone can
do it.

God bless
ladies like
Craddock's
wife !

ffins.

[1] sone in the MS.—F.

["*When as I doe reccord*," *printed in* Lo. and Hum. Songs,
     p. 68–9, *follows here in the MS.*]

White rose & red: [1]

This is but a pedestrian composition, being nothing more than a passage of a dull and not very accurate history of England turned into yet duller and as inaccurate verse. It was written, or perhaps was revised and added to, after 1619, as the Queen of James I., Anne of Denmark, is spoken of as dead and gone (v. 198), and she died in that year. The principal hero is Henry VII., who is pronounced a paragon of virtue, and *inter alia* a most faithful and affectionate husband. *De mortuis nil nisi bonum*, has been the poetaster's motto; or rather *De Tudore mortuo nil nisi optimum*. The piece may have had its use in aiding and abetting the memories of the common people. Books were not yet so cheap and plentiful but that artificial memory-helps were welcome. The ballad form was in extreme requisition and popularity for all manners of subjects in the first half of the seventeenth century. Everything was be-balladed.

In the wars
of the Roses

WHEN yorke & Lancaster made warre
   within this ffamous Land,
the lines of all our Noble men
4   did in great danger stand.

many
kings were
left heirless,

7 Kings in bloodye ffeilde
   ffor Englands crowne did ffight,
& yett their heyres were, all but twaine,
8   of liffe bereaued quite.

---

[1] In the printed Collection of Old Ballads, 1726, Vol. 2. p. 206, N. xv.—P.   Written or recast in James I.'s time: see lines 78, 149.—F.

ther 30000 Englishmen
   were in one battell slaine;
yett all *that* English blood cold not
12   one setled peace obtaine.

and 30,000
lives

secured no
peace.

father[s] killed their owne deare sonne,
   the sonnes the ffathers slew,
& kinsmen ffought against their K*ing*,
16   & none eche other knew.

att Lenght, by Heneryes Lawfull claime,[1]
   these wasting warres had end,
for Englands peace he did restore,
20   & did the same defend.

But Henry
VII.

ffor tyrant Richard named the 3^d,
   the breeder of this woe,
by him was slaine nere Leister towne,
24   as chronicles doe shoe.

slew Richard
III.

all ffeare of warr was then Exiled,
   wh*i*ch Ioyed eche Englishman;
& dayes of long desired peace
28   w*i*thin this Land began.

and brought
peace

to the land.

he ruled this kingdome by true loue,
   to gaine his subiects lines;
then men lined quietly att home
32   w*i*th their children & their wiues.

K*ing* Henery tooke such princely care
   our ffurther peace to frame,
tooke ffaire Elizabeth to wiffe,[2]
36   *that* gallant yorkshire dame.

Henry

married

---

[1] One stroke of the *m* is wanting in the MS.—F.   [2] See *Ladye Bessiye* in vol. iii.—F.

4 Edwardes daughter, blest of god,
 to scape king Edwards [1] spight,
was thus made Englands peereles Queene,
40 & Heneryes hartes delight.

this Henery, ffirst of Tudors name
 & last of Lancaster,

York's
heiress ;

with Yorkes right heyre a true loues knott
44 did knitt & make ffast there.

the White
Rose bedded
with the
Red ;

renowned yorke, the white rose gaue ;
 braue Lancaster the redd ;
by wedlocke both ioyned were
48 to lye in one princely bed.

these roses grew, & buded fayre,
 & with soe good a grace,

and they are
a badge in
the Royal
Arms.

that Kings of Engl[a]nd in their armes [2]
52 affords a worthy place.

May they
flourish
still !

& fflourish may these roses still,
 that all they world may tell !
the owners of these princely fflowers
56 in vertue to Exell !

To glorifye these roses more,   [page 289]
 king henerye & his Queene
did place their pictures in red gold,
60 most gorgeous to be scene.

The King's
Guard wear

the Kings owne guard doe weare them now
 vpon their backe & brest,
where loue & loyaltye remaines,
64 & euermore may rest.

---

[1] That is, Richard's.—Adams.
[2] The Red and White Roses never
were, strictly speaking, in the Royal
Arms, but were and are a badge borne
with them.—G. E. Adams, *Rouge Dragon.*

the red rose on the backe is placed,
  theron a crowne of gold ;
the wh[i]te rose on the brest as rich,
68   and castlye [1] to behold,

the Red Rose on their backs,

the White on their breasts,

bedecket with siluer studdes,
  & coates of scarlett & redd,
a blushing hew, which Englands fame
72   this many yeeres hath spredd.

on their scarlet coats,

this Tudor & Plantaginett
  these honors ffirst devised
to welcome home a settled peace
76   by vs soe dearlye prized :

in honour of peace so prized

which peace now maintained is
  by Iames our gracyous Kinge ;
ffor peace brings plentye to this Land,
80   with many a blessed thing.

(which James preserves).

to speake of Heneryes praise againe :
  his princley liberall hand
gaue giufts & graces many wayes
84   vnto this ffamous Land.

Henry gave liberally,

wherfore the Lord him blessing sent
  for to encrease his store,
for that he left more welthe to vs
88   then any King before.

and the Lord blest him,

the ffirst blessing was to his Queene,
  a giuft aboue the rest,
which brought him sonnes & daughters faire
92   to make his Kingdome blest.

with sons and daughters

the royall blood, which was att Ebbe,
  soe encreased by this Queene,
that Englands heyre vnto this day
96   doth fflourish ffresh & greene.

(whose line continues now).

[1] costlye.—F.

His heir,
Arthur
prince of
Wales,
sailed to
Spain

the first blossome of this seed
 was Arthur, Prince of wales,
whose vertue to the Spanish court
100 quite ore the Ocean sayles,

and married
Ferdinand's
daughter
Katherine,

where fferdinando, *King* of Spayne,
 his daughter Katherine gaue
ffor wiffe vnto this English Prince
104 a thing w*h*ich god wold haue.

but died
young,
(April 1502,)

yett Arthur, in his loftye youth
 & blooming time of age,
resigned vp his sweetest liffe
108 to deathes imperyall rage.

who dying thus, noe Isue left,—
 the sweet of natures Ioy,—
to England's
grief.
did compasse England round w*i*th greeffe,
112 & Spaine w*i*th sadd annoye.

But Henry
VII. had
another boy,

Henry VIII.,

yett Henery, to increase his Ioy,
 a Henery of his name,
in ffollowing time 8 Henery called,[1]
116 a king of worthy ffame ;

who
conquered
French
towns,

he Conquered Bullein w*i*th his sword,
 & many townes of ffrance ;
his kinglye manhood & his fortitude
120 did Englands ffame advance.

then Popish Abbyes he supprest,
 & Pappistrye put downe,
put down
Papistry,
& bound their Land by Parlaiment
124 vnto his royall crowne.

---

[1] The *d* is made over an *l* in the MS.—F.

he had 3 Children by 3 Queenes,
   all Princes raigning here,
Edward, Marry, & Elizabeth,
128   A Queene beloued most deere.   [page 290]

and had
three
children,
who all
reigned,

yett these 3 branches bare noe fruite;
   noe such blessing god did send;
wherby the King by Tudors name
132   in England here hath end.

but left no
issue.

Plantaginett ffirst Tudor was
   named Elizabeth;
Ellizabeth Last Tudor was,
136   the greatest Queene on Earth.

The first and
last Tudors
were
Elizabeths.

This Tudor & Plantaginett,
   by yeelding vnto death,
haue made steward now the greates[t] King
140   *that* is now vpon the earth.

A Stewart
now reigns.

to speake of the 7 Henery I must,
   whose grace gaue ffree consent
to haue his daughters marryed both
144   to kings of his descent.

Henry VII.

married his
eldest
daughter to

his Eldest daughter Margarett
   was made great Scottlands Queene,
as wise, as ffaire, as vertnous,
148   as euer[1] was Ladye scene.

the King of
Scotland,

of this faire *Queene* our royall King
   by Lineall course descended,
which weareth now the Imperyall crowne,
152   which god now still defendeth.

and James
is her
descendant.

---

[1] Only one stroke for the *u* in the MS.—F.

his second daughter, Marye called,
 as Princelye by degree,
was by her ffather worthy thought
156 the Queene of ffrance to bee;

& after to the Duke of Suffollke
 was made a Noble wiffe;
& in this ffamous English court
160 shee led a virtuous liffe.

thus Henery & his louely Queene
 reioced to see that day,
to haue their Children thus advancet
164 to honors euery way,

which purchased pleasure & content
 with many a yeeres delight,
till sad mischance by cruell death
168 procured them both a spighte.

this worthy Queene, this gracyous dame,
 this mother meeke and mild,
to add more number to their Ioyes,

172 againe proued bigg with child;

wheratt the King reioced much,
 & against that carefull hower

he lodged his deere & louelye Queene
176 in Londons stately Tower.

which Tower proued ffatall once
 to Princes of degree;

itt proued ffatall to this Queene,
180 for therin died shee,

in Child bed [she] lost he[r] sweet liffe,
 her liffe estemed soe deere,
which had beene Englands Louely Queene
184 many a happy yeere.

therfore the *King* was greeued sore,
 & many monthes did mourne,
 & wept & sighet, & said " like her
188 he cold not flind out one ;

Henry
mourned,

" nor none he wold in ffancy chuse
 to make his wedded wiffe,
but a widdower he wold remaine
192 the remnant of his liffe."

and vowed

to remain a
widower.

his latter dayes he spent in peace
 & quiettnesse of mind.
like *King* & *Queene* as these 2 were,
196 the world can hardlye flind !

Two like
these can
scarce be
found.

yett such a *King* as now wee haue,
 & such a *Queene* wee had,
who hath heauenly powers from aboue,
200 & giusts ¹ as the 2 hadd.

God saue our Prince, & *King* & Land,
 & send them long to raigine !
in health, in welth, in quietnesse,
204 amongst vs to remaine !   ffins.

God bless
our King
and land !

¹ ? ghosts, spirits; *or miswritten for* giufts.—F.

Bell my Wiffe.[1]

THE Folio version of this song is here printed in its integrity for the first time; for in the copy given in the *Reliques*, "the corruptions" "are removed by the assistance of the Scottish edition"—that in Ramsay's *Tea-Table Miscellany*. Our readers will not be sorry to see these "corruptions." They give, indeed, a somewhat different turn to the piece. Whereas in the ordinary version, the temptation against which the good man is warned is vaguely "pride," it takes in the Folio MS. a more definite shape. He is tempted to abandon his agricultural life and turn courtier. He vows:

> I'll go find the court within,
> I'll no longer lend nor borrow,
> I'll go find the court within,
> For I'll have a new cloak about me.

Bell, his wife, rejoins:

> —good husband, follow my counsel now:
> Forsake the court and follow the plough.
> Man, take thy old coat about thee.

This definiteness inclines us to believe that this version is older than the current one. The poem naturally grew vaguer as it grew generally popular.

That it enjoyed an extensive popularity is shown by the appearance of one of its verses in *Othello*, and the delight with

[1] This Song is in Ramsay's Tea-table Miscellany, p. 105. [1753]. The printed copy is much better than this, if it has not had some modern Improvements. This seems to have been strip'd of its Scottisms by some English hand: which is observable of some other in this Collection.— P.

which Cassio hears Iago troll it out. "'Fore God, an excellent song," says the lieutenant of "And let the canakin clink, clink;" and of "King Stephen was a worthy peer," "Why, this is a more exquisite song than the other."

The dialect in which it is written, and the general character of the piece—its scenery, its economy, its canniness — clearly imply a northern origin. As to the time at which it was written, all that can be said is, that it clearly reflects an age of social disturbance and alteration—an age growing "so picked that the toe of the peasant comes so near the heel of the courtier he galls his kibe." The piece is something more than a mere humorous domestic altercation as to the replenishing of a husband's wardrobe. It is, in fact, a controversy between the spirits of Social Revolution and Social Conservatism. The man is anxious to better himself, no longer content to tend cows and drive the plough; his neighbours are rising and advancing around him; the clown is not now distinguishable from the gentleman. The old arrangements have had their day. Metaphorically, the old scarlet cloak, which some four-and-forty years ago was so satisfactory, and kept out so well the wind and rain, is now but a "sorry clout," looks right mean and shabby among the spruce black, green, yellow, blue garments that flaunt around it, and must certainly be cast off for something new and fashionable. In answer to all these grumblings, the other reminds him how well their old life has suited them, how their employments (though humble) have been sufficient for their needs, how they have lived and loved together for many a long year and been blessed with many children and the happiness of seeing them grow up in the nurture and admonition of the Lord, how Royalty had contented itself with the smallest of tailor's bills and yet thought that excessive, and, generally, how pride undermines a country. Her advice is, that he should not disquiet himself with efforts to rise

in the world, but should rest content with the state wherein he
is. The goodman, weary of controversy, lets his wife's counsel
prevail. He sees, in the version now given (the ordinary form
of the last verse is much less striking), what his wife cannot
see—that is, how times have altered; but he consents to acquiesce in his present position—θῆσσαν τράπεζαν αἰνέσαι—

> O Bell my wife! why dost thou flyte?
>   Now is now, and then was then;
> We will live now obedient life,
>   Thou the woman and I the man.
> It's not for a man with a woman to threap
>   Unless he first gives over the plea.
> We will live now as we began,
>   And I'll have mine old cloak about me.

As to the author, nothing is known. Undoubtedly he was one
who had noted the signs of his times. He would seem to
have sympathised with those who regarded the social changes
transpiring as dangerous and to be deprecated. To us he is a
mere voice crying.

It freezes hard,

"THIS winters weather itt waxeth cold,   [page 291]
  & ffrost itt ffreeseth on euery hill,
  & Boreas blowes his blasts soe bold

and the cattle are likely to die.

4 that all our cattell are like to spill.
  Bell[1] my wiffe, shee[2] loues noe strife,

My wife Bell says "Get up and save the cow's life. Put your old cloak on."

  she sayd vnto my quietlye,[3]
  'rise vp, & saue Cow crumbockes liffe!
8 man! put thine old cloake about thee!'

"Steady, wife. My cloak's very old,

[4] "O Bell my wiffe! why dost thou fflyte[5]?
  thou kens my cloake is verry thin;

---

[1] Then [Bell].—P.
[2] who.—P.
[3] to me right hastily.—P.
[4] This stanza not in print:—and yet

seems necessary to support the dialogue.
—P.
[5] A.-S. flitan, to strive, quarrel.—F.

itt is soe sore ouer worne,

12   a cricke [1] theron cannott runn :

Ile goe ffind the court w*i*thin,

Ile noe longer lend nor borrow ;

Ile goe ffind tho court [2] w*i*thin,

I shall get a new one."

16   for Ile haue a new cloake about me."

"Cow Crumbocke is a very good cowe,

"The cow's a good cow,

shee has alwayes beene good to the pale,

shee has helpt vs to butter & cheese, I trow,

20   & other things shee will not fayle ;

for I wold be loth to see her pine ;

don't let he die ;

therfore, good husband, ffollow my councell now,

forsake the court & follow the ploughe ;

24   man ! take thine old coate about thee ! "

put your old coat on."

[3] "My cloake itt was a verry good cloake,

it hath beene alwayes good to the weare,

itt hath cost mee many a groat,

28   I have had itt this 44 yeere ;

sometime itt was of the cloth in graine, [4]

"I've had my cloak forty-four years,

itt is now but a sigh [5] clout, as you may see ;

It will neither hold out winde nor raine ;

and mean to get a new one."

32   & Ile haue a new kloake [6] about mee."

"It is 44 yeeres agoe

"Yes, we've been together forty-four years,

since the one of vs the other did ken,

& wee haue had betwixt vs both,

36   children either nine or ten ;

---

[1] *Cricke*, most probably an old word for a louse. Jamieson. Compare the description of Avarice in Langlande's Vision of Piers Ploughman, Passus V. l. 107-113, p. 58, Vernon Text, ed. Skeat:

Þenne com Conetyse . . .
In A toren Tabert of twelue Wynter Age.
But ȝif a lous couþe lepe, I con hit not
I-leue

Heo scholde wandre on þat walk, hit was so þred-bare.—F.

[2] Only half the *u* in the MS.—F.

[3] This Stanza is very different from that in print.—P.

[4] Fr. *Cramoisi* : m. crimson colour. *Sot en cramoisi.* An Asse in graine. Cotgrave.—F.

[5] ? sorry, miserable.—F.

[6] ? a *c* made over the first *k* in the MS.—F.

<table>
<tr><td>

and brought
ten children
up.

</td><td>

wee haue brought them vp to women & men
    in the feare of god I trow they bee ;

</td></tr>
</table>

and brought ten children up.

> wee haue brought them vp to women & men
>> in the feare of god I trow they bee ;
> & why wilt thou thy selfe misken ?

Don't be proud ; put your old cloak on."

40   man ! take thine old cloake about thee ! ' "

"O Bell my wiffe ! why doest thou flyte ?
    now is nowe, & then was then ;
seeke all the world now throughout,
    thou kens not Clownes from gentlemen ;

" Old times are old ; all people dress fine now,

44

they are cladd in blacke, greene, yellow, & blew,[1]
    soe ffarr aboue their owne degree ;

and I'll have a new cloak too."

once in my liffe Ile take a vow,[2]
    ffor Ile haue a new cloake about mee."

48

" King Harry thought his breeches too dear at 5s.

"King Harry was a verry good K[ing ;]
    I trow his hose cost but a Crowne ;
he thought them 12ᵈ ouer to deere,
    therfore he called the taylor Clowne.

52

he was King & wore the Crowne,
    & thouse but of a low degree ;

Don't be proud ; put your old cloak on."

itts pride *that* putts this cumtrye downe ;

56   man ! put thye old Cloake about thee !

" Well, it's no good

[3] "O Bell my wiffe ! why dost thou fflyte ?
    now is now, & then was then ;
wee will liue now obedyent liffe,

60   thou the woman, & I the man.

for a man to dispute with his wife.

itts not ffor a man with a woman to threape [4]
    vnlesse he ffirst giue ouer the play ;
wee will liue noue [5] as wee began,

I will put my old cloak on."

64   and Ile haue mine old Cloake abaut me."
        ffins.

---

[1] Some letter marked out following the *b* in the MS.—F.

[2] ? MS. *tew*, a rope (or line) : Nares. I'll giue myself some rope, license.—F.

[3] Different from the print : as indeed is almost every Line of the whole.—P.

[4] A.-S. *þreapian*, to threap, reproue, afflict. Bosworth.—F.

[5] ? MS. 'none' for 'on'.—F. Better 'now'; compare l. 58, 59.—H.

𝕴 𝖑𝖎𝖚𝖊 𝖜𝖍𝖊𝖗𝖊 : 𝕴 𝖑𝖔𝖚𝖊 :

THE affected, strained style of this piece tells pretty clearly to what period it belongs. "True conceit be still my feeding," says the lover; so evidently says this author too. His is the *ars ostentandi artem.*

WITH my hart my loue was nesled [1]   [page 292]
    into the sonne of happynesse ; [2]   I was happy with my
ffrom my loue my liffe was rested [3]   love, and then was
4   into a world of heauinesse ;   torn from her.
    O lett my loue my liffe remaine, [4]
    since I loue not where I wold. [5]

Darksome distance doth devyde vs,   We are apart now,
8   ffarr ffrom thee I must remaine ;
    dismall planetts still doth [6] guide vs,
    ffearing wee shold meete againe ;
    but ffroward ffortune once remoued, [7]   but Fortune may change, and join us.
12   then will I liue where I wold. [8]

Iff I send them, doe not suspect mee ;   Do not suspect me,
    but if I come, then am I seene ;
    O let thy wisdome [9] soe direct mee
16   *that* I may blind Argus eyen !
    for my true hart shall neuer remou[e,]   though I am away from you.
    tho I liue not where I loue.

[1] Read *nested*, to rhyme with *rested.* —Skeat.
[2] In a sunme of happinesse.—P.
[3] wrested.—F.
[1] O let me soon from life remove.—P.
[5] Since I live not where I love.—P. Since I live not where I would faine.—H.
[6] do.—P.   [7] remove.—P.
[8] love.—P.   [9] MS. wisdone.—F.

What grief
haue I
suffered!

Sweete! what greeffe haue I sustained
20   in the accomplishing my desires ! [1]
my affections are not flained,
    tho my wish be nere the nere.[2]
if wishes wold substantiall proue,
24   then wold I liue where I loue.

With
bleeding
heart, I pray

to be with
thee again.

True conceit be still my feeding,
    & the flood being soe [3] conceipted,
whilest my hart for thee lyes bleeding,
28   sunne & heauens to be intreated ;
perhaps my orisons then may moue,
that I may liue where I loue.

When
heaven
grants this,

we'll smile
at past
troubles.

Loue & ffaction still agreeing,
32   by the consent of heauens electyon,
where wee both may haue our being,
vnderneath the heauens protectyon,
& smiling att our sorrowes past,
36   wee shall enioye [4] our wishe att Last.

                                         ffins.

---

[1] To accomplish my desire.—P.
[2] nigher.—P.
[3] After this is written *contented*, with the *tente* only marked out, then follows *ceipted*.—F.
[4] may enjoy.—P.

Younge : Andrew : [1]

This touching ballad is unhappily somewhat imperfect in parts; and we have not met with any copy elsewhere, with which it might be collated.

The story would be too painful and disgusting to read, but for the extreme gentleness of the poor sadly abused lady. This, while it aggravates our loathing of the monster whose prey she became, and makes her wrongs the more hideous, yet renders the tale tolerable. That gleam of light reconciles our eyes to the Stygian darkness. Otherwise it would be too horrible. We could not endure even to read of such a fiend as he who appears in it.

This atrocious ruffian is apparently a Scotchman (so his name seems to imply, and vv. 69, 92), who concludes a moonlight meeting with a fond, weak, credulous woman by deliberately robbing her, not only of her father's gold which she had fetched at his request, but of every article of dress she had on, in spite of her piteous pleadings, and this with brutal declarations that the spoil is intended for his own lady who dwells in a far country, till at last remains to her only such covering as nature gave—her long flowing hair. Then he gives the poor wretched creature the choice of dying there and then on his sword's point, or going home as she was. She goes home, to be greeted by her father's curse, and die of a broken heart at his door. The story is too frightful to be told as a reality; it is told as a dream.

[1] Shewing his disloyalty to an Earl's daughter. This Song in some Places is imperfect.—P.

I dreamt of
young
Andrew.

AS: I was cast in my ffirst sleepe,
　　　a dreadffull draught [1] in my mind I drew ;
ffor I was dreamed of one [2] yong man,
4　　some men called him yonge Andrew.

A lady tells
him she's
loved him
long.

the moone shone bright, & itt cast a ffayre light ;
　　　sayes shee, "welcome, my honey, my hart, & my
　　　　　sweete !
for I haue loued thee this 7 long yeere,
8　　& our chance itt was wee cold neuer meete."

He kisses
her.

then he tooke her in his armes 2,
　　　& k[i]ssed her both cheeke & chin ;
& 2ce or 3ce he pleased this may [3]
12　　before they tow did part in twinn ;

She reminds
him of his
promise to
marry her.

saies, "now, good Sir, you haue had your will,
　　　you can demand no more of mee ;
Good Sir, Remember what you said before, [4]
16　　& goe to the church & marry mee."

He says he'll
do it
if she brings
him her
father's
gold.

" ffaire maid, I cannott doe as I wold ;
　　　[Till I am got to my own country [5]]
goe home & fett [6] thy fathers redd gold,
20　　& Ile goe to the church & marry thee."

She gets her

this Ladye is gone to her ffathers hall,
　　　& well she knew where his red gold Lay,

father's 500l.
and jewels,

[7] and counted fforth 5 hundred pound
24　　besides all other Iuells & chaines,

and takes
them to
young
Andrew.

& brought itt all to yonge Andrew ;
　　　itt was well counted vpon his knee.
then he tooke her by the Lillye white hand,
28　　& led her vp to one [8] hill soe hye ;

---

[1] sketch, picture.—F.
[2] a.—P.
[3] maid.—P.
[4] you sware.—P.
[5] Percy's line.—F.
[6] fet. Vid. fol. 514. Note.—P.
[7] she.—P.
[8] a.—P.

shee had vpon [1] a gowne of blacke veluett ;—
  a pittyffull sight after yee shall see ;—
"put of thy clothes, bonny wenche," he sayes,   He makes her take off
32   " for noe ffoote further thoust gang with mee."

but then shee put of her gowne of veluett [2]   her velvet gown,
  [3] with many a salt teare from her eye,
And in a kirtle of ffine [4] breaden silke   [page 293]
36   shee stood beffore young Andrews eye.

sais, " o put off [5] thy kirtle of silke ;
  ffor some & all shall goe with mee :
& to my owne Lady I must itt beare,
40   who [6] I must needs loue better then thee."

then shee put of her kirtle of silke   her silken kirtle,
  with [7] many a salt teare still ffrom her eye ;
in a peticoate of scarlett redd   her scarlet
44   shee stood before young Andrewes eye.

saies, " o put of [5] thy peticoate ;
  for some & all of itt shall goe with mee ;
& to my owne Lady I will itt beare,
48   which dwells soe ffarr in a strange countrye."

but then shee put of her peticoate   petticoat,
  with many a salt teare still from her eye ;   her white silk smock
& in a smocke of braue white silke
52   shee stood before young Andrews eye.

saies, " o put of [5] thy smocke of silke ;
  for some & all shall goe with mee ;
vnto my owne Ladye I will it beare,
56   that dwells soe ffarr in a strange countrye."

---

[1] vp bracketted for omission by P.   braided.— F.
[2] velvet gown.—P.   [5] Put off, put off.—P.
[3] while many . . . ran.—P.   [6] whom.—P.
[4] a fine kirtle.—P. ? breaden,   [7] while . . . . ran from.—P.

(though she
prays to keep
it),

sayes,[1] "o remember, young Andrew !
 once of a woman you were borne ;
 & ffor *that* birth *that* Marye bore,
60 I pray you let my smocke be vpon ! "

"yes, ffayre Ladye, I know itt well ;
 once of a woman I was borne ;
 yett ffor noe birth *that* Mary bore,
64 thy smocke shall not be left here vpon."

and her head
dress.

but then shee put of her head geere ffine ;
 shee hadd billaments [2] worth a 100.li ;
 the hayre *that* was vpon this bony wench head,[3]
68 couered her bodye downe to the ground.

Then he asks
her whether

then he pulled forth a scottish brand,
 & held itt there in his owne right hand ; [4]

she'll die on
his sword or
go naked
home.

saies, "whether wilt thou dye vpon my swords
  point, Ladye,
72 or thow wilt [5] goe naked home againe ? "

She chooses

"my liffe is sweet, then Sir," said shee,
 "therfore I pray you leaue mee with mine ;
 before I wold dye on your swords point,

walking
naked home,

76 I had rather goe naked home againe.

but warns
young
Andrew that
her father
will hang
him if he
catches him,

"my ffather," shee sayes, " is a right good Erle
 as any remaines in his countrye ;
 if euer he doe your body take,
80 your sure to fflower a gallow tree ;

and her
brothers will
take his life.

" & I haue 7 brethren," shee sayes,[6]
 " & they are all hardy men & bold ;
 giff euer the doe your body take,
84 you must neuer gang quicke ouer the mold."

---

[1] she sayes.—P.
[2] habilliments, dress, cloaths.—P.
[3] but . . . upon her head.—P.

[4] And there he held it forth amaine.
—P.   [5] wilt thou.—P.
[6] And seven brethren I haue she says.
—P.

"if your ffather be a right good Erle
　　as any remaines in his owne countrye,
tush! he shall neuer my body take,
88　Ile gang soe ffast ouer[1] the sea!

Young
Andrew says
he'll

sail from her
father,

"if you haue 7 brethren," he sayes,
　　"if they be neuer soe hardy or bold;
tush! they shall neuer my body take;
92　Ile gang soe ffast into the scottish mold!"

and take
refuge in
Scotland
from her
brothers.

Now this Ladye is gone to her fathers hall
　　when euery body their rest did take;
but the Erle which was her ffather [dear][2]
96　lay waken for his deere daughters sake.

The lady
goes home,

"but who is that," her ffather can say,[3]
　　"that soe priuilye knowes that pinn[4]?"
"its Hellen, your owne deere daughter, ffather[5]!
100　I pray you rise and lett me in."

her father
hears her,

[6] "noe, by my hood[7]!" quoth her ffather then,
　　"my [house] thoust[8] neuer come within,
without I had my red gold againe."

but won't let
her in till
she brings
back his
gold.

104　"nay, your gold is gone, ffather!" said shee.[9]
　　"then naked thou came into this world,
and naked thou shalt returne againe."

She says it's
gone.

"nay! god fforgaue his death, father!" shee sayes,
108　"& soe I hope you will doe mee."
"away, away, thou cursed woman!
　　"I pray god an ill death thou may dye!" [page 294]

He curses
her.

---

[1] hence o're. –P.
[2] dear.—P.
[3] to say.—P.
[4] pinn. Compare vol. i. p. 249, l. 38,
' he thirled vpon a *pinn*.'—F.
[5] here.—P.

[6] O no, O no, I will not rise.—P.
[7] Rood.—P.
[8] my House thou.—P.
[9] O pardon, pardon me, she says,
　　For all your red gold it is taen.—P.

Her heart
bursts, and
she falls
dead.

112 shee stood soe long quacking on the ground
       till [1] her hart itt burst [2] in three,
       & then shee ffell dead downe in a swoond;
       & this was the end of this bonny Ladye.

In the
morning her
father

sees her
corpse.

116 ithe morning when her ffather gott [3] vpp,
       a pittyffull sight there he might see [4];
       his owne deere daughter was dead [5] without [6] Clothes!
       they teares they trickeled fast ffrom his eye;

He curses
his love of
gold,

120 sais, " fye of gold, and ffye of ffee ! [7]
       for I sett soe much by my red gold
       that now itt hath lost both my daughter and mee !"

and fades as
a flower in
frost.

       but after [8] this time he neere dought [9] good day,
       but as [10] flowers doth fade in the ffrost,
124 soe he did wast & weare away.

As to young
Andrew,

       but let vs leaue talking of this Ladye,
       & talke some more of young Andrew, [11]
       ffor ffalse he was to this bonny Ladye ;
128 more pitty *that* itt had [12] not beene true.

he hadn't
gone half a
mile into
Wales

       he was not gone a mile into the wild forrest, [13]
       or halfe a mile into the hart of wales,
       but there they cought him by such a braue wyle
132 *that* hee must come to tell noe more tales.

[1] untill.—P.
[2] truly.—P.
[3] rose.—P.
[4] might he see.—P.
[5] there lay dead.—P.
[6] *any* follows in the MS., and is crossed out.—F.
[7] O fye O fye now on my gold
  O fye on gold & fye on fee.—P.
[8] Thus having lost his daughter fair,
  He after &c.—P.
[9] dought—A.-S. *dugan*, valere, hinc *dohtig* Sax. i. e. doughty, fortis, strenus, Gloss. ad G. Doug! —P.

[10] [insert] the.—P.
[11] And once more tell of young Andrew.—P.
[12] he had.—P.
[13] He scarse was from this Lady gone,
  or
  As he did from this Lady go
  And thro' the forest past his way
  A furious wolf did him beset
  And there this perjured *knight*
  did slay.—P.
  And tow'rd the woods had gang'd away.—P.

ffull soone a wolfe did of him smell,
    & shee came roaring like a beare,
& gaping like a ffeend of hell ;

before a wolf attacked him,

136 soe they ffought together like 2 Lyons [there],[1]
    & fire betweene them 2 glashet out ;
thé raught eche other such a great rappe,
that there young Andrew was slaine, well I wott.

killed him,

140 but[2] now young Andrew he is dead ;
    but he was neuer buryed vnder mold ;
for ther as the wolfe devoured him,
there[3] lyes all this great erles gold.

and eat him up.

                    ffins.

---

[1] Percy has added *there*, and marked the line as part of the verse above.—F.

[2] And.—P.
[3] And there &c.—P.

Percy has marked in red ink brackets, for omission, the following words or parts of them :

    as, l. 142.
    u, *of* neuer, l. 141.
    father, l. 107.
    but, l. 97.
    deere, l. 96.
    in *of* into, l. 92.
    with, l. 74.

point, Ladye, l. 71.
this bony wench, l. 67.
vp *of* vpon, l. 64, 60, 29.

In line 8 he marks *cold neuer* to be transposed to *neuer cold.* In other poems I have not noticed these red ink marks. They would have swelled the notes too much, and there are plenty of Percy's alterations already.

𝔄 : 𝔉𝔦𝔤𝔤𝔢 : [1]

"A JIG," says Nares, "meant anciently not only a merry dance, but merriment and humour in writing, and particularly a ballad. Thus when Polonius objects to the Player's speech, Hamlet sarcastically observes,

He's for a *jigg* or a tale of bawdry or he sleeps.—(Haml. ii. 2.)

He does not mean a dance (which then players did not undertake), but ludicrous dialogue or a ballad. . . . In the Harleian collection of old ballads are many under the title of *jigs*; as 'A Northern Jige, called Daintie, come thou to me,' 'A merry new Jigge or the pleasant Wooing between Kit and Pegge,' &c. So in the *Fatal Contract* by Hemmings,

We'll hear your *jigg* :
How is your ballad titled?—(Act iv. sc. 4.)

Thus :

A small matter! you'll find it worth Meg of Westminster, although it be but a bare jig.—(Hog hath lost, &c. O. Pl. vi. 385.)

It appears that this jig was a ballad."

The following specimen of the Jig Dialogical is a sort of vulgar reproduction of the *Nut-Brown Maid*. The mode and circumstances of life depicted in the original ballad had passed out of date; the old order had given place to a new. A new audience—new chronologically, new socially—demanded a new version—a "people's edition," so to speak. The lover who here tests his mistress is no knight, but a common soldier; the mistress is no highborn lady, but a common woman. And these personal changes are characteristic of the others which the old ballad has undergone, to take its present shape. No such transmutations

[1] Pepys. iv. 42. A Poetical Dialogue between a Soldier & his Mistress, not unlike the Nut-brown Maid.—P.

are likely to be, from a literary point of view, successful. This
one is not. But the beauty of the original is too great to be
altogether destroyed, however rude the hands that handle it.
Something of the charm of the *Nut-Brown Maid* lingers around
this *Jig*.

Other handlers of the old ballad turned it to a religious sense.
See the *New Notbrowne Mayd upon the Passion of Christ* in
Mr. Hazlitt's Early Popular Poetry of England.

"MARGRETT, my sweetest margett! I must goe!   *Margaret,*
                                                I must leave
most dere to mee *that* neuer¹ may be soe;   *you.*
as ffortune willes, I cannott itt deny."
4   "then know thy loue, thy Margarett, shee must dye."   *"Then I'll die."*

"Not ffor the gold *that* euer Crœssus hadd,   *Not for the*
                                                world would
wold I once² see thy sweetest lookes soe fade;   *I make you*
                                                sad,
nor³ ffor all *that* my eyes did euer⁴ see,
8   wold I once part thy sweetest loue from mee;

"The King comands, & I must to the warres."   *but I must*
                                                to the wars.
"thers⁵ others more enow to end those cares."
"but I am one appointed ffor to goe,
12 & I dare not ffor my liffe once say noe,"

"O marry mee, & you may stay att home!   *"Marry me*
                                                and stay at
ffull 30 weekes you know *that* I am gone.⁶"   *home!"*
"theres time enough; another ffather take;   *Get another*
                                                father for
16 heele loue thee well, & not thy child forsake." *your child.*

"And haue I doted ouer thy sweetest fface?   *"No, I love*
                                                you
& dost infring the things I haue in chase,
thy ffaith, I meane? but I will wend with thee." *and will go*
                                                with you.
20 "itt is to ffar ffor Pegg to goe with mee."

---

¹ i.e. never hereafter.—H.   ⁴ Only half the *u* or *e* in the MS.—F.
² There is a mark like an *i* undotted   ⁵ There's.—P.
before the *o*.—F.   ⁶ i.e. with Child.—P.
³ nor yet.—P.

I'll carry
your sword,

"I will goe with thee, my loue, both night and day,
& I will beare thy sword like lakyney; Lead the way!"[1]
"but wee must ryde, & will you ffollow then
24 amongst a troope of vs thats[2] armed men?"

clean your
horse,

"Ile beare thy Lance, & grinde thy stirropp too,
Ile rub thy horsse, & more then that Ile doo."
"but Margretts flingars, they be all to ffine
28 to stand & waite when shee shall see mee dine,"

wait on you,

"Ile see you dine, & wayte still att your backe,
Ile giue you wine or any thing you Lacke."
"but youle repine when you shall see mee haue
32 a dainty wench that is both ffine & braue."

love your
wench,

"Ile loue thy wench, my sweetest loue, I vow, [page 295]
Ile watch the time when shee may pleasure you!"
"but you will greene to see vs lye in bedd;
36 & you must watch still in anothers steede."

see you sleep
with her,

"Ile watch my loue to see you take your rest;
& when you sleepe, then shall I thinke me blest."
"the time will come, deliuered you must bee;
40 then in the campe you will discredditt mee."

and leave
you before
my own
baby
comes."
You mustn't
go with me.

"Ile goe ffrom thee beffor that time shalbee;
when all his well, my loue againe Ile see."
"all will not serue, ffor Margarett may not goe;
44 then doe resolue, my loue, what else to doe."

"Then I'll
die, loving
you still."
No, I'll stop
with you,

"Must I not goe? why then, sweete loue, adew!
needs must I dye, but yet in dying trew!"
"a! stay[3] my loue! I loue my Margarett well,
48 & heere I vow[4] with Margarett still to dwell!"

---

[1] along the way.—P.   [3] Ah! stay.—P.
[2] all.—P.   [4] vow.—P.

" Giue me thy hand ! thy Margarett liues againe ! "

" heeres [1] my hand ! Ile neuer breed thee paine ! and never
pain you.

I kisse my loue in token *that* is soe ;

52 wee will be wedd : come, Margarett, let vs goe." We'll be
we

ffins.

---

[1] here is.—P.

Eglamore : [1]

[In Six Parts.—P.]

THIS romance has been printed among the Thornton Romances
for the Camden Society from a MS. in the Public Library of
Cambridge (Ff. ii. 38), the copies of it and *Degrevant* made by
Thornton "unfortunately being imperfect." There is another
copy among the MSS. Cotton (Calig. A. 11). The Percy Folio
copy is here printed for the first time : " A single leaf of another
early copy," as Mr. Halliwell, the editor of the Thornton Ro-
mances, informs us, "is preserved in a MS. belonging to Lord
Francis Egerton. It was printed at Edinburgh in 1508 by
Walter Chapman, and subsequently at London by Copland and
Walley. Shakespeare may possibly have had this hero in his
mind when he calls one of his characters by his name in the
Two Gentlemen of Verona : 'What think'st thou of the fair Sir
Eglamore ?' The name, however, appears to have passed into
a kind of proverb. So in Dekker's *Satiromastix*: 'Adieu, Sir
Eglamore! adieu, lute-string, curtain-rod, goose-quill!' The
name of Torrent of Portugal is partly founded upon the story
related in *Sir Eglamore*. The names are changed, but the resemblance is too striking to have been the result of chance. The
treachery of the sovereign, the prowess of the knight, the indis-
cretions and misfortunes of the lady, and the happy conclusions

---

[1] The readings marked T. are from
the Thornton MS., 'Sir Eglamour of
Artois' (MS. Syr Egyllamowre of Artas)
as edited by Mr. Halliwell for the
Camden Society in 1844. Very few of
the very many differences between the
two texts are given.—F.

of her misfortunes—these form the leading incidents of each romance. Torrent of Portugal is preserved in an unique manuscript of the fifteenth century, in the Chetham Library at Manchester:

> Here bygynneth a good tale
> Of Torrente of Portingale :

and although somewhat disfigured by the errors of the scribe, contains much that is curious and valuable. As this poetical tale has recently been published, there is no necessity for proving in this place a similarity that will be at once detected by the reader; but there is perhaps a secret history attached to the source of these romances that remains to be unravelled."

Ellis makes the abstract he gives of *Eglamore* from the copy printed by Walley. All at all important differences between the Thornton copy and ours are recorded by Mr. Furnivall in the notes.

The romance is certainly of more than usual merit—less prolix and garrulous, or rather of more interesting garrulity. Many of its " positions " are indeed of the kind commonest in romantic literature, as the passage of the squire's love for his lord's daughter, the combat with the giant, the unconsummated marriage of a son and his mother. No one of them perhaps can be pronounced novel. The stories of a woman's exposure to the mercy of the winds and seas, and of the carrying off of her son by a great bird, are well known elsewhere—in Chaucer's *Man of Law's Tale*, and among the legends of the house of Stanley—and are undoubtedly of extreme antiquity. But there are other charms besides novelty of incident. These can make old things new, can endow with spirit and vigour the form that is worn and wasted. The minstrel who wrote, or rather translated, this piece, if a minstrel he was, as verses 1227–9 might suggest, told an old tale freshly,—a tale of love much crossed and thwarted, but prosperous in the end—of treachery, potent

and prevailing for a while, but at last shown futile and fatal—
of strange partings and yet stranger meetings.

> Full true it is, by god in heaven,
> That men meet at unset steven.

Thrice old themes these; but in the hands of this romance-writer
made juvenescent.

Such an union between mother and son as that which occurs
in *Eglamore* is a very favourite arrangement with the old
romance-writers. It immediately precedes and generally brings
about the ἀναγνώρισις. Thus the extremest alarm and horror
immediately introduce the extremest delight. Fear and joy are
brought into the closest juxtaposition. The romance-writer could
conceive of no more terrible disturbance and overthrow of the
order of nature than that fearful conversion of a mother into a
wife, a son into a husband—that ruin of the most beautiful of
the domestic relations. Though bold enough to describe it as
possible, and, indeed, imminent, he never dares to let it actually
come to pass. He never lets the ghastly shade become a living
thing. The Greek poets too regarded this same connection as
the culminating horror. In their eyes, too, conflicts between
father and son, love other than pious between son and mother,
appeared the most frightful of all possible frightfulnesses. But
they went further than the old romance-writers. They were not
content with the apprehension; they did not shrink from the act.
What in the romances is only threatened, is in the Greek legend
perpetrated. Hideous possibilities become there yet more hideous
realities. Eve in the one case only fingers the apple; in the
other she plucks and eats it. Medieval feeling was the more
delicate and sensitive in this respect. Its poet ever averts the
horrible catastrophe. As the storm is on the point of bursting,
and the nymphs with wild frantic faces stand ready to " shriek
on the mountain," suddenly the sky clears, there are pious
embracings, the domestic sanctities are preserved and ratified.

[Part I.]

[How Eglamore loved Christabell, and undertook three Deeds of Arms to win her.]

1

IESUS : christ, heauen king!
  grant vs all his deere blessinge,
    & builde vs [in] [1] his bower [2]!
4 & giue them [ioye] [3] *that* will heare
  of Elders *that* before vs were,
    that liued in great honor.[4]
I will tell you of a Knight
8 *that* was both [5] hardye & wight,
  & stiffe in euerye stower;
  & wher any deeds of armes were,
  hee wan the prize with sheeld & speare,
12   & euer he was the fflower.

Christ, bless us,

and give joy to those that love old heroes!

I'll tell you of a hardy knight

who always won the prize.

2

In Artoys the Knight was borne,
  & his ffather him beforne;
    listen; I will you say.[6]
16 Sir Prinsamoure the Erle hight;
  & Eglamore thé hight [the] Knight [7]
    that curteous was alway;
  & he was for a man [8] verament,
20 with the Erle was he bent,[9]
    to none he wold say nay.[10]

He was born in Artoys,

his name was Eglamore;

he was a man, and never refused a fight.

---

[1] in.—T. in.—P. builde, shelter, as in vol. i. p. 27, l. 11.—F.
[2] boure.—P.
[3] ioye.—T. joye.—P.
[4] honoure.—P.
[5] bolde.—P. hardy.—T.
[6] Percy marks to come after this :

For that he was a man full bolde
With the Erle was he holde
In housholde nyght & day.

The Thornton MS. has :

To dedes of armes he ys wente,
Wyth the Erle of Artas he ys lente,
He faylyth hym not nyght nor daye.
[7] Sir Eglam[re] than hyght the knyght.
—P. Syr Egyllamowre men calle the knyʒt.—T.
[8] And for he was a man.—P.
[9] lente.—P. he ys lente.—T.
[10] To no man he wolde.—P. T. has:

Whylle the erle had him in holde,
Of dedes of armes he was bolde,
For no man seyde he nay.—F.

The Earl of
Artoys
has a lovely
daughter,
the Erle had noe Child but one,
a maiden as white as whalles bone,[1]
24   *that* his right heyre shold bee ;

Christabell,
Christabell was the Ladyes name ;
a ffairer maid then shee was ane
was none [2] in christentye.

28   Christabell soe well her bore ;
the Erle loued nothing more
then his daughter ffree ;

Eglamore
loves her,
soe did *that* gentle knight
32   *that* was soe full of might ;
it was the more pittye.

3

the knight was both hardy & snell,
& knew the ladye loued him well.

and she
loves him.
36   listen a while & dwell :
Lords came ffrom many a Land

Strange
lords come
to woo her.
her to haue, I vnderstand,
with fforce ffold [3] and ffell.

40   Sir Prinsamoure then did crye

A tourney is
held,
strong Iusting & turnamentrye [4]
for the loue of Christabell.
what man *that* did her craue,

and
Eglamore
unhorses all
her suitors.
44   such stroakes Eglamore him gaue,
that downe right he ffell.

4

to his chamberlaine [5] then gan he saw,[6]

He opens his
heart to his
chamber-
lain,
" ffrom thee I cann hyde nought away,"
48   (where they did together rest [7] ;)
" ffaire ffrand, nought to laine,
my councell thou wold not saine ;
On thee is all my trust."   [page 296]

---

[1] ivory.—F. as faire.—T.
[2] not.—P. Ther was none soche.—T.
[3] ferse folke.—T.
[4] Syr Egyllamowre he dud to crye
Of dedes of armys utterly.—T.

[5] squyer, (with altered lines).—T.
See squier, st. 9. l. 111 below.—F.
[6] say.—P.
[7] rest.—P. *Rell* altered into *rest* in
the MS.—F.

52 "Master," hee said, "per ma fay,
  what-soeuer you to me say,
    I shall itt neuer out cast."
  "the Erles daughter, soe god me saue,

56 the loue of her but *that* I haue,
    my liffe itt may not Last."

*and says he
shall die
unless he
can win
Christabell's
love.*

5

 "Master," said the young man ffree,
  "you haue told me your priuitye ;

60 I will giue you answere
  to this tale: I vnderstand
  you are a knight of litle Land,.
    & much wold haue more ;

64 If I shold to *that* Ladye goe
  & show your hart & loue,
    shee lightlye wold let me fare ;
  the man *that* heweth ouer hye,

68 some chipp ffalleth on his eye ;
    thus doth it euer fare.

*The cham-
berlain*

answers

*that
Eglamore is
too poor,*

*the lady
wouldn't
listen to
him ;*

*those
hewing too
high get
chips in
their eye.*

6

 "remember Master, of one thing,[1]
  that shee wold haue both Erle & King,

72 & many a bold Barron alsoe ;
  the Ladye will haue none of those,
  but in her maidenhead hold ;[2]
  ffor wist her ffather, by heauen King,

76 *that* you were sett on such a thinge,
    right deere itt shold be bought.
  trow yee shee wold King fforsake,
  & such a simple knight take,

80 but if you haue loued her of old ? "

*But yet she
refuses her
rich suitors,*

*and that
must be for
Eglamore's
love.*

[1] Syr, than unbe-thanke on thys
thyng.—T.
[2] ȝyt wylle sche not haue of thoo,
But in godenes hur holdyth so,

The which y trowe ys for thy loue
and no mo.—T.
  T. also transposes the next two
triplets.—F.

7

the knight answerd ffull mild :
" euer since I was a Child
thou hast beene loued of [1] mee.

84 in any iusting or any stower,
saw you me haue any dishonor
in battell where I haue bee ? "

" Nay, Master, att all rights

88 you are one of the best knights
in all Christentye ;

in deeds of armes, by god aliue,
thy body is worth other 5."

92   " gramercy, Sir," sayd hee :

8

Eglamore sighed, & said noe more,
but to his Chamber gan hee ffare,
that richelye was wrought.

96 to god his hands he held vp soone,
" Lord ! " he said, " grant me a boone
as thou on roode me bought !

the Erles daughter, ffaire & ffree,

100 *that* shee may my wiffe bee,
ffor shee is most in my thought ;
that I may wed her to my wiffe,
& in Ioy to lead our liffe ; [2]

104   from care then were I brought."

9

on the morrow *that* maiden small
eate with her ffather in the hall,
that was soe faire & bright.

108 all the knights were at meate sane hee ;
the Ladye said, " for gods pittye !
where is Sir Eglamore my *Knight?*

[1] lento wyth.—T.   [2] and sethen reches in my life.—T.

his squier answerd with heauye cheere,

112 " he is sicke, & dead ffull neere,

he prayeth you of a sight ;

he is now cast in such a care,

but if he mends not of his fare

116 he liueth not to night."

" He is
nearly dead,
and prays to
see you."

10

the Erle vnto his daughter spake,

" damsell," he said, " for god sake

listen vnto mee!

120 after me, doe as I thee hend ; [1]

to his chamber see thou wend,

ffor hee was curteous & ffree ;

ffull trulye with his intent,   [page 297]

124 with Iusting & in Turnament,

he said vs neuer nay ;

if any deeds of armes were,

he wan the prize with turnay [2] cleere ;

128 our worshippe for euer and aye."

The Earl
charges
Christabell

to go and see
Eglamore,

who never
refused a
tourney,

and always
won the
prize.

11

then after meate that Ladye gent

did affter her fathers comandement,[3]

shee busked her to wend.

132 forth shee went withouten more,

for nothing wold shee spare,

but went there as hee Lay.[4]

" Master," said the squier, " be of good cheere,

136 heere cometh the Erles daughter deere,

some words to you to say."

After Hall,

Christabell

goes to
Eglamore,

---

[1] After mete do ye as hynde.—T. See
'After meate,' st. 11, l. 129. But 'after
me' may mean, by my direction, see l.
130, though I do not know hend in the
sense of tell, bid.—F.

[2] jurney.—T.

[3] Only half the first n in the MS.—F.

[4] T. puts in three lines in which Christabell asks the squire how Eglamore is.
—F.

12

& then said *that* Ladye bright,

and asks how he is.

"how fareth Sir Eglamore my Knight,

140   *that* is a man right ffaire?"

"forsoothe, Ladye, as you may see,

"Dying for love of you."

with woe I am bound for the loue of yee,

in longing & in care."

144   "Sir," shee said, "by gods pittye,

"I'm very sorry to grieve you."

if you be agrreeued [1] ffor mee,

itt wold greeue me full sore!"

"damsell, if I might turne to liffe,

"Then be my wife."

148   I wold haue you to my wiffe,

if itt *your* will were."

13

"Sir," shee said, "soo mote I thee,

"You're a noble knight,

you are a Noble Knight and ffree,

152   & come of gentle blood;

and manful in fight.

a manfull man you are in ffeild

to win the gree with speare & sheeld

nobly by the roode;

Ask my father,

156   Sir, att my ffather read you witt, [2]

& see what hee will say to itt;

or if his will bee good,

and if he agrees,

& if *that* hee be att assent,

160   as I am true Ladie & gent,

I will."

my will it shalbe good."

14

the Knight desired noe other [3] blisse

Eglamore is in bliss,

when he had gotten his grantesse, [4]

164   but made royall [5] cheere;

he comanded a Sqiuer to goo

---

[1] The *rr* is much like *u* in the MS.— F.

[2] T. makes the lady take the 'Ask Papa' on herself, and when they are agreed, she'll not fail Eglamore.—F.

[3] kepte no more.—T.

[4] geton graunt of thys.—T.

[5] hur fulle gode.—T.

to ffeitch gold, a 100 [1] or towe,
    & giue the [2] Maidens cleere.

and gives
Christabell's
maidens
100£.

168 Sir Eglamore said, "soe haue I blisse !
to your marriage I giue you this,
    ffor yee neuer come heere yore."
the Lady then thanked & kissed the Knight;

Christabell
kisses him,

172 shee tooke her leaue anon-right,
    "farwell, my true sonne deere." [3]

15

then homeward shee tooke the way. [4]
"welcome ! " sayd the Erle, " in ffay,

goes back to
her father,

176   tell mee how haue yee doone.
say, my daughter as white as any flower,
how ffareth my knight Sir Eglamore ? "
    & shee answered him soone:

and tells him
Sir
Eglamore is
quite well,

180 " fforsooth, to mee he hartilye sware
he was amended of his care,
    good comfort hath hee tane ;
he told me & my maidens hende,

184 *that* hee vnto the riuer wold wend
    with hounds & hawkes right."

and is going
out
hawking.

16

the Erle said, " soe Mote I thee,
with him will I ryde *that* sight to see,

188   to make my hart more light." [5]
on the morrow, when itt was day,
Sir Eglamore tooke the way
    to the riuer ffull right.

Next day
Eglamore

192 the Erle made him redye there,
& both rode to they riuer

and the Earl
hawk

---

[1] and take an hundurd pownd.—T.
[2] hur.—T.
[3] And seyde ' Farewelle my fere.'—T.
[4] Crystyabelle hath takyn hur way. —T.
[5] For comforte of that knyght.—T.

to see some ffaire fllight.

and are
pleasant
together.
all they day they made good cheere :

196   a wrath began, as yon may heare,

long ere itt was night.[1]

17

But coming
home,
Eglamore
asks if the
Earl will
hear him.
as they rode homeward in the way,

Sir Eglamore to the Erle gan say,

"Certainly,
200   " My lord, will you now [2] heare ? "   [page 298]

"all ready, Eglamore ; in ffay,

I like to
hear you :
whatsoeuer you to me say,

to me itt is ffull deere ;

you're the
best knight
in the land."
204   ffor why, the doughtyest art thou

that dwelleth in this Land now,

for to beare sheeld & speare.[3] "

"When will
your
daughter be
betrothed ? "
" my Lord," he said, " of charitye,

208   Christabell your daughter ffree,

when shall shee haue a ffeere ? "

18

"I know no
one whom
she would
have."
the Erle said, " soe god me saue,

I know noe man that shee wold haue,

212   my daughter faire and cleere."

" Give her
to me."
" now, good Lord, I you pray,

for I haue serued you many a day,

to giue me her withouten nay."

"I will, and
all Artois
too, if you'll
do 3 deeds of
arms for
her."
216   the Erle said, " by gods paine,

if thou her winne as I shall saine,

by deeds of armes three,

then shalt thou haue my daughter deere,

220   & all Artois ffarr & neere."

" Thank
you !
" gramercy, Sir ! " said hee.

[1] long ere night it were.—P.   [3] Awnturs ferre or nere.—T.
[2] ye me.—T.

19

Sir Eglamore [sware [1]], "soe mote I thee,
att my iourney [2] ffaine wold I be!"

224 right soone he made him yare.
the Erle said, "here by west
dwelleth a Gyant in a fforrest,—
ffowler neuer saw I ere;—
228 therin be trees ffaire & [3] long,
3 harts [4] run them [5] amonge,
the fairest *that* on ffoot gone.
Sir, might yee bring one away,
232 then durst I boldly say
that yee had beene there."

let me go to
work at
once."

The Earl
sets
Eglamore
his first
feat :
to go to a
giant's
forest,
and fetch
him one of
three harts
running
about there.

20

[6] "fforsooth," said Eglamore then,
"if *that* hee be a Christyan man,
236 I shall him neuer fforsake."
the Erle said in good cheere,
"with him shalt thou flight in feere ;
his name is Sir Marroccke."
240 the Knight thought on Christabell ;
he swore by him *that* harrowed hell,
him wold he neuer fforsake.
"Sir, keepe well my Lady & my Land !"
244 therto the Erle held vp his hand,
& trothes they did strike.

Eglamore
undertakes
to fetch the
hart,

and fight
the giant
Marrocke.

He commits
Christabell
to her
father's care,

21

then afterwards, as I you say,
Sir Eglamore tooke the way

---

[1] The knyght sweryd.—T.
[2] The *o* looks like *a* in the MS.—F.
[3] Cypur trees there growe owte.—T.
[4] The *h* is like an *l* in the MS.—F.
[5] Grete hertys there walke.—T.
[6] T. has for this stanza :

Bo Jhesu swore the knyght than,
 "Yf he be ony Crystyn-man,
 Y schalle hym nevyr forsake.
Holde well my lady and my londe."
"3vs," seyde the erle, "here myn honde !"
 Hys trowthe to hym he strake.

248   to *that* Ladye soe ffree :

" damsell," hee said to her anon,

" ffor your Loue I haue vndertane

deeds of Armes three."

252   " good Sir," shee said, " be merry & glad ; [1]

ffor a worsse Iourney you neuer had

in noe christyan countrye.

if god grant ffrom his grace

256   *that* wee [2] may ffrom *that* Iourney apace,

god grant it may be soe [3] !

                              22

" S*i*r, if you be on hunting ffound,

I shall you giue a good greyhound

260   *that* is dun as a doe ;

ffor as I am a true gentle woman,

there was neuer deere *that* he att [4] ran

that might scape him ffroe :

264   alsoo a sword I giue thee,

that was ffound in the sea [5] ;

of such I know noe moe.

if you haue happ to keepe itt weele,

268   there is no helme of Iron nor steele

but itt wold carue in 2.

[Part II.[6]]

[How Eglamore kills the giant Marrocke and a big Boar.]

                              23

Eglamore kissed *that* Lady gent ;

he tooke his leaue, & fforth hee went.

---

272   his way now hath hee tane ;

The lye streetes held he west   [page 299]   rides to the forest,

till he came to the fforrest ;

ffarrer saw he neuer none,

276   with trees of Cypresse lying out.

2ᵈ Parte. the wood was walled round abowt

with strong walles of stone ;

fforthe he rade, as I vnderstand,

280   till he came to a gate *that* he ffand,   enters it by a gate,

& therin is he gone.

24

his horne he blew in that tyde ;   blows his horn,

harts start vpp on euery side,

284   & a noble deere [1] ffull prest ;

the hounds att the deere gan bay.   and his hounds bay at the deer.

with *that* heard the Gyant where he lay ;   The giant Marrocke

itt lett him of his rest ;

288   "methinketh, by hounds *that* I heare,

that there is one hunting [2] my deare ;

it were better *that* he cease [3] !

by him *that* wore the crowne of thorne,   swears it' be the worst blowing the man euer made,

292   in a worse time he neuer blew a horne,

ne dearer bought a messe [4] ! "

25

Marrocke the Gyant tooke the way

thorrow the fforrest were itt Lay ;

296   to the gate he sett his backe.   and goes to his gate.

Sir Eglamore hath done to dead,

---

[1] Twety does not use the word *deer* in speaking "of the Hert. Now wyl we speke of the hert ; and speke we of his degres : that is to say, the fyrst yere he is a calfe, the secunde yere a broket, the iij. yeare a spayer, the iiij. yere a stagg, the v. yere a greet stagg, the vj. yeare a hert at the fyrst hed ; but that ne fallith not in jugement of huntersse, for the gret dyversyte that is fownde of hem, for alleway we calle of the fyrst hed tyl that he be of x. of the lasse. *Reliq. Antiq.* i. 151.—F.

[2] Yondur is a thefe to stele.—T.

[3] He were welle bettur to be at the see.—T.

[4] Neythur hys bowe bende in no manys fee.—T.

Eglamore
kills a stag,
cuts his head
off,

slaine a hart, & smitten off his head;

the prize [1] he blew ffull shrill;

300 & when he came where the gyant was,

and asks
Marrocke to
let him pass.

"good Sir," he sayd, "lett me passe,

if *that* itt be your will."

Marrocke

"nay, traitor! thou art tane!

304 my principall [2] hart thou hast slaine!

thou shalt itt like ffull ill."

26

strikes at
him

the Gyant att the chase [3],

a great clubb vp hee takes,

308 *that* villanous was and great [4];

such a stroke hee him gaue

that into the earth went his staffe,

a ffoote on euery side.

and says he'll
keep him
there.

312 "traitor!" he said, "what doest thou here

in my fforrest to slay my deere?

here shalt thou now abyde."

Eglamore
hits the
giant in the
eye, and
blinds him,

Eglamore his sword out drew,

316 & in his sight made such a shew, [5]

& made him blind *that* tyde.

27

but he
fights on for
two days and
more;

how-be-itt he lost his sight,

he ffought w*i*th Sir Eglamore *that* K*nigh*t

320 2 dayes & some deale more;

till the 3ᵈ [6] day att prime

then
Eglamore
kills him,

Sir Eglamore waited his time,

& to the hart him bare.

---

[1] And whan the hert is take, ye shal blowe iiij. motys . . . and the hed shal be brout hom to the lord, and the skyn . . . Than blow at the doro of halle the *pryse*. . . . And whan the buk is i-take, ye shal blowe *pryse*, and reward your houndes of the paunch and the bowellis. Twety, in *Relig. Ant.* i. 153. Fr. *Prise* a taking . . . also, the death or fall of a hunted beast. Cotgrave.—F.

[2] chefe.—T.

[3] to the knyȝt ys gon.—T.

[4] mekylle and fulle unweelde.—T.

[5] And to the geant he gafe a sowe. —T. *Sough*, a stroke or blow. Jamieson.- F.

[6] Tytle on the todur.—T.

324 through gods might, & his kniffe,
there the Gyant lost his liffe;
    ffast he began to rore.

and he
roars.

  ffor certaine sooth, as I you say,
328 when he was meaten[1] there he Lay
    he was 15 ffoote[2] & more.

He measures
fifteen feet.

28[3]

  through the might of god, & his kniffe,
thus hath the Gyant Lost his liffe;
332 he may thanke god of his boone!
the Gyants head with him hee bare

Eglamore
takes the
giant's head

  the right way as hee ffound there,
    till hee came to the castle of stone.
336 all the whole court came him againe;
"such a head," they gan saine,
    "saw they neuer none."
  before the Erle he itt bare,

to the Earl
of Artoys,
and says he
has been to
the giant.

340 "my Lord," he said, "I haue beene there,
    in witnesse of you all[4]!"

29

  the Erle said, "sith itt is done,
Another Iourney there shall come soone,— [page 300]

The Earl
sets him his
second deed
of arms:

344 buske thee & make thee yare,—
  to Sattin, that[5] countrye,

to go to
Sattin

  ffor therin may noe man bee
    for doubt[6] of a bore;

and kill a
big boar
there,

348 his tuskes are a yard[7] long;
what fflesh that they doe come among,
    itt coucreth[8] neuer more;

---

[1] meted, measured.—F.
[2] xl. fote.—T.
[3] Mr. Halliwell makes two stanzas of 28, the rhyme-lines varying.—F.
[4] For *there*, l. 339, compare l. 233. T. adds (in italics):

Make we mery, so have we blys,
Thys ys the furste fytt of thys
That we have undertane.—F.

[5] In Sydon, in that ryche.—T.
[6] fear.—F. drede.—T.
[7] fote.—T.   [8] recovers.—F.

which kills
everything
it gets hold
of.

both man & beast itt slayeth,
352   all *that* euer hee ouer-taketh,
    & giueth them wounds sore."

30

Sir Eglamore wold not gaine-say,
he tooke his leaue & went his way,
356   to his Iourney went hee.
towards Sattin, I vnderstand,
a ffortnight he went on Land,
  & alsoe soe long on sea.
360 itt ffell againe in the euen tyde,
in the fforrest he did ryde
  wheras the bore shold bee ;
& tydings of the bore soone hee ffound ;
364 by him men Lay dead on many a Land,[1]
  that pittye itt was to see.

31

Sir Eglamore *that Knight* awoke,[2]
& priuilye lay vnder an oke ;
368   till morrow the sun shone bright,
in the fforrest ffast did hee lye ;
of the bore he hard a crye,[3]
  & neerer he gan gone right.
372 ffaire helmes he ffound in fere
that men of armes had lefft there,
  that the bore had slaine.
Eglamore to the cliffe went hee,
376 he saw the bore come from the sea,
  his morne draught [4] had he tane.

Eglamore
starts again,

journeys

fourteen
days over
land and sea,

and then
comes on
traces of
the boar,

dead men all
about.

Next
morning

he hears the
boar's cry,

and sees it
come from
the sea.

---

[1] Tho Lawnd in woodes. *Saltus nemorum*. Baret. *Saltus*, woodland pasture.—F.

[2] The last words of these lines are interchanged. T. has :

Syr Egyllamowre restyd hym vndur an oke ;
Tylle on the morowe that he can wake.
[3] on the see he harde a sowe.—T.
[4] morne drynke.—T.

32

the bore saw where the K*night* stood,   The boar

his tuskes he whetted as he were [1] wood,

380   to him he drew *that* tyde.   comes
                                                            towards
Si*r* Eglamore weened well what to doe,   him ;
                                                            Eglamore
with a speare he rode him to   rides at it,

as ffast as he might ryde.

384   all if hee [2] rode neuer soe ffast,

the good speare assunder brast,   but breaks
                                                            his spear,
it wold not in the hyde.

that bore did him woe enoughe,   and the
                                                            boar kills
388   his good horsse vnder him he slough ;   his horse.

on ffoote then must hee byde.

33

Eglamore saw no boote *that* tyde,   He puts his
                                                           side to an
but to an oake he sett his side   oak,

392   amongst the trees great ;

his good sword he drew out then,

& smote vpon [3] the wild swine   cuts at the
                                                           boar two
2 dayes & some deale more ; [4]   days,

396   till the 3ᵈ day att noone

Eglamore thought his liffe was doone   till he's
                                                           nearly dead,
for flightting with that bore ; ̣

then Eglamore with Egar mood

400   smote of the bores head ;   but then
                                                           kills it.
his tuskes he smote of thore.

34

[5] the K*ing* of Sattin on hunting fare   The King of
                                                          Sattin
with 15 armed men & more ;

---

[1] The first *e* is made over an *h* in the   mowr*e* only break off the boar's tusks in
MS.—F.   the preceding stanza, omits lines 2, 5, 7,
[2] Gyf he.—T.   of this, and has here :
[3] fyghtyth with.—T.   He thankyd God that ylke stownde,
[4] Thre dayes and more.—T.   And gaf the bore hys dethys wound,
[5] The Thornton version makes Egy̆la-   The boke of Rome thus can telle.—F.

404   the bore loud hard he yell;

he camanded a squier to fare,

and sends a
squire to see
who's in
danger.

"some man is in his perill there!

I trow to long wee dwell."

408   no longer wold the squier tarry,

but rode fast thither, by S! Marye,

he was therto ffull snell [1];

vp to the cliffe rode hee thore;

412   Sir Eglamore ffought ffast with the bore   [page 301]

with stroakes ffeirce & ffell.

35

the squier stood & beheld them 2,

hee went againe and told soe,

He tells the
King the
boar is
slain
by a knight

416   "fforsooth the bore is slaine."

"Lord! S! Mary! how may this bee?"

"a Knight is yonder certainlye

that was the bores bane;

420   "of gold he beareth a seemly sight,

in a ffeeld of azure an armed Knight,

to battell as hee shold gone;

& on the crest vpon the head is

424   a Ladye made in her likenesse;

his spures are sable eche one."

36

the King said, "soe mote I thee,

those rich armers I will see:"

428   & thither hee tooke the way.

by that time Sir Eglamore

had onercome the sharp stoure,

& ouerthawrt the bore lay.[2]

432   the King said, "god rest with thee!"

"my Lord," said Eglamore, "welcome be yee,

---

[1] query MS. siell.—F.   [2] And to reste hym down he lay.—T.

of peace now I thee pray!
I haue soe ffoughten with the bore   exhausted ;
436 *that* certainlye I may noe more ;
     this is the 3ᵈ day."

37

they all said anon-right,
" great sinn itt were with thee to ffight,
440   or to doe thee any teene ;
manffully thou hast slaine this bore   praises him
that hath done hurt sore,   for killing
     & many a mans death hath beene ;   the boar
444 thou hast manfully vnder sheeld
slaine this bore in the ffeild,
     that all wee haue seene !
this haue I wist, the sooth to say,   that had
                                       slain so
448 he hath slaine 40 ¹ on a day   many
     of my armed knights keene ! ²   knights ;

38

meat & drinke they him brought,   provides him
rich wine they spared nought,   meat and
452   & white clothes they spread.   wine ;
the King said, " soe mote I thee,
I will dine for loue of thee ;   dines with
     thou hast been hard bestead."   him,
456 " forsooooth," then Sir Eglamore saies,
" I haue ffought these 4 dayes,³
     and not a ffoote him ffledd."
then said the King, " I pray thee
460 all night to dwell with mee,   and asks
     & rest thee on a bedd."   him home to
                                           sleep.

---

¹ syxty.—T.
² Welle armyd men and clene.—T.
³ The three days have grown to four.
T. has :

     " Ye," he seyde, " permafay,
     Now hyt ys the fyrste day
       That evyr oon fote y fledd."—F.

39

Eglamore
tells the
King
what his
name is,

& after meate, the soothe to say,

the K*ing* Sir Eglamore did pray

464 " of what country hee was."

" my name," he said, " is S*ir* Eglamore [1] :

I dwell alsoe w*ith* Sir Prinsamoure,

that Erle is of artoys."

468 then Lords to the K*ing* drew,

" this is hee *that* Sir Marroccke slew,

the gyants brother Mamasse. [2]

and the
King tells
him of a

" Sir," said the K*ing*, " I pray thee

472 these 3 dayes to dwell with mee,

from mee thou shalt not passe ;

40

Giant near
who wants
to seize his
daughter,

" there dwelleth a Gyant here beside ;

my daughter *that* is of micklell pride,

476 he wold haue me ffroe ;

I dare to no place goe out

but men of armes be me about,

for dread of my foe. [3]

480 the bore thou hast slaine here,

that hath liued here this 15 yeere [4]

christen men for to sloe,

Now is he gone with sorrow enough [page 301] [5]

and is
Marroeke's
brother.

484 to [berye [6]] his brother *that* thou slough."

[that evyrmore be hym woo ! [7]]

41

No one can
cut up the
boar

to break [8] the bore they went ffull tyte ;

there was noe kniffe *that* wold him bitte, [9]

[1] He said "My name is Syr Awntour."
—T.
[2] Yondur ys he that Arrok slowee,
 The yeauntys brodur Maras.—T.
[3] Fulle soldome have y thus sene soo.
—T.
[4] He hath fedd hym xv yere.—T.

[5] There are two pages 301 in the MS.,
and no page 302.—F.
[6] berye.—T.
[7] From the Thornton MS.—F.
[8] splatt.—T.
[9] Query MS.; it may be *kitte*.—F.
byte.—T.

488   soe hard of hyde was hee.

     "Sir Eglamore,[1] thou him sloughe;

     I trow thy sword[2] be good enough;

     haue done, I pray thee."[3]

492   Eglamore to the bore gan gone,   *but Eglamore,*

     & claue him by the ridge[4] bone,

      that ioy itt was to see;

     "Lordings," he said, "great & small,[5]   *who claims only his head.*

496   giue me the head, & take you all;

     for why, *that* is my ffee."

42

     the King said, "soe god me saue!

     the head thou shalt haue;

500   thou hast itt bought full deere!"[6]

     all the countrye was ffaine,   *The people rejoice at the boar's death.*

     for the wild[7] bore was slaine,

      they made ffull royall cheere.

504   the Queene said, "god send[8] vs from shame!

     ffor when the Gyant cometh home,

     new tydings shall be here.[9]"

43

     against euen the King did dight

508   a bath ffor *that* gentle Knight,

---

[1] Syr Awntour, seyde the kyng.—T.

[2] knyfe.—T.

[3] Gyf that thy wylle bee.—T.

[4] A.-Sax. *hricg, ricg,* the back.—F.

[5] Lorde, seyde the kuyght, y dud hym falle.—T.

[6] Aftur cartys can they sende;
Ageyn none home with that they wende,
  The cyte was them nere.—T.

[7] wekyd.—T.

[8] schylde.—T.

[9] gete we sone.—T., and it adds, p. 142:
For he ys stronge and stowte,
And therof y haue mekylle dowte
  That he wylle do us grete dere or we have done.

XLV.

Syr Egyllamowre, that nobylle knyȝt,
Was sett with the kynges doghtyr bryght,
  For that he scholde be blythe.
The maydenys name was Organata so fre;
Sche preyeth hym of gode chere to bee,
  And besechyd hym so many a sythe.
Aftur mete sche can hym telle
How that geant wolde them quelle:
  The knyght began to lagh anone;
"Damyselle," he seyde, "so mote y thee,
And he come whylle y here bee,
  Y schalle hym assay sone!"

that was of Erbes [1] good.

Sir Eglamore therin Lay

till itt was light of the day,

Eglamore
lies in a
bath all
night.

512   *that* men to Mattins [2] yode.

[Part III.[3]]

[How Eglamore kills another Giant, and a Dragon near Rome, and
begets a Boy on Christabell.]

Next
morning
the Giant
comes,

By the time he had heard masse,

the Gyant to this place come was,

& cryed as hee were wood ;

and demands
the King's
daughter
Aruada.

516   "Sir King," he said, " send vnto mee

3ᵈ Part.   Arnada [4] thy daughter ffree,

or I shall [5] spill thy blood."

44

Eglamore

Sir Eglamore anon-right [6]

520   in good armour he him dight,

& vpon the walles he yode [7] ;

tells a squire

to show the
Giant the
boar's head.

he camanded a squier to beare

the bores head vpon a speare,

524   *that* the Gyant might itt [8] see.

& when he looked on the head,

The Giant

"alas! " he said,[9] "art thou dead ?

my trust was all in thee !

swears he'll
avenge its
death,

528   now by the Law *that* I liue in,[10]

my litle speckeled hoglin,[11]

deare bought shall thy death bee ! "

---

[1] Sibes.—P. The MS. is indistinct,
and the Bishop explains it. See the
way to prepare a bath in Russel's Boke
of Nurture, *Babees Boke &c.* E. E. Text
Soc. 1868, p. 182-5.
[2] mete.—T.
[3] T. ends its *seconde fytt* with stanza 52,
l. 611 below.—F.
[4] Orgauata.—T.

[5] thou schalt.—T.
[6] that nobylle knyght.—T.
[7] for ' yode he.'—F. wendyth hee.—T.
[8] Maras myght hym.—T.
[9] my bore.—T.
[10] leve yune.—T.
[11] spote hoglyn.—T. Fr. *cochonnet,* a
shote or shete pigge, a prettie big pig.
—Cotgrave.

45

the Gyant on the walls donge ;
532 att euery stroke fyer out spronge ;
for nothing wold he spare.
towards the castle gan he crye,
" false traitor ! thou shalt dye [1]

536 for slaying of my bore !
your strong walles I doe [2] downe ding,
& with my hands I shall the hange [3]
ere *that* I fforther passe. [4] "

540 but through the grace of god almight,
the Gyant had his ffill of fight,
& therto some deale more. [5]

and threatens to kill Egla-more.

46 [6]

Sir Eglamore was not agast ;
544 on might-ffull god was all his trust,
& on his sword soe good.
to Eglamore said the K*ing* then,
" best is to arme vs euerye man ;
548 this theefe, I hold him woode."

Eglamore trusts in God and his good sword,

47 [6]

Sir Eglamore sware by the roode,
" I shall him assay if hee were wood ;
mickle is gods might ! "
552 he rode a course to say his steed,
he tooke his helme & forth hee yeede ;
All men prayed for *that* K*n*ight. [page 303]

gives his steed a gallop,

48

Sir Eglamore into the ffeild taketh ;
556 the Gyant see him, [7] & to him goeth ;

takes the field,

---

[1] Thevys, traytures, ye schalle abye. —T.
[2] schalle.—T.   [3] hynge.—T.
[4] fare, qu.—P. Or that y hens fare. —T.   [5] mair.—P.
[6] T. makes one stanza, XLIX, of these, p. 144–5, and alters the arrange-ment of the lines, &c.—F.
[7] *him* has a line through it.—F.

"welcome," he said, " my ffeere !
thou art hee *that* slew [1] my bore !
that shalt thou repent ffull sore,
560   & buy itt wonderous deere ! "

Sir Eglamore weened well what to doe;
with a speare he rode him to,
as a man of armes cleere.

564 against him the Gyant was redy bowne,
but horsse & man he bare all downe,
that dead he was ffull nere.

49

Sir Eglamore cold noe better read,
568 but what time his horsse was dead,
to his ffoote he hath him tane ;

& then Eglamore to him gan goe ;

the right arme he smote him froe,
572 euen by the sholder bone ;
& tho he [2] had lost his hand,

all day hee stood a ffightand
till the ssun to rest gan goe ;
576 [3] the sooth to say, withouten lye,
he sobbed & was soe drye

that liffe him lasteth none.

50

all *that* on the walles were,
580 when they heard the Gyant rore,
ffor ioy the bells thé ring.

Edmond was the K*ing*s [4] name,
swore to Sir Eglamore, " by St. Iame,
584 here shalt thou be K*ing* !

---

[1] Y trowe thou halpe to sle.—T.
[2] Thowe the lorelle.—T.
[3] Then was he so wery he my3t not
stonde,

The blode ran so faste fro hym on
every honde,
That lyfe dayes hadd he nevyr oon.
—T.
[4] kynges.—T.

"to-morrow thow shalt crowned bee,
& thou shalt wed my daughter ffree
 with a curyous rich ringe!"

and marry him to his daughter.

588 Eglamore answered with words mild :
"god [1] giue you ioy of your child!
 ffor here I may not abyde longe. [2]"

Eglamore declines the young lady,

51

"Sir Eglamore, for thy doughtye deede
592 thou shalt not be called lewd
 in noe place where thou goe!" [3]
then said Arnada, [4] *that* sweete thing,
"haue here of me a gold ring

though she gives him a charmed ring

596 with a precyous stone;
where-soe you bee on water or Land,
& this ring vpon your hand,
 nothing may you slone."

52

600 "gramercy!" sayd Eglamore ffree.
"this 15 yeeres will I abyde thee,
 soe *that* you will me wed;
this will I sweare, soe god me saue,

and offers to wait fifteen years for him,

604 King ne Prince nor none will haue,
 if they be comlye cladd!"
"damsell," he said, "by my ffay,
by *that* time I will you say

He puts her off,

608 how *that* I haue spedd."
he tooke the Gyants head & the bore,
& towards Artoys did he ffare,
 god helpe me att neede! [5]

and starts towards Artoys.

---

[1] Syr.—T.   [2] may ye not lende.—T.
[3] Y schalle geve the a nobylle stede,
 Al so redd as ony roone;
Yn yustyng ne in turnement,
Thou schalt never soffur dethys
 wound
Whylle thou syttyst hym upon.
    —T.
[4] Seyde Organata.—T.

[5] The knyght takyth hys leve and
 farys.
Wyth the geauntys hedd and the
 borys,
The weyes owre Lord wylle hym
 lede.
Thys ys the seconde fytt of thys :
Make we mery, so have we blys,
For ferre have we to rede.—T.

53

In seven
weeks Egla-
more reaches
Artoys,

612   by *that* 7 weekes were comen to end,
     euen att Artoys he did lend,
       wheras Prinsamoure was.
     the Erle therof was greatly faine
616   *that* Eglamore was come againe;
       soe was both more[1] and lesse.

is greeted by
Christabell),

     when Christabell as white as swan,
     heard tell how Eglamore was come,
620   to him shee went full yare;[2]

54

whom he
kisses,

     the K*night* kissed *that* Lady gent,
     then into the hall hee went
       the Erle for to teene.

but her
father says,
" Devil take
you, will
nothing kill
you ?

624   The Erle answered, & was ffull woe   [page 304]
     " what devill! may nothing thee sloe ?
       forsooth, right as I weene,
     thou art about, as I vnderstand,

You want
my land and
my daughter
I suppose."

628   for to winn Artoys & all my Land,
     & alsoe my daughter cleane."

55

" I do," says
Eglamore.

     Sir Eglamore said, " soe mote I thee,
     not but if I worthy bee;
632   soe god giue me good read !"[3]

" Oh !
perhaps
you'll get
killed yet."

     the Erle said, " such chance may ffall,
     that one may come & quitt all,
       be thou neuer so prest."

Eglamore
asks for
twelve weeks
rest ;

636   " but good Lord, I you pray,
     of 12 weekes to giue me day,

---

[1] One stroke too many in the MS. *m.*
—F.

[2] T. adds:
'Syr," sche seyde, "how haue ye
  faryn ?"

" Damycelle, wele, and in travelle byn
To brynge us bothe owt of care."

[3] Helpe God that ys beste.—T.

my weary body to rest."
12 weekes were granted then
640 by prayer of many [1] a gentleman.
   & comforted him with the best.

56

Sir Eglamore after supper

after supper goes to Christabell's chamber.

   went to Christabells chamber
644   with torches burning bright.
the Ladye was of soe great pride,[2]
shee sett him on her bedside,
   & said, " welcome, Sir Knight ! "
648 then Eglamore did her tell
of adventures *that* him befell,
   but there he dwelled all night.

stays there all night, and begets a son on her.

" damsell," he said, " soe god me speed,
652 I hope in god you for to wedd !"
   & then their trothes they plight.[3]

57

by *that* 12 weekes were come & gone,

In twelve weeks Christabell

Christabbell *that* was as faire as sunn,[4]
656   all wan waxed her hewe.

grows wan,

shee said vnto her maidens flree,

and begs her maids to keep her secret.

" in *that* yee know my priuitye,[5]
   looke *that* yee bee trew ! "
660 the Erle angerlye gan flare,

The Earl orders Egla-more off,

he said to Eglamore, " make thee yare
   for thy Iourney a-new ! "
When Christabell therof heard tell,[6]

and Christa-bell mourns.

664 shee mourned night & day,
   that all men might her rue.

---

[1] Only half the *n* is in the MS.—F.
[2] was not for to hyde.—T.
[3] T. adds :
  So graeyously he come hur tylle,
  Of poyntes of armys he schewyd
    hur hys fylle,
  That there they dwellyd alle nyȝt.

[4] as whyte as fome.—T.
[5] Sche prayed hur gentylle women so
   fre,
  That they would layne hur privyte.
       .. T.
[6] say.—P.

58

Eglamore's
Third Deed
of Arms is to
kill a strong
Dragon near
Rome.

the Erle said, " there is mee told long,

beside Roome there is a dragon strong ;

668   forsooth as I you say,

the dragon is of such renowne

there dare noe man come neere the towne

by 5 miles and more ; [1]

672   arme thee well & thither wend ;

looke *that* thou slay him with thy hand,

or else [2] say mee nay."

59

Eglamore
takes leave

Sir Eglamore to the chamber went,

676   & tooke his leaue of the Ladye gent,

white as fflower on ffeelde [3] ;

of Christa-
bell,

" damsell," he said, " I haue to doone ;

I am to goe, & come againe right soone

680   through the might of Marry mild.

gives her a
gold ring,

a gold ring I will giue thee ;

keepe itt well for the loue of mee

if christ send me a child."

684   & then, in Romans as wee say,

and goes to
Rome.

to great roome he tooke his way,

to seeke the dragon wild. [4]

60

if he were neuer soe hardye a *Knight*,

688   when of the dragon he had a sight,

his hart began to be cold. [5]

The Dragon
throws down
him and his
horse.

anon the dragon waxed wrothe,

he smote Sir Eglamore & his steed bothe,

692   *that* both to grownd they ffell. [6]

---

[1] Be xv. myle of way.—T.
[2] ellys thou.—T. After *nay* T. adds
six lines not in our text.—F.
[3] in may.—P.
[4] The Thornton text adds :

Tokenynges sone of hym he fonde,
Slayne men on every honde ;
  Be hunderdes he them tolde.—F.
[5] to folde.—T.
[6] To the grounde so colde.—T.

Eglamore rose, & to him sett,
& on *that* ffowle worme hee bett
with stroakes many and bold [1] ;

[page 305]

Eglamore attacks the Dragon,

61

696 the dragon shott fire with his mouth
like the devill of hell ;
Sir Eglamore neere him gan goe,
& smote his taile halfe him ffroe [2] ;
700 then he began to yell,
& with the stumpe *that* yett was leaued
he smote Sir Eglamore on the head ;
that stroake was ffeirce and ffell.

cuts half its tail off,

is wounded himself in the head,

62

704 " Sir Eglamore neere him gan goe,
the dragons head he smote of thoe,
fforsooth as I you say,
his wings he smote of alsoe,[3]
708 he smote the ridge bone in 2,
& wan the ffeild *that* day.
the Emperour of Roome Lay [4] in his tower
& ffast beheld Sir Eglamore,
712 & to his K*nigh*ts gan say,
" doe cry in Roome, the dragons slaine !
a knigh[t] him slew with might & maine,
maufully, by my ffay ! "
716 through Roome they made a crye,
euery officer in his baylye,
" the dragon is slaine this day ! "

but kills the Dragon.

The Emperor Constantine of Rome

orders the Dragon's death to be proclaimed,

63

& then the Emperour tooke the way
720 to the place where Eglamore Lay,

then goes to Eglamore,

---

[1] Wyth byttur dynte and felle.—T.
[2] Halfe the tonge he stroke away.—T.
[3] The knyght seyde, " Now am y schente ! "
Nere that wyckyd worme he went ;
Hys hedd he stroke away.—T.
[4] stode.—T.

beside *that* ffoule thing,
w*i*th all *that* might ride or gone.
S*i*r Eglamore they hane vp tane,

brings him
to Rome,
and the
people meet
him in
procession.

724   & to the towne they can him bring;
ffor ioy *that* they dragon was slaine,
they came w*i*th procession him againe,
and bells they did ringe.

728   the Emperour of Roome brought him soone,
Constantine, *that* was his name,
a Lord of great Longinge.

64

[1] all *that* ener saw his head,
732   th*é* said *that* Eglamore was but dead,
that Knight S*i*r Eglamore.

Constan-
tine's
daughter
Vyardus

the Emperour had a daughter bright,
shee vndertooke to heale the Knight,
736   her name was vyardus.[2]

heals Egla-
more's head,
and saves
his life.

[3] with good salues shee healed his head
& saued him ffrom the dead,
that Lady of great valours:

740   & there w*i*thin a little stond
shee made S*i*r Eglamore whole & sound;
god giue her honor! [3]

---

[1] T. omits the next three lines.—F.
[2] ys Dawntowre.—T.
[3-3] The Thornton text has for these:
Scho savys hym fro the dedd,
And with hur handys sche helyth hys
    hedd
A twelmonth in hur bowre.

It then adds two stanzas of twelves,
(LXVII, LXVIII, p. 153-4) telling how
the Emperor had the Dragon's body
fetched into Rome, and put in "seynt
Laurens kyrke." As to this church, see
Stacions of Rome, p. 13; *Pol. Rel. & Love
Poems*, p. 132. p. xxxv.—F.

[Part IV.]

[How Christabell's child is born, and a Griffin flies away with it.]

65

744   Anon word came to Artois
how *that* the dragon slaine was:
a K*night that* deede had done.
soe long at the Leeche-craft he did dwell,

4 parte   *that* a ffaire sonne[1] had Christabell

748   as white as whales bone.[2]
then the Erle made his vow,
" daughter ! into the sea shalt thou
in a shipp thy selfe alone !

752   Thy younge sonne shall be thy fere,[3]
christendome[4] getteth itt none here ! "
her maidens wept eche one.

While Eglamore is under the doctor's hands, Christabell has a son.

Her father vows he'll send her and her brat out to sea alone.

66

[5] her mother in swoone did ffall,

756   right soe did her ffreinds all
that wold her any good.
" good Lord," she said, " I you pray,
let some prest a gospell say,

760   ffor doubt of ffeendes in the fllood.
ffarwell," shee said, " my maidens ffree !
greet well my Lord when you him see."
they wept as they were woode.

764   Leaue wee now Sir Eglamore,
And speake wee more of *that* Ladye fflower
that vnknown wayes yeelde.[6]

Christabell prays that a priest may say a gospel for them,

and takes leave of her maidens.

[page 306]

---

[1] A man-chylde.—T.

[2] Some ancient writers imagined ivory, formerly made from the teeth of the walrus, to be formed from the bones of the whale. Halliwell's Gloss.—F.

[3] And that bastard that to the ys dere.—T.

[4] christening.—F.

[5] T. inserts a stanza and a quarter here, p. 154-5, but leaves out the mother's swooning.—F.

[6] yeede.—P.

67

Her ship
comes to a
rock,

the shipp droue fforth night & day

768 vp to a rocke, the sooth to say,

where wild beasts did run.[1]

shee was ffull ffaine, I vnderstand,

she lands,

shee wend shee had beene in some [known [2]] Land,

772 & vp then gan shee wend.

noe manner of men ffound shee there,

finds only
birds and
beasts there,

that ffoules & beasts *that* were there,

ffast they flled ffrom Land.

and a griffin
carries her
boy off to a
strange
country,

776 there came a Griffon [3] *that* ronght her care ;

her younge child away hee bare

Into a countrye vnknowne.[4]

68

the Ladye wept, & said " alas

780 *that* euer shee borne was !

my child is taken me ffroe ! "

the King of
Isarell's

the *King* of Isarell on huntinge went ;

he saw where the ffoule lent ;

784 towards him gan he goe.

a griffon, the booke saith *that* he hight,

land.

that in Isarell did light,

that wrought *that* Ladye woe.

788 the ffoule smote him with his bill,

the child cryed and liked ill ;

the griffon then lefft him there.

69

A Gentle-
woman picks
up the boy.

a gentlewoman to *that* [child [5]] gan passe,

792 & lapp[t] itt in a mantle of Scarlett was,

& with a rich pane.[6]

---

[1] feede.—P.

[2] there had be a kende londe.—T.

[3] a grype.—T. Fr. *griffon*, a grype or griffon.—Cotgrave. Grype, byrde, *vul-tur*; Promptorium: see Mr. Way's note to it, p. 212-13.—F.

[4] unknowe.—P.

[5] a squyer to the chylde.—T.

[6] Pane of furre, *panne* (Palsgrave); *Panne* a skinne, fell or hide (Cotgrave); from L. *pannus*, Way. Cp. counterpane. —F.

the child was large of lim & lythe,
a girdle of gold itt was bound with,
796   with worsse cloth itt was cladd.
the King swore by the rood,   *The King*
" the child is come of gentle blood,
whersoeuer *that* hee was tane ;
800 & for he froe the Griffon fell,
they named the child degrabell,   *christens*
                          him Degra-
that lost was in wilsome way.   *bell,*

70

the King wold hunt noe more *that* tyde,
804 but with the child homeward gan ryde,
that ffrom the Griffon was hent.   *and takes*
                          him home to
" Madam," he said to his Queene,   *his wife,*
" ffull oft I haue a hunting beene ;
808 this day god hath me lent."
of *that* Child he was blythe ;
after nurses shee went beliue ;   *who gets*
                          nurses for
the child was louelye gent.   *him.*
812 leaue wee now of this chylde,
& talke wee of his mother mild,   *Meantime,*
                          Christabell
to what Land god her sent.

71

all *that* night on the rocke shee Lay ;   *leaves her*
816 a wind rose vpon the [1] day,   *rock,*
& ffrom the Land her driueth.
in *that* shipp was neither mast nor ore,
but euery streame vpon other   *is driven*
                          about the
820 *that* flast vpon her driueth.   *sea,*
& as the great booke of Roome saies,
shee was without meate 5 dayes   *fasts five*
among the great cliffes. [2]   *days,*

---

[1] ageynys.—T.   [2] MS. cliitles.—F.

824   by *that* 5 dayes were gone,
        god sent her succour soone ;

and then reaches Egypt.   in œgipt [1] shee arriued.

72

The King   the King of Ægipt [1] lay in his tower,
828   & saw the Ladye as white as fllower
        that came right neere the Land ;

sends a squire to her.   he comanded a Squire ffree
        to ' Looke what in *that* shipp might bee
832   *that* is vpon the sand.'
        the Squier went thither ffull tite,
        on the shipbord he did smite,
        a Ladye vp then gan stand ;

Christabell cannot speak to the squire,   836   Shee might not speake to him a word,   [page 307]
        but lay & looked ouer the bord,
        & made signes with her hand. [2]

73

        the squier wist not what shee ment ;
who goes back to the King,   840   againe to the King he went,
        & kneeled on his knee :
        " Lord, in the shipp nothing is,
        sauing one in a womans Likenesse
844   *that* ffast looked on mee.

and tells him what a lovely foreign woman he has seen.   but on [3] shee be of fllesh & bone,
        a ffairer saw I neuer none,
        sane my Ladye soe ffree ! [4]
848   shee maketh signes with her hand ;
        shee seemeth of some ffair Land ;
        vnknowen shee is to mee. [5]

---

[1] The MS. may be either Œ or Æ in this and other cases.—F.

[2] The Thornton text adds:
Make we mery for Goddys est ;
Thys ys the thrydd fytte of owre geste,
That dar y take an hande.—F.

[3] an, if.—F.

[4] But hyt were Mary free.–-T.

[5] Beyonde the Grekys see.—T.

74

Sir Marmaduke [1] highet the King, [2]

852 he went to see *that* sweet thing,

    he went a good pace.

    to the Ladye he said in same,

    " speake, woman, on gods name ! "

856 against him shee rose.

    the Lady *that* was soe meeke & milde,

    shee had bewept sore her child,

    that almost gone shee was. [3]

860 home to the court they her Ledd,

    with good meates they her ffedd ; [4]

    with good will shee itt taketh. [5]

King Marmaduke goes to Christabell, speaks to her,

takes her home to Court, feeds her well,

75

    " Now, good damsell," said the King,

864 " where were you borne, my sweet thing ?

    yee are soe bright of blee."

    " Lord, in Artois borne I was ;

    Sir Prinsamoure my ffather was,

868 *that* Lord is of *that* Countrye ;

    I and my maidens went to play

    by an arme of the sea ;

    Iocund wee were and Iollye :

872 they wind was lithe, a bote there stood,

    I and my squier in yode,

    but vnchristened was hee.

and asks her who she is.

Christabell tells him,

and says she

got into a boat with her boy,

76

    " on land I lefft my maidens all,

876 my younge squier on sleepe gan ffall,

    my mantle al on him I threw ;

wrapped him in her mantle,

---

[1] Marmaduke seems to have been from Marmaluke.—Pencil note.

[2] Be Ihesu swere that gentylle kynge. —T. T. doesn't give " The kyng of Egypt " a name.—F.

[3] Sche was wexyn alle horse.—T.

[4] Dylyevus metys they hur badd.—T.

[5] sche them tase.—T.

and a griffin
flew away
with him.

a griffon there came *that* rought me care,

my younge squier away hee bare,

880   southeast with him hee drew."

"All right,
you shall be
my niece
then:"

"damsell," he said, "be of good cheere,

thou art my brothers daughter deere."

ffor Ioy of him shee longe ;

and Christa-
bell stays in
Egypt.

884   ¹ & there shee did still dwell

till time *that* better beffell,

with ioy and mirth enoughe.¹

[Part V.]

[How Eglamore comes back to Artois, and goes to the Holy Land for
fifteen years ; and how Christabell marries her own son.]

77

As soon as
Eglamore
recovers,

888   Now is Eglamore whole & sound,

& well healed of his wound ;

he leaves
Rome,

homeward then wold hee ffare.

of the Emperour he tooke leaue I-wis,

5.ᵈ **parte**   of the daughter, & of the Empresse,

892   & of all the meany *that* were there.

Christabell was most in his thought :

to go home
to Christa-
bell.

the dragons head hee home brought,

on his speare he itt bare.

896   by *that* 7 weekes were come to end,

He reaches
Artois,

in the land of Artoys can he Lend,

wheras the Erle gan ffare.

78

in the court was told, as I vnderstand,

900   how *that* Eglamore was come to Land

with the dragons head.

his Squier rode againe him soone,

and his
squire tells
him that
Christabell
is dead.

"Sir, thus hath our Lord doone ; ²

904   ffaire Christabell is dead !

---

¹⁻¹ Kepe we thys lady whyte as flowre,   Now comyth to hym care y-nogh.—T.
And speke we of syr Egyllamowre ;   ² Lo ! lorde, what the erle hath done !—T.

a ffaire sonne shee had borne ;

¹ bothe they are now fforlorne

through his ffalse read ; ¹

908 In ² a shipp hee put them 2,   [page 308]

& with the wind let them goe."

then swooned ³ he where hee stood.

Her father
sent her and
her boy

out to sea in
a ship.

Eglamore
swoons,

79

"alas ! " then said the Knight soe ffree,

912 " Lord ! where may my maidens bee

that in her chamber was ? "

the Squier answered him ffull soone,

" as soone as shee was doone,

916 ech one their way did passe."

Eglamore went into the hall

before the Squiers & knights all :

" & thou, Erle of Artoys !

920 take," he said, " the dragons head !

all his mine that here his lead !

what dost thou in this place ? " ⁴

asks after
Christabell's
maidens,

goes to the
Earl of
Artois,
gives him
the Dragon's
head,
claims all
his goods,
and asks him
what he's
doing there.

80

great dole itt was to heere

924 when he called Christabell his fere :

" what ! art thou drowned in the sea ?

god that dyed on the rood bitterlye,⁵

on thy soule haue mercye,

928 and on that younge child soe ffree ! "

the Erle was soe feard of Eglamore

that he was ffaine to take his tower ; ⁶

Eglamore
laments over
Christabell
and her boy,

---

^{1—1} The erle hath hys lyfe forlorne,
He was bothe whyte and rede.—T.

² Im in MS.—P.

³ Swooning was the correct thing for a knight, and on very much less provocation than this. See many instances in Seynt Graal, &c. &c. It betokened the possession of delicate feelings.—F.

⁴ Alle ys myn that here ys levydd.
Thou syttyst in my place.—T.

⁵ on crosse verye.—T.

⁶ The erle rose up and toke a towre.
—T.

that enermore woe him bee !

932 Eglamore said, "soe god me saue,

all *that* the order of Knight-hoode will haue,

rise vp & goe with mee ! "

81

they were ffull faine to do his will ;

936 vp they rose, & came him till ;

he gaue them order soone.

the while *that* he in hall abode,

32 [1] knights he made,

940 ffrom morne till itt was noone.

[2] those *that* liuing had none,

he gaue them liuing to liue vpon,

ffor Christabell to pray soone.

944 then anon, I vnderstand,

he tooke the way to the holy Land,

where god on the rood was done.

82

Sir Eglamore, as you heare,

948 he dwelled there 15 yeere

the heathen men amonge ;

ffull manffullye he there him bare,

where any deeds of armes were,

952 against him *that* liued wronge.

in battell or in turnament

there might no man withstand his dent,

but downe right he him thronge.

956 by *that* 15 yeeres were gone,

his sonne *that* the griffon had tane,

was waxen both stiffe and stronge.

[1] V. and thretty.—T.
[2] And he that was the porest of them
  alle,
He gaf for Crystabellys soule
  Londys to leve vpon.

A thousand, as y vndurstonde,
He toke with hym, and went into
  the Holy Londe,
There God on cros was done.—T.

83

now was degrabell waxen wight ;
960　the K*ing* of Isarell dubbd him a K*night* is dubbed knight,
　　and Prince with his hand.
　　Listen, Lords great and small,
　　of what manner of armes he bare, and these are his arms :
964　　& yee will vnderstand :
　　he bare in azure, a griffon of gold on a shield of azure
　　richlye portrayed in the mold, a golden griffin
　　on his clawes hanginge
968　a man child in a mantle round carrying a boy with a
　　& with a girdle of gold bound, girdle of gold.
　　without any Leasinge.

84

the K*ing* of Isarell, hee waxed old ; The King of Isarell asks
972　to degrabell his sonne he told, Degrabell to marry.
　　" I wold thou had a wiffe
　　while *that* I liue, my sonne deere ;
　　when I am dead, thou hast noe ffere,
976　　riches is soe riffe." [1]
　　a messenger stoode by the K*ing* : They are told of Christabell
　　" in Ægipt is a sweet thing, in Egypt ;
　　I know noe such on liue ;
980　the K*ing*, fforsooth, this oath hath sworne,
　　there shall none her haue *that* is borne but he who wins her
　　　But he winne her by striffe." 　[page 309] must fight for her.
　　the King said, " by the rood,
984　wee will not Lett if shee bee good ;
　　haue done, & buske vs swythe."
　　anon-right they made them yare, They make ready,
　　& their armour to the shipp the bare,
988　to passe the watter beliue. sail off,

---

[1] When y am dedd, thou getyst no pere,
　　Of ryches thou art so ryfe.—T.

85

by tthat 7 dayes [1] were comen to end,
in ægipt Land they gan Lend,
  the vncouthe costes to see.[2]

992   messengers went before to tell,
  " here cometh the King of Isarell
    with a ffaire Meany,
  & the Prince with many a Knight,
996   ffor to haue your daughter bright,
    if itt your wil be."
  the King said, " I trow I shall
    ffind Lodging [3] ffor you all ;

1000   right welcome yee are to mee ! "

86

then trumpetts in the shipp [4] rose,
& euery man to Land goes ;
  the Knights were clothed in pall.
1004 the younge Knight of 15 yeere,
  he rydeth, as yee may heere,
    a ffoote aboue them all.
  the King of Isarell on the Land,

1008 the King of Ægipt takes him by the hand
    & Ledd him into the hall :
  [5] " Sir," said the King, " ffor charitye,
  will you lett mee your daughter see,[5]
1012   white as bone of whall ? "

87

the Lady ffrom the chamber was brought ;

with mans hands shee seemed wrought
  & carued out of tree.

1016 her owne sonne stood & beheld :

[1] Be th[r]e wekys.—T.
[2] Ther forsus for to knowe swythe.
—T.
[3] redy yustyng.—T.

[4] Trumpus in the topp-castelle.—T.
[5] Y prey the thou gyf me a syght
Of Crystyabelle, yowre doghtyr
bryght.—T.

" well worthye him *that* might weld ! "
thus to himselfe thought hee.
the K*ing* of Isarell asked then
1020   if that she [1] might passe the streame,
his sonnes wiffe ffor to bee.
" Sir," said the K*ing*, " if *that* you may

and may
have her if
he wins her

meete me a stroake to-morrowe,
1024   thine asking grant I thee."

88

Lords in hall were sett,

They dine,

& waites blew to the meate.
they made all royall cheere ;
1028   the 2 K*ings* the desse began,[2]

and Degra-
bell and his
mother have
the high
seat.

Sir Degrabell & his mother then,
the 2 were sibb ffull neere.
then K*nigh*ts went to sitt I-wis,
1032   & euery man to his office,
to serue the K*nigh*ts deere ;
& affter meate washed they,[3]
& Clarkes grace gan say
1036   in hall, as you may heere.

89

then on the morrow when day sprong

Next day

gentlemen in their armour [4] throng,
Degrabell was dight ;

Degrabell
arms,
and the
King of
Egypt tries
him.

1040   the K*ing* of Ægipt gan him say
in a ffaire ffeeld *that* day
with many a noble Knight.
what time the great Lord might him see,
1044   they asked, " what Lord *that* might bee
with the griffon soe bright ? "

---

[1] MS. the. Yf she.—T. (with other changes).—F.

[2] had the chief seats on the dais.—F.

[3] See the operation described in *The Boke of Curtasye &c.* (E. E. Text Soc.

1867).—F. T. has:
Aftur mete, than seyde they
Deus pacis, clerkys canne seye.

[1] to haruds.—T.

the ruler of *that* game gan tell,
　　　"this is the Prince of Israell!
1048　　　beware! ffor he is wight."

　　　　　　　　90

　　　the King of Ægipt tooke a shafft;
Degrabell
sits firm,　　the Prince saw *that*, & sadlye sate,
　　　　　if he were neuer soe keene.[1]
1052　against the King he made him bowne,
unhorses the　And on the ground he cast him downe,　　　[page 310]
King,
　　　　　the ground *that* was soe greene.
wins Christ-　they King said, " soe god me saue,
tabell,
1056　thou art worthy her to haue ! "
　　　　　soe said they all by-deene.

　　　　　　　　91

　　　euerye Lord gan other assay,
　　　& squiers on the other day,
1060　　*that* doughtye were of deede.
　　　S*ir* Degrabell his troth hee plight ;
　　　& Christabell, *that* Ladye bright,
　　　　to church they her ledd.
and by God's　1064　through the might of god he[2] spedd,
might
marries his　his owne mother there he wedd,
mother.
　　　　　in Romaus as wee reade.[3]
She sees his　shee saw his armes him beforne[4] ;
arms,
1068　shee thought of him *that* was forlorne,
　　　　　shee wept like to be dead.

　　　　　　　　92

　　　"what cheere," he said, " my Lady cleere[5] ? "
　　　what weepe you, & make such heauye cheere ?
1072　　methinkes you are in thought."

---

[1] ? MS. keere.—F.
[2] Thus gracyously he hath.—T.
[3] Thus harde y a clerke rede.—T.
[4] MS. beforme.—F.
[5] The word may be *cleerre*. T. omits
this and the next two lines.—F.

" Sir, in your armes now I see
a ſſoule *that* [rafte] on a time ſſrom mee
a child *that* I deere bought,[1]

1076 *that* in a scarlett mantle was wound,
& in a girdle of gold bound
that richely was wrought."

the K*ing* of Isarell said ſſull right,
1080 " in my ſſorrest the ſſoule gan Light ;
a griffon to Land him brought."

and tells him
how a bird
took her boy
away,

in a mantle,
and with a
gold girdle
on.

The King of
Isarell says
the Griffin
alighted in
his land,

93

he sent a squier ſſull hend,
& bade him ffor the mantle wende
1084 that hee was in Layd.
beſſore him itt was brought ſſull yare,
the girdle & the mantle there,
that richlye were graned.
1088 "alas ! " then said *that* Lady ffree,
" this same the Griffon tooke ſſrom mee."
in swoning downe shee braid.
" how long agoe ? " the K*ing* gan say.
1092 " S*ir*, 15 yeere par ma ffay."
they assented to *that* shee said.

and the boy
was brought
to him.

Christabell
says the boy
was hers,

and it's
fifteen years
ago.

94

" ſſorsooth, my sonne, I am afraid
that tó[2] sibb maryage wee haue made
1096 in the beginninge of this moone."
" damsell, looke,—soe god me saue !—
wh*i*ch of my K*nights* thou wilt haue."
then degrabell answered soone,
1100 " S*ir*, I hold you[r] Erles good,
& soe I doe my mother, by the roode,
that I wedded before they noone ;

She tells her
son-husband
that their
marriage is
void.

The King
offers her
any husband
she'll choose.

No, says
Degrabell,

[1] That sometyme rafte a chylde fro me,
A knyght fulle dere hym boght.—T. [2] When *to* stands for *too*, the *o* will be
accented hereafter.—F.

the knights
must fight
for her.

there shall none haue her certainlye
1104 but if he winne her with maisterye
as I my-selfe haue doone."

95

All the lords
agree to
do so.

then euery Lord to other gan say,
" ffor her I will make delay [1]
1108 with a speare & sheeld in hand ;
who-soe may winne that Lady clere,
ffor to be his wedded ffere,
must wed her in that Land."

[Part VI.]

[How Eglamore won back his lost loue Christabell, and married her.]

96

Eglamore,

1112 Sir Eglamore was homward bowne,
he hard tell of that great renowne,
& thither wold hee wend.[2]

many lords,

6ᵈ Parte

great Lords that hard of that crye,
they rode thither hastilye,
as ffast as they might ffare.

and the
King of
Sattin, come
to the
tourney.

the King of Sattin [3] was there alsoe,
& other great Lords many more
1120 that royall armes [4] bare.

Lists are
prepared,

Then ringes were made in the ffeeld
that Lords might therin weld ;

and all the
lords make
ready.

thé busked & made them yare.
1124 Sir Eglamore, thoe he came Last,
he was not worthy out to be cast ;
that Knight was clothed in care.

97

ffor *that* Christabell was put to the sea,
1128 new armes beareth hee,
  I will them descrye :
  he beareth in azure a shipp of gold,
  ffull richlye portrayed on the mold,   [page 311]
1132 ffull well & worthylye ;
  the sea was made both grim & bold ;
  a younge child of a night old,
   & a woman Lying there by ;
1136 of siluer was the mast, of gold the ffane[1] ;
  sayle, ropes, & cables, eche one
   painted were worthylye.

Eglamore bears as arms, on a blue shield a gold ship, with a child, and a woman lying by it.

98

heralds of armes soone on hye,
1140 euery Lords armes gan descrye
  in *that* ffeeld soe broade.[2]
  then Chr[i]stabell as white as fflower,
  she sate vpon a hye tower ;[3]
1144 ffor her *that* crye was made.
  the younge kn*ig*ht of 15 yeere old
  that was both doughtye & bold,
   into the ffeeld he rode.
1148 who-soe *that* Sir Degrabell did smite,
  w*i*th his dint they ffell tyte,
   neuer a one his stroake abode.

Christabell sits in a high tower :

her son Degrabell rides into the field,

and fells all who attacks him,

99

Sir Eglamo*r*e houed[4] & beheild
1152 how the folke in the feild downe feld
  they Kn*ig*hts all by-deene.

Eglamore looks on.

---

[1] Fane, a Weather-cock, which turns about as the Wind changes, and shews from what Quarter it blows. Phillips. —F.

[2] The three lines above are not in T.

[3] Was broght to a corner of the walle.—T.

[4] halted, stood still. The first three lines of this stanza are not in T.—F.

when Degrabell him see, he rode him till,[1]
& said, " Sir, why are you soe still
1156   amonge all these Knights keene ? "

Eglamore said to him I-wis,[2]
"I am come out of heathenesse,
    itt were sinne mee to meete.[3] "
1160 Degrabell said, " soe mote I thee !
more worshipp itt had beene to thee,
    vnarmed to haue beene."

100

the ffather on the sonne Lough ;

1164 " haue yee not Iusting enoughe [4]
    where euer that you bee ?
that day ffall haue I seene,
with as bigg men haue I beene,
1168   & yett well gone my way.

& yett, fforsooth," said he then,
" I will doe as well as I can,
    with you once to play."

1172 heard together they knights donge
with great speares sharpe and longe ;
    them beheld eche one.

Sir Eglamore, as itt was his happ,[5]
1176 giue his sonne such a rappe [6]
    that to the ground went hee.

101

" alas ! " then said that Ladye ffree,
" my sonne is dead, by gods pittye !
1180   the keene knight hath him slaine ! "
then men said wholy on mold,

" the Knight that beares the shipp of gold
    hath wonne her on the plaine."

---

[1] He sende a knyght anon fulle stylle.
—T.
[2] He seyde, Syr recreawntes.—T.
[3] tene, T., which is better.—F.

[4] T. alters this and the next nineteen
lines.—F.
[5] turnyd hys swerde flatt.—T.
[6] patte.—T.

102

1184   Heralds of armes cryed then,

     " is there now any manner of man

       will make his body good,

     that will iust any more ?

1188   say now while wee be here ! "

     then a while they still stoode.

     Degrabell said, " by god almight !

     methinkes *that* I durst with him flight,

1192   if he were neuer soe wood."

     Lords together made a vow,

     " fforssooth," they said, " best worthy art thou

     to haue thy ffreelye ffood ! "

Right margin: Heralds ask if any one else will fight Eglamore.

Right margin: None answer

Right margin: so Christabell is adjudged to him.

103

1196   ffor to vnarme him Lords gan goe ;

     ¹ clothes of gold on him they doe,

     & then to meate thé wende.

     Sir Eglamore then wan the gree,

1200   beside the Lady sett was hee :

     shee frened him as her ffreind,¹

     " ffor what cause *that* he bore

     a shipp of gold with mast & ore."

1204   he said with words hende,

     " damsell, into the sea was done

     my Lady & my younge ² sonne ;

     & there they made an ende."

Right margin: Eglamore is clad in cloth of gold,

Right margin: and sits in the chief place with Christabell. She asks him why his arms are a ship.

Right margin: " Because my lady and son were put to sea, and died."

104

1208   ³ knowledge to him tooke shee thoe ;

     " now, good Sir, tell me soe,

     where they were brought to ground ? " [page 312]

Right margin: Where were they buried?

¹⁻¹ In cortyls, sorcatys, and schorte clothys,
That doghty weryn of dede.
Two kyngys the deyse began,

Syr Egyllamowre and Crystyabelle than ;
Ihesu us alle spede !—T.

² lemman and my yongest.—T.

³ T. omits the next six lines. —F

"I was away. Her father sent her to sea to drown."

"while I was in ffarr countrye

1212   her ffather put her into the sea,

with the waues to confounde."

with honest mirth & game

What is your name?

of him shee asked the name ;

1216   & he answered that stond,

"men call mee, where I was bore,

"Sir Egla-more of Artois."

of Artoys Sir Eglamore,

that with a worme was wound."

105

Christabell swoons, then welcomes Eglamore,

1220   in swooning ffell *that* Lady ffree ;

"welcome, Sir Eglamore, to mee !

thy Loue I haue bought full deere ! "

then shee sate, & told full soone

and tells what she has suffered.

1224   how into the sea shee was doone ;

then wept both lesse and more.

[1] minstrills had their gifts ffree,

wherby the might the better bee ;

1228   to spend they wold not spare.[2]

ffull true itt is, by god in heauen,

that men meete att vnsett steven,[3]

(People meet when they least expect it.)

& soe itt beffell there.

106

The King of Isarell tells how he found Degrabell,

1232   the King of Isarell gan tell

how *that* hee found Sir Degrabell ;

Lordings, Listen t' en : [4]

---

[1] This gentle reminder to the hearers of their duty to the singers of the Romance is repeated with some variation at the end.—F.

[2] For the former part of this st. 105, T. has, st. cxi. p. 171:
There was many a robe of palle;
The chylde seruyd in the halle
At the fyrste mete that day.
Preuely scho to hym spake,
" ȝondur ys thy fadur that the gate ! "
A grete yoye hyt was to see ay

When he knelyd downe on hys kne,
Ther was mony an herte sore,
Be God that dyed on a tree !—F.

[3] unfixed time, time not appointed. Compare Chaucer, in The Knightes Tale, l. 666, v. ii. p. 47, ed. Morris:
It is ful fair a man to bere him euene,
For al day meteth men atte vnset stevene.
Ful litel woot Arcite of his felawe,
That was so neih to herken of his sawe.
—F.

[4] Knyghtys lystenyd ther-to than.
—T.

Sir Eglamore kneeled on his knee,
1236 "my Lord!" he said, "god yeeld itt thee!
yee haue made him a May.[1] "

 and gives him half his kingdom.

the King of Isarell said, "I will the[e] giue
halfe my kindome while I doe liue,
1240 my deere sonne as white as swan."
"thou shalt haue my daughter Arnada,"
the King of Sattin sayd alsoe,
"I remember, since thou her wan."

 The King of Sattin also gives his daughter Arnada to Degrabell.

107

1244 [2] Eglamore prayed the Kings 3
att his wedding ffor to bee,
if *that* they wold vouch[s]afe.

 Eglamore invites every one to his wedding.

all granted him *that* there were,

 All accept,

1248 litle, lesse, & more;
Lord Iesus christ them haue!
Kings, Erles, I vnde[r]stand,
with many dukes of other Lands,
1252 with Ioy & mirth enoughe.
the trumpetts in the shipp blowes,
that euery man to shipp goes,

 sail off,

the winde them ouer blew.

108

1256 through gods might, all his meany
in good liking passed the sea;
in Artois they did arriue.
the Erle then in the tower stoode,

 and reach Artois safely.
 The old Earl

1260 he saw men passe the fflood,
& ffast [3] to his horsse gan driue.

---

[1] man.—T. *May* generally means maiden; but *mawe, maze*, is a kinsman; A.-Sax. *mæg*, a son, kinsman.—F.
[2] T. shortens and alters this stanza and part of the next.—F.
[3] So in printed copy, but very different in *the* Cotton MS.— Pencil note in MS.

when he heard of Eglamore,

falls out of his tower and breaks his neck,

he ffell out of his tower

1264 & broke his necke beliue.

the messenger went againe to tell

of *that* case, how itt beffell:

by a merciful providence.

with god may no man striue.

109

The Emperor is sent for,

1268 [1] thus in Artois the Lords thē Lent;

after the Emperour [2] soone thē sent,

to come to *that* Marryage;

every one in the land is bidden to the Feast,

in all they land they mad crye,

1272 who-soe wold come to *that* ffeast worthye,

right welcome shold they bee;

and Eglamore weds Christabell, Degrabell weds Arnada.

Sir Eglamore to the church is gone,

degrabell & Arnada they haue tane,

1276 and his Lady bright of blee.

the King of Isarell said, "Ile giue

halfe my land while I liue;

brooke well [all [3]] after my day."

110

The Feast lasts forty days,

1280 with mickle mirth the feast was made,

40 dayes itt abode

amonge all the Lords hend;

and then forsooth, as I you say,

and then all the guests go home.

1284 euery man tooke his way   [page 313]

wherin him liked to dwell.

---

[1] T. alters these concluding stanzas a good deal.—F.

[2] An Emperor was thought necessary to give the proper eclat to a wedding:

> Ther com tyl hir weddyng
> An *emperoure* and a kyng,
> Erchebyschopbz with ryng
> Mo then fyftene!

The mayster of hospitalle
Come over with a cardinalle,
The gret kyng of Portyngalie,
With knyȝthus ful kene.
Sir Degrevant, p. 252-3, Thornton Romances.—F.

[3] all. p.c.—Pencil note. T. has not the line. *Brooke* is A.-S. *brucan*, to enjoy.—F.

minstrells had good great plentye,
that euer they better may thé bee,
1288 and bolder ffor to spend.
in Romans this Chronickle is.
dere Iesus! bring vs to thy blisse
that lasteth without end ! [1]

ffins.

[1] T. winds up with "Amen. Here endyth syr Egyllamowre of Artas, and begyn-neth syr Tryamowre."—-F.

[" *When Scortching Phœbus*," *printed in* Lo. and Hum. Songs,
pp. 70–3, *follows here in the MS.*]

The Emperour & the Childe.[1]

THE following piece is here printed for the first time. Percy describes it as an old poem "in a wretched corrupt state, unworthy the press." Selecting from it "such particulars as could be adopted," he composed himself a poem on the subject of it,— a poem in Two Parts, altogether some 400 lines long, beginning in this wise:

> When Flora 'gins to decke the fields
> With colours fresh and fine,
> The holy clerkes their mattins sing
> To good Saint Valentine! &c.

Is this style so very much worthier of the press than that of

> Within the Grecian land some time did dwell
> An Emperor, whose name did far excell, &c. ?

We doubt whether either piece is particularly worthy of the press. But that which suited best the taste of the eighteenth century is certainly the less worthy of the two. That century could see the mote in the eye of a preceding age, but not the beam in its own eye.

This piece is evidently of very late origin, written at a time when the period of professional ballad-makers had well set in.

The story was, in prose, extremely popular. This prose version was a translation from the French. Of the old French romance an analysis is given in the *Bibliothèque des Romans*, which ranks it among *Romans Historiques* : [1]—

[1] The Old song of Valentine & Ursin or Orsin.
This song or Poem seems to be quite modern by the Language & versification.
N.B. This Poem only suggested the subject of that I printed on Valentine and Ursin.—P.

[2] Histoire des deux nobles et vaillans Chevaliers Valentin et Orson, fils de l'Empereur de Grèce et neveux du très-chrétien Roi de France Pépin, contenant 74 chapitres, lesquels parlent de plusieurs et diverses matières très-plaisantes et récréatives. Lyon, 1495, in-folio, et 1590 in-octavo, et depuis à Troyes, chez Oudot, in-quarto.

Nous avons annoncé dans notre avant-dernier volume que nous avions encore à parler d'un roman singulier et intéressant concernant Pépin, Roi de France, premier de la seconde race et père de Charlemagne ; c'est celui dont on vient de lire le titre. Il est bien constamment historique, quoique l'histoire y soit défigurée ; que Pépin y voyage dans des pays dont il n'a jamais approché, tels que Constantinople et Jérusalem, qu'on l'y fasse prisonnier d'un Roi des Indes, ainsi que les douze pairs de France ; qu'on ajoute à cette prétendue captivité les circonstances les plus ridicules ; qu'on suppose à Pépin deux fils, une sœur et deux neveux, qui n'ont jamais existé ; enfin, quoique les commencements de l'histoire de Charlemagne que l'on trouve dans ce roman-ci soient aussi éloignés de la vérité que ce qui est dit du règne de Pépin, tout cela, cependant, se fait lire avec plaisir ; et nous croyons que nos lecteurs ne trouveront point trop long l'extrait très-détaillé que nous allons en faire, chapitre par chapitre, sans rien changer à sa marche, et respectant presque également le style, qui n'est pas si gaulois que celui des autres romans de chevalerie que nous avons extraits jusqu'à présent, car celui-ci peut être rangé dans la même classe : on peut aussi, si l'on veut, le compter parmi les romans d'amour, car malgré les ridiculités dont il est rempli, la marche en est très-régulière. L'histoire des deux frères qui en font les héros y est conduite depuis l'instant de leur naissance jusqu'à leur mort ; tous deux sont amoureux et épousent enfin leurs maîtresses. Rien ne nous prouve que ce roman soit fort ancien. Nous n'en connaissons aucuns manuscrits ; et ne pouvant parler d'après nous-mêmes de la première édition (in-folio), qui est très-rare, nous ne trouvons rien dans la seconde (qui est celle de 1590) qui porte une certaine marque d'ancienneté, non-seulement dans le style, mais même dans les détails, et nous ne croyons pas qu'on puisse en faire remonter l'époque plus haut que le règne de Charles VIII, temps où beaucoup de romans de ce genre virent le jour, les uns étant tirés de quelques manuscrits plus anciens, les autres étant tout à fait nouveaux. Ne poussons pas plus loin nos recherches et nos observations préliminaires sur Valentin et Orson, et commençons notre extrait en suppliant nos lecteurs d'avoir de l'indulgence pour la simplicité et la bonhomie avec lesquelles cet ouvrage a été composé. On y trouvera bien des traits curieux et des situations très-intéressantes, mêlés avec mille circonstances ridicules. La singularité de tout cela pourra, du moins, amuser.

L'auteur raconte, d'abord, en peu de mots, la touchante histoire de Berthe au grand pied, qui a fait la matière d'un roman entier,

dont nous avons donné l'extrait dans notre premier volume du mois
dernier. Il suppose seulement que les deux fils de Pépin et de la fausse
Berthe vécurent, et se trouvèrent en état, à la mort de Pépin, de combattre le roi Charlemagne et de lui disputer la couronne ; que celui-ci,
après avoir été chassé de son royaume par eux, y rentra, pourtant, et
les vainquit à son tour.   Il suppose encore que Pépin avait une sœur
nommée Béligrane ou Bélissante, qu'elle épousa un Empereur de
Constantinople nommé Alexandre, et c'est ici que commence le
roman.

As the matter of a chap-book, the story was very common both
in France and in England.   How it was generally treated will
be shown by the following headings of chapters from the *Histoire
de Valentin et Orson, très-nobles et très-vaillants chevaliers, fils
de l'Empereur de Grèce et neveux du très-vaillant et très-
chrétien Pépin, Roi de France.*

Cap. I.—Comme le très-noble roi Pépin épousa Berthe, dame de
très-grande renommée et prudence.

Cap. II.—Comme l'Empereur fut trahi par l'Archevêque de Constantinople.

Cap. III.—Comme l'Archevêque étant éconduit de Bellisant pour
son honneur sauver, machina grande trahison.

Cap. IV.—Comme l'Archevêque se mit en habit de chevalier, et
monta à cheval pour poursuivre la dame Bellisant, laquelle était
bannie.

Cap. V.—Comme Bellisant enfanta deux enfants dans la forêt
d'Orléans, dont l'un fut appelé Valentin et l'autre Orson, et comme
elle les perdit.

Cap. VI.—De l'ourse qui emporta de Bellisant parmi le bois.

Cap. VII.—Comme par le conseil de l'Archevêque furent élevées
de nouvelles coutumes en la cité de Constantinople, et comme la
trahison fut connue.

Cap. VIII.—Comme l'Empereur Alexandre, par le conseil des
sages, envoya quérir le roi Pépin pour savoir la vérité de la querelle
du marchand et de l'Archevêque.

Cap. IX.—Comment le marchand et l'Archevêque se combattirent
au champ de bataille.

Cap. X.—Comme le roi Pépin prit congé de l'Empereur et partit
de Constantinople pour retourner en France, et comme après il alla
à Rome contre les Sarrasins qui la cité avaient prise.

Cap. XI.—Comme Hauffroi et Henri eurent envie sur Valentin pour le grand amour que lui portait le roi.

Cap. XII.—Comme Valentin conquit Orson son frère dans la forêt d'Orléans.

Cap. XIII.—Comme après que Valentin eut conquis Orson, il partit de la forêt pour retourner à Orléans vers le roi Pépin.

Cap. XIV.—Comme Hauffroi et Henri, par envie, résolurent de tuer Valentin en la chambre de la belle Esglantine.

Cap. XV.—Comme le duc de Savary envoya vers le roi Pépin pour avoir aide contre le vert chevalier qui voulait avoir sa fille Fezonne pour épouse.

Cap. XVI.—Comme plusieurs chevaliers vinrent en Aquitaine pour avoir la belle Fezonne.

Cap. XVII.—Comme Hauffroi et Henri firent guetter Valentin et Orson sur le chemin pour le faire mourir.

Cap. XVIII.—Comme le roi Pépin commanda que devant son palais fût appareillé le champ pour voir Orson et Grigard combattre ensemble.

*   *   *   *   *   *

Cap. LVI.—Comme Valentin fit la pénitence qui lui avait été imposée pour expier le meurtre de son père.

Cap. LVII.—Comme le roi Hugon fit demander Escharmonde pour femme, et comme il trahit Orson et le vert chevalier.

Cap. LVIII.—Comme Bellisant et Escharmonde surent la trahison et fausse entreprise du roi Hugon.

Cap. LIX.—Comme Orson et le vert chevalier furent délivrés des prisons du roi de Syrie, et comme le roi Hugon, pour éviter la guerre, se soumit à eux.

Cap. LX.—Comme, au bout de sept ans, Valentin, finit ses jours dans son palais de Constantinople, et écrivit une lettre par laquelle il fut connu.

WHITHIN the Grecyan land some time did dwell
    an Emperour, whose name did flar excell;
    he tooke to wiffe the Lady B[e]llefaunt,
4 the only sister to the Kinge of ffrance,
    with whome he lined in pleasure & delight
    vntill that ffortune came to worke them spight.

ffor within the court a bishoppe [1] there did rest,

8   the which the Emperour held in great request ;

his enuious hart itt was soe sore enfllamed

vpon the Empresse, *that* gallant dame,

[2] *that* he wold perswade her many [3] a wile

12   her husbands marriage bed for to defile.

but shee denyed *that* vnchast request,

as to her honor did beseeme her best ;

which when the Bishopp saw, away he went

16   vnton the Emperour with a fell intent,

& then most ffalselye her he did accuse,

how *that* shee wold his marryage bed abuse ;

& thervpon he swore the same to proue,

20   which made her husbands loue in wrath to proue.

then the Emperour went to her with speed,

ffor to accuse her of this shamefull deede.

and when shee saw how shee was betrayd,

24   her inocency shee began to pleade ;

The
Emperor
wouldn't
hear her,
but banished
her at once ;

but then her husband wold not heare her speake,

which made her hart with sorrow like to breake ;

but straight the Emperour he gaue command

28   *that* shee shold be banished [4] out of his land.

but when *that* shee ffrom them did goe,

before them all shee did reccount [5] her woe,

& said *that* shee was banished wrongffullye ;

32   & soe shee went with sorrow like to dye.

now is shee gone, but with one Squier alone,

vnto her brother in ffrance to make her Mone.

And being come within the realme of ffrance,   [page 315]

36   O there beffell a very heauy chance !

ffor [6] as shee trauelled through a wild fforrest,

the labor of Childhood did her sore oppresse,

---

[1] An Archpriest, says the Story Book.
—P.
[2] That her he would persuade with.
—P.
[3] with many, qu.—P.

[4] banish'd be.—P.
[5] recount.—P.
[6] all follows in the MS., marked out.
—F.

& more & more her paines increased still

40 *that* shee was fforced to rest against her will.

now att the lenght her trauell came to end,

ffor the Lord 2 children did her send,

the w*h*ich were ffaire & *proper* boyes indeed,

44 wh*i*ch made her hart w*i*th Ioy for to exceede.

but now behold how ffortune gan to Lower,[1]

& turned her Ioy to greefe w*i*thin an hower!

ffor why, shee saw an vgly beare as then,

48 the wh*i*ch was come fforthe of some lothesome den;

& when the beare did see her in *that* place,

he made towards her w*i*th an Egar pace,

& ffrom her tooke one of her children small,

52 a sight to greeue the mothers hart w*i*th-all.

but when shee saw her child soe borne away,

shee Laid the other downe, & did not stay,

& ffollowed itt as ffast as euer shee might;

56 but all in vaine! of itt shee lost the sight.

but soe itt chanced, att *that* verry tyde

the K*i*ng of ffrance did there a hunting ryde;

& in the fforrest as he rode vp and downe,

60 the other child he ffound vpon the ground.

& when he saw the child to be soe ffaire,

to take itt vp he bade his men take care,

& keepe itt well as tho itt were his owne,

64 vntill the ffather of the child where [2] knowne.

the Empresse returned there backe againe,

when as shee saw the beare w*i*thin his den;

but when shee saw her other sonne was lost,

68 her hart w*i*th sorrow then was like to burst.

then downe shee sate her with a heauy hart,

& wishes [3] death to ease her of her smart;

shee wrong her hands w*i*th many a sigh full deepe

72 *that* wold haue made a fflyntye hart to weepe.

Right margin notes:

she was taken in labour,

and bore two boys.

A bear

carried off one of them.

She laid the other down, and ran after the lost one, but couldn't find it.

The King of France finds the boy laid down,

and has him carried off.

The Empress comes back for him,

but finds him gone.

Her heart nearly breaks.

[1] lour.—P.   [2] were.—P.   [3] wish'd for.—P.

She leaves
the place,

then shee departed from *that* woefull place,
& fforth of ffrance shee went away apace ;
ffor why, as yett shee wold not there be knowen

76 vntill some newes of her young sonnes were shone.[1]

and goes to
a castle
for help.

but shee beheld a Castle ffaire & stronge,—[2]
shee had not trauelled ffrom *that* place not Long,—
wheratt shee knocket, some succour for to find.

80 but itt ffell out contrary to her mind ;
ffor why, with-in *that* castle dwelt as then

But a giant
lives there

a monstrous gyant, ffeared of all men,
who tooke this Ladye into his prison strong,

and puts her
in prison,

84 & there he kept her ffast in prison long.
but when he saw her lookes to be soe sadd,
& hauing knowen what sorrowes she had had,

but doesn't
hurt her.

he kept her close, but he hurt her not ;

88 & soe shee liued in prison long, god wotte.
the child the *which* the beare had borne away,
amongst her younge ones was brought vp alway,
& soe brought vp vntill att length as then

a huge wild
man,

92 he there became a monstrous huge wild man,
& [d]aylye ranged about the fforrest wilde,

who kills all
that pass by
his den.

& did destroy man, woman, beast and child,
& all things else *which* by his den did passe,

96 *which* to the country great annoyance was.

The other
boy is
christened
Valentine,

the other child *which* they King[3] had ffound,[4]
he christened was, & valentine was his name ;
& when he grew to be of ripe yeeres,

100 he was beloued both of King and peeres ;
in ffeates off armes he did himselfe advance,
that none like him there cold be ffond in ffrance ;
& ffor *that* same, the King did dub him Knight ;

is knighted,
and is
valiant.

104 he allwaies was soe vallyant in his fight.

Poor men
complain of
the Wild
Man.

then to the court did many pore men come
to show what hurt the wild man there had done ;

---

[1] shown.— P.
[2] The *o* and *a* are squeezed together
in the MS.— F.

[3] the *which* the King.— P.
[4] tane ; qu.— P.

but when the King did heare the moane they made,[1]
108   he sent fforth men the monster to inuade ;

but all in vaine ; ffor why, hee crusht them soe
that none of them with-in his reach durst goe.

Then valentine vnto the King did sue   [page 316]
112   *that* he might goe the Monster to subdue.

then fforthe he went the Monster ffor to see,
whom he saw come bearing a younge oke tree ;
& when the wild man of him had a sight,
116   he went vnto him & cast him downe right.

& when he saw his strenght cold not prevaile,
he praid to god his purpose might not fflayle ;
then a poinard presently he drew out,
120   & peirct his side, wherwith the blood gusht out.

but when the wild man did behold his blood,
he [2] quicklye brought him ffrom his ffuryous mood ;
then ffrom the fforrest both together went
124   towards the Emperour,[3] & with ffull intent

of [him] desired leaue by sea to sayle
into an Ile *that* Lyeth in Portingall,
wheras thé hard [4] with-in a Castle was
128   a Ladye ffaire *that* kept a head of brasse,

the which cold tell of any questyon asket.
& thither came braue valentine att Last ;
& when *that* they to [5] the castle came,
132   they thought ffor to haue entered the same ;

but itt ffell out not vnto their mind,
because the porters there were much vnkind ;
ffor why, thé ffound 2 gyants att the gate,
136   with [w]home [6] they ffought or they cold in theratt.

then went they vpp wheras they head did stand ;
& by itt sate the bewtyous Claramande,

Marginal notes:

The King sends men to kill him,

but he kills them.

Valentine goes to subdue him ;

the Wild Man knocks him down with an oak,

but gets stabbed in return.

Then they make it up, and ask the Emperor leaue to go to an island in Portingall,

to consult a brass head.

They go there,

fight two giants to get in,

see the head and fair Claramande,

---

[1] The *m* has one stroke too many in the MS.—F.
[2] It.— P.
[3] King of Fraunce, qu.—P.
[4] heard.—P.
[5] unto.—P.
[6] whom.—P.

whom, when the noble valentine did see,

140   he swore his hart ffor euer there shold bee.

then did shee speake vnto the head of brasse,

& bade itt tell whose sonne valentine was,

& whom the wild man there shold bee.

144   to whom the head gaue answer presentlye :

    " ffirst be it knowen, he is thy brother deere,

    & you are both sonnes to the Greeyan peere ;

    & your mother wrongffullye banished was,

148   & you were both borne in a wild fforrest ;

    & that [1] by a beare vrsin was nurst vpp,

    & valentine by [2] his vnckles court ;

    & your mother lyeth in prison stronge

152   with King fferagus,[3] where shee hath beene long.

    alsoe I say, looke vnder vrsines tounge ;

    there shall you ffind a string both bigg & stronge ;

    cut that in tow, & then his speech shall breake ;

156   & this is all ; & I noe more can speake."

then vrsin to his speeche restored was hee,

& valentine had CLAREMONDE soe ffree.

soe al together [4] on their Iourney went

160   towards their mother being in prison pent ;

    & soe they came vnto the place att Last

    wheras their mother was in prison ffast ;

    & him they slew that did their mother keepe,

164   & soe they brought her out of prison deepe.

    & when that they were al together come,

    vnto their mother they then made them knowne ;

    which when shee saw her owne sonnes sett her ffree,

168   no ioye to her there might compared bee.

    then presentlye they purpose to take read,[5]

    into the Land of greece to hye with speed.

    & when that they had many a storme ore past,

172   they did arriue with-in that Land att last ;

---

[1] there.—P.

[2] in.—P.

[3] This is the name of one of the Charlemagne heroes.—F.

[4] MS. altogether, and in l. 165.—F.

[5] counsel.—P.

then on their Iourney towards they court they went,

& to the Emperour a messenger they sent,

to tell him ffreinds of his were comen vpon land,

176 & did intreat some ffavor att his hand.

when the Emperour was come vnto them there,

& knew the woman to be his wiffe most deere,

& *that* the other 2 were his owne deare sonnes,

180 he then bewailed their happ with bitter moanes,

ffirst *that* because his wiffe was wronge exilde,

& ffor the greeffe when as shee traueled with child.

& soe att lenght, in spight of ffortunes happ,

184 they liued in ioy, & ffeared noe after clappe.

ffins.

to the Court.

When the
Emperor
finds his
wife
and sons,

he bewails
their past
sufferings;

and they
live happily
thereafter.

𝔖𝔦𝔱𝔱𝔦𝔫𝔤𝔢 : 𝔏𝔞𝔱𝔢 : [1]

THIS piece declares that women will have their own way, and further, that that way will frequently be wanton. It attempts to reconcile husbands to the loss of their supremacy, and their other consequent troubles. The argument is not always thoroughly satisfactory; as, when we are taught that because Paris of Troy got into such trouble for running away with another man's wife, therefore we cannot expect to enjoy any immunity from trouble in respect of our own wives. We cannot, if we would, says the poem, exercise a sufficiently sharp surveillance over them. In all ranks of life they " have their own will ;" beggars' wives, and the wives of better men, all elude and mock their husbands. The only place where this is not the rule is Rome, and it is not so there simply because a woman-pope would not let it be so. Thus woman's will reigns supreme everywhere.

But perhaps the only interest this sorry composition possesses is its illustrating *Hudibras* (Part I. canto ii. vv. 545–552):—

> Some cried the Covenant, instead
> Of pudding-pies and ginger-bread ;
> *And some or brooms, old boots, and shoes,*
> *Bawl'd out to purge the Commons' House ;*
> Instead of kitchen-stuff, some cry
> A Gospel-preaching Ministry ;
> And some for old suits, coats, or cloak,
> No surplices, nor Service-book :—

and Falstaff's remark on the worthy Justice Shallow, that " a came ever in the rearward of the fashion, and *sung those tunes* to the overscutched huswives *that he heard the carmen whistle,* and sware they were his fancies or his good-nights." Many

---

[1] A Satire on the Women.—P.

other references to the sibilant powers of the sixteenth and seventeenth century carmen are given by Mr. Chappell, in his *Popular Music of Olden Time*, à propos of the air called " The Carmen's Whistle."

SITTINGE: late, my selfe alone,   [page 317]
     to heare the birds sweete harmonye,
     one sighed sore with many a grone,   *I heard a man bewailing that his wife would be his master ;*
4   "my wiffe will still my *master* bee ! "
     his sig[h]es eeclipsed bright Phebus beames,
     his hart did burne like ætna hill,
     his teares like Nilus fllowing streames,[1]   *he wept, and cried shrilly,*
8   his cryes did peirce the Eccho shrill.
     with *that* I drew my care aside
     to heare him thus complaine of ill ;
     his greefe & mind were both a-like,   *and said his filly would have her will.*
12   *that* ginnye[2] his fllilly wold haue her owne will.

     The King of Sirya mad a law,   *Men won't keep the King of Syria's law, that men shall keep their wives in order.*
     that euery[3] man with-in his land,
     that he shold lordlye keepe in awe
16   his wiffe, & those *that* did with-stand.
     which acte is cleane gone out of mind
     of all degrees, & will be still ;
     pore silly husbands are soe kind,
20   they let their wiues haue their owne will.

     When Princely Paris, pride of Troye,   *Paris got*
     had stolen away King Menelaus wiffe,
     10 yeeres of warr was all his Ioy,   *ten years war and his death for stealing his wife. If then kings get into trouble,*
24   & afterwards bereaued of liffe.
     by this wee see *that* Kings are tyed,
     as well as subiects, to much ill ;
     why shold wee poore men thinke itt scorne
28   to let our wiues haue their owne will ?

[1] *streaus* in the MS.—F.   [2] MS. may be *grimye*.—F.   [3] for *every*. —P.

All *that* lookes blacke, diggs not ffor coles ;
how shold our chymneys then be swept ?
& he *that* thinkes to Iumpe ore Powles,[1]
32   may once a yeare be well out leapte ;
ffor vulcan wore a head of horne [2]
when least misprision was of ill.

lett no man liuing thinke itt scorne
36   to let his wiffe haue her owne will !

But shee *that* lines by nille [3] & tape,
& with her bagge & lucett [4] beggs,
oft makes her husband many a scape [5]
40   although shee goes in simple raggs ;
ffor hungry doggs will alwayes range,
& vnsauory meate will staunch their fill ;
& they *that* take delight in change
44   will, Nolens Volens, haue their owne will.

But he *that* goes ffrom dore to dore,
& cryes " old buskins ffor new broome ;"
althoo his liuing be but poore,
48   another must supply his roome.
" old bootes & buskins ffor new broome !
come buy, ffaire maids, & take your fill !
there are no Cucholds made att Roome ;
52   Pope Ione hath sett itt downe by will."

---

[1] Powles, *i. e.* St. Paul's.—P.

[2] Note [2] in *Brand's Popular Antiquities*, ed. 1841, vol. ii. p. 126, col. 1, says, "In ' Paradoxical Assertions and Philosophical Problems, by R. H. 8vo. Lond. 1664, p. 5, ' Why Cuckolds are said to wear Horns ?' we read : ' Is not this monster said to wear the Horns because other Men with their two forefingers point and *make Horns* at him ?' " "*Cuckold*. Cuckolled, treated in the way that the cuckow (Lat. *cuculus*) serves other birds, viz. by laying an egg in their nest." Wedgwood.—F.

[3] MS. *iulle*, but as the dot over the *i* is very often misplaced in the MS. and *nill* means *needle*, I print *nille*.—F.

[4] perhaps budget.—P. Fr. *lucet* or *luchet* is a spade.—F.

[5] 1. A misdemeanour . . . 3. A trick, shift, or evasion. Halliwell.—F.

The Carman whistles vp & downe ;
    another cryes " will you buy any blacke [1] ? "
the cuntryman is held a clowne,
50   when better men haue greater lacke.
thus whiles they cards are shuffled about,
    the knaue will in the decke [2] lye still ;
& if all secretts were found out,
60   I doubt a number wold want their will.

It's well that all wives' secrets are not known.

ffins.

---

[1] ? Fr. *noir*, blacking, or *pierre noire*, Black Oaker, or the blacke marking-stone.—Cotgrave. It can't mean soot or mourning. —F.

[2] A pack of cards. Halliwell.—F.

𝕷𝖎𝖇𝖎𝖚𝖘 : 𝕯𝖎𝖘𝖈𝖔𝖓𝖎𝖚𝖘: [1]

[In nine Parts.—P.]

PERCY thought so well of the plot of this Romance that he chose it for analysis in his *Reliques* (v. iii. p. xii.–xvi. ed. 1765). Speaking of " these old poetical Legends," he says, " it will be proper to give at least one specimen of their skill [that is, the skill of the writers of them], in distributing and conducting their fable, by which it will be seen that nature and common sense had supplied in these old simple bards the want of critical art, and taught them some of the most essential rules of Epic Poetry. I shall select the Romance of LIBIUS DISCONIUS, as being one of those mentioned by Chaucer, and either shorter or more intelligible than the others he has quoted.[2] If an Epic Poem may be defined, ' [3] A fable related by a poet, to excite admiration and inspire virtue, by representing the action of some one heroe, favoured by heaven, who executes a great design, spite of all the obstacles that oppose him :' I know not why we should withhold the name of EPIC POEM from the piece which I am about to analyse."

---

[1] This Piece may be considered perhaps as one of the first rude Attempts towards the Epic or Narrative Poem in Europe since the Roman Times. [See v. i. p. 417, l. 4.] Nor is it deffective [so] in the most essential Parts of Epic Poetry. The Hero is one. The great action to which every thing tends is one: there is little interruption of episode; & it [b]egins nearer the [E]vent than most of that age.—P.

This appears to be more ancient than the Time of Chaucer. See The Rhyme of Sir Thopas quoted below, St. 22[d].—P.

N.B. The Rhyme of Sir Thopas seems to be intended in Imitation of this old Piece. N.B. This is a translation from *the* French. Vid. p. 327, st. 15 [of MS. p. 441, l. 706 here].—P

[2] Men speken of Romaunces of Price,
Of Horne-Child and Ipotis,
Of Bevis and Sir Guy,
Of Sir Libeaux and Blandamoure,
But Sir Thopas bereth the floure
Of riall chevallrie.—*Rel.* iii. p. viii.

[3] Vide " Discours sur la Poësie Epique," prefixed to TÉLÉMAQUE.—P.

The Bishop then gives a sketch of each of the nine Parts of the Romance, and winds up with, " Such is the fable of this ancient piece : which the reader may observe, is as regular in its conduct as any of the finest poems of classical antiquity. If the execution, particularly as to the diction and sentiments, were but equal to the plan, it would be a capital performance ; but this is such as might be expected in rude and ignorant times, and in a barbarous unpolished language." Poor times! Why hadn't you a bishop with a blacking-brush to make you shine ?

The subject of the story is one that, told in the language and clothed with the feelings of each successive age, can never fail to interest that age at least,—the adventures of a young unknown man on his dangerous road from poverty to success in life, from nameless obscurity to rank and fame, from the consciousness of power existing only in the youth's own brain, to the full manifestation of that power, in the sight and with the applause of all beholders, who rejoice to see it receive its fitting reward.

In the present instance, Lybius comes from his mother's apron-strings, not knowing his father (he is Gawain's bastard [1]) to Arthur's court. He asks for knighthood, and the first adventure that comes in. He gets both ; and his task is to free the Lady of Sinadowne from prison. Though scorned for his youth by her messengers, he conquers, one after another, thirteen formidable opponents, of whom the first nine are Sir William de la Braunch, his three cousins, two giants, Sir Gefferon, Sir Otes de Lisle, and the Giant Mangys. A more insidious foe is behind, the sorceress of the Golden Isle, whom our hero has rescued from Mangys. For a year she keeps him from fulfilling his task ; but at last he breaks

---

[1] That story of rising from an obscure beginning is a very common one in mediaeval literature, and belongs to a principle of mediaeval sentiment, that noble blood was never lost, (bastardy was considered no real stain ;) and that if a knight, for instance, met with a woman in a wood, and got her with child, however ignoble the woman, or however low the circumstances under which the child received its first nurture, the blood it had received from the father would inevitably urge it onward till it reached its natural station. There are stories illustrating this feeling in all its forms. —T. Wright.

away from her, and goes to Sinadowne. There he conquers one knight, Sir Lambers, and then two necromancers who have turned the Lady of Sinadowne into a serpent. The serpent kisses him, and at the kiss turns into a lovely princess, who offers him herself and her lands. He accepts both, marries the Lady, and carries her off to King Arthur's court.

The English Romance was first printed by Ritson from the Cotton MS. Caligula A. ii. This text refers several times to its original, " the Frenssch tale " (l. 2122, *Ritson*, ii. 90; l. 222, *ib.* 10, &c.). On this, Ritson remarked, " The French original is unknown," ii. 253. The same statement continued true for many a year. Like the original of *Sir Generides* (which I edited from Mr. Tollemache's MS. for Mr. Gibbs as his gift-book to the Roxburghe Club in 1865, and the French of which is still to seek), the original of *Lybeaus Disconus* could not be found. But a lucky purchase by one of our subscribers, the Duc d'Aumale, of a MS. volume of French poems, and a luckier placing by him of it in the hands of Professor Hippeau of Caen in 1855, led to the discovery of the long-hidden French Romance, *Li Biaus Desconneus*, and also the name of its writer, RENALS DE BIAUJU, or,—as M. Hippeau modernises it,—RENAULD DE BEAUJEU. In 1860 M. Hippeau published the poem as *Le Bel Inconnu*, dating its writer as of the thirteenth century. It is not certain that De Biauju's text is the one that the English translators or adapters worked from; for in the two passages above referred to, where the English text refers to the French tale as the authority for its statements, De Biauju's text contains no such statements. But that is not conclusive, for we know that our English versifiers were seldom translators only : like our modern play-wrights, they treated their French (or French-writing) originals with great freedom, cut out what they didn't want, altered what they didn't like, and put in incidents at discretion. As one instance, take Robert of Brunne's treatment of William of

Wadington's *Manuel des Pechiez*, detailed in my preface to the *Handlyng Synne*. De Biauju's text *may* have given rise to some lost later version which the English adapters handled; but I see no reason why the early French text which M. Hippeau has printed may not have been before our early men. The motive is the same in both stories, and the chief incidents are the same, though in one—the way in which the Fairy of the Golden Isle, or *La Damoiselle as Blances Mains*, is represented, and the latter part of the story told—they differ markedly. And as in this part of the French poem M. Hippeau finds the original of part of the story of Tasso's *Gerusalemme Liberata*, it may be as well to give M. Hippeau's abstract, remembering that the English version makes the lady a mere sorceress who detains Lybius twelve months from pursuing the task that he had vowed to accomplish, and then appears no more in the story. The French text makes her keep him only a day before he has freed the Lady of Sinadowne; but after he has done this, and she has offered herself and her lands to him, De Biauju introduces the Fairy again—the English text saying nothing of her—and makes Lybius halt at the Lady of Sinadowne's offer thus :

The offer is tempting ; but the laws of chivalry are opposed to his pledging his troth without having received the authorisation of King Arthur. All the barons of the *pays de Galles* arrive at the *Cité Gastée*; bishops and abbots also come to purify by their pious ceremonies and their processions the places over which the infernal spirits have cast a spell ; and, before all her baronage, *Blonde Esmerée* declares that she has decided on taking Giglain as her spouse. A deputation of lords goes to him, and the knight still answers to the long request addressed to him, that he can do nothing without the consent of King Arthur. It is the king who, in granting the princess the help of one of his knights, has the right to all his gratitude. She ought then to go to his court, with all her barons, to thank him.

The queen prepares to set out, in the sweet anticipation that the valorous knight will accompany her in her journey. But widely different feelings now move *le Bel Inconnu*. He cannot drive from his heart the recollection of the beautiful fairy of the *Ile d'Or*.

The description of this unconquerable passion occupies a large space in the story of our trouvère. He finds happy expressions to describe those torments of love which he appears, from the frequent reference he makes to himself, to know only too well. Readers will be astonished to see with what pliancy the language of the thirteenth century lent itself to the developement of the most delicate shades of feeling. Giglain knows not at what point to stop. He dares not return to the *Ile d'Or*, which he left so abruptly; he cannot, on the other hand, drive away the too seductive image which besieges him night and day. The advice of Robert, his faithful squire, decides him on letting the daughter of the king of *Galles* set out alone. She parts from him with the sadness of resignation, and he sets out for the *Ile d'Or*. But there his perplexities begin again. Shall he go and present himself to the woman whose love he has seemed to disdain? He weeps, he laments, he is grievously distressed. But happily Robert is always at his side : he has much more confidence than his master in the kindly feelings of the fairy. She wanted to keep him, she was angry at his going, she will then see him again with joy.

At length the dreaded interview takes place. Having reached the magnificent fruit-garden (*verger*), which leads to the palace of the *Ile d'Or*, a delightful garden which contains all of most perfect that God has created upon earth, Giglain and his companion perceive the Fairy of the White Hands (*fée aux blanches mains*), and the former at once directs his steps towards her. The fairy receives him with an appearance of anger, which soon vanishes under the tender protestations of love with which Giglain accompanies the explanations that he gives her. She asks nothing better than to forgive him, and she conducts the happy knight into her castle.

If the passion of Giglain was violent when he was far from the Fairy of the Golden Isle, how can he resist it when he finds himself in the middle of her palace, where all the attendants, keeping discreetly at a distance, soon leave him alone with her?

We are, you will perceive, in the midst of the palace of Armida. The situation of our knight in this charming abode, recalls, in fact, quite naturally, that which made Rinaldo forget, in the bosom of the delights in which an enchantress held him, his most sacred duties and the glory of combat. How, and by means of what changes, have the adventures of Giglain in the castle of the Golden Isle become one of the most interesting episodes of the *Gerusalemme Liberata*?[1] It is

---

[1] On *La Dame d'Amore* of the Cotton text (and ours, p. 470, l. 1508), Ritson observes, v. ii. p. 263, " This lady bears a strong resemblance to the no less

a study which would require long unfoldings (*dévelopements*), and which we may try elsewhere when we have to occupy ourselves with the translations or imitations of which the poems of our trouvères have been the object among the different nations of Europe.

However that may be, we shall only follow with reserve the French poet in this part of his story, where he indulges a little too much, like his brethren of the same epoch, in the descriptive style. The fairy would not have been a woman if, notwithstanding her tenderness for *le Bel Inconnu*, she had completely forgotten the insult done to her charms, however honourable might have been the cause which took him the first time from the Golden Isle. She forgives him, but only after having revenged herself slightly. It is not in vain that he inhabits an enchanted palace. During the night he is twice a prey to a frightful illusion. He wakes and starts up; he seems to be bearing on his head the whole roof of the hall; he calls to his help all the attendants of the fairy. They run to him and find him struggling with his pillow, which is over his head. The second time, he gets out of bed and arrives at a torrent, which he crosses on a narrow plank; terror seizes him; he thinks that the quivering waves draw him in; he clings to the plank with all his might, and then calls the whole house to his help. They find him grasping with his two hands a sparrow-hawk's perch.

The Lady of the Golden Isle thinks him sufficiently punished. We will here leave our author a second time to add, to his glory, that we find again in his poem the means employed by the Italian poet to snatch his hero from the seductions of Armida.

We left the daughter of the king of *Galles* journeying but joylessly towards King Arthur's court. She there experiences a reception worthy of her; all the knights share her grief when she informs them that the warrior to whom she owes her deliverance, has not accompanied her, and that she knows not whither he has directed his steps.

Arthur knows well how to bring back to him the most illustrious of the knights of the Round Table. He has a grand tournament proclaimed all over the country. One day two players (*jongleurs*) present themselves at the castle of the Golden Isle, and penetrate even to *le Bel Inconnu*. They announce to him the feast of arms prepared by King Arthur. At this news, Giglain hesitates not an instant; he forgets his love, to think only of glory. In vain does

magical than beauteous fairys, the Calypso of Homer, and the Alcina of Ariosto; both of whom detain'd Ulysses and Rogero in the manner *la dame d'amore* here treats Lybeaus."

the beautiful fairy try to hold him back. She knows beforehand, in her double quality of woman and fairy, that the love of the handsome knight cannot be eternal. She has had to prepare herself long since to lose him. I like better, I declare, the jealous fury of Armida than the easy resignation of the Fairy of the White Hands.

At break of day, Giglain, who had gone to bed the night before in the palace of the Golden Isle, wakes and finds at his side his horse and his squire Robert, in the middle of a dark forest, whither the all-power of the fairy had transported him. Though he is a little surprised at what has happened, he takes his fate bravely, and sets forward without delay towards the place assigned as the rendezvous of the paladins (adventure-seeking heroes) who are to take part in the tournay.

Though the narratives which have as their subject these brilliant jousts are generally the parts treated by the authors of our poems with a partiality justified by the desire of pleasing the noble lords for whom they wrote, it would be difficult to find a tournament which could sustain comparison with that of *Valedon*. Walter Scott would seem[1] to have been inspired by it in his account of the famous passage of arms at Ashby. It is needless to say that all the honour of the day belongs to *le Bel Inconnu*. The heat of the battle has dissipated the last vestiges of his love for the Fairy of the White Hands. Having married the princess of *Galles*, he delays not to go and take possession of the crown which so many high deeds have rendered him worthy of.

All this tantalising of the Lady of Sinadowne, keeping her waiting for her lover after she had been so many years serpentised or wivernised by the two necromancers, the English adapter has thought unfair, and cut out. Must not we sympathise with him? What should we have said to Mr. Tennyson if he had kept The Sleeping Beauty waiting a year for her husband after she had been kissed? Voted him a hard-hearted Frenchman, clearly. But of course he has done nothing so wrong. Well, besides this, the adapter has, as remarked in the notes, cut out all about Renals de Biauju's own lady-love, for whom he composed the poem—had the poor Englishman no sweetheart?—all about

---

[1] As he died in 1832, and the French Romance was not published till 1860, there is some difficulty in this *semblerait s'en être inspiré*.

Robers, Lybius's squire, an important personage in the French Romance; and all about the French tale of the Falcon (though the English Part IV. may be taken to represent this), &c. &c.

On the other hand, the adapter introduces a fresh Part (IV.) into the English text; puts in the incident of Lybius's diving down at a knight and slicing his head off (p. 492) as a sort of refresher before encountering the necromantic perils of the Castle of Sinadowne ; and also alters the place of the adventure with Sir William de la Braunch's (or Blioblcris's) three cousins, putting it before, instead of after, the fight with the two giants (p. 433-7, and p. 438-41), besides many minor variations. The telling of the story varies all through ; but so far as I can judge, the original French of De Biauju is a far better piece of work than that of any of his adapters.

Of English MSS. of *Lybius* I know only five: the Cotton Caligula A ii., printed by Ritson and M. Hippeau ; the fragment in the Lincoln's Inn MS. 150; the Lambeth MS. 306 ; our Percy folio, and the Ashmole MS. 61, leaf 38, back, of which Mr. Coxe, Bodley Librarian, has just told me. Of these I judge the Lincoln's Inn vellum one to be the oldest, both in writing (ab. 1430-40 A.D.), and in its preservation of the early double vowel for the later single one, *þeo, scoþþe, heold, feol.* The paper Cotton MS. comes next (ab. 1460 A.D.); third, the Ashmole 61, on paper, written towards the end of the 15th century, says Mr. Coxe, containing 2200 lines more or less, and beginning "Ihesu Cryst owre Sauyowre"; then the Lambeth one, also on paper (? about 1480 A.D.), and lastly the Percy. The Cotton text is interesting on account of its changes of *d* and *th*[1], which I suppose to be of Berkshire origin,—if one may judge from

---

[1] The *d* is substituted for *th* in the following, among other instances :—*durstede*, thirsted, l. 1336 ; *durste*, thirst, l. 1313; *clodede*, clothed, l. 1107; *yclodeth*, clothed, l. 1776 ; *dydyr*, thither, l. 1668; but *thyder*, l. 2082 ; *dare*, there, l. 1870;

de, thee, l. 673. On the other hand, *th* is put for *d*, in *unther*, under, l. 1039, l. 1002, l. 1191 ; *thoghtyer*, doughtier, l. 1091 ; but *doghty*, l. 1578, and *thoughty*, l. 1851 ; *theer*, deer, l. 1133 ; *there*, dearly, l. 1158 ; *thores*, doors,

Mr. Tom Hughes's books,—or some county near.[1] The infinitive in *y* also shows that the text is Southern [2]: *army*, arm, l. 216; *justy*, joust, l. 909, l. 951, but *juste*, l. 1542; *schewy*, show, l. 746; *spendy*, spend, l. 986, &c.

Grateful as I feel to M. Hippeau for his discovery and printing of the French text, I owe him a slight grudge for describing "l'auteur du *Canterbury Tales*" as "le poétique traducteur de nos trouvères," and therefore note that his print of the Cotton MS. is full of those mistakes that "a remarkably intelligent foreigner" would naturally make, *u* for *n*, and *n* for *u*, &c.[3]; to say nothing of other forms like *pryue* for þryue, thrive; *kepte* for lepte, l. 2039; *be* for he, l. 1388; *thogh tyer* for thoghtyer, doughtier, l. 1091; *he* for here, her, l. 887; *gwych* for swych, such, l. 712; *Sweyn* for Eweyn, l. 219; *lymest*, for lyme &, lime and, l. 713.

It may look rather spiteful to print these things, but editors are bound to consider the language they study rather than other editors' feelings: and with the full conviction that I invite similar treatment for the French as well as the English texts I have edited and may edit, and that in all there are and will be mistakes,[4] I hold it best to point out the misreadings in Early English that come across me, for the sake of the language and

---

[1] l. 1705; *tho*, do, l. 531, &c., and in many other places. I just copy the few that I noted years ago on a blank leaf, when reading part of M. Hippeau's edition.

[1] Probably Dorsetshire. I heard *drow* for *throw* near Weymouth this autumn, and Mr. Barnes says in his *Grammar and Glossary of the Dorset Dialect*, 1863, p. 16, "*Th* of the English sometimes, and mostly before *r*, becomes *d*, as *drow* for *throw*. Conversely, *th* (ð) is substituted in Dorset for the English *d*. as *blader*, a bladder, *lader*, a ladder." Mr. Hughes says he does not remember hearing this *th* and *d* change in Berkshire.

[2] "In the Dorset the verb takes *y* only when it is absolute, and never with an accusative case. We may say, 'Can ye

zewy?' but never, 'Wull ye zewy up theäse zeam?'"—*Barnes*, p. 28.

[3] *deutes* for *dentes*, l. 1304; *fou* for fon, foes, l. 1530, l. 1950; *sauvgh* for saunȝ, Fr. *sans*, without l. 1860 [In þat felde saunȝ fayle. MS. leaf 55, back, col. 1, line 18. See the last lines of the pieces in note, p. 413]; *hau* for han, have, l. 1263; *woneth* for woneth, dwells, l. 657; *gau* for gan, did, l. 343; *deseryne* for deseryue, describe, l. 1330, l. 1428; *houede* for houede, halted, l. 1502; *kenere* for keuere, recover, l. 1983; *leuede* for leuede, lived, l. 2125.

[4] Claude Platin's confession, "*mon ignorance, laquelle n'est pas petite*" (page 415 here), is the motto for many of us, adding carelessness.

its students. But to return from this digression ; the Lambeth MS. is in " The Wright's Chaste Wife " volume, and seems to be a later copy of a text like the Cotton. Some readings from it are given in the notes from Mr. Warwick King's transcript of it for the Early English Text Society. By way of exhibiting some of the differences of the five English texts, I put beside the first bit of the Lincoln's Inn fragment the passages corresponding to it in the other MSS.,[1] and at the end of the Romance as

[1] *Lincoln's Inn MS.* 150, *Art.* 1,
    faded, begins.

þan sir libeus ran
þar Manges scheld lay,
  And vp he con hit fange :
fast he ran to him,
And smot him wiþ mayn,
  And other gon asa[ilo.]
vnto þeo day was dyme . .
Bysyde þeo water
  þeo kynges heold bataile.
Libeus was warryour wy3t,
And 3af a strok of my3t
  þoww3 gepoun [?] plate and maile,
þoru3 his scholdur bon,
þat his ry3t arm anon
  feol in þeo feld saunfaile.

MS. Lambeth 306, *leaf* 94, *back.*
Than lybeous ranne aw-waye
There Mangis shelde laye,
  And vp he gan hit fange,
And ran a-gayne to hym.
With strokys sharpe and gryme
  Eyther other ganne assayle.
Till the day was dyme,
Vpon the watir brym
  By-twene hem was bataylle.
Lybeous was werrcour wight,
And smote a stroke of myght
  Throwe lepowne, plate, and mayle,
Thorowe the shulderbone,
That his Right Arme A-none [leaf 95]
  Ffell in the felde saunce fayle.

Cot. Calig. A. ii. leaf 50, *col.* 1.
þanne lybeauns ran away
þere þat mangys scheld lay,
  And vp he gan hyt fonge,
And Ran a-gayn to hym.   [col. 2]
With strokes strout & grym
  To-gydere þey go*n*ne a-sayle.
Be-syde þat rynere brym,
Tylle hyt derkede dym,
  Be-twene hem was batayle.
Lybeauns was werroure wy3t,
And smot a strok of my3t
  þoru3 gypelle, plate, & maylle,
Furþ *with* þe scholdere bon,
Mangys arm fylle of a-noon
  In-to þe feld saun3 fayle.

Percy Folio, p. 337.
then Sir Lybius rann away
thither were Mangis sheild Lay ;
  & vp he can itt gett,
& ran againe to him,
with stroakes great and grim
  together they did assayle ;
there beside the watter brimne
till it vaxed wonderous drimn,
  betweene them lasted *that* battell.
Sir Lybius was warryour wight,
& smote a stroke of much might ;
  through hawberke, plate and maile,
hee smote of by the shoolder bone
his right arme soone and anon
  into the ffeild with-out ffaile.

Ashmole MS. 61, *leaf* 52.
Than lybeus ranne A-wey
There mag*us* scheld ley,
  And vp he gan*e* it fong*e* ;
And libeus ra*n*ne to hy*m* A-3ene, [leaf 52ᵇ]
And smote hy*m with* meyn*e* ;
  Aythere o*þer* gan*e* A-seyle.
To þe dey was dy*m*me,
Be-syde þe wat*e*r bry*m*me

The kny3ht*es* held bat*e*yle.
Syre libeus was weryour*e* wy3ht,
And gaue strokes of my3ht
  Throu3ht plate *and* male,
And throw his schuld*er* bone,
That hys ry3ht Arme A*n*on*e*
  Fell in þe feld *with*-oute*n* feyle.

printed here, p. 497, will be found the endings of the Lincoln's Inn, Cotton, Lambeth, and Ashmole texts, for further contrast with the language of the Percy folio. I have not had time to collate them throughout, and Mr. Brock, who began the collation with the Cotton MS., soon gave it up as involving too much time and trouble for an adequate result, the second volume of Ritson being easily accessible to all readers.

Ritson says that this Romance

was certainly printed before the year 1600, being mention'd by the name of "*Libbius*," in "Vertues common wealth : or The highway to honour," by Henry Crosse, publish'd in that year; and is even alluded to by Skelton, who dye'd in 1529 :

> And of sir *Libius* named *Disconius*. . . .

A story similar to that which forms the principal subject of the present poem may be found in the "Voiage and travaile of sir John Maundeville" (London, 1725, 8vo. P. 28). It, likewise, by some means, has made its way into a pretendedly ancient Northhumbrian ballad intitle'd "The laidly worm of Spindleston-heugh," writen, in reality. by Robert Lambe, vicar of Norham, authour of *The history of chess*, &c., who had, however, hear'd some old stanzas, of which he avail'd himself, sung by a maid-servant. The remote original of all these storys was, probablely, much older than the time of Herodotus, by whom it is relateëd (*Urania*).

In French there was a prose translation of a Spanish romance mixing up a Charlemagnian hero with our Arthurian Gyngelayn, printed in 1530, which Brunet (ed. 1814) enters thus :

Giglan (l'histoire de), fils de messire Gauvain, qui fut roi de Galles ; et de Geoffroy de Mayence, son compaignon : translaté d'espaignol en françois par Claude Platin, *Lyon, Cl. Nourry*, 1530, *in-4. goth. fig.*

This is, says M. Hippeau, a fairly correct reproduction of the French *Li Biaus Desconneus*, "sauf quelques additions peu heureuses." His extract from Claude Platin's prologue is so pretty that I give it here :

Pour éviter oysiveté, mère et nourrice des vices, et aussi pour complaire à tous ceulx qui prennent plaisir à lire et à ouyr lire les livres des anciens, qui ont vescu si vertueusement en leur temps, que la renomée en sera jusques à la fin du siècle, lesquelles œuvres vertueuses doivent esmouvoir les cœurs des humains de les ensuyvir en vertus en haultz faitz, moi Frère Claude Platin, humble religieux de l'ordre monseigneur sainct Anthoine, ung jour, en une petite librairie où j'estoye, trouvay un gros livre de parchemin bien vieil, escript en rime espaignole, assez difficile à entendre, auquel trouvay une petite hystoire laaqelle me sembla bien plaisante, qui parloit de deux nobles chevaliers qui furent du temps du noble roi Artus et des nobles chevaliers de la Table-Ronde. . . J'ay donc voulu translater la dicte hystoire de cette rime espaignole, en prose francoyse, au moins mal que j'ay peu, selon mon petit entendement, à celle fin que plus facilement peust estre entendue de ceulx qui prendront plaisir à la lire ou ouyr lire : ausquelz je prie que les faultes qui y seront trouvées, ils les vueillent corriger, et excuser mon ignorance, laquelle n'est pas petite ; et aussi de ne se arrester ausdictes faultes, mais s'il y a riens de bon, qu'ilz en facent leur prouffit.

With what better commendation to the reader can I close this rambling Introduction, or leave him to study the poem of " The Fayre Unknown "?

[1] Iesus christ, Christen Kinge,[2]   Christ and Mary
    & his mother *that* sweete thing,[3]
    helpe them att their neede   help my hearers!
4   *th*at will listen to my tale !
    of a knight I will you tell,[4]   I'll tell you
    a doughtye man of deede,

---

[1] The Romance in the Cotton MS. Caligula A ii. begins thus:

INCIPIT LYBEAUS DISCONIUS.

¶ Ihesu cryst oure sauyoure,
And hys modyr *þat* swete flowre,
Helpe hem at here nede
þat harkeneþ of a *co*nqueroure,
Wys of wytte, & why3t werro*ur*,
And dou3ty man yn dede.

Hys name was called Geynleyn ;
Be-yete he was of syr Gaweyn
Be a forest syde.
Of stoutere kny3t & profytable

With artoure of þe Rounde table,
Ne herde ye neu*er* Rede.

¶ þys Gynleyn was fayre of sy3t,
Gentylle of body, of face bry3t,
Alle bastard 3ef he were.
Hys modyr kepte hy*m* yn clos
For doute of wykkede loos,
As dou3ty chyld & dere.—F.

[2] oure sauyoure.—C.
[3] flowre.— C.
[4] *þat* harkeneþ of a *co*nqueroure
wys of wytte & why3t werro*ur*.—C.

[page 318]

his name was cleped [1] Ginglaine ;

of Ginglaine,	his name was cleped [1] Ginglaine ;

bastard son of Sir Gawaiue.	8 gotten he was of *Sir* Gawaine
	     vnder a fforrest side ;
	   a better [2] knight w*i*thout ffable, [3]
	   W*i*th Arthur att the round table,
	12 yee heard neuer of read.

His mother tried to prevent him seeing a knight,	Gingglaine was ffaire & bright, [4]
	   an hardye man and a wight, [5]
	     bastard thoe hee were.
	16 [6] his mother kept him w*i*th all her might,
	   ffor he shold not of noe armed K*nigh*t
	     haue a sight in noe mannere.

because he was savage.	but he was soe sauage,
	20 & lightlye wold doe outrage
	     to his ffellowes in ffere. [6]
	   his mother kept him close
	   ffor dread [7] of wicked losse,
	24 as hend [8] child and deere.

His mother called him Beaufise because he was handsome.	ffor [9] hee was soe ffaire & wise, [10]
	   his mother cleped him beufise, [11]
	     & none other name ;
	28 & himselfe was not soe wise [12]
	   that hee asked not I-wis
	     what hee hight [13] of his dame.

One day	soe itt beffell vpon a day 32 Gingglaine [14] went to play,

---

[1] called.—C.
[2] stoutere.—C.
[3] & pro*f*ytable.—C.
[4] of sy3t.—C.
[5] Gentylle of body, of face bry3t.—C.
[6—6] *From* his *to* ffere *omitted in* C.—F.
[7] doumte.—C.
[8] dou3ty.—C.

[9] [And] for, i.e. because.—P.
[10] And fore loue of hys fayre vyys. —C.
[11] Beau-vise.—P. bewfis.—C.
[12] was full nys. C.
[13] what he was called ; what his Name was. See St. 11.—P.
[14] To wode he.—C.

wild deere to hunt ffor game ;
& as he went ouer the Lay,

he sees a knight, kills him,

he spyed a knight was stout & gay,
36   *that* soone he made ffull tame.[1]

then he did on [2] *that* Knights weede,
& himselfe therin yeede,[3]
into *that* rich armoure ;

puts on his armour, goes to Glastonbury, to King Arthur,

40   & when he had done *that* deede,
to Glasenbury swithe [4] hee yeede,
there Lay King Arthur.
& when he came into the hall
44   amonge the Lords and Ladyes all,
he grett [5] them with honore,
And said, " King Arthur, my Lord ! [6]

and asks Arthur

suffer me to speake a word,
48   I pray you par amoure [7] :

[8] " I am a child vncouthe ;
come I am out of the south,
& wold be made a knight.

to knight him, as he's fourteen, and can fight.

52   14 yeere old I am,
& of warre well I cann,
therfore grant me my right."
then said Arthur the King strong

Arthur

56   to the child *that* was soe younge,[9]

---

[1] The Cotton MS. reads:
He fond a kny3t, whare he lay,
In armes þat were stout & gay,
I-sclayne & made fulle tame.—F.
[2] þat chyld dede of.—C.
[3] And anon he gan hym schrede.—C.
[4] prompte, Jun.—P.
[5] did greet.—P.
[6] Mais cil li dist: " Ains m'escoutés.
Artu, venus sui à ta cort ;
Car n'i faura, comment qu'il cort,
Del primier don que je querrai :

Aurai-le je, u le j' faurai?
Donne-le moi et n'i penser
Tant esprendre ; ne l' dois véer."
" Je le vos dons : ce dist li rois."
            Le Bel Inconnu, l. 82–9, p. 4.
[7] par-amour, or perhaps pour amour ;
it is not here a compound word, signifying *Mistress* ; but is a Phrase equivalent to that [in] St. 14, lin. 3.— P.
[8] This stanza is omitted in C. The Lambeth MS. 306 has it.— F.
[9] A-noon withoute any dwellyng.—C.

asks him his
name.

" tell me what thou hight [1] ;

for neuer sithe I was borne

sawe I neuer heere beforne [2]

60   noe child soe ffaire of sight."

Ginglaine
says he
doesn't
know,

the child said, " by St. Iame,[3]

I wott not[4] what is my name !

    I am the more vnwise[5] ;

but his
mother
calls him
Beaufise.

64   but when I dwelled att home,[6]

my mother in her game

cleped mee beaufise."

then said[7] Arthur the King,

Arthur says
" by God it's
odd you

68   & said, " this is a wonderous thing,

by god & by S: Denise,

don't know
your own
name!

that thou wold be a Knight,

& wott nott what thou hight,

72   & art soe ffaire and wise[8] !

I'll give you
one

" now I will giue thee a name

heere amonge all you in-same ;

for thou art soe ffaire and free,—

that your
mother
never called
you,

76   I say, by god & by S: Iame,

soe cleped thee neuer thy dame,

what woman *that* euer shee bee ;—

and that is
Lybius
Disconius "
(the fair
unknown,
or handsome
stranger).

call yee him all thius,[9]

80   Lybius Disconius [10] ;

ffor the loue of mee

looke yee call him this name ;

both in ernest & in game,

84   certes, soe hight shall hee.[11] "

---

[1] þyn name aplyȝt.—C.
[2] Ne fond y me be-fore.—C.
[3] Cil li respont : "Certes ne sai,
Mais que tant dire vos en sai,
Que *biel fil* m'apieloit ma mère;
Ne je ne sai se je oi pere."
     Le Bel Inconnu, l. 115-18, p. 5.
[4] I not.—C.   [5] nys.—C.
[6] hame, idem.—P.   [7] spake.—F.
[8] fayre of vys.—C.   [9] thus.—P.

[10] lybeau desconus.—C.   The French
has, p. 6:
    " Et por ce qu'il ne se connuist,
    Li Biaus Desconnéus ait non !
    Si l'nommeront tot mi baron."
Le beaux Desconus, i.e. the fair unknown.—P.
[11] þan may ye wete a rowe
þe fayre vnknowe
Sertes so hatte he.—C.

King Arthur anon-right
  with a sword ffaire & bright,[1]
    trulye *that* same day

88 dubbed *that* Child a knight,[2]
  And gaue him armes bright[3];
    fforsooth as I you say,
  hee gaue to him in *that* ilke

92 a rich sheeld all ouer gilte
  with a griffon soe gay,[4]
  & tooke him to Sir Gawaine[5]
  ffor to teach him on the plaine

96   of euery princes[6] play.[7]

Then Arthur knights Lybius.

[page 319] *gives him arms*

and a shield,

and asks Gawaine to teach him.

when hee was made a knight,
  of the boone[8] he asked right,[9]
   & said, " my Lord soe ffree,

100 in my hart I wold be glad
  the ffirst battell if I had
    that men asked of thee."
  then said Arthur the King,

104 " I grant thee thine askinge,
  whatt battell *that* euer itt bee ;
  but euer methinke thou art to young
  ffor to doe a good[10] ffighting,

108   by ought *that* I can see.

Lybius

asks Arthur

to let him have the first fight that turns up.

Arthur grants this,

but thinks he's too young to fight well.

when he had him thus told,
  Dukes, Erles, and Barons bold,[11]

---

[1] Made hym þo a knyȝt.—C.
[2] And yaf hym armes bryȝt.—C.
[3] Hym geritto with swerde of myȝt.
—C.
[4] gryffoun of say.—C.
[5] And hym be-tok hys fadyr gaweyn.
—C.
[6] eche knyȝtes.—C.
[7] An *a* seems to have been blotted out
after the *y* in the MS.—F.
[8] Other boone, or another boone, or
One other D⁰.—P.
[9] Anon a bone þer he bad.—C.
[10] *thing*, which follows, has been
marked out in the MS.—F.
[11] With oute more resoun
  Duk, Erl & baroun.—C.

<table>
<tr><td>

Then all dine off wild fowl and venison.

</td><td>

112

</td><td>

washed & went to meate ;
of wild ffoule [1] and venison,[2]
as lords of great renowne,
inoughe they had to eate.

they had not sitten not a stoure,

</td></tr>
</table>

Then all dine off wild fowl and venison.

112　　washed & went to meate ;
of wild ffoule [1] and venison,[2]
as lords of great renowne,
inoughe they had to eate.

they had not sitten not a stoure,

Soon

116　　well the space of halfe an hower,
talking att their meate,[3]

come in hot haste a damsell and a dwarf.

there came a damsell att *that* tyde,[4]
& a dwarffe [5] by her side,

120　　all sweating [6] ffor heate ;

Her name is Hellen ; she brings a message from a lady,

the Maidens name was Hellen ;
sent shee was vnto the King,[7]
a Ladyes messenger.

124　　the maiden was ware & wise,
& cold doe her message att devi ce,[8]
shee was not to ffere [9] ;
the maid was ffaire & sheene,

and is clad in green.

128　　shee was cladd all in greene [10] ;
& ffurred [11] with Blaundemere [12] ;

---

[1] take y[e] heddes of [=off] all felde byrdes and wood byrdes, as fesande, pecocke, partryche, woodcocke, and curlewe, for they ete in theyr degrees foule thynges, as wormes, todes, and other suche. *Boke of Keruynge* in Babees Book &c., E. E. T. Soc. p. 279. See the capital bit about venison from Andrew Borde, *ib.* p. 210-11.—F.

[2] Of alle manere fusoun.—C.

[3] Ne hadde artoure bote a whyle þe mounntaunce of a myle At hys table y-sete.—C.

[4] a mayde Ryde.—C.

[5] dwerk.—C.

[6] be-swette.—C.

[7] Gentylle bry3t & schene.—C.

[8] i.e. Will, Pleasure. See Chau[r] Gloss.—P.

[9] þer nas contesse ne quene So semelyche on to sene þat my3te be here pere.—C.

[10] Sche was clodeþ in tars Rowme & nodyng skars.—C.

[11] pelured.—C.

[12] *Blaunchmer*, a kind of fur.

He ware a cyreote that was grene ;
With *blaunchmer* it was furred, I wene.
Syr Degoré, 701 in Halliwell's Glossary.

This word comes in so oddly that I could almost be tempted to think that Chaucer in his burlesque Romance of Sir Thopas might allude to it sportively, as thus :
Sir Libeaux and the[*] Blaundemere Scil: the Blaundemere Furr mentioned in his Romance &c. But after all perhaps this construction is too forced.
N.B. It might be the other Version which Chaucer alludes to.
See Chaucer's Rhyme of Sir Thopas, where this word seems to be mistaken, viz. :
Men spoken of Romaunces of Pris,
Of Horne-child and of Ipotis
Of Bevis & Sir Gie
Of Sir Libeaux and Blaindamoure
But Sir Thopas bereth the flowre
Of rich Chivalrie.—P.

---

[*] (or his)

her saddle was ouergilte,
& well bordered w*i*th silke,[1]

132 & white [2] was her distere.[3]

the dwarfe was cladd w*i*th scarlett fline,   The dwarf wears scarlet,
& ffured well w*i*th good [4]Ermine ; [5]
stout he was & keene [6] ;   is stout,

136 amonge all christen kind
such another might no man find [7] ;
his cercott [8] was of greene [9] ;
his haire was yellow as fllower on mold,[10]   has long yellow hair,

140 to his girdle hang [11] shining as gold,[12]
the sooth to tell in veretye ;
all [13] his shoone w*i*th gold were dight,
all as gay as any [14] knight,

144 there sseemed no pouertye.

Teddelyne was his name,[15]   is named Teddelyne,
wide sprang of him the fame,[16]
East, west, North & south ;

148 much he cold of game & glee,

---

[1] Here sadelle & here brydelle yn fere
Fulle of dyamandys were.—C.
The author of the French Romance gives
a fuller description of Maid Hellen, or
Hélie as he calls her. Doubtless it is
his own love, for whom he composed the
Romance, whom he sketches.
Gente de cors et de vis biele :
D'un samit estoit bien vestue ;
Si biele riens ne fu veüe.
Face et blance com flors d'esté,
Come rose et vis coloré,
Le iouls et vairs, bouce riant,
Les mains blances, cors avenant ;
Bel cief avoit, si estoit blonde :
N'ot plus biel cief feme del monde !
En son cief et un cercle d'or;
Ses perles valent un trésor
Sor un palefroi cerauçoit. (p. 6.) F.
[2] Melk.- C.
[3] apud Chauc. *Destrer*, a War-horse, or

Led Horse. Vid. Gloss.—P.
[4] One stroke too few in this word in
the MS.—F.
[5] Þe dwerke was clodeþ yn ynde
Be-fore & ek be-hynde.- C.
[6] pert.—C.
[7] fimd in the MS.—F.
[8] Surcoat—A gown & hood *the* same,
an upper coat, Ch. Gloss.—P.
[9] was ouert.—C.
[10] as ony wax.—C. Not in the French.
—F.
[11] hung.—P.   [12] henge þe plex.—C.
[13] als. also.—P.
[14] And kopeþ as a.—C.
[15] The French Romance doesn't name
him till he and Hellen leave the court,
and it calls him *Tidogolains*, l. 256,
p. 10.—F. Teaudelayn.- C.
[16] MS. same.—F. fame.- P. welle
swyde sprong hys name.—C.

Is a good
fiddler,

ffiddle, crowde,[1] and sowtrye,

    he was a merry man of mouth [2] ;

harpe, ribble [3] & sautrye,

minstrel
and jester

152 he cold much of Minstrelsye,

    he was a good Iestoure,

there was none such in noe country ;

a jolly man
with ladies.

a Iolly man fforsooth was hee

156   with Ladyes in their bower.

Hellen gives
Arthur her
message ;

then he bade maid Hellen

    ffor to tell her tale by-deene,

      & kneele before the King.

160 the maid kneeled in the hall

    among the Lords & Ladyes all,

      & said, " my Lord ! without Leasing

" There is a strong case toward ;   [page 320]

164 there [is] none such, nor soe hard,

her lady, of
Sinadone,
is in distress,

    nor of soe much dolour.

my [4] Lady of Sinadone

    is brought to strong prison,

168   that was of great valoure ;

and begs for
a knight to
fight for her.

shee prayes you of [5] a Knight

    ffor to win her in flight

      with ioy & much honor." [6]

Lybius at
once

172 vp rose that younge Knight,

---

[1] A kind of fiddle.—F.

[2] Myche he couþe of game,
with sytole sautyre yn same
harpe fydele & croupe.—C.

[3] There is none of this in the French.
—F. Al can they play on gitterne and
rubible. *Cook's Tale.* The giterne was
a small guitar, and the ribible a small
fiddle played by a bow, and not by hand
as the giterne was. Jerome of Moravia
says of the ribble, Ribible, or Ribibe :
—" Est autem *rubeba* musicum instru-
mentum habens solum duas cordas sono
distantes a se per diapente, quod quidem,

sicut et viella, cum arcu tangitur."—W. C.
ribble, a fiddle or guittern, Gl. Ch.—P.

[4] MS. ny.—F.

[5] of you.—P.

[6] The French adds some lines about
the kiss, on which so much turns at the
end :

" Certes moult auroit grant honnor
Icil qui de mal l'estordroit,
Et qui le FIER BAISIER feroit.
Mais pres que il li a mestier !
Onques n'ot tel à chevalier.
Jà mauvais hom le don ne quière ;
Tot en giroit en vers en bière !" (p. 8.)

in his hart he was ffull light,
    & said, "my Lord Arthur,

claims the fight.

"my couenant is to haue that fight
176 ffor to winne that Lady bright,
    if thou be true of word."
the King said without othe,
  "thereof thou saiest soothe,
180   thereto I beare record;

Arthur assigns it to him.

"god thee giue strenght & might
ffor to winne that Ladye bright
    with sheeld & with speare dint!"
184 then began the maid to say,
    & said, "alas that ilke day
    that I was hither sent!"

Maid Hellen grumbles,

shee said, "this word will spring wyde;
188 Sir King, lost is all thy pride,
    and all thy deeds is shent,[1]

and says it's a disgrace to Arthur

when thou sendest a child
    that is wittlesse & wild,
192   to deale doughtilie with dint!

to send a witless child to fight,

thou hast Knights of mickle maine,
Sir Perciuall & Sir Gawaine,
    ffull wise in Turnament."

when he has knights like Gawaine &c.

196 tho[2] the dwarffe with great error[3]
went vnto King Arthur,
    & said, "Sir! verament

Dwarf Teddelyne

"this child to be a warryour,
200 or to doe such a Labor,
    itt is not worth one ffarthing!
or[4] hee that Ladye may see,
hee shall haue battells 5 or three
204   trulye without any Leasinge;

says the child isn't worth a farthing. He'll have to fight five battles before reaching Sinadone;

---

[1] are shent, i. e. disgraced.—P.
[2] then.—P.
[3] Errour course, running. Halliwell.—F.
[4] i. e. before.—P.

the first at
the Bridge
of Perils.

"att the bridge of perill
beside the aduenturous chappell,
there is the flirst begining."

Lybins says
he's not
afraid;

208 Sir Lybius anon answered
& said, "I was neuer affeard
ffor no mans threatninge!

he can
fight,

"somewhat haue I lerd [1]
212 ffor to play with a sword
there men hath beene slowe.[2]
the man *that* flleethe ffor a threat
other [3] by way or by streete,
216   I wold he were to-draw.
I will the battell vndertake;

and will
never give
in: such is
Arthur's
law.

I ne will neuer fforsake,
fflor such is Arthurs Lawe."

220 the made [4] answered alsoe snell,[5]
& said, " *that* beseemeth thee well!
who-soe looketh on thee may know

Hellen
sneers at
Lybins,

"thou ne durst for thy berde
224 abyid [6] the wind of my [7] swerde,
by ought *that* I can see!"
then said *that* dwarffe in *that* stond,

and Tedde-
lyne tells
him

"dead men *that* lyen on the ground,
228   of thee affrayd may bee;
but betweene ernest & game,

to go and
suck his
mammy.

I counsell thee goe souke [8] thy dame,
& winne there the degree."

Arthur says
"By God
you shall
have nobody
else."

232 the King answered anon-right,
and said, "thou gettest noe other Knight,
by god *that* sitteth in Trinytye!

---

[1] lered, i.e. learned. see Ch. Gl.—P.
[2] Where—have been slaw, Qu.—P.
[3] i.e. either. So they still speak in Shropshire.—P. *Or* is the contraction of *other*. F.
[4] The Maid.—P.
[5] snel, i.e. presently, immediately.

see Gl. ad Ch.—P. Al soe *is* alsoo *in* MS.—F.
[6] abyde.—P.
[7] perhaps any: or perhaps she taunts him, as not a Match for a Woman.—P.
[8] souke, i.e. suck, Chauc.—P.

If thou thinke he bee not wight,

236 Goe [1] and gett thee another Knight   [page 321]

    that is of more power."

the maid ffor ire still did thinke,[2]

shee wold neither eate nor d[r]inke

240 ffor all *that* there were;

shee sate still, without ffable,

till they had vncouered the table,

she and the dwarffe in ffere.

244 *King* Arthur in *that* stond

comanded of the table round,

    4 knights in ffere,

of the best *that* might be found

243 in armes hole [3] & sound,

    to arme *that* child ffull right;

& said " through the might o Christ

that in ffome [4] Iordan was baptiste,

252 he shold doe *that* he hight,[5]

& become a Champyon

to the Lady of Sinadon,

& ffell her ffoemen in flight."

256 to arme him they were flaine,[6]

S*ir* Perciuall & S*ir* Gawaine,

    & arrayed him like a knight;

the 3.d was S*ir* Agranaine,[7]

260 & the 4.th was S*ir* Ewaine,[8]

Marginal notes:

Hellen gets angry, won't eat or drink anything,

nor will the dwarf.

Arthur orders

his four best knights to

arm Lybius,

as he'll do what he says, and be the Lady of Sinadone's champion.

Lybius is armed by Percival, Gawaine,

Agravaine, and Ewaine;

---

[1] The MS. curl to the *G* is like *w.*—F.

[2] The French Romance makes her leaue the court at once in disgust, and Lybius ride after her and overtake her, p. 10, 11.—F.

[3] whole.—P.

[4] i.e. River; Ital. fiume.—P.

[5] i.e. promised, engaged.—P.

[6] glad.—P.

[7] See the note on him in vol. i. p. 145, —F.

[8] Ewaine or Uwayn was the son of Arthur's sister, Morgan le Fay, and had a bad opinion of his mother: "'A,' sayd syr Uwayn, 'men saith that Merlyn was begoten of a deuylle, but I may saye an erthely deuylle bare me.'" This was when he stopt " my lady " his " moder " from killing " the kynge " Vryens, his " fader, slepynge in his bed." *Caxton's Malfor,* i. p. 107. The Cotton MS. has: The þyrþ was syr Eweyn, [Oweyn, below]

The ferþde was syr agrrafrayn,

So seyþ þe Frenȝsche tale.—F.

them right ffor to behold.

they cast on him right good silke,

a sercote as white as any [1] milke

264   *that* was worth 20, of golde ;

alsoe an hawberke ffaire & bright,

w*h*ich was ffull richelye dight

w*i*th nayles good and ffine.

268   S*i*r Gawaine, his owne ffather,

hange about his necke there

a sheeld w*i*th a griffou,[2]

& a helme *that* was ffull rich,

272   in all the Land there was none such.

Sir Perciuall sett on his crowne,

S*i*r Agrauaine brought him a speare

that was good euery where

276   & of a ffell ffashion.

S*i*r Ewaine brought him a steede

that was good in euery neede,

& as ffeirce as any Lyon.[3]

280   S*i*r Lybyus on his steede gan springe,

& rode fforth vnto the King,

& said, "Lord of renowne !

"giue me your blessinge

284   w*i*thout any Letting !

my will is fforth me to wend."

the K*i*ng his hand vpp did lifft,

& his blessing to him gaue right

288   as a K*ni*ght curteour[4] & hende,

& said, "god *that* is of might,

& his mother Marry bright,

---

[1] One stroke too few in the MS.—F.
[2] griffyne, qu.—P.
[3] The French Romance only makes
Gawain order Lybius's armour to be

brought, and Gawain give him a squire
"Robers: moult esteit sages et apers,"
p. 11.—F.
[4] ? *for* curteous.—F.

that is flowre of all women,

292 giue thee gracce ffor to gone

ffor to gett the ouerhand of thy fone,

& speed thee in thy iourney! Amen!"

will grant him grace to conquer his foes.

[The Second Part.]

296 Sir Lybius now rideth on his way,

& soe did that ffaire may,

the dwarffe alsoe rode them beside,

till itt beffell vpon the 3ᵈ day

2ᵈ parte. vpon the Knight all the way

300 ffast they gan to chide,

& said, "Lorell¹ and Caitiue!

tho thow were such ffine,

Lost is all thy pride!

Lybius starts with Hellen and the dwarf.

They begin

abusing him,

304 This way keepeth a Knight

that with euery man will ffight,

his name springeth wyde;

and say that a knight near,

"his name is William de la Braunche,²

308 his warres may noe man staunche,³

he is a warryour of great pride;

Both through hart & hanch

swithe⁴ hee will thee Launche,

312 all that to him rides."⁵

then said Sir Lybius,

"I will not Lett this nor thus

to play with him a ffitt!

316 ffor any thing that may betide,

I will against him ryde

to looke if that he can sitt!"

Sir William de la Braunche,

[page 322]

will soon spear him through.

Lybius says

whatever happens he'll ride at him.

---

¹ Lewd base fellow, Homo perditus. Lye.—P.

² Wylleam Celebronche (leaf 44 b.) here, and wylleam selebraunche, l. 342,

(leaf 45, col. 1) Cotton MS.—F.

³ stop, stay, resist.—P.

⁴ soon.—P.

⁵ and all that—ride, qu.—P.

F F 2

thé rode on then all 3:

320 vpon a ffaire Cansye.

Near the
Adventurous
Chapel
they see a
knight
on the
Bridge of
Peril,

beside the aduenturous chappell [1]

a knight anon they can see

with armes bright of blee,

324 vpon the bridge [2] of perrill.

he bare a sheeld all of greene

with 3 Lyons of gold sheene,

right rich and precyous.

well armed.

328 well armed [3] was *that* Knight

as he shold goe to flight,

as itt was his vse. [4]

The knight
tells Lybius

when he saw Sir Lybius with sight,

332 anon he went to him arright,

& said to him there,

he must
fight or
leave his
harness
there,

" who passeth here by day or night,

certer [5] with me must flight,

336 or leaue his harnesse here."

Lybius

then answered Sir Libyus

begs leave to
pass.

& said, " ffor the loue of Iesus

lett vs passe now here !

340 wee be ffarr ffroe our ffreind,

& haue ffarr ffor to wend,

I and this mayden in fere. [6] "

Sir William
refuses, and
says

Sir William answered thoe

344 & said, " thou shalt not scape soe !

soe god giue me good rest,

he *must*
fight him.

thow & I will, or wee goe,

deale stroakes betweene vs tow

348 a litle here by west."

---

[1] Ryght to chapell Auntours.—Lambeth MS. Be a castelle aunterous.—C.

[2] Fr. *le Gué Périlleus.*—F. Poynt perylous.—Lambeth MS. vale perylous.—C.

[3] arned in the MS.—F.

[1] The French adds, p. 13, l. 330–3:
Maint chevalier l'ont trouvé dure,
Que il avoit ocis al gué ;
Moult étoit plains de cruauté,
BLIOBLIÉRIS avoit non.

[5] certes.—P. [6] together.—P.

Sir Libyus sayd, "now I see

*th*at itt will none other bee;

goe fforth and doe thy best;

352 take thy course w*ith* thy shafft

if thou can ¹ well thy crafft,

ffor I ame here all prest.² "

Lybius says

Charge away!

· then noe longer they wold abyde,

356 but the one to the other gan ryde

w*i*th greatt randaun.³

S*i*r Libyus there in ⁴ that tyde

smote S*i*r will*i*am on his side

360 w*i*th a speare ffelon ⁵ ;

but S*i*r will*i*am sate soe ffast

*th*at his stirropps all to-brast,

he leaned on his arsowne ;

364 S*i*r Lybius made him stoupe,

he smote him over the horse croupe

in the ffeeld a-downe ;

They charge ;

Lybius hits Sir William on the side,

drives him over his saddle-back,

and grounds him.

his horsse ran ffrom him away.

368 S*i*r will*i*am not long Lay,

but start anon vpright,

and said, " S*i*r, by my-in ffay,

neuer beffore this day

372 I ffound none soe wight !

now is my horsse gone away !

ffight on [foot],⁶ I thee pray,

as thou art a K*ni*g*h*t worthye."

376 then sayd S*i*r Lybins,

" by the leane of Sweete Iesus

therto ffull ready I am.⁷ "

Sir William starts up

and asks Lybius to fight on foot.

¹ con.—P.
² i. e. ready.—P.
³ Ap*d* G. Doug. *randoun*. The swift Course, Flight or Motion of any thing. Fr. *randon*, idem. Gl. G.D.—P.
⁴ MS. therein.—F.

⁵ *fel*, *felon*, *feloun*, wicked, also cruel, fierce. Gl. Chauc.—P.
⁶ on [foot] I &c.—P. a fote.—C. on fote.—Lam.
⁷ am I.—P.

They do so	then together they went as tyte,[1]
	380 & with their swords they gan smite ;
	they ffonght wonderous Longe ;
	stroakes together they lett fflinge [page 323]
till the fire flies from their helms.	*that* they ffyer out gan springe
	384 ffrom of their helmes strong.
Sir William	but Sir will*ia*m de [2] la braunche
	to Sir Lybius gan he launche,
cuts off a corner of Lybius's shield.	& smote on his sheild soo ffast
	388 *that* one cantell [3] ffell to the ground ;
	& S*ir* Lybius att *that* sonde [4]
	in his hart was agast.
Lybius	then S*ir* Lybius with all his might
	392 defended him anon-right,
	was [5] warryour wight & slye ;
cuts off the coif and crest of Sir William's helm,	coyfe [6] & crest downe right,
	he made to ffly with great might,
	396 of S*ir* Will*ia*ms helme on hye ;
	& with the point of his sword
and his beard.	he cut of S*ir* will*ia*ms berd,
	and touched him ffull nye.
Sir William's sword breaks in two ;	400 S*ir* William smote S*ir* Lybius thoe
	[7] as *that* his sword brast in tow
	[8] *that* many men might see with eye.
he prays for his life.	then S*ir* William began to crye
	404 & sayd, " ffor the Loue of Marrye,
	on liue let mee weelde !
	itt were great villanye
	ffor to make a K*ni*ght dye
	408 weponlesse in the feeld."

[1] quickly.—F.
[2] MS. do.—F.
[3] cantle, a Piece, a part. Gl. Ch.—P.
[4] Perhaps stounde, time, mom*ent*, space.—P. Sonde is message.—F.
[5] as, qu.—P. as.—C. and L.
[6] *coif-de-fer*, the hood of mail worn by knights in the twelfth century. *Fair-*

holt. The second seal of Henry I. represents him without a helmet, the cowl of mail being drawn over a steel cap called a *coif-de-fer* in contradistinction to the *chapelle-de-fer* worn over the mail. *Planché*, i. 94.—F.
[7] That his, &c.—P.
[8] As men, &c.—P.

then spake Sir Lybius
& sayd, " by the leaue of Iesus !
of liffe gettest thou no space [1]

412 but if thou wilt sweare anon,
or thou out of the ffelld gone,
here before my fface,

Lybius grants it him

on condition

" & on knees kneele downe,
416 & swere by my sword browne
that thou shalt to Arthur wend,
& say, 'Lord of great renowne !
I am in battell ouerthrowne ;

420 a knight me hither doth send
that men cleped thus,
Sir Lybius Disconius,
vnknowen kn*igh*t and hend.' "

424 Sir will*ia*m mett [2] him on his knee ;
& the othe there made hee,
& fforward gan he wend.

that he swears to go to Arthur

and say that Lybius sends him.

Sir William swears,

thus departed all the rout.
428 Sir will*ia*m to Arthurs court
he tooke the ready way ; [3]
a sorry case there gan ffall :
3 knights [4] proude and tall

432 Sir will*ia*m mett *that* day ;
the 3 Kn*igh*ts all in ffere
where his emes [5] sonnes deere,
stout they were and gay.

and starts for Arthur's court.

His three cousins meet him,

---

[1] For the next stanza and a half, the French has, p. 18 :

  " Ens à la cort Artu le roi,
  A lui en irés de par moi."

[2] ? sett.—F.

[3] The French Romance sends him home wounded, puts him to bed, and there he sees the three knights.—F.

[4] The French makes them only his "compaignons," and him their "signor." Their names are :

  Elus li blans, sires des Aies,
  Et li bons chevaliers de Graies
  Et Willaume de Salebrant.

[5] *eme*, Uncle. See Jun. *eame*. See Gl. ad Chauc. &c.—P. A.-Sax. *éám*, uncle.—F.

436   when they saw Sir william bleed,
    &alway hanged downe his head,
      they rode to him with great array,

and ask him
who has
wounded
him.

    & said, " Cozen will !
440   who hath done to you this shame ?
    & why bleedest thou soe long ? "
    hee said, " Sirs, by St. Iame !
    one *that* is not to blame ;

444   a stout Knight & a stronge—

" Sir Lybius
Disconius,

    Sir Lybius disconius hee hight—
    to ffell his enemyes in flight ;
    he is not flarr to Learne ;

448   a dwarfe rydeth with him in fere
    as he was his Squier ;
    they ride away ffull yarne.[1]

and he has
made me
swear

    " but one thing greeueth me sore,
452   *that* he hath made me sweare
    on his sord soe bright,
    that I shold neuer more,

not to stop
till I get to
Arthur's
court,

    till I come to King Arthur,
456   Stint by day nor night ;   [page 324]
    and alsoe to him I ame yeelde
    as ouercome into the fleelde
    by power of his might ;

and never to
bear arms
against
him."

460   nor against him ffor to beare
    neither sheeld nor speare ;
    thus I haue him hight."

His cousins
promise to
avenge him:

    then said the Knights 3 :
464   " well auenged shalt thou bee
    certes without ffayle !
    ffor hee one against vs 3,

Lybius isn't
worth a flea;

    hee is not worthe a fllee
468   ffor to hold battell [2] !

---

[1] yerne, inter al. nimble, Ch. Gl.—P.   [2] battayle.—P.

goe fforth & keepe thine othe
tho*ugh* thou be neuer soe wroth;
   wee will him assayle.

472 or he this fforrest passe,   they'll soon
   wee will his armour vnlace,   unlace his
     tho itt were double maile."   armour.

theroff wist nothing *that* wight
476 Sir Lybius, *that* gentle K*nig*ht,   Lybius
   but rode a well good pace;   rides on
   he & that maiden bright   with Hellen.
   made together *that* night
480   game & great solace.
   shee cryed him mercye   She begs his
   ffor shee had spoken him villanye;   pardon for
                               having
   shee prayed him to fforgiue her *that* tyde; abused him.
484 the dwarffe was their squier,
   & serued them both in ffere
   off all *that* they had need.

on the morrow when itt was day,   Next day
488 fforthe thé rode on their way
    towards Sinadowne.
   then they say [1] in their way
   3 K*nig*hts stout and gay   the three
492   came ryding ffrom Caerleon;   cousins
                              meet Lybius,
   to him they sayd anon-right,[2]   and call on
   " Traitor, turne againe and flight!   him to fight.
   thou shalt lose thy renowne!
496 & *that* maide ffaire & bright,
   wee will her lead att night
   herby vnto a towne."

---

[1] saw.—P. ? Perhaps the MS. has a
w made over the *y*, or an *e* after it.—F.
[2] The French puts the fight with these
three knights (p. 34) after that with the
two giants (p. 23).—F.

<table>
<tr><td>Lybius is</td><td></td><td>Sir Lybius to them gan crye,</td></tr>
<tr><td>ready,</td><td>500</td><td>" ffor to flight I am all readye</td></tr>
<tr><td></td><td></td><td>against you all in-same.[1] "</td></tr>
<tr><td>✦</td><td></td><td>a [2] prince proude of pride,</td></tr>
<tr><td>charges</td><td></td><td>he rode against them that tyde</td></tr>
<tr><td></td><td>504</td><td>with mirth sport and game.</td></tr>
<tr><td>the eldest,</td><td></td><td>the Eldest brother then beere</td></tr>
<tr><td></td><td></td><td>to Sir Lybius with a Spere,</td></tr>
<tr><td>Sir Baner,</td><td></td><td>Sir Baner was his name.[3]</td></tr>
<tr><td></td><td>508</td><td>Sir Lybius rode att him anon</td></tr>
<tr><td>and breaks
his thigh in
two.</td><td></td><td>& brake in tow his thigh bone,</td></tr>
<tr><td></td><td></td><td>& lett him Lye there lame.[4]</td></tr>
<tr><td></td><td></td><td>the Knight mercy gan crye</td></tr>
<tr><td></td><td>512</td><td>when Sir Lybius certainely</td></tr>
<tr><td></td><td></td><td>had smitten him downe.</td></tr>
<tr><td>Dwarf
Teddelyne
rides Baner's
horse</td><td></td><td>the dwarffe that hight Teodline</td></tr>
<tr><td></td><td></td><td>tooke his horsse by the raine,</td></tr>
<tr><td></td><td>516</td><td>he lept into the arsoone [5];</td></tr>
<tr><td></td><td></td><td>he rode anon with that</td></tr>
<tr><td>to Hellen,</td><td></td><td>vnto the mayd where shee sate</td></tr>
<tr><td></td><td></td><td>soo ffayre of ffashyon.</td></tr>
<tr><td>and she says
Lybius is a
good
champion.</td><td>520</td><td>then laughed that Maiden bright,</td></tr>
<tr><td></td><td></td><td>& said, "fforssooth this young Knight</td></tr>
<tr><td></td><td></td><td>is a ffull good Champyon ! "</td></tr>
</table>

[1] i.e. all together; it seems a contraction of the Fr. ensemble. See G.D. Gl. alsame, sub. verb, same.—P.

[2] As, q.—Pencil note.

[3] Willaumes vint à lui premiers, l. 1052, p. 38. The French Rom. remarks on the knights attacking singly, in the good old times, as contrasted with the cowardice of the then modern ones:

Et à cel tens, costume estoit
Que quant i hom se combatoit,
N'avait garde que de celui
Qui faisoit la bataille à lui.
Or va li tens en febloiant
Et cis usages decaans,
Que XX et V en prendent un!
Cis afaires est si commun

Que tuit le tienent desormès ;
La force fait le plus adiès,
Tos est mués en autre guise,
Mais dont estoit fois et francise,
Pitiés, proesse et cortoisie,
Et largesse sans vilonnie.
Or fait cascuns tot son pooir,
Tos entendent au decevoir. (p. 38.)

[4] The French makes Lybius kill Willaume (or Sir Baner):
Mort le trebuce del ceval.
Il ne li fera huimais mal ! (p. 40.)
Then Helin de Graies attacks Lybius, and gets his right arm broken.—F.

[5] Fr. Arçon, a saddle bow, Per Meton. Saddle.—P.

[1] the 2ᵈ brother, he beheld   *The second cousin*

524 how is brother lay in the ffeild

    & had lost strenght & might;

    he smote Sir Lybius in *that* tyde   *charges Lybius.*

    on the sheeld with much pride,

528 with his speare ffull right.   *Lybius unhelms him.*

    Sir Lybius away gan beare   [page 325]

    with his good speare

    the helme of *that* knight.

532 the youngest brother [2] then gan ride,   *The third cousin*

    & hitt Sir Lybius in *that* tyde

    as a man of much might,

    & said to him then anon,   *says he should*

536 "Sir, thou art by St. Iohn

    a ffell Champyowne;

    by god *that* sitteth in trinitye,

    flight I will with thee,   *like to fight Lybius,*

540 I hope to beare thee downe." [1]

    as warryour out of witt,

    on Sir Lybius then hee hitt   *and cuts through*

    with a ffell ffanchyon;

544 soe stifllye his stroakes hee sett,

    that through helme [3] & basenett [4]   *his helm and bascinet into his head.*

    he carued Sir Lybius crowne.

    Sir Lybius was served in *that* stead   *Lybius*

548 when hee ffelled [5] on his head

    that the sword had drawen blood;

[1-1] þe myddelle broþer com ȝerne
Vp-on a stede sterne
Egre as lyoun.
Hym þoȝte hys body wolde berne
But he myȝt al so ȝerne
Felle lybeaus a-doun.—C.

[2] Sir Gramadone, the French calls
him, l. 1122, p. 40.—F.

[3] helmet or head-piece, Fr. D? *Galea.*
—P.

[4] *Bascinet,* a light helmet, shaped
like a skull-cap, worn with or without a
moveable front. *Fairholt.*—F.

[5] felt.—P. The Lambeth MS. reads:
Tho wax Lybeous a-greued
When he felt on his hed.
The Cotton has:
Tho was ly-beaus agreede
Whan he felde on hedde.—F.

waves his sword,

about his head the sword he waued,—
all *that* hee hitt, fforsoothe hee cleeued,
552　　as warryour wight and good ;—
Sir Lybius said swithe thoo,

says two against one isn't fair (the second cousin having joined in again ?),

" one to flight against 2
is nothing good."
556　ffast they hewed then on him
with stroakes great and grim ;
against[1] them he stifllye stood,

and cuts off the second cousin's right arm.

[2] & through gods grace
560　he smote the eldest in *that* place
vpon the right arme thoo ;
hee hitt him soe in *that* place,—
to see itt was a wonderous case,—
564　his right arme flell him ffroe.[2]

The third cousin

the youngest saw *that* sight,
& thought hee had noe might
to flight against his ffoe ;

yields to Lybius,

568　to Sir Lybius hee did vp-yeeld
his good Speare & sheeld ;

and cries for mercy.

mercy he cryed him thoo.[3]

Lybius grants it

anon Sir Lybius said, " nay,
572　thou shalt not passe this away—
by him *that* bought mankind—

on condition that he and his two brothers go to Arthur,

but thou & thy brethren twayne
plight your trothes without Layine
576　*that* yee will to K*ing* Arthur wende,
& say, ' Lord of great renowne !
in battaill wee be ouercome ;

---

[1] 'gainst.—P.
[2]–[2] The Cotton text omits these lines, and in the next ones makes both brothers yield to Lybius.—F.
[3] The French makes the battle with the third knight last all night till next day; then the horse of Sir Gramadone des Aies slips and falls, Lybius seizes the prostrate rider, and he is obliged to yield, p. 41-2.—F.

a Knight vs hither hath send
580 ffor to yeeld thee tower & towune,
& to bee att thy bandowne [1]
euermore withouten end.'

and give up their all to him.

" & but if you will doe soe,
584 certes I will you sloe
as I am true Knight."
anon they sware to him thoe;
that they wold to Arthur goe,

They swear to do this,

588 their trothes anon thé plight.
Sir Lybius & that ffaire May
rode fforth on the way
thither as they had hight;

and Lybius rides on with Hellen.

592 till itt beffell on the 3ᵈ day
thé ffell together in game & pley,
hee and *that* Maiden bright.

On the third day

they rode fforthe on west
596 into a wyde fforrest,
& might come to noe towne;
thé ne wist what way best,
ffor there they must needs rest,

they are benighted in a forest

600 & there they light a-downe.
amonge the greene eues [2]
they made a lodge with bower & leaues,
with swords bright and browne.

and camp out.

604 Sir Lybius & that maiden bright [page 326]
dwelled there all night,[3]
that was soe ffaire of ffashyon.

---

[1] Fr. bandon, "A son bandon," i. e. at
his will and Pleasure. Gl. G. Doug.—P.
[2] eaues. Metaph. from a house build-
ing.—P.
[3] The French picture is prettier:

Li Desconnéus se dormoit
Sur l'erbe fresce ù reposoit;
Dalés lui gist la damoisèle,
Desenr son brac gist la pucèle;
Li uns dalés l'autre dormoit,
Li lousignols sor els cantoit. (p. 23.)

The dwarf
keeps watch,

then the dwarffe began to wake,

608 ffor noe theenes shold take

away their horsses with guile ;

then ffor ffeare he began to quake ;

sees a great
fire,

a great ffyer hee saw make

612 ffrom them but a mile.

wakes
Lybius,
and says
they must be
off,

" arise," he said, " worthy K*night* !

to horsse *that* wee were dight

ffor doubt of more perill !

616 certes I heare a great bost [1] ;

as he smells
roast meat.

alsoe I smell a savor of rost,

by god & by S[t] Gyle ! "

[The Third Part.]

Lybius

Sir Lybius was stout & gay,

620 & leapt vpon his palffrey,

& tooke his sheeld & speare

rides off,

3[d] **part.** & rode fforth ffull ffast.

and finds
two
giants,

2 gyants hee ffound at Last,

624 [that] [2] strong & stout were.

The one was blacke as any sole,[3]

the other as red as ffyerye cole,

& ffoule bothe they were.

a black one
holding a
maid by the
bosom,

628 the blacke Gyant held in his [4] arme

a ffaire mayd by the barme,[5]

bright as rose on bryar [6] ;

[1] burst, report, like *the* discharge of a gun : It is still called *bost* in Shropsh. —P.

[2] Who.—P.

[3] A.-S. *sol*, soil, filth, mire, dirt. Bosworth. Fr. *souiller*, to soyle, slurrie, durtie, smutch, beray, begrime. Cotgrave. The Cotton stanza is :

þat on was Red & loþlyche,
And þat oþer swart as pyche,
    Grysly boþe of chere.
þat oon helde yn hys barme
A mayde y-clepte yn hys arme,
    As bryȝt as blosle on brere.—F.

[4] *hus* in the MS. with a dot.—F. The French is :

Car uns gaians moult la pressoit,
A force baisier le voloit,
Mais cele ne l' pooit soufrir,
Mais se voloit laissier morir.

[5] Sinus, gremium.—P. A.-S. *bearm*, the womb, lap, bosom. Bosworth.—F. A mayde i-clypped in his barme.—L.

[6] brere, so in Chauc.—P. *Bryar* is one of the words entered under *care* in Levins's Manipulus or Rhyming Dictionary, p. 209, col. 1, ed. 1867.—F.

the red Gyant ffull yarne
632 swythe about can turne
a wild bore on a spitt ;
ffaire the ffyer gan berne.
the maid cryed ffull yerne,
636 for men shold itt witt ;
shee said, "alas & euer away
that euer I abode this day
w*i*th 2 devills for to sitt !
640 helpe, Mary *that* is soe mild,
for the loue of the[1] child,
that I be not fforgett ! "

Si*r* Lybius said, "by S: Iame !
644 ffor[2] to bring *that* maid ffrom shame
itt were ffull great price ;
but ffor to fight w*i*th both in shame[3]
it is no childs game,
648 they be soe grim and grise.[4] "
he tooke his course w*i*th his shaft
as a man *that* cold his crafft,
& he rode by right assise :
652 the blacke he smote all soe smart
through the liuer, long[5] & hart
that he might neue*r* rise.

then ffled *that* maiden sheene,
656 & thanked[6] Marye, heauens queene,
that succour had her sent.
then came mayd Ellen
& the dwarffe by-dene,[7]
660 & by the hand her hent,

Side notes:

a red one

roasting a boar on a spit.

The maid cries out

for help.

Lybius says

it's no child's play to fight both giants,

but he charges the black one,

and runs him right through the heart.

The maid flees ;

Hellen takes her

---

[1] perhaps thy.—P.
[2] for.—P. qu. MS. ffea.—F.
[3] in same, i. e. together, ensemble, Fr. —P.
[4] id. ac grisly, horrid, horrible.—P.
[5] lung.—P.
[6] *d* added by Percy.—F.
[7] MS. "& by the dwarffe dene," but the tmesis must be a copier's mistake. — F. And the Dwarf by-dene.—P. Sehe & here dwerk y-mene.—Col.

<table>
<tr><td>

into the forest,

</td><td>

& went into the greaues,[1]
& lodged them vnder the leaues
in a good entent ;

</td></tr>
</table>

into the forest,

& went into the greaues,[1]
& lodged them vnder the leaues
in a good entent ;

and she prays for Lybius's safety.

664   & shee besought Iesus
flor to helpe Sir Lybius
that hee was not shent.

The red giant hits at Lybius with the boar,

the red Gyant smote thore[2]
668   att Sir Lybius with the bore
as a woolfe *that* were woode ;
his Dints he sett soe sore,

and knocks his horse down.

that Sir Lybins horsse therfore
672   downe to the grond yode.[3]

Lybius fights with his sword.

then Sir Lybius with ffeirce hart,
out of his saddle swythe he start
as spartle[4] doth out of fyer ;

676   feir[c]ely as any Lyon
he ffought with his flawchyon
to quitt the Gyant his hyer.

The giant lays on Lybius with his spit,

[5] the Gyants spitt sickerlye
680   was more then a cowle tree[6]
that he rosted on the bore ;
He laid on Sir Lybius ffast,
all the while the spitt did last,

[page 327]

684   euer more and more.

covers him with boar's grease,

the bore was soe hott then,
that on Sir Lybius the grease ran

---

[1] i.e. Groves, Bushes. So in Chauc. —P.

[2] i.e. there, *metri gratiâ.* so in Chauc. —P.

[3] went.—P. The French makes Lybius kill the other giant first :
  Il . . fiert celui premierement
  Qui esforçoit la damoisele.
  Si la feru lès la mamiele.
  Le fer li fist el euer serrer ;
  Les ioils del cief li fist torbler;
  Mort le trebuce el feu ardant. (p. 27.)
The Cotton text (leaf 46 back, col. 2)

follows the French :
  þe blake geaunt he smote smert
  þorgh the lyuere, longe, & herte,
  þat neuer he myȝte aryse.—F.

[4] sparkle.—P. sparkyll.—L. sperk. —C.

[5] This stanza is not in C. or L.—F.

[6] ? Phillipps's *coul-staff*: " Coul, a kind of Tub, or Vessel with two Ears to be carry'd between two Persons with a *Coul-staff.*" See Lambarde's Perambulation, p. 367, and Strutt, ii. 201, says Halliwell, under *Cowlstaff.*—F.

right ffast thore.[1]

688　the gyant was stiffe & stronge,
　　15 ffoote he was Longe ;
　　　hee smote Sir Lybius ffull sore.

and batters him till

　　Euer still the gyant smote
692　att Sir Lybius, well I wott,
　　　till the spitt brast in towe.
　　then as man *that* was wrath,
　　ffor a Trunchyon fforth he goth

the spit breaks. Then he gets a truncheon,

696　to flight aga[i]nst his ffoe,
　　　& w*i*th the End of *that* spitt
　　Sir Lybius sword [2] in 3 he hitt.
　　　then was Sir Lybius wonderous woe.

and splits Lybius's shield with it,

700　or he againe his staffe vp caught,
　　Sir Lybius a stroke him rought
　　　that his right arme ffell him ffroe.

but drops his staff. Lybius cuts off his right arm,

　　the Gyant ffell to the ground,
704　& Sir Lybius in *that* stond
　　　smote of his head thoo:
　　in a ffrench booke itt is ffound.[3]
　　　to the other he went in *that* stond,[4]
708　& serued him right soe.

then his head,

　　he tooke vp the heads then
　　& bare them to *that* ffaire maiden
　　　that he had woone in flight.

and gives both heads to the maiden.

712　the maid was glad & blythe,
　　& thanked god often sithe
　　　that euer he was made a Knight.

She

　　Sir Lybius said, "gentle dame,
716　tell me now what is your name

---

[1] There is nothing of this grease business in the French and Cotton texts. —F.

[2] scheld.—Cot. The French has not the passage.—F.

[3] Renals de Biauju's text omits the cutting off of the right arm, but makes Lybius split the giant's head to the teeth.—F.

[4] stound.—P.

& where *that* you were borne."

tells him
that her
father is

"Sir," she said, "by S⸍ Iame,

my ffather is of rich flame,

720 & dwelleth here beforne ;

he is a Lord of much might,

an earl,

an Erle & a Noble Knight ;

Sir Arthore,

his name is S[ir] Arthore,

and her
name is
Violet.

724 & my name is Vylett,[1]

that the Gyant had besett

for the Castle ore.

She was out
walking

" as I went on my demeaning [2]

728 to-night in the eueni[n]ge,

none euill then I thought ;

when the
giant sprang
on her,

the gyant, w*i*th-out leasing,

out of bush he gan spring,

732 & to the ffyer me brought.

and would
have
destroyed
her,
had it not
been for
Lybius.
Christ
reward him !

of him I had beene shent,

but *that* god me succour sent

that all this world hath wrought.

736 Sir *Knight*! god yeeld thee thy meed,

ffor vs *that* on the roode did bleed,

& w*i*th his blood vs bought ! "

They all ride
to

w*i*thout any more talking

740 to their horsses they gan spring,[3]

---

[1] Vilett, Violette.—P. Vyolette.—Cot.
The French gives the name and story
differently :

. . nòmmée sui Clarie . .
Et Saigremors si est mes frère,
Li jaians me prist cés mon père.
En un vergier hui mais entrai
Et por moi déduire i alai.
Li jaians ert desous l'entrée,
Trova la porte desfremée ;
Iluec me prist, si m'enporta,
Ici son compaignon trova. (p. 32.)—F.

[2] probably *going a walking*, demener,
the same as promener, qu.—P.

Yesterday yn the mornynge
Y wente on my playnge.
  Cot. MS. in Ritson.

[3] The French text makes them first
have a grand feast on the grass off the
giants' food. Squire *Robers* distinguishes
himself as cook, seneschal, butler, marshal, chamberlain, and squire, helped by
the dwarf, p. 32–34. *Robers* is a most
useful personage all through the French
story.—F.

& rode fforth all in-same,

& told the Erle in euery thing [1]

how he wan in ffighting

744 his Daughter ffrom woe & shame.

Sir
Arthore's,

then were these heads sent

vnto King Arthur ffor a present

with much mirth & game,

748 *that* in Arthurs court arose

of Sir Lybius great Losse [2]

& a right good name.

and Lybius
sends the
giants' heads
to King
Arthur.

[3] the Erle, ffor *that* good deede,

752 gaue Sir Lybius for his meede

sheeld and armour bright,

& alsoe a noble steede

that was good in euerye need,

756 in trauayle & in flight.

Sir Arthore
gives Lybius

armour

and a noble
steed.

[The Fourth Part.]

now Sir Lybius and his May

tooke their leaue, & rode their way

thither as they had hight.[4]

Lybins' rides
on towards
the Waste
Land,

760 ⌜Then they saw in a parke   [page 328]

a Castle stiffe & starke,[5]

that was ffull maruelouslye dight;

4ᵈ parte.

wrought itt was with lime & stone,—

764 such a one saw he neuer none,—

⌞with towers stiffe & stout.

and sees a
castle

---

[1] erl tydynge.—Cot.
[2] lose, praise.—F.
[3] The Cotton text has an extra stanza
here, in which Sir Arthore offers Lybius
his daughter Vyolette to wife, but the
offer is declined, leaf 47 b. MS., p. 30,
Ritson. The French has neither of the
stanzas.—F.
[4] þey Ryde forþ alle þre

Toward þe fayre cyte,
Kardeuyle fore soþ hyt hyȝt.—C.
Here follow in the French a page and
a quarter of what M. Hippeau terms
" Digression de l'Auteur: Il sera fidèle
à celle qu'il ne peut encore nommer
s'amie, mais qu'il appelle *la moult aimée*."
The next adventure with Sir Geffron,
or Part IV, is omitted.—F.
[5] i. e. strong.—P.

which he thinks very strong.

Sir Lybius said, "soe haue I blis!
worthy dwelling here itt is
768   to them *that* stood in doubt!"

Hellen tells him that a brave knight lives there:

then laughed *that* Maiden bright,
& sayd, "here dwelleth a Knight,
the best *that* here is about.
772   who-soe will with him flight,—
be he Baron or be he knight,—
he maketh him to loute.

whoever brings him a lady

" soe well he loueth his Leman
776   *that* is soe ffaire a woman,
& a worthy in weede,

fairer than his own, gets a white falcon :

who-soe bringeth a ffairer then,
a ioly flawcon as white as swan
780   he shall haue to his meede.

but if she is not so fair, Sir Gefferon

& if shee be not soe bright,
with Sir Gefferon he must flight ;
& if he may not speed,

cuts his head off.

784   ¹ his [head] shall be ffrom him take,
& sett ffull hye vpon a stake,
trulye withouten dread.

" the sooth you may see and heere ;
788   there is on euery corner ²
a head or tow ffull right."

Lybius declares he'll fight Gefferon,

Sir Lybius sayd al soe soone,
"by god & by Sͩ Iohn !
792   with Sir Gefferon will I flight,
& chalenge the lolly flawcon,
& say *that* I haue one in the towne,
a lemman al soe ³ bright ;

and produce Hellen as his love.

796   & if hee will her see,
then I will bring ⁴ thee,
be itt day or by night." ⁵

¹ his [head] shall.—P.
² Percy has added an *e* at the end. —F.
³ MS. alsoe, and in line 790.—F.   al
soe.—P
⁴ Only half the *n* in the MS.—F.
⁵ by day or night, or *dele* by.—P.

the dwarffe sayd, "by Sweete Iesus ! The dwarf
800 gentle Sir Lybyus [1] Disconiys, warns him
thou puttest thee in great perill.
Sir Giffron La ffraudeus,[2] of Gefferon's
in ffighting he hath an vse wiles.
804 Knights ffor to beguile."
Sir Lybius answered and sware, Lybius
& said, "therof I haue no care ! doesn't care
for 'em ; he
by god & by S! Gyle, will fight.
808 I will see him in the fface
or I passe out of this place,
ffor all his subtulle wile ! "

without any more questyon
812 thé[3] dwelled still in the towne
all night there in peace.
on the morrow he made him readie Next day
ffor to winne him the Masterye Lybius
816 certes[4] withouten Lease.
he armed him ffull sure arms
in the sayd Armor
that King Arthurs[5] was,
820 & his horsse began he to stryde ; and rides to
the dwarffe rod by his syde
to that strong palace. Gefferon's
castle.

Sir Gyffron la ffraudeus Gefferon
824 rose vp, as itt was his vse,
in the morrow tyde
ffor to honor sweete Iesus.
then he was ware of Sir Lybius ; sees him,
828 as a prince of much pryde

---

[1] There is a stroke too many after the u in the MS.—F.
[2] Syr Gyffroun le flowdous.—Cot.
[3] they.—P.
[4] MS. certer.— F.
[5] erl autores.—Cot., which must be right.— F. sir Arthores, or Knight Ar-thores.—P.

ffast he rode into *that* place.
Sir Ieffron maruailed att *that* case,
    & loud to him did crye
832 with voyce loud and shrill :
    " comest thou ffor good or ill ?
      tell me now on hye."

[page 329]

Sir Lybins said al soe ¹ tyte,
836 " certes I haue greate delight
    with thee ffor to ffight !
    thou hast [said] great despite ; ²
    thou hast a Leman,³ none so whyte
840 by day or by night
    as I haue one in the towne,
    ffairer of ffashyon
      for to see with sight.
844 therfore thy Iolly ffawcowne,
    to King Arthur with the crowne
      bring I will by right."

Sir Geffron said al soe right,
848 " where shall wee see *that* sight,
    whether the ffairer bee ? "
Sir Lybius said, " wee will ffull right
    in Cardigan see *that* sight,⁴
852 there all men may itt see ;
    in the middes of *that* Markett,
    there shall they both be sett
      to looke on them soe ffree ⁵ ;
856 & if my Leman be browne,
    ffor thy Iolly ffawcowne
      iust I will with thee."

Side notes:

and asks why he comes.

" To fight you," says Lybius ;

" you have no such fair maiden as I have ;

give me your falcon for King Arthur.

My lady is in Cardigan ;

we'll set yours and mine in the market, and see which is the fairer."

---

¹ MS. alsoe, and in l. 847.—F.
² Thou seyste a foule dispite.—Lam.
³ Lennan in the MS.—F.
⁴ In Cardenyle cyte ryȝt.—Cot.
⁵ bothe bond & fre.—Cot.

Sir Geffrou said alsoe then,

860 " I wold ffaine as any man

to-day att yondertyde.[1]

all this I grant thee well,

& out of this Castell

864 to Cardigan [2] I will ryde."

their gloues were there vp yold,

*th*at fforward [3] to hold,

as princes proud in pryde.

868 Sir Lybius wold no longer blinn,[4]

but rode againe to his inn

& wold no longer abyde.

Gefferon agrees.

Lybius rides back, and

he said to maid Ellen

872 *th*at was soe bright & sheene,

" looke thou make thee bowne !

I thee say, by S! Quintin,

Sir Gefferons Leman I will winn :

876 to-day shee will come to towne,

in the midds of this cytye,

*th*at men may you see,

& of you bothe the ffashyon ;

880 & if thou be not soe bright,

w*i*th Sir Geffron I shall flight

to winne the Iollye ffawcowne."

tells Hellen to get ready,

as she is to be shown against Gefferon's love.

the dwarffe answered, " for-thy [5]

884 *th*at thou doest a deed hardye [6]

. ffor any man borne.

thou wilt doe by no mans read

The dwarf tells him it's a foolhardy business ;

---

[1] *forte* ondertyde.—P. þys day at vnderne tyde.—C. This daye at vnder-tide.—L.

[2] Karlof.—Cot. Kardyle.—Lam.

[3] A.-S. *foreweard*, agreement.—F.

[4] blim in the MS.—F.

[5] for thy, *therefore*, according to Gl. Ch. & G.D., here it should seem to be *forthwith*.—P. Cot. omits this stanza.

The Lambeth MS. has :
The Dwerff answerd and seid,
" Thow doste a savage dede !
ffor any man i-borne,
Tow wilt not do by Rede,
But faryst with thi madd hede
As lorde that will be lorne."

[6] hardye, qu.—P. MS. not clear.—F.

for thou fforest in thy child head

888 as a man *that* wold be lorne!

he'd better go on his way.

& therfore I thee pray

to wend fforth on thy way,

& come not him beforne."

Lybius won't hear of this. 892 Sir Lybius said, "*that* were great shame!

I had lever with great grame [1]

with wild horsses to be torue."

Hellen decks herself

maid Ellen, ffaire and free,

896 made hast sickerlye

her ffor to attyre

in Keicheys [2] *that* were white,

for to doe all his delight,

900 with good [3] gold wyer.

with a violet mantle,

a vyolett mantle, the sooth to say,

ffurred well with gryse gay,[4]

shee cast about her Lyer [5];

and precious stones, 904 the stones shee had about her mold

were precyous & sett with gold,[6]

the best in *that* shire.

Sir Lybius sett *that* ffaire May

and rides on a palfrey 908 on [7] a right good [8] Palffrey,

& rode fforth all three.

euery man to other gan say,

"heere cometh a ffaire May,

912 And louelye ffor to see!"   [page 330]

to Cardigan market.

into the Markett hee rode,

& boldly there abode

---

[1] i.e. grief, sorrow; vexation, anger; madness: trouble, affliction, Gl. ad Chauc.—P.

[2] Kercheffs, qu.—P. keucchers.—C. kerchevys.—L.

[3] arayde wyth.—Cot.

[4] Pelured with grys & gray.—Cot.

[5] swyre (neck).—Cot.

[6] A sercle vp-on here molde, Of stones & of golde.—Cot. *Mold*, the suture of the skull; form, fashion, appearance.—Halliwell.

[7] *om*, or ? *one*, in the MS.—F.

[8] Vp-on a pomely.—Cot.

in the middes [1] of *that* citye.

916   anon thé saw Geffron come ryde,   To them
     & 2 squiers by his side,   comes
       & na more meanye [2] :   Geffron,

     he bare a sheelde of greene,
920 richelye itt was to be seene [3] ;
     of gold was the bordure,
     dight itt was with fflowers
     & alsoe with rich colours,

924   like as itt [4] were an Emperour.   with two
     the [5] squiers did with him ryde ;   squires
     the one bare by his side
     3 shafts good & stoure, [6]   (one bearing
                            a falcon)
928 the other bare, his head vpon,
     a gentle Iolly ffawcon [7]
     that was laid to wager ;

     & after did a Lady ryde,   and his fair
932 ffaire & bright, of Much pryde,   lady,
     cladd in purple pall.   clad in
     the people came ffarr & wyde
     to see *that* Ladye in *that* tyde, [8]
936 how gentle [9] shee was and small ;
     her mantle was of purple ffine,   purple,
     well ffurred with good Armine,
     itt was rich and royall ;
940 a sercotte sett about her necke soe sweete   her surcoat
     with dyamond & with Margarett,   set with
                              diamonds,
     & many a rich Emerall ;   pearls,
                              and
                              emeralds ;

---

[1] niddes in the MS.—F.
[2] attendants.—P.
[3] He barr þe schelde of goules,
Of syluer thre whyte oules.—C.
He bare the shelde gowlys,
Off syluer three white owlys.—L.
[4] hoe.—P.
[5] two.—P.

[6] Idem ac *sture, ingens,* crassus, Lye.
—P.
[7] I *would* read Ier-faucon. see st. 37
[l. 977] below.—P. gerfawcone.—C.
[8] To se here bak & syde. — Cot.
(which has many variations in the following lines).—F.
[9] forte, *gimp.*—P.

her hue
rose-red,
her hair
golden,

her colour was as the rose red ;
944 her haire *that* was on her head,
as gold wyer itt shone bright ;

her brows
like silk,

her browes were al soe [1] silke spread,
ffaire bent in lenght & bread ;
948 her nose was ffaire and right ;

her eyes
grey.

her eyen gray as any glasse ;
milke white was her fface.
the said *that* sawe *that* sight,

The lookers-
on

952 her body gentle and small,
' her beautye ffor to tell all,
noe man with tounge might.'

put two
chairs for
the ladies,

unto the Markett men gan bring
956 2 Chaires ffor to sitt in,
their bewtye ffor to descrye.
then said both old & younge,—

and decide
that
Gefferon's
is the fairer.

fforssooth without Leasing
960 betweene them was partye,—[2]
Geffrons Leman was ffaire & cleere
as euer was any rose on bryer,[3]
fforsooth without Lye.

Hellen is
only fit to be
her laundry-
maid.

964 Maid Ellen, the Messenger,
seemed to her but a Launderer [4]
in her nurserye.

Lybius then
challenges
Gefferon to
fight.

then said Sir Geffron la ffraudeus,[5]
968 " Sir Knight, by Sweet Iesus,
thy head thou hast fforlore [6] ! "
" nay ! " said Sir Lybius,
" *that* was neuer my vse !
972   iust I will therfore ;

---

[1] MS. alsoe.—F.
[2] This Line in a Parenthesis.—P.
[3] brere.—P. There is no short stroke
to the *y* in the MS.—F.
[4] i. e. Launderess, Laundress.—P.

[5] le fludous.—Cot.
[6] lost.—P. The Cotton MS. reads :
     Syr lybeaus Desconus,
     þys hauk þou hast for-lore.

"& if thou beare me downe,
take my head on thy ffawchyon,
& home with thee itt lead ;
976 & if I beare downe thee,
the Ierffaucon shall goe with mee
maugre thy head indeed.

"what needeth vs more to chyde ?
980 but into the saddle let vs glyde,
to proue our mastery."
either smote on others sheeld the while   *They charge*
with crownackles [1] *that* were of steele,
984 with great envye.
then their speares brake assunder ;   *and their*
the dints flared as the thunder   *spears break.*
that cometh out of the skye.
988 trumpetts & tabours,
herawdyes & good desoures,[2]
Their stroakes ffor to [3] descrye.   [page 391]

Geffron then began to speake :
992 "bring me a spere *that* will not breke,   *Gefferon*
a shaft with one crownall !   *calls for a*
    spear that
ffor this young ffeley ffreke   *won't break,*
sitteth in his saddle steke [4]
996 as stone in Castle wall.
I shall make him to stoope   *and he'll*
    soon unhorse
swithe ouer his saddle croope,   *Lybius !*
& giue him a great ffall,
1000 tho he were as wight a warryour
as Alexander or Arthur,
Sir Lancelott or Sir Perciuall."

---

[1] coronals.—Cot. *Coronel*, the upper
part of a jousting-lance, constructed to
unhorse, but not to wound, a knight.
Fairholt, p. 426 (with a cut of one).
—F. This seems to be the same as Crownall, st. 40 [of MS., l. 993 here]. both
seem to signify the heads of *the* spears.
—P.
[2] disours, tellers, narraters.—F.
[3] gon.—Cot.
[4] steke for stuck, rhithmi gratia.—P.

They charge again.

      then the Kni*ght*s both tow

1004   rode together swithe thoe

      with great ren[d]owne [1] :

      S*i*r Lybius smote S*i*r Geffron soe

Gefferon loses his shield.

      that his sheild ffell him ffroe

1008   into the ffeeld againe. [2]

      then laughed all *that* was there,

      & said without more,

      Duke, Erle, or Barron,

1012   *that* " thé saw neuer a Kni*ght*,

      ne noe man abide might

      a course of S*i*r Geffron."

The third course, Gefferon does nothing.

      another course gan thé ryde :

1016   S*i*r Geffron was aggreeued *that* tyde

      ffor hee might not speede.

The fourth,

      he rode againe al soe [3] tyte,

      & S*i*r Lybius he gan [4] smite

1020   as a doughtye man of deed.

Lybius

      S*i*r Lybius smote him soe ffast

      that S*i*r Geffron soone he cast

      him and his horsse a-downe ;

1024   S*i*r Ieffrons backe bone he brake

breaks Gefferon's back,

      that the ffolkes hard itt cracke ;

      lost was his renowne.

      then they all said, lesse & more,

1028   *that* Sir Geffrons had Lore

and wins his falcon.

      the white Gerffawcon. [5]

      the people came S*i*r Lybius before,

      & went w*i*th him, lesse & more,

1032   anon into the towne ;

---

[1] With welle greet Raundoun.—Cot.
[2] I *would* read *adowne.* see below, st. 45.—P. a-doun.—Cot. a-downe.—L.
[3] MS. alsoe.—F.
[4] MS. gam.—F.
[5] Only half the *w* in the MS.—F.

& S*i*r Geffron ffrom the ffeeld

was borne home on his sheild

w*i*th care and rueffull mone.

1036 the Gerffawcon sent was,

by a knight *that* hight Chaudas,[1]

to bring to Arthur w*i*th the crowne ;

& rote[2] to him all *that* dead,[3]

1040 & w*i*th him he gan to leade

the ffawcon *that* S*i*r Lybius wan.

when the K*i*ng had heard itt read,

he said to his kn*i*g*h*ts in *that* stead,

1044 " S*i*r Lybius well warr can !

he hath me sent w*i*th honor

that he hath done battells 4

since *that* he began ;

1048 I will him send of my treasure,

ffor to spend to his honor,

as ffalleth[4] ffor such a man."

a 100[li] ready[5] prest

1052 of ffloryins to spend w*i*th the best,

he sent to Cardigan towne.

then S*i*r Lybius held a feast

that lasted 40 dayes att Least

1056 w*i*th Lords of renowne.[6]

& att the 6: weeke end

hee tooke his leaue, ffor to wend,

of duke, Erle, and Barron.

---

[1] There was one Chandos a herald, whose book is preserved in Worcester College Library, Oxon.—P.

[2] He wrote, sic legerim.—P.

[3] deed.—P.

[4] fitteth, qu.—P.

[5] ready, speedy.—P.

[6] The Cotton text sends the falcon by a knyght that hyght Gludas, to King Arthur; and Arthur sends Lybius back a hundred pound of florins to Cardelof, where Lybius holds feast forty days. (MS. leaf 49, col. 2 ; ed. Ritson, p. 42). —F.

[The Fifth Part.]

[The Adventure of the Hound, and the Fight with Sir Otes de Lile.]

Lybius rides on

towards Sinadon.

He hears a horn,

and the dwarf says it's

5ᵈ parte

> Sir Lybius and his ffaire May
> rode fforth on their way
>   towards Sinadon.
> then as they rod in a throwe,[1]
> hornes heard they lowd blowe,
>   & hoinds [2] of great game.
> the dwarffe said in *that* throwe,[3]
> "*that* horne I well know
>   many yeeres agone ;

1060

1064

1068

Sir Otes de Lile's.

"Thatt horne bloweth Sir Ortes de lile,
That serued [4] my Ladye a while   [page 332]
   seemlye in her hall ;
& when shee was taken with guile,
he fled from *that* perill
   west into worrall.[5] "

1072

Then they see a beautiful hound

but as they rode talking,
they saw a ratch [6] runinge
   ouerthwart the way.
then said both old & young,
"ffrom the ffirst begining
   they saw neuer none soe gay."

1076

1080

---

[1] a short space, sed vid. infra, perhaps in a row.—P. A.-S. *þrah*, a space, time. —F.

[2] hounds.—P.

[3] a cast, a stroke. It. short space, Chauc. Gl.—P.

[4] seruede.—Cot.

[5] Wyrhale.—Cot.

[6] Ratches. Genus Canum : Braccones, Lye. Jun.—P. A.-S. *ræce*, a rach, a setting dog? Lye, in Bosworth. ? a dog hunting by scent.—F.

hee was of all couloures
that men may see on flowers
betweene Midsummer & May.

of all sorts
of colours.

1084 the Mayd sayd al soe [1] soone,
"soe faire a ratch I neuer saw none,
nor pleasanter to my pay [2] !

Hellen
wishes she
had it.

"wold to God *that* I him ought [3] !"
1088 Sir Lybius anon him caught,
& gaue him to maid Elen.[4]
they rode fforth all rightes,
& told of flighting w*i*th K*ni*ghts
1092 ffor ladyes bright & sheene.
they had rydden but a while,
not the space of [a] Mile
into *that* fforrest greene ;

So Lybius
catches it
and gives it
her.

Soon they

1096 then they saw a hind sterke,[5]
& 2 grayhounds *that* were like
the ratch *that* I of meane.

see a stag
followed by
two grey-
hounds,

thé hunted [6] still vnder the Lind [7]
1100 to see the course of *that* hind
vnder the fforrest side.
there beside dwelled *that* K*ni*ght
that Sir Otes de lile hight,
1104 a man of much pride ;
he was cladd all in Inde,[8]
& ffast pursued after the hind

and stop to
watch her.

Sir Otes de
Lile

---

[1] MS. alsoe.—F.
[2] satisfaction, liking.—P.
[3] owned, possest.—P.
[4] The French text makes the hound
stop with a thorn in its foot ; Hellen
takes it out, rides off with the dog, and
a huntsman sees it under her cloak.
She refuses to give it up to him or his
master, and so Sir Otes, or *L'Orguillous
de la Lande*, rides off for his armour, and

fights Lybius.—F.
[5] stout Hind.—P.
[6] hovede (stopt).—Cot.
[7] Properly a Teil or Lime tree, but
in these ballads it seems to be used for
Trees in general.—P.
[8] i.e. azure or blue as used by Lydg.
—black according to Sp. Gl. and Ch.
—P.

rides by on a
bay,

vpon a bay distere ;

1108   loude he gan his horne blow,

for the hunters shold itt know,

& know where he were.

as he rode by *that* woode right,

sees Lybius
and Hellen,

1112   there he saw *that* younge K*night*

& alsoe *that* ffaire May ;

they dwarffe rode by his side.

Sir Otes bade they shold abyde,

1116   they Ledd [1] his ratch away :

and
remonstrates
with them
for taking
his hound.

" ffreinds," he said, " why doe you soe ?

let my ratch ffrom you goe ;

good for you itt were.

1120   I say to you without Lye,

this ratch has beene my

all out this 7 yeere."

Sir Lybius said anon tho,

Lybins says
he means to
keep it.

1124   " I tooke him with my hands 2,

& with me shall he abyde ;

I gaue him to this maid hend [2]

that with me dothe wend

1128   riding by my side."

then said Sir Otes de lile,

Sir Otes
warns him
to look out
for his life.

" thou puttest thee in great perill

to be slaine, if thou abide."

Lybius calls
him a churl.

1132   Sir Lybius said in *that* while,

" I giue right nought of thy wile,

churle ! tho thou chyde."

then spake Sir Otes de lile,

Sir Otes
rebukes him;

1136   & said, " thy words be vile !

churle was neuer my name !

I say to thee without ffayle,

the countesse of Carlile

1140   certes was my dame ;

---

[1] The last *d* has a tag to it.—F.   [2] gentle, kind.—P.

" & if I were armed now
as well as art thou,
wee wold ffight in-same.

if he were
armed, he
would fight
him.

1144 or thou my ratch ffrom me reue,[1]
we wold play, ere itt were one,
a wonderous strong game."
Sir Lybius said al soe [2] prest,

1148 "goe fforth & doe thy best;
Thy ratch with mee shall wend." [page 333]
they rode on right [3] west
througe a deepe fforrest,

Lybius says
"Do your
best,"

and rides on.

1152 then as the dwarffe them kend.[4]

Sir Otes de lile in *that* stower
rode home into his Tower,
& ffor his ffreinds sent,

Sir Otes

tells his
friends

1156 & told them anon-rights
how one of Arthurs K*nigh*ts
shamely had him shent,
& had his ratche away Iuome.[5]

how badly
Lybius has
treated him.

1160 then thé sayd all and some,[6]
*th*at " theese shall soone be tane ;
& neuer home shall hee come
tho he were as grim a groome

They say
they'll soon
take Lybius.

1164 as euer was S*ir* Gawaine." [7]

they dight them to armes
with gleaues [8] and gysarmes,[9]
as they wold warr on take ;

They and
their friends
arm,

1168 Knights and squiers

[1] bereaue, take away.—P.
[2] alsoe, MS.—F.
[3] *th* is crossed out between *t* and *w*. —F.
[4] taught, made known. Gl. Ch.—P.
[5] y-nome, taken. Sax. *niman*, to take, hinc *nim*. ¹Lye.—P.
[6] sone in MS.—F.

[7] þau₃ he were þo₃tyere gome
   Than Launcelot du lake.— Cot.
M. Hippeau prints "thogh tyer," which doesn't look much like "doughtier" at first. MS. is clear, leaf 50, col. 2, l. 5.—F.
[8] gleaue, a sword, cutlace, Fr. *glaire.* —P. swerdes.—Cot.
[9] gysarme, a halbert or Bill. Sk.—P.

leapt on their disteres
ffor their Lords sake.

vpon a hill trulye

1172   S*i*r Lybius they can espye,
ryding a well good pace.

to him gan they loud crye,
& said, "thou shalt dye

1176   ffor thy great trespas!"

S*i*r Lybius againe beheld
how ffull was the ffeild,
for many people there was;

1180   he said to Maid Ellen,
"ffor this ratch I weene
to vs commeth a carefull case.

"I rede *that* yee withdraw

1184   yonder into the woods wawe,[1]
your heads for to hyde;
ffor here vpon this plaine,

tho I shold be slaine,

1188   the battell I will abyde."

into the fforrest thé rode;
and S*i*r Lybius there abode
of him what may betyde.

1192   then thé smote at him with crossebowes,
with speare, & with bowes turkoys,[2]

that made him wounds wyde.

S*i*r Lybius with his horsse ran,

1196   & bare downe horsse and man;

Marginal notes (left column):

mount,

see Lybius.

and say they'll kill him.

Lybius

advises Hellen

to hide in the forest.

He will abide the battle.

Lybius's foes

fire at him with bows

and wound him.

He rides down men and horses,

---

[1] wode schawe.—Cot. *wawe* is used in Chauc*e*r for a *wave*, but that can hardly be the sense here.—P. ? *Waw*, wall. Jamieson.—F.

[2] i. e. longbowes. Fr. *Turquois*, Turkish, such as the Turks use. Gl. ad G.D.—P. See Strutt, p. 66, ed. 1830. —F.

With bowe and wi*th* arblaste
To hym they schote faste.—Cot.

ffor nothing wold he spare.
euery man said then
that hee was the ffeend Sathan   like Satan,
1200   *that* wold mankind fforfare [1] ;

ffor he *that* Sir Lybius raught,
his death wound there he caught,
  & smote them downe by-deene.
1204   but anon he was besett,   but is beset
as a ffish in a nett,
  with groomes [2] ffell and keene ;

for 12 Kn*igh*ts verelye   by twelve
1208   he saw come ryding redylye   knights
in armes ffaire & bright ;
all the day they had rest,   who have
for thé thought in the fforrest   waited for
                                        him,
1212   to see Sir Lybius *that* Knight.
in a sweate they were all 12,—
one was the Lo*rd* himselfe
  in they [3] ryme to read right :—
1216   they smote att him all att once,   and all
ffor they thought to breake his bones attack him
  & ffell him downe in flight.   at once.

ffast together can thé ding ;
1220   & round they stroakes he gan fflinge   Lybius
among them all in fere ;
fforsooth w*i*thout Leasing
the sparkells out gan springe
1224   of sheeld and harnesse [4] cleere.
Sir Lybius slew of them 3,   kills three
  & 4 away gan fflee   of them ;
                                         four flee.

---

[1] perdere, perire. A.-S. *furfuran.*   [3] the.—P. There is nothing of this
Lye.—P.   incident in the French.--F.
[2] men.—P.   [4] Only half the *n* in the MS.—F.

[page 334]

And wold not come him nere ;

Sir Otes and his four sons

1228   the Lord abode in *that* stoure,

    & soe did his sonnes 4,

        to sell their liues deere.

strike at Lybius.

then they gaue [1] stroakes riue,[2]

1232   he one against them 5,

    & flought as they were wood,

        nye downe they gan him bring ;

His blood flows,

as the water of a Spring

1236   of him ran the bloode ;

his sword breaks,

his sword brake by the hilte ;

    then was he neere spilt ;

        he was ffull madd of moode.

Sir Otes cuts into his head,

1240   the Lord a stroake on him sett

    through helme and Basnett,

        in the skull itt stoode.

and he swoons ;

then in a swoone he lowted lowe ;

1244   he leaned on his saddle bow

    as a man *that* was nye slake ;

        his 4 sonnes were all a bowne [3]

        ffor to perish [4] his Acton,[5]

1248   double Maile and plate ;

but soon he revives,

but as he gan to smart,

    againe he plucked vp [6] his hart,

        as the Kinde [7] of his estate ;

seizes his axe,

1252   & soone he hent in his ffist

    an axe *that* hanged on his sadle crest,

        almost itt was too late.

and kills three horses.

then he ffought as a Knight ;

1256   their horsses ffell downe right,

---

[1] gan.—P.
[2] riue, To thrust, stab, to rend, &c. Gl. ad Ch.—P. ? rife, all about.—F.
[3] ready.—P.
[4] perce.—Cot. persyne.—Lam. MS.

[5] Fr. Hocqueton.—P.
[6] Vp he pullede.—Cot. (leaf 50, back, col. 2.) He pulled vp.—Lam.
[7] Four strokes for *in* in the MS.—F.

he slew att stroakes 3.

& when the Lord saw the flight,

of his horsse a-downe gan light,[1]

1260   away hee ffast gan fllee.

Sir Lybius noe longer abode,

but after him ffast he rode,

& vnder a chest of tree [2]

1264   there he had him killed ;

but the Lord him ȝeelded

att his will ffor to bee,

& ffor to yeeld him his stent,[3]

1268   treasure, Land, and rent,

Castle, hall, & tower.

Sir Lybius consented therto

in [4] fforward that he wold goe

1272   vnto King Arthur,

& say, " Lord of great renowne !

in battell I am ouerthrowne ;

& sent thee to honor."

1276   the Lord granted theretill,

ffor to doe all his will.

they went home to his tower,

& anon Maiden Ellen

1280   with knights ffiueteene

was ffeitched into the Castle.

shee & the dwarffe by-deene

told of his deeds Keene,

1284   & how that itt befell

that hee had presents [5] 4

sent vnto King Arthur,

Side notes:

Sir Otes flees;

Lybius catches him,

and Sir Otes yields up himself

and all his lands and goods,

and agrees to go to King Arthur

and honour him.

They go to Sir Otes's castle. Hellen is brought there,

and tells Sir Otes that he is Lybius's fourth present to Arthur.

---

[1] And on hys courser lyȝt.-- Cot.

[2] a chesten tree, i.e. a Chesnut Tree. Sic legerim. vid. Gl. ad Chauc.—P. chesteyn.—Cot. chesteyne.— Lam.

[3] his stint, apud Salopienses, signifies his measure, his quantity, his share. —P. be sertayne extante.—Cot.

[4] MS. him.—F. in.—Cot.

[5] presentes.— Cot. persones.—Lam.

that he had woone ffull well.

1288 the *Lord* was glad & blythe,
& thanked god often sithe,
& alsoe S! Michall,[1]

that such a noble Knight
1292 shold ffor that Ladye ffight
that was soe ffaire and ffree.
in the towne dwelled a K*night* :
att the ffull ffortnight

Lybius

1296 S*ir* Lybyus[2] there gan bee,

recovers from his wounds

& did heale him of his wounds
bothe hole and sound
by the 6 weekes end.

and rides on towards Sinadon.

1300 then S*ir* Lybius and his May
rode fforthe on their way,
to Sinadon to wend ;
and alsoe the Lord of *that* tower

Sir Otes goes to Arthur,

1304 went vnto K*ing* Arthur,
& prisoner him did yeeld,
& told how a K*night* younge
in ffighting had him woone,

[page 335]

1308 & ouercome him in the ffeeld ;

and tells him how Lybius beat him.

& said, " L*ord* of great renowne !
I am in battell brought a-downe
with a K*night* soe bolde."
1312 K*ing* Arthur had good game,
& soe had they all in-same
that heard that tale soe told.[3]

---

[1] The Cotton text omits the rest of this part. The French of the whole part is very different.—F.

[2] One stroke too many for *u* in the MS. *There* means, I suppose, the house of the knight of l. 1294. The Lambeth MS. has :

Lybeous a fourtenyght
Then with him came lende,

He did helen his wounde,
And made him hole and sownde.
Corresponding nearly with our text.—F.

[3] The French puts in here its tale of the Falcon or Sparrow-hawk, which M. Hippeau summarises thus, p. x. :

L'Inconnu, Robert, Hélie, et son nain aperçoivent, en sortant du bois [where Lybius has vanquished *l'Orguillous de*

[The Sixth Part.]

[Lybius's Adventure at the Ile Dore.]

1316	Now let vs rest awhile of S*ir* Otes de lile, & tell wee other tales.	
6ᵈ parte 1320	S*ir* Lybius rode many a mile, sawe ¹ aduentures many & vile in England ² & in Wales,	Lybius fres adventures in England and Wales.
	till itt beffell in the monthe of June, when the ffenell ³ hangeth in the towne all greene in seemlye manner,⁴	
1324	The midsum*mer*⁵ day is ffaire & long ; merry is the ffoules songe, the notes of birds on bryar ⁶ ;	On Mid- summer day

la Lande, our Sir Otes], un castel d'où descend, pour venir à leur rencontre, une dame richement vêtue et d'une beauté ravissante. Elle leur apprend que celui qu'elle aimait a été tué par un chevalier redoutable qui habite le château. Là se trouve, dit-elle, un épervier perché sur un bâton d'or. La damoiselle qui pourra s'en emparer sera proclamée la plus belle ; mais elle devra se faire accompagner par un chevalier assez hardi pour oser se mesurer avec le maître de l'épervier. La pauvre damoiselle, désireuse d'obtenir le prix de la beauté, avait conduit à ce chateau son ami qui avait succombé dans une lutte inégale. "Je le vengerai, et vous serez reconnue comme la plus belle !" dit l'Inconnu, qui trouve l'occasion d'un nouveau triomphe. *Gifflet, le fils d'O*, est terrassé au effet ; et, comme l'Inconnu apprend que la jeune fille pour laquelle il vient de se battre est Marguerie, la fille du roi d'Écosse, Agolant, il l'a fait conduire chez son père par un chevalier dont la valeur et la loyauté sont éprouvées. Hélie reconnaît en elle sa cousine ; elle lui fait de tendres adieux. "Je ne sais," dit-elle avec sensibilité, " si jamais je vous re-

verrai, mais je vous aimerai toujours ! " --F.

¹ One stroke too many for the *w* in the MS.—F.

² Among aventurus fyle
In Yrland.—Cot.
and sey awntours the while
and [in] Irlande.—Lam,
Vile = fele, numerous.—F.

³ *cerfille and* fiunle | Chervil & fennel
fela mihtigu twa | Two very * mighty
(ones)
þa wyrte gesceop | These worts formed
witig drihten | (The) wit-full† Lord
halig on heofenum | Holy in heavens
þa he hongode sette | Them he set hung-
up ‡
and sænde on vii. | And sent to the 7
worulde | worlds
carmum *and* eadi- | For the poor & the
gum | rich
eallum to bote. | For a remedy § for
all.

Leechdoms, iii. 31-7, ed. Cockayne.

⁴ P. has added au *e* to the *r.*—F. sales.—Cot. saale.—Lam.

⁵ One stroke too few in the MS.—F.

⁶ briere.—P.

As notes of the ny3tyngales.—Cot. And notis of the nyghtyngale.—Lam.

* fair and.—Cockayne.
† Wise he and witty is.—C.

‡ he suspended. -C.
§ Panacea.—C.

Lybius

1328

Sir Lybius then gan ryde
along by a riuer side,
    & saw a ffaire Citye

sees a fair
city,

with pauillyons of much pride,
& a castle ffaire & wyde,

1332

and gates great plentye.

which
Hellen
tells him

he asked ffast what itt hight:
the maid said anon-right,
    "Sir, I will tell thee;

is Ile d'Ore,

1336

men clepeth itt Ile dore;[1]
there hath beene slaine Knights more
then beene in this countrye

and that a
lovely lady
is kept there

"ffor a Ladye *that* is of price,

1340

her coulour is red as rose on rise.[2]
    all this cuntry is in doubt

by the giant
Mangys,

ffor a Gyant *that* hight Mangys,[3]
there is noe more such theenes![4]

1344

that Ladye hee lyeth about;
he is heathen, as blacke as pitch;
now there be no more such
    of deeds strong & stout;

to whom
every knight
must bow,
and lay down
his armour.

1348

what Knight *that* passeth this brigg,
his armes he must downe ligg,
    & to the gyant Lout.[5]

1352

    "he is 20[6] ffoote of lenght,
& much more of strenght

---

[1] Isle Dor, Fr. Yledor.—Cot. Il-deore.—Lam. The French has a long description of the Castle, but nothing about the giant Mangys. It is a knight, *Malgiers li Gris* (p. 77), who there defends the entrance to the castle; and if he conquers every comer for seven years (or nine according to M. Hippeau) he is to wed *La Dame aux blanches Mains.* The knight has killed 143 opponents, and cut their heads off (p. 71, l. 1985), when he is overcome by Lybius.—F.

[2] sprig, twig, shrub, Jun. Lye.—P.

[3] Maungys.—Cot.

[4] Nowhere hys pere ther nys.—Cot. Nowhere is non suche.—Lam.

[5] MS. Cot. omits the next twelve lines. —F.

[6] thirty.—Lam.

then other K*nigh*ts ffiue.

S*i*r Lybius! now [1] bethinke thee,

hee is more grim*mn*er ffor to see

She warns
Lybius not
to fight him.

1356   then any one aliue; [2]

he beareth haires on his brow

like the bristles of a sow;

    his head is great & stout [3];

1360 eche arme is the lenght of an ell,

his ffists beene great & ffell,

    dints ffor to driue about."

S*i*r Lybius said, " maiden hend !

Lybius says

1364 on our way wee will wend

ffor all his stroakes ill.

if god will me grace send,

that by
God's help
he'll kill
him before
the day ends.

or this day come to an end

1368   I hope him ffor to spill. [4]

tho I be young & lite, [5]

I will him sore smyte,

    & let god doe his will.

1372 I beseech god almight

*th*at I may see w*i*th him ffight,

    *th*at giant [6] ffor to kill."

then they rode fforth all 3

Near

1376 vnto *th*at ffaire cytye,

    men call itt Ile dore [7];

Ile d'Ore

anon Mangy can they see

they see
Mangys

    vpon a bridge of tree,

1380 as grimm as any bore;

---

[1] well.—Lam.
[2] That thou with him no macched bee,
    He is gryme to Diseryue.—Lam.
[3] grete as an hyve.—Cot.
[4] Cot. inserts here:
    I haue y-seyn grete okes
    Falle fore wyndes strokes,

þe smale han stonde stylle,
and omits the last three lines of the
stanza. Lam. does the same, altering
the words a little.—F.
[5] lite, little.—P.
[6] MS. grant.—F. giant, qu.—P.
[7] Ylledore.—Cot. Hedolour.—Lam.

[page 336]

<table>
<tr><td>with a black shield,</td><td></td><td>his sheild was blacke as ter [1];</td></tr>
</table>

with a black shield,

     his sheild was blacke as ter [1] ;

     his paytrill,[2] his crouper,[3]

        3 mammetts [4] there-in were ;

1384   thé were gaylye gilt with gold ;

a spear and sword.

     & a spere in his hand he did hold,

     & alsoe his sword in ffere.

     He cryed to him in despite,

Mangys asks Lybius who he is,

1388   & said, "ffellow, I thee quite ! [5]

     now what thou art, mee tell;

and advises him to turn back.

     & turne againe al soe [6] tyte

     ffor thine owne proffitt,

1392   if thou loue thy selfe well."

Lybius

     Sir Lybius said anon-right,

     "King Arthur made me a Knight.

     vnto him I made my vow

refuses.

1396   *that* I shold neuer turne my backe

     ffor noe such deuill in blacke.

     goe ! make thee readye now ! "

They charge

     Now Sir Lybius & Mangys,

1400   Of horsses [7] proud of price

     together they rode full right;

(Lords and ladies

     both Lords & Ladyes there

     Lay on pount tornere [8]

1404   to see *that* seemlye sight,

---

[1] tar.—F. perhaps as *Aster*, *Haster*, or *Aster* is a word still used in Shropshire, signifying the back of the chimney. "As black as the Haster" is a common expression with *them*.—P. pych.—Cot. pycche.—Lam. The French knight's shield is *Sinople*, greene colour (in Blazon).—Cotgrave :
Les escus à sinople estoit,
Et mains blances parmi avoit (p. 73).—F.

[2] Poitrel, peytrel, *antilena* : The breast-armour for a horse. Jun.—P.

[3] croupere.—P.

[4] Mammet, a puppet, an Image, a false-god. Jun.—P. One stroke too many in the MS.—F.

[5] Say, þou felaw yn whyt.—Cot. & Lam.

[6] MS. alsoe.—F.

[7] On Horses.—P. On stedes.—Cot. & Lam.

[8] ? *Pont Tornere*, the name of the bridge.—F.
Leyn out yn pomet tours.—Cot.
Laynen in her toures.—Lam.
The French text brings them all out of the castle, except La Dame aux blanches Mains.—F.

    & prayed to god loud & still,   pray that

    " if *that* itt were his will,

       to helpe *that* cristyan Knight;   Lybius may

1408   & the vile Gyaunt   kill Mangys).

    *tha*t beleeueth in Termagant,

    that he might dye in ffight ! "

    theire speres brake assunder,   Their spears break;

1412   their stroakes flared as the thunder,[1]

    the peeces gan out spring.

    euery man had great wonder

    that Sir Lybius had not beene vnder

1416   att the flirst begininge.

    anon they drew sords bothe ;   they draw their swords;

    as men *that* were ffull wrothe,

    together gan they dinge :

1420   Sir Lybius smote Mangyes thoe   Lybius cuts away

    *tha*t his sheild ffell him ffroe,   Mangys's shield ;

    in the ffeild he gan itt flling.

    Mangyes gan smite in *that* stead   Mangys kills Lybius's

1424   Sir Lybius horse on the head,   horse,

    & dashed out his braine ;

    his horsse fell downe dyinge.

    Sir Lybius sayd nothing,

1428   but start vp againe ;

    an axe in his hand he hent anon   and Lybius

    that hunge on his sadle arson,[2]

    & smote a stroake of maine

1432   through Mangis horsse swire,[3]   kills his.

    carued him throug long[4] & liuer,[5]

    & quitt him well againe.

---

[1] The first part of *thunder* is blotted in the MS.—F. donder.—Cot. thonder. —Lam.

[2] arçon. Fr. i.e. saddle bow.--P.

[3] swire, swere, the neck. Gl. ad Ch. —P.

[4] through lung.—P.

[5] P. has added an *e* to the end of *liuer*.—F.
fore-karf bon and lyre.— Cot.
forkarve bone and lyre. Lam.

descriue the stroakes cold no man

1436   *that* were giuen betwene them then ;

¹ to bedd peace was no boote thee ;

deepe wounds there they caught,

ffor they both sore ffought,

1440   & either was others ffoe.

ffro : the hower of prime

till it was euensong time,

they ffought together thoe.

1444   Si*r* Lybius thirsted then sore,

& sayd, " Mangyes, thine ore ² !

to drinke lett me goe ;

" & I will grant to thee,

1448   what loue ³ thou biddest mee,

such happe if thee betyde.

great shame itt wold bee

a K*night* ffor thirst shold dye,

1452   & to thee litle pryde."

Mangies granted him his will,

ffor to drinke his ffill

wi*th*out any more despite.

1456   as Si*r* Lybius lay ouer the banke,

through his helme he dranke ;

Mangyes gan him smite

that into the riuer he goes.

1460   but vp anon he rose ;

wonderffull he was dight

wi*th* his armour euery deale ;

"now by S! Micaheel

1464   I am twise as light !

---

¹ It was no boot then to bid (propose)
peace.—P. Cot. and Lam. have different lines.—F.

² mercy.—F.
³ bone.—C. & Lam.

what weenest thout ffeend fere ?

that I vnchirstened were

or thou saw itt with sight ?

1468   I shall, ffor thy baptise,   [page 337]

well qu[i]tte thee thy service,

by the grace of god almight."

a new battell there began ;

1472   either ffast to other ran,

& stroakes gaue with might.

there was many a gentleman,

and alsoe Ladyes as white as swan,

1476   they prayed all ffor the Knight.

but Mangis anon in the ffeild

carued assunder Sir Lybius sheild

with stroakes of armes great.

1480   then Sir Lybius rann away

thither were Mangis sheild Lay ;

& vp he can itt gett,

& ran againe to him [1] ;

1484   with stroakes great and grim

together they did assayle ;

there beside the watter brimne

till it waxed wonderous dimm,

1488   betweene them lasted *that* battell.[2]

Sir Lybius was warryour wight,

& smote a stroke of much might ;

through hawberke,[3] plate and maile,

1492   hee smote of by the shoolder bone

his right arme soone and anon

into the ffeild with-out ffaile.

---

[1] One stroke too many in MS.—F.
[2] battayle.—P.

[3] coat of mail, *thro' plate & mail*, is used both by Milton & Spencer.—P.

Mangys

¹ when the gyant *that* gan see

1496   *that* he shold slaine bee,

flees,   hee filled w*ith* much maine.

Lybius   Sir Lybius after him gan hye,
pursues him,
and cuts his   & w*ith* strong stroakes mightye
back in two,

1500   smote his backe in twaine.

thus was the Gyant dead :

and his head   Sir Lybius smote of his head ;
off.
then was the people flaine.²

Lybius goes   1504   Sir Lybius bare the head to the towne ;
into the
town,   thó mett him w*ith* a ffaire procession,

the people came him againe.

and is   a Ladye white as the Lyllye fllower,
received by
the beautiful 1508   hight Madam de Armoroure,³
Madam de
Armoroure,   receiued *that* gentle Knight,

& thanked him in *that* stoure

---

¹ The Ashmole MS. 61 reads :

Tho gyant*e* gan*e* to se
That sleyne schuld [he] be :
He stode to fense A-ȝeyne,
And at þe second stroke
Syr*e* lybeus to hy*m* smote,
And brake hys Arme in tweyne.
The gyante þer he lenyd,
lybeus smote of bys hede,
   There-of he was full feyne ;
He bore þe hed in-to þe tou*n*e.
W*ith* A feyre prosessyou*n*
   The folke co*m*e hy*m* A-ȝone.
That lady was whyte As flowre
That men callyd denamowre.
                    &c. &c.

² glad.—P. And of þe batayle was
fayn.—Cot.
   ³ The French text has a glowing description of the lady's beauty (p. 78-9):

Sa biauté tel clarté jeta,
Quant ele ens le palais entra,
Com la lune qu'ist de la nue . .
Plus estoit blance d'une flor,
Et d'une vermelle color
Estoit sa face enluminée:
Moult estoit bele et colorée.
Les oels ot vair, boce riant,

Le cors bien faict et avenant ;
Les levres avoit vermelletes,
[one Line wanting in the MS.]
Boce bien faite por baisier,
Et bras bien fais por embracer.
Mains ot blances com flors de lis,
Et la gorges, desous le vis.
Cors ot bien fait, et le cief blont ;
Onques si bele n'ot el mont.
Ele estoit d'un samit vestue,
Onques si bele n'ot sous nue,
La pene en fu moult bien ouvrée
D'ermine tote eschekerée ;
Moult sont bien fait li eschekier,
Li orles fu mout a prisier ;
Et deriere ot ses crins jetés ;
D'un fil d'or les ot galonés.
De roses avoit i capel
Moult avenant et gent et bel ;
D'un afremail son col frema,
Quant ele ens el palais entra.
Molt i ot gente damoisele,
Onques nus hom ne vit tant bele.
La dame entre el palais riant,
Al Desconnéu vint devant . .
There is a further description of her
in her *cemise* at p. 84-5.—F.
    ⁴ la dame damore.—Cot.
      la dame Amoure.—Lam.

that hee wold her succour

1512 against *that* ffeend to flight.

into the chamber shee him ledd, who clothes him in purple,

& in purple & pall shee him cledd,

& in rich royall weede ;

1516 & profferred him with honor and offers him her lands and herself.

ffor to be lord of towne & tower,

& her owne selfe to meede.

Sir Lybius ffrened [1] her in hast,

1520 & loue to her anon he cast, He gives her his love,

ffor shee was ffaire and sheene.

alas, *that* hee had not beene chast !

ffor afterwards att the Last

1524 shee did him betray & teene.[2] but she betrays him at last. Lybius stays twelve months there,

12 monthes and more

Sir Lybius tarryed thore,[3]

& his mayden with renowne,

1528 *that* he might neuer out scape

ffor to helpe & ffor to wrake[4]

the Ladye of Sinadone ;

ffor *that* ffaire Lady beguiled by the Lady's sorcery,

1532 told[5] more of Sorcery

then such other fliue ;

shee made him great melodye,

of all manner of minstrelsye

1536 *that* any man cold discreeue.

---

[1] asked.—P. gräntede.—Cot.

[2] curage, vex, grieve, Gl. ad G.D.
N.B. This does not appear from anything which follows in this Ballad: unless it be her detaining him by her enchantments in these stanzas.—P.

[3] there: so in Chauc.—P. The French Romance keeps Lybius only a night in the castle. The Lady comes to him in her chemise, leans on his breast :
Ses mameles et sa poitrine
Furent blauces comme flors d'espine ;

Se li ot desus son pis mis. (p. 85-6.)
She desires his love. He wants to kiss her, but she draws back, as that would be lechery till he had married her, and leaves his room. He has troubled dreams, thinking he holds her all night in his arms, and next morning he resolutely rides away, but returns after freeing the Lady of Sinadowne.—F.

[4] wreak, i. e. revenge.—P.

[5] for *cold*, knew.—F.

for, when
looking on
her,
he thinks
himself in
Paradise.

when he looked on her fface,
him thought certainlye *that* hee was
in paradice aliue,
1540 with ffantasye and fayrye;
& shee bleared his eye
with ffalse sorcerye.

[The Seventh Part.]

At last,
Hellen meets
him,

1544   till itt beffell vpon a day
he mett with Ellen *that* may
betwene the Castle and the tower;

and
reproaches
him
with his
faithlessness
to Arthur

Then vnto him shee gan say,   [page 338]
"thou art ffalse of thy ffay [1]
vnto King Arthur!
ffor the loue of that Ladye
that can soe much curtesye,
thou doest thee dishonor!

1548
7ᵈ Parte.

and the Lady
of Sinadon.

1552   My Ladye of Sinadon
may long lye in prison,
& *that* is great dolour!"

Lybius is
touched to
the heart,

Sir Lybius hard her speake,
1556   him thought his hart wold breake
ffor sorrow & ffor shame.

and they
ride off that
night.

att a posterne there beside
by night they gan out ryde
1560   ffrom *that* gentle dame.

Lybius

hee tooke with him his good steede,
his sheeld & his best weede,
& rode fforth all in-same;
1564   & the [2] steward stout in ffere,

makes Sir
Geffelett his
steward,

he made him his Squier,
Sir Geffelett [3] was his name.

---

[1] faith.—P.   [2] Her.—Cot. Hir.—Lam.   [3] Gyfllet.—Cot. Gurflete.—Lam.

they rode fforth on their way,

1568   but lightly on their Iourney,

on bay horsses and browne ;

till itt beffell vpon a day

they saw a Citye ffaire and gay,

1572   men call itt Sinadowne,[1]

with a Castle hye & wyde,

and pauillyons of much pride

that were of ffaire ffashyon.

1576   then said Sir Lybius

"I haue [2] great wonder of an vse

that he saw [3] in the towne ; "

they gathered dirt & mire ffull ffast :

1580   wh*i*ch beffore was out cast,[4]

they gathered in I-wis.

Sir Lybius said in hast,

"tell me now, mayd chast,

1584   what betokeneth this ?

they take in all their hore [5]

that was cast out beffore !

methinke they doe amisse."

1588   then sayd Mayd Ellen,

"Sir Lybius, w*i*thout Leasing

I will tell thee why itt is.

"there is no K*i*ng soe well arrayed,

1592   tho he had before payd,

that there shold take ostell,[6]

ffor a dread of a steward

that men call Sir Lamberd ;

1596   he is the constable of the Castle.

Margin notes:

and they ride on

till they see Sina-downe.

Lybius asks why they are

drawing into the city the dirt that was before cast out of it :

What does it mean ?

Hellen answers

that no one can lodge there

for fear of Sir Lamberd.

---

[1] synadowne.—Cot. Lam. *La Cité Gaste* is the French name of Sinadowne ; but this preliminary castle is called *Galigans.*—F.

[2] He had (or).

[3] I see.—P. The Cotton MS. reads: But lybeaus desconus

He hadde wonder of an vus *þat* he saw do yn tonne.

[4] For gore, and fen, and full wast, That there was out y-kast.— Cot.

[5] Sax. *horh*, fimus, scruta, phlegma. limus. Bens. Voc.—P.

[6] Fr. *hostel*, hospitium, Domus.—P.

but ride into the Castle gate,

& aske thine inne theratt

both flaire and well ;

1600   & or he bidd thee nede,

lusting he will thee bedd,

by god & by S! Michaell !

" & if he beare thee downe,

1604   his trumpetts[1] shalbe bowne,

their beangles[2] ffor to blow ;

then ouer all this towne,

both mayd & garsowne[3]

1608   but dirt on thee shall throwe ;

& but thou thither wend,

vnto thy lines end

cowarde thou shalt be know ;

1612   & soe may King Arthur

losse all his great honor

for thy deeds slowe ! "

Sir Lybins sayd, " *that* were despite !

1616   thither I will goe ffull tyte,

if I be man on line ;

ffor to doe Arthurs delight,

& to make *that* Lady quite,

1620   to him I will drine.

Sir Geffelett, make thee ready,

& lett vs now goe hastilye,

anon *that* wee were bowne."

1624   they rode fforth on their gate

till they came[4] to the Castle gate

That was of great renowne,

[page 339]

---

[1] Trumpetters.—P.
[2] bugles, hunting horns ; from bugle,
a wild bull, Lye.—P.

[3] Fr. Garçon, Boy.—P.
[4] *cane* in the MS.—F.

& there they asked Ostell
1628 in *that* ffaire Castell
  ffor a venturous knight.

and ask for lodging.

the porter ffaire & well
lett them in ffull snell,

The porter

1632 & asked anon-right,
"who is *your* gouernour?"

asks who their Governor is.

they sayd, "King Arthur,
a man of much might.

"King Arthur,

1636 to be a king he is worthye,
he is the fflower of Chiualrye,
  his ffone to ffell in flight."

the flower of chivalry!"

the porter went without ffable

The porter

1640 to his lord the Constable,
  & this tale him told:

tells Lamberd

"Sir, without any flable,
of Arthurs round table

that two of Arthur's knights have come.

1644 be comen 2 knights bold.
the one is armed ffull sure
with rich & royall armoure,
  with 3 Lyons of gold."

1648 the Lord was gladd & blythe,

Lamberd

& said to them ffull swythe,
  Iust with them hee wold:

says they

"bidd them make them yare [1]

are to get ready to fight.

1652 into the ffeeld ffor to ffare
  without the Castle gate."
the porter wold not stent,[2]

The porter

but euen anon went
1656 to them lightlye att the yate,
  & sayd anon-rightes,

tells them

"yee aduenturous knights,

---

[1] ready, Sax. *Gearwe.*—P. *se gearwa,* Bosworth.—F. [2] stint, stop.—P.

ffor nothing *that* yee Lett ;
1660 Looke yo*ur* sheelds be good & strong,
& yo*ur* speres good and long,
sheild, plate, & Basnett,

to ride into
the field,
and his
lord will
fight them.

" & ryde you into the ffeild ;
1664 my Lord w*i*th speare and sheild
anon w*i*th you will play."
Sir Lybius spake words bold,
& said, " this tale is well told,
1668 & pleasant to my pay.[1] "

They ride in,
into the feld th*e* rode,
and wait for
& boldlye there abode
in their best array.[2]

Lamberd,
1672 S[ir] Lamberd armed ffull weele
both in Iron and in steele
that was both stout & gay ;

whose shield
his sheeld was sure & ffine,
1676 3 bores heads was therin
is black,
as blacke as brond brent,[3]
the bordure was of rich armin,—
there was none soe quent[4] a ginn[5]
1680 ffrom Carlile into Kent,—
& of the same paynture
his armour
too.
was his paytrell & his armoure.
in lande where ener he went,
Two squires
attend him,
1684 2 squiers w*i*th him did ryde,
& bare 3 speares by his side
to deale w*i*th doughtye dint.

then *that* stout stewared
1688 *that* hight Sir Lamberd

---

[1] liking.—P.
[2] As best bro3t to bay.—C.
  As bestis brought to baye.—Lam.
[3] i.e. burnt brand.—P.
[4] quent, queint.—P.
[5] ginne, trick, contrivance.—P.

armed him ffull well & bright,
& rode into the ffeild ward—

and he rides
into the
field as fierce
as a leopard.

ffeircely as any Libbard—
1692   there abode him *that* knight.
him tooke a speare of great shape;[1]
he thought he came to Late.
when he him saw w*i*th sight,

Lybius
charges him,

1696   soone he[2] rode to him *that* stond
w*i*th a speare *that* was round,
as a man of much might.

Either smote on others sheeld

and both
shatter their
spears.

1700   *that* the peeces ffell in the ffeild
of theire speares long.
euery man to other tolde
"*that* younge K*n*ight is ffull bold."
1704   to him w*i*th a speare he fllounge;
S*i*r Lamberd did stifflye ssitt;
he was wrath out of his witt
ffor Ire and ffor teene,[3]   [page 340]
1708   & sayd, " bring me a speare !
ffor this Knight is not to Lere,
soone itt shalbe scene."[4]

then they tooke shaftes round,

They charge
again with
fresh spears.

1712   w*i*th crownalls sharpe ground,
& ffast to-gether did run ;
either proued other in *that* stond
to give either theire deaths wound,
1716   w*i*th harts as ffeirce as any Lyon.
Lamberd smote S*i*r Lybius thoe

Lamberd
knocks
Lybius's

that his sheeld ffell him ffroe

---

[1] He smote hys schaft yn grate.—C.
He sette his sheldo in grate.—Lam.
[2] Lybeanus.- C. Lyboous.—Lam.
[3] anger, madness, vexation.—P.

[4] He cryde, " Do come a strangere
schaft !
 ȝyf artours knyȝt kan craft,
 Now hyt schalle be sene.— Cot.

into the ffeild a-downe ;

1720 S*i*r Lamberd him soe hitt

shield on the ground,

that vnnethes [1] hee might sett

vpright in his arsowme,[2]

and nearly unhorses him.

his shaft brake with great power.

1724 S*i*r Lybins hitt him on the visor

that of went his helme bright ;

the pesanye,[3] ventayle,[4] & gorgere,[5]

Lybius cuts off Lamberd's helm,

with the helme fllew fforth in fere,

1728 & S*i*r Lamberd vpright

sate rocking[6] in his sadle

as a chyld in a cradle

without maine & might.

and makes him rock in his saddle like a child in a cradle.

1732 euery man tooke other by the lappe,

& laughed and gan their hands clappe,

barron, Burgesse, and K*n*ight.

Lamberd gets another helm,

S*i*r Lamberd, he thought to sitt bett ;

1736 another helme he made to ffett,[7]

& a shaft ffull meete.

and they charge againe.

& when they together mett,

either other on their helmes sett

1740 strokes grim & great.

then S*i*r Lamberds speare brast,

Lybius

& S*i*r Lybius sate soe ffast

---

[1] scarcely.—P.

[2] saddle.—P. arsoun.—C.

[3] pysane.—C. pesanie.—Lam. In *The Anturs of Arthur*, st. xlv. ed. Robson, p. 21, is:

He girdus to Syr Gauane
Throзhe ventaylle and *pusane* ;

on which Dr. Robson observes, p. 99, "This was either the Gorget or a substitute for it. In the Acts of Parliament of Scotland (anno 1429) vol. ii. p. 8, it is ordered that every one worth 20*l.* a year, or 100*l.* in moveable goods, 'be wele horsit and haill enarmyt as a gen-

till man aucht to be. And uther sympillare of X lib. of rent, or L lib. in gudes haif hat, gorgeat or *pesaune*, with rerebrasares, vambrasares, and gluffes of plate, breast plate, and leg splentes at the lest, or better gif him likes.'"—F.

[4] auentayle.—C. ventail, The Part of the Helmet wh*i*ch lifts up. Johns.—P.

[5] Gorgere, id. ae Gorget. The Piece of Arm*o*ur which defends the throat. Johns.—P.

[6] One stroke too many in this word in the MS.—F.

[7] fett, fetch.—P.

in the saddle there hee [1] sett,

1744 that they Constable Sir Lamberd

ffell of his horsse backward,

soe sore they there mett.

unhorses
Lamberd,

Sir Lamberd was ashamed sore.

1748 Sir Lybius asked if he wold more.[2]

he answered and said " nay !

ffor sithe *that* euer I was bore,

saw I neuer here beffore

and asks
him if he
wants any
more.
" No," says
Lamberd,

1752 none ryde soe to my pay !

by the faith *that* I am in,

thou art come of Sir Gawayines kin,

thou[3] art soe stout and gay.

"you must be
of Gawaine's
blood ;

1756 if thou wilt flight ffor my Ladye,

welcome thou art to mee,

by my troth I say ! "

will you
fight for
my lady ? "

Sir Lybius sayd, " sikerlye

1760 I will flight for my Ladye ; [4]

I promised soe to King Arthur ;

but I ne wott how ne why

who does her *that* villanye,

" Certainly I
will.

1764 ne what is her dolor ;

but this maid *that* is her mesenger,

certes has brought me here

her ffor to succour."

Hellen has
brought me
here to help
her."

1768 Sir Lamberd said in *that* stond

" welcome, Sir Kniyht of the table round,

into my strong tower ! "

Lamberd
welcomes
him to his
tower.

then mayd Ellen anon-rightes

1772 was ffetched fforth with 5 Knights

---

[1] One stroke too many in this word in the MS.—F.

[2] The French omits this question ; makes *Lampars* go to Lybius and say :
" Sire," fait-il, " ça. descendés ;
Par droit avés l'ostel conquis :
Vos l'auerés a vo devis,"

then embrace Hellen or *Hélie*, and ask her what she did (at Arthur's court).—F.

[3] A letter is crossed out at the end of this word in the MS.—F.

[4] fleyȝte y schalle for a lady.— C. flyght y shall for thy ladye.—Lam.

                    beffore Sir Lamberd.

        shee & the dwarffe by-deene
        told of 6 battells [1] keene

1776   that he had done thitherward :

        thé sayd that Sir Lybius then
        had ffought with strong men,
            & beene in stowers hardye.

1780   then they were glad & blythe,
            & thanked god alsoe sithe [2]
            that he were soe mightye.

        they welcomed him with mild cheere,

1784   & sett them to supper
            with much mirth and game.

        Sir Lybius & Sir Lamberd in ffere
        of ancyents that beffore were

1788   talked both in[3]-same.

Lybius asks
what knight
has im-
prisoned the
Lady of
Sinadowne.
        Sir Lybius sayd, " with-out ffable,[4]   [page 341]
        tell me now, Sir Constable,
            what is the Knights name

1792   that hath put in prison
            my Ladye of Sinadon
            that is soe gentle a dame ? "

        Sir Lamberd said, " soe mote I gone,

1796   Knights there beene none
            that dare her away Lead ;

        2 Clarkes beene her ffone,
        ffull ffalse in body & in bone,

1800   that hath done this deed.
        they be men of Masterye

            their artes ffor to reade of Sorcerye ;

---

[1] Tolde seven dedes.—Cot.   [3] im in the MS.—F.
[2] fele syde.— C. fele sythe.—Lam.   [4] There is none of this in the French.
' Swithe' is quickly.-- F.   - F.

Mabam [1] thé hight one in deede,   Mabam

1804 & Iron hight the other verelye,[2]   and Iron,

cla[r]ckes [3] of Nigromancye,   necro-
                                        mancers,

of them wee haue great dread.

" this Mabam & Irowne

1808 haue made in the towne   have made a
                                        curious
                                        palace that
a palace of quent gin [4] ;   no one dare
                                        enter,
there is no Erle ne barron

that has hart as Lyon

1812 *that* dare come therin ;

itt is all of the ffaierye   as it's
                                        wrought by
wrought by Nigromancye,

that wonder it is to winne.

1816 there they keepe in prison   necromancy;
                                        and there
my Ladye of Sinadowne,   they keep the
                                        Lady of
that is of K*nigh*ts kinn.[5]   Sinadowne,

" oftentimes wee her crye ;

1820 ffor to see [6] her with eye,

therto we haue no might.

this Mabam & Iron trulye

had sworene to death trulye   and will put
                                        her to death,
1824 her death ffor to dight,

but if shee grant vntill   unless she

ffor to do Mabams will,

& giue him all her right   gives up her
                                        dukedom to
1828 of all *that* Dukedome ffayre,   Mabam.

therof is my ladye heyre

that is soe much of might.

" shee is soe meeke & soe ffaire ;

1832 therfore wee be in dispayre

---

[1] Syr Maboune.—C.
  'syr Irayn hys brother.—C. Irayne.
—Lam.
[3] Clarkes.—P.

[4] Curious contrivance.—P.
[5] The *n* is made over an *e*, or *vice
versâ*, in the MS.—F.
[6] A *v* follows and is crossed out.—F.

ffor the dolour *that* shees in."
then sayd Sir Lybius,

1836 "through the helpe of Iesus
 that Ladye I will winne ;
& Mabam & Iron,
smite of there anon

he'll cut off
the heads of
Mabam and
Iron,

 theire heads in *that* stoure,
1840 & winne that Lady bright,
& bring her to her right

 with ioy & much honor." [1]

then there was no more tales to tell

1844 in *that* strong Castle.
 to supp & make good cheere,[2]

the Barrons & Burgesse all
came to *that* seemlye hall

1848 ffor to listen & heare

how Sir Lybius had wrought;
& if the Kni*ght* were ought,

 his talking for to harke.[3]
1852 they ffound them sitting in ffere
talking, att their supper,
 of Kni*ghts* stout and starke.

---

[1] C. omits the next twelve lines, (and alters many before).—F.

[2] Tho was no more tale

I the Castell grete and smale,
But stouped and made hym blythe.
 —Lam.

[3] His crafte for to kythe.—Lam.

[The Eighth Part.]

[Of Lybius's Adventures in Sinadowne, and how he conquers the Lady's Enchanters.]

   & after they went to rest,   All go to bed.

1856 & tooke their likeing[1] as them list[2]

   in *that* Castell all night.

   On the morrow anon-right   Next

   Sir Lybius was armed bright;   morning

1860   ffresh he was to flight.

   Sir Lamberd led him algate[3]   Lamberd

8ᵈ parte   right vnto the Castle gate;   takes

   open they were ffull right;   Lybius to

                       the castle

1864   no man durst him neere bringe   gates,

   fforsooth, with-out Leasing,   but no man

   Barron, Burgess, ne *Knight*,   dares go in

                       with him.

   But turned home againe.

1868   Sir Gefflet his owne swaine[4]   His sqmire

   wold with him ryde,   wants to,

   but Sir Lybius ffor certaine   but Lybius

   Sayd he shold backe againe,[1] [page 342] forbids him.

1872   and att home abyde.

   Sir Gefllett againe gan ryde[5]

   with Sir Lamberd ffor to abyde;

   & to Iesu christ they[6] cryed,   All pray for

                       the sorcerers'

1876   ffor to send them tydings gladd deaths.

   of them *that* long had

   destroyed their welthes wyde.

---

[1] Only half the *n* in the MS.—F.

[2] þo toke þeye hare reste,
In lykynge as hem leste.—C.
Tho toke they case and Reste,
And lykynges of the beste.—Lam.

[3] at all events, by all means.—P.
The French makes *Lampars* descrile

to Lybius what he will see, and what
he is to do, in *la Cité Gaste*, (p. 98-100).—F.

[4] youth, servant. Jun.—P.

[5] The Cotton text makes Gefllett stop
at the castle, l. 1754.—F.

[6] sc. the People.—P.

880 Sir Lybius, Knight curteous,
  rode into that proud palace,[1]
   & att the hall he light.
  trumpetts, hornes, & shaumes[2] ywis
  he ffound beffore the hye dese,[3]

1884 he heard, & saw with sight.
  a ffayre ffyer there was stout & stowre
  in the midds of the flore,
   brening ffaire and bright.[4]

1888 then ffurther in hee yeed,
  & tooke with him his steede
   that helped him to flight.

  ffurthermore he began to passe,

1892 & beheld then euerye place
   all about the hall ;

  of nothing, more ne lesse,
  he saw no body that there was,

1896 but minstrells cladde in pall,
  with harpe, ffidle & note,[5]

  & alsoe with Organ note,—
   great mirth they made all,—

1900 & alsoe fiddle and santrye[6] ;
  soe much of minstrelsye
   ne say[7] he neuer in hall.

  before euery man stood

1904 a torch ffayre and good,
   brening ffull bright.

  Sir Lybius Euermore yode[8]
  ffor to witt[9] with Egar mood

1908 who shold with him flight.

---

[1] The French text describes the
palace, p. 101.—F.
 [2] shaumes, a Psaltery : a Musical In-
strument like a Harp. Cham.'Gl.—P.
 [3] Dese, Deis. The high table.— P.
 [4] Was lyȝt & brende bryȝt.—C.

That tente and brende bright.—Lam.
[5] rote.—C. lute and roote.—Lam.
[6] a Psaltery, vid. Supra.—P.
[7] saw.—P.
[8] went.—P.
[9] know.—P.

hee went into all the corners,
& beheld the pillars
 that seemelye [1] were to sight;
1912 of Iasper ffine & Cristall,
all was fflourished in the hall;
itt was ffull fflaire & bright.

the dores were all of brasse,
1916 & the windowes of ffaire glasse,
 that ymagyrye itt was driue.
the hall well painted was;
noe ffairer in noe place;
1920 maruelous ffor to descriue.
hee sett him on the hye dese:
then the minstrells were in peace
 that made the mirth soo gay,
1924 the torches that were soo bright
were quenched anon-right,
 & the minstrells were all away;

the dores & the windowes all,
1928 thé bett [2] together in the hall
 as it were strokes of thunder;
the stones in the Castle wall
about him downe gan ffall;—
1932 thereof he had great wonder;—
the earth began to quake,
& the dese ffor to shake
 that was him there vnnder [3];
1936 the hall began for to breake,
& soe did the wall eke,
 as they shold ffall assunder.

as he sate thus dismayd,
1940 he held himselfe betrayd.

Side notes:

but only sees jasper pillars,

brass doors, &c.,

in the decorated hall.

He sits on the dais, and at once the music stops,

the torches go out,

the minstrels vanish,

the doors and windows clash together,

all the stones of the wall fall down,

the earth quakes,

the hall and walls begin to crack.

---

[1] In line 1910 in the MS.—F. [2] They beat.—P. [3] there vnder.—P.

Then he
hears horses
neigh. He
says there's
some one to
fight,
and sees

then horses heard hee nay :

to himselfe then he sayd,

"now I am the better apayd,

1944   for yett I hope to play."

hee looked fforth into the ffeild,

saw there with speare and sheild [1]

two men of
arms

men of armes tway,[2]

1948   in purple & pale armoure

well arrayed.

well harnished in *that* stoure,

with great garlands gay.

One rides
into the
hall,
and tells
Lybius he
must fight
them.

The one came ryding into the hall,   [page 343]

1952   & to him thus gan call,

"*Sir Knight* aduenturous !

such a case there is befall ;

tho thou bee proude in pall,

1956   ffight thou must with vs.

I hold thee quent of ginne [3]

if thou my Ladye winne [4]

that is in prison."

Lybius

1960   Sir Lybius sayd anon-right,

is quite
willing,

"all ffresh I am ffor to ffight,

with the helpe of goddes sonne."

Sir Lybyus with good hart

mounts,

1964   ffast into the saddle he start ;

in his hand a speare he hent,

& ffeircly he rode him till,

his enemyes ffor to spill ;

1968   ffor *that* was his entent.

---

[1] There is a stroke between the *e* and
i in the MS.—F.

[2] The French postpones the darkness,
&c., and makes Lybius first see and fight
a single knight (p. 103, *Evrains li fiers*,
p. 119), and put him to flight ; then fight
another (*Mabons*, p. 119), on a horse with
a horn in his forehead, and fire shooting
out of his nostrils, (p. 105-8). Then
comes the darkness, and a horrible noise ;

Lybius thinks of *La Damoiselle aux
blances melas*, and commends himself
to God ; the *Wivre* (Lat. *vipera*) appears,
comes near him, and kisses him ; he is
stupefied ; a voice tells him who he is ;
he dreams ; and on waking sees the
lovely *Esmeree*, who tells him her story.
-- F.

[3] clever of contrivance.—P.

[4] wime MS.—F.

but when they had together mett,
either on others helme sett
with speares doughtye dent.

1972 Mabam his speare all to-brast ;
then was Mabam euill agast,
& held him shamefully shent.

& with *that* stroke ffelowne [1]
1976 Sir Lybius bare him downe
oner his horsse tayle ;
ffor Mabams saddle arsowne
brake there-with, & fell downe
1980 into the ffeild without ffayle.
well nye he had him slone ;
but then came ryding Iron
In a good hawberke of mayle ;
1984 all ffresh he was to flight,
& thought he wold anon-right
Sir Lybius assayle.

Sir Lybius was of him ware,
1988 & speare vnto him bare,
& left his brother still.
such a stroke he gaue hime thore
that his hawberke all to-tore ;
1992 *that* liked him ffull ill.
their speares brake in 2 ;
swords gan they draw tho
with hart grim and grill,[2]
1996 & stifllye gan to other flight ;
either on Other proued their might,
eche other ffor to spill.

then together gan they hew.
2000 Mabam, the more shrew,[3]

---

[1] felon stroke, i.e. a murderous stroke.
—P.
[2] idem ac grisly. Gl. ad Ch.—P.

[3] shrew, *apud Chaucer est*, a *Villaine* ;
here it seems to signify shrewd, cunning,
artful.—P.

vp he rose againe ;

he heard & alsoe knew

Iron gaue strokes flew ;

2004   therof he was not flaine ;

but to him he went ffull right

ffor to helpe Iron to flight,

& auenge him on his enemye.

2008   tho he were neuer soe wroth,

Sir Lybius fought against them both

and kept himselfe manlye.

when Mabam saw Iron,[1]

2012   he flought as a Lyon

the knight to slay with wreake.

beffore his ffardar arsowne

soone he carued then downe

2016   Sir Lybius steeds necke.

Sir Lybius was a worthy warryour,

& smote a 2 his thye [2] in that stoure,

skine,[3] bone, and blood.

2020   then helped him not his clergye,

neither his ffalse Sorcerye,[4]

but downe he ffell with sorry moode.

Sir Lybius of his horsse alight,

2024   with Mabam ffor to flight.

in the ffeild both in ffere

strong stroakes they gaue with might,

that sprakeles [6] sprang out ffull bright

2028   ffrom helme and harnesse cleere.

as either ffast on other bett,[6]

both their swords mett,

---

[1] Yrayn saw Mabonn.—Cot. Lam.

[2] There is the long part of another *h*
in the MS.—F.

[3] ? skime in the MS.—F.

[4] þo halp hym noȝt hys armys,
Hys chauntement, ne hys charmys.
—Cot.

Ne halpe hym not his Armour,
His chauntements, ne his chambur.
—Lam.

[5] ? MS. spankeles.—F.

[6] did beat.—P.

As yee may now heare. [page 341]

2032 Mabam, *that* was the more shrew,
the sword of S*ir* Lybius he did hew
in 2 quite and cleare.

Mabam
cuts Lybius's
sword in
two.

then S*ir* Lybius was ashamed,
2036 & in his hart euis[1] agramed[2]
ffor he had Lost his sword,
& his steed was lamed,
& he shold be defamed
2040 to K*ing* Arthur his lord.

Lybius

gets angry,

to Iron lithelye[3] he ran,
& hent vp his sword then
that sharpe edge[4] had & hard,
2044 & ran to Mabam right
& ffast on him gan ffight,
& like a madman he ffared.

catches up
Iron's sword,

runs to
Mabam

but euer then ffought Mabam,
2048 as he had beene a wyld man,
S*ir* Lybius ffor to sloe.
but S*ir* Lybius earued downe
his sheild w*ith that* ffawchowne
2052 *that* he tooke Iron ffroe :
true tale ffor to be told,[5]
the left hand w*ith* the sheild
away he smote thoe.

and cuts off
his shield

and left
hand.

2056 then sayd Mabam him till
" S*ir*! thy stroakes beene ill !
gentle K*nigh*t, now hoe,[6]

Mabam

" & I will yeeld me to thee
2060 in loue and in Loyaltye

offers to
surrender
himself,

[1] for euir, or evil.—F. sore.—Lam. Cot. omits it.—F.
[2] *agramed*, displeased, grieved. Gl. ad Chauc. rather (*agramed*) angered. A.-S. *Gram.* Furor. Lye.—P.
[3] lithely. gently, (nimbly).—P.
[4] The *d* has two bottoms in the MS., or the word is *eidge*.—F.
[5] teld, rhythmi gratia.—P.
[6] i.e. now stop.—P.

att thine owne will,

and to give
np the Lady
of Sina-
dowue,

& alsoe *that* Lady ffree

that is in my posstee,[1]

2064 take her I will thee till ;

ffror through *that* sh[r]uced dint

my hand I haue tint[2] ;

for Iron's
sword was
poisoned,
and will kill
him.

the veinim will me spill ;

2068 fforsooth without othe

I venomed them both,

our enemyes ffor to kill."

S*i*r Lybins sayd, "by my thrifft

2072 I will not haue of thy gift

ffor all this world to w[i]nn !

therfore lay on stroakes swythe !

the one shall cut the other blythe

2076 the head of by the Chin[3] ! "

then S*i*r Lybins and Mabam

ffought together ffast then,

& lett ffor nothing againe ;

2080 *that* S*i*r Lybins *that* good K*night*

earned his helme downe right,

& his head in twayne.[4]

.

[1] posté, apud Chauc. est Power. Vid.
Gl.—P.

[2] lost.—P.

[3] One stroke too many in the MS.—F.

[4] The French adds (p. 108):
Del cors li saut i fumiere,
Qui molt estoit hideuse et fiere,
Qui li issoit parmi la boce, &c.—F.

[The Ninth Part.]

[How Lybius disenchants and weds the Lady of Sinadowne.]

2084

9ᵈ Parte
2088

> Now is Mabam slaine ;
> & to Irom he went againe,
>   with sword drawne to flight ;
> ffor to haue Clouen his braine;
> I tell you ffor certaine
>   he went to him ffull right ;
> but when he came there,[1]
> away he was bore,
>   into what place he nist.[2]

Lybius goes to kill Irou,

but he has vanished,

2092   he sought him ffor the nones[3]
wyde in many woones[4] ;
    to flight more him List.

and can't be found.

as he stood, & him bethought[5]
2096   *that* itt wold be deere bought
    that he was ffrom him fare,
ffor he wold with sorcerye
doe much tormenrtye,
2100   & *that* was much care.
he tooke his sword hastilye,
& rode vpon a hill hye,

Lybius

thinks he may give him trouble.

Lybius

---

[1] thore.— P.
[2] MS. list. ? nist, knew not.—F.
nyste.—Cot. nuste.—Lam.
[3] the *nones,* or *nonce,* on purpose ; de
industria. Jun. purposely.—P.
[4] *wone,* a house, habitation.—P.
[5] Neither the French, nor Cot., nor
Lam., has the seeing and slaying of the
knight which follows here. Cot. reads :
And whanne he ne fond hym noȝt,
  He held hymself be-cauȝt,
    And gan to syke sare,
And seyde yn word and þouȝt,
" þys wyll be sore a-bouȝt

þat he ys thus fram me y-fare."
⸿ On kne hym sette þat gentylle knyȝt,
And prayde to marie bryȝt,
  Keuere hym of hys care.
For the last three lines, Lam. substi-
tutes :
    " He will with sorcerye
    Do me tormentrye
      That is my moste care."
    Sore he sat and sighte ;
    He muste whate do her myght ;
      He was of blysse all bare.
(l. 2122-7 here).—F.

& looked round about.

sees a
knight in a
valley,
2104　then he was ware of [a] valley ;
　　　thitherward he tooke the way
　　　　as a sterne K*night* and stout.

　　　as he rode by a riuer side
2108　he was ware of him *that* tyde
　　　vpon the riuer brimm :

rides to him,
and cuts his
head off,
　　　He rode to him ffull hott,　　　　　　　[page 345]
　　　& of his head he smote,
2112　ffast by the Chinn ;
　　　& when he had him slaine,

then comes
back,
　　　ffast hee tooke the way againe
　　　　for to haue *that* lady gent.

2116　as soone as he did thither come,
　　　of his horsse he light downe,

and goes to
the hall
　　　　and into the hall hee went

to look for
the Lady of
Sinadowne.
　　　& sought *that* ladye ffaire and heud,
2120　but he cold her not find ;
　　　therfor he sighed ffull sore.[1]

He mourns,
because he
can't find
her.
　　　still he sate mourni[n]g
　　　ffor *that* Ladye ffaire & young;
2124　for her was all his care ;
　　　he ne wist what he doe might ;
　　　but still he sate, & sore he sight,
　　　　of Ioy hee was ffull bare.

A window
opens,
2128　but as he sate in *that* hall,
　　　he heard a window in the wall,
　　　ffaire itt gan vnheld ;—
　　　great [wonder[2]] there with-all
2132　in his hart gan ffall ;—
　　　as he sate & beheld,

---

[1] sair. Scotice.—P.　　[2] fear or dread.—P.　wonder.—Cot.　wondyr.—Lam.

a worme [1] out gan pace
with a womans fface
2136   *that* was younge & nothing old.
the wormes tayle [2] & her winges
shone flayre in all thinges,
& gay ffor to beholde.

2140   grislye great was her taile,
the clawes large without ffayle ;
Lothelye [3] was her bodye.
Sir Lybius swett for heate,
2144   there sate in his seate
as all had beene a ffire him by.[4]
then was Sir Lybius euill agast,
& thought his body wold brast.

2148   then shee neighed him nere ;
& or Sir Lybius itt wist,
the worme with mouth him Kist,
& colled about his lyre.[5]

2152   & after *that* kissing,
the wormes tayle & her wing

---

[1] Fr. *wivre*. Phillips gives " *Wyver*,
the Name of a Creature little known
otherwise than as it is painted in Coats
of Arms and described by Heralds : 'Tis
represented by Gwillim as a kind of
flying Serpent, and so may be deriv'd
from *Vipera*, as it were a winged Viper
or Serpent ; but others will have it to be
a sort of Ferret call'd *Viverra* in Latin."
De Biauju's description of it may be
compared with the English :

  A tant vit i aumaire ouvrir
  Et une Wivre fors issir,
  Qui jetoit une tel clarté
  Com i cierge bien enbrasé.
  Tot le palais enluminoit,
  Une si grant clarté jetoit.
  Hom ne vit onques sa parelle,
  Que la bouce ot tot vermelle ;
  Parmi jetoit le feu ardent ;
  Moult par estoit hideus et grant ;

  Parmi le pis plus grosse estoit
  Que i vaissaus d'un mui ne soit ;
  Les iols avoit gros et luisans,
  Comme ii escarbocles grans ;
  Contreval l'aumaire descent,
  Et vint parmi le pavement.
  Quatre toises de lonc duroit,
  En la queue iii neus avoit.
  C'onques nus hom ne vit greignor,
  Ains Dius ne fist cele color,
  Qu'en li ne soit entremellée,
  Dessous sambloit estre dorée.
(pp. 110–11).—F.

[2] Hyre body.—Cot. Lam.
[3] i.e. loathsome.— P.
[4] Maad as he were.—Lam.
As alle had ben in fyre.—Lam.
[5] apud Scot. flesh. Apud Chauc. *lere* is
the Complexion or Air of *the* face.—P.
Swyre.—Cot. Lam. *Coll* is to embrace ;
Fr. *collée*, an imbracing about the necke.
Cotgrave.

ffell away her ffroe ;

she was ffaire in all thing,

and a lovely woman 2156   a woman without Leasing ;

fairer he saw neuer or thoe.[1]

stands naked before him. shee stood vpp al soe [2] naked

as christ had her shaped.

2160   then was Sir Lybius woe.

She tells him shee sayd, " god _that_ on the rood gan bleed,

Sir Knight, quitt thee thy meede,

ffor thou my ffone wold sloe.[3]

he has slain two sorcerers, 2164   " thou hast slaine now ffull right

2 clarkes wicked of might

that wrought by the ffeende.

East, west, north and south,

2168   they were _masters_ of their mouth ;[4]

many a man they haue shend.

who turned her into a serpent through their inchantment,

to a worme thé had me meant,[5]

2172   ne woe to wrapp me in

till she should kiss Gawaine or one of his kin. till I had k[i]ssed Sir Gawaine

that is a noble Knight certaine,

or some man of his kinn.

---

[1] De Bianju sends her back into her cupboard after the kiss, stupefies Lybius, and reveals his name and parentage to him.—_Giglains_, son of _Gauvains_ (Gawaine), and _la fée as Blances Mains_, then sends him to sleep, and on his waking shows him the lady at her toilet (p. 115), fairer than any one else in the world, except she of the _Blances Mains_ (who excels Paris's Elaine, Isex la blonde, Bliblis, Lavine de Lombardie, and Morge la fée, (p. 152). This all takes place in _L'Ille de la Monthestée_ (p. 116); and the lady declares herself as the daughter of _le bon roi Gringars_. She narrates how _Mabons_ and _Eurains_ enchanted the 6000 inhabitants and made them destroy the city, and then turned her into a worm. Of the town she says:

. . ceste ville par droit non
Est appelée Senaudon ;

Por ce que Mabons l'a gastée,
Est GASTECITÉS apelée. (p. 120.)

But as the story has been sketched in the Introduction, I only note here that the lady's name, BLONDE ESMERÉE, is not given till p. 130, when she is starting for Arthur's court.—F.

[2] MS. alsoe.—F.

[3] God yelde þe dy whyle,
þat my fon þou woldest slo.—Cot.
God yelde the thi wille,
My foon thou woldest sloo.—Lam.

[4] Be wordes of hare mouthe.—Cot.
With maystres of her mouthe.—Lam.

[5] this word signifies mingled, mixed, apᵈ G. Doug. Chauc. &c.—P.
To warme me hadde þey y-went
In wo to welde and wend.—Cot.
To a worme they had me went,
In wo to leven and lende.—Lam.

2176   ffor [1] thou hast saued my liffe,

Castles 50 and [2] ffiue

    take to thee I will,

& my selfe to be thy wiffe

2180 right without striffe,

    if itt be your will." [3]

She promises Lybius fifty-five castles

and herself as his wife.

then was he glad & blythe,

& thanked god often sythe [4]

2184 That him *that* grace had sent, [page 346]

& sayd, "my Lord [5] faire & ffree,

all my loue I leaue with thee,

    by god omnipotent!

2188 I will goe, my La*dye* bright,

to the castle gate ffull right,

    thither ffor to wend

ffor to feitch your geere

2192 *that* yee were wont to weare,

    & them I will you send.

Lybius is blithe,

and proposes to fetch the lady's clothes from the castle,

"alsoe, if itt be your will,

I pray you to abyde still

2196 till I come [6] againe."

"Sir," shee said, "I you pray

wend fforth on your way, [7]

    therof I am ffaine."

if she will stay till he comes back.

2200 Sir Lybius to the castle rode,

there the people him abode;

Lybius rides to the castle

---

[1] because.—P.   [2] MS. amd.—F.

[3] 3yf hyt ys artours wylle.—Cot.

And hit be Arthures will.—Lam.

[4] Time—also, since, afterwards. Gl.
Chauc.—P. Cot. has for this and the
next sixteen lines:

And lepte to horse swyþe,

  And lefte þat lady stylle.

But euer he dradde yrayn,

For he was no3t y-slayn,

With speche he wolde hym spylle.

Lam. has nearly the same words, but
omits the last line but one.—F.

[5] Ladye.—P.

[6] cone in MS.—F.

[7] "I you pray" the writer of the MS.
was going to repeat, and got as far as
p: then he stopt, put in *on* after *I*,
added *r* to *yo*, and *way* to the *p*, so
that the words are "I on your pway."
—F.

to Iesu chr[i]st gan they crye
ffor to send them tydings glad

2204 of them *that* Long had
done them tormentrye.

Sir Lybius is to the Castle come,
& to Sir Lamberd he told anon,

and tells the
people that
Mabam and
Iron are
slain.

2208 and alsoe the Barronye,[1]
how Sir Mabam was slaine
& Sir Iron, both twayine,
by the helpe of mild Marye.

2212 when *that* Knight soe keene
had told how itt had beene
to them all by-deene,

a rich robe good & ffine,

He sends a
rich robe

2216 well flurred with good Ermine,
he sent *that* Ladye sheene ;

and garlands
to the lady,

Kerchers and garlands rich
he sent to her priuiliche,[2]

2220 *that* mayd he wold home bring.[3]
& when shee was readye dight,
thither they went anon-right,
both old and young,

and all the
people of
Sinadowne
go and
fetch her
home.

2224 & all the ffolke of Sinadowne
with a ffaire procession
the Ladye home they ffett.
& when they were come to towne,

They crown
her,

2228 of precyons gold a rich crowne
there on her head thé sett.

and thank
God.

they were glad and blythe,
& thanked god often sithe

---

[1] i. e. The Barrons collectively.—P.
[2] i. e. privily.—P.

[3] A-non with-out dwellynge.—Cot.
 A byrd hit ganne hir bringe.—Lam.

2232 *that* ffrom woe them had brought.

all the Lords of dignitye
did him homage and ffealtye,
 as of right they ought.

2236 they dwelled 7 dayes in the tower
there Sir Lamberd was gouernor,
 with mirth, Ioy, and game ;
& then they rode with honor

2240 vnto King Arthur,
 the Knights all in-same.

Lybius and
the lady stay
seven days
there,
and then
ride off to
Arthur.

ffins.[1]

[1] It is so very wrong of the copier or translator to have broken off the story without giving the wedding between Lybius and his love, that I add it here from the three unprinted MSS. as well as the Cotton one. The Lincoln's Inn and Ashmole MSS. have more stanzas than the Cotton and Lambeth ones.

Lincoln's Inn MS. Hale, No. 150, art. i.,
last leaf.

þay þonkyd god almyȝt,
Boþe Arthour and his knyȝt,
 þat heo [ne] hadde* schame.
Arthour ȝaf as blyue
Libeus þat may to wyue
 þat was so gent a dame.

ȝeo murthe of þeo brydale,
Nomon con wiþ tale
 Telle hit in no geste.
In þat semly sale
Weore lordes monye and fale,
 And ladyes wel honeste.
þer was ryche seruyse
Boþe to fool and wyse,
 To leste and to meste.
þer wan þay yche ȝifthes, [back of leaf]
veho mynstral a ryȝhtis,
 And somme þat weore vnprest.

Sir Gawayn, knyȝt of renoun,
saide to þeo lady of synaydoun,
 "Madame, treonely,
he þat weddid þe wiþ pruyde,
y gat him by a forest syde
 On a gentil lady."

Ashmole MS. 61, leaf 58b.

They thankyd god of his myȝhtes,
Kynge Arthour And hys knyȝhtes,
 That sche had no schame.
Arthour ȝaue be-lyue [leaf 59]
Syre lybeus þat mey to wyue,
 That was so jentyll A dame.

The my[r]the of þat brydall
May no man tell with tale
 No sey in no geste :
Yn þat sembly sale
Where brydes grete and smale,
 And lades full honeste ;
There was many A mane,
And seruys gode wone
 Both to most and leste.
Fore soth þe mynstrallus Alle
That [were] with-in þat halle
 And † ȝyftes of þo beste.

Syre lybeus moder so fro
Come to þat mangerre ;
 Hyre rudd was rede as ryse ;
Sche knew lybeus wele be syȝht,
And wyst wele A-none ryȝht
 That he was of mych pryse.
Sche went to sir gawene,
And seyd, "with-outen leyne

---

* An *s*, blotted, stands here in the MS.—F.   † had.—F.

þanne þat lady blyþe was,
And ful ofte kyssed his fas,
And haylsel [*sic*] hym sykyrly.
Sir Libeus þan wold kyþe:
he wonte to his fader swyþe,
And kyssed him tymes monye.

he kneoled in þat stounde,
And saide, kneoland on grounde,
" for godis loue al weldand,
þat made þeo world so round,
fayre fadir, or y fonde,
blesse me wiþ þyn hond."
þat hynde knyȝt Gawayn
blessyd þeo child wiþ mayn,
And made him scoþþe vp stande.
he comaunndyd knyȝt and sweyn
To clepe Libeus " Gengelayne,"
þat was lord of lond.

fourty dayes þay dwellyd,
And heore feste faire heold
wiþ Arthoure þeo kynge.
As þeo gest vs tolde,
Arthour wiþ knyȝtis bolde
hom gonne þay brynge.
twenty yere þay lyued in-same
wiþ muche gleo and game,
he and þat swete þynge.
Ihesu Cryst oure saueour,
And his modir þat swete flour,
spede vs at our nede!

Explicit Lebiuns de-sconius [? MS.]

Thys is owre chyld so fre."
Than was he glad *and* blyth,
And kyssed hym many A sythe,
And seyd, " þat lykes mo."

Syre gawen, knyȝht of renowne,
Seyd to þe lady of synadoun,
" Madame, treuly
Ho þat hath þe wedyd with pride,
Y gate hym vnd[er] A forest syde
Off a gentyll lady."
Than þat lady was blyth,
And thankyd hym many A syth,
And kyssed hym sykerly.
Than lybeus to hym wan,
And þer he kyssed þat man;
Fore soth treuly

He fell on kneys in þat stound,
lybeus knelyd on þe ground,
And seyd, "fore god All weldinge
That made þe werld rownd,
Feyre fader, wele be ȝe fownd!
Blysse me with ȝour blyssynge! "

That hend knyȝt gawene
Blyssed hys sone with mayne,
And made hym vp to stond,
And comandyd knyȝht *and* sweyne
To calle hym gyngelyane,
That was lorde of lond.

Forty deys þer they duellyd,   [leaf 59b.]
And grete fest þei held
With Arthour þe kynge.
As þe gest hath told,
Arthour with knyȝhtes bold
Home gane hym brynge.
X ȝere þei lyued in-same
With mekyll gle *and* game,
He *and* that suete thynge.
Ihesu cryst owre sauyour,
And his moder þat suete floure,
To heuene blys vs brynge!

Here endes þe lyfe—
Y telle ȝow with-outen stryfe—
Off gentyll libeus disconeus.
Fore his saule now byd ȝe
A pater noster And An Aue,
Fore þe loue off Ihesus,
That he of hys sawle haue pyte,
And off owrys, iff hys wyll be,
When we schall wend þer-to.
And ȝe þat haue herd þat talkynge,
ȝe schall haue þe blyssinge
Of Ihesu cryst All-so.

[*Finis.*]

And þonkede godes myʒtes,
Artoure and hys knyʒtes,
Þat he ne hadde no schame.
Artoure yaf here al so * blyue,
Lybeauus to be hys wyfe,
Þat was so gentylle a dame.

Þe Ioye of þat bredale
Nys not told yn tale,
Ne rekened yn no gest.
Barons and lordynges fale
Come to þat semyly sale,
And ladyes welle honeste.

Þer was ryche seruyse
Of alle þat men kouþ deuyse,
To lest & ek to mest.
Þe menstrales yn boure & halle
Hadde ryche yïtes with-alle,
And þey þat weryn vnwrest.

Fourty dayes þey dwellede
And hare feste helde
With artoure þe kyng.
As þe frenssche tale teld,
Artoure with knyʒtes beld
At hom gan hem brynge.

Fele ʒere þey leuede yn-same
With moche gle & game,
Lybeauus & þat swete þyng.
Ihesu cryst oure sauyoure,
And hys modere þat swete floure,
Graunte vs alle good endynge.
Amen.

Explicit libeauus desconus.

They thanked god with al his myghtis,
Arthur and alle his knyghtis,
That he hade no shame.
Arthur gave als blyve
Lybeous that lady to wyfe,
That was so gentille a dame.

The myrrour of that brydale
No man myght telle with tale
In Ryme nor in geste.
In that semely Saale
Were lordys many and fale,
And ladies fulle honeste.

There was Riche Service
Bothe to lorde and ladyes,
To leste and eke to moste.
Thare were gevyn riche giftis,
Euche mynstrale her thriftis,
And some that were vnbrest.

ffourty dayes thei dwelden,
And ther here feste helden
With Arthur the kynge,
As the ffrensshe tale vs tolde.
Arthur kyng, with his knyghtis bolde,
Home he gonne hem brynge.

Sevyn yere they levid same
With mekylle Ioye and game,
He and that swete thynge.
Nowe Ihesu Criste oure Savioure,
And his moder, that swete floure,
Grawnte vs gode Endynge! Amen.

Explicit libious Disconyus.

---

* MS. also.

Childe Maurice:[1]

THIS piece has been already printed from the Folio, just as it is by Jamieson in his *Popular Ballads and Songs* (1806).

The other versions of the old ballad are, *Gil Morice* given by Percy in the *Reliques* from a printed edition current in Scotland, *Child Noryce* and *Chield Morice* given by Motherwell from recitations, 3 stanzas of a traditional version given by Jamieson. The number of these versions shows how popular the ballad was. Another proof is its use by Langhorne, by Home, and others, as the basis of longer, more pretentious works. Of the said versions *Gil Morice* and *Chield Morice* closely resemble each other, and are infinitely less forcible than the other two. They are intolerably prolix. The fire is quenched with much water. They are the offspring of men who possessed the faculty of Midas with a difference—they turned everything they touched into dross. The other two versions are admirably terse and vigorous, and have a right to places in the first ranks of our ballad-poetry. Undoubtedly the less corrupted is the Folio version; but, unhappily, it is somewhat imperfect.

This is indeed a noble specimen of our ballad-poetry in all its strength. For the overpowering vigour of its objective style it may be compared with *Little Musgrave and Lady Bernard*. How vivid every picture it paints is! how effective every stroke! Not a word is wasted. The writer is too absorbed in the action of his piece to indulge in any comments, or moralisings, or superfluities of any sort.

Semper ad eventum festinat, et in medias res,
Non secus ac notas, auditorem rapit.

[1] vid. Scottish Edition which is evidently a modern Improvement.—P.

This abstinence from all reflections and sentimentalities is indescribably impressive. The ballad-writer of later times is too often like the guide who introduces the traveller to a fine cathedral, and disturbs the glorious effect of the sight with his intrusive conceited garrulity. This old writer presents us with a wonderful spectacle without putting in ever a word of his own. You forget the guide, and are given up wholly to the effect of the spectacle. If we could never consider the heavens without having suggested to us the names of the stars and their sizes and distances from the earth! This old writer is content to let his tale produce its own effect. He conceives it in all its tremendous force, too really to permit him to criticise or dally with it in any way. Feeling much, he says little. Hence the intensity of his narration.

What strange wild pictures he paints! The Child in the silver wood,

> sitting on a block
> With a silver comb in his hand,
> Kembing his yellow lock.

—the foot-page hasting on his errand with the presents of the grass-green mantle and of the gold and precious stone rings— the husband and his wife's son drying on the grass or a sleeve their bright brown swords—the victor, his supposed rival's head cut off, how he

> pricked it on his sword's point,
> Went singing there beside,
> And he rode till he came to the lady fair
> Whereas this lady lied,
> & says " Dost thou know Child Maurice head
> If that thou dost it see?
> And lap it soft and kiss it oft,
> For thou lovedst him better than me.

—the mother recognising in her slain lover her one only son. That terrible passage in the *Bacchæ* of Euripides, where the scales fall from Agave's eyes, naturally suggests itself as one looks at that last picture; though there, indeed, the horror of

the situation is deepened by the fact that her own hands have
done the deed :

ἔα, τί λεύσσω ; τί φέρομαι τόδ' ἐν χεροῖν ;

Then answers Cadmus :

ἄθρησον αὐτὸ καὶ σαφέστερον μάθε.
ΑΓ. ὁρῶ μέγιστον ἄλγος ἡ τάλαιν' ἐγώ.
ΚΑ. μῶν σοι λέοντι φαίνεται προσεικέναι ;
ΑΓ. οὔκ · ἀλλὰ Πενθέως ἡ τάλαιν' ἔχω κάρα.

CHILDE Maurice hunted ithe siluen [1] wood,
    he hunted itt round about,
& noebodye *that* he ffound therin,
4   nor none there was with-out.

[2] & he tooke his siluer combe in his hand,
    to kembe his yellow lockes ;
he sayes, "come hither, thou litle ffoot page,
8   *that* runneth [3] lowlye by my knee ;
ffor thou shalt goe to Iohn stewards wiffe
    & pray her speake with mee.

" & as itt ffalls out many times,
12   as knotts beene knitt on a koll,[4]
or Marchant men gone to Leene London
    either to buy ware or sell,

" I, and greete thou doe *that* Ladye well,
16   euer soe well ffroe mee,—
And as itt ffalles out many times   [page 347]
    as any hart can thinke,

Sidenotes: Child Maurice, while hunting, / tells his footpage / to go to John Steward's wife, / greet her as many times as there are knots on a net, / and ask her

---

[1] The downstroke of the *r* of *siluen* is
made twice over.— F.

[2] Prof. Child dots two lines as missing, before lines 5, 15, & 21, and after
line 64. *Ballads* ii. 313-16.—F.

[3] MS. runneth.— F.

[4] Kelle, *reticulum, retiaculum* (Catholicon). *Reticula* a lytell nette or kalle.
Reticinellum, a kalle (Ortus) . . . The
fashion of confining the hair in an orna-
mental network, which occasionally was
jewelled, seems to have obtained in
England from the time of Henry III.
until that of Elizabeth, and an endless
variety of examples are afforded by
illuminated MSS. and monumental effi-
gies. It was termed *calle* or *kelle*, a
term directly taken, perhaps, from the
French *cale*. Latin *calantica* or *callus*.
Way in *Promptorium*, p. 270, note [1].—F.

"as schoole masters are in any schoole house
20   writting with pen and Iinke,—
ffor if I might, as well as shee may,
    this night I wold with her speake.

"& heere I send her a mantle of greene,
24   as greene as any grasse,
& bidd her come to the siluer wood
    to hunt with Child Maurice;

to come and hunt with him.

"& there I send her a ring of gold,
28   a ring of precyous stone,
& bidd her come to the siluer wood;
    let ffor no kind of man."

He sends her a ring.

one while this litle boy he yode,
32   another while he ran;
vntill he came to Iohn Stewards hall,
    I-wis he neuer blan.

The footpage goes to John Steward's hall,

& of nurture the child had good;
36   hee ran vp hall & bower ffree,
& when he came to this Lady ffaire,
    sayes, "god you saue and see!

and gives the lady

"I am come ffrom Ch[i]ld Maurice,
40   a message vnto thee;
& Child Maurice, he greetes you well,
    & euer soe well ffrom mee.

Child Maurice's message:

"& as itt ffalls out oftentimes,
44   as knotts beene knitt on a kell,
or Marchant men gone to leeue London,
    either ffor to buy ware or sell,

he greets her as many times as there are knots on her cap,

"& as oftentimes he greetes you well
48   as any hart can thinke,
or schoolemasters in any schoole
    wryting with pen and inke;

" & heere he sends a Mantle of greene,

52   as greene as any grasse,

& he bidds you come to the siluer wood,

to hunt with Child Maurice.

" & heere he sends you a ring of gold,

56   a ring of the precyous stone,

he prayes you to come to the siluer wood,

let ffor no kind of man."

" now peace, now peace, thou litle ffootpage,

60   ffor Christes sake, I pray thee !

ffor if my lord heare one of these words,

thou must be hanged hye ! "

Iohn steward stood vnder the Castle wall,

64   & he wrote the words euerye one,

& he called vnto his horskeeper,

"make readye you my steede ! "

I, and soe hee did to his Chamberlaine,

68   "make readye then my weede!"

& he cast a lease [1] vpon his backe,

& he rode to the siluer wood ;

& there he sought all about,

72   about the siluer wood,

& there he ffound him Child Maurice

sitting vpon a blocke,

with a siluer combe in his hand

76   kembing his yellow locke.

he sayes, "how now, how now, Child Maurice ?

alacke ! how may this bee ? "

but then stood vp him Child Maurice,

80   & sayd these words trulye :

[1] ? leash, thong, cord. See lees, lese in Halliwell.—F.

" I doe not know your Ladye," he said,
  " if *that* I doe her see."
" ffor thou hast sent her loue tokens,
84   more now then 2 or 3 ;

The Child says he doesn't know John's wife. "And yet you've sent her love-tokens,

" ffor thou hast sent her a Mantle of greene,
  as greene as any grasse,
& bade her come to the siluer woode
88   to hunt with Child Maurice ;

a green mantle,

" & thou [hast] sent her a ring of gold,
  a ring of precyous stone,
& bade her come to the siluer wood,
92   let ffor noe kind of man.

and a gold ring,

and bade her come to the wood to you!

" and by my ffaith, now, Child Maurice,
  the tone of vs shall dye ! "
" Now be my troth," sayd Child Maurice, [page 318]
96   " & *that* shall not be I."

One of us shall die."

but hee pulled forth a bright browne [1] sword
  & dryed itt on the grasse,
& soe ffast he smote att Iohn Steward,
100   I-wisse he neuer rest.

then hee pulled fforth his bright browne sword,
  & dryed itt on his sleeue ;
& the ffirst good stroke Iohn stewart stroke,
104   Child Maurice head he did cleeue ;

John draws his sword, splits the Child's head,

& he pricked itt on his swords poynt,
  went singing there beside,
& he rode till he came to *that* Ladye ffaire
108   wheras this ladye Lyed ;

carries it on his sword-point to his wife,

[1] Only half the *n* in the MS.—F.

and sayes, "dost thou know Child Maurice head
 if *that* thou dost itt see ?

and tells her
to kiss it.

& lapp itt soft, & kisse itt offt,
· 112 ffor thou louedst him better then mee."

She says
he has
killed her
only child.

but when shee looked on Child Maurice head,
 shee neuer spake words but 3,
"I neuer beare no Child but one,
116 & you haue slaine him trulye."

John
Steward
reproaches
his men for
not staying
him in his
wrath ;

sayes, " wicked be my merrymen all,
 I gaue Meate, drinke, & Clothe !
but cold they not haue holden me
120 when I was in all *that* wrath ?

he has slain
his wife and
her son.

" ffor I haue slaine one of the curteouse[s]t K*nigh*ts
 that euer bestrode a steed !
soe haue I done one [of] the fairest Ladyes
124 *that* euer ware womans weede ! "

        ffins.

Phillis hoe:

HERE apparently one endeavours to reconcile an offended swain to his offending mistress. He had begged a kiss, it would seem, and been denied it; had concluded that his Phillis cared nothing for him. Deaf to all the pleas urged in her behalf, he rejoices that he has escaped from her. We do not know any other copy of the song.

SHEPARDES hoe! Shepards hoe!
harkes how Phillis[1] calles thee! La: La: La:
Philis hoe: Phillis hoe!
4 " shall I lose my Phillis ? noe, noe, noe! "
" what ailes thee Shepard [that thou] looke soe sadd ?   *Why are you sad ?*
where is thy louely lasse shold make thee gladd ? "
" ay me ! my *mistress* proues vntrue,   *"My love is false."*
8 & my louely lasse bidds me adew ! "

" Shepards, flye ! Sheperds, flye !
doe not wrong thy lasse, & noe cause whye."   *No, she is not.*
" Phillis noe, Phillis noe !
12 but if shee proue light in loue, Ile let her goe."
thus wee poore mayds must beare the blame,
w*h*ich[2] incoustant men deserue the same.
if ought be ill, tis our amisse,
16 but a womans word is noe iudge in this.

" Come away ! Come away !   *Come and look at her.*
see ! the louelye lasse tripps ore the lay."
" lett her goe ! lett her goe !   *" Not I, let her go.*
20 neuer more shall my loue say mee noe."

---

[1] The first *l* is much like an *s* in the MS. The colons in lines 2 and 3 are those of the MS. Before the first *La* Percy inserts *hoe*.—F.   [2] while.—P.

L l 2

"ffye shepard! thou thy loue dost wrong!
flor maides, thé dare not doe amidst a throng."

She
wouldn't
kiss me!"

24 "O, beg I did but one pore kisse;
but shee with coy disdaine said noe by Iys.[1]"

Don't be
jealous,

"Iclous loue, Iclous loue,
herafter doth vnconstant proue."
"many flind,[2] many flind

28 women & their words are like the winde.
men sweare thé loue, & do protest;
but when a woman sweares, shee doth but Iest.
who Iestes with loue, playes with a bayte

32 *that* doth wound the hart with slye deceipte."

love your
love again;

"Shepards swaine, Shepards swaine,
let thy lasse inioy thy loue againe!
Iff maids pray, if maids pray,

women must
have their
way.

36 women in their wants will haue noe nay;
thus women they must learne to wooe,
when men fforgetts what nature bidds them do."
"if women wooe, tis much abuse,

40 tho cuningly they coyne[3] a coy excuse."

"Haples shee, hapless shee
that doth loue[4] soe base a swaine as thee!"

"No, I'm not
such a fool.

"happye I, happye I:

44 *that* ffortune haue such ffolly for to fflye!
base minds to basenes still will fflee,
but honor in an honored hart doth lye.

We shep-
herds are as
coy as
kings."

tho base, my mind true honor brings; ffins.

48 [w]ee shepards in our loues are as coy as Kings."

---

[1] noe Iwis.—P.
[2] There is a tag to the *d*.—F.
[3] MS. coyme.—F.
[4] Three strokes for the *u*.—F.

Guy & Colebrande : [1]

[In 3 Parts.—P.]

"GUY & PHILLIS" is simply a *résumé*, with some slight additions from other sources, of the old romance of *Guy of Warwick*; "Guy & Amaranth" and "Guy & Colbrand" are versions, one modern, by Samuel Rowlands, the other much older, of scenes in that romance.

The presence in the MS. Folio of three pieces dealing with Sir Guy is a sign of the immense popularity he enjoyed, if any sign were needed. But indeed there is no lack of evidence of his warm acceptance with the Middle Ages as well in foreign countries as in England. Certainly among the heroes of romance he was one of the most popular. At home, Arthur, and Sir Bevis, and he, surpassed all others in the extent and endurance of the admiration they attracted. There is nothing more touching anywhere than the story of the last moments of Guy. Such was its intrinsic interest, that it won the ear of the world solely on the strength of it; for the story seems never to have been worthily told. Not one of the three poems treasured up in the Folio is of any considerable literary value. Nor can higher praise be bestowed on the old romance. "Guy of Warwick," says Ellis, "is certainly one of the most ancient and popular, and no less certainly one of the dullest and most tedious of our early romances." Dull and tedious it emphatically is. This jewel then has never yet been skilfully set. But its preciousness was appreciated in spite of the rude craftsmen into whose hands it

---

[1] A curious old Song, but very incorrect.—P.

had fallen. Its lustre glorified its clumsy encasements as the
beauty of the beggar-maid her unworthy dress.

> As shines the moon in cloudy skies
> She in her poor attire was seen.

The oldest form in which we have the story is that of an Anglo-
Norman romance, Romanz de Gui de Warwyk, extant, as Ritson
informs us, in the library of Corpus Christi College, Cambridge
(1. 6), and in the University Library (More 690), Harl. MSS.
No. 3775, King's MSS. 8 F. ix. There are two fragments of it
in the Bodleian (printed in the *British Bibliographer*, iii. 268 ;
see Introduction to the Abbotsford Club edition of the copy of
the English romance in the Auchinleck MS.). Other fragments
were found in the cover of an old book by Sir Thomas Phillips.
There is also a copy in the Bibl. Impériale (MSS. de Colbert,
4289), Paris. There was a copy at Bruges in 1467, at Brussels
in 1487, as we learn from Barrois' account of the Librairies du
Fils du Roi Jean Charles V., &c. (See Guy de Warwick,
Abbotsford Club, Introduction.) This French work was composed probably in the thirteenth century. Its composer may
possibly have been Walter of Exeter, as is stated by Carew in his
Survey of Cornwall. Whoever composed it, and wherever, it
was done into English early in the fourteenth century, which
English version is mentioned in the Prologue to Hampole's
Speculum Vitæ, or Mirrour of Life, written about 1350, amongst
the popularities of the day :

> I warne you firste at the begynnynge
> That I will make no vayne carpynge
> Of dedes of armes, ne of amours,
> As does mynstellis & gestours,
> That maketh carpynge in many a place
> Of Octavione & Isenbrace,
> And of many other gestes
> And namely when they come to festes,
> Ne of the lyf of Bevis of Hamptonne
> That was a knyght of grete renoune,
> Ne of Syr Gye of Warwyke.   (*apud* Warton. II. Eng. P.)

and by Chaucer in the *Rime of Sir Topas* (about 1380) as one of the romances of price of his day. Of it the oldest copy extant is preserved in the Auchinleck MS. There are others in Caius College and the Public Libraries, Cambridge. It was still in demand in the sixteenth century, and was then printed by Copland, and by Cawood. The romance was then condensed, as was the custom, into a ballad. In 159½ Richard Jones has entered on the Register of the Stationers' Company " A pleasante songe of the valiant actes of Guy of Warwicke to the tune of *Was ever man so tost in love.*" This is the " Guy & Phillis " of the present volume. The common title, says Percy, is " A pleasant song of the valiant deeds of chivalry atchieved by that noble knight Sir Guy of Warwick, who for the love of fair Phelis became a hermit & dyed in a cave of craggy rocke, a mile distant from Warwick." Of this ballad there are copies in the Bagford, the Pepys, and the Roxburghe Collections. The legend was afterwards rendered into prose, and in that shape printed again and again down to very recent times. In the British Museum Library there is a copy of the 7th edition of a cheap printed prose version, 1733. Ellis speaks of this popular form as " to be found at almost every stall in the metropolis." The Anglo-Norman romance was converted into prose in 1525.

But the story was not given up wholly to the romance-writers and their followers. The oldest other recital of it now extant may possibly be that ascribed to Gerard of Cornwall, printed by Hearne in the Appendix to his edition of the *Annales de Dunstable.* This *Historia Guidonis de Werwyke* is preserved in MS. 147, Magd. Coll. Oxford. "There is not however anything else of Gerard's in the Magd. MS. (which the compiler has seen), and the short piece which has been printed is written at the end of Higden's Polychronicon, on the same page with it, and preceding its copious index." (See *Macray's* Manual of British Historians.) Of Gerard's date and life nothing whatever is known. " He is said to have written a book *De Gestis Britonum,* and another *De Gestis Regum West-Saxonum,* which are referred to three times by Th. Rudburn in his History of Winchester. Thin also mentions him in his catalogue of historians in Holinshed, p. 1590." This piece, whenever written and by whomsoever, describes the famous fight with Colbrand much as the Folio MS. version narrates it. An entry in the Registry of the priory at Winchester, quoted by Warton in his *History of English Poetry,* tells us that when Adam de Orleten, bishop of Winchester, visited his cathedral priory of St. Swithin in that city, " Cantabat joculator quidam, nomine Herebertus, *Canticum Colbrondi,* necnon gestum Emme regine, a judicio ignis liberate in aula prioris." The first certain historical mention of the great Saxon champion is to be found, as Ritson points out, in the Robert de Brunne's translation with additions, made *circ.* 1338, of Peter Langtoft's Chronicle, written *circ.* 1308.

> That was Guy of Warwik, as the boko sais,
> There he slouh Colbrant with haebe Daneis.

The story of Guy's abnegation of his wife, and his lonely uncomforted end in the cell he had hewn for himself, is told in chapter clxxii. of the *Gesta Romanorum,* compiled in all probability about the same time with Langtoft's Chronicle. This compilation, made to serve mediæval preachers for purposes of illustration, naturally took that part of the story that exemplified their favourite teachings. Towards the end of the same, the fourteenth century, Henry Knighton, Canon of Leicester, in his *Chronicon de Eventibus Angliæ ab anno 950 ad 1395,* recounted the old tale at full length. He introduces it with a sort of apology. " Set quia historia dicti Guidonis," he writes, " cunctis seculis laudabili memoria commendanda est, in presenti historia immiscere curavi." Then he relates, with circumstances, how " Olavus rex Daciæ," " Golanus rex Norwegiæ," and " dux Neustriæ," invaded England and besieged King Athelstan for a space of two years in Winchester. They had enlisted in the service of their expedition a vast Saracen, "de Africâ quendam gigantem, Colebrandum nomine, qui eo tempore fortissimus et elegantissimus reputabatur in orbe," described subsequently as "diabolicæ staturæ," and by Guy when he stands face to face with him as "non homo, immo potius spiritus diaboli in effigie hominis latens." Eventually a truce, "treuga," was agreed to, and the determining of the war by a single combat. But there seemed scant hope of finding a match for Colebrand, who was of course put forward to maintain the Scandinavian cause. Then follows, as in "Guy & Colbrand," an account of the vision that appeared to the perplexed King Athelstan, and how, obeying it, and posting himself "ad altam primam" at one of the city's gates, he saw amongst the entering crowd "virum elegantem cursantem, de una sclauma alba vestitum, et unum sertum de albis rosis in capite tectum, fustemque grandem in manu ferentem; set multum erat debilitatus et discoloratus anxietateque minoratus, eo quod nudipes laboravit, barbamque prolixam habuit." This wild woe-begone figure was Guy—Guy in deep distress for his sins, and caring only to escape from hospitalities to pray for indulgence and pardon. But he is moved at last to undertake the combat with the giant. "Fecit se armari de melioribus armaturis regis, et cinxit se gladio Constantini [the sword of Constantine the Great and the spear of Charlemagne were among the presents given to Athelstan by Hugh, Duke of the Franks] lanceamque sancti Mauricii in manu tulit." Then the fight is described with extreme minuteness. Colbrand seems overpowering till Guy cuts off his sword-arm; "Quod Dani videntes, multum ex hoc contabuerunt, et Deos suos in Colubrandi adjutorum cum ejulatu magno invocare cœperunt." And then comes the final scene in the hero's life.

In 1410, as Dugdale (Baron. i. 243) relates on the authority of Rous, to whom we shall come presently, Guy's fame was well spread abroad at Jerusalem; for the Soldan's lieutenant hearing

that Lord Beauchamp, then travelling in the Holy Land, " was
descended from the famous Guy of Warwick, whose story they
had in books of their own language, invited him to his palace ;
and royally feasting him presented him with three precious stones
of great value, besides divers cloaths of silk and gold given to his
servants." The history of Sir Guy, as Percy points out (*Reliques*,
vol. iii.), " is alluded to in the old Spanish romance, ' Tirante
el blanco ' which, it is believed, was written not long after the
year 1430." About the middle of the fifteenth century Rudburn,
who has been mentioned above in a quotation, a Benedictine
of Winchester, called *Junior* to distinguish him from another
chronicler of the same name who died Bishop of St. David's in
1441, gives some account of the great combat. Leland in his
Collectanea, fol. 595, quotes " ex chronicis Thomæ Rudbourne
monachi Wintonensis " this amongst other passages : " Tertio
Ethelstani anno, duellum inter Colbrondum Dauum & Guidonem
comitem de Warwik, extra borealem civitatis Wintoniensis pla-
gam, in loco qui modo Hidemede, olim Denmarsch appellatus est,
prope monasterium de Hida. Insignum vero victoriæ servatur
sica prædicti Colbronde gigantis, cumqua truncatum erat ; caput
ejus a Guidone comite de Warwik in eccl. cathedrali Wintoniæ
usque in hodiernum diem.[1] Rudbourne describes the fight more
fully in his *Historia Major Wintonensis* (*apud* Wharton's *Anglia
Sacra*). There the " Rex Dacorum " is " Anelaf ;" the scene of
the combat is Hyde Mede ; the " gigas " is " miræ longitudinis,
invisus, inhumanus ac non malæ meditationis ignarus." Lydgate,
contemporary with Rudbourne, versified the above-mentioned *Historia Guidonis de Werwyke* just as Samuel Rowland, something
more than a century after him, retold the conflict of Guy with
Amaranth in the form given in this volume. Lydgate's work,
never yet printed, is preserved among the Bodleian MSS. and

---

[1] " This history remained in rude
painting against the walls of the north
transept of the cathedral till within
my memory." Warton, H. E. P.

in Harl. MS. 7333 f. 35. b.[1] Revised by one Lane, it was
licensed to be printed in 1617 (Harl. MSS. 5243),[1] but the licence
seems never to have been acted upon. Later on, in the latter
half of the fifteenth century, John Rous, appointed priest, or one
of the two priests, at the chapel at Guy's Cliff near Warwick
(erected, with a statue of Guy, by Richard Beauchamp in 1422),
" labored and finished " a " roll " (now in the Ashmolean Museum,
Oxford, numbered 839) containing a biography of him in whose
honour he held his office, for whose soul he offered daily prayers.
Dugdale pronounces him " a diligent searcher after antiquities,
and especially of this county," and one that " hath left behind
him divers notable things, industriously gathered from many
choice manuscripts, whereof he had perusal in sundry monastries
in England and Wales, which now, through the fatal subversion
of those houses, are for the most part perisht." Rous narrates as
sober facts the story of the romance:

Dame Felys, daughter and heire to Erle Rohand, for her beauty called
Felyle belle, or Felys the fayre by true enheritance, was countesse
of Warwyke, and lady and wyfe to the most victoriouse Knight, Sir
Guy, to whome in his woinge tyme she made greate straungenes, and
caused him for her sake, to put himself in meny greate distresse, dangers
and perills; but when they wer wedded and bñ but a litle season
togither, he departed from her to her greate hevynes, and never was
conversaunt with her after, to her vnderstandinge; and all the while she
kept her cleane and trew lady and wyf to him, devout to godward, and
by way of Almes, greatly helpinge them that wer in poore estate. Sir
Gy of Warwyke, flower and honor of Knighthode, sonne to Sir Seyward,
baron of Walingforde, and his lady and wyfe Dame Sabyn, a florentyne
in Italy of the noble bloode of the contrey, translate from Italy vnto
this lande, as Dame Genches, Saynt Martyns sister, borne in Greke
lande, was maryed here, and had in this lande noble Saynct Patryke,
that converted Irelande to the Christian faythe. This worshipfull
Knight Sir Gy, in his actes of warre ever consydered what parties had
wronge, and therto wold he draw, by which doinge his loos spred so

farre that he was called the worthiest Knight lyvinge in his dayes.
Then his most speciall and chief Lady that he had sette his hart of
most, Dame Felys, applied to his will and was wedded to him.   This
noble warryor Sir Gy, after his mariage consideringe [what] he had
don for a womans sake, thought to besset the other part of his lyf
for Goddes sake, departed from his lady in pilgrymeweede as hir
shewys, which rayment he kept to his lyves ende, and did menyi greate
battells, of the which the last was the victory of Colbrond at
Winchester by the warninge of an angell. And from thence, vnknowen
savinge to the Kinge only, come to Warwyke, receyved as a pilgryme
of his owne lady, and by her leave at his abydinge at Gibclif, and his
livery by his page dayly sett at the Castell. And two dayes afore his
deathe, an angell enformed of his passage oute of this world, and of his
ladyes the day fourtnight after him.   And at Gibelyf wer they bothe
buryed, for ther cowld no man fro thence Remofe him till his sworn
brother com, Sr Tyrry, wᵗʰ whome he was translate without lett. And
to this day God for her sake, to tho that devoutely seeke him for hur
sakes, with other Greuis as by miracle seen remedied. And in remem-
brance of his habit it wer full convenient yoᵿ yᵗ it pleased som good
lord or lady to fynde in the same place ij. poore men that cowde help
a priest to singe, one of theim to be ther continually present, wearinge
his pilgrime habyte, and to shew folke the place ; and their habitacion
might be full well sett over his cave in the rocke.

The story of Sir Guy then had evidently long before Rous's
time found a local habitation, both at Warwick and at Winchester.
Leland, in his *Itinerary*, says of Gibclife or Guycliffe : " Ould
Fame remaineth with the People there that Guido Earl of
Warwike in King Athelston's Dayes . . . lived in this place like a
Heremite, unknowen to his wife Felice, untill at the Article of his
Death he shewed what he was. . . . Here is a house of Pleasure, a
Place meet for the Muses. There is sylence, a praty Wood, *antra
in vivo saxo*, the River rowling over the stones with a praty
noyse, *nemusculum ibidem opacum, fontes liquidi et gemmei,
prata florida, antra muscosa, rivi leves et per saxa discursus,
necnon solitudo et quies multis amicissima.*" The heart of the
antiquary warms towards the lovely spot.

Such are the authorities, if the word may be used in this case, for the legend. At any rate, they may serve to show how old it is, and how widely and generally popular it was. In the Elizabethan literature allusions to it abound, though, strangely enough, not one occurs in the plays of Shakespeare, familiar as he must have been with it and the locality to which the more touching part is attached. Puttenham, in his *Art of Poetry* (1589), speaks of " places of assembly where the company shall be desirous to hear of old adventures and valiances of noble knights in times past, as are those of King Arthur and the Knights of the round table—Sir Bevis of Southampton, Guy of Warwick, and others like." In Dr. King's *Dialogues of the Dead* (quoted by Mr. Chappell), " It is the negligence of our ballad singers," a Ghost remarks, " that makes us to be talked of less than others; for who almost besides St. George, King Arthur, Bevis, Guy and Hickathrift, are in the chronicles ? " The Little French Lawyer in Fletcher's play of the name, and Old Master Merrythought in the *Knight of the Burning Pestle* sing snatches of the *Legend*. Corbet in his *Iter Boreale* wishes,

> May all the ballads be call'd in & dye,
> Which sing the warrs of Colebrand & Sir Guy.

Butler tells us of Talgol, one of Hudibras' supporters (who, according to L'Estrange, represented a certain Newgate Market butcher),

> He many a boar & huge dun-cow
> Did, like another Guy, o'erthrow;
> But Guy with him in fight compar'd
> Had like the boar or dun-cow far'd.

Such has been the popularity of this story. The oldest literary form of it preserved to us is, as we have seen, an Anglo-Norman romance, composed probably in the thirteenth century. This, no doubt, was founded on songs and traditions that were then commonly in vogue in the country, that had then already been so for many a generation. These were dressed and decorated by the romance-writer according to the fashion of his age :

the old Saxon hero transformed into a Norman knight, dispatched to the crusades, conducted from tournament to tournament throughout Europe, and carried through all the adventures
proper for a hero of chivalry. One most prominent feature
of the romance is its monastic feeling, which, indeed, is so
strong that one may well believe it to be the work of a monk.
A terrible remorse seizes Guy at last for all the blood he has
shed, and his love for the woman who has incited him to his
blood-shedding career passes away. Is this penitential element
part of the original tale? Was this sung of by old pre-Norman
gleemen? Or is it rather to be ascribed to the translator and
editor of the thirteenth century? Probably so. In the old Saxon
poetry, so far as is known, women occupy but an unimportant
place. Neither there, nor indeed in the life which that poetry
reflects, do they "rain influence and adjudge the prize." Moreover, one can well conceive such an addition being made to the
story in the thirteenth century, a period of a great monastic
revival—a period of much doubt as to matrimony, an uneasy
suspicion prevailing that it was an indulgence which the truly
pious man would scarcely allow himself. Such a suspicion enters
the soul of Guy, when at last, after waiting and longing and
serving so long, he is at last crowned with the happiness of his
heart; he resolves to abandon the treasure gained. How noble
and devout such an abandonment was held to be by the mediæval
monks may be seen from endless instances, notably from the
story of Saint Alexios, of whom Alban Butler thus writes [1]:

Having, in compliance with the will of his parents, married a rich
and virtuous lady, he on the very day of the nuptials, making use of
the liberty which the laws of God and his church give a person before
the marriage be consummated, of preferring a more perfect state,
secretly withdrew, in order to break all the ties which held him in
this world. In disguise he travelled into a different country, em-

---

[1] See Appendix at the end of this Introduction.

braced extreme poverty, and resided in a hut adjoining to a church dedicated to the Mother of God. Being after some time there discovered to be a stranger of distinction, he returned home, and being relieved as a poor pilgrim, lived some time unknown in his father's house, bearing the contumely and ill-treatment of the servants with invincible patience and silence. A little before he died he by a letter discovered himself to his parents.

Guy's wife-desertion then, and his severe asceticism, may be later additions to his original story. There can be little doubt that that original story belongs to a remote age,—possibly, as has been suggested, to an age anterior even to that assigned to it in the romance—the age of Athelstan. With this age of Athelstan it would seem to have been connected from a very early time. There is no kind of historical basis for it in what records we have of that age. There was certainly a great Northern invasion in the reign of Athelstan. Northumbria, lately annexed by him, allied itself with Scots, Danes, Welsh, and essayed to recover its independence. "They fought with Athelstan," writes Milton, " at a place called Wenduse [which might easily have been confounded with Wynton]; others term it Brunnnbury, others [as William of Malmesbury] Bruneford; which Ingulgh [who calls it Brunford] places beyond Humber; Camden in Glendale of Northumberland on the Scottish borders—the bloodiest fight, say authors, that ever this island saw." Ellis suggests that Guy —he should say Egil—may be identical with one Egils, " who did in fact contribute very materially " to the victory. If this be so, then the legend must be rather Scandinavian than Saxon; for this Egil was a northern viking enlisted on the side of Athelstan. But, indeed, if the legend be an old Saxon one, there need be no difficulty in accounting for its later connection with the reign of Athelstan. That was the most glorious reign in the history of Saxon England. Athelstan reaped the rich fruits of his illustrious grandfather's wisdom and policy. He was enabled to consolidate the kingdom, and to maintain its unity unimpaired. At home

and abroad his name was known and feared.   His crowning
victory at Brunanburgh produced a profound impression.   Even
the Saxon imagination was stirred by such power and glory.
" To describe his famous fight," says Milton, " the Saxon annalist,
wont to be sober and succinct, whether the same or another writer,
now labouring under the weight of his argument and overcharged,
runs on a sudden into such extravagant fancies and metaphors as
bear him quite beyond the scope of being understood."   Strangely
enough, the great poet did not recognise in the passage he thus
characterises the work of an older bard ; for it is in fact one of
the few Saxon poems that survive.   There are many signs of a
rich ballad literature, besides that spirited piece, appertaining
to this great monarch's reign.   There is the story of Analaf
belonging to that same battle, which is evidently taken by
Malmesbury from some old ballad.   Then there are the stories of
the King's mother's dream, and of his brother Edwin's punish-
ment for taking part in a conspiracy against him, both which
that chronicler confessedly found in old ballads.   Naturally
enough, the story too of the great combat with the giant was
attached to his reign ; for legends attract each other, so to speak.
The name given in later times to the national combatant was
Guy.

Other romances in course of time grew around that of Guy,
treating of his son Ruisburn, of his tutor Herand and his son.

Harl. MS. 7333, fol. 35 b.

þe ermyte with Inne litil spase
By dethe is past þe Ende of his laboure
Aftir whome Guy was þer successoure
Space of twoo yere by grace of crist Ihesu
Dauntyng his flesho by penaunce and Rygour
Ay more and more encressyng in vertev
¶ God made him knowe þe dayo þt he shold dyce
þorowe his gracious vesitacioune

By an Aungel his spirit to conveye
Aftir his bodyly Resolycioune
For his merit is to þe hevenely mansyoune
þan in alle haste he sent his weddyng Ryng
Vn to his wyff of trewe Affeccioune
Prayd her to come|And beo at his conding
¶ That she sholde doone þere hir besyn cure
As by A maner wyflly deligense
In haste to ordeyne for his Cepulture

With noo þret coste ne with no grete
dispence
Sheo hasted hir til sheo cam in presence
Wher þat Guy lay dedly pale of face
Bespreynt with teeres kuelyng with
Reuerence
þe dede body Felyce did ther iubrace
¶ This uotable & Famouse worthi kuyght
Sent her to sayne bi his messagier
In þilke place to burye hym auoone
Right
Wher that he lay to fore in A smal
Awter
And Afftir this doe trewly hir deveyre
þer for her selfe dysposyū and provide
Fyfftene dayes Folowyng þe same ȝere
She to be buried þere by Guyes syde
¶ His holy wyf of al this toke good hede
Like as he badde and liste no longer
tarye
Tacquyte hir selfe of wyffly womanhede
For she was loþᵉ frome his desire to
varye
Sent in Al haste for þe ordenarye
Wiche ocupied in þat dyosyse
She was not founde in oone poynt
contrarye
Eche thyng tacomplyshe / as ye haue
herde devise
¶ And alle þis cronicle / For to conclude
At hes Exequyes old & younge of age
Of diuerse folke cam grete multitude
With grete devocioune vn to þat her-
mitage
Lyche A prynse with al þe surplusage
þei tooke hym vppe / and leyde him in his
grave
Ordeynid of god be marcyal curage
Ageinst þe Danys þis Regioune to saue
¶ Whos sowle I truste restight nowe in
glorie

With holy Spiretis Above þe Firmament
Felice his wyf callyng to her memorye
þe daye gaue neghe of her enterremeut
To forne provided in her testan.ent
Reynborne þeire heyre / iouslely to succede
By title of hir and lyncalle discent
þeorldume of warwike trewly to possede
¶ þe stok descendyng douue by þe pee
dugree
To Guy his fadir by title of mariage
Afftir whos dethe / of lawe and equyte
Reynborne to entre in to his Eritage
Cleimeyng his Ryght / his moder of good
age
Haþe yolde hir dette by dethe vnto
nature
By side her lorde in þat Ermitage
Wiche couded feyre was made hir
Sepulture
¶ For to auctorise better þis matere
Whos translacioun sheweþe þe sentence
Oote of latyne made by þe Cronniculier
Callid of olde Gyrard Cronnbyence
Wiche whilome wrot with gret deligence
Dedis of hem in westesex crowned kynges
Gretly comendyng for kneyghtly ex-
cellence
Guy of werrewike in heos famouse
wreytingis
¶ Of whos nobelesse ful gret hede he toke
His kneyghtly fame to putten in Re-
memberavuse
þe eleventþe chapitre / of his historialboke
þe parfite lyf þe vertuouse gouernaũnce
His wilfulle pouertee / harde ligginge and
penaunce
Al sent to me in Euglishe to translate
If owght be wrong in metre or substance
Put al þe wyte / for dulnesse oñ lydegate

Harleian MS. 5243, fol. 4.

To all heroical knightes, and illustrious
Ladies, both in Court, and Countrie
for virtewe, love, bewtie, chivalrie,
prowes, bowntie : & of other com-
pleate departmentes most eminent
and honorabl, John Lane in all
dutie wisheth gratious perfection to
felicitie eternal.
After, nay before all your secular affaires,
vouchsafe to accepte, to your recreations

the pleasant historie of this vertuous
paire instanced in the most noble pair of
frendes, and lovers, the Ladie Felis, and
her exemplarie sparck of christian honor,
Sir Gwy Earle of warwick, surnamed
the heremite; reckoned for more then
twoe hundred yeeres togeather, the last of
the Nine worthies: albeit in that heroical
ranck, hee standeth indignified, or neglected, but without anie known cause,

by some foraine heraultes, for theire Duke Gothfreyes sake, wheareof expostulation is made after a modest fasshion in this Poem. His deedes have lately bin renewed in verse, and published in a litle tract ; neverthelos for brevitie sake, (as it seemeth) it omitteth much of the original historie, left vnto vs by all the ancient English pooetes: whose historie I take to bee meerly english, and not delt withall by anie straungers. (vnlesse by Ariosto) as kinge Arturs hath bin by the Italien Boeas, in honorable manner, and by some French, and Spanish, as it is reported. But all our ancientes, fallinge in love with the high-pitchd vertew, which our noble Guyon bore in martial prowes, have in divers successive ages, as Poetes historical, reillustrated the same ; as well is observed by our learned, and farthest traveiled antiquarie Mr Camden, whoe with approved poetical iudgment, of givinge discreet accompte to the Muses, calleth him Guidonem warwicensem decautatum illum heroem. And him have they sunge in deed into the fabrick of sownd poetrie, although in termes obsolete ; the which, posteritie muie againe, and againe, (as listeth Poetes) refine, in lines more polite, accordinge as our language is become refined, and more copious, equal (at the least) to anie circumstant vulgar: as with reason, and learned demonstration, is wittnessed by our noble, and highlie ingenious knight Sir Philip Sidney, but in sublimitie of conceipt, cann passe them never, for that they (dealinge in own loomes as poets historical) have ever since, built on the same model, either expressely, or transposedly, which also is punctualy. It beinge by them idealie layd, after the laudabl. & lawfull manner of poetical fiction, doe serve out Guions trewe real historie, vnder the signature of Misterie; which hath to drawe with it Allusion, Circumstance, Discourse, Speculation, Sentence, Immitation : all sommd vp in these twoe vz Invention, Demonstration . as well knoweth the Classis of poetes laureat, to whome I produce Chaucers tale by the Squier, never yet told out by anie in the same straine ; the which formes, I also in this poem shall, and in my poetical visions, first and second partes, and in my Twelue monethes observe, and exemplifye . the name Poeta, being derived

of ποιέω, signifieth to make as a maker ; howbeit to define the art it selfe is all as hard, as to doe it indeede, but not to doe it rightly I cannever define yt soundly: No though her practise doe thus extend yt : vz Primo, into the Satyrical, which proveth so offensive to the meridien wheare yt confineth ! as that her back cannever beare half the enimies shee begetteth to her self. Secundo, it maie be laid in ye Lyrical which hath to praise or despraise ; which satisfyeth not the best wittes ; sith flotinge topp of the wave for the gull to feed on particulars. Tercio, it maie bee carried in the kind called heroical, or Allegorical ; the which (allegorical waie anglinge at the bottom) implieth those other twaine, and all notions ells, beinge exercised in such different descant, and varietie of verse in kind, as discreete art findeth most congruent to the muse: is thearefore most delightfull to the most iudicious, as having in yt an heroical powr of callinge the highest vnderstandinges of all others, as namely our master Aristotel, Alexander magnus, Scipio Affricanus, Octauius Augustus Cesar, Jacobus Angliæ rex, with manie moe, whoe are by so much the more often honorablie remembred, as theire bownteous favors to the ingenious in this faculty, have bin shewed, and theire own iudicious dexterities in it abownded, but is no meate for paperpeckinge In rimers — out poetasters, sith — muse-traducinge, — witt abusinge, —Poesie-missysinge Pieridistes. In which last, szt heroical kind ; Homer bestirred him selfe to lead the dawnce. Virgil blasoned the riches of his learninge in the same cloth of arras . the ancient English Poetes (meaninge allwaies the sownd ones) have delivered them of heroical birthes in this kind ; which doe survive of theire deceased parentes glorie, all of them adducinge a complete knight, in the personations of twoe in number ; and maie as lawfullie bee instanced in one : and all as well in twoe, as pleaseth the ingenious. For so Mr Edm: Spencer in his allegorical declaratorie, faerely declameth. Now, for my own part (vnder correction) I endevour to call a general muster of all our noblest Guions whole historie, in the same kind also, as beinge most proper for it, and him ; but without derogatinge from the desert of our ancient

English poets first plott: the *which* (representinge excellent) was written allmo>t three hundred yeeres gonn, by Don Lidgate, and since him, by John Rowse & Pepulwick. But wheare all they had theire first president! is now by the ancient historiens verie hard to prove; for that in our greate combustion of antiquitie, they suffred shippwrack: Notwithstandinge, some of them escaped yᵉ distroier, and are yet extant, & well preserved by the singular industries of osm, that waie both studious, and learned: amongst whome, Mʳ Thomas Allen, in the learnedst ranckes hath reputation; as Sir Robert Coton knight his industrie in this kind, hath singular commendation. All these ancient Cronoclers wrote of Guies person, & greate prowes; namely, Henricus Knighton, Thomas Radburn, Giraldus Cornubiensis, Johannes Strench, Johannes Hardinge, Johannes Gresley, Johannes Powtrel: all beinge manuscriptes, never printed, with many moe, as saith John Rosse, whoe dilligentlie in K. Hen: the seavnths time collected them on the point of Gwy, while the recordes weare yet extant, every of them avonchinge his overcominge of Colbrand on the same conditions, *which* tradition hath ever since that time maintained. Cronica cronicorum affirmeth the same, though at the second hand, and with missuaminge of Giraldus Cambrensis, for Giraldus Cornubiensis. Yet all this notwithstandinge! our valient Guy is so vnfortunate amongste our late Croniclers, as that they are pleased to saie lesse of him, then Hanibals epitaph, amounted vnto. Amongst whome! som of oures, (but vnkindlie for th'innocent English penn, and that to this worthies dishonor) whose person they confesse; yet after holdinge his own for many ages in his grave ex concesso, woold faine decline the credite of all yᵉ ancientes, concerninge the conditions of Guyes fightinge the Duello for this kingdom, when hee slewe Colbrand the Affrican giant challenginge for the Danes: as yf Sir Guy, beinge then a man retired to obscuritie, and besides overtaken of old age; shoold, or woold runn at a masterie so daungerous for glorie, *which* hee contemned : and not vppon the necessitie of that occasion, but this presumptuous kind of novitious writinge, maie rest assured, that onlie

one of yonder ancientes, livinge neerer the time of the famous Guy by some hundreds of yeeres, will carrie more credite! then one thowsand such newe, offringe so forwardly, *which* must needes bee ignorantlie, sith not havinge seene anie of the manuscriptes before mentioned. Howbeit, John Stowes note of Guy, is perfecter then all the rest of the newe. Against *which* manner of historifyenge, *which* intendeth but to vex the credite of antiquity, (speakinge this vnder correction, and without taxinge the good endevoure of anie man, or the person it selfe) Poetrie hath to bringe her action of encrochment, for vsurpinge on her licence of allusion in matter of fact, and it applienge to historic of longe before our new writers times: *which* manner, scarce is historicum dicendi genus, but is goodly to shewe with what eloqution such endewe them selves with all, and to enlarge tomes beyond movinge, without the helpe of a porter. In the meane time, the precise naked integritie of the ancientes. gave (with more brevitie) accompt, rather of plaine fact, as it was indeede, then of affected eloquence poeticalie interlined (but vnlawfullie) in historic. Which new fluence, breeding affluence, will shortlie leave in evidence, that what Poetrie doth idealie deliver for fiction! is trewe; constant truith standing vp her perpetual ensigne: and what this novel kind of historifienge affirmeth for trewe! is false, sith mixed. For, marck if theire affected insinuations doe not purposely wooe these three common concubines Partialitie! feare! flattery! and on them begetteth the bastard falsity! a chaungelin, the *which* mote these faeries overlive them selves! and the parties they have with theire mowth glewe starched! they woold not faile so to stripp off theire old skinn, cast all theire loose haier, and rectifie theire new sett countenaunce att annother glasse; as that Proteus him selfe woold not bee able to knowe them. How then may such bee trusted to bee cited in other discentes de futuro? yf not as trewly reportinge! as doth positive divinitie in schooles: with whome, to growe to particulars, woold surelie provoke theire passion, but theire integritie never. On thother side, sownd Poetrie of the ancient manner, suffreth no alter-

ation, but as a beakoun, or land marcke,
standeth vp from age to age impregnable,
against all wittes invectives, to drive
them home to theire vocatiuo caret.
Againe, yet som others, contrario to
thallegeance dewe to tho muses, and
thearfore impardonable, sith blabbinge
theire secretes left in trust without
leave, vncleaulie, (yet as it weare iocund-
lie) denie Guy, and his actes to bee at
all ; but how these doe better know it
now ! or whie woe must take theire
wordes for aucthentical, against tho
soberer & chaster ancientes, livinge
neerer that time by many ages ! wee no
more dare belive, then them selves are
suer to bee belived, regarded, or ought
esteemed, when they also have takenn
farewell of the world : though now seem-
inge to bee fallen out but with Lidgate
onlie, and his poetrie ; doe yet in effect,
through his sides, word censor like let
drive at her, but not as Aristotels
scholers, naie rather his masters, in not
obayeuge his iniunction concerninge fa-
cultie, of oportet discentem credere.
Wheareas Lidgate hath respectivelie followed the advise of the same Aristotl
given for Poetry szt of fownding yt on
ann historie, and the same determininge
in a short time : both which preceptes,
Lidgate hath dewlie performed in this
manner, viz that touchinge time ! Manns
whole lief is but short, and touchinge
truith of storie ! Lidgate fownd this of
Guy, first recorded by Giraldus Cornubiensis, and by manie other cronielers
before named. Besides, that the noblest
Normanes, whoe came in with the Conquerour, and weare carles of Warwick
after earle Newbreghte, above six score
yeeres after Guy, namely the familie of
Beauchamp, or Bellocampe, many yeeres
after that ; reioiced to ioine them selves
to the memorie of such ann ancestor :
and did not onlie repaire those monumentes weare fownd of Guy, but added
somewhat elles. Thus Lidgat fuierlie
discharginge him selfe, leaveth it apparent, that the meere historien, is of all
other infestus ! the most malignant toward the Poet historical : whome hee
vnderstandeth not : though him the
Poet doth, at ann haier, is thearefore the
most vnfitt to accuse, or censure the
industrious, in the same case, that Prince
Hector, and kinge Artur maie also bee

doubted of, because they likewise have
binn poeticalie historified by poetes pro-
sequutinge ideal veritie, as the historien
pretendeth positive truith. But now
alas so sickly ! sith tempted by yonder
three fountaine troublinge faeries, that
(as the world waggeth,) it is harder to
find ann ancient poet false, then a new
historien trowe ; while hee imbibeth that
rancke penn swoln humor, newly cleaped
the art of reformation : meaninge tho
same art, which our excellently learned
knight Sir Henrie Sauyl in his annota-
tions vppon Tacitus, inett stealinge over-
sea hitherward, vppon whose bold forehead, hoe scoreth a lecture, wheareof shee
is hardlie capable szt of more modestie.
Weare it not thearefore better, that Don
Barckley (the ferriman) bee delt with all,
to shipp her back againe ? sith none that
knowes, trustes her for strawes ; rather
then thus, through her envious suppress-
inge the heroes, to discourage the fertile
wittes of our Englishe nation, which weare
readie to comme into the deservinge ranck
with the Greekes, Latines and Italienes,
to renewe that poetical reputation it in-
herited of old, but for this odd fashion
of presumed-sinceare wisdom, down
strikinge with her lightned thunderbolt
the deceased. Whoe in theire times
(without comparison) sored on no com-
temptible opinion, an hartninge of the
foraner, to detract also. But if it shold
bee imposed on the meere historiens (so
well beeseene in antiquities, and glistringe
of the reformatives aforesaid) to reconcile those Poemes of Chaucer, and Lidgate, & of somme other later English
(even the best of that kind, which
staieth not yt selfo on particulars only,
the which kind was, is, and ever wilbee
scandalous) to bee all one thinge vari-
ously transposed ! it mote chaunce to
pose them all though to the poet it bee
possible to give a tract, which cann
satisfy all men, on what kinds of learninge soever they insist ! And further
demonstrate, how that a forano poet
(esteemed excellent, but dealinge with
holie scripture in the Letter) hath from
trewe poetries waiese (meaninge the ancient) not a litle erred : forasmuch as it is
well known to the Academick Classis
Laureate, that not good verse alone, nor
prose alone, ne store of similes, or some
discription with allusion onlie, and the

like, doe make poetrie complete. Yet beinge of it! cann at the most amount but to Sermocination, of prose turnd verse. Thus yf Poetes bee of my iury! I hope I have not provoked anie discreete manns choler, in thus showldringe (though weakely, to poetries behoof) for tho same roome for her, which Porphirie in schooles collateth szt habet esse in genere demonstrantium; and thearfore without leave, is worthie of own ingenious reputation as well now, as then; to whome ancient learninge woold never give the lye, for doubt of pledginge the new in apium risus. Otherwise, even Cornelius Agrippa, ipse aries (for all his occult philosophick lookes) maie chaunce in this straine, to sitt beatinge his heeles without the muses gates, singinge to own vanity, Beati qui non intelligunt. more mote bee brought how lustie some historiens deport them on own glorious ostentation, as yf theare weare none to them! sith vncivilie tauntinge, discreditinge, degradinge, and controwlinge deiected poetrie (the ideal model of moral demonstratives) which ever was rara auis in terris, and knoweth what shee doth, without such as publish ann ignorance, never ingendred in schooles: for Poetrie hath waies by her selfe. Whearfore such angrie quillmen maie, (when they knowe more) blush of own shame, yf shee acquitt her self from beinge either ward! or tenent

at will to them! Howbeet love predominatinge with vs, concealeth names, that by this litle (gentlie ment,) they woold bee pleased to amend much; which more woold commend their own learninge, yf not indignlie baiting sound poetrie of virtuous institute; and thearfore so much the more esteemed by the most noble, most honorable, most valient, wise, and learned, as thinge (by som maintained) which none maie teach to other: Least elles shee complaine her to all her ingenious pupills, whoe cann byte home yf bytten. I never had the philosophers stone, whearwith to promise our Guyon, in suche daintie limned worck, as Ariostoes orlando hath fownd since hee came into England; nevertheles this meanethe historicalie with the ancientes, to present Sir Gwies youth, manwood, and old age: his love, warr, & mortification, all sommed vp in his liefe, and death, and that accordinge to our most ancient historiens, poetes, heraltes recordes, publick monumentes, and tradicion also, which somtime is a never dienge trewe cronicler. Thus not havinge whearewith to expresse my poore service vnto you then in this expense of times leasure with takinge humblest leave doe recommend it vnto you, and you all, to thalmightie.
this   of
　　　Your verie lovinge frend
　　　　Jo: La:

See Mrs. Jameson's *Sacred and Legendary Art.* Alexis' father wishes him to marry, and chooses him a bride. " On the appointed day the nuptials were celebrated with great pomp and festivity; but when the evening came the bride-groom had disappeared, and they sought him everywhere in vain; and when they questioned the bride, she answered, 'Behold, he came into my chamber and gave me this ring of gold, and this girdle of precious stones, and this veil of purple, and then he bade me farewell, and I know not whither he is gone.' And they were all astonished; and seeing he returned not, they gave themselves up to grief: his mother spread sackcloth on the earth and sprinkled it with ashes, and sat down upon it; and his

wife took off her jewels and bridal robes, and darkened her windows, and put on widow's attire, weeping continually; and Euphemian sent servants and messengers to all parts of the world to seek his son, but he was nowhere to be found. In the meantime, Alexis, after taking leave of his bride, disguised himself in the habit of a pilgrim, fled from his father's house, and throwing himself into a little boat, he reached the mouth of the Tiber; at Ostia he embarked in a vessel bound for Laodicea, and thence he repaired to Edessa, a city of Mesopotamia, and dwelt there in great poverty and humility, spending his days in ministering to the sick and poor, and in devotion to the Madonna, until the people who beheld his great piety, cried out 'A saint!' Then fearing for his virtue, he left that place and embarked in a ship bound for Tarsus, in order to pay his devotions to St. Paul. But a great tempest arose, and after many days the ship, instead of reaching the desired port, was driven to the mouth of the Tiber, and entered the port of Ostia. When Alexis found himself again near his native home, he thought, 'It is better for me to live by the charity of my parents than to be a burden to strangers,' and hoping that he was so much changed that no one would recognise him, he entered the city of Rome. As he approached his father's house, he saw him come forth with a great retinue of servants, and accosting him humbly besought a corner of refuge beneath his roof, and to eat of the crumbs which fell from his table; and Euphemian, looking on him, knew not that it was his son, nevertheless he felt his heart moved with unusual pity, and granted his petition, thinking within himself, 'Alas for my son Alexis! perhaps he is now a wanderer and poor, even as this man.' So he gave Alexis in charge to his servants, commanding that he should have all things needful. But, as it often happens with rich men who have many servitors and slaves, Euphemian was ill obeyed; for, believing Alexis to be what he appeared—a poor ragged wayworn beggar—they gave him no other lodging than a hole under the marble steps which led to his father's door, and all who passed and repassed looked on his misery; and the servants, seeing that he bore all uncomplaining, mocked at him, thinking him an idiot, and pulled his matted beard, and threw dirt on his head; but he endured in silence. A far greater trial was to witness every day the grief of his mother and wife; for his wife, like another Ruth, refused to go back to the house of her fathers; and often, as he lay in his dark hole under the steps, he heard her weeping in her chamber and crying, 'O my Alexis! whither art thou gone? Why hast thou espoused me only to forsake me?' And hearing her thus tenderly lamenting and upbraiding his absence, he was sorely tempted; nevertheless he remained steadfast. Thus many years passed away, until his emaciated frame sunk under his sufferings, and it was revealed to him that he should die. Then he procured from a servant of the house pen and ink, and wrote a full account of all these things, and all that had happened to him in his life, and put the letter in his bosom, expecting death. It happened about this time, on a certain feast day, that Pope Innocent was celebrating high mass before the Emperor Honorius and all his court, and suddenly a voice was heard, which said, 'Seek the servant of God who is about to depart from this life, and who shall pray for the city of Rome.' So the people fell on their faces; and another voice said, 'Where shall we seek him?' And the first voice answered, 'In the house of Euphemian the patrician.' And Euphemian was standing next to the emperor, who said to him, 'What! hast thou such a treasure in thy house, and hast not divulged it? Let us now repair thither immediately.' So Euphemian went before to prepare the way, and as he approached his house a servant met him, saying, 'The poor beggar whom thou hast sheltered has died within this hour, and we have laid him on the steps before the door.' And Euphemian ran up the steps and uncovered the face of the beggar, and it seemed to him the face of an angel, such a glory of light proceeded from it; and his heart melted within him, and he fell on his knees; and as the emperor and his court came near, he said, 'This is the servant of God of whom the voice spake just now.' And when the pope saw the letter which was in the dead hand of Alexis, he humbly asked him to deliver it; and the hand relinquished it forthwith, and the chancellor read it aloud before all the assembly."

[The First Part.]

[How Guy undertakes to fight a Danish Giant.]

WHEN : meate & drinke is great plentye, [page 349] At feasts
then lords and Ladyes still wilbe,
& sitt, & solace lythe [1] ;
4 then itt is time ffor mee to speake
of keene knights & kempes [2] great,
such carping ffor to kythe, [3]

I tell of knights and warriors

how they haue conquered, for Englands right :
8 with helme vpon head, with halbert [4] bright,
ffull oft & many a sithe [5]
they [6] haue burnt by dale and downe,
citye, castle, tower, & towne,
12 & made bearnes vnblythe ;

who have

burnt towers and towns,

made Ladyes ffor to weepe with dreery mood,
when theire ffreinds ought ayled but good,
their hands [7] to wring and writhe. [8]
16 of all cronicles ffarr and neere,
were [9] any deeds of armes weere, [10]
the most I prayse Sir Guy

and made women weep for their friends.

Above all heroes

I put Guy of Warwick,

of warwicke! that noble knight
20 oft times ffor Englands right
hath done ffull worthylye ;
yett hee kept itt as priuilye
as tho itt had neuer beene hee,
24 without noyse or crye.

who kept secret his noble deeds for England.

& when he came ouer the salt ffome
ffrom Sir Terrey of Gorwaine, [11]

When he came back

---

[1] soft, gentle.—P. listen to.—F.
[2] *kempa*, a soldier, Champion; *kemp*, to contend. Scot. vid. Gl. ad G.D.—P.
[3] A.-S. *cyðan*, to make known, relate. —F.
[4] hauberk.—P.
[5] *sithe*, vices (time) Lye ; Chaucer. —P.
[6] The Danes.—P.
[7] MS. lands.—F. hands.—P.
[8] The author wrote "wry."—Dyce.
[9] where.—P.
[10] There is a tag to the *e*.—F.
[11] Sir Thierry of Gurmoise, in the Affleck Romance as analysed by Ellis, first Guy's opponent, then the friend rescued by him. See Ellis, p. 204, 214, 218, 223 (ed. Bohn).—F.

a knight of maine and moode,
28 ffor ffeare lest any one shold him know,
he kept him in silly beggars rowe

where euer hee went or stood ;

& euer he sperred [1] priuilicke

32 how they ffared att warwicke,
& how they liued there.

King Athels[t]one, the truth to say,
att the towne of winchester there he lay
36 with one soe royall a ffare.

the King of Denmarke, Auelocke, [2]
he into England brought a fflocke
of bearnes as breeme as beare [3] ;

40 & with him a Gyant stiffe & starke,
a Lodlye devill out of Denmarke :
such another you neuer saw yore :

hee was rayed richlye with royall plate
44 both legg & arme, you may well wott, [4]
in armor bright to be seene ;
he brought weapon,—who list ffor to read—
more then any cart could lead, [5]
48 to ding men downe by-deene ;

& swore othes great and grim,
that all England shold hold of him,
or he would kindle their care.

52 then in England there was neuer a knight
that once with him durst flight,—
ffull sore [6] he did them dread, [7]—

neither with Auelocke nor Athelstone.
56 then our King, to Christ he made his moane,

---

[1] i.e. enquired.—P. There are two
strokes for the second *i* in *priuilicke*.—F.
[2] Anlaf, in the Affleck MS. The
change here is due, no doubt, to the
Romance of Havelok the Dane.—F.

[3] boare, q.—P. *Bore* is the regular
word.—F.   [4] wate, weet, q.—P.
[5] forte pro (lade, i.e.) load, A.-S.
hladan, B. læden.—P.
[6] soe sore.—P.   [7] dare, q.—P.

& to his mother bright to be scene.

then one Night as our K*ing* lay in a vision,

there came an Angell downe ffrom heauen

60 to lett him vnderstand [1] :

an angel comes to him in a vision,

he sayd, " rise vp in the morning by prime,[2]

& goe to the gates in a good time ;

an old man shall you ffind there,

64 both with his scripp and his pike,

as *th*at hee were palmer like,

lowring [3] vnder his here.[4]

and tells him to go early to the gates, where he'll find an old man like a palmer.

vpon thy knees, S*i*r K*ing*, looke thou kneele him to,

68 & pray him the battell to doe,

ffor his loue *th*at Marry bore.[5] "

Him he must pray to fight the giant.

w*i*th *th*at the Angell vanished away.

but more of this Gyant I haue to say.

72 as I haue heard my Elders tell,

he was soe ffoule & soe great course,[6]

That neither might beare him steed nor horsse ;

men thought he came ffrom hell.

[page 350]

76 the[n] bespake a Squier priuilye :

" where is the K*night* men call S*i*r Guy,

some time [7] in this land did dwell?

or S*i*r Arrard [8] of arden alsoe ?

80 the one of these might thither goe

the Gyant ffor to quell."

(A squire says Sir Guy

or Sir Arrard of Arden would fight him.

then bespake him an Erle in *th*at while,

& sais, " S*i*r Guy is now in Exile,

84 no man knowes wh[i]ther or where ;

he had but one sonne, & he hight Rainborne ;

a merchant stold him ffrom wallingford towne,

ouer the seas w*i*th him to ffare ;

"Ah! but Guy is in exile.

His son Rainborne is stolen ;

---

[1] him ken aright, q.—P.

[2] *Prime*, the first houre of the day (in Summer at foure a clocke, in Winter at eight). Cotgrave.—F.

[3] Only half the *n* in the MS.—F.

[4] hair, q.—P.   here = hair.—F.

[5] bare, q.—P.

[6] i. e. Corpse.—P.

[7] *tine* in the MS.—F.

[8] Sir Heraud, Guy's trusty companion, then " in a dungeon on the coast of Africa." Ellis, p. 198, 234.—F.

88   " the Erle & the Countesse beene both dead,

and his wife,
Felix,

Dame ffelix is sore adread

    of [1] her Lord, Sir Guye.

" her ffather and mother beene dead her ffroe ;

thinks he,
Guy, is
dead.")

92   & soe shee thinkes Sir Guy is alsoe,

    the flower of knighthood bold."

Next
morning,
Athelstan
goes to the
gates,

then Earlye, as soone as itt was day,

our King to the gates tooke his way,

96   his fforward [2] ffor to hold.

right certaine truth to tell,

finds an old
man in
palmer's
dress,

he ffound [3] a man in the same apparell

    as the Angell before had him told.

100   vpon his knees the King kneeled him to,

and prays
him to fight
the giant.

and prayd him the battell doe,

    ffor his loue that Iudas sold.

The Palmer
says

then answered the Palmer right,

104   & sayd, " in England you haue many a Knight

    the battell that may doe.

I am brused in my body, & am vnyeeld [4] ;

he is too
weak.

alas, I may no wepons welde !

108   behold, & take good heede [5] ! "

Athelstan
says
God wills
that he
should fight.

our King sayd the palmer vntill,

" well I wott itt is gods will

    you shold helpe me in my need [6] ! "

"Then I
will,"
answers he.

112   " If that be soe," the palmer did speake,

" by the might of Christ I shall thee wreake, [7]

    if I had armour & sheild."

Athelstan

our King of this hee was ffull ffaine,

116   & soe were all his lords certaine.

---

[1] for, q.—P.
[2] agreement: with the angel?—F.
[3] MS. faund.—F.
[4] unwielde or unweld, q. Chauc.—P.

[5] Then take good heed thereto, q. —P.
[6] in the field, q.—P.
[7] revenge.—P.

to a Chamber they cold him Lead ;
they sought vp Armour bright and flaire,
inough ffor any King to haue in store,[1]
120   & they best they did him bidd.

offers him
armour,

but meete for his body there was none,
he was soe large of blood and bone,
    the fferssest[2] *that* euer was fledd.
124 the day of battell drew neere hand ;
but 5 dayes before, as I vnderstand,
    our king was sore affrayd.

but none
will fit him,
he is so big.

The day of
battle draws
near.

then bespake the palmer priuilye,
128 "where is the Knight men call Sir Guye ?
sometimes in this land he dyd dwell[3] ;
once I see him beyond the sea ;
his Armoure I thinke wold serue mee
132   in battell stifllye to stand."

The Palmer
suggests
that Guy's
armour will
fit him.

the King did thereto assent ;
the Kings messenger to warwicke went,
    the Countesse soone he ffound.[4]
136 before her he kneeled him on his knee,
prayed her of the armor belonged to Sir Guy
    when he was a-liue liuande.[5]

• Athelstan
sends to the
Countess for
it,

shee saught vp armoure ffaire to bee seene :
140 Sir Guyes sword was sharpe & keene,
    himselfe was wonnt to weare.
to the towne of winchester they did itt bring ;
ffull gladd therof then was the King,
144   & many *that* with him there were.

and she
sends it
back, with
Guy's sword.

then the rayed the palmer anon-right
with helme vpon head, with halbert[6] bright ;

They arm
him.

[1] to wear, q.— P.
[2] MS. fferffest.—F.
[3] he did dwell in this land. q.—P.
[4] fand, q.—P.
[5] alive on ground, q.— P.
[6] hauberk, q.—P.

they raught him sheild and speare.

he mounts,
and rides
forth.

148 Then he lope on horsbacke with good entent, [p. 351]
& fforth of the gates then hee went,
    his ffoes ffor to ffeare.

When he
gets to the
field

then al be-spread [1] was the ffeild
152 with helme vpon head, with shining sheild,[2]
    as breeme[3] as any beare.[4]

Guy dis-
mounts,

& when the palmer all the armes sawe,
he lighted downe, & list not lauge,

and prays

156   but he mad his prayers arright[5]:

to Christ

    " Christ! _that_ suffered wounds 5,
    & raised Lazarus ffrom dath to liffe,[6]
        to grant mee speech & sight,—

160 & saued danyell the Lyons ffroe,
    & borrowed[7] Susanna out of woe,—

to grant him
strength to

        to grant vs strenght & might,

free England
from the
Danish yoke.

    "_that_ I may England out of thraldome bring
164 & not let vnder[8] the danish _King_
    haue litle England att his will."

Then he
springs into
the saddle,

then without any stirropp verament
into the saddle he sprent,

168   & sate there sadd and still.

and Athel-
stan says

our _King_ said, " by gods grace
this riseth ffrom a light liuerues,[9]
and of an Egar will.

he never
saw any one
do that
except Sir
Guy.

172 I neuer keww no man _that_ soe cold haue done,
    but old Sir Guy of warw[i]cke towne,
    that curteous knight himselfe.[10] "

---

[1] MS. albe spread.—F. all bespread.
—P.
[2] With Hauberk glitterand bright,
query.—P.
[3] MS. breene.—F.
[4] boar, qu.—P. _Bore_ is the old word;
but the rhyme with _feare_ makes the
change necessary. See too l. 39.—F.
[5] prayers thore.—P.

[6] from dead on liue, q.—P.
[7] borrow, ab. A.-S. _beorgan_; servare,
custodire.—P.
[8] delend.—P.
[9] nimbleness. See _liuer_, vol. i. p. 17,
l. 46. Fr. _delivre de sa personne_, an
active nimble wight. Cotgrave.—F.
[10] himsel. Boreal. D.—P.

[The Second Part.]

[How Sir Guy fights and kills the Danish Giant.]

176

2ᵈ parte

The Gyant was the ffirst *that* tooke the place ;
vglye he was, and ffoule of fface ;
the danish men began to smile.
he wold neither runne nor leape,
but layd all his weapons vpon a heape,
& dryd ¹ himselfe for guile
that he might choose of the best,
that who-soeuer with them hee hitt,
w*hi*ch warr *that* hard while.

The foul Giant comes,

stands still,

and tries his weapons.

184 Trumpetts made steeds to stampe & stare ;
the K*ing* of denmarke, he was there,
the K*ing* of England alsoe.
then the K*ing* of Denmarke a booke out breade,²
188 & sware theron, as the story sayes,—
behold & take good heed :—

King Avelocke

swears

"if the Gyant had the warre,³
of England he wold neuer cleame more,
192 neither nye nor ffurr.⁴ "
the kinge of England was there alsoe ;
the same othe he sware alsoe,—
behold and take good heede,⁵—

that if the Giant is beaten, he'll never claim England again. Athelstan swears that if

196 "if the pore palmer had the wore,
of England he wold neuer claime more,
while his liffe dayes last wold."
& thus their trothes together they strake,
200 they said their poyntment shold not slake,
nor exile out off Arr.⁶

his Palmer is beaten he'll not claim England.

¹ fort è *dress'd.*—P.   tried.—F.
² breide, braide, arose, &c., also pulled
out, drew, Gl. ad Chauc.—P.
³ werre for werrs.—P.
⁴ *i.e.* nigh nor far.—P.
⁵ corrupt.—P.
⁶ mold, q.—P.

The Giant
says that
he'll

then the Gyant loud did crye :
to the King of Denmarke [1] these words says hee,

204 "behold & take good heede !
yonder is an Iland in the sea ;
ffrom me he can-not scape away,
nor passe my hands indeed ;

kill or drown
Guy,

208 "but I shall either slay him with my brand,
or drowne him in yonder salt strand [2];
ffro me he shall not scape away.

and crown
Avelocke
King of
England.

then I will with my owne hand
212 crowne thee king of litle England
ffor euer and ffor aye."

that was true, as the King of denmarke thought ;

The Giant
and Guy
cross to an
island
in two barges.

comanded 2 barges fforth to be brought,
216 & either into one was done.
the Gyant was [3] the ffirst that ore did passe.

Guy pushes
his barge off

& as soone as hee [4] to the Iland come was,
his barge there he thrust him ffrom ;

220 with his ffoote & with his hand
· he thrust his barge ffrom the Land,
with the watter he lett itt goe,

into the
stream,

he let itt passe ffrom him downe the streame.
224 then att him the Gyant wold ffreane [5]
why he wold doe soe.

saying that

then bespake the Palmer anon-right,
"hither wee be come ffor to flight
228 till the tone of vs be slaine ;
2 botes brought vs hither,

one is
enough to
carry the
victor back.

& therfore came not both together,
but one will bring vs home. [6]

---

[1] MS. Demmarke.—F.
[2] Cp. "then I was ware of a runing strand." Eger & Grime, vol. i. p. 360, l. 187.—F.
[3] It should be 'Sir Guy was.'—P.
[4] Guy.—F.
[5] frein, fraine, interrogare, Jun.—P.
[6] Percy adds (againe) ? Home is for hame.—F.

232 " ffor thy Bote thou hast yonder tyde,   [page 352]
    ouer in thy bote I trust to ryde ;
    & therfore Gyant, beware ! "
    trumpetts blew, & bade them goe toote,   *The*
236 the one [on] horsbacke, the other on ffoote [1] ;   *trumpets sound,*
    but Guy to god was darre.[2]

    Sir Guy weened well to doo,   *and Sir Guy*
    he tooke a strong speare & rode h[i]m too,   *charges.*
240 he was in a good intent :
    althoe he rode neuer soe ffast,
    his strong speare on the Gyant hee brast,   *He shivers*
    that all to shiuers itt went.   *his spear on the Giant,*

244 & then Sir Guy anon-right
    drew out his sword *that* was soe bright,   *draws his*
    that many a man beheld,   *sword,*
    & on the Gyant he smote [3] soe   *and cuts off*
248 *that* a quarter of his sheild fell him ffroe,   *part of his shield.*
    euen vntill the fleild.

    the Gyant against him made him bowne [4] ;   *The Giant*
    horsse & man & all came downe   *knocks Guy over,*
252 vpon the ground [5] soe greene.
    throughout Sir Guyes steede   *and cuts his*
    the Gyants sword to the ground yeed [6] ;   *horse right through.*
    such stroakes haue seldome [7] beene seene.

256 then Sir Guy started on his feete ffull tyte,[8]   *Guy cuts*
    & on the Gyant cold hee smite
    as a man *that* had beene woode ;
    & vpon the Gyant he smote soe ffast   *through the*
260 *that* the Gyants strong armour all to-brast ;   *Giant's armour,*
    there-out sprang the bloode.   *and draws blood.*

---

[1] There is a mark between the *f* and *o* in the MS.—F.
[2] deare, q.—P.
[3] *snote* in the MS.—F.
[4] ready.—P

[5] One stroke too many in the MS.—F.
[6] passed.—P.
[7] seld or seeld, q.—P.
[8] Light, q.—P.

then the Gyant hitt Sir Guy vpon the helme ;
aboue on his head the stroake itt ffell ;
264   itt was with stones sett,
itt was with precyous stones made ;
Sir Guys helmett neere assunder yode[1] ;
such stroakes of men beene drade.

268 then the Gyant thirsted sore ;
some of his blood he had lost thore[2] ;

    & this he sayd on hye :
" good Sir, & itt be thy will,

272 giue me leaue to drinke my ffill,
ffor sweete St Charytye ;

" and I will doe thee the same deede
another time, if thou haue neede,
276   I tell the certainlye."

" why, vpon that couenant," Sir Guy can sayine,
" goe & drinke thy ffill, & come againe,
and heere Ile abyde thee."

280 beside them there the riuer ran ;
the Gyant went & reffresht him then,
    & came ffull soone againe.

ffrom that itt was lowe prime
284 till itt was hye noone,
the delten strokes with maine.[3]

but the sword that Sir Guy had lead,
therewith he kept his head,
288   stoode oft in poynt ffor to be slaine.

then Sir Guy thirsted sore ;
he had rather haue had drunke there
    then haue had England & almaigne[4] :

---

yade.—P.
[2] So Chaucer R R 1853, pro tho, vel
there, metri gratia.—P.

[3] amaine, q.—P.
[4] Germany.—P.

292 " good S*i*r, iff itt be thy will,
lett me goe now & drinke my ffill,
beffore as I did thee."

and asks the Giant to let him drink.

" nay," then sayd the Gyant, " I were to blame
296 vnlesse *that* I knew thy name,
I tell thee certainlye."

" You may if you'll tell me your name."

" why then," quoth hee, " Ile neue[r] swicke [1];
my name is Guy of warwicke;
300 what shold I longer layne [2] to thee ? "
the Gyant sayd, " soe might I swinke,[3]
doest thou thinke Ile let thee drinke ?
no ! not ffor all Cristentye !

" Guy of Warwick."

" Then you sha'n't drink.

304 " Ah ha ! " quoth the Gyant, " haue I S*i*r Guy here ?
in all this world is not a [4] peere.
ffor ought *that* thou can doe or deale,[5]
thy head [I] shall present my Lady the Queene,
308 I tell thee certainlye [bedeene.] [6] "
then S*i*r Guy towards the riuer came.

I'll give your head to my queen."

However, Guy goes into the river,

the Gyant was not light, but after him went ;
the Gyant Layd after Guy w*i*th strokes strong,
312 but Guy was light, & lope againe to the Land [7];
ffor ere he cold any stroke of Sir Guy wooue,[8]
Guy had beene in the riuer [9] to the chune,[10]
& dranke *that* did him gaine.

[page 353]

up to his chin, and drinks.

316 & vp he start, & sayd there :
" thou ffoule traitor ! I will thee loue noe more [11] !
ffor thy trechery, traytor, thou shalt abuy [12] ! "

Then he reproaches the Giant for his treachery,

[1] *swik*, fallere, decipere. Lye. G.D. 102, 38.—P.
[2] *laine* celare.—P.
[3] labor, toil.—P.
[4] his.—F.   [5] delend, q.—P.
[6] Added by Percy.—F.
[7] The Giant did not lag behind him long,

But layd after Guy with strokes strong.
Guy lope on *the* Land againe.—P.
[8] winne, q.—P.
[9] Only half the *u* in the MS.—F.
[10] chinne.—P.
[11] leaue no mair, q.—P.
[12] reel, q.—P. Perhaps " kneele ": compare l. 327.—Dyce.

these words spake good S*i*r Guy,

320 & liffted vp his swordd on hye,

& saies, "good stroakes thou shalt ffeele."

and hits him
a stroke

then S*i*r Guy att the Gyant smote

a dint *that* wonderffull byterlye bote :

that cuts

324 he smote assunder Iron & steele ;

S*i*r Guys sword through the basnett [1] ran,

down to his
skull.

& glased [2] vpon his braine pan,

& the Gyant began to kneele.

The Giant
knocks Guy
down.

328 & then the Gyant att S*i*r Guy smote

a dint *that* wonderffull [3]bitterlye bote ;

he smote S*i*r Guy downe to the ground.

S*i*r Guy was neu*er* soe discomffitted before ;

332 but through [4] the might of him *that* Marye bore,

releeued him againe in *that* stonde.

Guy thinks
on Christ,

he thought on Christ *that* suffered wounds 5,

& raised Lazarus ffrom d[e]ath to liffe,

336 & vpon the crosse was wound,

to giue him grace to quitt *that*.

& then his sword in his hand he gatt,

& narr [5] the Gyant did hee stand,[6]

sticks the
Giant
through the
breast-plate,

340 & att the Gyant there he smote

a dint *that* wonderffull bitterlye bote ;

through his brest-plate his sword he stake.[7]

& as S*i*r Guy wold haue wrested itt out,

but breaks
his sword.

344 his good sword broke w*i*th-on[t] all [8] doubt,

w*i*thin the hiltes itt brake ;

---

[1] *Bassnet*, Helmet, or Head-piece (French) Gl. ad G. D.—P. A light helmet, shaped like a skull-cap. Fairholt.—F.

[2] glanced or grazed, q.—P.

[3] *bu* with one dot for *hi* in the MS.—F.

[4] delend.—P.

[5] i.e. nearer.—P.

[6] stond, q.—P.

[7] strake, Qu.—P.

[8] without all, q.—P.

& theratt loughe the Danish King,
& Athelstone made much mour[n]ing
348   to heare how the Gyant spake :

"now thou hast broken thy sword & thy sheeld,   The Giant tells him
here is no wepons ffor to weld ;
therfore yeeld thee to mee swythe,[1]
352   & I will thy arrand soe doo,   he had better yield at once, and
& to Auelocke our King Ile speake ffor thee,   Avelocke will grant him land and life.
to grant thee land and liffe,
that thou durst ffor thy Chiualrye
356   be soe bold as ffight with mee
that am [2] soe stiffe and stithe.[3] "

"nay ! " sayd Sir Guy, "by heauen Queene,   Guy refuses.
that sight by me shall neuer be seene,
[forsooth I do thee tell.]
360   ffor I shall kindle thy Kings cares [4] :
through the Might of him that Marry bare,
with stroakes I shall thee ffell."

the Gyant laught, & loud gan crye,   But, says the Giant,
364   "why speakest thou masterffullye ?
hearke what I shall thee tell :
thou hast broken thy sword & thy sheeld,
& thou hast noe weapons thy selfe to weld,   you've no weapons to fight with.
368   nor [5] here is none to sell."

"no," sayd Sir Guy, "I know better cheape ;   "I'll help myself from your heap."
yonder lyes a great cart-load on a heape,
that thou thy-selfe hither did bring."
372   "then the wold laugh me to scorne, my Lords manye,
if of my wepons I shold let thee take anye,
my selfe downe ffor to dinge."

---

[1] soon, instantly.—P. There is a
stroke between *to* and *mee.*—F.
[2] *ann* in the MS.—F.

[3] Stithe, *rigidus, validus, strenuus.*
Lye.—P.
[4] care, q.—P.   [5] ? MS. now.—F.

Guy seizes a
Danish axe,

then Sir Guy to the weapons went :
376 a danish [1] axe in his hand hee hent,
   & lightlye about his head he can itt ffling.

cuts off the
Giant's
sword-arm,

the Gyant vpon the sholder he smote ;
the sword and arme ffell to hys [2] ffoote,
380 this was noe leasinge.

and then, as
he stoops,

then as he wold haue stooped, as I vnde[r]stand,
to haue taken vp his sword in his other hand
   to haue wreaked him of *that* wrathe,

his head.

384 Sir Guys axe was sharpe, & share,
the Gyants head he smote of there,
   bremelye [3] in that breath.

The Danes

& then the Danish men gan say
388 to our Englishmen, " well-away   [page 354]
   that euer wee came in *your* griste [4] ! "

flee,

they ran & they rode ouer hill & slade [5] ;
much haste home-ward they made
392   with sorrow & care enough.

and take
their king
home,

they hyed them ouer the salt ffome
to bring the K*ing* of denmarke hame
   with sorrow and mickle care ;
396 ffor they haue left behind them slaine
a ffull ffoule Lodlye [6] swayne,
   both of head and hayre.

as they
swore to
claim
England no
more.

ffor their trothes they had truly plight,
400 *that* ' as they were true K*ing* and Knight,
   of England neuer to clayme more.'
& then to the body they sett his head ;
his sword in his hand was lead,[7]
404   [8] the strongest *that* euer man bo[re].

---

[1] See note * to l. 169, p. 68, vol. i.
—F.
  [2] The *y* is dotted as in old MSS.—F.
  [3] breme, *ferox, atrox.* Lye.—P.
  [4] ? MS. grisle.—F.
  [5] A.-S. *slæd*, a slade ; plain, open tract

of country. Bosworth.—F.
  [6] filthy.—P.
  [7] laid, q.—P.
  [8] *& stanke as did the tike* is crossed
out at the beginning of this line in the
MS.—F.

the Gyants blood was blacke & red,   The Giant's

his body was like the beaten lead,

& stanke as did the tyke.[1]

408 then thé Layd the head to the corse,   corpse

& the arme againe to the bodye alsoe,

& buryed them both in a diche.[2]   is buried.

great hanocke our Englishmen made.   The English make fun

412 of[3] the great cart-loade of weapons *that* were made,[4]   over his weapons.

they loughe, & good game they made.[5]

that the axe out of Denmarke was brought,

the Gyants head of to smyte,[6]

416 thé thanked christ *that* tyde.

& then the K*ing* beffore the palmer did kneele,   Athelstan thanks Guy.

sayes, "thou art blest, I wott itt weele,

of god and our Ladye."

420 the palmer, in his hart hee was full sore   Guy

when he saw our king kneele him before;

"stand vp, my lord!" sayd hee,

"ffor well I wott itt was his deede   gives the victory to Christ.

424 *that* ffor vs vpon a crosse did bleede

vpon the mount of Caluarye."

& then our king after *that*,   Athelstan

in the honor of this battell great,

428 this deed hee caused to be done :

gard them to take vp the axe & the sword,   has the Giant's sword and axe hung up in

& keepe them well in royall ward,

& bring them to winchester towne,

432 & hang them vp on St. Swythens church on hye   St. Swithin's Church in Winchester.

that all men[7] there may see,

---

[1] tike, *Ricinus*, [tick,] a dog-louse. 'n Shakespear it is used for a little dog. Johnson.—P.

[2] Dyke, q.—P.

[3] at.—P.

[4] laid, q.—P.

[5] & did deryde, q.—P.

[6] that smote, q.—P.

[7] *mem* in the MS.—F. There is no tradition in Winchester of Guy's axe and sword ever having been in St. Swithin's church.—Bailey.

thither if they wold ffare.[1]

I tell you the weapons be there & there

436 but of this matter Ile tell you more,

hastylye and soone.

[The Third Part.]

[How Sir Guy turns Hermit, and sends for his Wife as he dies.]

A procession of monks,

Then all religious of the towne,

they mett the King with ffaire procession;

440 & other psalmes amonge,[2]

singing *Te Deum*, meets Athelstan,

3ᵈ parte

te deum was theire song,

& other praises there amonge,

that plaused[3] the Lords to pray.

who offers Guy castles and towers.

444 the profferred the palmer att *that* tyde,

castles hye & towers wyde,

good horsses to assay.

Guy asks only for his staff and pike.

"Nay," saies he, "giue me *that* is mine,

448 my scripp & my pike & my slauen,[4]

& lett me wend my way."

ffor all they profferred him there,

he fforsooke them : wold haue no more[5]

452 but *that* with him he brought.

The King goes with him and asks his name.

& then our King with him forth on his way went;

to know his name was his entent;

" but all," he sayd, " is ffor nought,

Guy tells

456 without you wilbe sworne vnto me,

ffor 12 monthes in councell itt shalbe,

---

[1] gone.—P.

[2] all their *Psa*lms 'gan say, q.—P.

[3] It pleased, q.—P.

[4] *Slaveine*, a pilgrim's mantle. *Sara-harda*, Anglice a sclavene. Halliwell. Fr. *Esclavine* as *Esclauune* (a long and thicke riding cloake to beare off the raine ;

a Pilgrims cloake or mantle ; a cloake for a traueller ;) or a sea-gowne ; or a course high-collered, and short-sleeued gowne, reaching downe to the mid-leg, and vsed most by seamen and Saylors. Cotgrave, A.D. 1611.—F.

[5] mair, q.—P.

by him *that* all this world has wrought."
& when our *King* had sworne him too,

him under a
vow of
secresy.

460 "why, my name," he sayes, "is Guy of warwicke, loe!
& this ffor thee I haue ffought."

"O," said our *King*, "Sir Guy, abyde with mee,
& halfe of England I will giue thee,

Athelstan
offers him
half of
England
to stay.

464   & assunder wee will neuer."
"nay, I thanke you my lord curteous & kind,[1]
I haue a pilgramage great to wend,
ffrom sinne my soule to couer.[2]

Guy refuses,
he must go a
pilgrimage

468 Sometimes I was one of *your* Erles wight,[3] [page 355]
but now age & trauell hath me dight;
ffarwell, my Lord, ffor euer!
for to warwicke wend will I,

472 to speake with fayre ffelix[4] my wiffe, before I dye,
for nothing I had leauer."

to Warwick,

to see his
wife.

he had beene in battell stiffe & strong,
& smitten with wepons *that* were long,

476   & bidden many a drearye day:
when thé parted, they both did weepe.
Sir Guy held downe the hye street,[5]
in [6] warwicke where he lay.

Guy
journeys

480 & when he came to warwicke towne,
his owne countesse to dinner was bowne
& all masses were sayd.
ffor ffeare lest any man shold him Ken,

to Warwick,
finds his
Countess at
dinner,

484 he sett him downe among the poore godsmen,
& held him well pleased.[1]

and
sits down
among the
poor
godsmen.

---

[1] hend, q.—P.
[2] pronounced *kiver*; perhaps *sever*.
—P.
[3] stout, active.—P.
[4] Felice, in Ellis.—F.

[5] i.e. the High-way. Qu. the high
Roman Road.—P.
[6] to, q.—P.
[7] well-apaid, q. (eodem fere sensu.)
—P.

The
Countess
feeds daily
13 palmers.

his owne Ladye euerye day att her gate
13 palmers in cold shee take
488   to dine with her att noone.

Guy goes in
as one,

Sir Guy was leane of cheeke & chin,
& thereffore the porter lett him in,
& 12 after him did goe.[1]

and his
Lady gives

492   the Ladye see hee was ill att ease ;
shee ffounded[2] ffast him to please,
[and did him make good cheere ;[3]]

him wine :
he gives it to
his mates.

shee ffett him a pott of her best wine :
496   he dealt[4] itt about him at that time,
all to his ffellowes there.

then after dinner, as saith the booke,

He takes
leave of his
Lady.

leaue of his owne Ladye he tooke
500   before them in the hall.

She bids her
steward

the Ladye called her steward vnto ;
shee sayd, " my bidding looke thou doe."
" Madam," hee sayd, " I shall."

504   " why then, goe to yonder[5] pore palmer,

tell him to
come to
dinner every
day.

& bidd him come euerye day to dinner
before me in this hall ;
ffor an honest man[6] he hath beene
508   when he was younge & kept cleane,
as may be well seene."[7]

The steward
gives Guy
the message.

the steward wold no longer abyde,
but went after the palmer that tyde,

---

[1] gone, q.—P.
[2] fond, found, to try, endeavour.
.S. fandian, tentare. Urry, Jun.—P.
[3] A Line wanting :
' And bade (or did) him make good
cheere." q.—P.

[4] him follows, marked out.—F.
[5] yonder in the MS.—F.
[6] MS. me. A.-S. mæg is a relation,
friend, neighbour.—F.
[7] as may be seene of all, q.—P.

512   & did as the Ladye him bede;[1]
says, "well greetes you my Ladye mild of cheere,
prayes you euery day to come to dinner,[2]
giffe *that* itt be your will."

516   the palmer made answer her steward vnto[3];   Guy says
say, "I pray to christ grant her *that* meede
that welds both welth and witt!
a litle ffurther I haue to ffare,   he must go
on to an
520 to speake with an hermitt here,
giff I can with him hitt."

"an hermitt is dead, I vnderstand,   empty
hermitage
& here a hermitage stands vacand,   near.
524 as [I] doe vnderstand."[4]

& there he liued, the truth to say,   He goes,
lives on
till itt was his ending day,
& serued christ our King;
528 he neuer cate other meate
but herbes and rootes greate,   herbs, roots,
and water,
& dranke the water of a springe.

then he hyred him a litle page   and his
page
532 *that* was but 13 yeeres of age,
he was both ffayre and ffeate[5];
& euery day when the noone bell rang,   daily at
noon
the litle ladd to the towne must gang,   fetches the
Countess's
536 to ffeitch[6] the Ladyes liuerye.[7]   allowance to
him.

---

[1] as ye Lady did him tell.
As the Ladye bade him till or tell.
q.—P.
[2] dinnere, q.—P.
[3] to her Steward answer made, q.—P.
[4] Half a Stanza or more wanting.
These seem to be the Steward's words.
—P.
[5] MS. may be *feale.*—F. feate, q.—P.
"both ffayre and ffeate was he."—Dyce.
[6] to fet, q.—P.

[7] delivery, allowance of food. Fr.
Livrée, A deliuerie of a thing thats
giuen; and (but lesse properly) the thing
so giuen; hence, a Liuerie; Ones cloth,
colours, or deuice in colours worn by his
servants, or others. *La Livrée des
Chanoines.* Their liuerie, or corrodie;
their stipend, exhibition, daillie allowance in victualls or money. Cotgraue.
—F.

the Ladye was gladd, as I vnderstand ;
shee gaue itt with her owne handes,[1]
    and gladd itt soe shold bee.

At last a
death-sick-
ness takes
Guy ;

540 but there he liued, as sayth the booke,
till a sicknesse there him tooke,
    that needlye[2] he must dye.

an angel
comes to
him

one night as Sir Guy lay in vysion,
544 there came an Angell downe from heauen
    to lett him vnderstand.

to warn him
he shall
die—

he was as light as any leame,[3]
as bright as any sunn beames.
548   with that wakened Sir Guy.[4]

[page 356]

He sayes, " I coniure in the power of Iesus christ [5]
to tell me wether thou be an euill angell or a good!"

St. Michael,
from God.

he sayd, " I hett Michall.
552 I came ffrom him that can both loose and bind
both mee, and thee, and all mankind,
    both heauen, earth, and hell."

Sir Guy
sends his
page

& then Sir Guy his ring out raught
556 to the litle ladd, and him taught,
    & bidd he shold " goe snell [6]

to tell his
wife to
come to him.

to her that hath beene true to mee,
& pray her to come, my end and see ;
560 ffor nothing that shee dwell.[7] "

The page
goes to the
Countess,

the litle lad made him bowne
till he came to warwicke towne.

---

[1] hand.—P.
[2] so Chaucer, for needs must.—P.
[3] Leame, leme, a flame, a Light, a blaze.
Chauc. Urry. Jun.—P. A.-S. leoma.
—F.
[4] Sir Guy wakende, q.—P.

[5] Jesus' blood, q. I conjure thee
    by ye Roode. Qu.—P.
[6] snell, celer, pernix, citus, agilis. A.-S.
snel. Lye.—P.
[7] dwelle, to stay, tarry. Chauc. Isl.
dwelia, est cessare, morari. Jun. Lye.
—P.

the Countesse soone hee ffound ;
564 before her he kneeled on his knee ;
saith, "well¹ greeteth you my Lord, Sir Guy !
but he is dead neere hand,²

tells her that Guy is dying,

" & heere he hath sent to you his ringe,—
568 ffull well you know this tokeninge,—
& bidds you hye him till."
a squier wold haue brought her a palffrey,
but shee tooke a neerer stay ;

and bids her come to him.

572 ffor knight ne squier none wold shee haue,
but ffollow shee did the litle knaue³ ;
the way was ffayre and drye ;
ffollow shee did the litle ffoot page
576 till shee came to the hermitage
wheras her lord did lye ;

She follows the page to the hermitage,

& then the lady curteous & snell,
vpon his bed-side downe shee ffell
580 with many a greeuous groue.
hee looked vpon her with eyes 2,⁴
he neuer spake more words but these,
saying, "Madam, lett be thy ffare⁵ ! "

and falls down by Guy, groaning grievously.

He tells her to be still.

584 a man that had scene the sorrow shee had,
& alsoe the contrition that shee made
ffor her Lord, Sir Guy,
they wold haue shed many salt teares⁶ :
588 soe did all that with them were,
both lords eke and Ladyes.

You'd have cried to see her sorrow.

---

¹ *greeth* follows, marked out, in the
MS.—F.
² hond, q.—P.
³ cnafa, puer.—P.

⁴ with his eyes, q.—P.
⁵ mone.—P.
⁶ many a teare, q.—P.

She says
she and Guy
were
together
only 40
lays;

    then shee told them how they had loued long,
    & were marryed together when they were younge,
592   & liued together but dayes 40 :
    & afterward shee neuer him see,
    by no knowledge *that* cold bee,
    of 30 winters and three.

their child
was stolen,

596   then shee told them of much more woe :
    theire younge child was stolen them froe ;
    they had neuer none but one.

and Sir
Arrarde
went to
seek it.

    S*i*r Arrarde of Arden after him went
600   to seeke the child with good intent,
    that was true of borne blood.[1]

    & as shee can [2] these tales tell,
    in swooning downe shee ffell
604   vpon the ground soe greene ;
    & when shee was reuarted againe,

The
Countess
goes to King
Athelstan,

    shee wold neuer rest nor rowe [3]
    till shee came our king vnto,
608   her to wishe and read.
    before our king when shee was brought,

who tells her
how Guy
slew the
giant.

    the king told her how S*i*r Guy had fought
    & smitten of the Gyants head :

612   "ffast his name I did ffreane,[4]
    but he sware me *that* I must leane [5]
    ffor a 12 month and a day."

Athelstan
vows he'll
bury Guy in
Winchester.

    the king said, "soe christ me saue !
616   this Erle to winchester I will haue ;

---

[1] of true blood borne, q.—P.   [4] ask.—P.
[2] i. e. gan.—P. did.—F.   [5] conceal.—P.
[3] A.-S. *row*, sweet, quiet, repose.—F.

his body there I will interre."

but all *that* about him there cold stand,

they cold not remoue him with their hands

620   nor ffurther thence him beare.

But his corpse cannot be moved,

a new purpose there thé tooke ;

they made a graue, as saith the booke,

   before the hye Altar,

624 & buryed him in warwicke, the truth to say.

the ladye liued after him but dayes 40:

   And there was buryed alsoe.[1]   [page 357]

and is therefore buried in Warwick, with his wife, who soon dies.

& then they ffounded a ffayre abbey,

628 & moukes ffor them to singe.

. . . .

thus came the k*nigh*t out of his cares,[2]

that had beene in land wyde where,

that came to England safe againe.

632 now all you *that* haue heard this litle Iest,[3]

I betake your soules to Iesus christ,

   [4] [to save from endless pain,]

& *that* wee may on doomesday

come to the blisse *that* shall ffor aye,

636   with Angells to remaine.   ffins.

Bless you, all my hearers! May you go to heaven!

---

[1] *alswa*, Chauc. idem.—P.

[2] care.—P.

[3] Properly Gest.—P.

[4] a Line wanting.—P.

John : De[1] Reeue :[2]

[in 3 Parts.—P.]

THIS piece, now for the first time published, represents Royalty
mixing freely and genially with one of its lowest subjects. All
the splendours of majesty are for the nonce laid aside, the crown
done off, the sceptre laid down; and the King wanders forth as a
common man, and fraternizes with common men. Such a descending from its height down to the level of the humblest, was,
as we have said in the Introduction to the *King and Miller*, a
picture of monarchy highly agreeable to the popular taste—(see
p. 147 above). The value of the following piece, however, does not
lie so much in the picture of such a fellowship as in the por-
trayal of a villain's life and circumstances that it gives. The
hero of this piece is not the King; it is the villain. The King
appears, but as a good-humoured genial presence, who can forget
his dignity and enjoy a frolic with the best. All the powers of
the poet are devoted to the description and portraiture of the
villain. He understands best the life of the villain; his sympa-
thies go with it; his great delight is to depict it.

I incline to believe that the piece was originally written
about the middle of the fifteenth century.[3] It professes to
describe an incident that took place in the days of King Edward.
It adds:

> Of that name were Kings *three*;
> But Edward with the long shanks was he,
> A lord of great renown.

---

[1] *De* is of course &c, i.e. *the*.—H.

[2] or John the Reeve, i.e. Bailiff, vid.
St. 23. See also St. 7, P.t 3. An Old
Song of King Edward Longshanks, not
unlike the King and the Millar.—P.

[3] Mr. Wright assigns it to the latter
part of the fourteenth century.—H.

The poem then was written after the death of Edward III., that is, after 1377 and before the accession of Edward IV., that is, before 1461. Its general character shows that it was written at a period when the position and prospects of the villain were brightening. It was evidently written in the decadence of feudalism, when the darkest ages of villenage were fast passing away. The bare notion of making a villain a knight could scarcely have occurred to any man's mind before the fifteenth century; nor yet the bare notion of a villain's delighting in his position. The lower classes had already felt their strength, and made their strength felt, when John de Reeve was described with so much respect and pride. The great rising of Richard II.'s reign, however abortive, however completely foiled it might have seemed at the time, had produced a lasting effect. In the course of events, kings were presently to assume in earnest that position of leadership which Richard had taken lyingly in Smithfield in 1381. This is a poem of mirth and of hope, not a wild angry satire, not a deep bitter moan. That mighty exodus which the fifteenth century witnessed is being accomplished. The house of bondage is being left. The land of freedom is coming into sight.

The knight had had poems sung and written in his honour for many a long year. A whole literature had celebrated him; he is the one star and glory of the old romances. The yeoman, too, had had his praises sung. His services at Crecy and Poictiers had given him an importance and a celebrity that could not be forgotten. He had become a name. And now, at last, the villain had raised himself so far out of the depths of his abasement, that he too was found worthy of poetic celebration.

John de Reeve, one of the King's bondmen, is represented here as extremely well-to-do and comfortable in his circumstances, of a highly independent spirit, with a supreme contempt

for penniless courtiers, convivial, and indulging his disposition
in that respect. He is indeed a somewhat coarse-grained fellow,
apt to brag of his prosperity when he can do so securely,
illiterate, prejudiced. Altogether, he is very much what the
average Englishman of to-day is—a good-hearted Philistine.
But one thing mars his felicity—his fear of the King and the
King's purveyor. This constrains him to conceal his riches,
to simulate poverty, to shrink from intercourse with wayfarers
and strangers.

This picture of a villain's life may seem surprisingly bright
and cheerful. No doubt it would be unwise to conclude that all
the members of his class were as sleek and affluent as this
John de Reeve. On the other hand, it is unwise to conclude
from the laws that regulated it, that the position of that class
was, at least in the latter feudal days, for the most part
beggarly and wretched. The wall of partition that separated
the villain from the freeman was often very slight. The
arbitrary services, the exaction of which characterized his condition, assumed in course of time a definite shape, so that his
tenure was as little galling as those of his neighbours. He
could prosecute his own interests as undisturbedly as they. His
social state would be nominally inferior to theirs; but his oppor-
tunities of growing rich would be as good, with few drawbacks.
Probably there would be often little to choose between the small
yeoman and the villain.[1] Villains too had fought in the English
ranks on the famous battle-fields of the fourteenth and fifteenth
centuries. That fearful pestilence that ravaged the land in
1349 may be said to have dealt villenage a blow from which it
never recovered. Free labourers, as Eden (in his *State of the
Poor*) remarks, are first specifically recognised by the legislature
in 1350. The First Act of Richard the Second (cap. 6) has
reference to complaints urged by the Lords and Commons, that

[1] Cf. v. 307 of the ballad.

villains and land-tenants withdraw their services " under pretext
of exemplifications from the Book of Domesday, and by their
evil interpretation of the same they affirm themselves to be quit
and utterly discharged of all manner of servage, due as well
of their body as of their said tenures, and will not suffer any
distress or other justice to be made upon them, but do menace
the ministers of their lords, and gather themselves together in
great routs, and agree by such confederacy that every one shall
aid other to resist their lords with strong hand, to the great
damage of these said lords, and evil example to other to begin
such riots." These combinations did much to advance the
position of the working classes, as unions, with whatever admixture of evil, have done since. How tremendous was their
power some four years after those complaints were submitted to
the royal ear and measures taken to satisfy them, is illustrated
by the eagerness of the King to grant the four points of the
charter the assembled mob then demanded of him. The roar
of that mob was remembered for many a day. (See Chaucer's
Nonne Prest his Tale.) Nor were there wanting at the same
time those who advocated the claims of those insurgents on the
most general grounds, who dealt with the question radically.
Ideas fatal to the notion of thraldom were now growing into
predominance in France, in Flanders, in England and elsewhere.
The Church, however lax its practice, had again and again raised
its voice against it. There is nowhere a nobler rebuke of it
than that given by Chaucer's *Parson*—" Thilke that thay clepe
thralles," he says, in that division of his discourse that treats of
Avarice ("an adaptation of some chapters" of Frère Lorens'
Somme des Vices et des Vertus: see Mr. Morris's *Ayenbite of
Inwyt*, Pref. p. ii.), " ben Goddes people; for humble folk ben
Cristes frendes; thay ben contubernially with the Lord. Thenk
eek as of such seed as cherles springen, of such seed springe
lords; as wel may the cherl be saved as the lord. The same

deth that takith the cherl, such death takith the lord. Wherfor
I rede do right so with thi cherl as thou woldist thi lord dide
with the, if thou were in his plyt. Every sinful man is a cherl
as to synne. I rede the certes, thou lord, that thou werke in
such a wise with thy cherles that they rather love the than drede
the." Such words as these said more perhaps than their utterer
intended. Certainly, they enable us to understand how the
position of the villain grew to be much more tolerable than its
expressed conditions would have led us to expect.

Moreover, the villain's hardships must have been greatly
alleviated by that resolute independence which forms so prominent a feature in the native English character. The Englishman
would prove but a stiff-necked, obstinate, troublesome slave—his
self-willedness would go far to protect him from the worst
excesses of the hardest master—his surliness would often serve
him for a shield.

This ballad gives us a view of both the private and public life
of the churl. We see him as he goes abroad, and we see him in
the security of his domestic comfort. He makes no secret of the
cause of those fears which make him so chary of his hospitality,
which induce him to cut such a sorry figure when out of doors.
See v. 103 et seq., v. 199 et seq. &c. His personal appearance
is described with great care in vv. 52–57, and again in vv. 593–
650. He offers his guests the poorest food and liquor at first.
(Compare the account of the poor widow's "sclender meel" in
the Nonne Prest his Tale.) No doubt his fears were well grounded.
"Thurgh his cursed synne of avarice," says the Parson whom we
have already quoted, "comen these harde lordschipes, thurgh
whiche men ben destreyned by talliages, custumes, and cariages
more than here ducte of resoun is; and elles take thay of here
bondemen amercimentes, whiche mighte more resonably ben
callid extorciouns than mercymentis. Of whiche mersyments
and raunsonyng of bondemen, some lordes stywardes seyn that it

is rightful, for as moche as a cherl hath no temporel thing that it nys his lordes, as thay sayn. But certes thise lordeshipes doon wrong that bireven here bondemen thinges that thay never gave hem." When the abolition of slavery was proposed in the first Parliament that met after Wat Tyler's insurrection, "with one accord," writes Knight (in his *Popular History of England*), "the interested lords of the soil replied that they never would consent to be deprived of the services of their bondmen. But they complained of grievances less inherent in the structure of society—of purveyance ; of the rapacity of law officers ; of maintainers of suits, who violated right and law as if they were kings in the country ; of excessive and useless taxation." "I have no doubt," says Eden, "that the tax-gatherers were extremely partial to the rich and oppressive to the poor ; for notwithstanding the above instance of their scrupulous attention to levy the utmost farthing on petty tradesmen [certain instances he has quoted from the valuation of movable property made at Colchester in 1296, see *Rot. Parl.* i. 228], we find that the master and brethren of an hospital, besides their cattle and corn, only accounted for one household utensil, a brass pot, and an Abbot and a Prior paid only for their corn and their live stock. The Rector of St. Peter's seems to have been equally fortunate."

But, on whatever account John de Reeve may make whatever pretence of direful penury, he is in fact a man of wealth. He may say with Horace's miser, "At mihi plaudo ipse domi." He says:

> "I go girt in a russet gown,
> My hood is of homemade browne,
>   I wear neither burnet nor green,
> And yet I trow I have in store
> A thousand pounds and some deal more,
>   For all ye are prouder and fine.
>
> Therefore I say, as mote I thee,
> A bondman it is good to be,
>   And come of carles kin ;

For and I be in tavern set,
To drink as good wine I will not let
   As London Edward or his Queen."

The Earl said: "By godes might,
John, thou art a comely knight
   And sturdy in every fray."
"A knight!" quoth John, "do away for shame!
I am the King's bondman:
   Such waste words do away.

"I know you not in your estate;
I am misnurtured, well I wot;
   I will not thereto say nay.
But if any such do me wrong
I will fight with him hand to hand
   When I am clad in mine array."

We must now commend this most interesting ballad to our readers.[1]

[1] The Editors have received the following letter from Archdeacon Hale, whom they here beg to thank:

Charterhouse, Dec. 18, 1867.

Dear Sir,—I am obliged to you for the opportunity of reading the interesting ballad of "John de Reeve." That he designates himself as the King's bondman, seems to me to imply that he was of villain rank. I think it probable that the king's bondmen, nativi and villains, were proud of their position, as being attached to royalty, and as having the privilege of tenants in ancient demesne, of not being impleaded or distrained except in the king's courts. It would seem from the Act of Richard the Second, of which mention is made in the preface, p. 552, that they made use of this privilege to withdraw their services from the lords of manors in which they were tenants, and that they were in reality leaders of that resistance to the rights of the lords which produced the disturbances of Tyler and Cade. Except *taillage ad voluntatem domini*, none of the services due from the various classes of villains appear to me cruel or unjust,

prædial service being the rent paid for the possession of land by the villain class. I am inclined to think that as trade increased in the fourteenth and fifteenth centuries, the tradesmen became possessors of villain land, and that as those lands were accumulated in fewer hands, the prædial service became more difficult to be rendered, as well as more unsuitable to the personal position of the tenant, who might himself be a freeholder, *liber tenens*, and yet possess villain land. John de Reeve had become rich; his name implies that he had come from a family who held office, possibly in a royal manor; the house in which he lived having a hall and a dais, indicates the superior character of his tenement. I may also remark that his abode was in the south-west country, and that, to the best of my recollection, royal manors, and consequently tenants in ancient demesnes, abound in Wilts and Somerset. The description of his house would lead to the idea that he dwelt in the hall of the demesne. He was of the same freeledge (p. 564) as his two neighbours; but it was afterwards (p. 593), that they were made

[The First Part.]

[How John at first avoids the King, and then takes him home.]

God : through thy might and thy mercy,   God bless all
all *that* loueth game and glee,   who love
    their soules to heauen bringe !   merriment!
4   best is mirth of all solace ;
    therfore I hope itt betokens grace,
    of mirth who hath likinge.

as I heard tell this other yeere,   A Lanca-
8   a clarke came out of Lancashire :   shire clerk
    a rolle [1] he had reading,   this story
    a bourde [2] written therein he ffound,[3]
    that some time ffell in England,[4]   of Edward
12   in Edwards dayes our King.

by East, west, north, and Southe,
all this realme well run [5] hee cowthe,[6]
    castle, tower, and towne.

---

freemen. I shall be very glad if what I have written should seem to throw light upon the condition of John de Reeve.

    And I remain,
        Yours very faithfully,
           W. H. Hale.

Mr. Toulmin Smith, in a communication made to the Editors, is of opinion that the Reeve "was the King's collector of local dues—in other words the Farmer of the taxes. He was in bond to the King (as all collectors still are) to remit truly, and hence, and not as a vassal, his bondsman. The collector would only be afraid of the King because he did not want it known what a capital bargain he had made, lest the price paid by him for his office should be raised." But there is nothing whatever in the ballad to justify this interpretation of the Reeve's fear. Nor are we prepared to acquiesce in the confusion of the terms "bondman" and "bondsman."—H.

[1] rolle.—P. Qu. MS. rolde.—F.
[2] i.e. Jest. Junius.—P.
[3] fonde.—P.
[4] Englonde, qu.—P.
[5] i.e. run over.—P.
[6] couthe, could. So, 'he ne couth,' He could not. Gloss. ad G. Doug.—P.

Longshanks.

16   of *that* name were Kings 3 ;
       but Edward with the long shankes was hee,
       a Lord of great renowne.

One day, out
hawking, the
King loses
all his

       as the K*ing* rode a hunting vpon a day,
20   3 ffawcons [1] fflew away ;
       he ffollowed wonderous ffast.
       thé rode vpon their horsses *that* tyde,
       they rode forth on euery side,
24   the country they ont cast ;

       ffrom morning vntill eueninge late,
followers
       many meun abroad they gate
           wandring all alone ;
28   the night came att the last ;
       there was no man *that* wist
           what way the King was gone,

except a
Bishop and
an Earl.
       saue a Bishopp & an Erle ffree
32   *that* was allwayes the king ffull nye,
           & thus then gan they say :
The three
lose their
way,
       " itt is a ffolly, by St. Iohn,
       ffor vs thus to ryde alone
36   soe many a wilsome [2] way ;

       " a K*ing* and an Erle to ryde in hast,
       a bishopp ffrom his coste [3] to be cast,
           ffor hunting sikerlye.[4]
and the
weather is
very bad.
40   the whether happned [5] wonderous ill,
       all night wee may ryde vnskill,[6]
           nott wotting where wee bee."

---

[1] 3 [of his] fawc?   Qu.—P.
[2] *wilsome, wilsum.* Desert, solitary,
wandering. i.e. Wild : (Scotch) Gloss. to
Ramsay's Evergreen, q.d.*wildsome.* Gloss.
to G.D.—P.

[3] province, district.—F.
[4] surely, certainly : *sicker,* sur, certain.   Johns?—P.
[5] happneth, query.—P.
[6] i.e. unskill'd.—P.

then the *King* began to say,

44   "good S*i*r Bishopp, I you pray

some comfort, if you may."

as they stoode talking [1] all about,   They see
a man

they were ware of a carle [2] stout :

48   "good deene, ffellow ! " can [3] they say.

then the Erle was well apayd [4] :

" you be welcome, good ffellow ! " hee sayd,

" of ffellowshipp wee pray thee ! "

52   the carle ffull hye on horsse sate, [5]   on horseback

his leggs were short and broad, [6]

his stirropps were of tree [7] ;

a payre of shooes were [8] stiffe & store, [9]

56   on his heele a rustye spurre,   riding away
from them.

thus fforwards rydeth hee.

the Bishopp rode after on his palfrey: The Bishop
asks him to
stop,

" abyde, good ffellow, I thee pray,

60   and take vs home with thee ! "

The carle answered him *that* tyde,   [page 358]

" ffrom me thou gett oft noe other guide,   but the man
won't,

I sweare by sweete St. Iohn [10] ! "

64   then said the Erle ware and wise,

" thou canst litle of gentrise [11] !

say not soe ffor shame ! "

---

[1] *forté* were stalking.—P.

[2] Carle (*ceorl.*) Vir tennioris atque obscuræ sortis. idem ac *churl* &c. Jun.—P. The shape of the initial *c* in the MS. begins to change here frequently. It is made like an *l* instead of a foreigner's *c*, accented. It might be printed C, but that the old form of the C is retained, as in *Curteouslye*, l. 121.—F.

[3] can, delend.—P. can *is* did.—F.

[4] glad. *lætus.* Jun.—P.

[5] The rhyme requires *rode.*—Dyce.

[6] [some deal] *brade* or *braid*—Lancasshire Dialect.—P

[7] i.e. wood.—P. *treene*, wooden, p. 181, l. 1.—F.

[8] *Forté* The shoes he ware were &c.—P.

[9] *stour, sture*, great, thick, ingens crassus, Jun., stiff, strong, robust. Gloss. ad G. D.—P.

[10] Jame, see st. 22ᵈ [l. 132]—P.

[11] *Genteriee* is still in use in Scotland, for gentility, honourable birth. See Gloss. to Ramsay's Evergreen.—P.

the carle answered the Erle vnto,

he has
nothing to
do with
courtesy.
68 "with gentlenesse [1] I haue nothing to doe,
       I tell thee by my flay."
the weather was cold & euen roughe [2] ;
the King and the Erle sate and loughe,
72 the Bishopp did him soe pray.

The King
and Earl
the King said, "soe mote I thee [3] !
hee is a carle, whosoeuer hee be !
I reade [4] wee ryde him neere."
76 thé sayd [5] with words hend, [6]
beg the man
to stop,
"ryd saftlye, gentle ffreind,
       & bring vs to some harbor."

then to tarry the carle was lothe,
but he still
rides on.
80 but rode forth as he was wrothe,
       I tell you sickerlye.
The King
tells them
the king sayd, "by mary bright,
I troe [7] wee shall ryde all this night
84 in wast vnskillffullye [8] ;

to pull the
man down.
"I ffeare wee shall come to no towne ;
ryde to the carle and pull him downe
       hastilye without delay."
The Bishop
asks him to
stop.
88 the Bishopp said soone on hye,
"abyde, good ffellow, & take vs with thee !
       ffor my loue, I thee pray."

---

[1] gentrise, qu.—P.
[2] evening rough.—P. pronounced row.

þe Amyral bende ys browes rowe,
  & clepede is consaile.
Kyng Sortybrant & oþre ynowe
  ther come wyþ-oute fayle.

Sir Ferumbras, MS. Ashmole 33, fol. 26.

. Thow a Sarsens hed ye here,
Row, and full of lowsy here.

Skelton, Poems against Garnesche, l. 124.

Works, ed. Dyce, vol. i. p. 123.—F.
[3] *thee*, i.e. thrive. Lye.—P.
[4] i.e. counsel : *reade* is counsel, con-
silium. Junius.—P.
[5] sayd [to him].—P.
[6] i.e. kind, *hend, hende*, i.e. feat, fine,
gentle, *forté*, q.d. handy or handsome.
Skinner, ab Isl. henta, i.e. decere. Lye.
MS.—P.
[7] trow, confido, opinor. Lye.—P.
[8] without reason. O. N. *skil*, reason.
--F.

the Erle said, " by god in heauen !
92 oft men meete att vnsett steuen [1] ;
to quite thee well wee may."

The Earl
says he'll
pay him out
some day.

the carle sayd, " by St. Iohn
I am [2] affraye of you eche one,
96 I tell you by my ffay ! "

The man
explains
that he is
afraid of
them.

the carle sayd, " by Marye bright,
I am afrayd of you this night !
I see you rowne [3] and reason, [4]
100 I know [5] you not & itt were day,
I troe you thinke more then you say,
I am affrayd of treason.

" the night is merke, [6] I may not see
104 what kind of men *that* you bee.
but & you will doe one thinge,
swere to doe me not [7] desease, [8]
then wold I ffaine you please,
108 if I cold, with any thinge."

If they'll
swear not to
hurt him,

he'll help
them.

then sayd the Erle with words ffree,
" I pray you, ffellow, come hither to mee,
& to some towne vs bringe ;
112 & after, if wee may thee kenn,
amonge Lords and gentlemen
wee shall requite [9] thy dealinge."

The Earl
says, if he
will, they'll

reward him
among
Lords.

" of lords," sayes hee, " speake no more [10] !
116 with them I haue nothing to doe,
nor neuer thinke to haue ;

The man
says he'll

---

[1] i. e. unexpectedly : at a time un-
appointed. *Steven*, tempus statutum.
Jun.—P. See p. 386, note [3], above.—F.
[2] MS. ann.—F.
[3] *rowne*, i. e. whisper.—P.
[4] t. i. talk, as in Shakspere, &c.—Dyce.
[5] *forté* knew.—P.
[6] i. e. dark.—P.
[7] no disease.—P.

[8] prejudice, to make uneasy. see
Johnson.—P.
[9] *forté*, quite.—P.
[10] moe.—P. Compare
Aqueyntanse of lordschip wyll y noght,
For, furste or laste, dere hit woll be
bowght.— Proverbs from MS. Ii. iii.,
back of last leaf. Camb. Univ. Lib., in
Reliq. Antiq., vol. i. p. 205.—F.

ffor I had rather be brought in bale,

my hood or *that* [1] I wold vayle, [2]

never crouch to Lords.

120   on them to crouch or crane. [3] ”

the K*ing* sayd Curteouslye,

The King asks him who he is.

“ what manner of man aree yee

att home in your dwellinge ? ”

The King's bondman,

124   “ a husbandman, fforssooth I am,

& the Kings bondman [4];

thereof I haue good Likinge."

“ S*ir*, when spake you w*ith* our King ? ”

tho' he never spoke to him.

128   “ in ffaith, neuer, in all my liuing !

he knoweth not my name ;

& I haue my Capull [5] & my crofft [6];

if I speake not w*ith* the K*ing* oft,

132   I care not, by St. Iame ! ”

---

[1] or that, i. e. before that.—P.

[2] vail, to let fall ; to suffer, to descend, in token of respect. Fr. *avaller le bonet*. Johnson.—P.

[3] Was John. like Chaucer's Reeve, 'a sklendre colericke man'? Among the marks of persons of 'Chollericke complexion' are: 'The sixth is, they be stout stomacked, that is, they can suffer no injuries, by reason of the heate in them. And therefore Aviceñ sayth, That to take every thing impatiently signifieth heate. The seauenth is, they be liberall to those that honour them,'—as John says in lines 169, 243, he'll give the wanderers all they want, so that they be thankful :—'The fourteenth is, he is wily,'—cp. the first bad supper, below ;—'The eleuenth is, he is soone angry, through his hote nature'—as the King's porter experiences, l. 731;—'The thirteenth is, he is bold. for boldnesse commeth of great heat. specially about the heart,'—cp. l. 304;—John's cowardice at first, l. 97, was but prudence, the better part of valour. Also, he must have had a beard. 'The ninth is, a Cholericke person is hayry, by reason of

the heate that openeth the pores, and moueth the matter of hayres to the skinne. And therefore it is a common saying, *The Cholericke man is as hayrie as a Goat*.' On the other hand John must have had a cross of ' the sanguine person' in him, for ' Secondly, the Sanguine person is merry and jocond, that is to say, with merry words he moueth other to laugh, or else he is glad through benignity of the sanguine humour, prouoking a man to gladnesse and jocondity, through cleare and perfect spirits ingendred of bloud. Thirdly, he gladly heareth fables and merry sports, for the same cause. . Fifthly, he gladly drinketh good Wine. Sixthly, he delighteth to feede on good meate, by reason that the sanguine person desireth the most like to his complexion, that is, good Wines and good meates.' *Regimen Sanitatis Salerni*, ed. 1634, p. 169–71.—F.

[4] i. e. Vassall.—P.

[5] capull, i. e. *keyfil*, Welch for a Horse. Lye.—P.

[6] Croft est agellus prope domum rusticum. Lye.—P.

"what is thy name, ffellow, by thy leaue?"

"marry," quoth hee, "Iohn de Reeue [1];

 I care not who itt heare;

136 ffor if you come into my inne,[2]

 with beeffe & bread you shall beginn

 soone att your supper [3]; [page 359]

His name is
John de
Reeve;

he can feed
them

"salt Bacon of a yeere old,

140 ale *that* is both sower & cold,[4]—

 I vse neither braggatt [5] nor beere, —

 I lett you witt withouten lett,

 I dare eate noe other meate,

144 I sell my wheate ech yeere."

with stale
bacon and
sour ale:

he brews no
beer, for

he sells his
wheat,

"why doe you, Iohn, sell your wheate?"

"ffor [I] dare [6] not eate *that* I gett.

 therof I am ffull wrothe;

148 ffor I loue a draught of good drinke as well

 as any man *that* doth itt sell,

 & alsoe a good wheat loffe.

he dare not
keep it,

though he
likes
good drink
and bread.

"ffor he *that* ffirst [7] starueth Iohn de reeue,

152 I pray to god hee may neuer well [8] cheeue,[9]

 neither on water nor land,

 whether itt be[10] Sherriffe or King

 that makes such statuinge,[11]

156 I outcept [12] neuer a one!

May all who
starve him
come to
grief!

---

[1] Query, John the Reeve, i.e. Bailiff. Jun. See St. 7, Pt. 3.—P.

[2] *inne*, Sax. est cubiculum, caverna, diuersorium domus. Inne, a house, habitation.—P.

[3] suppere.—P.

[4] *Non sit acetosa cervisia, sed bene clara* . . . This text declareth fiue things, by which one may know good Ale and Beere. The first is, that it be not sower, for that hurteth the stomacke. A sower thing (as Avicen saith in many places) hurteth the sinewes. And the stomacke is a member full of sinewes, especially about the brim or mouth. *Regimen Sanitatis Salerni*, ed. 1634, p. 59.—F.

[5] Chauc. *Brakit*, Camb. Br. *bragod*. A sweet drink made of honey & spices, used in Wales, &c. Urry's Gloss,—P.

[6] I dare, Qu.—P.

[7] first, *delend*, Qu.—P.

[8] well, *delend*, Qu.—P.

[9] thrive, qu.—P. Fr. *chevir*, to bring a business to a head, get well through it; from *chef*.—F.

[10] MS. ber.—F.

[11] statuing.—P.

[12] *forté* except.—P. An odd hybrid. *Outtake* is the older word.—F.

"ffor and the Kings penny were Layd by mine,
 I durst as well as hee drinke the [1] wine
  till all my good [2] were gone.

He asks
where they
live.

160 but sithence *that* wee are mett [3] soe meete,
 tell mee where is your recreate,[4]
  you seeme good laddes eche one."

The Earl
says,
In the
King's
house.

 the Erle answered with words ffaire,
164 " in the kings house is our repayre,[5]
  if [6] wee bee out of the way."

John pro-
mises to
lodge them if

 " this night," quoth Iohn, " you shall not spill;
 such harbour I shall bring you till ;
168 I hett [7] itt you to-day.

they are
thankful,

 " soe *that* yee take itt thankeffullye
 in gods name & St. Iollye,
  I aske noe other pay ;

but if they're
saucy he'll
keep 'em out,

172 & if you be sturdy & stout,
 I shall garr [8] you to [9] stand without,
  ffor ought *that* you can say.

with the
help of his
two neigh-
bours,

 " for I haue 2 neighbors won [10] by mee
176 of the same ffreeledge [11] *that* am I,
  of old band-shipp [12] are wee :

owned by
the Bishop of
Durham
and the Earl
of Glo'ster,

 the Bishopp of Durham this towne [13] oweth,
 the Erle of Gloster—who-soe him knoweth—
180 Lord of the other is hee.

---

[1] the, delend.—P.
[2] goods, qu.—P.
[3] One stroke too many in the MS.—F.
[4] ? MS. retreate, home.—F.
[5] *repair*, resort, abode, the act of betaking oneself anywhither. Johnson.—P.
[6] ? but.—F.
[7] i. e. I promise, assure.—P.
[8] cause.—F.
[9] To, delend. Qu.—P.
[10] i. e. dwell.—P.
[11] *frelege*, freedom, power, privilege : a quo forte corrupt. It is yet used in Sheffield. Ray. Gloss. ad G. Doug. who has render'd *Cui tanta Deo permissa potestas*, Quhat God has to him grantit, sic *frelege*, St. 9, v. 97.—P. A.-Sax. *freolac* is A free offering, a sacrifice : but -*lac* and -*ledge* have the meaning of state, condition.—F.
[12] à *band*, Vinculum, retinaculum, ligamen, nexus ; A.S. *banda*.—P.
[13] Perhaps Toune, viz. the one of his Companions was vassal to the Bishop, vid. p. 66, V. 251 [of MS. ; vol. i. p. 159, l. 466 of text].—P.

"wist my neighbors *that* I were thratt,[1]
I vow to god thé wold not lett
ffor to come soone to mee ;

184   if any wrong were to mee done,
    wee 3 durst flight a whole afternoone,
      I tell you sikerlye."

who'd fight all afternoon for him.

the King sayd, "Iohn, tell vs not this tale ;

188   wee are not ordayned ffor battell,[2]
    our weeds are wett and cold ;
    heere is no man *that* yee shall greeue.
    but helpe vs, Iohn, by *your* leaue,

192   with bright a ffeeare[3] and bold."

The King says their clothes are wet,

they want a good fire.

"Ifaith," sayd Iohn, "*that* you shall want,
ffor ffuell heere is wonderous scant,
    as I heere haue yee told.

196   thou getteth noe other of Iohn de Reeue ;
    ffor the kings statutes,[4] whilest I liue,
      I thinke to vse and hold.

John says he can't give them that,

as he is a bondman.

"If thou find in my house payment ffine,[5]

200   or in my kitchin poultry slaine,
    peraduenture thou wold say
    that Iohn Reeue his bond hath broken :
    I wold not *that* such words weere spoken

204   in the kings[6] house another day,

If he were to feed them well,

---

[1] A.-S. *þreatian*, to threaten, disquiet, distress.—F.

[2] battayle. Chauc.—P.

[3] with a bright fire &c.—P.

[4] ? referring to William the Conqueror's law that fires and lights were to be put out at the 8 o'clock curfew, and people go to bed. The evening must have been far advanced when John spoke.—F.

[5] I *would* read 'If thou find in my house Pain de main,' fortassè corruptè pro pain de maine, i.e. white bread.

So Chaucer, 'White was his face as paine de maine.' Rime of *Sir* Thopas. Lye. —P. 'Payman, a kind of cheese-cake.' Halliwell. Pyment or Piment was both a special honeyed and spiced wine,—see a recipe in Halliwell,—and also the general name for sweet wines : see *Henderson's Hist.*, p. 283, and *Babees Book*, &c., p. 202. If 'payment' is used here for bread, as in l. 428. part ii. below, then I suppose it means 'spiced bread.'—F.

[6] To the King an :—P.

it might get
to some
officials'
ears, and
injure him.

"ffor itt might turne me to great greeffe [1] ;
such proud ladds *that* beare office
wold danger a pore man aye ;
208 & or I wold pray thee of mercy longe,
yett weere I better [2] to lett thee gange
in twentye twiine devills way.[3] "

thus thé rode to the towne :

John takes
the King,
Bishop, and
Earl to his
hall.

212 Iohn de Reeue lighted downe
beside a comlye hall.[4]
4 men beliue [5] came wight [6] ;
they hasted them ffull swyft
216 when they heard Iohn call ;
thé served him honestly and able,
And [led [7]] his horsse to the stable,   [page 360]
& lett noe terme misfall.

His wife
welcomes
them.

220 some went to warne their dame
that Iohn had brought guests home.[8]
shee came to welcome them tyte [9]
in a side [10] kirtle of greene,[11]
224 her head was dight all by-deene,[12]
the wiffe was of noe pryde ;

her kerchers were all of silke,

Her hair is
white.

her hayre as white as any milke,
228 lone-some of hue [13] and hyde ;

---

[1] Two letters are marked out after the
g.— F.
[2] Yt were better.—P.
[3] 'twenty devil way' is the ordinary
phrase.—F.
[4] Cp. Chaucer's description of the
Reeve's 'wonying fair upon an heth.'
Prol. Cant. T. l. 609.—F.
[5] *belive,* instantly. Lye.—P.
[6] *wight,* swift, nimble. Johnson; also
stout, valiant, clever, active. Gloss? ad
G.D.—P.
[7] And [led] his &c.--P.

[8] I *would* read thus (St. 38)
To welcome *them* that tyde
Shee came in a side Kirtle &c.—P.
[9] brót [3] guests hame. Qu.—P.
[10] all. or, that tyde.—P. *tyte,* quickly.
—F.
[11] i. e. long.- P. A.-S. *sid,* wide.—F.
[12] *bedene,* Scotch, is, immediately.
Gloss? to Ramsays Evergreen; a Germ.
bedienen præstare officium. Gloss. ad
G.D.—P. Dutch *by dien,* by this.—F.
[13] ? MS. huid.—F. hue, Qu. See Egar
& Grime, pa.—P.

shee was thicke, & some deal broad,
of comlye ffashyon was shee made,
 both belly, backe, and side.

She is comely.

232 then Iohn called his men all,
sayes, "build me a ffire in the hall,
 & giue their Capulls meate ;
lay before them corne and hay ;
236 ffor my loue rubb of the clay,
 ffor they beene weary and wett ;

John orders a fire for his guests, and food for their horses.

"lay vnder them straw to the knee,
ffor courtyes [1] comonly wold be Iollye,
240 and haue but litle to spend."

then hee said, "by St. Iohn,
you are welcome euery one,
 if you take itt thankefullye !
244 curtesye I learned neu[e]r none,
but after mee, ffellowes, I read you gone."
 till a chamber they went all 3 ;

John bids them welcome,

a charcole [2] ffire was burning bright,
248 candles on chandlours [3] light,
 Eche ffreake [4] might other see.
"where are your sords [5] ?" quoth Iohn de
 Reeue.
the Erle said, "Sir, by your leaue,
252 wee weare none, pardye."

and shows them into a room with a fire and candles.

---

[1] courtyers.—P.
[2] Charcoal fires were used to avoid the smoke from wood or coal getting into men's eyes, as there were no chimneys. See *Ladye Bessiye*, vol. iii., and cp. *Kinge and Miller*, p. 150, l. 40, above.—F.
[3] chandlours. Fr. *chandelier*, a Candlestick.—P.
[4] freke, man. Jun.—P.
[5] swords.—P.

John asks
the Earl
who the
long-legged
fellow is.

then Iohn rowned [1] w*i*th the Erle soo ffree :

"what long ffellow is yonder," quoth hee,

"*that is* [2] soe long of lim and lyre [3] ?"

256   the Erle answered w*i*th words small,

"yonder is Peeres pay-ffor-all,

"The
Queen's head
Falconer."

the Queenes Cheefe ffawconer. [4] "

"ah, ah!" quoth Iohn, "ffor gods good,

"If I had
his gay hood,

260   where gott hee *that* gay hood,

glitering as gold itt were?

& I were as proud as hee is like,

there is no man in England ryke [5]

I'd keep no
man's
hawks.

264   shold garr me keepe his gleads [6] one yeere.

But who's
that
next the
Falconer?"

"I pray you, s*i*r, ffor gods worke,

who is yond in yonder serke [7]

that rydeth [8] Peeres soo nye ?"

268   the Erle answered him againe,

"yonder is a pore chaplaine,

"That's
a poor
Chaplain,

long aduanced or hee bee ;

and I am a
Sumpter-
man."

"& I my selfe am a sumpter man, [9]

272   other craft keepe I none,

I say you w*i*thouten Misse."

"Gay
fellows, and
penniless
too, I
suppose!"

"you are ffresh ffellowes in your appay, [10]

Iolly Ietters [11] in your array,

276   proud ladds, & I trow penyles."

---

[1] whispered.—F.
[2] that is, delend.—P.
[3] lim, i.e. limb: lyre, i.e. flesh, quicquid carnosum & nervosum in homine. Lye. Also Lire, is complexion or air of *the* face. Gloss. ad G. D.—P. "Lyke the quhyte lyllie wes her *lyre*." Lyndesay's *Hist. of Squyer Meldrum*.—F.
[4] fawconere.—P.
[5] ryke, A.-Sax. *rice* regnum, imperium.—P.
[6] *gleads*, i.e. Kites.—P.

[7] *serke*, Indusium, a shirt or such garment. Jun.—P.
[8] ? standeth.—F.
[9] *forté* mon.—P.
[10] ? content, self-satisfaction.—F.
[11] To *jet*, inter alia, signifies to strut, to agitate the body by a proud gait. So the Turky-Cock is said to *jett*, when he bridles &c. See Johnson, from Shakesp. 12th Night. *Jetters* then are strutters &c. See pag. 237 [of MS.; p. 155, l. 178 of text, above].—P.

the King said, " soe mote I thee,
there is not a penny amongst [1] vs 3
to buy vs bread and fllesh."

" We haven't
a penny to
pay for our
food," says
the King.

280 " ah, ha! " quoth Iohn, " there is [2] small charge ;
280* ffor courtyes [3] comonlye are att large,
if they goe neuer soe ffresh.

" Ah,
courtiers
generally
live on other
people ;

" I goe girt in a russett gowne,
my hood is of homemade browne,
284 I weare neither burnett [4] nor greene,
& yett I troe I haue in store
a 1000 and some deale more,
ffor all yee are prouder and ffine ;

but though
I wear
russet,

I've 1000l. in
store.

288 " therfore I say, as mote I thee, [5]
a bondman itt is good [6] [to] bee, [7]
& come of carles kinne ;
ffor and I bee in tauerne [8] sett,
292 to drinke as good wine I will not Lett,
as London [9] Edward or his Queene."

It's well to
be a bond-
man,

for I drink
as good wine
as the King."

the Erle sayd, " by gods might,
Iohn, thou art a comly knight,
296 and sturdy in euerye ffray."
" a knight! " quoth Iohn, " doe away, ffor shame !
I am the King's bondman.
Such wast words doe away ! [page 361]

" You're a
comely
knight,
John."

" Knight!
nonsense !

300 " I know you not in your estate ;
I am misnurtured, well I wott [10] ;
I will not therto say nay.

---

[1] annongst in the MS.—F.
[2] forte that is.—P.
[3] courtyers.—P.
[4] burnet, a kind of colour, whether
that of the Pimpernel, which is called
Burnet, or a dark brown (French bru-
nette) stuff worn by Persons of quality.
Gloss? ad G. Doug.—P.

[5] St. 49, as mote I thee. Thee,—to
thrive. Vid. Jun. & Lye.—P.
[6] forte " as good."—P.
[7] bee, or to bee. Qu.—P.
[8] Only half the n in the MS.—F.
[9] forte delend.—P.
[10] forte wate ; G. Doug! wete, weet.
Chauc,—P.

But if any
one
wrongs me
I'll fight
him."

but if any such doe me wrong,[1]

304   I will flight with him hand to hand,[2]

when I am cladd in mine [3] array."

"Have you
travelled
beyond sea,
John?"
"Not I!

the Bishopp sayd, "you seeme sturdye:

travelled you neuer beyond the sea?"

308   Ihon sayd sharplye "nay!

I know none such strange guise,

But I can
hold my own
on the road
at home,

but att home on my [4] owne wise

I dare hold the hye way;

and have got
into trouble
by it."

312   "& that hath done Iohn Reeue scath,

ffor I haue made such as you wrath

with choppes and chances [5] yare."

"Iohn de Reeue,[6]" sayd our King,

"Have you
any armour
or weapons,
John?"

316   "hast thou any armouringe,

or any weapon to weare?"

"None but
a two-
pronged
pitchfork,

"I vow, Sir, to god," sayd Iohn thoe,[7]

"but a pikefforke with graines 2—

320   my ffather vsed neuer other [8] speare:—

a rusty
sword,

a rusty sword that well will byte,

and a broad
knife,

& a handffull, a thyttille [9] syde

that [10]sharplye will stare,[11]

324   "an acton [12] & a habargyon a ffoote side;

tho' perhaps
I can fight
as well as
you.

& yett peraduenture I durst abyde [13]

as well as thou, Peeres, ffor all thy painted geere."

---

[1] forté wrang. Dialect. boreal.—P.

[2] forté hond to hond.—P.

[3] ? mine in the MS.— F.

[4] forté in my.—P.

[5] Changes, Qu. yare, ready. dextrous, ready. —P.

[6] John the Reeve.—P.

[7] thoe, i.e. then.—P.

[8] had no other. (Qu.—P.

[9] thuitil, a knife. Halliwell. A.-Sax. þwitan, to cut off.—F. thytill, some weapon. perhaps a Dagger, so named from its being worn upon the thigh, thigh-till. syde is long; perhaps the verse should be read "And a thytill a handful

syde," i.e. a handful long: so a foot side, is a foot long. Vid. Stan. 26, P[t] 3[d] —P. Syde is also broad, wide.—F.

[10] will full sharplye share.—P.

[11] share.—P.

[12] Acton, Fr[ench] Hoequeton, sagum militare: a kind of armour made of Taffity or leather, quilted thick, and stuck full of thread, fringe, &c. reaching from the neck to the knee, worn under the Habergeon, to save the body from Bruises &c. Skene's exposition of difficil words contain'd in the 4 buiks of Regiam Magestatem, 1611 Q[to]—ubi plura.—P.

[13] stand a charge, fight; last out.—F.

quoth Iohn, "I reede wee goe to the hall,

328 wee 3 ffellowes; & peeres pay=for=all
    the proudest before shall fare."

But let's go
to supper."

thither they raked[1] anon-wright[2] :
a charcole ffyer burning bright

332 with manye a strang[3] brand.
the hall was large & some deale wyde,
there bords were[4] couered on euerye syde,
there mirth was comanded.[5]

They go to
the Hall,
which has a
fire in it,

and tables
laid.

336 then the good wiffe sayd with a seemlye cheere,
"your supper is readye there."
    "yett watter,[6]" quoth Iohn, "letts see."
by then came Iohn's neighbors 2,

340 hobkin[7] long and hob alsoe :
    the ffirst ffitt here ffind wee.

John's
neighbours,
Hobkin and
Hodgkin,
come in.

[1] went.—F.
[2] right.—P.
[3] strong.—P.
[4] *werer* in the MS.—F.
[5] *forté,* at command.—P.
[6] This was for washing hands. See

Babees Book, p. 5, l. 129, &c.
Whenne that ye se youre lorde to mete
  shalle goo,
Be redy to feeche him *water* sone.—F.
    [7] Hodgkin, vid. infra.—P.

[The Second Part.]

[How John feasts the King, and dances with him.]

John arranges his guests:

the King at top, the

344

Bishop next his wife,

2.ᴵ parte.

Iohn sayd, "for want of a marshall, I will take
   the wand :[1]
Peeres fflauconer before shall gange ;
   begin the dish[2] shall hee.
goe to the bench, thou proud chaplaine,
   my wiffe shall sitt thee againe ;
   thy meate-fellow[3] shall shee bee."

the Earl near the King,

348

he sett the Erle against the King ;
they were ffaine att his bidding.
   thus Iohn marshalled his meanye.[4]

his prettiest daughter next the King, the other by the Earl ;

352

Then Iohn sperred[5] where his daughters were :
"the ffairer shall sitt by the ffawconere ;
   he is the best ffarrand[6] man :
the other shall the Sompter man haue."
the Erle sayd, "soe god me saue !

356

of curtesye, Iohn, thou can.[7] "

and says that if

"If my selfe," quoth Iohn, "be bound,[8]
yett my daughters beene well ffarrand,
   I tell you sickerlye.

the King married one,

360

Peeres, & thou had wedded Iohn daughter reeue,
there were no man *that* durst thee greeue
   neither ffor gold nor ffee.

---

[1] John *said* as marshal I'll take the wand &c.—P. Compare *The Boke of Curtasye*, Sloane MS. 1486, ed. Halliwell. Percy Soc., ed. Furnivall in *Babees Book* &c. E. E. Text Soc. 1868.

Fowre men þer ben þat ȝerdis schalle bere,
Porter, marshalle, stuarde, vsshere ;
The porter schalle haue þe lengest wande,
The marshalle a schorter schalle haue in hande.

l. 352-6; *Babees Book, &c.* p. 309.
In halle, marshalle alle men schalle sett

After here degre, with-outen lett.
         l. 403-4.—F.

[2] deese. dais.—F.

[3] i.e. Mess-mate.—P.

[4] familia, multitudo. Lye.—P.

[5] i.e. enquired.—P.

[6] *farrand*, perhaps the same as *far-rantly*, a word in Staffordshire signifying sufficient, handsome, proper &c. T.P. *farand, farrant*, beseeming, becoming, courteous, handsome. Gloss. to G. Doug.—P.   [7] knowest.—F.

[8] bende, or bande.—P.

"Sompter man, & thou the other had,[1]
364 in good ffaith then thou were made
ffor euer in this cuntrye;
then, Peeres,[2] thou might[3] beare the prize.
yett I wold this chaplaine had a benefize,
368 as mote I[4] thariue[5] or three[6]!

and the Earl the other, they'd be made men.

And as for the Bishop,

"in this towne a kirke there is;
& I were king, itt shold be his,
he shold haue itt of mee;
372 yett will I helpe as well as I may."
the King, the Erle, the Bishopp, can say,
"Iohn, & wee liue wee shall quitte thee."

if he, John, were king, he'd give him their parish church.

They all 3 promise to reward him.

when his daughters were come to dease,[7]
376 "sitt ffarther," quoth Iohn withouten Leaze,[8]
"ffor there shalbe no more.[9]   [page 362]
these strange ffellowes I doe not ken;
peraduenture they may be some[10] gentlemen;
380 therfore I and my neighbors towe,

"att side end bord wee[11] will bee,
out of the gentles companye[12]:
thinke yee not best soe?
384 ffor. itt was neuer the Law of England[13]
to sett gentles blood with bound[14];
therfore to supper will wee goe.[15]"

John and his two neighbours sit at a side table.

[1] yee—had, Qu.—P.
[2] Tho' Peeres, &c.—P.
[3] mought, mote.—P.
[4] so mote I.—P.
[5] Qu. MS. There is one stroke too few for *thariue.* "Thrive or thee" is the phrase intended.—F.
[6] all three, Qu.—P.
[7] *Deis,* eral altior & eminentior mensa in aula. The high table. See Jun. *Deis,* desk, bench, seat, table. Per metonym. adj., a feast, banquet, or entertainment Et per al. meton. to set at deis with one

(Lat. *hospitium*) is taken for friendship, alliance, or [cov]enant. . . . .—P.
[8] *Lese,* Lying, falsehood, treachery. Urry, Gloss. to Chaucer.—P.
[9] moe.—P.
[10] some *defend.*—P.
[11] At side berd end wee &c. Vid. St. 15. At siden borde we &c. So withouten for without. Shenstone.—P.
[12] Only half the *n* in the MS.—F.
[13] Englonde.—P.
[14] bonde.—P.
[15] wee'll go.—P.

The supper is bean bread, salt bacon, broth,	by then came in beane bread,[1]
	388 salt Bacon rusted and redd,
	& brewice[2] in a blacke dish,
lean beef,	leane salt beefe of a yeere old,
sour ale.	ale *that* was both sower & cold :
	392 this was the flirst service :
	eche one had of that ylke[3] a messe.
The King doesn't like it.	the king sayd, " soe haue I blisse,
	such service nerest[4] I see."
John says	396 quoth Iohn, " thou gettest noe other of mee
	att this time but this."[5]
	" yes, good fellow," the King gan say,
	" take this service here[6] away,
	400 & better bread vs bringe ;
	& gett vs some better drinke ;
	we shall thee requite, as wee thinke,
	without any letting."
he'll give him no better, unless they all swear	404 quoth Iohn, " beshrew the morsell of bread
	this night *that* shall come in your head
	but thou sweare me one thinge !
	swore to me by booke and bell
not to tell the King.	408 *that* thou shalt neuer Iohn Reeue bettell
	vnto Edward our kinge."
The King vows he'll never tell him,	quoth the king, " to thee my truth I plight,
	he shall nott witt our service[7]
	412 no more then he doth nowe,
	neuer while wee 3 liue in land."
	" therto," quoth Iohn, " hold vp thy hand,
	& then I will thee troe."

---

[1] Compare the loaves of beans and bran baked for his children by the Ploughman. *Vision*, p. 89, l. 270 ed. Skeat.—F.

[2] Brewice, i.e. Broth, Pottage. Jun.—P. The *ice* stands over *ish* marked out. —F.

[3] ilk, *ipse* that ilk, *idem* that same. Lye.—P.   [4] never, or ne'er.—P.

[5] Forté other [Meate or other Service] Qth John, at this Time, but this Thou gettest none of me.—P.

[6] MS. herer.—F.

[7] our service witt. Qu.—P.

416 "loe," quoth the king, "my hand is heere!"

"soe is mine!" quoth the Erle with a merry cheere, *and so say the Earl*

 "thereto I giue god a vowe."

 "haue heere my hand!" the Bishopp sayd. *and Bishop.*

420 "marry," quoth Iohn, "thou may hold thee well
  apayd,

 ffor itt is ffor thy power.[1]

 "take this away, thou hobkin [2] long, *John orders the bad supper off,*

 & let vs sitt out of the throng

424 att a side bords end ;

these strange ffellowes thinke vncouthlye

this night att our [3] Cookerye,

 such as god hath vs sent.[4]"

428 by them [5] came in the payment bread, *and then has in the good : spiced bread, and good wine.*

wine *that* was both white and redd

 in siluer cupp[e]s cleare.

"a ha!" quoth Iohn,[6] "our supp*er* begins with
 drinke!

432 tasste itt, ladds! & looke how [7] yee thinke,[8] *He tells them to taste his wine.*

 ffor my loue, and make good cheere!

 "of meate & drinke you shall haue good ffare ; *There is plenty of it,*

& as ffor good wine, wee will not spare,

436 I goe [9] you to vnderstand.[10]

ffor euerye yeere, I tell thee thoe,[11]

I will haue a tunn or towe *and the best that can be got.*

 of the best *that* may be ffound.[12]

440 "yee shall see 3 Churles heere

drinke the wine w*i*th a merry cheere ;

 I pray you doe you soe ;

---

[1] Forté,
 Qu*th* John yee may be well ap*d*
 For it is in my power now.—P.
Power is for Prowe, profit, advantage ;
Fr. prou.—F.

[2] Hodgkin, vid. Infra.—P.

[3] of our &c.—P.

[4] God doth us send.—P.

[5] ? MS. then.—F.

[6] Quoth John, &c. (a ha *defend*).—P.

[7] Forté tell how &c.—P.

[8] Qn. slink, perhaps thinke.—P.

[9] Qu. give.--P.

[10] understonde.—P.

[11] thee now or true.—P.

[12] fonde.—P.

They'll all
sup, and
then dance.
& when our supper is all doone,

444 you and wee will dance soone;

letts see who best can doe."

The Earl
says the
King
can drink no
better wine.
the Erle sayd, "by Marry bright,

wheresoeuer the King lyeth this night,

448 he drinketh no better wine

then thou selfe[1] does att this tyde."

"infaith," quoth Iohn, "soe had leeuer[2] I did

then liue ay in woe & payne.[3]

452 "If I be come of Carles kinne,

part of the good that I may winne,   [page 3 68]

some therof shall be mine.

he that neuer spendeth but alway spareth,

456 comonlye oft[4] the worsse he ffareth;

others will broake[5] itt ffine.[6] "

by then came in red wine & ale,

the bores head[7] into the hall,

Next come
the boar's
head,
460 then sheild[8] with sauces scere[9] ;

Capons both baked & rosted,[10]

capons,
woodcockes, venison, without bost,

venison,
& dish meeate[11] dight ffull deere.

swans,
464 swannes they had piping hott,

curlews,
Coneys, curleys,[12] well I wott,

herons, &c.
the crane, the hearne[13] in ffere,[14]

---

[1] thyself.— P.

[2] i.e. rather: 1 leeuer, legend.—P.

[3] pine or pyne. Chauc. idem.—P.

[4] oft, de'end.— P.

[5] to brouke, broke, to brook, bear;
To use, enjoy. Urry in Chauc.—P.

[6] fine for finely.—P.

[7] See the Carol, The boris hede furst,
in Mrs. Ormsby Gore's Porkington MS.
No. 10. The carol is printed in Reliq.
Antiq. vol. ii., Babees Book &c. p. 397.- F.

[8] The sword of Bacon is call'd the
Shield: and the horny Part of brawn in
some places. -P.

[9] scere, sere, several; many; contract.

from sere, or several. Gloss. ad G. D.
—P.

[10] roste.—P.

[11] sweet dishes, &c. Russell says in
his Boke of Nurture, l. 513–14,
Some mau r cury of Cookes crafft sotelly
y haue espied,
how peire dischmetes ar dressid with
homy not claryfied.—F.

[12] curlews.—P.

[13] heron. See Russell, in Babees Book,
p. 143-4. Compare this feast with Russell's Fest for a Franklen, B.B. p. 172-3.
—F.

[14] i.e. together, along.--P.

pigeons, partrid[g]es, with spicerye,
468 Elkes,[1] fflomes,[2] with ffroterye.[3]
Iohn bade them make good cheere.

partridges, tarts &c.

the Erle sayd, "soe mote I thee,
Iohn, you serue vs royallye!
472 if yee had dwelled att London,[4]
if king Edward where here,[5]
he might be a-payd [6] with this supper,[7]
such ffreindshipp wee haue ffound."

The Earl says it's a royal feast; the King might be pleased with it.

476 "Nay," sayd Iohn, "by gods grace,
& Edward wher in [8] this place,
hee shold not touch this tonne.
hee wold be wrath with Iohn, I hope;
480 thereffore I beshrew [9] the soupe [10]
that shall come in his mouth [11]!"

"If he were here, he shouldn't have a scrap," says John.

theratt the King laughed & made good cheere.
the Bishopp sayd, "wee fare well heere!"
484 the Erle sayd as him thought.
they spake lattine amongst them there [12]:
"infayth," quoth Iohn, "and yee greeue mee,
ffull deere itt shalbe bought.

They talk Latin together. John tells them to

488 "speake English euerye-eche one,[13]
or else sitt still, in the devills name!
such talke loue I naught.[14]
Lattine spoken amongst Lewd [15] men,
492 therin noe reason ffind I can;
ffor ffalshood itt is wrought.

talk English,

[1] '*Elk*, a wild swan. Northern.' Halliwell. ? *yelk*, some dish of eggs.—F.
[2] ? *flauns*, a kind of cheesecake.—F.
[3] *fruterye*, fruit collectively taken, *fruiterie* Fr. Johnson.—P. Fritters, I have no doubt. See them in Russell's *Boke of Nurture* (p. 168-70 *Babees Book*) and many other Bills of Fare.—F.
[4] *Forte* As ye at London won'd.—P.
[5] Edward's self were heere.—P.
[6] to appay, to satisfy, to content, hence

'well appaid' is pleased. 'ill appayd' is uneasy (Fr. *appayer*). Johns.—P.
[7] suppere.—P.
[8] MS. wherin.—F. wero in.—P.
[9] *beshrew*, verbum male precantis. Jun. —P.
[10] sup, soupe.—P.
[11] That in his Mouth sholde come.—P.
[12] perhaps "three."—P.
[13] everiche one.—P.
[14] not, or hold I naught.—P.
[15] Lewd, i.e. Laymen. Johnson.—P.

he doesn't
like whisper-
ing.

       "row[n]ing,[1] I loue itt[2] neither young nor old ;
       therefore yee ought not to bee to bold,
496   neither att Meate nor meale.

it's traitors'
work

       hee was ffalse *that* rowning began ;
       theerfore I say to you certaine
       I loue itt neuer a deale:

and not to
be tolerated
by any
courteous
host.

500   "that man can [nought] of curtesye
       that lets att his meate rowning bee,[3]
       I say, soe haue I seile.[4]"

The Earl
promises to
leave off.

       the Erle sayd right againe,
504   "att your bidding wee will be baine,[5]
       wee thinke you say right weele."

Then sweets
come in,

       by this came vp ffrom the kitchin
       sirrupps[6] on plates[7] good and ffine,
508   wrought in a ffayre array.

and John
proposes
that they
shall be
merry

       "Sirrah,[8]" sayth Iohn, "sithe wee are mett,
       & as good ffellowes together sett,
       lett vs be blythe to-day.

and he and
his mates
shall

512   "Hodgkin long, & hob of the Lath,[9]
       you are counted good ffellowes both,[10]
       now is no time to thrine[11] ;

---

[1] rowning, they are used promiscuously in Chauc! —P.

[2] *in*, qu. ; or loued neither.—P.

[3] John is right here. Whispering is strictly forbidden by the old Books of Courtesy, &c.
"Loke þou *rownde* not in no mannys ere."
          Babees Book, p. 20, l. 54.
Looke that ye be in rihte stable sylence,
Withe-oute lowde lauhtere or langelynge,
Rovnynge, Iapynge or other Insolence.
          ib. p. 253, l. 93-5.
Bekenyng, fynguryng, noω þou vse,
And prvne *rownyng* loke thou refuse.
Boke of Curtasye, 1. 250, Bab. Book, p. 306.

[4] *seil*, Scotch, i.e. prosperity, happiness. Gloss: to Ramsay's Ever-green. à Teut. *seliy.* &c., beatus, felix. Gloss.

ad G. D.—P.

[5] so *bane* in G. Doug. is ready. Æ. 3, v. 96, Antiquam exquirite matrem : 'to seik zour auld moder, mako ze bane.' perhaps for *bowne*, metri gratia. Gloss. ad G. Doug.—P.

[6] Compare Russell, 1. 509, (in *Babees Book &c.*) speaking of cooks:
Some with Sireppis (Sawces), Sowes and soppes.—F.

[7] *forté* platters.—P.

[8] *Forté* Sirs.—P.   Sirrahs.—Dyce.

[9] Lathe.—P.   [10] baith.—P.

[11] The German *thränen*, to run over, weep, is the only word I can suggest for this, though it could hardly become *thrine*. A.-S. *þringan* is to throng, crowd, press. *Trine*, to hang. Halliwell.—F.

this wine is now come out of ffrance ;

516   be god ! me list well to dance,   *dance.*

      therfore take my hand in thine ;

    " ffor wee will ffor our guests sake

    hop and dance, & Reuell make."

520   the truth ffor to know,

    vp he rose, & dranke the wine :   *John stands*

    " wee must haue powder of ginger therein,"   *up*

    Iohn sayd, as I troe.

524   Iohn bade them stand vp all about,

    " & yee shall see the carles stout

     dance about the bowle.

    Hob of the lathe [1] & Hodgkin long,   *with Hob*

528   in ffayth you dance your mesures wrong !   *and Hodgkin,*

    methinkes *that* I shold know.   *and they dance*

    " yee dance neither Gallyard [2] nor hawe,[3]

    Trace [4] nor true mesure, as I trowe,[5]   [page 364]

532   but hopp as yee were woode."

    when they began of ffoote to ffayle,

    thé tumbled top ouer tayle,   *till they*

     & *Master* and *Master* they yode.   *tumble down.*

536   fforth they stepped on stones store [6] ;

    Hob of the lathe lay on the fflore,

     his brow brast out of blood.

    " ah, ha !" Quoth Iohn, " thou makes good game ! *John laughs*

540   had thou not ffalled, wee had not laught ;   *at Hob,*

    thou gladds vs all, by the rood."

---

[1] *lathe* est horreum ; a Corn-house, a Grange. Jun.—P.

[2] A quick and lively dance introduced into this country about 1541. Halliwell.—F.

[3] *Hay*, Qu. Dance tho Hay.— P. A round country dance. Halliwell.—F.

[4] *Trasinge*, ap! G. Douglas, is explain'd in ye Gloss., 'stepping, walking softly,' from the Fr. *trace*, a step ; but it is join'd with dancing in ye following Passage :

The harpis & gythornis playis attanis,
Upstert Troyanis, & syne Italianis
And gan do doubil brangillis & gambettis
Dansis & roundis *trasing* mony gatis.—P.

[5] *Forté*, as I say.— P.

[6] *store*, *stour*, *sture*, ingens, crassus. Lye.—P.

and pulls
him up.

Iohn hent [1] vp hobb [2] by the hand,[3]

says, "methinkes wee dance our measures wronge,

544 by him *that* sitteth in throne."

They begin
to play at
kicks,

then they began to kicke & wince,[4]

Iohn hitt the king ouer the shinnes

w*i*th a payre of new clowted shoone.

and the
King has a
merry night.

548 sith K*ing* Edward was mad a knight,

had he neuer soe merry a night

as he had w*i*th Iohn de Reeue.[5]

to bed thé busked them auon,

552 their lineryes [6] were serued them vp soone

w*i*th a merry cheere;

Next
morning

& thus [7] they sleeped till morning att prime [8]

in full good sheetes of Line.

they hear
Mass,

556 a masse [9] he garred them to haue,

breakfast,

& after they dight them to dine

w*i*th boyled capons good & fline.

the Duke sayd,[10] "soe god me saue,

promise
John a
reward,

560 if euer wee come to our abone,[11]

we shall thee quitt our Barrison [12];

thou shalt not need itt [13] to craue."

---

[1] i.e. held. Lye.—P.

[2] The first *b* is made over a *p* in the MS.—F.

[3] hond or wrang.—P.

[4] *Winche*, to kick. Halliwell.—F.

[5] the Reeve, *or* John Re*e*ve there.—P.

[6] Allowances of meat and drink &c. ' *Lyueray* he hase of mete and drynke.' *Boke of Curtasye*, 1. 371, *Babees Book*, p. 310. Bouge of Court it is called in *Household Ordinances*, t. Edw. IV.—F.

[7] there.—P.

[8] prime sic legerit. Lye. D. *forté* morn*g* prime, or morn at prime.—P.

[9] perhaps *Mess.*—P. Mass was heard by all in the morning.—F.

[10] The Erle *said*.—P.

[11] *Fortasse* Wone.—P. *Abofe* is abode, dwelling (Halliwell); *abone*, above.—F.

[12] *Warrison* [gift, reward] see P! 3rd St. 40.—P.

[13] *it* delend.—P.

[The Third Part.]

[How the King invites John to court, and rewards him.]

the king tooke leaue att man & mayde [1];
564 Iohn sett him in the rode way;
    to windsor can hee [2] ryde.

and take their leave.

Then all the court was ffull faine
that the king was comen againe,
568   & thanked chr[i]st *that* tyde.

King Edward is welcomed at Windsor.

3ᵈ parte

the Ierfawcons were taken againe
in the fforrest of windsor without laine,[3]
    the Lords did soe provyde,
572 they thanked god & S! Iollye.
to tell the Queene of their harbor [4]
    the lords had ffull great pryde.

They tell the Queen about John de Reeve,

The Queene sayd, " Sir, by your leaue,
576 I pray you send ffor *that* Noble Reeue,
    that I may see him with sight."
the Messenger was made to wend,
& bidd Iohn Reeue goe to the King
580   hastilye with all his might.

and she asks the King to send for him.

A messenger tells John to come to the King.

Iohn waxed vnfaine [5] in bone & blood,
saith, " dame, to me this is noe good,
    my truth to you I plight."
584 " you must come in your best array."
" what too," sayd Iohn, " Sir, I thee pray ? "
    " thou must be made a Knight."

He is put out at first,

---

[1] may.—Dyce.
[2] gan he &c.—P. *Can* means did.—F.
[3] MS. laine.—F. Vid. Stanz. 45.—P.

[4] *forte* harborye, or harberye.—P. lodging.—F.
[5] displeased, literally ' unglad.'—P.

thinks his
late guests

"a knight," sayd Iohn, "by Marry myld,

588 I know right well I am beguiled

with the guests I harbord late.

have got him
into a
scrape ;
" but never
mind,

to debate they will me bring;

yett cast [1] I mee ffor nothinge

592 noe sorrow ffor to take;

wife, fetch
my armour,

"Allice, ffeitch mee downe my side Acton,

my round pallett [2] to my crowne,

is made of Millayne [3] plate,

pitchfork,
and sword."

596 a pitch-fforke and a sword. [4] "

shee sayd shee was affrayd [5]

this deede wold make debate.

Allice ffeitched downe his Acton syde;

600 hee tooke itt ffor no litle pryde,

yett must hee itt weare.

The
scabbard
is torn.

the Scaberd was rent withouten doubt,

a large handfull the bleade [6] hanged out:

604 Iohn the REEUE sayd there,

John calls
for leather
and a nail to
mend it,

"gett lether & a nayle," Iohn can say,

"lett me sow itt [7] a chape to-day,

Lest men scorne my geere.   [page 365]

608 Now," sayd Iohn, "will I see

[w]hether [8] itt will out lightlye

or [9] I meane itt to weare."

and tries to
pull the
blade out.

Iohn pulled ffast att the blade :

612 (I wold hee had kist my arse *that* itt made !)

he cold not gett itt out.

---

[1] to cast, to calculate, to reckon, compute. Item, to contrive, to turn the thoughts. Johnson.—P.

[2] Pallat, in G. Doug? is used for *caput*. Scot. bor. *pallet* or *pallat* is the crown of the Head or Skull. Gloss. ad G. Doug? Hence it should signify here an Helmet or Skull-cap.—P.

[3] See note [2], vol. i. p. 68.— F.

[4] *forte* sweard.— P.

[5] affear'd.—P.

[6] blade.—P.

[7] *Forte* sow in. in, qy.—P. Chape, the hook of a scabbard; the metal part at the top. Halliwell.—F.

[8] whether.—P.

[9] or, i.e. before.—P.

Allice held, & Iohn draughe,[1]
either att other ffast loughe,[2]
616　I doe yee out of doubt.

his wife
holds, he
pulls,

Iohn pulled att the scaberd soe hard,
againe a post he ran backward
　& gaue his head a rowte.[3]
620　his wiffe did laughe when he did ffall,
　& soe did his [4] meanye all
　　that were there neere about.

and he falls
back against
a post.

His wife and
men laugh at
him.

Iohn sent after his neighbors both,[5]
624　Hodgkine long & hobb of the lath.[6]
　　they were beene[7] att his biddinge.
　3 pottles of wine[8] in a dishe
　they supped itt[9] all off, as I wis,
628　all there att their partinge.

He sends for
Hodgkin
and Hob,

to drink and
take leave of
him.

Iohn sayd, " & I had my buckler,[10]
theres nothing that shold me dare,
　I tell you all in ffere.[11]
632　ffeitch me downe," quoth he, " my gloues ;
they came but [12] on my [13] hands but once
　this 22 [14] yeere.

Then he calls
for his

gloves,

" ffeitch mee my Capull," sayd hee there.
636　his saddle was of a new manner,[15]
　his stirropps were of a tree.[16]
" dame," he sayd, " ffeitch me wine ;
I will drinke to thee [17] once againe,
640　I troe I shall neuer thee see.

his horse,

and more
wine.

---

[1] drowghe, Chaucr, i.e. drew.—P.
[2] lough, or lowghe, i.e. laughed. Chaucr.—P.
[3] Great or violent stir. Devon. Hall.—F.
[4] his in the MS.—F.
[5] baith.—P.
[6] Lathe.—P.
[7] Qu. bowne, bane, bayne, Vid. Pt 2. St. 29 [f. i. 28 of MS., l. 504 above].—P.
[8] MS. wime.—F.
[9] itt, delend, censeo.—P.
[10] bucklere.—P.
[11] in fere, together, intire, wholly. Gloss. ad G.D.—P.
[12] delend. Qu.—P.
[13] came upon my.—P.
[14] two & twentye.—P.
[15] mannere.—P.
[16] of tree.—P. wood.—F.
[17] An upright stroke, which may be for l. stands between thee and once.—F.

JOHN DE REEVE.

He,
Hodgkin,
and Hob

"Hodgkin long, & hob of the lathe,
tarry & drinke with me bothe,[1]
ffor my cares are flast commannde.[2]"

drink five
gallons;
644 they dranke 5 gallons verament :
"ffarwell ffellowes all present,
ffor I am readye to gange ! "

Iohn was soe combred in his geere
and
Hodgkin
heaues him
on to his
mare.
648 hee cold not gett vpon his mare
till hodgkinn heaue vp[3] behind.

"Now ffarwell, Sir, by the roode ! "
to neither Knight nor Barron good
652 his hatt he wold not vayle
When he
gets to
Windsor
Castle, the
porter won't
let him in,
till[4] he came to the Kings gate :
the Porter wold not lett him in theratt,
nor come within the walle,

656 till a Knight came walking out.
they sayd, "yonder standeth a carle stout
in a rusticall arraye."
on him they all wondred wright,[5]
660 & said he was an vnseemelye wight,
& thus to him they[6] gan say :

"hayle, ffellow ! where wast thou borne?
and the
servants
chaff him.
thee beseemeth ffull well to weare a horne !
664 where had thou that ffaire geere?
I troe a man might seeke ffull long,
one like to thee ar that hee ffound,[7]
tho he sought all this yeere."

---

[1] bathe or baith.—P.
[2] i.e. are coming fast. comand, idem
ar coming.—P.
[3] hove up.—P.
[4] when. Qu.—P.
[5] right.—P.
[6] they deland.—P.
[7] fonde.—P. ? ffong, got hold of.—Dyce.

668 Iohn bade them kisse the devills arse[1]: *John says*
  "ffor you my geare is much the worsse[2]!
  you will itt not amend,
  by my ffaith, *that* can I lead!
672 vpon[3] the head I shall you shread *he'll crack their crowns if they don't go.*
  but if you hence wende!

  " the devill him speede vpon his crowne *The devil take the fellow who brought him there!*
  that causeth[4] me to come to this towne,
676 whether he weare Iacke or Iill!
  what shold such men as I doe heere
  att the kings Manner[5]?
  I might haue beene att home still."

680 as Iohn stoode fflyting[6] ffast, *Then John sees his guest, the Earl,*
  he saw one of his guests come at the last;
  to him he spake ffull bold,
  to him he ffast ffull rode,[7]
684 he vayled neither hatt nor hood;
  sayth, " thou hast me betold! [page 366] *and reproaches him with having told of him.*

  " full well I wott by this light
  that thou hast disdainde mee right;
688 ffor wrat[h] I waxe neere wood!"
  The Erle sayd, " by Marry bright, *The Earl says he won't be hurt,*
  Iohn, thou made vs a merry night;
  thou shalt haue nothing but good."

692 the Erle tooke leaue att Iohn Reue,
  sayd, " thou shalt come in without greefe;
  I pray thee tarry a while."

---

[1] Erse, Chauc.—P.
[2] werse, Chauc.—P.
[3] MS. vpan *or* vpom.—F.
[4] *Forté* caused.—P.
[5] Mannere.—P. Dwelling, mansion.
—F.

[6] To flyte, i.e. to chide, is still in use in Scotland. Gloss? to Ramsay's Evergreen. *flyt*, to scold, chide. A.-S. *flitan*, contendere, rixari. Gloss. ad G. Doug*.*
—P.
[7] full faste rode.—P.

and goes to
tell the King
that John is
at the gate.

the Erle into the hall went,

696   & told the *King* verament

     that [1] Iohn Reeue was att the gate ;

   " to no man list hee lout.

   a rusty sword gird [2] him about,

700   & a long flawchyon, I wott. [3] "

King
Edward
orders John
to be brought
in to table.

the *King* said, " goe wee to meate,

   & bringe him when [4] wee are sett ;

    our dame shall haue a play."

The Earl
describes
John's

704   " he hath 10 arrowes in a thonge,

   some are short & some are long,

    the sooth as I shold say ;

armour,

   "a rusty sallett [5] vpon his crowne,

708   his hood were made home browne [6] ;

    there may nothing him dare ;

his knife,

   a thytill hee hath ffast in his hand

   that hangeth in a peake band, [7]

712   & sharplye itt will share.

   " he hath a pouch hanging ffull wyde,

   a rusty Buckeler on the other syde,

gloves,

    his mittons [8] are of blacke clothe.

716   who-soe to him sayth ought but good,

    [9] [I swear it to you by the rood,]

and temper.

    ffull soone hee wilbe wrothe."

John tells
the porter to
let him in.

then Iohn sayd, " Porter, lett mee in !

720   some of my goods thou shalt win ;

    I loue not ffor to pray."

---

[1] That *delend.*—P.

[2] girdeth.—P.

[3] weet. Item. wate, wat, i.e. know, knew, wot. Gloss. ad G. D.—P.

[4] him in, when.—P.

[5] Aliter *salad*, a Gallic. *Salade*, a Headpiece. *Celada*, or *Zelada*, Spanish. Lye. vid. St. 6, Pt 3d [l. 594 above].—P.

[6] of homespun brown : or rather, was of homemade brow[n]. See Pt 1, St. 48 [l. 284 above].—P.

[7] See the Picture of Chaucer.—P.

[8] Cp. Twey mitteynes as meter. *Piers Plowman's Crede.*—F.

[9] A line wanting.—P.

the Porter sayd, "stand abacke !

& thou come neere I shall thee rappe,

724 thou carle, by my ffay ! "

Iohn tooke his fforke [1] in his hand,

he bare his fforke on an End,

 he thought to make a ffray ;

728 his Capull was wight,[2] & corne ffedd ;

vpon the Porter hee him spedd,

 and him had welnye slaine.[3]

he hitt the Porter vpon the crowne,

732 with *that* stroke hee ffell downe,

 fforsooth as I you tell ;

& then hee rode into the hall,

& all the doggs both great & small [4]

736 on Iohn ffast can thé yell.[5]

Iohn layd about as hee were wood,

& 4 hee killed as hee stood ;

 the rest will now be ware.

740 then came fforth a squier hend,

& sayd, " Iohn, I am thy ffreind,

 I pray you light downe heere."

another sayd, " gine me thy fforke,"

744 & Iohn sayd, " nay, by S! William of Yorke,[6]

 ffirst I will cracke thy crowne ! "

---

[1] forke. Perhaps *stocke*, which is used by Gawain Douglas for a dagger, rapier, Æn. 7, 669, "veruque sabello" being render'd "with stokkis sabellyne." ab Ital. *stoico*, *ensis longior*. Gloss. ad G. D. *Stock*, caudex, Truncus. Jun. It signifies also the handle of anything. Johnson. A staff or long Pole.—P. John's tool is of course his two-grained pitchfork that he describes in line 319, and asks for in line 596 above.—F.

[2] Vid. Pt. 1, St. 36.—P.
[3] did well-nye slay.—P.
[4] Dogs had possession of the whole of the houses in Early English days. See the directions for turning them out of the lord's bedroom in Russell, the Sloane MS. Boke of Curtasye, &c. in *Babees Book*, p. 182, l. 969 ; p. 283, l. 93, p. 69.—F.
[5] gan to yell.—P.
[6] ? what saint.—F.

A third, his sword

another sayd, "lay downe thy sword [1];
sett vp thy horsse; be not affeard;

748 thy bow, good Iohn, lay downe;

and helmet.

"I shall hold your stirroppe;
doe of your pallett & your hoode
ere thé ffall, as I troe.

He must be very stupid not to see in whose presence he is.

752 yee see not who sitteth att the meate;
yee are a wonderous silly ffreake,
& alsoe passing sloe [2] !"

"What the devil's that to you?" says John. "I shall wear my sword."

"what devill," sayd Iohn, "is *that* ffor thee [3]?

756 itt is my owne, soe mote I thee!
therfore I will itt weare."

The Queen asks who he can be.

the Queene beheld him in hast:
" my lord,[4] " shee sayd, "ffor gods ffast,

760 who is yonder *that* doth ryde?
such a ffellow saw I neuer yore [5]!
shee saith, "hee hath the quaintest geere,
he is but simple of pryde." [page 367]

John rides on,

764 right soe came Iohn as hee were wood;
he vayled neither hatt nor hood,
he was a ffaley [6] ffreake;

with his pitchfork at the charge,

he tooke his fforke as hee wold Iust;

768 vp to the dease [7] ffast he itt thrust.
the Queene ffor ffeare did speake,

and frightens the Queen.

& sayd, "lords, beware, ffor gods grace!
ffor hee [8] will ffrowte [9] some in the fface

772 if yee take not good heede!"

---

[1] swerde.—P.
[2] slow.—P.
[3] ye deuill . . is that to thee.—P.
[4] my Lords. Qu.—P.
[5] yore, jamdudum, jam olim. Jun. perhaps here.—P.
[6] perhaps *stately.*—P. ? *Ferley,* wonderful.—F.

[7] Dease, or Deis. See P! 2^d S! 6. —P.
[8] MS. thee.—F.
[9] Perhaps from Fr. *froter,* in the sense of to bang or beat (*battre, frapper*), or in its original sense to rub. To *frote* is in use in this sense in Shropshire.—T. P.

thé laughed without doubt,
& soe did all *that* were about,
to see Iohn on his steede.

The rest
laugh.

776 then sayd Iohn to our Queene,
"thou mayst be proud, dame, as I weene,
to haue such a ffawconer [1] !
ffor he is a well ffarrand man,
780 & much good manner [2] hee can,
I tell you sooth in ffere.
[3] [.   .   .   .   .]
"but, lord," hee sayd, "my good, its thine;
my body alsoe, ffor to pine,
784 ffor thou art king with crowne.
but, lord, thy word is hono*rable*,
both stedffast, sure, and stable,
& alsoe [4] great of renowne !

John tells
the Queen
she may be
proud of her
falconer.

He's a fine-
looking
man.

[Then
finding that
it's King
Edward I.,]
to whom his
goods and
body belong,

788 "therfore haue mind [5] what thou me hight
when thou with me [harbord [6]] a night,
a warryson [7] *that* I shold haue."
Iohn spoke to him with sturdye mood,
792 hee vayled neither hatt nor hood,
but stood with him checkmate.[8]

he reminds
him of the
pledge he
made the
night he
lodged with
him.

the King sayd, "fellow mine,
ffor thy capons hott, & good red wine,
796 much thankes I doe giue thee."
the Queene sayd, " by Mary bright,
award him as his [9] right ;
well aduanced lett him bee ! "

Edward
thanks him
for his
capons and
wine,

---

[1] fawconere.—P.
[2] manners.—P.
[3] Some lines wanting here, containing the discovery of the King's rank. Some lines seem wanting here.—P.
[4] also *delend.*—P.
[5] *nind* in the MS.—F.
[6] me [passedst] a.—P.
[7] *warison*, reward. Scottish. See

Gloss. to Ramsay's Ever-green.—P.

[8] Qu. Check-mate : *mate* is companion, *Socius, sodalis,* q.d. cheek by Jole This passage may also be explain'd from the Term in chess; checkmate being when the king is hem'd in by some inferiour Piece ; so that he cannot stir.—T. P.

[9] forte *as is,* or *as it is.*—P.

800   the King sayd vntill him then,
            "Iohn, I make thee a gentleman;
                thy manner place [1] I thee giue,
                & a 100[ll] to thee and thine,[2]
804   & euery yeere a tunn of red wine
                soe long as thou dost liue."

but then Iohn began to kneele:
            "I thanke you, my Lord, as I haue soule,[3]
808   therof I am well payd.[4]"
thee King tooke a coller bright,
            & sayd, "Iohn, heere I make thee a knight
                with worshippe."   when hee sayd,

812   then was Iohn euill apayd,[5]
            & amongst them all thus hee sayd,
                "full oft I haue heard tell
                that after a coller comes a rope;
816   I shall be hanged by the throate;
                methinkes itt doth not well."

[6] "sith thou hast taken this estate,
            that euery man may itt wott,[7]
820   thou must begin the bord."
            then Iohn therof was nothing ffaine—
            I tell you truth with-outen laine,[8]—
                he spake neuer a word,

824   but att the bords end he sate him downe;
            ffor hee had leeuer beene att home
                then att all [9] their ffrankish [10] ffare;

---

[1] *place* delend.—P. dwelling place.
—F.
[2] *aud thime* in the MS.—F.
[3] sele or seil.—P.
[4] forte apayd, i.e. content.—P.
[5] i.e. sad, *tristis*. (See Jun[s]) uneasy.
P.

[6] something is wanting here.—P.
[7] wate, or weet.—P.
[8] lean, celare, occultare, ab. Isl. *leina,*
launa, occultare. Lye.—P.
[9] *All* is redundant.—P.
[10] frank, *liber, liberalis.* Jun.—P.

ffor there was wine, well I wott;

828 royall meates of the best sortes

were sett before him there.

a gallon of wine was put in a dishe;

Iohn supped itt of, both more & lesse.

832 "ffeitch," Quoth the King, "such more.[1]"

"by my Lady,[2]" Quoth Iohn, "this is good wine!

lett vs make merry, ffor now itt is time;

Christs curse on him *that* doth itt spare[3]!"

He drinks off a gallon of wine,

and wants to make merry.

836 w*i*th *that* came in the Porter[4] hend

& kneeled downe before the King,

was all[5] berunnen[6] with blood.

then the King in hart was woe,

840 sayes, "Porter, who hath dight thee soe?

tell on; I wax neere wood."

The porter comes in

all over blood.

"Who did this?" says the King.

"Now infaith," sayd Iohn, "*that* same was I,

for to teach him some curtesye,

844 [7] ffor thou hast taught him noe good.   [page 368]

for when thou came to my pore place,

with mee thou fonnd soe great a grace,

[8] noe man did bidd thee stand w*i*thout;

"I," says John, "to teach him manners.

When you came to me, if anyone had told you to

848 "ffor if any man had against thee spoken,

his head ffull soone I shold haue broken,"

Iohn sayd, "with-outen doubt.

therfore I warne thy porters ffree,

852 when any man [comes] out of my[9] Countrye,

another[10] [time] lett them not be soe stont.

stop outside, I'd have broken his head.

Your porters mustn't be so saucy next time."

---

[1] mare or mair.—P.

[2] *forté* our Lady.—P.

[3] on them that spare.—P.

[4] MS. Porters.—F.

[5] Ono was all &c.—P.

[6] MS. berumen.—F.

[7] For none thou hast him taught. Qu. —P.

[8] None bade thee stand w*i*thout.—P.

[9] Any come out, or comes from my &c.—P.

[10] *defend* another.—P.

"if both thy porters goe walling [1] wood,
begod I shall reaue [2] their hood,
856　　　or goe on ffoote boote.
but thou, Lord, hast after me sent,
& I am come att thy commandement
hastilye withouten doubt."

The King neknow- ledges that his porter was in fault,

860　　　the King sayd, "by St. Iame!
John, my porters were to blame;
yee did nothing but right."
he tooke the case into his hand;

but makes John kiss him

864　　　then to kisse [3] hee made them gange;
then laughed both King and Knight.
"I pray you," quoth the King, "good ffellows bee."

and be friends.

"yes," quoth Iohn, "soe mote I thee,
868　　　we were not wrathe [4] ore night."

The Bishop promises to put John's two sons to school,

then they [5] Bishopp sayd to him thee,
"John, send hither thy sonnes 2;
to the schoole [6] I shall them ffind,
872　　　& soe god may for them worke,
that either of them haue a kirke
if ffortune be their ffreind.

and says the King will find his daughters good husbands.

"also send hither thye daughters both [7];
876　　　2 marryages the King will garr them to haue, [8]
& wedd them with a ringe.

---

[1] walling, i.e. boiling, fervent; S. wellan. Lye.—P.

[2] reave, i.e. bereave (like as reft is for bereft) to take away by stealth or violence. Johnson. (used rather for riv, i.e. cleave.)—P.

[3] Cp. Chaucer's making the Host and Pardoner kiss. Cant. Tales, end of The Pardoneres Tale:

'And ye, sir host, that ben to me so deere,
I pray yow that ye kisse the pardoner;

And pardoner, I pray you draweth yow ner,
And as we dede, let us laugh and playe.'
Anon thay kisse, and riden forth her waye.
v. iii., p. 105, l. 502-6, ed. Morris.—F.

[4] wrothe.—P.
[5] the.—P.
[6] Fortè At schoole.—P.
[7] baith.—P.
[8] gar them have.—P.

went [1] fforth, Iohn, on thy way,
looke thou be kind & curteous aye,
880   of meate & drinke be neu[e]r nithing. [2]"

then Iohn tooke leaue of King & Queene, [3]   John takes leaue of the Court.
& after att all the court by-deene,
& went fforth on his way.

884   he sent his daughters to the King,   The King marries his daughters to two squires;
& they were weded with a ringe
vnto 2 squiers gay.

his sonnes both hardye & wight,   knights one of his sons,
888   the one of them was made a Knight,
& fresh in euery ffray ;
the other a parson of a kirke,   gives the other a living,
gods seruice ffor to worke,
892   to god serue [4] night & day.

thus Iohn Reeue and his wiffe
with mirth & Iolty [5] ledden their liffe ;
to god they made Laudinge.
896   Hodgikin long & hobb [6] of the lathe,   and makes Hodgkin and Hob freemen.
they were made ffreemen bothe [7]
through the grace of the King hend. [8]

then thought [John] [9] on the Bishopps word,   John de Reeve keeps open house
900   & euer after kept open bord
ffor guests that god him send ;
till death ffcitcht him away   till he dies.
to the blisse that lasteth aye :
904   & thus Iohn Reeue made an end.

---

[1] wend.—P.
[2] Nithing, nequam, naught, It. a dastard poltron: here it seems to mean niggardly.—P. A.-S. niðing, a wicked man, an outlaw,—Bosworth,—later, a niggard.—F.
[3] Only half the n in the MS.—F.

[4] to serve God.—P.
[5] Jollity.—P.
[6] A stroke like a t follows in the MS. —F.
[7] baith.—P.
[8] Perhaps hend King.—P.
[9] thought [he].—P.

　　　　　　　thus endeth the tale of Reeue soe wight.[1]

God save all
who
　　　　　　god *that* is soe ffull of might,
　　　　　　　　to heauen their soules bring

have heard
this story!
908　*that* haue heard this litle story,
　　　　　　　that lined [2] sometimes in the south-west countrye
　　　　　　　iu long [3] Edwards dayes our K*ing*.

　　　　　　　　　　　　　　　　　　ffns.

---

[1] See Page 210 [of MS.] top of y°
Page (fell some time, &c.).—P.

[2] Forte *happned*.—P.
[3] long-[shanks] or without *long*.—P.

Appendix.

— ◆ —

I.

Agincourt Ballads.

(See p. 159, Nos. 3 and 4.)

1. Agincourt, or the English Bowman's Glory.

A spirited black-letter ballad, of early date, the only existing copy of which was, however, "printed for Henry Harper in Smithfield," not long anterior to the Civil Wars; it bears for title "Agincourt, or the English Bowman's Glory," purporting to have been sung "to a pleasant new tune." *Collier's Shakespeare*, ed. 1858, vol. iii. p. 538.

> Agincourt, Agincourt!
> Know ye not Agincourt?
> Where English slue and hurt
>   All their French foemen?
> With our pikes and bills brown,
> How the French were beat downe,
>   Shot by our bowmen.
>
> Agincourt, Agincourt!
> Know ye not Agincourt,
> Never to be forgot
>   Or known to no men?
> Where English cloth-yard arrows
> Kill'd the French like tame sparrows,
>   Slaine by our bowmen.
>
> Agincourt, Agincourt!
> Know ye not Agincourt,
> Where we won field and fort?
> French fled like wo-men
> By land, and eke by water;
> Never was scene such slaughter,
>   Made by our bowmen.

Agincourt, Agincourt!
Know ye not Agincourt?
English of every sort,
  High men and low men,
Fought that day wondrous well, as
All our old stories tell us,
   Thanks to our bowmen.

Agincourt, Agincourt!
Know ye not Agincourt?
Either tale, or report,
  Quickly will show men
What can be done by courage,
Men without food or forage,
   Still lusty bowmen.

Agincourt, Agincourt!
Know ye not Agincourt?
Where such a fight was fought,
  As, when they grow men,
Our boys shall imitate;
Nor need we long to waite;
   They'll be good bowmen.

Agincourt, Agincourt!
Know ye not Agincourt?
Where our fifth Harry taught
  Frenchmen to know men:
And when the day was done,
Thousands there fell to one
   Good English bowman.

Agincourt, Agincourt!
Huzza for Agincourt!
When that day is forgot
  There will be no men.
It was a day of glory,
And till our heads are hoary
   Praise we our bowmen.

Agincourt, Agincourt!
Know ye not Agincourt?
When our best hopes were nought,

Tenfold our foemen.
Harry led his men to battle,
Slue the French like sheep and cattle :
Huzza! our bowmen.

Agincourt, Agincourt!
Know ye not Agincourt?
O, it was noble sport!
    Then did we owe men ;
Men, who a victory won us
'Gainst any odds among us :
    Such were our bowmen.

Agincourt, Agincourt!
Know ye not Agincourt?
Dear was the victory bought
    By fifty yeomen.
Ask any English wench,
They were worth all the French :
    Rare English bowmen ! [1]

───────

2. King Henry V. his Conquest of France
In Revenge for the Affront offered by the French King ;
In sending him (instead of the Tribute) a Ton
of Tennis Balls.

(From the copy in Chetham's Library, Manchester, obligingly transcribed
by Mr. Jones, the Librarian. Dr. Rimbault has a copy of this ballad
"Printed and sold in Aldermary Church Yard." He says that traditional versions of it also appeared in the Rev. J. C. Tyler's *Henry
of Monmouth*, 8vo. vol. ii. p. 197, and in Mr. Dixon's *Ancient Poems,
Ballads, and Songs of the Peasantry of England*, printed by the Percy
Society in 1846. *Notes and Queries*, No. 23, Jan. 25, 1851, vol. iii.
p. 51, col. 1.)

As our King lay musing on his bed,
    He bethought himself upon a time,
Of a tribute that was due from France,
    Had not been paid for so long a time.
        Fal, lal, &c.

───────

[1] In the original it is " Rare English *women*," but probably a mistake
for " bowmen," the printer having been misled by the word " wench "
above. All the other stanzas end with " bowmen."—J. P. Collier.

He called for his lovely page,
  His lovely page then called he ;
Saying, you must go to the King of France,
  To the King of France, sir, ride speedily.
O then went away this lovely page,
  This lovely page then away went he ;
Low he came to the King of France,
  And when fell down on his bended knee.
My master greets you, worthy sir,
  Ten ton of gold that is due to he,
That you will send him his tribute home,
  Or in French laud you soon will him see.
        Fal, lal, &c.

Your master's young and of tender years,
  Not fit to come into my degree :
And I will send him three Tennis-Balls,
  That with them he may learn to play.

O then returned this lovely page,
  This lovely page then returned he,
And when he came to our gracious King,
  Low he fell down on his bended knee.
What news? what news? my trusty page,
  What is the news you have brought to me ?
I have brought such news from the King of France,
  That he and you will ne'er agree.
He says, you're young and of tender years,
  Not fit to come into his degree ;
And he will send you three Tennis-Balls,
  That with them you may learn to play.
Recruit me Cheshire and Lancashire
  And Derby Hills that are so free :
No marry'd man or widow's son,
  For no widow's curse shall go with me.
They recruited Cheshire and Lancashire,
  And Derby Hills that are so free :
No marry'd man, nor no widow's son,
  Yet there was a jovial bold company.

O then we march'd into the French land,
  With drums and trumpets so merrily ;
And then bespoke the King of France,
  Lo yonder comes proud King Henry.

The first shot that the Frenchmen gave,
  They kill'd our Englishmen so free.
We kill'd ten thousand of the French,
  And the rest of them they run away.
And then we marched to Paris gates,
  With drums and trumpets so merrily ;
O then bespoke the King of France,
  The Lord have mercy on my men and me,
O I will send him his tribute home,
  Ten ton of gold that is due to he,
And the finest flower that is in all France
  To the Rose of England I will give free.

II.

King Estmere.

(See p. 200, note 1.)

WE give here reprints of this ballad as it appeared in the 1st and 4th editions of the *Reliques*, putting in italics all the words changed in spelling or position, or for other words, in the two editions, so as to make Percy's acknowledged changes apparent. His unacknowledged ones we must leave to the critical power of our readers to ascertain.

FIRST EDITION, 1765.	FOURTH EDITION, 1794.
HEARKEN to me, gentlemen, Come and you shall heare : He tell you of two of the boldest brethren, That ever *born* y-were.	HEARKEN to me, gentlemen, Come and you shall heare ; He tell you of two of the boldest brethren [1] That ever *borne* y-were.
The tone of them was Adler *yonge*, 5 The tother was kyng Estmere ; The were as bolde men in their *deedes*, As any were farr and neare.	The tone of them was Adler *younge*, The tother was kyng Estmere ; The were as bolde men in their *deeds*, As any were farr and neare.
As they were drinking ale and wine Within kyng Estmeres halle : 10 *Whan* will ye marry a wyfe, brother, A wyfe to *gladd* us all?	As they were drinking ale and wine Within kyng Estmeres halle [2] : *When* will ye marry a wyfe, brother, A wyfe to *glad* us all ?
Then bespake him kyng Estmere, And answered him hastilee : I knowe not that ladye in any *lande*, 15 *That is able* [1] *to marry* with mee.	Then bespake him kyng Estmere, And answered him hastilee [3] : I know not that ladye in any *land* *That's able* [4] *to marrye* with mee.
Kyng Adland hath a daughter, brother, Men call her bright and sheene ; If I were kyng here in your stead, That ladye *sholde* be queene. 20	Kyng Adland hath a daughter, brother, Men call her bright and sheene ; If I were kyng here in your stead, That ladye *shold* be my queene.

Ver. 3. brother. fol. MS.
Ver. 10. his brother's hall. fol. MS.

[1] Ver. 11. hartilye. fol. MS.
[4] He means fit, suitable.

FIRST EDITION, 1765.

Sayes, Reade me, reade me, deare bro-
ther,
Throughout *merrye* England,
Where we might find a messenger
Betweene us *two* to sende.

Sayes, You shal ryde yourselfe, brother, 25
He beare you *companie* ;
Many throughe fals messengers are de-
ceivde,
And I feare lest soe shold wee.

Thus the renisht them to ryde
Of twoe good renisht *steedes*, 30
And when *they* came to *kyng* Adlands
halle,
Of *red golde* shone their *weedes.*

And *whan* the came to kyng Adlands
halle
Before the goodlye *yate*,
Ther they found good kyng Adland 35
Rearing himselfe theratt.

Nowe Christ thee save, good kyng Ad-
land ;
Nowe Christ *thee* save and see.
Sayd, you be welcome, *kyng* Estmere,
Right hartilye *unto* mee. 40

You have a daughter, *sayd* Adler *yonge*,
Men call her bright and sheene,
My brother wold marrye her to his wiffe,
Of Englande to *bee* queene.

Yesterdaye was *at* my *deare* daughter 45
Syr Bremor the kyng of Spayne ;
And then *she* nicked him of naye,
I *feare* sheele doe *youe* the same.

The kyng of Spayne is a foule paynim,
And 'leeveth on Mahound; 50
And pitye it were that fayre la lye
Shold marrye a heathen hound.

But grant to me, sayes kyng Estmere,
For my love I you praye,
That I may see your daughter *deare* 55
Before I goe hence awaye.

FOURTH EDITION, 1794.

Saies, Reade me, reade me, deare bro-
ther,
Throughout *merry* England,
Where we might find a messenger
Betwixt us *towe* to sende.

Saies, You shal ryde yourselfe, brother,
He beare you *companye* ;
Many throughe fals messengers are [1] de-
ceived,
And I feare lest soe shold wee.

Thus the renisht them to ryde
Of twoe good renisht *steeds*,
And when *the* came to *king* Adlands
halle,
Of *redd gold* shone their *weeds.*

And *when* the came to kyng Adlands
hall
Before the goodlye *gate*,
There they found good kyng Adland
Rearing himselfe theratt.

Now Christ thee save, good kyng Ad-
land ;
Now Christ *you* save and see.
Sayd, You be welcome, *king* Estmere,
Right hartilye *to* mee.

You have a daughter, *said* Adler *younge*,
Men call her bright and sheene,
My brother wold marrye her to his wiffe,
Of Englande to *be* queene.

Yesterday was *att* my *deere* daughter
Syr Bremor the kyng of Spayne ; [2]
And then *she* nicked him of naye,
And I *doubt* sheele *do you* the same.

The kyng of Spayne is a foule paynim,
And 'leeveth [3] on Mahound;
And pitye it were that fayre ladye
Shold marrye a heathen hound.

But grant to me, sayes kyng Estmere,
For my love I you praye ;
That I may see your daughter *deere*
Before I goe hence awaye.

[1] Ver. 27. Many a man . . . is. fol. MS.   [2] Ver. 46. The king his sonne of Spayn. fol. MS.
[3] Misprinted 'leeve thou.

FIRST EDITION, 1765.

Alth nghe itt is seven yeare and more
  Syth my daughter was in halle,
She shall come downe once for your sake
  To glad my guestès all.   60

Downe then came that mayden fayre,
  With ladyes lacede in pall,
And halfe a hundred of bolde knightes,
  To bring her from bowre to hall ;
And eke as manye gentle squieres,   65
  To waite upon them all.

The talents of golde, were on her head
    sette,
  Hange lowe downe to her knee ;
And everye rynge on her smalle fingèr,
  Shone of the chrystall free.   70

Sayes, Christ you save, my deare madàme ;
  Sayes, Christ you save and see,
Sayes, You be welcome, kyng Estmere,
  Right welcome unto mee.

And iff you love me, as you saye,   75
  So well and hartilèe,
All that ever you are comen about
  Soone sped now itt may bee.

Then bespake her father deare :
  My daughter, I saye naye ;   80
Remember well the kyng of Spayne,
  What he sayd yesterdaye.

He wold pull downe my halles and
    castles,
  And reave me of my lyfe :
And ever I feare that paynim kyng,   85
  Iff I reave him of his wyfe.

Your castles and your towres, father,
  Are stronglye built aboute ;
And therefore of that foule paynim
  Wee neede not stande in doubte.   90

Plyght me your troth, nowe, kyng Est-
    mère,
  By heaven and your righte hand,
That you will marrye me to your wyfe,
  And make me queene of your land.

Then kyng Estmere he plyght his troth 95
  By heaven and his righte hand,
That he wold marrye her to his wyfe,
  And make her queene of his land.

FOURTH EDITION, 1794.

Although itt is seven yeers and more
  Since my daughter was in halle,
She shall come once downe for your sake
  To glad my guestès alle.

Downe then came that mayden fayre,
  With ladyes laced in pall,
And halfe a hundred of bold knightes,
  To bring her [from] bowre to hall ;
And as many gentle squiers,
  To tend upon them all.

The talents of golde were on her head
    sette,
  Hanged low downe to her knee ;
And everye ring on her small fingèr,
  Shone of the chrystall free.

Saies, God you save, my deere madàm ;
  Saies, God you save and see."
Said, You be welcome, kyng Estmere,
  Right welcome unto mee.

And, if you love me, as you saye,
  Soe well and hartilèe,
All that ever you are comen about
  Soone sped now itt shal bee.

Then bespake her father deare :
  My daughter, I saye naye ;
Remember well the kyng of Spayne,
  What he sayd yesterdaye.

He wold pull downe my halles and
    castles,
  And reave me of my lyfe :
I cannot blame him if he doe,
  If I reave him of his wyfe.

Your castles and your towres, father,
  Are stronglye built aboute ;
And therefore of the king of Spaine [1]
  Wee neede not stande in doubt.

Plight me your troth, nowe, kyng Est-
    mère,
  By heaven and your righte hand,
That you will marrye me to your wyfe,
  And make me queene of your land.

Then kyng Estmere he plight his troth
  By heaven and his righte hand,
hat he wolde marrye her to his wyfe,
  And make her queene of his land.

---

[1] Ver. 89, of the King his sonne of Spaine. fol. MS.

And he tooke leave of that ladye fayre,
　To goe to his owne countree,　　　100
To fetche him dukes and lordes and
　　knightes,
　That marryed the might bee.

They had not ridden scant a myle,
　A myle forthe of the towne,
But in did come the kyng of Spayne, 105
　With kempès many a one.

But in did come the kyng of Spayne,
　With manye a *grimme* barône,
Tone day to marrye kyng Adlands daugh-
　　ter,
　Tother daye to carrye her home.　110

Then shee sent after kyng Estmère
　In all the spede might bee,
That he must either *returne* and fighte,
　Or goe home and *lose* his ladyè.

One whyle then the page he went,　115
　Another *whyle* he ranne;
Till he had oretaken *kyng* Estmere
　I-wis, he never blanne.

Tydinges, tydinges, kyng Estmere!
　What tydinges nowe, my boye?　120
O tydinges I can tell to you,
　That will you sore annoye.

You had not ridden scant a *myle*,
　A *myle* out of the towne,
But in did come the kyng of Spayne 125
　With kempès many a one :

But in did come the kyng of Spayne
　With manye a *grimme* barône,
Tone daye to marrye king Adlands
　　daughter,
　Tother daye to carrye her home.　130

That ladye fayre she greetes you well,
　And ever-more well by mee :
You must either turne againe and fighte,
　Or goe home and *lose* your ladyè.

Sayes, Reade me, reade me, *deare* brother, 135
　My reade shall ryde[1] at thee,
Whiche waye we best may turne and
　　fighte,
　To save *this fayre* ladyè.

And he tooke leave of that ladye fayre,
　To goe to his owne countree,
To fetche him dukes and lordes and
　　knightes,
　That marryed the might bee.

They had not ridden scant a myle,
　A myle forthe of the towne,
But in did come the kyng of Spayne,
　With kempès many one.

But in did come the kyng of Spayne,
　With manye a *bold* barône,
Tone day to marrye kyng Adlands daugh-
　　ter,
　Tother daye to carrye her home.

Shee sent *one* after kyng Estmère
　In all the spede might bee,
That he must either *turne againe* and
　　fighte,
　Or goe home and *loose* his ladyè.

One whyle then the page he went,
　Another *while* he ranne;
Till he had oretaken *king* Estmere,
　I wis, he never blanne.

Tydings, tydings, kyng Estmere!
　What tydinges nowe, my boye?
O, tydinges I can tell to you,
　That will you sore annoye.

You had not ridden scant a *mile*,
　A *mile* out of the towne,
But in did come the kyng of Spayne
　With kempès many a one :

But in did come the kyng of Spayne
　With manye a *bold* barône.
Tone daye to marrye king Adlands
　　daughter,
　Tother daye to carry her home.

My ladye fayre she greetes you well,
　And ever-more well by mee :
You must either turne againe and fighte,
　Or goe home and *loose* your ladyè.

Saies, Reade me, reade me, *deere* brother,
　My reade shall ryde[2] at thee,
Whether it is better to turne and fighte,
　Or goe home and *loose my* ladyè.

---

[1] *Sic.*　[2] *Sic* MS. It should probably be "ryse," i.e. my counsel shall arise from thee. See ver. 140.

Now hearken to me, sayes Adler yonge,
  And your reade must rise[1] at me, 140
I quicklye will devise a waye
  To sette thy ladye free.

My mother was a westerne woman,
  And learned in gramarye,[3]
And when I learned at the schole,   145
  Something shee taught itt mee.

There *groweth* an hearbe within this
  fielde,
And iff it were but knowne,
His color, which is whyte and redd,
  Itt will make blacke and browne : 150

His color, which is browne and blacke,
  Itt will make redd and whyte ;
That sworde is not in all Englande,
  Upon his coate will byte.

And you shal be a harper, brother,   155
  Out of the north *countrie*;
And Ile be your *boye*, so faine of fighte,
  To beare your harpe by your knee.

And you *shall* be the best harper,
  That ever tooke harpe in hand ;   160
And I *will* be the best singer,
  That ever sung in this *land*.

Itt shal be written in our forheads
  All and in *gramarye*,
That we towe are the boldest men,   165
  That are in all Christentye.

And thus they renisht them to ryde,
  On *towe* good renish steedes ;
And *whan* they came to king Adlands
  hall,
  Of redd gold shone their weedes.   170

And whan the came to kyng Adlands
  hall
Untill the fayre hall yate,
There they found a proud porter
  Rearing himselfe *thereatt*.

Sayes, Christ thee save, thou proud
  porter :   175
Sayes, Christ thee save and see.
Nowe you be welcome, sayd tho porter,
  Of what land soever ye bee.

Now hearken to me, sayes Adler yonge,
  And your reade must rise[2] at me,
I quicklye will devise a waye
  To sette thy ladye free.

My mother was a westerne woman,
  And learned in gramarye,[3]
And when I learned at the schole,
  Something shee taught itt mee.

There *growes* an hearbe within this
  field,
And iff it were but knowne,
His color, which is whyte and redd,
  It will make blacke and browne :

His color, which is browne and blacke,
  Itt will make redd and whyte ;
That sworde is not in all Englande,
  Upon his coate will byte.

And you shal be a harper, brother,
  Out of the north *countrye*;
And Ile be your *boy*, see faine of fighte,
  And beare your harpe by your knee.

And you *shal* be the best harper,
  That ever tooke harpe in hand ;
And I *wil* be the best singer,
  That ever sung in this *launde*.

Itt shal be written in our forheads
  All and in *grammarye*,
That we towe are the boldest men,
  That are in all Christentye.

And thus they renisht them to ryde,
  On *tow* good renish steedes ;
And *when* they came to king Adlands
  hall,
  Of redd gold shone their weedes.

And whan the came to kyng Adlands
  hall,
Untill the fayre hall yate,
There thoy found a proud porter
  Rearing himselfe *thereatt*.

Sayes, Christ thee save, thou proud
  porter ;
Sayes, Christ thee save and see.
Nowe you be welcome, sayd tho porter,
  Of what land soever ye bee.

---

[1] *Sie.*   [2] *Sie* MS.   See at the end of this ballad, Note *.* [not reprinted here.—F.]

FIRST EDITION, 1765.

We been harpers, sayd Adler younge,
  Come out of the northe countree; 180
We beene come hither untill this place,
  This proud weddinge for to see.

Sayd, And your color were white and
    redd,
  As it is blacke and browne,
Ill saye king Estmere and his brother 185
  Were comen untill this towne.

Then they pulled out a ryng of gold,
  Layd itt on the porters arme :
And ever we will thee, proud portèr,
  Thow wilt saye us no harme. 190

Sore he looked on kyng Estmère,
  And sore he handled the ryng,
Then opened to them the fayre hall yates,
  He lett for no kind of thyng.

Kyng Estmere he light off his steede 195
  Up att the fayre hall board ;
The frothe, that came from his brydle
    bitte,
  Light on kyng Bremors beard.

Sayes, Stable thou steede, thou proud
    harpèr,
  Goe stable him in the stalle ; 200
Itt doth not beseeme a proud harpèr
  To stable him in a kyngs halle.

My ladd he is so lither, he sayd,
  He will do nought that's meete ;
And aye that I cold but find the man, 205
  Were able him to beate.

Thou speakst proud wordes, sayd the Pay-
    nim kyng,
  Thou harper here to mee ;
There is a man within this halle,
  That will beate thy lad and thee. 210

O lett that man come downe, he sayd,
  A sight of him wolde I see ;
And whan hee hath beaten well my ladd,
  Then he shall beate of mee.

Downe then came the kemperye man, 215
  And looked him in the eare;
For all the golde, that was under heaven,
  He durst not neigh him neare.

FOURTH EDITION, 1794.

Wee beene harpers, sayd Adler younge,
  Come out of the northe countrye ;
Wee beene come hither untill this place,
  This proud weddinge for to see.

Sayd, And your color were white and
    redd,
  As it is blacke and browne,
I wold saye king Estmere and his brother
  Were comen untill this towne.

Then they pulled out a ryng of gold,
  Layd itt on the porters arme :
And ever we will thee, proud portèr,
  Thow wilt saye us no harme.

Sore he looked on kyng Estmère,
  And sore he handled the ryng,
Then opened to them the fayre hall yates,
  He lett for no kind of thyng.

Kyng Estmere he stabled his steede
  Soe fayre att the hall bord ;
The froth, that came from his brydle
    bitte,
  Light in kyng Bremors beard.

Saies, Stable thy steed, thou proud
    harpèr,
  Saies, Stable him in the stalle ;
It doth not beseeme a proud harpèr
  To stable 'him' in a kyngs halle.[1]

My ladde he is so lither, he said,
  He will doe nought that's meete ;
And is there any man in this hall
  Were able him to beate.

Thou speakst proud words, sayes the king
    of Spaine,
  Thou harper here to mee :
There is a man within this halle,
  Will beate thy ladd and thee.

O let that man come downe, he said,
  A sight of him wold I see ;
And when hee hath beaten well my ladd,
  Then he shall beate of mee.

Downe then came the kemperye man,
  And looked him in the eare ;
For all the gold, that was under heaven,
  He durst not neigh him neare.

---

[1] Ver. 202. To stable his steede. fol. MS.

FIRST EDITION, 1765.	FOURTH EDITION, 1794.

And how nowe, kempe, *sayd* the kyng of
    Spaⁿ,
  And how what aileth thee?   220
He *saies, It is written* in his forhead
  All and in gramarye,
That for all the gold that is under
    heaven,
  I dare not neigh him nye.

Kyng Estmere *then pulled* forth his harpe, 225
  And playd theron so sweete:
Upstarte the ladye from the kynge,
  As he sate at the meate.

Now stay thy harpe, thou proud harper,
  Now stay thy harpe, I say: 230
For an thou playest as thou beginnest,
  Thou'lt till my bride awaye.

He *strucke* upon his harpe *agayne,*
  And playd *both fayre and free;*
The ladye was so pleasde theratt, 235
  She laught loud laughters three.

Now sell me thy harpe, *sayd the kyng of*
    Spayne,
  Thy harpe and stryngs eche one,
And as many gold nobles thou shalt
  have,
  As there be stryngs thereon. 240

And what wold ye doe with my harpe,
  he sayd,
Iff I did sell *it ye?*
To playe my wiffe and me a FITT,
  When abed together *we* bee.

Now sell me, *syr kyng,* thy bryde soe
  gay, 245
  As shee sitts *laced in pall,*
And as many gold nobles I will give,
  As there be rings in the hall.

And what wold ye doe with my bryde
  so gay,
  Iff I did sell her *yee?* 250
More seemelye it is for her fayre bodye
  To lye by mee *than* thee.

He played agayne both loud and shrille,
  And Adler he did syng,
"O la lye, this is thy owne true love; 255
  "Noe harper but a kyng.

And how nowe, kempe, *said* the kyng of
    Spaine,
  And how what aileth thee?
He *saies, It is writt* in his forhead
  All and in gramarye,
That for all the gold that is under
    heaven,
  I dare not neigh him nye.

Then kyng Estmere *pulld* forth his harpe,
  And *plaid a pretty thinge:*
The ladye upstart from the *borde,*
  And wold have gone from the king.

Stay thy harpe, thou proud harper,
  For Gods love I pray thee
For *and thou playes* as thou *beginns,*
  Thou'lt till¹ my *bryde from mee.*

He *stroake* upon his harpe *againe,*
  And playd *a pretty thinge;*
The ladye *lough a loud laughter,*
  As shee sate by the king.

Saies, sell me thy harpe, *thou proud*
    harper,
  And thy stringes all,
For as many gold nobles, 'thou shalt
  have'
  As heere bee ringes in the hall.

What wold ye doe with my harpe, 'he
  sayd,'
  If I did sell *itt yee?*
"To playe my wiffe and me a FITT,²
  When abed together *wee* bee."

Now sell me, *quoth hee,* thy bryde soe
  gay,
  As shee sitts *by thy knee,*
And as many gold nobles I will give,
  As leaves been on a tree.

And what wold ye doe with my bryde
  soe gay,
  Iff I did sell her *thee?*
More seemelye it is for her fayre bodye
  To lye by mee *then* thee.

Hee played agayne both loud and shrille,³
  And Adler he did syng,
"O ladye, this is thy owne true love;
  "Noe harper, but a kyng.

---

v. Entice. Vol. Gloss.

... a tune, or train of music. See Gloss.

V. r. ?... in liberties have been taken in the following stanzas; but wherever this edition
... refer to the preceding, it hath been brought nearer to the folio MS.

FIRST EDITION, 1765.

" O ladye, this is thy owne true love,
    " As playnlye thou mayest see ;
" And Ile rid thee of that foule paynim,
    " Who partes thy love and thee." 260

The ladye *louked*, the ladye blushte,
    And blushte and lookt agayne,
While Adler he hath drawne his brande,
    And hath *sir Bremor* slayne.

Up then rose the kemperye men, 265
    And loud they gan to crye :
Ah! traytors, yee have slayne our kyng,
    And therefore yee shall dye.

Kyng Estmere threwe the harpe asyde,
    And swith he drew his brand ; 270
And Estmere he, and Adler yonge
    Right stiffe in stour can stand.

And aye their swordes soe sore can *byte*,
    Throughe help of gramaryè,
That soone they have slayne the kempery
    men, 275
    Or forst them forth to flee.

Kyng Estmere tooke that fayre ladyè,
    And marryed her to his *wyfe*,
And brought her home to *merrye* England
    With her to leade his *lyfe*. 280

FOURTH EDITION, 1794.

" O ladye, this is thy owne true love,
    " As playnlye thou mayest see ;
" And Ile rid thee of that foule paynim,
    " Who partes thy love and thee."

The ladye *looked*, the ladye blushte,
    And blushte and lookt agayne,[1]
While Adler he hath drawne his brande,
    And hath *the Sowdan* slayne.

Up then rose the kemperye men,
    And loud they gan to crye :
Ah! traytors, yee have slayne our kyng,
    And therefore yee shall dye.

Kyng Estmere threwe the harpe asyde,
    And swith he drew his brand ;
And Estmere he, and Adler yonge
    Right stiffe in stour can stand.

And aye their swordes soe sore can *fyte*,
    Throughe help of Gramaryè,
That soone they have slayne the kempery
    men,
    Or forst them forth to flee.

Kyng Estmere tooke that fayre ladyè,
    And marryed her to his *wiffe*,
And brought her home to *merry* England
    With her to leade his *life*.

These lines must be Percy's own.—F.

III.

Beginning of Guy and Phillis, *p.* 201.

PERCY says in his *Reliques*, iii. 105, 1st ed., that his text of "The Legend of Sir Guy" is "Printed from an ancient MS. copy in the Editor's old folio volume, collated with two printed ones, one of which is in black letter in the Pepys collection." As he tore the beginning of it out of his Folio, I applied to the Librarian of Magdalene to correct by the Pepys copy a transcript of the first twenty-two stanzas of Percy's text; but as I could not give a reference to the volume and page where the ballad is, and the Librarian's catalogue is not yet complete, he has not sent me the collation. I am therefore obliged to print the beginning of the "inferior copy in Ritson's *Ancient Songs and Ballads*, ii. 193" (Child).

SIR GUY OF WARWICK.

WAS ever knight, for ladys sake,
  So toss'd in love, as I, Sir Guy,
For Phillis fair, that lady bright
  As ever man beheld with eye?
She gave me leave myself to try
  The valiant knight with shield and
    spear,
Ere that her love she would grant me;
  Which made me venture far and near.

The proud Sir Guy, a baron bold,
  In deeds of arms the doughty knight,
That every day in England was,
  With sword and spear in field to
    fight;
An English man I was by birth,
  In faith of Christ a Christian true;
The wicked laws of infidels
  I sought by power to subdue.

Two hundred twenty years, and odd
  After our saviour Christ his birth,
When king Athelstan wore the crown,
  I lived here upon the earth.

Sometime I was of Warwick earl,
  And, as I said, on very truth,
A ladys love did me constrain
  To seek strange ventures in my youth:

To try my fame by feats of arms,
  In strange and sundry heathen lands;
Where I atchieved, for her sake,
  Right dangerous conquests with my
    hands.
For first I sail'd to Normandy,
  And there I stoutly won in fight,
The emperours daughter of Almain,
  From many a valiant worthy knight.

Then passed I the seas of Greece,
  To help the emperour to his right,
Against the mighty soldans host
  Of puissant Persians for to fight:
Where I did slay of Saracens
  And heathen pagans, many a man,
And slew the soldans cousin dear,
  Who had to name, doughty Colbron.

Ezkeldered, that famous knight,
 . To death likewise I did pursue,
And Almain, king of Tyre, also,
  Most terrible too in fight to view :
I went into the soldans host,
  Being thither on ambassage sent,
And brought away his head with me,
  I having slain him in his tent.

There was a dragon in the land,
  Which I also myself did slay,
As he a lion did pursue,
  Most fiercely met me by the way.
From thence I pass'd the seas of Greece,
  And came to Pavy land aright,
Where I the duke of Pavy kill'd,
  His heinous treason to requite.

And after came into this land,
  Towards fair Phillis, lady bright ;
For love of whom I travel'd far,
  To try my manhood and my might.
But when I had espoused her,
  I stay'd with her but forty days,
But there I left this lady fair,
  And then I went beyond the seas.

All clad in gray, in pilgrim sort,
  My voyage from her I did take,
Unto that blessed holy land,
  For Jesus Christ my saviours sake :
Where I carl Jonas did redeem,
  And all his sons, which were fifteen,
Who with the cruel Saracen,
  In prison for long time had been.

I slew the giant Amarant,
  In battle fiercely hand to hand:
And doughty Barknard killed I,
  The mighty duke of that same land.
Then I to England came again,
  And here with Colbron fell I fought,
An ugly giant, which the Danes
  Had for their champion hither brought.

I overcame him in the field,
  And slew him dead right valiantly ;
Where I the land did then redeem
  From Danish tribute utterly ;
And afterwards I offered up
  The use of weapons solemnly,
At Winchester, whereas I fought,
  In sight of many far and nigh.

In Windsor-forest, &c.

Ritson. *A Select Collection of English Songs,* vol. ii. p. 296–299.
Part IV., *Ancient Ballads.*

INDEX.

END OF THE SECOND VOLUME.

SPOTTISWOODE AND CO., PRINTERS, NEW-STREET SQUARE AND PARLIAMENT STREET.